BIRDS FLYING IN THE DARK

Also published by Midnight Fire Media

Your Own Fate
Night on Earth

The Janus Clan series:

The Defenseless
The Slaves

Next book At the End of the Rainbow for sale October 31, 2012

Poems:

Amos Keppler: Complete poems 1989 - 2003

(A few of the) other works to be published:

The Afterglow trilogy
Season of the Witch
Alarums of Reality
Dreams Belong to the Night
ShadowWalk
Thunder Road: Ice and Fire
Falling
Black Dragon

For a «complete» list of current and current future Amos Keppler and Midnight Fire Media projects see the back of the book and the Midnight Fire/Midnight Fire Media web pages.

The Janus Clan, Book Three

«The first twenty years - Book Three»
The years 1975 - 1976

Birds Flying in the Dark

By

Amos Keppler

MIDNIGHT FIRE MEDIA
2011

Midnight Fire Media

http://midnight-fire.net/mfm
For more about Birds Flying in the Dark and the Janus Clan:
http://midnight-fire.net/sw

E-Mail:
ak@midnight-fire.net
manofhood@yahoo.com

Cover, text, design, premedia, art and photos Amos Keppler

ISBN 978-82-91693-10-1

«The desire for power has always been among humanity's worst qualities. Through recorded history it shows up in many forms. In our days, with our smaller world, super-communications and ever more «improved» databanks the people crying for power have better provisions than ever before. Technology is inherently oppressive. The people you have just read about, those calling themselves The High Ones exploited these methods systematically. But their ideas about training braindead slaves and adapting them to their needs are nothing new or exceptional. On the contrary, it's quite common. Their kind is the vast majority in economic power centers, multinational corporations, governments and parliaments across the world».

Excerpts from author's word, the non-fiction novel The Slaves by Eric Carr

Doors won't keep them out,
Lightning won't keep them back,
Like snakes they slip through doors,
Like wind they enter by the hinges,
They keep the woman away from the man's arms,
And tear the son off the father's knee.

Sumerian proverb about the evil ones

«Life is more than you can see around you. This is something we don't learn in school, at home... You must learn it yourself. That was my life's most important lesson... Don't sell yourself short».

Bruce Springsteen

«The Universe isn't just stranger than we believe, but stranger than we can imagine».

Professor J. B. S. Haldane

«The system should be changed, I think, to begin with. It's hard, really, the way our system operates now, for a truly frank, honest man to stay in that system indefinitely without being weeded out, or fired, or made apathetic or in fact corrupted in the end».

Daniel Ellsberg, interview with Walter Cronkite June 23rd 1971

PART ONE
TED

CHAPTER ONE

It was another gray day. The clouds hung low over the land. It was raining hard, and the snow that had fallen just a few days before was washed away. On a stretch somewhere in the English countryside, there was a cluster of modern buildings. They had been unnoticed for quite a while. They belonged to the government, possibly the army. Tall, barbed wired fences surrounded the property. Soldiers guarded the place, both inside and outside the fences. No one knew what went on inside, even though many had some ideas. No one spoke about it. One didn't speak about such matters. Dots of mist drifted between the dark buildings, away from them, and through the many-layered electrical fences.

Reaching for the red car turning off the main road. The icy water covered the asphalt like a blanket, flowing through the air behind the car. On several turns the car was just a notch or two from ending up on the field. The man behind the wheel - Mark Stewart - smiled grimly. He saw patrol cars everywhere. They were stationed along the road, along his route like ants. He hoped they would stop him, making him show them, them and the people in the dark buildings how things had changed.

His years in hiding were at an end. Those in power had no longer anything they could use against him. He decided his own fate from now on.

The car drove on ever-smaller roads. The exception was the last stretch. It was broad as a main road, even though it was just covered by gravel. He saw the buildings. It was as if the sky above them was even darker than usual. This was one of the Masters' places of power.

It had stopped raining. He was glad for that, at least. In front of the main gate had gathered a crowd. People with notebooks, cameras and tape-recorders. Several TV-cars were placed at strategic spots on the terrain. He observed his eyes in the mirror, his excited, glowing eyes. And that, too, pleased him. He wanted to cause a stir, wanted to herald his return to life.

Behind the gate a dozen soldiers with expressionless faces stood straight and unmovable. They were unarmed, a state of being clearly created for the «benefit» of the present journalists.

Stewart stopped well before the gate. The pack of dogs rushed towards him in an uneven stream. He departed the car and jumped up on its hood. He stood there, as they gathered in front of him, as they fired question after question at him, as all semblance of intelligible words drowned in the buzz from the many voices. There was no reply. He just stood there, waiting, good-humored and seemingly infinitely patient.

The voices eventually quieted, as they finally got the point. They even stopped taking pictures. Stewart looked at his watch, waited ten seconds of silence before speaking.

– Listen up, he said forcefully. – You'll get everything you came here for.

And then he smiled enigmatically.

– And more. Much more.

There was a quiet buzz, then, of excitement and expectation. They knew he was in control, and they accepted it, because of everything they stood to gain by it.

He took in their heat, used it and multiplied it, knew he could stand like this for hours, unhampered by the cold and freezing of limbs.

This was the end, the end of the years of forgetting and loneliness.

– Mr. Fontaine…

– Stewart, he corrected, – Mark Stewart.

– Mr. Stewart, when you left this morning you refused to speak to us. What made you change your mind?

– Let's say I was a bit more… vulnerable then.

– So… the confirmation has come? All charges have been dropped?

A paper glowed in the light from the flashes. There was a murmur surging through the gathering.

– My secretary will give you copies later.

Stunned silence greeted his words.

– I was kidding…

More stunned silence followed by uncertain laughter. He played them, played them like he would a fiddle.

He pulled a pile of sheets from his coat, and began distributing them among the crowd. There was a lot pushing and muffled protests as they scrambled to get the first look, but everything eventually calmed down. He calmed them, with small gestures and reproaching glances. They turned from a pack of wolves to tame dogs eating off his hand.

– That's better. He nodded. – I've had enough bullshit lately.

– From various government representatives?

A man in the front picked up the cue in an instant.

– You hit that one right on the head, Stewart grinned ironically. – They were quite angry with me, especially because of the public spectacle I've made of all this. They wanted to give their own, balanced version of it all, I guess.

– Does this have a connection to the fact that the youths are being treated in such a remote facility, in a military hospital?

That was one of the Americans. Probing journalism was quite popular there these days. He did his best to ape Stewart's ironic voice.

– You should ask the decision-makers that question…

They laughed. They «liked» Stewart, especially these days when he was the flavor of the day.

– But if I'm allowed to speculate, and I am, I would say that the expression «out of sight, out of mind», applies here. Almost all members of the Abraxas Omega are also members of The Thousand Feet, a respected organization in today's world, respected members of the so-called elite. They can't cry wolf this time, because there's hardly anybody but perceived white sheep currently filling up the prisons around the world. By placing the visible, tangible part of their problem, their embarrassment out here they hope that the electorates will eventually forget about this, too… and unfortunately, they're correct.

They wrote so fast that pens seemed to fly over the paper. Cameras clicked and hummed.

– You may quote me word by word on this, he added sweetly.

But there wasn't a mild-mannered man standing there, before them, by any stretch of the imagination. A lifetime of frustration and rage was exposed this day, raw and uncompromising.

– A persistent rumor claims your hair and eye color has changed. That was an Englishman, clearly a man more government friendly inclined. – The same rumor says you're not the real Mark Stewart…

Loud and spontaneous and true laughter erupted across the gray and white landscape.

– It's not that difficult to say where this rumor originates from… is it?

More laughter from the spectators, louder and friendlier.

– The government claims it has weighty reasons for treating the patients out here. It was the same Englishman. – That they're in dire need of protection, and that this is the best place for that.

– There is danger, no doubt, even though this particular world-spanning branch of the Abraxas Omega has been pretty much dismantled. But most of the threat comes from the government itself. Basically, the «patients» don't need more protection than most others. They need rest, and true healing. Not to be surrounded by public servants disguised as physicians.

– You're implying that certain parts of the government are using the situation to… learn something?

– Implying, yes…

It was like the sun broke through the clouds, even though it clearly didn't. They looked up at the sky, and it was still the same, gray ceiling. But down here, right in their midst, was the fire. Later, many of them swore they had seen shadows in the others' faces.

– Are you a communist? Mr. Stewart?

A thin voice from the crowd, completely devoid of the usual condemnation.

And at that moment it turned silent, everything. They imagined they actually heard the snow melt.

– I'm very pleased to get the opportunity to answer that question», he mocked. – I expected that. No, I'm not a communist.

– But you're quite critical towards our society and its government?

– And I'm therefore a communist, right? How typical, how sad.

Stewart shook his head in contempt.

– I'm far more radical and critical than those pretenders.

He moved a bit, took a long, hard look at them all, and began speaking.

– Communism and Capitalism are, to put it simply, merely two sides of the same coin. Or two almost identical coins in a world where there shouldn't be any coins at all. Both are based on power, hierarchies not very different from other dictatorships throughout history. The only difference between a democracy and a dictatorship is that in a democracy people are fooled into believing that they have a say in how things should be done. A democracy is a clever dictatorship, nothing more. Overt dictatorships are on their way out. It's bad for business. Today's tyrants are sneakier, far more dangerous than all of history's Hitlers and Victorias and such. Law and Order are hailed as the triumph of free will and humanism while they're nothing of the sort. Law and Rule are made by the rich and powerful to benefit the rich and powerful, against those who have little or nothing. We're living in a totalitarian society unparalleled in history, and this is being hailed as progress. And that is, of course, how the people above want it. They are, for the very first time, close to being master of all they survey, but they still aren't content. They want total control. Not a single drop of rain shall fall without their control. So they're constantly seeking to improve their system, and learn even more about ways to pacify unruly subjects, learn better behavior control and such. And people are fooled all the time.

– And your alternative is?

It was a guy with a Scandinavian accent, clearly agitated.

– There are literally thousands of alternative ways for humans to live. Stewart shrugged, deliberately, very deliberately. – One of the truly great achievements, seen from the tyrants' point of view in today's world, is that they have succeeded to such an uncanny degree at convincing people that there are no alternatives. To most people today reality isn't much bigger than a television set, and that's just the half of it. The Sixties showed some of it, some temporary progress, but it's all being squandered already.

– *Squandered?* What about women's rights, colored people right's to vote in United States and everything?

– One step forward. Ten leaps behind.

Stewart grinned then, and the journalist had difficulty breathing, hiding his anger.

– It's strange, he spat. – Nothing I've read about you… and I've read a lot, even suggested you were political.

– One thinks. Stewart shrugged again. – One lives. One learns. One's biding one's time. And now…

There was a rush in the crowd.

– … the time is nigh.

2

– There are headlines, Stewart told Zoe Stella Espershin. – This is too big, too gross to tone down. This is no longer a forgotten place. The kids are no longer gone from people's mind. Humanity has been wakened from apathy… at least for a few days.

Long, dark corridors. Hallways stretching on forever. Not so different from what Mark had seen in the Verheyen Mansion's cellar or in the youths' souls.

She walked by his side clearly frustrated, clearly out of it.

– You wanted to say something, Zoe?

– It's the patients, she said in wonder and almost irritation. – I don't understand it. The reports from the states… the victims there, their beyond dim prospects… I wrote most of our people off, too, reckoned they would spend the rest of their lives in padded cells. But now… It's unbelievable.

– I told you, Mark said lightly. – They're tough, and they're fighters. It will take time, but they will recover. After a time even the bad dreams will fade. Humans forget easily, perhaps too easily.

– You have been a big help, I admit that. She spoke as if clenching her teeth. – You must have learned somewhere…

I have certainly helped, he thought. More than you can imagine.

– I told you. A Gypsy witch taught me, taught me things you never learn at your prestigious academies.

– I've seen you with them, she said. – The effort and concern you put into your time with them. It takes its toll on you. I think you care too much. You're not very professional.
He had taxed himself, and had been forced to take frequent breaks lately.
– Do you want me to be? He asked her.
– No, she replied hesitatingly. – No!
Her hands touched his. His skin was cold, cold as ice.
They were interrupted. A man rushed towards them with quick, determined steps. The medals flashed on his uniform.
– Where the hell have you been, Stewart? The man snarled. – I've tried to get hold of you since early this morning.
– You know very well where I've been today, General...
– And what was that stunt you pulled in front of the gates?
– Do you know what, General…
– *What?*
– You can go and fuck yourself.
The high and mighty General looked like he had been struck by lightning.
– W-what? What kind of liberties are you granting yourself?
– All the kinds I want, General. Mark's body was like a steel spring. His voice filled with repressed rage. – I told you people from the very beginning that I wouldn't stand for any of your nonsense. Just now we're playing something called democracy. Do you understand that word, General? It means I can tell anything to anybody without explaining myself to anyone.
– It's like I suspected, Stewart. You're a threat to society's structure and the defense of the realm.
– As I said, General.
Stewart grinned and stared him down. He evaded the burning eyes in seconds, and shrank in his tracks, and Mark felt the putrid hatred within the man.
– Most people are like sheep, the general said low and timid, with his small chinks of eyes. – They don't know their own good. They must be shepherded. You made a mistake when you went public with this. A big mistake.
– The way I kept you guys from sending out the approved version, you mean?
– I can still have you *reprimanded,* the General screamed, suddenly cracking like a shell, his small eyes bulging.

– Try, General, Mark challenged him, totally unafraid, his rage burning like a song within him. – Try! There's still a lot I know and haven't published. That I have solid proof of. And people will listen to me. Now.

Mark saw the man crack, saw him disintegrate, and Mark longed to contribute further to that, to prove himself, to go deep within the asshole and open him up, expose all the vulnerability in there.

There was another interruption. Mark felt it like the roaring buzz within pulled back, pulled back just a little, but never truly quieting, not anymore.

A soldier approached. He ran and he was out of breath. He stopped between Stewart and the General, greeting both of them, clearly confused, taught as he was, to acknowledge authority in all things.

Stewart nodded mercifully to him.

– There's a… visitor at the gate, sir.

– A visitor?

Both Stewart and the General eyed him, and he turned very nervous.

– A relative, sir. She insists on coming in, sir. In fact she says she won't leave until she's granted access, and she says this much to the journalists, sir.

Slowly Stewart began smiling.

As he walked away, the general and the doctor stared at his back. None of them would ever be the same. They would always feel the need to look behind them, to see if he was there.

Mark looked at the girl in amusement, showing nothing of his boiling insides. He studied her without studying her, another of his kin, his distant thunder.

Elizabeth Warren was young, vulnerable, open. Her face was very similar to how Ted's face had been. She had shoulder-length brown hair, like Ted's had used to be. Her eyes were blue, blue like the sky and ocean, deep and shallow.

She rose from the chair as he entered the room, and the chair seemed to be pulled back, without her being near it. The rush within Stewart rose high again.

– Liz… isn't it?

– Liz it is, she replied.

– Welcome.

– Mark…

She reached out her hands. He didn't take them. Her hands fell.

– My, how you have grown…

She was tall. As expected she had grown a lot in the three years since he had last seen her. She reached him above the shoulders, taller than Betty and Tilla, but not as tall as Ted. She reddened under his close scrutiny. She was not yet sixteen, mature for her age, but still a girl.

– I've been expecting you, he said.

– You have? Insecurity and confidence warring within her, like virtually everything else.

– I have indeed, and I have to say it is downright impressive how you managed to find this place and how you got inside it.

– It was easy, she said haughtily. – If I hadn't had my ingenuity and beauty I would… I would have *sniffed* my way here. It's like a *beacon* in my mind, a torch in the blackest darkness.

– A fire in the night, he nodded.

She shook.

– And what about him? She asked, her worry carefully masked, open like a wound to him. – Has he been expecting me?

A shaking of his head.

– No.

– I must see him, she said passionately, hiding herself no longer.

– He doesn't know you're here, Stewart said. – And that's also how it should be.

She began pacing. For every step her feet slammed against the wooden floor. Her eyes sending lightning of rage and frustration and need against him.

– Look, I can sympathize. The unrest, insecurity and boundless frustration, all those things you feel are something I've felt for many lonely years.

And he didn't tell her about the need they both felt, to destroy, to tear at everything he felt dominated him more and more, what he felt grow in her.

– I must speak to him. She whirled around to face him. – I have to.

– And you will. He will. But not yet, not now. Be patient and he will come to you.

There was something about her, something uniquely her that gave… gave him the *willies*. Shocked beyond words he realized he had his hand on the Peacemaker inside his jacket. Slowly, slowly he let go of it, pulling the hand back out. He kept his eyes on her. She didn't notice, distracted as she was, distracted beyond words.

– He will come? You know this for a fact?

He nodded, closing and opening his eyes.

– Yes, he will come. You belong together. In what way I don't know, but you *do*.

– I can see us, she mumbled. – See us together…

He heard the flapping of wings, and he saw her eyes widen.
– Your eyes are so very pretty, now, she said breathlessly. – Yours and his, I would venture. I wish…
– There's no need for that, he revealed to her. – And that's a shame… since your eyes are so pretty already.
He sensed understanding, acceptance and joy flow within her. Gooseflesh broke out on his arms and legs. So far he had never come. So far he would never come.
– You must go back. When he's ready he will come to you.
– I will do it, she said forcefully. – I will follow your advice.
And for unfathomable reasons those very words made a chill flow down his spine.
She stepped close to him and kissed him on the cheek, and he was helpless to stop her. There was a flash, a flash of Shadow. They both staggered back, away from each other.
– Goodbye, Mark, she said softly.
He saw her leave, saw her walk out of the door, observed her as she walked to the gate, her long, dark hair blowing in the wind.

3

He stared blindly at the woman on the bed. Jean slept peacefully.
Images haunted him. Her in the chopper with Gidman, what had never happened. If she had been he knew she wouldn't have survived.
Nightmares haunted him, in the bright, dark day.
Her eyes opened. Her face cracked in a wide smile. She reached out with a hand, and he accepted it. Her small hand rested in his big, coarse.
– I dreamed, she said sleepily. – And it was peaceful, restful. Thank you. Thank you.
There were the crawling ants of fear inside him, and he strived with everything he could muster to hide it.
She knew him, now, knew his secret, the secret he had been hiding for her all these years, and he was glad.
– Your hand is so warm, she whispered. – I feel it all over my body, deep within my soul.
One time healing her, and he had let go, sharing himself with her.
– It's over, now, he said, – the years in hiding.
And he did sense worry in her, even as she attempted to conceal it.
He emphasized his words by giving her small, short bursts of the heat he carried inside. It calmed and convinced her further. Comforted her. Every time the silent scream in her faded a bit more.

There were other girls in the room with them. He sensed their curiosity, their interest, their perception of his weirdness. But he didn't share himself with them. He gave them heat, but not illumination beyond that.

– We have our entire life ahead of us, he whispered.

They embraced. He sensed her surprise over his intimacy, his show of emotion, of vulnerability. With a hopeful smile she let her head rest on his shoulder. She didn't notice the two lonely tears wetting his cheeks.

4

Eric Carr scratched his chest, or he tried to, tried scratching it through the large bandage covering most of his upper body.

Resting in his lap was the notebook Stewart had given him. He sat upright on the bed and wrote, took notes as they appeared in his still somewhat fever-hot mind. He was alone. They had given him an entire room of his own to recuperate… or rather to die. He shrugged and grinned and felt cold penetrate him.

He felt fine. His mind worked overtime, that's all. It felt alive with theorems and concepts and words and images. Vivid images from the surgeon's operating room, of Zoe Espershin's grim face, of her stunned surprise when it was clear that he would survive. He remembered heat, and a couple of burning eyes, and he couldn't tell whether or not it was real. And the unreality of it all haunted him.

Espershin entered the room. Her cold eyes fixed on him, still unable to hide her perplexing look.

– So, you've finally started on the Big Novel, huh?

She kinda surprised him with that one. He didn't, generally speaking, see her as a person who cared, about anything. It did seem like more than just an attempt at polite conversation.

– Quite right, ma'am. Did he see things or was she actually reddening? – I kinda *lost* the chance to file the Great Article, and even if someone still probably wants it, given my twenty minutes of fame and all, I also want to give a more detailed report of everything. I see a vast tapestry unfold.

– One of the girls also used that expression. Espershin frowned.

– I know that, Eric said. – It was Iris, wasn't it?

– Yes, how did you…

She trailed off, as she approached him.

– I'm going to check on your wounds and change your bandages, now, she said sternly. – There might be some pain and discomfort.

Her voice, paper dry and cutting like metal.

Her delicate surgeon hands began removing the bandages. To Eric it was like she was touching wood, and just as personal. She worked fast and effective, confident to the point of arrogance.

– I guess I should be grateful you don't leave me in the hands of those brutal military Amazon nurses, he joked.

She pulled, pulled hard, and pain shot through his shoulder. He yelped and wondered if he saw the shadow of a smile in her face.

The bandages were off. He stared at her. Whatever expression she had had in her face previously was supplanted with something he easily recognized as incredulity and… and fear. A thrill shot through him.

His wounds… what had to have been ghastly wounds… were practically gone. Memories assaulted him. He recalled the heat from Stewart's body, Stewart's hands.

– I guess we're looking at a long and hard recuperation here, Doctor. How many years before I can walk again?

– Beyond the grave, she sniffed.

There was some inflammatory tissue here and there, but aside from that he wasn't really in any bad way at all anymore. He met her eyes, and he saw the same fear there he felt inside himself.

– You look fine, she said, pulling herself together with an effort. – You should rest a few more days, just to be on the safe side, but I would say you're off the critical list.

He wanted to ask her if she was always understating things this much, but his voice failed him.

She left, leaving the fresh, unused bandages at the night table. To him it looked like she was running.

5

He was practically up and running the next morning, walking the round with his notebook and pen.

Linda sat upright on the bed, deeply engrossed in a book. The other beds were temporarily empty. The other girls had taken a walk.

He coughed. She lifted her head, and smiled when she saw who it was.

– Visiting me, are you? That's so sweet of you.

– I would like to speak with you, he began.

Bluish eyes sought his. If not for that bluish taint they would have been as colorless as the hair. They had changed. Stewart had showed him an old photo of her and the brothers. The eyes had been deep blue then, like the sky. The photo had been disturbing in more ways than one. He wondered why Stewart had showed it to him.

– And you're going to make us all famous, I hear…

He reddened. She was dressed in a bland hospital gown, buttoned all the way to the neck, but it did no good to conceal her sensuality. Neither did the sight of her still injured, bandaged arm in the sling, and the dark bags under her eyes.

– I've spoken to most of the others…

He tried to keep an even tone, failing miserably. His wounds were still itching, itching a lot.

– So you saved me for last? What an honor.

– I hoped Tilla could tell me something about Betty, but she couldn't, really.

– Neither can I. None of us knew her, truly knew her.

– But you can tell me about almost everything else. You were there, living through it all.

– And I guess you wanted to speak to me alone? That was why you came while the other girls were out… right?

He tried to reply, but couldn't, just couldn't. Not with his voice.

She put away the book and jumped out of the bed, grabbing his hand. Like Tilla and Betty she was a bit taller than him.

– In that case we should get out of here. They will be back soon. Come with me.

She pulled him with her, led him out in the hallway. They met a couple of the girls on their way back. Not long after that he heard one of them, Iris giggle, giggle a lot.

Linda led him into an empty room, and locked the door behind them. There were beds there, lots of beds. She let the arm slip out of the sling and put the palm of her hand at his chest… and it didn't itch anymore. As if by magick it no longer itched.

He unbuttoned the upper part of her gown, and exposed her naked shoulder. It was like with him. Only slightly inflammatory skin broke the symmetry of white skin. There was no wound.

– That's it, now I like you better, she said.

– No more bullshit, now, he snarled. – What is it with Stewart and your brother? There is something. I know that much. I'm not stupid.

– You're the one who must stop the bullshit, she said huskily. – You're crazy. Stop denying it to yourself, and all will be well. Many are. It isn't wrong.

She unbuttoned the gown completely, exposing her breasts. He swallowed when he saw how swollen they were and when seeing the expression in her eyes.

– Do you remember? She whispered, reaching out with a hand to his groin, pushing it at it, closing her eyes. – You remember. I'm so happy, so very happy.

He was unable to think. Hardly noticing her pushing him down on the nearest bed. He tried to, as she crawled on top of him, but all he could think of was blood, blood filling all his senses.

– My shoulder is still a bit stiff, she apologized, she joked. – You'll have to remove your pants unaided.

But he couldn't do it. He was paralyzed. She used her left hand and managed to open his fly. He moaned towards the beautiful dark angel, the white rose. He felt her smooth softness embrace him. Blood filled him. And her as well. She pressed her palms at his chest. Pointed breasts stabbed him. He grabbed them. He could do that, now. Moans rose uncontrollable from them both. Her butt started moving in small pushes and pulls, up and down. The world changed for him, then. Forever. While the dark angel lowered herself on him, covered him, devoured him, devoured his will. And he no longer had a head.

6

Doctor Espershin made her round, made her chores, in a daze of indifference. She had to show her ID twice to cover the premises. She spotted Stewart outside one of the girls' dorms, tensed, and turned abruptly. She walked to the boys down the corridor, but the leering young males hardly gave her any peace.

– Hello, Zoe, Bruce Channon, greeted her cheerfully.

– Doctor Espershin, she corrected him. – How are you feeling today, Channon?

– Bruce, Zoe, he corrected her. – I've got a rather large problem, Doctor. I get a hard-on every time you enter the room…

The time she spent in there, before returning to her office just passed in a daze. Distraught she fumbled with her keys to the locked door, growing even more so when she realized that the lights were on in there, and she had left them off.

Stewart welcomed her inside that small space with his direct stare. He sat in her chair, his large frame virtually surrounding the chair, instead of the other way around. He saw her, saw straight through her.

He saw straight through himself, saw the entire picture within and without.

– Pretty, sexy Zoe, he said, – not ready to acknowledge that fact. Attempting to hide it with the way she dresses, but succeeding badly.

She upheld her mask of cool confidence, but to Stewart she was like a bundle of neurosis, as if she lit up on the spot.

– Is there anything I can help you with? She asked.

– Come with me, he nodded. – I want to show you something.

He rose, and was at the door before she even managed to turn. As she did turn she practically collided with him. She lost her footing. He grabbed her before she fell.

The large man led her off like he would a child. They walked down the twilight hallway. Everything was shadow here. There was no electrical light during daytime, and all illumination came from the distant windows in each end of the corridor or from doors in-between that happened to be open. There weren't that many of them. Those who were open seemed so very insufficient.

– You're a cold bitch, aren't you.

He said it lightly, totally out of the blue.

– I beg your PARDON.

She looked around her, for other people, wanting them to be there, not wanting them to be there. There was actual fear painted in her face.

There wasn't any. If she herself could hear voices, they were distant and immaterial.

– And a virgin to boot, he stated surprised. – It's easy to see that. What a waste. Do you know what they call you? Doctor Ice?

She tried to speak, tried to do more than move her lips, but she couldn't do it. He was so close to her, so horribly close.

– Something happened, didn't it? Either to you or someone close to you. And because of that you've buried yourself, discarded any fire within.

All kinds of thoughts raced through her mind. His voice was soft, but still threatening to her. She wanted to run away, to flee.

– What was it you wanted to show me? She wondered, returning to the cold, impassive mask.

– I'm the locomotive of a runaway train, he grinned, – and it's about to derail gloriously.

Was there anything in his voice beyond the glee, the contempt? It was hard to tell. He led her further down the dark tunnel.

He stopped her by a closed door.

– Listen, he bade her. – Be quiet and put your ear to the door.

She did. He put a hand to her head and pushed it closer.

There were… sounds. At first she didn't understand what they were. It seemed to her that those inside had been running, running far. They were breathing heavily… moaning.

And then she finally got it.

– Oh, God, she gasped.

She turned abruptly and stood face to face with him. Suddenly it was like all her blood in her body flowed to her groin. She pushed her hands at her ears in a hopeless attempt to keep out the beastly sounds. He kissed her lips. She fought. She did. But his hands were all over her body. His hands, everything about him was red hot. He pushed a hand to her groin. She moaned helplessly. Returned his kisses violently. Her legs failed under her. He lifted her up. Easily carrying her using one arm like others might use two. Carried her away. Through the door, into the room opposite the other. As if being very far away she heard the sound of a key turning in a lock, a sting of panic easily quelled.

He began tearing off her clothes, piece by piece. The pieces were like a trail behind them, flashes of reality where no reason resided. They were in bed. They pushed at each other in wild, powerful thrusts. He looked down on her, his prey, fully conscious of his glowing eyes. She was naked. He began undressing, taking his time. She lay in bed with her thighs pulled tight together, both hands moving up and down, as they were buried in her groin.

– Your eagerness pleases me, he said contemptuously. – It pleases me that you're *learning*.

He hardly heard his own voice. It didn't matter. He had problems removing his underwear. It didn't matter. He tore it down his thighs. It ruptured and his cock leaped from its confines, hard and pointing right at her. A soundless scream arose from her. He grabbed both her wrists in one hand and pulled them away, opening her up, smiling cruelly. She fought to liberate herself, but his hand was like a vice. She kept her thighs tight, but he opened her further up with just a light touch. The itch, the pain, the pleasure rose in her, turning *unbearable*.

– You're not totally unfamiliar with the good life, I see. He nodded, incredibly unmoved. Only the throbbing huge thing she couldn't stop looking at, revealed that he wasn't indifferent. – I guess you were involved in some girl play at school, huh.

The lips moved, but not a single sound flowed through them. She nodded, kept nodding and nodding until he stopped her with a stinging slap on her cheek. It wasn't necessary, but he wanted to do it.

He fondled her breasts. They were small, but round and firm. The nipples were hard and pointed straight at him, and had done so for quite some time. He turned her over on her belly, as he descended on the slim body. He was cold again. It dawned on Zoe in a flash of thought. Cold as death. Mark bit into the flesh in her neck, and then he penetrated her virgin shield. The coarse hand over her mouth quelled her scream. The taste of blood almost made him lose control, lose it completely. He held on by a thin thread. A part of him enjoyed himself. A part of him wanted to… to let go.

He felt her pain as a minor sting. Then there was only pleasure, joy in her as well. Her rational being dissipated under the onslaught of his charge. He longed to… longed to let go. But that would mean certain death for her. And to him it would mean… He just wanted to use the female's body and throw it away like the garbage it was.

7

Iris looked completely normal, almost plain at first glance, but at least to Stewart it was as if he was sucked into her sphere, her influence the moment she turned her plain looking eyes at him. Something stirred within him once again, within them both.

Pain touched her eyes. He saw it, saw it through his own hazy red vision.

She sat there alone on the bed, in the room, both timid and bold. Her pale face turned away from him, her eyes staring at the wall. He had no problems recognizing the haunted look in her windows to the soul.

– You don't need to touch me. I heal on my own.

Her voice also had those opposing qualities of apprehension and indifferent courage.

– I know that. I felt you when I touched you.

There was a smile, not quite true. Her pale face turned to him.

– So you want to learn more about me… is that it? Do you want to see what makes the witch… tick?

He was practically glowing. Energy crackled and sparked, and he knew she sensed that.

– From one witch to another, he said calmly.

– So you're not like everybody else. She smiled seductively, sickly. – You don't expect us to pick up the pieces and go home.

– I don't expect you will, he replied, noncommittal.

She rose, abruptly, and walked to the window. Her eyes at the back of her head looked at him, stared at him without pause. He saw her face, not her face.

– I… remind you of someone, don't I?

He didn't reply. His mouth opened several times, but he didn't speak.

– There are a lot of hungry gaps out there, she said, frost in her voice.

– They're standing in line, he nodded, fully aware that she saw him nod.

– And what pieces do you expect to pick up? She wondered. – When the smoke clears, where will you be?

She dissolved in front of him, and when the smoke cleared later the boy sat there with his back turned to him.

Ted Warren waited for him. Mark always called him that, in his mind, as a reminder.

– You wanted to speak to me.

Mark nodded, not surprised by the fact that Ted knew who it was with his back turned.

Yeah, I did.

– I thought we had said everything there is to say to each other.

Ted turned towards him.

– We haven't.

– Why must Tilla and I be here? It's boring.

– As stated, I need you here, as extra eyes and ears.

Stewart paused, deliberately.

– And strange as it sounds, this is a sort of safe haven, at least for the time being. I want to make sure you know all the forces that will be let loose upon you the moment you step out of here, both organized and not, both known and not.

– In London? Ted wondered. – In the midst of the world's attention.

– They will lay low for a while, but they will be there, in the shadows, waiting for their chance. I wouldn't overestimate their cautious approach, if I were you.

– I'm not, Ted said. – We aren't. We know they're coming, and we're ready for them.

– I see, Mark said quietly.

There was a pause. It never turned completely silent between them when they didn't speak, even though none of them was very communicative.

– Elizabeth was here, Mark said abruptly.

The reaction was strong. The eyes under the dark hair began glowing instantly.

– Oh, I see, and I guess you decided you were the only one «worthy» of talking with her?

– Well put, Stewart replied ironically. – Like I told her: You aren't ready for each other yet. You know I'm right.

– I know one thing, Ted said. – You must have done quite a snow job on her to make her leave. She came all this way, and you made her turn at the door. How many truths did you tell her to lie to her, Mark? What makes you qualified to make choices on our behalf? Are you psychic or what?

– That one is easy, Stewart said, masking the jolt he felt behind a grin. – Experience. I'm twice your age. I fought with knives while you were gestating in your mother's belly. Disregard my advice at your peril. And Liz isn't even sixteen yet. Throwing her into the mess, the cauldron you guys have fallen into at this point would be a grave mistake.

– As stated, you're very good, Ted snarled. – Such a slick customer. As often is the case it's impossible to tell what you're actually saying…

Stewart walked past the paragon of rage there on the bed and to the window. Ted's words echoed in his mind. He stared out and down, shaking within. Today was a nice, sunny day. Strong colors. The yellow grass should have been «tanned» in the light of the burning sun. At the very least there should have been grass there. Life.

Everything was black. The ground was black. It wasn't there. Only the black. The dark. There was no use closing his eyes. The dark was still there.

– I feel your fear, Mark. What are you hiding? *What?*

– That one is even easier, kid. I worry about you, your cocky attitude. It's about time you *listen,* and listen *good.*

Ted rose. Rising a fist half up.

– I might, if you begin *leveling* with me.

– Okay, Stewart sighed. – I'm gonna tell you this, and tell you once, in the hope that you'll get it. Let me tell you about the forces we have against us: The Abraxas Omega is a radical faction within the larger lattice of the Thousand Feet. They want more control, a tighter regime. They want an end to all pussyfooting, to the velvet glove.

And it sounded fake, so very fake, even in his own ears, even though that wasn't necessarily the case.

– *Is?*

– Its purpose is thousands of years' old. It doesn't just fold and disintegrate at the first signs of resistance, of a few servants falling out of favor. It's more resilient than that.

It was impossible to ignore Stewart's strangely pale complexion and the inherent desperation in the glowing eyes.

– This wasn't quite what you told the journalists, was it?

– I wanted room… to maneuver. I wanted those still secure in their vaunted positions to think they're safe.

He walked balk and forth between the walls a few times, pacing like Uncle Scrooge. It seemed so ridiculous that Ted almost smiled. Almost.

Stewart shrugged.

– Like there are factions within the Thousand Feet, there are also factions within the Omega. I believe ascending factions are now moving in to pick up the pieces, the vacuum left by those fallen from favor. Nothing has changed. There has been a ripple in the water. The world remains the same. Abraxas Omega and even the Thousand Feet are immaterial. They're quite simply one of many, more of the same. The entire world is our enemy, kid. Do you understand, now?

There was another pause, immaterial, useless.

– You're not telling me anything I don't already know.

Ted Warren said.

Stewart paced a few more times, before stopping, before stopping right in front of him, before he seemed to be reaching a conclusion, making a decision.

– One thing is more important than everything else: You must not, not under any circumstances reveal your paranormal abilities to the public, to all those that won't understand.

– That's the one good «advice» you've given me… I will heed it.

Ted's voice remained challenging, ironic, caustic.

– Good, good…

Mark didn't seem to notice. There was relief there, in his stormy eyes. He seemed strangely subdued, timid… fearful even.

– It's hard to keep yourself in check, to hide what you are, I know that. But try anyway. Your powers are your ace in the hole, the rabbit from the hat in your moment of utter need, of total desperation. There are other ways to defend yourself before it comes to that, methods that are also a great way of concealing what you do… when you do harm, when you fight, when you kill.

They stared at each other with a glimpse of perceived understanding.

– I've got something for you. You said no once before, but I know you've reconsidered a lot of stuff since then…

There was sand blowing outside the window, whispering sand.

He drew the Peacemaker. There was a slight hesitation before he handed it over. Ted accepted it, formed his hands around the cold metal, as he knew, knew beyond doubt that Stewart had done it again, done it with more smoke and mirrors, that the older man hadn't really told him anything.

– This is yours.

CHAPTER TWO

– I am the Oracle, The Storyteller. I see times long past, and times long coming. I see the Nights of Future Past, and I see the Tapestry.

A woman sits by the fire a dark night. An ageless woman. The color of her hair is shifting in the borderline between light and dark. Her eyes are like opaque pools of that darkest night. Her weaving hands shadows, reaching in and out of the flames. Everybody sitting around the fire is looking at her, curious and attentive and expectant. The fire is reaching into the night, into their hearts.

– You know about the forest people. You see them in your shadow, on the edge of your vision every day. Tonight's story is about their early life, their humble beginnings, in an age of unparalleled strife, suffering... and war.

2

Freedom, sweet and unbound emerged as they walked through the streets of London. The small group of people visited the crowded places. It was still early in the year, still cold outside, but as they moved, moved together, they felt the heat stir inside, felt it within themselves like they did in their friends. Pigeons rose in their path as they crossed Trafalgar Square, flapping their wings. The youths felt the pressure wave in their faces, sensed the flapping of wings, distant and close.

– I feel... *Life* here, Iris cried.

They looked at each other, now, when they had finally left the grim buildings, where all the bad memories had been exposed, exposed again. They looked at each other, in feeble attempts to look back, through the murky past, before... before everything happened, to remember how everybody, how all the strangers had been like in that distant city, so long ago.

Ted and Tilla studied Iris, bathing in the heat of her radiant being. She noticed and turned her head, scrutinizing them with her direct stare, slowly smiling.

They were all here, the youths from Denver that had been rescued on New Year's Eve, and also others who had been staying at the hidden-away facility in the English countryside. Carr had stayed, and Frank, so much thinner that they had to keep themselves from staring, had joined them. Stewart had left early. Caine and McKenzie they hadn't seen since early in the year.

Pete was here, and Sandy, and several others still living in the Soho building with them.
– Everything is different, Eric cried, his joy and youthful optimism hardly contained.
It was. That fact was also evident in other people around them, the longhairs and hippies, the still strong echoes of the Sixties. It was far more visible here, than it had ever been in Denver.
The rather large group made their way into the deep recesses of Hyde Park, where the cityscape was hardly visible. Especially these days of colorful costumes and exuberant behavior.
Tilla touched Ted's shoulder and pointed. He followed the line of her finger to a tree, a branch nearby, where they saw a raven. A thrill shot through them. Ice trickled down their spine.
There was a guy playing a guitar, surrounded by a widening, thickening circle. They went there and they joined the others making up the human ring of fire.
– It's so strange, Tilla said to Ted. – There's absolutely nothing obvious dividing us from all the others gathered here, but we're still different.
He saw it, saw them from above, saw their place in the circle, how they joined it, how they diverted from it. And as he did so he turned without turning, looked without looking, at a non-descriptive man sitting by a tree quite a distance away.
– They keep their eyes on us, he said.
Tilla stiffened by his side. Eric heard him, too, and after his eyes had swept the terrain he nodded to himself.
It was later that day. The guitarist had stopped playing. The gathering had stopped by the water edge, as the bright sky turned to twilight. Excited cries rose to the heavens as Iris, Sandy, Tilla and Ted gathered dry branches and lit a fire. There were worried glances, too, but the excited cries persisted. Iris moved close to the fire, while moving her hands above and around it, and those watching were tempted to believe she was actually touching it.
– There's a place, she began, – where there's always mist.
– Yeah, a girl said excited. – Where love is everything.
Iris reached out a hand, and then they heard it, the flapping of wings. And the raven landed on her arm. There were gasps of horror and excitement.
– No, she shook her head. – A place where there's everything. Just like here, but more intense, more pronounced. It's a place of Life… in all its shades.

She was nervous. Everybody could easily see that, see the fear, but the determination burned in her eyes, and she kept going.

– Frank has told me about it, Sandy said. – I can sense his ambiguity concerning it, his apprehension and interest both.

There was a bit of laughter, good hearted, from those who knew her.

– Frank? A boy wondered, looking at the Frank in their midst.

They laughed. Frank, too. It was a good joke.

– Who's Frank? The boy asked curious.

– One of my spirit guides, she grinned. – I'm not sure if he's a crazy as a loon spirit or not, but he claims to be coming from a solar system far far away, and he says he wants humanity to be like them, like his species, to join the Universal peace, that they've come here to save humanity from our baser instincts, our primitive aggression.

– That sounds a bit too good for comfort, a boy said.

– No, no. It was the girl again. – They bring love. They've come to save us.

There were cries of support, but also fairly vicious laughter. But before the situation was given time to escalate it was interrupted by a guy approaching them in something close to a run.

– The cops are coming, he gasped, before rushing on, to warn others.

The raven, spooked, left Iris' arm. Its cry sounded almost human.

The circle dissolved in a matter of seconds, its individuals vanishing in the dark. Grinning, they let the fire burn, generously leaving it to the approaching coppers.

Ted sent a smile to Iris, in an attempt to comfort her. She was clearly on edge, vulnerable, her resolve diminishing, now, when the determination faded.

– We will do it again, he told her. – We will never stop, never stop seeking answers.

The nervous look she sent him didn't exactly convince him he had done her a service.

– I feel them, you know, she whispered, – even when I can't easily spot them.

There was a slight pause.

They crossed through Marble Arch, on their way back east. There was a woman standing in front of the movie theater across the street. She stared at them. Tilla soothed him, calmed his rage, giving him comforting kisses.

– I do, too, he admitted. – They keep their eyes on us. Not close enough or brazen enough for us to react, but enough to convince us they're there. They want us to know. Occasionally, when we begin to feel «safe», they make sure we do.

The others heard him. He wanted them to. Tilla squeezed his arm.
Eric walked in front, his anger hardly concealed.
– I know them, know people like them.
And he seemed as young, as vulnerable as they all felt, perhaps even more so.
Bruce chuckled, shaking his head. He looked more than a little crazy, and they couldn't fault him for that. He looked very much like they all felt.
– What they did to us was nothing personal, to them. The current world didn't, doesn't conspire against us, not only against us, but against almost everybody.
They laughed a lot about that, a raw, brittle laughter. Their brief respite had been just that, another calm before the Storm.
– Thank the Goddess for the journalists, Jane said. – Without the attention we get from them the… others might have been… bolder.
Everybody could easily see the journalists. They, too, followed them, not so inconspicuous, though.
The sun rose. The sun set. That was all. That was all there is.
The very small group of young people walking through the big city sought close to each other, to the comfort of the circle, returning in a somewhat calm haste to their home, the dark fortress in the night.

3

Ted stared through the window. Through it he was able to see towards Leicester Square and Piccadilly Circus. The dust whirled around his feet in the former storage building in Soho. It was the Spring Equinox, The Ostara March 21st 1975. The day and the night, light and dark were even.
The sun set over London. The city's glitter and artificial lights were lit.
– I can feel your rage, Tilla said. – So strong that I could probably feel it from the other side of the world.
She stood somewhere behind him. He knew where, exactly on the spot. He turned, and she could observe first hand how distraught he was.
– I just wish I could make it all go away. He struck out with his hand towards the buildings outside. – All this, all the organized *suffering*.
– And it bothers you, she said softly. – Your dark thoughts bother you.
He nodded, frustration and fear clearly visible in his features.
She walked to him, gently grabbing his arms, staring him in the eyes.
– Remember what I told you, that we're feeling stronger than others, not different?
– How can a burning desire to tear and shred, and kill not be… bad?

– It's just rage, boundless frustration over the way the world works. It's perfectly natural. Everybody should feel that way. I certainly do. I would be worried if you weren't.

– I miss Stewart, he said. – Miss the bastard. I didn't think I would.

– Except for the part of him being kin, I don't think you do, she said softly. – You just miss the opportunity to have something to reach for, someone to measure up to. And there's the old fear, as well, the fear that there isn't, that there won't be anyone left to… to stop you.

He stared at her, and for a moment he couldn't hold back the hatred. The astute bitch!

Stewart had done one last thing for them before leaving. He had made sure they were all given permission to stay beyond the six-month «tourist visa». Another curious thing, another unfathomable act on his part. But with one, qualified result: They were in no hurry. They were free, within limits to make their own destiny.

– I know, now, what Mike felt, at least in part. Ted spoke hesitatingly, haltingly. – His eagerness to meet a challenge, the sense of being able to stop the wind. How he was drawn to the barren, remote areas of the land. He always told me how he loved the desert.

– I understand, she whispered, clinging to him. – I will always understand.

The large bird flapped its wings. They both felt it, sensed its wind.

He turned a bit away from her, pushing her away. On the floor, in front of him were a thick, square board, a hammer and a box filled with nails.

– It's growing stronger, isn't it? Building momentum… like a storm?

In her voice, in her being he sensed no fear. He sensed acceptance.

– It *is* a storm.

He came here every time something irritated him, every time he sensed the rush of rage, in an attempt to relieve the pressure, to stem the tidal wave, to delay the inevitable. He stared straight ahead, glassy eyed. The ember turned to glow, the glow to fire. Suddenly, without warning the three items on the floor were pulled up in the air. There was a loud crack as the board hit the ceiling. Four nails flew from the box. Their points were pushed against the four corners. One strike with the hammer and the first nail was buried to its head. Three more strikes and all the nails were done.

He heard steps in the stairs, female steps, more than one pair.

More nails rose from the box. He closed his eyes. It took less than a second, now, for him to adjust. The board was suddenly covered by metal. The nails were struck one by one. One strike, one nail buried to its head. It happened fast, like with a jackhammer. His second sight had become just as good, if not better than his normal vision. To him it wasn't frightening anymore.

A wind came from nowhere, pushing Iris and Sandy the last few steps up on the attic floor. Open-mouthed they watched the spectacle unfolding before their eyes.

– You've become good, Teddy, Iris whispered in awe. – In fact you've become great.

– You try, he told her, ordered her.

She did. And she did it, but she had to work harder, concentrate more. He sensed her fear, the inhibitions holding her back and wanted to smash them, break them like dry twigs, and he couldn't fathom why he was holding back. Iris sensed his rage and shivered under his stare, and she stopped levitating the items, and they hit the floor with several cracks.

– I'll try. She cried. – I'll do better, for you.

– I want you to do better for *you,* he said, frustration audible in his voice.

She made the attempt, tried so hard that sweat flowed from her brow, but didn't improve her performance much.

He comforted her, somewhat, caressing her cheek. She grabbed his hand and kissed it with wet lips.

They walked downstairs, to the hallway outside the little used living room. Tilla blindfolded him by tying a black scarf before his eyes. He walked inside, to yet another test of rearranged furniture. The objective was to cross the room without walking into anything… And he did so, fast and unhampered. It was like the blindfold wasn't there, wasn't there at all.

– Seeing without eyes, Iris whispered. – Hearing without ears. Smelling without smell. Tasting without taste. Sensing without skin.

Sandy looked at her. There was a strange look in her eyes when she looked at her. Even stranger than when she looked at Ted and Tilla.

– We came to tell you guys that dinner is ready soon, she said.

Tilla sniffed in the air.

– It smells delicious, she said.

– You gals run along, Ted said. – I'll be with you shortly.

He saw that Tilla was hurt for being included in that, and felt the instant pang of remorse, even as he strived to keep an impassive mask.

The girls left. Left him alone. Just as he had wanted. He stood there for a while, listening with the blindfold on, savoring using his enhanced hearing and other senses. Other people might not get enhanced senses when one was no longer there, as was claimed, but he did.

Steps in the stairs. Light, to the point of silent. No one would have heard anything, but he did. The steps didn't worry him. He knew them, as he did his own. A wind came from nowhere and caressed the long, red hair. Tilla felt a light, impatient push in her back. She laughed, and rushed up the last few steps. He stood there with his back turned. She walked close to him, and put her hands on his sinewy shoulders, rubbing them gently, teasingly.

– I can never hide from you, she whispered. – You'll know it's me no matter what.

– I can hear you, he said, – smell you, sense you, taste you, see you through the thickest walls. And that's just during normal circumstances, when I'm not doing anything in particular. When I concentrate everything turns that much sharper.

He turned his head slightly, letting her find his lips with her own. They kissed and he was certain their heat could be seen and felt for miles.

– I didn't want to leave you alone, she whispered. – I'll never do that.

There was more silence, but now it spoke to them louder then ever before.

– We have a good thing here, don't we?

The uncertainty in his voice didn't escape her.

– That's right. She pulled him even closer. – Let's stay for a while.

– I meant…

– I know what you meant. She drew breath deeply. – Most of those gathered here have, after all a home to return to. We don't. You and I… and Linda. What Mark revealed to us more than clinched that.

– That shit, Ted snarled. – He practically came out and told us that you and Betty are sisters, identical twins to boot, and it didn't seem to bother him at all, bother him that he kept it from us for so long. Isn't he aware of how that could have changed things?

– I think he's very much aware of that. She nodded solemnly. – As with many other things.

– I think he knows everything, he said passionately. – And he hides it from us, everything that means so much to us both. I can smell something, something dangerous…

He held back.

– Let's go downstairs, he said.

He pulled her with him. They descended the stairs. She let herself be pulled, but looked at him with a lewd expression moving her face.

– What is it? Tell Tilla.

– What is what? He countered.

– Don't try that with me, she grinned. – I know you. I know what lies beneath your cool exterior.

And more intensely:

– Don't hide anything from me. Not you.
She dug her nails into his arm. The gray eyes grew even more intense.
– Mark gave me the Peacemaker, he finally said. – Complete with domestic and international licenses… before pulling back, pulling out, to get a better *view,* I gather. He still hasn't told us everything he knows or suspect, and he never will. He bids his time, like a vulture, ready to pick up the pieces.
The words forced themselves out of him:
– I believe he has begun the walk… on the Path of Power.

4

The music from below rose at them. They met Frank as he was on his way up. To meet them, they reckoned. They looked at him, trying not to stare, still amazed by how changed he was.
The walk through the Mojave Desert had emaciated Frank Forester to the point of him being almost unrecognizable. It had burned away virtually all excess-fat on his body. But that was only the purely physical result. The more subtle results were far more pronounced.
Aside from his body fat it had burned away all the waste accumulated in his mind throughout his life. He had recounted the tale of the four men's walk through the desert numerous times, told of Stewart's seemingly miraculous role in it, how he had saved them all, seemingly with his force of will alone, and as the boy relived it, he seemed to grow even more set, more determined to throw away the garbage of his past life. Only in glimpses they spotted the old Frank. He had, admittedly, incredibly changed most of them all.
And he kept exercising, kept up his rock-hard desire to change himself.
– I got the first transfer today, Frank told them, grinning solemnly. – It will keep us going for a while.
The first money transfer.
– Mother couldn't stop me from inheriting my father's money, he said. – She couldn't stop me from using it, even though she has stopped me from getting it all by that preliminary court order, and she will undoubtedly keep trying in her schemes. I don't really want my father's fortune either. He lied to me, deceived me most of my life. But we do need the money, and the thought of him turning restlessly in his grave over the way I spend it is also a great comfort.
Passion. There was passion in his words, a passion beyond words in his eyes. Ted and Tilla rejoiced. They saw him being reborn, and it felt good, so very good.

– Money makes the world go around, Tilla said softly. – A very unfortunate state of affairs, but that's how it is.

They observed him, in the large dining room, as he helped Jane serve the food. How he related to her, and she to him, in ways he wasn't yet quite aware of, but they saw his joy, sensed it like a thick cloud surrounding him.

And it encouraged them. They danced as he and the girl danced, embraced as he and the girl embraced, and the fire sparked softly in their eyes.

They sat around the long table, the lot of them, enjoying each other's company, encouraged by each other's presence. This was the way things worked here.

– This is good. Jane giggled in Frank's ear. – You're not burning the meat anymore.

Her eyes were pools of desire. They saw him swallow hard.

There was laughter. They laughed with him, not at him.

They gathered below later that evening, at Eric's insistence, knowing fully well why he had asked them to come. A heavy heart warred with anticipation and hunger inside of them.

He had, for some time now, been teaching them self-defense.

– Welcome, he greeted them, – to the very first evening of Carr's deep course in Martial Arts and self-awareness.

Stunned silence greeted his words.

– Yes, that's right. The light sparring we've done so far was hardly even worthy of being deemed preparation to the real thing.

– It's a worthy pursuit. Ted nodded, nodded to them all. – And a necessity, not the least that.

The joy around the long table already felt faded, distant.

Carr nodded in acknowledgement to Ted.

– The Abraxas Omega program was burned into you all, Eric cried. – And it still lingers, in spite of everything Stewart did, everything that has been done to counter its effects. We'll pick its last pieces. When I'm done you'll be able to hold them in your hand, to pick and choose from its advantages.

– Advantages? Bruce said hoarsely.

Angry stares directed themselves at Eric, hurt and bewilderment evident in the youths' stance.

Eric signed for Bruce to come forward. He did, hesitatingly, carrying his fear on the outside like a heavy load. Eric stepped forward, fast as lighting, hitting him. Bruce and the others stared astonished at him. Eric hit him again. The boy's head was jerked sideways. Blood flowed from his mouth. Eric kept striking him. Bruce backed off. Eric kept hitting him, kept hounding him. Bruce fell, staring up at the man hovering above him, fighting himself on his feet. Eric kept pushing him back, pushing him into a corner. Hands moving fast as the wind kept beating Bruce, beating him up. The pain and horror Bruce felt was echoed in everybody present. Carr slapped Bruce's swollen cheek. Raised a hand to deliver the next crushing blow. And it came, like lightning. It was just as fast, just as cruel as the rest. Bruce parried it. Suddenly his hand moved, not merely in an ineffective attempt to stave off the attack, but in an amazing show of force and skill. Eric kicked out with his right foot. Bruce met the attack, took all the force out of it, and then, just like that, he counterattacked. There was rage in him, but there was also cold, measured calculation. Eric defended himself fairly easily, but he was still hit a couple of times. Bruce stopped, staring in amazement, and Eric stopped, too, smiling grimly.

There was another attack, but this Bruce defended himself against immediately. They stopped again. Bruce shivered violently, as his eyes grew wide and huge.

– Yes, you remember, Eric said softly. – You're reminded of what was done to you. With awareness comes pain. But it's only memories. They don't rule you. They don't define your reality, not anymore. You were supposed to be braindead soldiers in the service of the masters. Now you'll be warriors in the service of yourself, of freedom.

There was a jolt. Ted recalled the training sessions. They all did, all those who had been slaves, the slaves of Abraxas Omega. He sensed them do so, sensed their pain, and it was tenfold in him, in him, too. He heard Iris whimper and fall. He felt Tilla grab hold of him, comforting him, in spite of the horror she herself felt. And he returned her caresses, her deep-felt affection.

– Move! Eric snapped, and they all did.

Those who hadn't experienced what Ted and the others had, moved clumsily, of course. But Ted and the others went deep, and they moved, as Eric assaulted them one by one, as they pulled something from deep within themselves, far more than Abraxas Omega had taught them.

Eric stood there before them.

– Before I'm through with you, you will all have learned true self-defense. You will all have learned to kill. We can all hope you will never need to apply that skill, but we'll only be fooling ourselves if we do. You will learn eighty or so ways to kill, and several hundred methods of disabling opponents, and you'll learn to apply it all like a second skin. It will not be true to life. Exercise can never be that. The only way you can learn to kill… is to kill, but that will come soon enough.

And then, incredibly enough there was a change in him, a change in them.

– And of course, even though you'll learn more violence, you'll also learn, from me, from yourself far more than violence. By going deep you'll learn more about yourself. You will gain an increase in your capacity for violence, but that is, though important, incidental. The greater insight you'll gain is so much more than the mere physical.

He shrugged.

– I learned from my drill sergeant how not to do it, he added. – How to not teach students.

More brittle laughter, sore with life and pain.

The next days and nights passed in a blur, as Eric made his best to imitate his boot camp instructor. It was cruel and hideous, but also so very, very liberating. Seconds passed in a haze, and all they could see was red.

– He doesn't know what he's doing, Ted told Tilla, told her what she already knew, as he shook in her arms.

Very slowly he saw it, saw Iris hit Eric, strike him so hard that he rolled almost to the other side of the room. Ted studied Eric, studied his outward composure, his bewilderment, as he wondered what had happened, what he had seen. Ted had seen it, seen clearly that Iris' hand had never actually made contact with Eric's jaw. What had hit him was nothing but air, air turned hard.

– Wow! Eric rose, drying his lips. – Perhaps I should consider a career in this.

He spoke indistinct, his mouth filled with blood.

– Next, he grinned.

Iris sneaked off, her outward calm hiding a bundle of inward chaos and terror. Ted hurried inconspicuously after her. He doubted that anyone noticed. Except Tilla, of course. She noticed everything. Iris hurried down dark hallways. Her tears burned on his cheeks. Ted didn't see her, but he knew where she was, where she was heading.

Then he spotted Bruce ahead, and slowed down. Bruce was also following her. Ted felt his heart beat, felt it beat in tune with both of them. He stopped just around the corner from her bedroom, as he caught a glimpse of Bruce rushing inside. Ted didn't go any closer. He could easily hear everything going on in the room, hear a spider scratch on the worn wall.

Ted heard her, heard Iris choke as she spoke to Bruce, as they clung to each other.

– I can't go deep, I just can't. There's a monster inside me, hiding, waiting patiently for the day it gets out.

There was a flash. Ted cringed as he recalled the sight, the sense of a large, dark mouth in a shadowy room.

He pulled back, as the girl's crying slowly halted, changed, and she began moaning, moaning in need and despair. He heard them all the way back.

Days passed in a flash. There were base needs and hardly anything else.

– I can *feel* it. Jane cried excited. – I thought I was in good shape, but now it's *rising* within me, everything.

They sat in their circle, right there on the naked concrete floor, closer than ever. There were bruises, bad bruises on large parts of their body, but they felt strangely good.

– I had no idea. No idea at all.

Eric kept doing what he had done for weeks, now, teaching them what he knew, what they knew. Pete and Sandy and the others, too. They were far behind, but in spite of the soreness and unpleasantness and pain they, like the others stuck to the rigorous training program he devised for them.

– Strength isn't enough, he told them. – Your body and mind must be one, supple like a cat, a soaring eagle.

And they sucked up his words, because they knew they had to, because they needed to, desperately needed what he had to offer. And they felt the changes without and within.

Eric fought Linda with knives. It was such a startling sight, such a violent ballet that it looked very dangerous to those who were watching. She clearly did everything in her power to hurt him, as he did not to hurt her.

She lay there on the ground, in his grip, in his power, but she still looked dangerous, still looked deadly.

Eric fought Tilla. She was the best of them, even better than Ted and Linda. She had been good. Now she was lethal. He had to truly be at his best to keep her at bay. There was nothing he could teach her anymore that she wouldn't learn on her own, given time. She had begun to take part in the instruction, and he could stand back and relax a little, as if a great burden had been lifted from his shoulders.

– You may still have a stretch to go. He stood there, breathing hard, enjoying the laughter in his students' eyes. – But you're no pushovers anymore. Never believe you are.

– We won't, they mumbled, they assured him.

– The bad things you've experienced will always be with you, and it should, but it won't dominate your every waken hours anymore. I've done nothing but to unleash your potential and you know that. You know you're so much more than what the masters told you you are. You've never been worthless. They told you you are, but it has never been true. And now it's less true than ever. They told you you're nothing more than what they said you are, that they defined your reality. Now, you, yourselves are doing it, now, and until the end of time.

They sat there, taking it all in, breathing deeply, and the light in their eyes was the moon, was the sun.

The circle split for the evening, parted until meeting again. There was no welcome, no goodbye.

A while later Eric pulled Tilla aside.

– Where's Ted? He wondered. – He should be here, should be a part of the instructor team. He's almost as good as you, now.

– Oh, he didn't feel up to it tonight, she replied lightly. – Please don't doubt his dedication. He's struggling a bit, that's all. He will be back tomorrow.

– I don't, he said. – I'm sure he will.

Tilla waited until she was well outside his presence before allowing herself to reveal a bit of the anxiety playing inside her.

He's afraid, she thought.

5

Linda walked into the bedroom Ted shared with Tilla without knocking. The fabric of her white dress stuck to her skin, the damp skin. Her hair was still wet. Vapor surrounded it, turning to mist.

Ted lay still on the bed, with his eyes closed. He was nude and uncovered. There was a constriction in her throat. She had to swallow several times while she approached the bed.

She spotted the big, black revolver on the table. To her it stood out like a sore throat. She reached for it, but her hand closed only around air. It had slipped away, to the other side of the table. She threw herself at it, missing again. It slipped up in the air, the barrel pointing right at her.

– You're awake, she stated with a certainty she in no way felt.

The only response she received was that of the cock of the gun being pulled back. She froze. The cock fell. There was a click. Then five more in quick succession. She turned. He sat on the bed. Two eyes x-rayed her.

She felt the thrill, the familiar joy well up inside her.

– You scared me, she grinned.

She stared into the deep wells of his fires, and didn't waver a single moment.

A box at the table opened. Six shiny shells rose from it, towards the still levitating gun. Ted cocked it halfway, and opened the flap to the revolving barrel. In a matter of seconds the weapon was fully loaded. It descended slowly to the table and was put to rest there.

– Your skill has grown.

– It will grow even more, he said.

They were alone. There was loud music somewhere in the building, but it faded into inconsequence as she sat down on the bed by his feet. There was silence outside, and nothing but.

– I can meet your eyes now, the totality of your being, now, she said. – I was only a girl in Denver, afraid of everything. Now, I'm a woman, afraid of nothing, ready to take my place by your side.

She reached out with a hand, touching the closest of his.

– You're more powerful than Mike ever was, she said softly. – He knew you would be, and did everything in his feeble power to arrest your growth. I guess his eyes would also have changed, given time, but they would never have burned as hot as yours do.

She let the left strap of the dress slip down from the shoulder, down the arm. One of her pointed, supple breasts was exposed. The nipple was already hard and swollen. The mist in her eyes grew. She rubbed the nipple.

– I'm horny, she said distantly. – I want to fuck you. I want it so much.

She put a hand, a palm on his thigh, rubbing it back and forth, moving herself close to him, on him. There was a flash, where she saw him grab her, tear off her dress and put her on her back, where she was shivering in delight and desire.

He grabbed her hands, pushing her gently away. She looked at him, down on his soft and shrunken cock and her eyes turned wide and uncomprehending.

– Listen… he began, he tried softly.

– Ted, she whispered. – Why won't you fuck me? You've fucked just about everyone else here. Tilla has, too. But me you're honoring with your chastity.

– It's different with you, he said. – You know that. The others are different, because it's just sex. There are no… deeper emotions involved.

– So what? Her voice rose an octave or two. – I'm not out to «replace» Tilla, if that's what you're suggesting. I just want a goddamn fuck like all the others.

He laughed, an ugly, scornful sound making her shrink in her tracks.

– Your intentions are clear as day, he said harshly. – You're just attempting to hide them in plain sight. Quite an interesting strategy, really.

She pulled a bit back, the hurt in her eyes an open wound.

– Linda, listen to me, he tried, tried some more, – we've got a great place here, a place to seek and find and live. We can do so much here.

– Sanctimonious bullshit, she replied with a scornful, hateful grin. – So I'm alone then? Well, so be it. You impotent, scared *shit*.

His patience ended abruptly. His face twisted feature by feature. Twisted dark. His voice changed, becoming very much like hers.

– Well, as you can plainly see you're not exactly turning me on.

She snarled wordlessly, like an animal. Her hand with the long, sharp nails was stopped only by the smallest pf margins right above his crotch. And forced upwards again. His eyes burned, burned her. She screamed furiously, and jumped out of the bed, throwing herself at the gun. She practically froze in midair. He used no words, but she sensed a clear, persistent pressure in her back, pushing her at the door. It opened. She relaxed, her enraged face changing into a sick smile, and as she started walking, as she walked through the door, she turned, and spat some more venom.

– Don't think for a moment you're scaring me. You're much too *weak* for that.

There was a loud bang as he closed the door behind her. Closed it so hard that huge cracks appeared in several places. He sat in bed, shaking, shaking in rage for minutes afterwards. He shook and the entire room and its walls shook with him.

– You want this? He shouted. – Well, perhaps I'll give you this.

And somewhere, in the dark hallways, he knew she heard him, knew she was smiling.

The rage didn't abate, but was increasing by the second. He stepped out of the bed, and started pacing around the room, meditating as he moved, to find his center, as the saying went, in an attempt to calm himself, calm his rage, and it was all totally useless. The floor felt warm against his soles. Everything heated up, ready to explode. He burned energy, he knew he did. It flowed from him like a waterfall. And it was waxing, not waning. Relieving pressure might have helped others, but not him.

Stewart. A distraction, a focusing. Ted walked to the table. He picked up the gun. It filled his hand. Stewart had said this was an excellent diversion, something to be used if not the situation was absolutely critical. A few bullet holes were far easier to explain than if a person looked like a truck or something had crushed him or her. Ted remembered. Stewart had pushed him into using the gun. It had felt awkward, strange at first, but after just a day, an hour or so it had felt like he was clothing himself in a second skin. Ice and fire in his hand felt so natural, so right, and his aim, his ease in treating the tool had improved by the second. He recalled the recoil, the feeling of the bullets leaving the barrel, hitting the target, as if he was using the gun right now. It was as if he had always used it, as if he had never stopped using it.

– I'm… growing, he said to Tilla somewhere in Space and Time. – I discover ever more things about myself, and the power is like a song within me. I don't know if I can control it much longer, if I, in truth want to.

Tilla faded before his eyes, as she always did. Linda appeared, hard-eyed, seductive, willing, dangerous, as lethal as the black blade she wielded. But she, too, faded. They all did.

She was his. There was nothing she wouldn't do for him, except leaving him alone. Damn her!

He walked to the drawer. He kicked a naked foot right through the hard wood and screamed in pain. The wooden chips stuck in his skin like nails. Small droplets of blood appeared on the inflamed skin. He sat down on the floor and pulled out the chips, still holding the gun. The wound seemed bad, but he wasn't worried. He could make it vanish in minutes, if that was his desire.

Sounds. From the hall. Steps approaching. Abruptly he heard the ravens on the roof, the voices from the exercise below, as if the entire world rushed in to overwhelm him. A man. Steps were heavy and light at the same time. He who was out there attempted to push down the handle and open the door. It did him no good. He made another attempt. Harder. Useless. Ted slowly smiled.

– Ted, are you there?

Eric.

– What do you want?

– Talk to you, face to face. Voice was carefully modulated, resolute. – Open up.

– We hear each other just fine. Talk away.

The human being outside the door drew his breath hard. There was anger, just as tangible as the weight of the gun. Resolution increased. There was a distinct quality in Eric's voice. The song inside rose like the volcanic ash, the pyroclastic flow it was.

– Okay, Eric said. – I wonder. I can't help but wondering. About many things I've considered lately. About the miraculous recovery you all enjoyed, while many other victims of the Abraxas Omega machinations around the world have turned hopelessly insane. Stewart… did something to me, I know that. I'm not stupid. And there's more. You. Linda…

Ted directed the gun at the door and fired. Six shots in quick succession, in one, raging move.

Eric threw himself flat on the floor. He shook his head, staring incredulous at the door. The bullet holes were so tight that they made out a single, gaping hole. It was luck, pure luck that he hadn't been in the bullets' path. It dawned on him. He wasn't stupid. The kid hadn't cared if he was hit or not. He just didn't care. The Abyss opened up beneath Eric. He jumped to his feet and rushed off. Away from the secret he had been so sure of taking part in. But the interest faded quickly. He understood a warning when he got one, and this was one of the clearest he had ever been given. A message given to be obeyed.

Fuck off!

6

It was a dry, strangely clear and warm April evening. Tilla was alone in the lower living room. Most residents of the collective had taken a trip to the outside world or were busy. Ted, too. She was restless, and would have joined him if not for her bad shoulder. She had injured it during practice earlier today. It was purely a coincidence that she passed the window just then, and spotted the silver hair in the streetlight glow, the bag the figure carried over a shoulder.

She hurried, hurried fast down the stairs. She practically flew, her feet hardly touching the stairs or the floor. When arriving at the street she was breathing hard. It wasn't really a matter of physical fatigue. She was in better shape than she had ever been. But an anxiety in the soul she could hardly name. She reached the streets just in time to see Linda disappear around the corner. She set out in pursuit, fairly unnecessary as it turned out. Linda didn't stop, but didn't increase her speed either. She kept walking calmly. Tilla grabbed her shoulder and turned her around. She stood there, staring into the cold eyes, unable to utter a single word.

– What are you doing? Linda said with perplexity in her voice and stance.

– What are *you* doing? Tilla wondered hurt and bewildered. – Where are you going?

Linda pointed to herself with the same incredulous/wronged expression.

– I? I'm leaving. And before Tilla managed to say anything she added: – It is as you think. It's because you and Ted.

And then softly:

– Relax, it isn't your fault.

The patronizing made Tilla furious, but she remained somewhat calm. Linda wanted her to lose her cool.

– It's no one's fault, she insisted. – Please understand. It's just the way it is. You must learn to live with it.

– I'm leaving, Linda said. – With that injury you won't be able to stop me.

– Stop you? Are you nuts?

Linda backed off, not taking her eyes off the redhead. Tilla reached out with her hand, as if begging.

– Don't leave. Can't you sense the connection between everybody here, the rightness of it all?

– Ted will come to me, you know. Sooner or later he will come. Until then I will prepare myself, become worthy of him. When it happens I'll be ready.

She stopped and Tilla looked straight at the face that had become a rigid mask.

– Don't follow me, sister. I would rather not harm you.

Tilla swallowed and swallowed while staring after the silver haired girl as she made her way down the alley.

Sadness and an insane rage flowed through her. She rolled her hands into fists.

For a while she stood like that, a living statue. Then she shook imperceptibly and ran back to the house. To what Linda had refused to call home.

7

Ted and Pete led a team of six, themselves included, leaving the Underground at Baker Street Station. If one looked carefully, and knew what to look for, they clearly moved differently from the late afternoon commuters surrounding them. They strolled casually down the street while their eyes and ears and senses never rested, upholding a state of perpetual awareness.

Bruce drew breath deep and content, with a huge smile on his face.

– Behold these old streets, he exclaimed excitedly. – So much history, such a well of memories. It's always a pleasure leaving a London Underground station.

The boys and girls who had known him in Denver stared at him, half stunned, half amused, not surprised. He had changed, like they all had. A hard ball struck in the throat signified the powerful emotions running through them all.

And Ted sensed more. He truly sensed times past, impressions old and new. Sherlock Holmes had never lived here. Ted had learned that he often added things in his mind, added fantasy to what his powers told him, that he had to part facts from the confusion his mind created. He saw the street as it had been. Broad, then as now. But not tarmac, cars and electrical lights. Trees, horse cabs and similar. All that fit, but not the man in the window, smoking a pipe.

The large, dark Regent Park close by almost swallowed him, even when he didn't actually see it in his direct line of sight. The forest was close, even here. The forest was close all over London. It was a city of antiquity, a strange mix of now and then, young and old.

– This is a city, Iris said. – But it doesn't smell like one.

– Smell? Pete said, a bit more jaded, having spent years and years of his life in London.

– You know, Bruce said. – You know what she means.

And they all did.

They kept strolling on the right side of the street, behaving very much like any group of young people would do, trading jokes and insults in an equal manner.

– Eric is around here somewhere… isn't he?

Sandy looked mystified around her with both a wide and shaken smile.

– He is, Jane said. – Even though we can't see him.

There was laughter, nervous, excited and happy.

Ted sensed him. He knew Eric, knew his own «feeling» when Eric was close.

He had one feeling for Eric, one for every one he knew, but the Vietnam veteran was clearly more intense than most, a sort of beacon, easily differentiating him from others.

And then he forgot about Eric, totally forgot him. They passed a building. Both he and Iris froze cold, and couldn't keep going, couldn't rush past the building even though every instinct told them to.

Sandy looked at them both, looked long and hard.

– That's the old King George Hotel, she informed them. – It was closed in 1932. The building has been empty ever since. No one has lived there. No one goes there. It's said that even rats stay away.

They were five or six steps from the entrance. The doors were no longer there. Layers of wooden plates blocked the entrance and they were welded to the foundation by countless nails, but Ted saw the open door, and he felt the cold, cold draft from it, felt it reach out to touch him.

Before he was conscious of it they were way past the building. He looked back at it, and it was just a building, old and decrepit and dirty, not really that different from many other older buildings in town. Iris' flickering eyes echoed his own.

– Focus, now, people, he said. – We're near tonight's objective. – Everybody stay sharp.

His voice, shaken and brittle as it was, calmed her, calmed him.

– Christ, Pete joked. – You two look as skittish as yesterday's laundry…

There was more laughter, but far more contrived this time.

Twilight came. Night came.

Ted looked around him, looked at its shadows, and had to force himself to stop doing it. He didn't have to look at his hands to know they were shaking, shaking badly.

The group turned a corner and one more, and one more. In Chapel Street they passed Edgware Road Station, entering Praed Street, and knew they were close, and grew visibly more cautious. Inexperience burned them, burned Ted. Both in terms of what was ahead, and what was behind. Something had touched them, touched them *again*.

He knew he should have stopped and talked with the others about it, especially Iris, but he couldn't make himself do it, and he felt ashamed.

They found the right address, the right house without much trouble. There were no lights lit inside, as they had been told would be the case. They could only sense the silhouette towards the night sky. The six of them moved, spread out in a wide pattern, listening to the teacher's words, to Eric Carr's crude voice, listening to the quiet voices inside, to the instincts they had, at this point barely tapped.

Ted, Pete and Iris moved towards the main entrance. It was in shadow, in darkness. The terrain fit the map they had been given. Everything looked… looked right.

It was so dark that Pete stumbled several times. Iris and Ted reached the front door several seconds before he did.

– Solid door, he said nervously. – Impossible to break up without making serious noise.

A pair of glowing eyes burned at him. He shut up.

– As I've told everybody, Ted stated, – opening this lock will be child's play.

Most of the tenants in the Soho building thought that meant he would be using a picklock.

Ted Warren put a hand to the lock. It was a Yale, far more complicated than what he had trained on. He concentrated, as Iris put a hand on his shoulder, calming him, making him sweat less.

It was as if the skin on his hand… extended with the air being sucked into the tiny hole. A Yale lock was fine mechanics, easy to destroy instead of open, and his capacity for destruction had always exceeded that of construction.

And this is engineer work, he thought feverishly. This is…

A click. The lock turned. Ted exhaled, opening the door with his hand.

They rushed inside, to the trapdoor on the wall. Ted opened it and turned off a switch hidden there.

– Ten seconds, he said. – Easy.

There was enough light from the street outside, enough for Pete to see, too, as they made their way upstairs.

They had reached the upper part of the staircase when the alarm started howling.

– Damn! Ted swore. – DAMN!

– A dummy, Pete cried. – Assholes.

The loud sound hurt their ears. They turned bewildered. Pete stopped turning and signed towards the door downstairs, for them to leave, leave immediately. Ted and Iris kept turning, seeking eyes penetrating their surroundings, and then finally they stopped. And then there was a crack and sparks, sparks and smoke spat from the opposite wall downstairs. The alarm seemed to be cut off. The awful noise ended abruptly.

They reached the upper floor, moving silently, quickly from room to room. Ted signed to the other two, but kept walking, signed that a man was hiding behind the door to the next room. To him the man's silent breathing roared in the ears. Ted threw himself forward and kicked in the door. There was a dump sound as flesh was hit and flesh fell to the floor. The three rushed into the room, ready for anything, but the caution, in this case showed itself to be uncalled for. There was only the one man, and he was stretched out on the floor, unconscious, bleeding from a wound to his head.

The bag with the money waited for them at the table. Ted grinned wickedly. A useless bait. They opened it. There was a lot of cash there, wrinkled ten and twenty pounds bills. Ted grabbed the bag, and they hurried back down, back out. He closed the front door calmly behind them.

Bruce gave them the thumb up from the other side of the street, and they hurried off, away from there, homeward bound. Triumph and high spirits dominated the six as the two groups joined after a block or so.

Don't get overly confident, Ted thought bitterly. Don't get cocky.

He turned just outside Baker Street Station, as Eric waited for them inside. Ted turned, not to Eric, but towards the itch in his back.

– Someone following us? Pete asked casually.

– I don't know, Ted replied.

They hurried inside, hurried down to the trains, panic, calm and caution burning in their gut. During the next hour they made a series of complicated maze-inspired maneuvers in the Swiss cheese that was the London Underground, but the itch in Ted's gut didn't go away. He couldn't pinpoint it, couldn't say for sure if it was real, and he came to doubt his own senses. Again. They made all kinds of coordinated maneuvers to ditch followers, before finally leaving at Leicester Square Station.

– We're safe, now, Pete assured them, assured himself. – No one could have followed us through all this without us discovering him or her or them. Not the best tracker in the world. No one.

And Ted did imagine that the itch in his back let up, at least a bit.

But he couldn't say for sure.

After an uneventful trip they returned to their home, to their fortress. It embraced them, as they passed the guards, seen and unseen, as they were given howls of approval from a waiting crowd, and there were lots of hugging and kissing.

Dinner waited for them. Joy waited for them, as they all sat down around the long table.

Ted noticed the two absentees instantly. He couldn't avoid that.

– Linda and Tilla left just after you guys, Frank said. – They didn't say anything to anyone.

A worried frown crossed Ted's forehead, all their foreheads.

– They're adults, Ted said finally. – They can take care of themselves.

But that didn't make them impervious to harm. Ted knew that. They all did.

– You shouldn't be overly worried, Iris told him a while later, the two of them pulling a bit away from the rest. – There's reason to be worried, but I don't sense any immediate threat.

He looked at her, as they often looked at each other.

– Vast and terrible forces stand against us, she whispered.

– That's true. He nodded. – Even though the fear we experienced tonight might be just as much due to our inexperience in such matters that is true. But it doesn't matter. We'll deal with it, *deal* with all of it, seen and unseen.

And it was out in the open now, between them. They couldn't hide from it anymore.

He shook her, shook her hard.

– Okay?

– Ok-kay.

He let go of her, slowly, and the boiling fury inside increased another notch or two.

The night people, like they all were, sat up for a while, as they usually did. His mind touched briefly upon unpleasant truths, as he laughed and celebrated with the others. He wondered where to begin looking if they didn't return, and fear and more rage touched his frozen heart.

It was three o'clock when he walked to his room, to their room, and threw himself down on the bed, the cold bed, fully dressed. He slept with open eyes.

She returned about five. He didn't look at his watch. He didn't need to.

The red hair was set quite casual in a top. She looked teasingly at him.

– You've been waiting up for me. That's so sweet of you…

He realized with a shock that she was intoxicated. Her breath smelled. And he also smelled another, to him very distinct scent from her, telling him what she had been doing tonight. He didn't even need his olfactory sense for that. The sight of her was more than sufficient.

– Come to bed, he said curtly.

– I know that look, she grinned. – Don't think you have an exclusive there.

Her clothes, her shirt casually half stuck in the pants, half not, only confirmed the story. Only a few buttons were fastened, revealing more than a bit of what was hidden. He felt, with desperate scorn and humor, «sorry» for the poor guy she had met up with tonight… whoever it was.

She stumbled towards the bed while attempting, halfheartedly to unbutton her shirt. Easily penetrating her bright mood he sensed how fake it truly was.

– Where's Linda? He asked.

Rage flowed through him, directed at she who had left.

– She isn't with us anymore, Tilla said with a hollow voice. – She's gone.

Her good mood was gone, evaporated like the thin bubble it had been. Her eyes were like cut in stone. In that moment Tilla hated she who had left with everything she was.

– She‘s gone!

CHAPTER THREE

Walking streets late at night…

Linda had a goal. She knew where she was heading, but was in no hurry getting there. That would happen soon enough. There was no rush anymore.

She carried the bag in her left hand. It wasn't heavy. It contained only the white dress, the black blade and a few other essentials. On her body she wore, except for the running shoes, nothing but a coat. Nothing beneath. She had feared she would feel naked, but she didn't. Heat coursed through her in waves. Every time she touched the black blade there was another wave.

The Eros statue rose before her, rose one more time. She was positive she had passed this place at least ten times in the hours, the wretched eternity she had wandered these streets. People passed by her, back and forth on Piccadilly Circus. Lights and neon lights flashed at her on all sides, hurting her eyes. People were dressed in costumes and clothes looking like costumes, a variety of another world. A boy ascended the Eros statue naked. There was applause from an excited crowd.

She experienced London in all its variety and joy… and it meant nothing to her.

She walked through Berwick Street, zigzagged between the fruit stalls while observing how the half denuded girls sent seductive smiles to the passing men. Some even sent some to her. She pretended not to notice.

Several of the girls walked around with their breasts bared, as the most natural thing in the world.

Paul Raymond's nude dancers also advertised for the show, below a stylized sign bragging about the show's longevity. Food and people, dreams and life itself, everything was for sale.

Linda walked past it all.

She reached Oxford Street. This late it was abandoned, quiet, completely different from the hectic activity during daytime. Contrary to Soho, the area she had just left, there was nothing here at night.

A group of young boys appeared behind her. They had followed her for a while, from the fruit stalls in Berwick Street. She studied them without studying them, without turning, without giving any indication that she had noticed them.

– Her, boys? One of them wondered, with a loud and fake voice.

– Her, another, the leader nodded.

There were six of them. She allowed them to catch up to her, allowed them to pass her, to surround her.

– What's going on, boys? She asked reserved, calmly.

– You must be kidding… The leader again. The oldest. About her age. – We know what you are, so why don't we stop pretending.

She shrugged.

– Why not? You look like cute boys.

She touched his jaw, studying him like she would a prize animal or an exhibition object.

– I'm expensive, she added dryly, letting go of him, observing the glimpse of fear fading in his eyes.

– We can afford you, he grinned.

It was true. They rented a room at the almost new Hotel Selfridge. Newly constructed luxury.

She kicked off her shoes and removed her coat, revealing herself to them.

– Not much need for clothes, huh?

They giggled nervously. Boys, they were boys. The leader pulled her to him and kissed her on the lips, and she felt nothing.

The silence afterwards, caused by the triple windows was what she recalled best. Of the rest not very much. Only the shame, the contempt and the cold hatred, everything she desired.

She rested, somewhat on her belly on the bed. They dropped the rolls of money on her back as they passed her on their way out. The leader last.

– You were good, he said. – We'll see you around.

She lay like that without moving until dawn. Then she turned, gathered the money, put them in the bag. Then she showered, showered, showered… She used all available towels to dry herself. Then she went to bed and slept a few hours. She ate breakfast in the room, and then she sent for more towels, and showered some more. The gray, late morning light penetrated the room. She took her time brushing her hair, before re-administrating the coat, tying her shoelaces, and leaving the room.

She left the hotel without paying. The fake ID she had given them would avail them nothing, if they should attempt to locate her.

During dinner later, at an exclusive restaurant, she did enjoy herself, enjoyed the servants walking back and forth to please her. She cast a few glances south, but not more than that. She was outside his territory, now, and she didn't want to be found.

After dinner she walked right to the house that was her goal. She had prepared this thoroughly. It had taken her some time to locate the right place. No one at the collective had the slightest idea what she had been doing, what she was up to, and that was how she wanted it.

The door was not locked. She didn't knock, but walked right inside.

Inside was exactly like she had imagined it. Strong colors, deep chairs, tempting, fake. A man blocked her way.

– What do you want? He asked brusquely. – You don't belong here.

– I'm one of Auntie's nieces, she replied cockily.

– You don't look like one to me, he muttered. – Wait here!

She had no desire to leave the place, to change her mind. But even if she had, she wouldn't have been allowed to. They closed in on her from all sides, until surrounding her in a circle. Mostly women and a few men.

Auntie descended the staircase. A woman just as tall as Linda, but far larger. On her heels followed a woman that was almost as muscular. Auntie walked through the opening made for her. She stopped in front of Linda with a threatening scowl.

– Why did you say you were my niece? I don't have any fucking nieces.

– Isn't that what you're calling your employees? Linda asked innocently. – I see you have a few nephews as well…

A few seconds' silence. Auntie studied the blonde girl meticulously and with hard, stinging eyes.

– You want a job, she finally said.

Linda nodded, afraid that her voice would fail her. Dry in her throat at the other woman's scrutiny.

– Any experience?

– A b-bit.

– Okay, let's have a look at you, see if you have what it takes.

There was a vicious, scornful grin.

Linda slipped out of her coat. She removed her shoes with swift, gracious moves, resembling a little girl at a ballet school.

Auntie grabbed one of her breasts and squeezed it. The girl accepted it with hazy, half closed eyes.

– You like this?

– It feels good.

– Men are shit, huh?

– Yes.

Now the voice and eyes were clear as day.

– You're not using make-up?

– I don't need any.

– Good…

Suddenly a powerful arm reached for her, fast as lightning. Auntie grabbed Linda's hair and pulled, pulled hard. Linda's head was forced back, until she had no choice but to look right up in the brutal face.

– I've accepted you. Following that is a number of matters I will only say once. You work from eight to four at night, not more or less. There's one boss here and that is I. Oppose me or fail to obey me, and you'll be severely punished. And if I tell you to wear make-up, you will, understood?

– Yes, Auntie, Linda replied humbly. – Of course, Auntie.

A final pull made Linda moan. The Auntie let go. Linda swayed so much she was close to falling.

– A final word: Our enterprise is semi-official and hardly that. Officially there are no whorehouses in Great Britain. We're running an escort service. If the truth comes out not even the coppers I have in my pocket will be able to save my ass. I won't look with kind eyes at anyone that directly or indirectly makes that happen.

Linda kept quiet. Her eyes were glassy. Auntie gave her a motherly pat on the cheek.

– You're such a nice piece of meat, honey. You'll be quite popular. Grab your coat. Marlene will take you to your room.

Linda grabbed her coat and left her shoes.

The redhead led her up the stairs. Linda saw the hallway before her, and hardly much more. The room was surprisingly large and bright. Linda noticed that virtually all the lamps had colored bulbs. Everything here was done with the night in mind.

– You're not so superior anymore, are you know, skinny doll, Marlene said softly. – Most newcomers get quite a bit jacked down after being given a treat from Auntie. You've learned your lesson well, I gather. You will be obedient and respectful, and not cause too much trouble.

There was no reaction in Linda's hardened mask, no way to discern whether or not she had heard anything of what had been said.

– On the bed, Marlene commanded. – On your back.

Linda obeyed sleepily. She lay there, looking at the other girl while she opened the suitcase. Marlene pulled up the white dress, whistling in acknowledgement. She put it back and walked to the bed, sitting down on its edge.

– I know you've recognized me, Linda, she said seductively. – We never got to know each other very much…

A hand slipped under the coat, reaching one of Linda's warm breasts. Linda looked up at Marlene with shiny eyes. The coat was swept aside.

Hands played in curly hair. A moan pushed itself from between Linda's lips.

– I knew what kind you were.

Marlene undressed, slowly. She smiled triumphantly over the fact that Linda breathed faster.

– We'll become such good friends. The voice hardened. – As long as you know your place. I've got a leading position in this house. The girls pay half of their income to me. You will also do so. I'm very cross when it comes to insubordination. But know that I can be generous, too…

Linda moaned when the large, muscular body shadowed the light. She felt the other's kiss, and threw her head back. Felt the pain and pleasure when the hand squeezed her breasts. Then she sent four rigid fingers into the other girl's abdomen. She threw the dead weight off and away from her, towards the door. Marlene fought herself gasping and painfully on her feet. Linda stood straight on the bed, in full defense mode.

– C'mon, she snarled. – I surprised you, didn't I? I'm no match for you in a fair fight, am I?

– You made a grave mistake, now, skinny. I'll give you a lesson you'll never forget.

Linda jumped light-footed from the bed, charging the enraged opponent. She stopped the bigger girl from taking a step forward with a kick in the belly. Marlene gasped aloud, falling to her knees clutching the lower parts of her upper body, completely defenseless. Linda walked around her, laughing scornfully. Marlene gasped and gasped. She knelt forward with wide-open mouth, as if something was stuck in her throat. Linda grabbed her hair hard, and pulled her up. She grabbed one of Marlene's breasts - and dug her long, sharp nails deep into them. Marlene whined and begged. There was no breath left in her for a scream. But tears of pain jumped from her eyes. Linda pushed her down on the bed in contempt.

– Poor Marlene, you haven't exactly been lucky in your picks lately… encountering several people above your station.

The powerful body on the bed shook in tears, of humiliation, fear, pain. Linda sat down, rubbing her hands over it until she reached the face. She took the head in her hands and turned it towards her own. She kissed dry the tear-wet skin.

– Hush… Don't worry. No one will hurt you. Not even I. If you behave. I'll take care of you, look after you. Take care of what's yours. Because you've *learned,* now, haven't you?

An eager nod. Many nods.

– Where your place is. Everything I can do with you. Destroy you. Kill and torture you. I'll say this once: you better learn, if you haven't already, while you're still able.

Marlene kept nodding, terrified and timid. She attempted to speak, but her lips shook so much that she couldn't produce anything but low, childish sounds. Linda was so fast, so hard, so bad. Marlene attempted to think, but the fear paralyzed her mind, the soul, the will. When she sensed the tongue sliding down her belly, the moan of pleasure rose instantly.

– I'll treat you sooo nice…

Marlene stretched on the bed, surrendering herself to the Queen. The Queen commanded. The Queen was obeyed. The Queen was mighty. Could destroy her with a gesture, a kind word. Marlene responded to the passionate, demanding kisses, very conscious of how easily she had been destroyed. There was nothing but pieces left. She knew that fully, now. The face above her. Innocent, smiling. Kind. She had been fooled. Like many others would be. Satanic, evil. Impossible to escape.

Linda stood before the mirror. Marlene rested quietly on the bed. Only the chest moved up and down. Linda was dressed. The evening dress she had been given that showed a lot more than it hid. That suited her just fine. She studied her body with a pleased, tiny smile. They would come to her, saliva flowing from their mouth, crawling on their all fours. And she would do as she had done now: please herself first. There would be no reason for her to be carried away. She would be seductive and cuddly and observe the shame in their eyes when they had completed their task.

She needed one who understood her. Not only partly, but fully. Eric didn't. Neither did John. Those poor suckers. Ted did, the fiend. And she understood him, like no other, Tilla included. Sooner or later he would come to her. And if he never did… fuck him. There were others like him. One day she would encounter one of them. Until then she would prepare, become worthy of him. When that happened she would be ready.

2

When Tilla awakened, when she opened weary eyes, she spotted Ted in a chair. He sat there, staring out of the window, looking at the world down there. She saw an indistinct silhouette and nothing more. But she did feel his rage. It was so strong that she almost saw it, like a tangible frame surrounding his body. She frowned at first. Then a few seconds later, she experienced in full the frost surging through her veins.

She heard him, heard him uttering something unintelligible that others would probably not understand. But Tilla did.

– Stupid cow.

It wasn't directed at Tilla. She knew that. Ted didn't speak to her, if he was speaking to anybody at all, but to somebody else, far away, beyond his immediate reach.

He turned towards her, his voice crude and ugly.

– That wretched cunt. If she had stayed, been here now, she would have gotten the treatment she has been begging for. She would have gotten it in abundance.

The windows broke, broke in tiny pieces. The pieces and the disintegrated wood flew straight through the air across the street, and slammed into the neighboring building, into the concrete wall. Ground to powder and dust it fell slowly to the street below.

Tilla stared. She couldn't help the feeling rising in her, one of fear and expectation, and also a deeper sense of inferiority, the same she had felt for Mike.

Ted turned towards her, abrupt and scary.

That day there was a strange mood in the building. They all felt it, inevitably, even though very few could pinpoint the source. There were occasional cold spots, like in the otherwise hot kitchen. Jane and Frank, making dinner felt the cold, felt it as someone, someone they couldn't see passed them in the hallway. Not until they saw Ted, saw him like a shadow or a breath, the specter from the past, they realized what was happening, and fear gripped their hearts.

– They talk about me, Ted said to Tilla, – talk about me behind the walls, unable to face me, to speak to my face.

– They're silly, Tilla said. – Silly and ignorant. They're beneath you.

She knew what to say, knew it as the back of her hand. Half forgotten words and phrases from her time with Mike reappeared in the upper part of her consciousness. It was like swimming or riding a bike: you never forgot it.

He ran, ran straight out, through the entire central park area. St James's Park, Green Park, Hyde Park and Kensington Gardens. One time, two times, three times. It did little good. Eventually it did tire him physically, but the powers kept raging unabated within.

Linda was nowhere to be found. He ran through streets, attempting for hours to get a clue to her whereabouts, a kind of mental trace, in vain. He went to the attic, to its silence, concentrated hard in order to «see» her and her surroundings. There was nothing. He kept going at it. When the sun was about to set he had to realize that it was useless. His powers just didn't work this way.

He stared at the horizon, at the reddening sky. The sun had just vanished below the cityscape. He stared and kept staring at it.

– Keep concentrating, Tilla said. – Keep focusing.

He saw her without turning, saw her calm composure, the acceptance in her eyes.

Sweat began flowing from his brow, dissipating before reaching his eyes.

And then he saw it. It was as if the sun returned to the evening sky. Large and red and mighty beyond words it burned the city, the master of the world, over light and darkness, life and death. He saw nothing but red. Red was the color of life… and death, the knowledge burning in everybody riding down the river Styx.

It was dark beyond dark. The mist had descended on the streets right after sunset. It had, as it always did, penetrated walls to the training hall. Usually that didn't dissuade people, but tonight it did. No one ventured there tonight. There weren't many in the two living rooms or in other places of gathering either. The kitchen was empty. Everybody made sandwiches in their rooms or dined out. They crouched sore afraid, no matter where they hid.

Even in the brightest lit public place they felt the shadow descending on them.

The mist penetrated the walls, into the bedroom. Ted crouched in bed with Tilla by his side. Cold and heat surged through them both.

There was a knock on the door, careful and timid. Ted said nothing. He opened the door. The handle was pushed down, the door opened, as if by an invisible hand. Sandy stepped inside. She stared rigidly at the two on the bed. She stopped three hesitating steps into the room. Her lips quivered. She swallowed hard at the sight of the sweaty, nude bodies.

– You can trust me, she said. – I will never reveal anything… about you… never *betray* you.

– We know that, Ted said softly. – Come here.

The door closed with a bang behind her. She shook, but obeyed, obeyed the compelling voice, began her long walk towards the bed.

– Why am I dressed in this white dress? Can't you…

A forewarning look from Tilla silenced her.

The wind began. Began by her feet. Rising. Until it played with her hair. She looked at the window, the closed window. At Tilla's hair not moving.

– Relax.

Tilla met her on the edge of the bed, giving her a comforting kiss.

– Relax, don't resist.

The wind quieted. But then there was the cold, the icy cold. Sandy could see her own breath in the air. This was more than mist, more than ordinary moisture or drop in temperature. Something pushed at her shoulders. The dress' straps broke like twigs. She felt the dress slide down her body, until it crumbled by her feet. The pressure spread to her entire body. She was lifted up, high into the air. Her legs were pushed up until she floated horizontally above the bed. She was turned around and she looked down at the demon below. Holding her breath she was lowered down between the two waiting for her, down there, in the cold, molten flow of fire.

– *Look what we have here…*

The female's skin was glowing hot, but the demon's body was colder than ice, and Sandy burned. She gasped when she saw his hands, resembling paws. He grabbed her hair, pulling hard, so hard that she couldn't move her head without hurting herself. The other paw he used to rub her nipples, already hard nipples and swollen breasts. But he was all over her body. Her feet, her face, her belly, her thighs. In her bush. Not with his hands or any visible part of himself, but he was there. It was as if he… digested her, body and soul, his giant mouth chewing her and cutting her with his sharp teeth.

– Why is your mouth so big, grandma? She joked.

A few tears of pain and fear were pushed from her eyes and down her cheeks.

– The night doesn't care where it goes, he said. – The Storm doesn't care where it blows.

He touched her, and she gasped. She shifted her position slightly, and they fell on her, and she moaned. In the midst of the cold she burned in a mix of anxiety and pleasure unlike anything she had ever experienced.

And then something *happened.* The three of them froze.

– Your name is Penelope, Ted cried. – Penelope Middleton.

Suddenly she saw everything from his vantage point. He blinked. At the first blink there was nothing, just a deep, deep nothing of black, but by the second everything… everything changed. He felt the energy rise from her, felt it pour into him, and as that happened he, for the first time in his life, had the dreams he had suffered since childhood when being fully awake, both diluted and clear as day.

There was a campfire, a tall fire in the middle of the forest. There were a man and a woman there. The man stood over her, shaking badly. She sat with her back against a tree with her big belly, gasping, her gasps being loud as a storm.

The woman rode a horse. A smiling, confident woman, secure in her world and in the world. She didn't look the same, but it was her. The world changed, turning dark and foreboding, and the woman turned timid and small, shaking like a leaf. Suddenly she was with another man in a dark cave, and she was scared. She was frightened beyond her wits.

A group of people gathered around the campfire. In the twilight between light and dark, day and night they began chanting.

A man stood outside the forest. He waved to his men, and they began chopping down trees, chopping down the forest. The man rose to a giant in the dreamscape, in the nightmare.

The nightmare of the World Grinder. An enormous grinder in Space sucking in the Earth, transforming it. Out on the other side comes the Mega City, a planet covered in concrete, plastic, glass and steel.

The World Grinder… It's a metaphor, but also a terrifying reality.

The voice spoke in Ted Warren's mind, echoed inside Tilla Stevens and Penelope Middleton.

He saw himself step into a ring, a circle on the ground. Nothing grows in there, nothing at all, spoke the voice. It's barren, barren like the moon. He stepped inside, and he turned to fire, black and golden fire filling the circle.

There was an old and frail hooded woman walking in the Egyptian sand by the great pyramids. The three in the bed saw that clearly, as if they looked through a not so dirty window. The cars were not modern, but there were cars, decades old models.

And then… then they saw new, sleek cars ride through the desert, one desert, new cars unlike anything current. They saw a hooded figure walk on a desert road, a figure without face, form or fear. They glimpsed the face, the form, and they felt fear beyond fear, terror beyond terror.

Three forms writhed on the bed, gasping in pleasure, in desperate need. Words resembling chants rose from the male's throat, and suddenly from Sandy's as well, and the redhead followed as if in a dream, and the pleasure almost choked her in its intensity. In another room another girl twisted on her bed, caught in dreams, caught in terror beyond any nightmare.

The beast lowered itself on Penelope. She writhed in her pleasure, her pain, and she wanted it, wanted the Beast to cover her. Tilla stood on her knees above the two, swaying, swaying wide. Her eyes were empty, her arms hanging straight down. Ted blinked. He saw images, impressions from her early childhood, before she had been separated from her twin sister Betty. What she herself had practically forgotten, what he wanted to see, and he saw it, saw Sandy reach for him, begging him with wet eyes.

She wanted him, with all her desire, her burning body and her deepest instincts. There was a silent cry of joy and terror as the human beast descended on her, the way it had happened a thousand times before.

He saw, they all saw a jumble of images, impossible to ignore or deny. The ravens on the roof cried out, called to them, fervently flapping their black wings. The girl in the other room sat up in bed, wide eyed and terrified. Penelope cried out. The cold skin surrounded her. The heat burned her, hotter than a thousand suns.

The first thing the female noticed when she opened her eyes was the broken window. Memory returned instantly, of the previous night, terrorizing her, bringing it all back. The shaking began, uncontrollable in seconds. There were hands on her shoulders. There were whispers in her ears. She wanted to shake herself free, to escape the claws cutting her skin, but was too weak. She could hardly do anything more than turn a bit, and stare into Tilla Stevens' clear, gray eyes. That smile. She didn't know how to interpret it. It was so kind, so very kind.

– T-ted, I don't see Ted. Voice raspy. Throat. Dry as sand, as desert sand. – Where is he?

– He's up in the attic, Tilla replied kindly. – He'll be back soon.

Sandy managed to raise her head a bit. She saw the sun. It was afternoon already. The time? She had slept for eighteen hours. Going to bed early she hadn't really been tired. Rather she had been in a state of extreme awareness. She put a hand on her heart. She hardly felt its beat.

– T-the attic? What's he doing there?

– Not what you think, Tilla replied, both cheerfully and somber. – He's attempting to clarify things to himself, I guess, but it does concern us all.

– What did he DO? TELL ME! What is he? What happened… what he did… it was HORRIBLE!

She attempted to grab Tilla's shoulder, but lost her hold immediately and nearly fell out of the bed. Tilla grabbed her and held her steady.

– I'm not sure he did it. Tilla shook her head in wonder, in fear. – At least it wasn't him alone…

Sandy, Penelope looked at her with huge eyes.

– … It was both of us as well. We contributed all of us, to something greater than the sum of the parts. We were *right* about you. What we did tonight was a test of sorts. You were a sacrifice contributing to a magick ritual with an origin far back in time. We knew you had a fair chance of surviving with your sanity in place, but you did far more than that. We suspected *strongly* you were different… and we were right.

Tilla dried sweat from the wet forehead under the sand-colored forelock. Sandy moaned in distress, the night's events still vivid in her mind. The memories didn't fade in the light of day. She put her fingers in the mouth and began chewing on her nails, something she hadn't done since she was a little girl. She was like that little girl again.

– I don't want to stay here. I want to l-leave.

– I don't think it matters where you go, dear girl. You can't hide, not from yourself… and certainly not from him.

There was a draft from the door. They both froze and turned. But it wasn't Ted standing there, as they had expected. Iris rushed inside, closing the door behind her with a haunted look in her wide eyes.

– I sensed you, she whispered. – I was awake. In fact I could not, dared not sleep, but I was still dreaming. I saw a hooded creature walking through an arid desert. In one hand it had a sword. In the other it held a wand with a skull on top. It scared me, it did, so very much.

Sandy turned to Tilla, grabbing her, and this time she held fast.

– You can get us all away from here, she begged.

– It's no use, Tilla said. – There's nowhere for us to run.

– You know. Iris nodded. – You know what may happen. You should be scared. You have to be.

– No. Tilla smiled, as she shook her head. – I'm not… because I can join him.

The two fell silent then. Iris leaned her back at the wall. Her eyes were open, but the visions nearly overwhelmed her.

– I see Its mouth, she mumbled, – the black, black lips in the darkness.

Sandy writhed on her back, wrinkling the sheets, staring at the ceiling. Tilla climbed out of the bed. She walked to the chair, where she had left her clothes and started dressing, dressing without haste.

– Stay here, she told the other two. – There's nothing we can do now but wait.

She began her exercise. It was crude, but strangely effective, calming her body and mind, and deepest Self. It began as relaxation techniques resembling those from the Far East, but it quickly departed from those confines. Sandy and Iris looked at her, at each other, and then they began moving, too, moving like she did.

– I feel something rise, Iris mumbled, as a sheet began moving, dancing by itself on the bed. – Rise from the Stygian depths.

He would come through the door soon. If not they would very soon hear loud ruckus. Screams. Death cries. Then it would take quite a bit longer before he came, came and fetched them.

Steps. Fateful. She bit her lip, didn't quite know what to feel. The steps stopped for a moment. An eternity. The door slid open. She glimpsed a hand on the handle. She saw his face.

And then she knew.

3

Ted changed then, changed again. Unnoticeable perhaps, to most of them. Not to Tilla, Pete, Penelope and Iris. Sandy didn't leave, didn't leave anywhere, but stayed close to Ted like so many of those others present in this miniature world. Ted's change pleased Tilla. She pondered her own feelings, and it still pleased her. The rage that had dominated him for months had quieted. It was still there, lingering, inevitable, forever, but he was no longer an erupting volcano. He stayed away from the attic and no longer used his powers actively. His eyes had the same color of dark ember. That would never change, but they no longer flared in fire.

He returned to his old hobby - reading newspapers. And as he reached out to the world, so did they all.

– To be informed is quite required. Pete nodded. – No matter where you bunk. You can't really believe anything you read, but if you read between the lines, you get to know at least some of the important things happening in the world.

April brought at least two days of happiness from the international stage to them. They cheered April 16th when the news of Pnon Phens capitulation in Cambodia reached them through their old black and white TV. They cheered even louder when Saigon, the South Vietnamese capitol capitulated. There was a grand celebration as they were watching the Americans' humiliating escape from the roof of their South Vietnamese embassy.

There had been 540 000 American soldiers in the country in 1969. Now, six years later the few who were left suffered as prisoners of war, victims of their government's failed policy, prisoners of people who wanted vengeance for years of slaughter, napalm bombs and downright genocide.

– That's a lot of poetic justice, Bruce commented.

Cheers of agreement followed his words.

– But nothing is really being done. Iris stood up and raised a fist. – Nothing about the actual reasons for everything that's wrong. The foundation isn't truly shaken, not even after everything that has happened in the world the last ten years.

– CIA, among many «firms» is still in business, Eric said. – The recent exposure hasn't changed shit. The news about assassinations of heads of state, other political murders, chemical experiments on students. They use a kind of poison arrows, a poison making the victim suffer violently before death occurs. «Words» of warning. I've heard these words from agents several times: «Those who fuck with us will pay for it». They're not even hiding their intentions. They want people to know, want us to know what happens to those who rock the boat. Nixon's fall did shock them, because it's practically unprecedented, but he's just one man, easily replaced by anyone supporting the system. And most people don't see that. They don't want to see it, wandering around in a haze of their own fevered dreams.

They began rearranging the tables in the lower, bigger living room. It began slowly, hesitatingly. Ted walked around with a visible wrinkle on his forehead. Tilla observed him. She saw illumination light his face, energy driving his movements. When his eyes began glowing it was in excitement, not rage.

– Let's make a round table, he said.

He didn't raise his voice, but everybody heard him. They looked at each other in amazement and joy, and began working. There was a noise of another world as furniture was shifted around in a seemingly chaotic pattern, until the dust finally settled, until the noise and the ruckus slowly faded, and everybody stood and stared. The effect was so immediate, so striking that they just stood there for a while, gawking in wonder.

– No one sits at the head of the table, Ted said poised. – No one at its feet. We deny the thought of the Hierarchy so dominating in the current world. Human Beings are equal in *all* things.

They all joined around the round table, as twilight set, as night set. Eric sat there, pondering, a bit distant, writing in his notebook.

Suddenly they noticed the rush of wind many of them had become familiar, even intimately familiar with. They realized that Ted and Tilla no longer were present in the room, and that several others were also missing. Lights dimmed, candle fire rose in the shadows, and then four masked figures dressed in dark robes and hoods entered the room.

– In this modern world we are birds flying in the dark, a voice coming from nowhere said, – flapping our mighty wings above ruins and wretched lives.

Mist rose from the floor. Smoke filled the room from every angle. The moist air had in inexplicable ways entered the building and the warm, cozy place they called home. The four people danced. One wielded a sword. He seemed to be cutting through the others, but they slipped away from the blade of fire and shadows like the dark mist they had become.

The four, Ted, Tilla, Iris and Sandy eventually unmasked, but it felt like they were still wearing masks. There were no applause, but warmth and affection and understanding and acceptance flowed towards the performers as they rejoined the others at the table.

The dark voice kept resonating within them all, as Eric wrote with energetic, excited moves. They sat there, looking at each other, pondering the strange mood, their powerful emotions as pinpricks of electricity pinched their skin, telling them they were *alive*.

Jane stood up, an image of confidence and passion. Those who had known her the longest, recalled her from Denver and from the cabin in the mountains, and they saw how she was more, more than ever.

– Begriffe sind actionen, actionen begriffe, she said. – Concepts are actions and actions concepts.

She paused a bit, letting her words linger.

– Gudrun Ensslin - German rhetoric student in the nineteen-sixties, leading member of Red Army Faction said that, Jane said passionately. – She and her three other founding members of the army are now being tortured and brainwashed in German prison cells. That's the way all freedom fighters are treated in this modern world. And most people don't know or don't want to know what's happening.

– Even words, the language itself, have been redesigned to aid the tyrants, Frank cried. – Just a few people are reacting to the pervasive injustice, looking through the haze of lies, deceit and oppression.

Cries of agreement echoed his sentiment. Years of frustration and suffering erupted in passion bathing them all.

– We need communication without words, Ted said. – Words become a part of society, and are thereby just as oppressive as society itself… except during extreme circumstances.

– By bypassing societies' accepted truths we discover the true reality.

That was Eric. And he looked strange as they studied him, as if he wasn't really there.

They sat there for hours, through the evening, through the night, and even as dawn fell on them the next morning, they didn't feel that they were through with it, realizing that they would never be through with it. They were tired, inevitably. Humans needed sleep. But they weren't *tired.*

Iris nipped Ted's arm, calling his attention to the door, the door Eric disappeared through. They both felt it, his restlessness and anxiety, but they didn't know why.

– They have to use gas masks to breathe in Tokyo's streets these days, Jane said quietly. – That's the future. That's where the world and humanity is heading, and if that isn't one of many reasons for being desperate, I don't know what is.

More cries of agreement, passionate and somber. The night ended. They embraced, they all embraced and went to bed, the day's ugly light marking them, but not as bad as it often did.

Tilla woke up sometimes in the afternoon, stretching, snuggling in bed, knowing immediately that Ted wasn't there, his warm skin not pushing at hers. She looked around. He wasn't in the room either. She knew that, not sensing his eyes on her. As she rose from the bed, the snuggling warmth, the cold surrounded her, almost embraced her. She walked around the room while dressing, distracted, before inevitably being pulled towards the closet. She found what she looked for under a heap of clothes. The Peacemaker, packed in a oily cloth. And the wooden medicine box Stewart had left, a smaller version of what the older man carried with him wherever he went.

– Mark, you sly dog, she said aloud. – Why are you being so generous?

The redhead sighed and put the gun and the box back in the closet. There were a few seconds she stood still, before leaving the room and closing the door quietly behind her.

She found Ted in the training room, exactly where she had expected him to be.

He stiffened, bending his back, bending forward.

– It's me, she said cheerfully. – Your light in the dark.

– I know that, he said.

She walked to him, embracing him from behind.

– This night passed us by all too briefly, she said, longing strongly present in her voice.

Turning somber and sad.

– They all do.

He kissed her hand in a rare show of affection. Her eyes widened. He didn't speak.

– It was all so great, she said dreamingly. – An island of life in a stream of death.

He still didn't speak.

– I know one thing, she said, hesitatingly at first, then with conviction. – Whatever kind of uncertainty that would otherwise haunt us…

She turned him around, looked at him, made him look at her.

– Ted and Tilla will never be what Mike and Tilla was, she said simply. – I *know* that, now, beyond doubt.

They kissed, so effortlessly, so somber. She noticed his reluctance or something close to it instantly, able to read his most minutia shifts in mood. And he could, too, hers. He pulled away, touching her cheek lightly. She did her best to convey understanding, acceptance, patiently waiting.

He fumbled in his right pants pocket, pulling up a note, handing it to her. It was neatly folded. She unfolded it and read:

I'M LEAVING. NOTHING PERSONAL. SEE YOU GUYS.
ERIC

– He has always had a flair for the dramatic, Tilla mused.

– He brought his notes and his manuscript, Ted said. – We will hear from him, one way or another.

– I'm glad, Tilla said.

– May he find his place… Ted said hesitatingly, – like we have.

There was a sigh in the wind, a falling of tears.

– We do have a place here, she stated. – A place where we may think, learn and grow on our own terms.

He smiled. Putting his hand on her shoulder. She twisted her head and kissed it. Its skin was dry and warm.

– It's almost enough to feel optimistic, he said.

– Almost, she nodded.

– A life, he whispered.

She took a step back, smiling teasingly at him, reaching out a hand to him.

– Come; let's turn the city upside down.

He did take her hand, and they walked to the door at the opposite part of the room, left the building through it, to the vast, endless world outside.

4

Tilla awoke when the sun's rays reached her fully. She stretched her body with a wide grin on her face, performing for him. He sat on the chair, looking at her. She never stopped being fascinated by his eyes. There seemed to be life there, independent of the body and face.

– Hi, she greeted him in a flare of joy.

– Hi, yourself, he grinned.

– It's such a beautiful morning.

She stretched her nude body some more.

Sensing more than seeing how it swayed and touched him.

She rose gracefully, sensually, dancing towards him, to him, sitting down in his lap. There were no words, only movement and heat. As she moved up and down on him, as he pushed and pulled inside her, as reality faded around them, as it asserted itself fully and undeniably. Sweat poured into her eyes. She didn't notice. Her hair filled his mouth. It felt like the purest air. She felt every drop. He felt every single strand. Heat exploded in their loins, spreading in an instant all over their bodies, to their entire being.

The heat and the summer came to London, the warmest summer in many years, reaching its peak in July/August. The ice in the youths' hearts melted a bit more. They began reaching out, beyond their confines, the confines of their fortress. They traveled and they received travelers. There was a «delegation» of two from a squatted house in Amsterdam, Janice and Ruth, inviting them to pay a visit sometime. The two girls stayed a week before leaving, before there were a lot of kisses and tears and then, subsequently departure.

– We'll have to get a phone. Communication through letters is unsatisfactory, really. The world is so big, and there is no easy way to do it.

Ted and Tilla stood with Frank and Pete, a bit ahead of the larger group, as they all watched Janice and Ruth leave. Frank and Pete both began to speak, before stopping and looking at each other.

– I'll handle it.

Frank shrugged.

– It's for the best. Pete shrugged as well. – My method would have been more… risky.

Tilla and Ted walked north one day, strolling up Tottenham Court Road and further. Tilla sensed both eagerness and dread in him, and both emotions made him speed up. She let herself be dragged along.

To the old King George Hotel. They held hands as they stared at it, from the other side of the street.

– What do you sense? She asked him carefully, curiously.

He turned towards her, very collected, very focused.

– What do *you* sense?

She looked at him, looked at the building.

– Menace, she shivered. – I sense menace.

– I do, too. He nodded. – Even though that word is insufficient to describe what I sense.

He grabbed her arm, a bit too hard. Her fear grew.

– Most people can pass this place without noticing anything out of the ordinary, he said. – To them it's just an old, abandoned building. The fact that we do notice whatever is in there makes it more dangerous to us. We can touch it… and therefore it can touch us.

He took her hand lightly… and then he walked on, then she followed him, and they crossed the street.

Finding a way in wasn't really that difficult. There was a window on the back. Not really open, but easy enough to pry open. He went through it first. She followed after a brief hesitation.

– I want to go with you, she stated. – I want to go wherever you go.

– Ditto, he said.
They stood there in the twilight darkness, holding hands, seeing each other clearly.
Both their surroundings, fairly easy to ascertain at first, changed into whirls of dust and featureless shapes.
– Concentrate, he said. – Nothing is really changing. Only our perception is.
She did. And the stairs ahead, and the window they crawled through returned. She could see both that… and the rest. What was revealed in the dust and the endless mist.
– Goddess! She exclaimed. – What a stench.
The mood changed then, instantly, turning even more menacing.
There was no further warning. A scratch appeared on Ted's cheek. Blood gushed from the wound. Ted snarled, and Tilla sensed the shock, the astonishment in the surroundings.
– You don't want to do that again, he warned.
The blood flowed, flowed like water, growing as it fell through the air, hissing as it hit the floor. There were whispers, whispers turning into gasps. And then Tilla felt it, felt the cold filling her. She saw herself through Ted's eyes, saw the face twist, saw the menace in the eyes, the eyes no longer her own.
Her hand flashed forward, towards Ted's face. He ducked. Her foot started to move, but then she froze. Ted froze her in midair.
– You get a few seconds, Ted cried. – If you're still fucking with us after that, there will be hell to pay.
– I believe you, a ghostly voice spoke as Tilla's lips moved. – You know, things are usually quite boring around here, but you two have truly lived things up, and you've been here less than a minute.
Ted's eyes glowed. He made a fist, and there were screams of rage and pain. Tilla turned limp in his grip, and he put her back on the floor.
– I feel like wet paper, she said frosty.
The world had just changed - again.
– Let's go, he said.
They returned quickly, but on steady feet, to the window. There were vibrations in the air, forming words. They both turned.
– This has been fun. Feel free to return at any time.
The «voice» cut them like a rusty saw.
– Don't «worry», Ted replied lightly. – We *will!*
Tilla crawled through the window first. Ted followed an instant later. The icy cold left them only slowly, as they hurried away.
– Are you sure…

She shivered as she turned towards him, as she looked at him with worry in her eyes.

– Are you positive there's no… *residue?*

– I would have felt it, he replied. – Felt it like a cancer. Nothing about you is different, compared to before we went inside.

But he wasn't the same. She sensed that. Something had clearly turned in him, making him even more feverish, even more intense and… haunted.

– Is there something you're not telling me? She asked him lightly later that day, as they bathed in the sunlight sitting on a bench by National Film Theater, surveying the Thames River and its traffic and surroundings.

– No, he replied. – You know what I know, that even though we've experienced something that would've been amazing to most others, so isn't it really that remarkable to us. You know that what we experienced in there is with us, here, far away from the actual place, as it will always be, that that isn't anything new either. It has always been thus, long before we visited the honorable King George Hotel.

And a swell of pleasure flowed through her, as they shared the moment, once again shared the incredible that was their life.

They went to Brighton the next day, to the piers and the beaches, to the warm sea, the joy-filled evenings and nights. It was fairly easy to avoid the crew on the trains, and they usually didn't pay the fare. Brighton was like a southern city, at least to them, on those hot summer nights. Others, known and unknown, friends and strangers joined them on their travels throughout southern England, both the South East and the entire southern coast, to the southern western shores.

The two of them journeyed far and wide, sometimes it was just the two of them, sometimes they were many.

They visited a house, an infamous haunted house.

Ted snarled and cried «foul». People around them looked puzzled at each other. Tilla laughed so hard that she feared she would burst.

After more than a few of such visits Tilla finally realized that Ted sought them, sought them deliberately. And for the first time in quite a while she began wondering what he was seeking.

On the Salisbury Plains, on the place called Stonehenge she knew something was up, knew it the instant he stepped into the circle.

– This place is old…

There was laughter, as other visitors reacted to the simpleton in their midst.

He raised his hands, until the arms pointed straight out from the body. Tilla, Pete and Sandy almost burst with curiosity, but didn't dare disturb him.

– We have been here…

Now most of the visitors looked puzzled and even angry at him. Some spoke to the guides. They didn't know what he meant, of course.

– When? Tilla asked excitedly. This was just as important to her as it was to him.

– … not sure. He spoke with a distant, very distant voice. – Tracks cross and crisscross. Four thousand years or so. Something terrible happened here. Blood flows everywhere.

People wondered some more. The angry voices increased in volume. The complaints increased as well. The guards approached them and asked them to leave. In spite of her excitement and joy, Tilla worried. But there was no need. Ted was uncharacteristically good-natured, and let himself be removed quite willingly.

There was the city and piers of Torquay. They walked there, too, at dusk.

– It's funny, Ted grinned. – I feel like I've been here before.

She looked at him, not needing to, to sense his sincerity, to know that, too, as the back of her hand.

– That iron gate. He pointed. – I remember it. The houses on the hill, encircling the bay… It's so very familiar.

She knew what he was talking about, what his words entailed, and a thrill shot through her.

They reached Padstow, a tourist trap in Cornwall. He walked a bit ahead of the group, and Tilla let him, as she walked a bit behind, with the others.

– Is he… sniffing? Rhee Kim said in wonder.

– I would say that's quite a correct description, Pete grinned, not offering any further explanation.

Tilla caught up with him a bit later, discretely, hardly able to contain herself.

– This is different, he said. – I don't know what it is. It feels totally, utterly… normal, but there's still a tingle inside of me that won't go away.

They took the trip north, to Tintagel, to more old buildings and more even older history. Frank rented some tents and a car, and they headed for Darthmoor and foggy nights and dark days. They sat there between fires, between tents and listened to the sounds of the night. A loud howl sounded across the moor.

– That was a wolf, Bruce said, clinging to Iris. – That gotta be a wolf… right?

And they laughed, and it did feel good to be alive. Once again they felt the rare joy given them by experiencing a special moment in time, the odd moment when they felt close, and close to everything.

– This is so great, Iris said, said to them all, and they all listened. – I sit here, and fear that it's all a dream, and that I will wake up one day, and that I'll never get the chance to experience this. We've reason to be grateful… haven't we?

They easily noticed the choking ambiguity in her voice, and they didn't hold it against her. The hard ball in her throat was in theirs as well.

The squatters traveled southern England in groups. There were always at least one day group left in the fortress. And the travelers called… home every day. And nothing particularly dangerous was happening. But the ants crawling through Ted's veins wouldn't let up. Tilla saw it, saw the eyes at the back of his head never cease their restless search.

– We've been left alone for quite some time now, Pete said, as they all watched Ted, as he stood between the darkness and the fire, almost hidden by the shadows he stared at. – It won't last. If anything is too good to be true it usually is.

They nodded. That lesson had been hammered into them from an early age. Ted heard them. He froze, there in the heated night. He couldn't stop freezing.

It was weeks later. They took one single, purpose-filled trip from London to the South East, to Kent, to a village called Pluckley.

– England is filled with haunted houses and places. Iris read from a booklet. – But Pluckley is the icing of the cake. There's a reason it's called «The City of Many Ghosts».

They all saw it, how Iris and Ted seemed to be struck already at the railway station. It was as if they ran into a wall. Blood flowed instantly from their nostrils, and there was so much of it. Their companions cringed in fear.

– It's all right, Ted mumbled. – It looks worse than it is. It always does. It will pass.

– Is this it, Teddy? Iris wondered. – Is this what you're looking for?

– Part of it, he nodded. – I don't know exactly, but I know enough.

He chuckled.

– It's funny, up to this moment I wasn't really conscious of the fact that I was looking.

Tilla rubbed his back, kissing him softly on the cheek, as she looked around her with jittery nerves.

– It's all right, he assured his companions. – It's mostly overwhelming, but not dangerous, at least not inherently dangerous.

They looked at each other with pale faces, laughing a bit, a brittle, uncertain laughter. And walked into the village. The locals passed them, looking at them, not unfriendly. As the group witnessed how the villagers strolled casually around, as they realized that these people lived here, actually lived here they visibly relaxed.

Iris stopped abruptly, at a crossroads turning white, absolutely white. Ted grabbed her hand, holding on, and then he saw it, too. One second, two seconds passed… and then they all saw it.

They saw a man hang from a gallows. His bloated tongue protruded from his mouth like a trunk. The corpse grinned to them. The grin was beyond horrible, beyond any sense of terror they might have had.

The image faded in their eyes, but in their mind it stuck, remaining forever.

Ted threw up as they passed a mill, but he pressed on, and they followed him.

– I won't claim it's all totally harmless, he said, – Under a certain set of circumstances it can prove very dangerous, but as a rule you can look at it as pictures in a book, echoes of time, of what has been.

They had just bordered the evening train back to London.

– It's true, Bruce stated excitedly. – The world is so much more than we can imagine.

And nods and smiles of agreement were exchanged between them all.

– That's right, Ted said. – It's nothing like we've been told, not even resembling the lies we have been sold from birth.

He stood there with his hands rolled into fists. His words were rage, but most of all they were passion, and they all felt that passion burn in their very bones.

– Yes, he nodded. – We've found what we were looking for.

And joy tainted all their smiles.

They were all more than they had been, and merely seconds later, joy completely overwhelmed any sense of horror they might have had.

The train passed a stone quarry. Ted pressed his hands to his ears. Sweat broke out all over his body. Cold sweat like fire. There was a scream somewhere, so loud, so piercing that it seemed to come from the deepest pit.

– It might have proved even more interesting to spend a night in Pluckley, Jane pondered, – but right now… I'm glad we didn't…

There was more laughter. They could joke about it. They could actually joke about it.

In many a night, in later years Ted would hear a scream, a loud, piercing sound causing sweat to break on his forehead, seemingly from nowhere, unable to recall where he recalled it from.

Together, sitting tight, sharing fears and horrors and joys beyond normal ken they returned to the hot London night.

5

The shock treatment continued unabated the coming day. They visited the London Dungeon, the medieval torture chamber by London Bridge. Dark lighting, ritual sacrifices, a church organ, an English family in the nineteen thirties eating the flesh of other humans. The entrance was decorated by a version of the French guillotine.

Ted's eyes glowed the entire time they spent there, but Tilla wasn't worried, at least not overly so. She felt excitement, too, over the sight of the murderers bathing in their victim's blood. But she realized that he forced himself to watch, to somehow inoculate himself from the quiver of pleasure it produced within. She sensed it in herself. It was working.

They visited London Zoo, more than a bit ambiguous. They loved being near the animals, but they didn't need to make much of an effort to see that the wee beasts were hurting, suffering beyond suffering.

Iris danced in front, a bit heavyset, as her «condition» became increasingly apparent, a bit in her own world, humming on a melody, a melody both Ted and Tilla knew well, provoking sadness and joy, and sadness and joy again, again and again. The people in the small group feared they would burst.

They stopped in front of the polar bear cage. It was quite big, with water and a cave and all. The poor big guy stretched flat out on the rocks, knocked out by the heat.

– I would like to meet the person who got the bright idea of bringing him here, Bruce said bitterly. – I would very much like that.

– I can hear them, Iris whimpered. – They call my name. They speak to me. They ask why the world has walls.

The tiger snarled behind the bars, walking restlessly back and forth. Ted felt its rage, felt it resound within himself… and then the tiger snarled louder, as Ted's rage resounded within him. Ted's eyes widened. He felt it, felt the sharp claws. The polar bear rose and began pacing in the unnatural heat. The mountain goats vanished into their caves. The gibbon monkeys went apeshit, jumping up and down in the large cage. Several of them hurt themselves. A large gorilla roared and hit his chest in a row of impressive drumbeats.

Iris clapped her hands. There were tears in her eyes. She turned and embraced Ted, choking in happiness.

– I knew it! She cried. – I'm right about you!

There was nothing sensual about her touch, nothing sensual at all. There was a beyond strange glare in her eyes. He felt the rays hit his skin, the power, the passion, the everything. Gooseflesh broke out all over his body, and when he looked at Tilla's skin it was there, too.

Total chaos erupted all over the zoo. The unrest spread to the other visitors. The «caretakers» went totally bananas.

– Please make your way to the exit in an orderly fashion, a man in a suit shouted insanely through a bullhorn. – THE ZOO IS CLOSED.

Some of the orderlies went more than a bit overboard and started pushing people forward. When people stopped to protest a man struck and kicked them in a savage rout. Somebody struck him from behind and he went down like a felled tree.

Somebody managed to open the gate wide just in time before the brunt of the crowd arrived, narrowly avoiding a bigger disaster. People rushed out into Regent Park, a wild, undisciplined stampede without reason or mind.

The smaller group from the Soho building walked south through the large park, shaking their heads, not certain what to think, what to feel.

– That was amazing.

Pete kept shaking his head.

– That was positively weird, Sandy grinned.

– That was beautiful, Jane whispered, stars in her eyes.

There were still lots of the people from the zoo around them. They were easily recognizable by their troubled behavior and the caustic look they sent the youths. Ted felt a sudden *surge* inside. He spontaneously turned, turned towards the massive crowd behind them.

– LISTEN UP! He shouted, a voice like thunder.

And many did indeed stop, staring at him in anger and fear.

– NATURE STRIKES BACK AT ITS ASSAILANT, STRIKES BACK TENFOLD. IGNORE THIS TRUTH AT YOUR PERIL.

And they stared openmouthed at him, scurrying away from there the fastest they could, keeping their eyes on the rattling snake, fearful, fearing it might strike at any time.

His friends stared at him, too, impressed, but with a bit if fear as well. It didn't faze him. He got a lot of that. Tilla snuggled close to him, kissing him. In her eyes was only respect, admiration.

– I got inspired, he admitted later.

And it felt so much later, as if they had walked for hours, as if only seconds had passed and the image and the voice were still vivid in their mind.

One night in June, when they were all gathered in the lower living room, watching television, something happened that no one understood the reason for, at least not when it happened.

A woman, Margaret Thatcher had, incredibly enough been elected leader of the Conservative Party. The youths were naturally curious. This was something different, and they watched and listened, but were quickly put off, really.

– She's just the old clothed in a new form.

Jane shook her head in dismay.

Ted walked to the TV, and turned it off.

– Hey, Frank cried, – I was watching that.

Others joined in in the choir of protests.

– Sorry, I can't watch that hag, Ted said, clearly more than a bit uncomfortable, cold sweat on his brow.

Tilla rushed to him, touching him tenderly, but this time she couldn't calm him down as she usually could.

– She *is* quite a figure. Pete nodded. – Just *listen* to her, the way she speaks, her intonation, her high and mighty stance. She's the epitome of the establishment. That's why she has made it this «far», why she will keep making it in the times to come. People are fooled into believing she's something new and fresh, but in truth she has long since died on the wine.

– Just like the Moonies, someone cried.

They all looked at Ted, strangely enough, not at Pete, nodding.

Smiling and shrugging.

There was evening, and there was night. They turned off the electrical lights and lit the candles, listening to low-key music, foreign rhythms and chords, giving them notions of another world. They sat there swaying, not doing much but listening. It was quite possible to have a conversation without screaming. Their words mixed with the music. Their voices didn't drown in the music and not in each other.

They had a late breakfast the next day, as they often had. The mood was both excited and subdued, peaceful. Ted remained restless, energetic.

He took Tilla aside, pulling her discreetly into another room. And she knew before she saw the tense expression painted on his face.

– There's one more stop to make…

He took her there, took her only.

To a public meeting in Hyde Park, one of many held there in recent years.

The park was filled with people, a buzz of expectation and fervor coursed through the hordes of people. The two of them spotted an artificial rise somewhere ahead, and their guts made more than one violent tipsy turvey.

– My skin crawls, she whispered.

– That's good, he said, looking at her in relief, – considering the alternative.

His eyes were locked on the man on the stage, the man in white.

– Brian Garrett, Tilla whistled, – the Bishop of California.

– I first encountered him with Linda in Chicago, Ted said. – He was a power to be reckoned with even back then. Now, he's even more so.

Tilla looked at the audience, studied them with a perception that didn't fail her, even though that this was one of the occasions she wasn't exactly comfortable with it.

It wasn't hard to see, not to an outsider, their glazed eyes, their rigid stance, the emptiness of mind that assaulted them.

– Christ, Tilla said, suddenly overwhelmed by terror. – *Look* at them, they're eating it up.

– Or he's eating them up…

He started shaking, and that stunning fact didn't even surprise her. She understood.

– I saw how he transfixed Linda, like he transfixed all the other people in that park in Chicago. She recovered fairly quickly, so I guess the effect is transitory… as long as they don't come under his… his… lasting influence.

He grabbed her hand, and it hurt, hurt terribly.

– The *World Grinder,* he said, his voice hardly more than a snarl.

And Tilla Stevens turned pale, turned white as milk.

– FELLOW HUMANS, the man on the stage cried. – I WISH YOU WELCOME, WELCOME TO THIS MEETING OF SEEKERS.

White-clad people, males and females, bodyguards and eager supporters, surrounded him. There was a surge from the crowd. Ted and Tilla watched chilled to their bones how faces turned shiny and flushed.

Ted turned towards the stage, looking at the man up there, staring at him, and then…

– CHILDREN OF LIGHT, Garrett cried, seemingly embracing them, taking them all in his arms. – TOGETHER WE WILL BUILD THE NEW WORLD PROPHESIZED FOR MILLENNIA. WE…

He… faltered. Ted and Tilla saw it, felt it. There was another surge, a surge between them, between them and Garrett. There was pain beyond pain, as the two of them gasped, as Garrett bent slightly forward and his face, too, was flooded in cold sweat. They saw him, saw how he surveyed the crowd, how his eyes searched and searched, finding nothing, nothing but the endless sea of faces before him.

– WE ARE GATHERED HERE TO USHER IN THAT NEW WORLD, THAT NEW AGE. His voice was strained. Others might not notice that, but Tilla and Ted did. – WE CAN DO IT. WE ONLY NEED TO WANT IT AND IT WILL HAPPEN.

– The number of his followers was high already in the sixties, Ted said, clenching his teeth. – And it has grown, and it keeps growing.

– But he's… afraid of us, Tilla said astonished. – He doesn't know us, doesn't know who we are, but he's still afraid of us.

– We're outside his realm of influence, Ted said, as if sniffing in the air, touching the very world surrounding them. – He's not insensitive. He knows there's something… something present here today, a reason for him to *worry*. We're harder to control, and thereby a threat to him, to his… his ultimate goal… And there's more…

She realized he… *tasted* every word, as if feeling his way around them, attempting to grasp their meaning, the meaning beyond the words.

– We're his Enemy, he said. – The Adversary of him and all his works. I know that much, and we will meet again.

His choice of words… So *weird*. Tilla stared at him, as she attempted to grasp their meaning, the meaning beyond the words.

Garrett kept speaking. He droned on and on.

– LOVE IS THE POWER SUPREME. LOVE WILL SET US FREE. THE WORLD IS FILLED WITH STRIFE, WITH UNREST AND WILLFUL PEOPLE. BUT HUMANITY IS GROWING UP AND THE NEW AGE IS LOOMING IN OUR FUTURE.

Ted pulled back, and Tilla hurried after him, quickly out of breath. It was as if none of them could leave the gathering and the park fast enough.

– It feels like running away. Tilla voiced both their concern, like she often did. – But experiencing this also feels like a kind of catharsis, a confirmation that this is just one more threat we sooner or later have to deal with.

They stopped at a kind of safe distance, knowing nowhere was safe.

– This… She indicated the stage and the crowd behind them with a swift moving hand. – This is horrible and fake beyond words.

She spoke in a low voice. Her body, the entire her whispered to him.

– When you shouted to people… outside the zoo… it felt… *mighty*.

– It felt right, he said. – Right as rain.
A thrill, a dread shot through them both.
– And behold, the rain came, she said softly, unable to keep either apprehension or expectation from manifesting in her voice.
Their bodies left the park. But their minds remained. They never truly left. They would always look behind them, and see if the man in white… if the man in white was *there*.
– He will come for us, he said. – I know that. When he's ready he will come for us all.
Filled with fear and an unnamed hatred, a sickening rage they turned their back on the man in white. And he loomed over them like a vulture, ceaselessly seeking their invisible forms.

CHAPTER FOUR

They spent a lot of time on the beaches of Brighton. His skin turned a darker hue of brown. They swam long hours on the long, southern coast of England. Her skin kept brightening, turning ever whiter, resembling ivory, ever more resembling that of Betty, the more sunrays bathing it. He looked worriedly at her, but she returned a calm look of expectation, of pride.
– It isn't bad, she assured him. – Not a bad thing. I'm finally becoming a big girl, that's all.
They floated on long waves, looking lazily towards the shore.
– I can hear the buzz from the crowd, she commented. – Like a gathering Storm in my mind.
He couldn't. In his mind was only the roar of the sea, drowning everything else.
The two of them left the fortress alone one afternoon, as they sometimes did, and ventured into the city only the two of them, the two of them alone. They dined at an inexpensive, what people in the money would call a cheap hippy vegetarian place north of Oxford Street.
The place… welcomed them, it did. This wasn't people «dining out». This was people coming here to eat, and meet other people, other people with similar tastes and preferences. Here, too were the glances, the looks at the two strangers in their midst, but there were less of them. They played music, loud, but not so loud making it impossible to engage in a conversation or two.
– What do you think? Tilla said, sometime later, as they were eating, sitting in the back of the locale.

– Think about what? He said, seemingly drawing a blank.
– The food, dummy, she grinned.
– Vegetarian food is great, he replied. – I think humans are basically meat eaters, but that's not all we are. We can and should enjoy a multitude of flavors.

And she took his hand, stars in her eyes, and he accepted her hand, fire in his eyes.

A jarring sound broke the moment. They smiled in regret, and kept eating. Sometime later they rose from their chairs, walking out in the hot sun, from the music inside to the music outside. People clapped their hands to the beat. There was a street theater group performing by a wall by the café. People laughed with them and enjoyed the play.

There was a mime doing her thing in the middle of the road. She was dressed in a classic mime costume. White mask, hidden hair and clothes resembling closely that of a clown. And mimes had been the clowns in the past - with a sting most clowns lacked.

Drivers pushed their horns as she played matador and bull with them. She placed herself in the middle of the road, holding up a large red carpet. Some of the cars slowed down, and she dutifully and graciously stepped aside. But when some speeded up, she stood her ground, and forced them to stop. Then, waving her red flag, she graciously stepped aside.

Tilla and Ted headed south and west with a smaller group of people. The spirits were high. They mingled among themselves like old friends, not strangers. The jigsaw group walked down the streets as if they owned it, and they did. They enjoyed the bright day. In a spell of euphoria Tilla broke loose from the main body and ran ahead, dancing, performing for them, for anyone watching, for him, only for him.

She danced, danced as if there was truly music filling the street, and not only what was inside her. For a brief moment there her hair seemed to catch fire, true fire, and the onlookers gasped in horror and a joy they attempted very hard to hide. Then it was gone, and they felt cheated somehow.

Firehair rushed back into his arm, and he felt her burn him in her wild abandon. She laughed giddily and throatily, and for a brief moment he imagined the fire was also de facto present in her eyes.

They headed for St James's Park again, amazed really how they enjoyed the relaxed mood there, the birds and the lake.

But not today.

He stiffened the moment they walked through Admirality Arch. She didn't have to look at him anymore to notice. And he easily noticed that she noticed. And the warm tingle rose inside her.

– Look, he said, nodding to a point ahead.
At first she didn't see it, because she didn't know what to look for. One of the others in their entourage, pointing spotted it before she did.
They looked at the royal castle, at the far end of the Mall, the broad road going all the way from Admirality Arch to the other end of St. James's Park. The castle was cast in shadow, which was weird since there wasn't a cloud in the sky, and the shadow moved, almost as if being alive… and then Tilla realized to her astonishment that it was.
– What is it? She wondered, cold and timid.
The others also looked at each other, bewildered and anxious.
– Flies, Ted Warren said, and Tilla Stevens was struck by the certainty in his voice. – Hordes of flies.
The others looked at him, sore afraid, looking at the Stranger in their midst.
– Come, he bade them.
– Oh, you didn't plan this, too?
Tilla playing the vamp.
– No. He shook his head. – I didn't know.
They walked down - or up - The Mall.
– The Lake is burning, he said.
She and the others had to turn and look, so convincing was his voice. The St. James's Park Lake rested there, peaceful and quiet, the birds and trees and light mist in the air the very image of serenity. Tilla imagined she saw the shadows deepening, and that fire rose from the water, that the very water burned, and she felt a cold dread.
All of them hurried quite the long distance to the castle, past the castle, into Green Park. The swarm was right above them now. They heard its buzz. Saw its darkness as it covered the Sun.
Ted was neurotic, irritable, as he pulled them along, but he was often like that. This was something more. He displayed urgency usually absent.
Green Park looked normal enough. They had actually never thought much about how it usually looked, and now, when they did, it looked strange and foreboding. And…
Then there was the matter of the Swarm.
– Do flies usually behave like this? A girl cried.
– Certainly not, a boy snorted.
– So does anybody know whether or not flies have ever behaved like this? The girl wondered.
– I… don't… know.
The girl looked up, timid and beyond apprehension.
– It's following us, she said in a thin, thin voice.

They rushed faster across Green Park, up Constitution Hill. The Swarm remained directly above them. The girl moaned.

She ran away. A scream rose from her, and she bolted to the right like a deer fleeing from a predator. Tilla turned cold all over. A boy bolted to the left. The swarm followed neither him nor the girl. The others looked at each other, and as if on cue, by telepathy they ran off in all directions. Ted stopped. Tilla did, too. The flies levitated, as if suspended in the air above them.

Their feet moved, slowly, so very slowly at first, but then faster anew, pulled them further towards Hyde Park Corner.

They began crossing the street, and then they heard it, heard the screeching of brakes, way too late.

Two cars collided, and the sound hurt in their ears. They had been alert, attentive and open, and the collision seemed to be exploding in their very faces.

They crouched in the street, blinking, the sound of thunder fading in and out of their consciousness, dust slowly rising and falling, obscuring, clearing their vision, hitting their wide open eyes. People were screaming.

– Help me, a man begged, cried to anybody, repeating it several times like a mantra. – *Help me!*

His voice was hardly audible, but Ted and Tilla heard him. They turned to him as one, to the gaping wound in his gut. They nodded to each other, and he closed the wound with his mind. What had been a gashing hole was pressed tight. He had stopped the bleeding, even though he knew well that his power couldn't heal the damaged skin. His attention wasn't really on the task, wasn't really here, but somewhere ahead. The sense of urgency persisted. He and Tilla tore apart their clothes and used them as bandages. At the very least it served to obscure the way he held the wound closed. The man looked feverishly and gratefully at them, attempting to speak, to voice his gratitude. It hurt and he nearly fell into shock, but he kept himself, somehow from doing that, or perhaps it was Tilla doing that, without truly knowing what she was doing, Ted didn't know.

The swarm kept lingering above them, adding to the loud, insisting buzz in his head. People pointed, sore afraid, but he didn't see them or hear them.

The ambulances with the paramedics finally arrived, probably, amazingly after just a few minutes. It felt like an eternity. Ted rose, and he and Tilla pulled back, nodding, continuing on their interrupted walk.

And then… then suddenly, finally, through the gate and the iron fence they saw it. They could no longer avoid seeing it.

Across the road, somewhat in the deeper part of Hyde Park there was a gathering of people, directing their attention to a smaller stage. Some there by chance, some by intention. The two crossing the road sensed the ambivalence quivering in the air, directing their attention to the giant redheaded man and the dark-haired brown-skinned woman on the stage. There were only the two of them, the woman remaining in the background. No trappings, except the minor stage.

– That's Martin Keller, the archeologist, one woman crossing the road with them said excitedly. – This appearance has been announced for weeks. I had completely forgotten. And I wanted to see him, hear him. His public appearances are rare.

– Archeologist, huh? I would venture a guess that that isn't all he is. A man spoke up sourly.

– I hear he's making Crowley look like small potatoes, another said.

Another slight shiver cursed through Ted.

They walked through the gate, and the park… appeared to them, as they rushed, as they kept rushing the final stretch to their destination.

– The world is large. He knew Tilla looked at him. – So very large.

Keller had spoken for quite a while. They surmised that easily, studying the speechless listeners.

And then it *happened,* as Ted and Tilla joined the audience. Gooseflesh raced across their skin. The swarm descended, falling like dry snow towards the crowd. A part of it surrounded Keller first. People cried out in alarm.

– Don't be afraid of Nature, the man reaching out to them all from the stage called. – Respect it, but don't fear it.

The swarm descended among them all.

– Yuck, Tilla exclaimed, helplessly fascinated.

We brought the flies, she thought. They arrived with us. And we brought him as well. Or perhaps he brought us.

– These creatures are large, the man on the stage cried. – The building blocks of life, of nature, of reality are far smaller, though we should all recognize that scale is an illusion. We live in an illusion, not in the sense that what surrounds us in our daily lives isn't «real», but in its importance. Our perception is formed by propaganda far older than those men in the ridiculous costumes. And today that propaganda is developed to a razor's edge. Joseph Goebbels would have been stunned, been practically ecstatic to see what is under way today.

And the stage dissolved, and he seemed to be among them, among his beloved tiny creatures. And they seemed to speak in his voice, telling everybody about the wretched kingdoms.

His words sparked an outcry and a silent whisper, but everybody had to listen. They had no choice.

The woman by his side produced something that was clearly a large, ceremonial knife. She danced slowly. She turned. And she burned. She cut the fleshy side of her left hand. One second passed, two… and droplets of blood fell from her hand. But it never hit the ground or the floor or the ground, but flew through the air with the flies, hovering like dust with wings, motes of eternity.

– Yes, Blood is the Life, Life is the Blood, he cried. – And blood shall set us free.

– Come, Ted said, Ted snarled. – *Come!*

– You're *hurting* me!

He held her arm so hard that she feared its bones would break.

He rushed towards the stage with her in tow, she caught up in his fervor, his urgency.

The stage had vanished, and the two on it were gone, gone with the wind, and the swarm dissolved, becoming flies again, staying for a while, attracted to the sweat, before flying away. Touches light as feathers faded, and nothing was left but the memory.

– Something…

She touched his shoulder, her hand light as a feather, attempting to comfort him, in vain.

– I can't hold on to it, he cried, beyond frustrated. – The more I reach for it, the more it slips away. It's important. He could have… he could have…

A cloud passed the sun. On a sky without clouds.

– He could have changed everything, he said, a cold, hollow voice.

And she realized that he had reached it, even as it kept slipping away.

– You will, she assured him. – You will grasp one from the pitiless wave.

– I know him. I know them both.

Turning swift as a shadow, he looked at her. He already looked at her, but now he *looked.*

– Not… the woman? She ventured, certainty rising in her gut.

He nodded.

– Him… and Garrett?

She hardly spoke the last name, only moved her lips.

They moved away from the place, caught in the high tide of the crowd. It was just as well. There was nothing there now, nothing now anymore.

– Keller isn't like… isn't like… is he?

– No, he shook his head. – Keller is imposing, even dangerous in many ways, even… related in some obscure way to the… to the… white king, but he isn't twisting my guts inside out.
– But… the man the other day did.
She shook. She couldn't stop shaking.
– I had to see him, see him again. I thought perhaps it was me as a still fairly innocent child reacting to him… the way I did, but it wasn't. He still makes my stomach turn.
– You see his «children» on every street corner. She nodded. – Just like you see the Moonies, the Scientology Church and others, youths that initially sought something new and fresh and were seduced by the old and trite and dangerous. Boys and girls very much… like us. He's catching them in his net like fish.
Her voice, so passionate and raw. He took her hands, uncannily tender.
– For that and many other things, *all* the other things waiting out there, we need to be… what we are, who we are born to be.
She paused, paused a long time, meeting his eyes, doing so very deliberately.
– We need mighty, she said. – We need the Storm.
He looked back at her. And in that look was everything she would ever know about him.
– You're… scared, she said. – Worried… about the Storm. The fear is still twisting your guts. Perhaps not the way it did in Denver, but it's still there.
– Perhaps it should be, he stated.
– NO! She stated, hammering her fists at his chest. – Never! Uncertainty and second-guessing were beaten into you, beaten into the boy, but you're a boy no longer.
He avoided her gaze.
– That night, he began. – I was awake all the time. I wasn't tired. I didn't eat. I wasn't hungry. Sandy… sated me.
There was a strange mix of fear and longing in his voice.
– I'm just afraid of what I might… become, he said, and deep, deep in his eyes ice put out the fire.
She kissed him passionately, desperately drawing blood.
– I see the fire in your eyes, and it warms me, she mumbled. – Your blood is burning in my veins, and I want it to, do you hear me?
– I hear you, his voice beyond hoarse.
– It is part of how you react towards adversity, she emphasized, very deliberately licking blood from her lips, – …the way you *should* react. You go deep within yourself where everything is, where your cauldron is

boiling and churning. The good and bad and ugly and fascinating and mysterious and unending joy.

They sat there, on a bench, a green one, among green and brown trees, in seconds of silence, never silent, as she struggled to express the burning voice inside.

And then:

– I feel it, too. I always have.

And there were no more words for a long time. And the silence spoke more volumes than any word.

They walked on the Embankment somewhere, and the river Thames seemed to roar instead of whisper, as its relatively calm water should indicate.

– So we hide… he stated. – Hide in plain sight… until we are the predator and he is and they are the prey.

– Yes! She replied.

– There's a darkness inside of me…

– Good! She stated. – I love you!

She sensed hesitation in him before he spoke, before he somewhat somberly replied to her passionate words.

– No matter what happens we'll meet it together.

They stopped, turning towards each other.

Holding up their palms, pushing them tight.

– We're one, she said.

– We're one, he repeated.

– I saw this in a dream, she said.

– I did, too, he nodded.

The sun warmed them. It almost burned them

– Most people curb their savagery, she said. – The way they've learned, the way they've been *neutered* from an early age. But we don't. We don't want to. The primitive, the primal is there, still present, ever there, under all the layers of civilization, of dehumanizing people are taught from birth. And this holds even truer for us… our family. We have a characteristic trait, carried, preserved through the centuries, the millennia. We have preserved what most of humanity has cast aside. They have lost something, something indescribably precious. We are Wild. *We* carry the treasure of mankind.

He smiled then, hesitatingly at first, then wider, much wider.

And they were pulled even closer together. They tasted, probed this new, these emotions, these dark passions deeper than the ocean. And they laughed out aloud, unafraid and unbowed. People stared worriedly at them. The fact that people dared to laugh openly this way clearly *terrified* them.

– I won't loose control again, he assured her. – I'll begin the training cautiously this time, preparing thoroughly, build knowledge and power slowly, but surely. And so will you. We'll learn together, learn everything there is to learn. And we'll pick the grains of the golden sand from the hand.

They didn't return at dusk, like they often did. Keeping their eyes open they had a snack or two at a sidewalk café off Leicester Square. The spices in the area tingled their sinuses, tickled their nose and the grin they sent each other, and the blushing cheeks they radiated spoke volumes. They took another stroll down and up Charing Cross Road, under the many trees, passing the many artists painting and drawing life as it happened. It was well into the night when they returned home. Everybody, except Iris had gone to bed. She rose from the couch. She wasn't the same, lithe girl. Her far progressed pregnancy made it difficult to move with any kind of her former grace. She looked at them. It was funny what one single look could convey. Their blushing cheeks blushed some more. She kissed them on those cheeks, giving them a wet kiss each. They understood. In oneself one recognized others.

That night they were in bed before they reached the bed. They touched without touching. The air moved as they moved, shook as the desert haze right above the ground. And their touches, when they finally happened, seconds later, as they fell on the bed, as they writhed and heaved on the wrinkled sheets were like volcanoes spewing fire in the night, making the darkness brighter than any day.

2

Ted looked into the mirror, at his half hidden face, hidden by his shoulder-length hair. He had breakfast, half lost in thought, half eating with Tilla and the rest, enjoying the lovely morning. He and Tilla were more in touch than not. It was funny in a way, experiencing the others' reactions, their good-hearted snickering.

He went to Rhee Kim and her «special» room right after breakfast, smiling in return to Tilla's curious look.

It was a special room. It was Kim's second room in a way. He sat in the chair before a cracked mirror. She stood above him with a scissor in her hand.

– Tell me this be a joke, she had gasped in her halting English.

Kim was a Vietnamese refugee. Kim was her «first name». She had anglicized it by turning it around, calling herself Kim Rhee, now.

She studied to be a hairdresser. They had met her in the place where she was an apprentice. And she had moved in with them fairly quickly. With a little help from Jane and Pete she now did the hair of the entire building. It wasn't as bad as it sounded. They hardly cut their hair these days, when even people in general walked around with long tresses.

Even though she was tall to be Vietnamese, she had to stand on a low stool to do the job. He realized he had grown even taller the last year, studying himself under the sheet she used to cover his body from the neck down. It felt strange to see the locks fall to the floor, like changing on the spot. And perhaps he was. Tilla entered the room with a bemused look on her face. She sat down. During the next minutes several others joined her to watch the spectacle.

A considerable time later the floor was covered by hair, and Kim was still not completely done.

– An ordeal to be sure, Bruce commented. – Poor Kim would have needed to retire early if this was commonplace.

There was laughter, not unkind.

And then the sea on the floor covered Kim's high heels, as she could finally dry her face and step down from the stool. What remained was the fairly short hair Ted had had before the abduction. Kim stared, and so did Tilla and the rest of the spectators. They had come here to have some fun, really, to take part in the spectacle, participation being quite common among them… and were totally unprepared of the result.

They, like Ted himself stared at the stranger in the mirror. He had been aware that he had changed to a certain degree the last two years, that his appearance had changed with his inner self. But this was shocking beyond words. Now, without the hair obscuring the changes they were far more pronounced.

Feature by feature it might be hard to see what the change actually consisted of, but looking at the whole, the soft jigsaw puzzle in the mirror, he was like transformed. He looked far more ethnic than Kim did, in all ways and none. It was strange beyond belief.

He rose slowly from the chair, giving the paralyzed Kim a kiss on the cheek.

– Thank you, he grinned. – This was just what I was looking for. You have a great future.

The joke fell somewhat flat. He walked to Tilla, taking her hand. She shook a bit, shaking free from her partial trance.

– You were far away, now, weren't you?

– It's nothing, she said, kissing him softly. – Come, let's go.

They left the room, locked in each other's eyes. Kim smiled and began brushing the floor, taking on the enormous task of cleaning the floor. The others' present, with a wide range of expressions visible in their face and eyes, began helping her.

They returned to the beaches of Brighton the next day, and stayed there on quite a few bright days during the remaining of the summer. Dodging the fare on the trains. Eating from garbage cans. There was a lot of food available from that source. They fed like beasts after midnight. They lit fires in the sand. And on rare occasions when people discovered them and saw fit to lessen their fun, they vanished like ghosts. The various public officials scratched their heads and wondered what had made them come, what dreams had lured them out of bed and down here to chase off people that weren't here. The three stood there before the bonfire, holding hands, growing stronger together. Iris glowed in joy as the power rose in her.

Tilla's skin turned even whiter. Ted's turned a darker hue of brown. She glowed in the silver moonlight, floating at the top of the frothing waves. He vanished there on the dark sea, like Shadow. They *lived* that brief summer, for the first time in their life. And that life was like the waves, carrying them on.

They swam through the tallest waves, the most unruly of waters, resting there on their back, between the sea and the sandy shore, breathing hard as their heart hammered in their chest, smiling with their entire body.

Except for the countless baths they didn't bother washing much, not washing their clothes either, and especially not in the searing heat, the cauldron the city had become. They drew more than one caustic and uncertain glance from more traditionally inclined people.

A girl whispered something to her boyfriend. He nodded.

– It stinks of sweat here, the girl cried in disgust.

The entire coach stared, and not at the girl.

– I can sympathize, Ted grinned. – I, for my part can't abide the overwhelming perfume stench in here…

She turned pale. The boy, too. Everybody present stared in shock.

– That shut her up, Tilla said, very loud.

The boy wanted to do something, like a dog pulling in his rope. The girl wanted to claw out their eyes. They stayed their hand, not sure why, but with a sickening feeling in their stomach.

– DIRTY GYPSIES, a woman shouted after them as they left the train platform in London Victoria Station.

– Thank, you, My Lady. Tilla curtseyed. – You say the nicest things.

Iris turned to her with eyes turning distant, turning dark.

– We're far older than the gypsies.

Her voice ice against ice a winter night. She cut through them with her razor's edge.

Her friends looked at her as her face slowly returned to normal, worried for her, worried of her, the same emotions they also read in her eyes.

They tried their best to kiss and make better the anxiety in those ebony eyes.

The good mood persisted, in spite of everything, through the weeks, through the beginning rain. They held on to it for their bare lives, filled with fire, filled with ice.

A morning, weeks later, they visited the Saturday market in Portobello Road. Tilla shook her head.

– Heaps of garbage, useless to boot, she said. – And people are buying it.

– Desperately looking for the jewels somewhere in the giant heap, Pete said. – Ever content by confirming their own, self-made illusions.

– The modern condition, Frank stated angrily. – The dreams of electric sheep.

There was a commotion somewhere ahead. At least mildly interested they pushed themselves forward through the crowd and the chaos, while attempting to not lose sight of each other.

Two salesmen quarreled like two dogs in a yard. They seemed to have lost all sense of place, not really seeing anything or anyone except each other, gearing up for what was doomed to get ugly.

– Look at that, Tilla grinned, pointing to an ugly looking mug between them. – Is that supposed to be antique?

The two men stopped their advances, and turned and looked flabbergasted and ashamed at her. They backed off and returned to behind their tables.

– That was quick thinking. A man praised and appraised Tilla.

– Thank you, sir, she replied.

– Tilla is a witch, Iris said, not unkind. – She casts her spells as easy as sand.

To his credit the man didn't back off, and shared in the hearty laughter, probably thinking it was a joke.

And it had to be. They laughed, didn't they?

– Yeah, Frank said. – She rides her broom through the night every full moon.

The group kept going on their light feet, laughing easily, laughing loud and unafraid at the world, followed with envious eyes by the crowd.

No one noticed the first yellow leaves falling on the ground.

As the summer elegy caught up with them.

3

As the days grew shorter and the nights longer it was evident to all that they wouldn't be left alone. The journalists, the publicity, attention were gone, now. The field was open to anybody who wanted to move in. And they did.

A reverend went for them during a television debate program. They weren't explicitly mentioned, but there was little doubt that they were the object of his rants.

– There's no doubt about it. The extended squatting in our proud city these days is immoral and an abomination to the Lord. Especially those youths that we have taken in and helped to heal their sorrows. They're drawing in the poor and the disenfranchised, and even worse: our bright and educated and upstanding youth. So many boys and girls under the same roof can't be good, and should cease this moment.

– That's what really buggers them, Jane said, – that the rich kids come here. They don't care shit about the others.

– He's frothing, Bruce giggled. – Look at him. He's actually frothing around his mouth.

They didn't really care about him, except as one more danger, distraction.

But they did decide to bother with him.

– People like him usually get away with saying anything, doing anything, Ted said, – because no one dares threaten their «moral superiority». Well, let's see about that…

So they put him under surveillance. And the result wasn't long in coming.

Late one night they followed him to a certain house in Kings Cross. They photographed him when a light-clad beauty welcomed him in the door for all to see, welcomed him with a sultry kiss and tight body-contact.

The next day the newspapers received the photos and a detailed background study.

The youths half expected their visas to be withdrawn after that, but they weren't, perhaps especially because of this, because of the bad press it would still create.

So the forces aligned against them stepped up the less obvious and evident pressure.

On September 30th the youths sat in their home and saw Mohammed Ali beat the living bearshit out of Joe Frazier. Their attention was, as it had been for some nights now, diverted by police cars driving by with their sirens on, and also other, less intrusive acts, like people throwing bricks through windows and such.

– Damn, they're doing it on purpose.

Bruce struck the armchair with an already sore palm.

– Yes, they haven't chosen this alternative route through the neighborhood out of practical reasons, Iris said mildly, rubbing his neck.

Summer already felt like a memory, distant and dull.

– Why don't they watch the match? One cried, in a false sourpuss tone.

They laughed, but behind the cheerfulness the uncertainty and worry haunted them.

– I guess they were ordered here tonight, Jane shrugged, – to make them even more irritable, an act encouraging them to be even more zealous in their duty.

– It has begun, Pete stated quietly.

Strangely enough everybody heard him.

Just before the referee stopped the match, when it was at its most exciting, a score of police cars practically closed off the street outside. They blocked both entrances. Ted had stood by the window for some time. He cried out in alarm:

– Pete, call Carl and ask him to come here right away. Iris and Kim, you stay. You know what to do. Half of the rest come with me, the rest go with Tilla.

Fast, but not panicked the two groups rushed to each of the two entrances. They placed themselves tight like sardines there, barring the expected intruders. They waited for the onslaught, but only one of the car-doors was opened.

Pete appeared by Ted's side, whispering is his ears.

– Phone is dead, dead as a doornail. There's no sound. What now?

– Be calm, Ted admonished. – Stay calm, everybody.

A man in a long coat appeared from the backseat of the front car, a limo. Ted had never seen him before, but he knew of him, of his kind. He disliked him at first sight. Two police officers flanked him. Ted knew one of them, knew him well. It was Ralph, Ralph, who had stayed in the collective until he had realized he could no longer bully people there.

– Move! Ralph snarled. – You're in the way.

– Hi, Ralphie, Sandy said sour and sweet, – you've moved up in the world, I see.

– Why? Ted asked him.

– We've been informed that there are illegal substances on the premises, Long Coat informed them softly. – If that isn't correct or is fraudulent, you've got nothing to fear. We'll do a thorough search, and then leave.
And the list of unfortunates in this world that had believed that and regretted it was long and steep.
– Oh, we know you'll do a *thorough* job, Pete said sarcastically. – You've brought enough cops to incriminate the entire building.
Long Coat turned slowly red.
– Do you have a warrant?
Long Coat turned purple when spotting the smile Ted didn't quite hide.
– Do you think we need a *warrant?* He suddenly shouted, totally besides himself. – You're nothing but trash. No one will believe any claim of yours.
– You've got a point there. Pete nodded, deliberately hiding his rage, his triumph. – It's always like that, isn't it? People believe what they want to believe. If they don't believe in the government they'll have to admit to themselves that they're living a lie, and thereby they'll be loosing their footing in life. You would have reached your aim easily, also with us… if we hadn't taken precautions.
Long Coat looked at Ted.
Ted pointed up. Long Coat looked up, at the pregnant Iris waving with one hand, holding a camera in the other. She took a lot of pictures.
– We have more people posted all over the place, Ted said icily. – With infrared film, too, if you want to know. We will remain here, on this spot. None of us will resist you, not in the slightest. But if you invade our home, I guarantee you that those photos will be on every newspaper's desk within the hour.
– Photographs are generally believed. A caustic voice spat from the crowd.
Ralph reached for the club he carried on his hip. Long Coat stopped him with a swift move of his hand. The good Coat grinned.
– We didn't have a search warrant this time, but that doesn't mean we won't have one the next time.
He nodded to his two lackeys, and all three returned to the limo. It was like a signal. The police cars began backing off, as if they were human, sentient. With red and blue lights and honoring the youths with full-blown sirens, they vanished one by one. The limo last. They glimpsed Ralph's hate-filled face.
– He probably takes it as another personal insult, Sandy said.

– I think we should go to the papers anyway, Ted drawled. – With the recordings we did in addition to the photographs we should be okay… for a while, at least.

The next day, miraculously this was the heading in the afternoon edition of a fairly notable paper:

WHAT BUSINESS HAD SIR WOLCOTT
IN SECRET SERVICE IN THIS BUILDING?

This paper was the first. The following day almost all had something about the story, in one form or another.

– You're good, Ted told Iris, looking at the front-page picture of the cars resembling vultures on the prowl.

– I was lucky, she said embarrassed.

– No, you're good, Tilla stated. – The composition and style is incredible. You have a future in this…

Major efforts were made to track down Sir Wolcott, but he was nowhere to be found. According to his press secretary he had left the country «for a long needed vacation». No, they did not know when he would be back.

In short, there was so much commotion that government officials, and others, who couldn't afford to be put under scrutiny decided to stay away from the building in question. The youths laughed giddily, enjoying the moment, knowing fully well that it wouldn't last.

– We were lucky, Ted told them, and his words made them nod solemnly. – The assholes underestimated us. It was too easy to get rid of Long Coat. Those pulling his strings will be far harder to discourage. It's about time to implement simple precautions. Get rid of all the drugs. And I mean everything. Don't use anything, here or elsewhere. And stop turning tricks. And no more filching. Let's not make it easy for them.

They nodded, smiling grimly, determined, and the fire, the joy within persevered.

October ninth, as five of them passed not far away the moment it happened, the Irish Republican Army blew up Green Park Station, killing one, wounding twenty.

Attention turned, in good and bad ways away from them.

Close to a month passed, as the small society began to hope against hope that it had ended for good, before it started up again, picked up momentum and gathered in strength. Different, more hidden, just as cruel and directed.

One night they sat crouched and tight in the large living room. The glowing fireplace warmed them while the cold autumn winds raged outside. The phone rang. Iris wanted to answer it… Ted rushed forward and grabbed it right in front of her.

– Hello.
– Tell the particular whore of yours whose time is soon that we will take good care of her spawn.
– We're going to take care of you, Ted said, deadly calm. His hand whitened around the phone. – And *you* in particular.
Just after *you* the other hung up. Ted put the phone down so hard that he almost broke it. Iris' eyes turned large and round.
– I heard, she said.
Unnecessary. Everybody had heard.
– Fuck, FUCK! Frank began to walk back and forth on the limited space. – How can anybody do something like this? They have no right. Damn me, *no right!*
– When will you learn? Pete asked him wearily. – Those having the power have the right.
They all started pacing, not saying much at first. Distress, very evident from the start grew.
Suns and moons rose and fell as twilight and night descended outside.
Frank entered the large living room as most of them had gathered around the couch and table, watching television, not really seeing what was on it. His left hand was curled into a fist.
– In a world of cruel daylight we struggle to find our footing, he said. – Something as mundane as dignity.
They looked at him, at his tight, enraged features.
– Those arrayed against us have a frightening influence in this world, he said, very calm, very centered. – But we're not without resources of our own.
He waited. They waited. They felt expectation and other, less identifiable emotions.
– We've got power, he said. – We're not powerless, not as individuals and not as a group, the tribe we've grown into. And… we also have some… untraditional means at our disposal.
There was silence. They grinned, but they looked solemnly at him.
– That's true, Iris said slowly, with only a hint of apprehension in her voice. – That's *true!*
It was strange. No one spoke. No one made any decisive gesture. But eyes met eyes, eyes deep and black, and when Iris rose almost everybody present shifted in their seats, and she headed for the door and walked out of the room, they rose, too, and they followed her into the darkness.
She walked ahead with a single candle in her hand. Tilla grabbed some more from the drawer, candles yet to be lit. They walked up the stairs.

Everybody knew that, well before they reached the older, dustier part of the building.

The attic breathed as they entered it, as if welcoming them.

– I can feel it, Iris mumbled. – Feel her.

She took a piece of chalk from her pocket, bent down and drew a pentacle, doing so with practiced ease, fully aware like the rest of them were that she had only done it a few times before.

Tilla placed the candles evenly across the floor, outside the… the perimeter. Dark fire lit the vast space, exposing the patchwork ceiling.

– Sit in a circle. Iris directed them with a voice already hollow. – Just about touching the sacred form.

– Behold the priestess, Sandy cried. – Behold Thalama, Goddess of Destiny.

They sat down, good humored and solemn both, turned inward, facing the center of the pentacle. Iris smiled, a bit strained.

– This is our Place of Power, she declared. – It has already been consecrated… consecrated to *Magick*. Now, all we need is to make use of it, to bind us to it, to bind it to us… forever.

– That's *all?*

Jane giggled nervously. And several others followed her.

– This is serious stuff, Iris corrected them sharply, a bit sharper than she had intended. The laughter died. – This will work. Magick is real. A force residing within, the one, true force of the Universe. I have dreams, you know. You wouldn't *believe* the dreams I have…

She trailed off, visibly shaking, before clenching her teeth, before pulling herself together. They looked at her, now. She made them look, as she pulled a large, two-edged knife from her robe. Turning to Frank, she handed him the knife. It rested in her palm.

– Take it, she commanded.

He looked anxiously at it, hesitating.

– You are the instigator, she told Frank. – You are first.

He took it.

– What do I do?

– Make the incision in the meaty part of your hand, she said dryly. – That way you won't have to strive clumsily for minutes…

There were gasps of horror, quickly fading, submerged in the buzz, the wind, the rising buzz, the increasing wind.

He held out his left hand over the floor, hesitating a bit more, before raising the knife…

– Don't do it! Iris said quickly. – Don't…

Her words came too late. He had already done it, done the irreversible deed.

He made a quick incision, both his hands clearly shaking. The blood hit the floor, hit the dust. A bit of mist rose from the ruby vapor. They saw it. They could all see it.

Iris sagged a bit, before straightening, before crumbling.

– The book is burning, she mumbled. – Everything is up for grabs.

They didn't hear her, didn't really, as black eyes turned on them again.

– Thalama, Mistress of Destiny, Iris cried, – we call you. We call you by blood, by mind and by fire. Send your Shadow to us, so we might know enlightenment.

Everything, even the most insensitive sensed it. Nothing happened. They heard the wind. There was no wind.

Ted took the knife and cut his hand. There was blood, a lot of blood flowing from the small incision. Compared to Frank it was like he should have cut a vein or something. The blood flowed, and as it hit the floor it boiled and hissed.

– Did it just turn colder in here, Kim whispered.

Suddenly she spoke without accent. As long as they had known her she had stumbled over the words and switched them around, making her non-English origin evident. Now, as fast as one strike of a match it was gone.

They noticed their breath in the air.

Iris' eyes rolled back in her skull, and turned white.

– Christ, a boy exclaimed. – I've seen people try something like this for years without making it work.

The girl beside him hushed him up.

Iris rocked a bit back and forth, hardly noticeable. Or it would have been, if not everyone in the room hadn't suddenly turned immensely sensitive to such small details. The air… moved. They saw it, saw it roll like waves. Suddenly there was wind, wind like there were no walls, no ceiling, as if they sat at the top of the mountain… and could see the vast fields below.

Tilla cut her hand. The blood flowed and landed in the dust.

– I see, Iris mumbled, as she cut her hand, as thick, thick, red, red blood gushed from her hand, splashing on the floor. – I see an old woman in the sands of Egypt. I see a younger woman with ruby eyes in a European city during wartime. She falls. The old woman falls in the sand. The young woman is hit by shrapnel from a nearby bomb, and disintegrated from another bomb. They die. They both die, at the very same moment, and they turn to mist and shadow. I see two young girls, twins, die in a car crash. I see them. I see them.

There were cries, numerous from the circle.
– I see, too. I see so much.
And there were echoes, and stir of echoes from the dark corners of the room.
Bruce was the last. He sat there with the knife, the bloody knife in his hand, waited for one second, two. He smiled and cut his hand.
The circle was complete. They all stared as the blood on the floor stretched and mingled, as it formed a circle within a circle, a thin, thin line, thickening, thickening, puling, and glowing, glowing in ruby red.
– This is just a brief look, Iris mumbled, rocking back and forth. – A brief like nothing look into infinity. Infinity will come to us. Eternity will come to us. There's a door slamming open. A book slams shut, for a while, a short while, or so it seems. The door, the wall itself disintegrates and everything… everything will become as it is… Infinite.
The air above, the floor below, the air and walls, not walls… opened up.
– This is incredible, a girl gasped. – This can't be happening… can it?
She almost begged.
But there was wonder in her eyes.
– There are teeth, Tilla said, in a ghostly voice. – Most people today miss the teeth, bloody and sharp, covered in meat and skin, because they don't want to see them, see them all around us, see reality in all its glory.
Music. They heard music from the street. Or they imagined it, and it didn't matter. They heard it. It was real.
It was true.
They walked, walked an ancient path across fields, through the forest, saw familiar faces around them. Beneath the unknown faces, the unfamiliar eyes, they recognized the masks they had always known. Two masked people, one male and one female danced in smoke and fire and Shadow.
An eternity passed and passed again. The wind died, the wind was born within the furnace of their heart.
– I see, Iris cried muted. – I see the two who are one walking through the desert, surrounded by their twenty and one. Our enemies will be vanquished eventually, I see this. I see the rising of mountains and falling of valleys. I see fire incarnated rise from the circle in the sand.
The circle of blood caught fire. They all screamed. At on a spot, a line, right in front of Iris the fire rose, rose to a dancing, dark flame. A face appeared in the fire. Iris screamed. There was a shadow in that fire. Ted saw it, and he couldn't look away. And in the mirror of that fire was a shadow surrounding Iris, a figure so vast that Ted could hardly imagine

its size. He saw its face, a female demon with long fangs and black eyes. It smiled to him.

The fire was put out in the course of a moment, as if by a mighty hand, and ice and mist supplanted it.

Iris fell forward. Ted grabbed her, caught her, keeping her from falling off the mountain.

– So fast, she whispered. – Just a glimpse, but in that glimpse was everything. I forget as I speak. Memory is fading like dust.

She reaches for Frank, reaches across the great divide.

– I'm sorry, she sniffs, tears in her voice. – I'm sorry.

They sat there, remained there for a while, all of them, frozen, moving while sitting still. They moved as much as the air. Their skin moved, fluid and slippery like water. They looked around them, shocked beyond words.

All the candles had been blown out. It was pitch black around them, but they could still see.

– This is just the beginning, Ted stated softly, and his words sounded both as a promise and a threat. – This is what we will become. This is who we are.

They filed back down eventually, filed down the stairs, in mute shock and astonishment. Some of them gathered back in the living room. Some went to their rooms. And there were those who left.

Candles burned high in the living room, creating vast shadows.

– The words I spoke, I uttered up there, Sandy began, still shaking.

The others shook with her.

– I can't for the very life of me say where those words were coming from, she whispered. – They just appeared on my lips… like Magick.

– I saw Eric, John said amazed. – At least I think I did. He spoke to me, and it was almost as if he was here, was back with us. I couldn't understand the words, but they sounded awfully important.

– I can't remember much about it, Frank said. – But there was so much. I saw so much.

– We all did, Jane said solemnly and heated, like a fire.

– Bits and pieces of the world…

Someone said. They couldn't tell whom.

– I think that's exactly right, Tilla said, making them all look at her. – I think what we saw was the world, in all its horror, complexity and glory. We all experienced it differently, but that was what happened. We saw ourselves, and our place in things, outside things. We're outsiders, and are thereby more a part of the world than we could ever imagine.

Smiles and cautious laughter. Incredulity.

– It's an accepted opinion that mankind has conquered nature, Ted said, – but nature will strike back. It's just a matter of time.

– The professional liars tell us so much. Jane cried agitated. – Society itself, the Machine the world has become tells us we are supposed to be one thing, while we can be and are many.

– They define what's human, Pete said. – And what's left after they have done all their slicing and dicing is a mere tiny slice in the middle, bleeding from all sides.

Tilla stood straight, there in front of them, seen by everybody present. Her left hand was raised like a fist.

– Everybody walking the Path of Power is destroying everything they touch. Humanity, all life on Earth is drowning in industrial waste, in poison, actual and spiritual, and they don't give a damn, don't give a damn if the Earth is a stinking waste disposal heap when they're through with it. We live so far away from home, all of us, so very far away from everything we're born to be.

The night deepened, as the gathered youths for perhaps the very first time allowed themselves to think the unthinkable.

Far into the night, when angry and passionate voices finally faded or was lowered the fire was still there, reflecting that in the fireplace, burning hotter than ever.

No one had left the room for hours, for centuries, for a million heartbeats. Those who had stayed to take part in the beginning of the loud discussion, stayed. Tilla's eyes… twinkled, as she excitedly put her arms around them all, one by one or in groups of four or five. She had long arms, such incredibly long arms.

– We have something here… something indescribably precious, this real, this true inside, that we must never allow to die or to fade. We must hold onto it with both hands. And never let go…

She grabbed two hands. One hand of each of those by her side. Turning clockwise in the circle, until she had touched them all. Never. Always. Forever. Those were huge words. Perhaps too big to ever use. They all clasped hands, and they touched, touched something they had hardly glimpsed earlier in their lives.

– I don't know about you, Frank said solemnly, something catching in his throat. – But I will remember this moment forever, beyond the gates of the kingdom of death itself.

He cried sometime later, but no one chastised him for it. They felt a strong urge to cry themselves, in grief, in joy, in desolation and passion. Everything just swelled inside, to something they had yet to truly grasp.

Night deepened. Sleep came. But they didn't sleep.

– I saw Eric, too, Ted told Tilla in a corner of the room, speaking in a hushed whisper, closing the two of them off from the rest. – He said: «I sat there for days, and nothing came to me, but then suddenly was clarity, bursts of imagination, of reality, the way life is, sometimes». I saw him, and I saw John, Frank, Iris, Sandy and Jane suffer and die. It was all in glimpses, but I saw it, clear as night.

He stared insanely at her.

– There's no way I will allow that to happen, he snarled. – Do you hear me? No way!

– Of course not, she whispered, and embraced him, kissed his brow.

After silence she spoke. Softly in his ear.

– We touched something once, touched it again tonight, touched it *more,* something fundamental, perhaps even beyond Magick, or at least a rare part of it. It's not good or bad or anything. It just *is*.

He heard her words and a huge, horrible pain tore at his insides.

Night deepened. Sleep came. But they didn't sleep.

Next afternoon, when Frank approached Ted and asked to speak to him in private it dawned on Ted that he had been following him around, shadowing him all day. They walked up the stairs to the bright room, to the attic. It looked as dusty, as abandoned as it had been doing for months. It looked like there hadn't been anyone there for a very long time.

– It's encouraging me, Frank said as he turned to face the other. – It's all so beyond encouraging. Do you understand?

– I understand, Ted replied hoarsely.

– I received a letter from my lawyer yesterday. Frank cut right to the chase. – Strangely loyal, that man. My mother has been re-marrying, with the before-mentioned First Loan executive, and in doing so achieved some pretty powerful allies in her struggle to wrest from me the control of the fortune.

He handed Ted an envelope. Ted took it and put it aside without looking at it. A grateful smile.

– I trust you, Ted said in his hollow voice. – Trust you beyond reason. You are my valued warrior in a vast struggle.

And they would have laughed a lot, both of them of such a ridiculous statement, perhaps as late as a month ago, but they did so no longer.

– I must leave. Frank spoke firmly. – I was going to let it slide, stay here, if necessary without money. But last night changed that, changed that inexplicably. Tilla spoke true. We have something invaluable here, something I've never been close to feeling before, and I want to feel many times more. But we need money. Money makes *this* world move.

So we need it. I can't let that go without fighting. None of you can help me. You must remain. If it's up to me mother won't be able to stop a single payout.

Ted, uncharacteristically, grasped his hand. It was just flesh, no flashes, no sense of immediate danger. Ted nodded.

So once again they were diminished, as they saw him leave, as they said: «until we meet again». Eyes were dry. There were no tears in the rain.

– I will strangle the bitch, he cried, as he entered the train, and raised a fist in greeting to the small group on the platform.

They made their way home, somewhat comforted, somewhat happy for him, on his behalf.

They made their weekly visit to the post office a few days later, neither surprised nor able to whip up much anger when they saw the sleaze-ball-grin painted on the robotic face behind the counter.

– No check today, she grinned. – No check tomorrow. No check the day after tomorrow.

The insane laughter followed them out on the streets, and blocks and blocks after that, twisting the knife in their gut until the pain and rage was just a dull thud somewhere deep inside, joining every sharp and dull cut that was already there, slowly, slowly tearing them to pieces.

CHAPTER FIVE

The pig rested on her, sending his hot mush into her. She knew him, his features, tall and well built, in his forties. Knew him intimately, his preferences, his inclinations, his weaknesses. He was one of the many in the city council howling against immorality and sin.

He pushed himself off her, leaving the bed, revealing his muscled body, his flat belly.

While dressing he seemed a bit puzzled. She knew why. She hadn't quite behaved as expected, even though he couldn't put his finger on what was wrong.

– You're such a sweet, little angel. He praised her. – I'll be happy to recommend you to others.

– Thank you.

She gave him one of her happiest and most innocent of smiles. Yet, he got the weird feeling again. There was something not quite right about her. But to admit that, he would have to admit to his own inadequacies, so he didn't.

– Give daddy a goodnight kiss, he commanded firmly.

She turned in bed, twisting her body slightly, and then she knelt before him. It was so easy. He bent down and she gave him a wet kiss on the cheek. Everything was done right. But it wasn't right now either. A chill ravaged his body, and he hurried off.

Linda heard the door slam shut. She rose from the bed in a gracious move, and walked to the bathroom. Took a towel and dried herself thoroughly. The face in the mirror. A mask. Weaved just as thoroughly, detailed.

– You want my perceived innocence, she said to the mirror. – You aren't the most sensitive person in the world, but you still felt the chills. I enjoy it, you know, seeing your shame and confusion, in all of you, every single one of you. Some of you are strong, too strong for me to reach. I'll use the knife on you one day. I'll introduce you to my wonderful, beloved black blade. I long, I live for that day.

It rested in the drawer. She pulled the drawer, reaching a hand into the silk stockings there, until skin and hard metal met. The black metal tingled. It always did.

She pulled up a hairbrush and started the extensive brushing. It was a pleasant sensation she had always enjoyed. It felt good, so good to have the brush slide through the hair, to sense its movement on dead skin.

There was a knock on the door. The brush stopped in the middle of the movement. She swore.

– Early, huh? You impatient pigs.

Wicked eyes burned the mirror, burned the innocent-looking girl there. She made a few corrections to her hair, and put the brush away. Leaving the mirror, the face. The mask twisted under the silver lining.

She walked to the door and opened it. Auntie stood there. Linda felt a sting of worry, of unrest.

The large woman entered the room.

– As I've told you more than once. You aren't supposed to greet the clients nude. The anticipation, the sense of successful hunting is half the game to satisfy them.

– Am I not successful then? Am I not your most popular… niece?

– You have other qualities. The innocence never leaves your face. Not even when you attempt to smile, it changes expression. The other girls wonder about you and are envious beyond belief. You aren't marked by what you do, not very vicarious at all, and I suppose you never will be. You're a treasure, dear girl.

Auntie stopped in front of her. Not that much taller, but still towering. There wasn't much excess fat on her muscular body. She was big as a man. Linda shook slightly.

– You are indeed my most popular girl, and it has happened so fast. I must say I underestimated you in several ways.

It was so quiet in here, so difficult to breathe. Linda felt frozen, like a deer in the forest.

– Tomorrow… Auntie spat, – you'll start using make-up.

– Why should I use it, Linda objected sourly, – when it isn't necessary?

A large, fleshy hand struck her cheek. Her head was pushed aside.

– Because *I* say so, puppet. Because *you,* like everybody else within these walls, belong to *me*.

– Don't *touch* me!

Linda backed off with tiny shakes of her head and lips, a tight wire, raising her hands in defense.

Auntie charged her. Linda struck her in the belly, but it didn't have any visible effect. And she got only that one chance. Auntie kicked her legs away from under her and kicked her in the chest, moving the bulky body uncannily fast. The pain paralyzed the thin body and Linda was unable to defend herself when her head was knocked at the floor. Dully she noticed that she was grabbed around the wrists and lifted up. She moaned when the strong grip fastened around her jaw, when she saw the indistinct, ruthless face. She started gasping in fright, couldn't help herself.

– Don't worry, puppet. I won't hurt you. Not where it shows. What I'm gonna do is to teach you obedience. Cure you of your silly obstinacy.

Auntie threw her on the bed. Hard. She almost hit the wall. Sniffing she kept her doe eyes on the large woman. Auntie undressed. Slowly, to make sure Linda saw every move.

– To show you how kind I can be, I'll allow you to keep the advantages you have claimed. You handle the girls far better than Marlene ever did. But I guarantee you won't be uppity against Auntie anymore.

– I won't, Auntie. I swear. Swear.

The bed creaked. Salty tears flowed from the puppet's eyes. Fearful, enraged eyes.

– I believe you, bitch. I do indeed.

Linda bit her lower lip to not scream. It was only a partly successful «tactic». The dragon, the wheezing dragon was so clever, so devilishly so. She knew well, very well what to do to make it hurt, to make it humiliating beyond words, to make the puppet she played moan in joy.

She tried to speak, to shout her protests, but she wasn't allowed to, not a single moment. The puppet on the bed writhed her inflamed, hurting body long after Auntie had finished with it. She didn't stop performing, courting Auntie's attention.

– You're truly a beautiful puppet. Auntie stroked the silver hair. – And so attentive, so obedient. My personal servant. You'll hear my whisper, obey my slightest signal. You don't mean anything, only I and my wishes mean something, right?

– Yes, Auntie. Whatever you want.

A fearful, respectful glance under the swollen eyelids.

– Sit!

Linda obeyed almost before the command was done.

– That's my girl.

A pat on the cheek, rewarding the puppet.

– Do you know what the other girls call you?

– The Ice P-princess, the girl replied, both proud and humble.

– That's right, Auntie said pleased. – Well, Princess, give Auntie a kiss.

Linda sensed nothing, felt nothing. She saw nothing, heard, tasted, smelled nothing. But she knew what was happening, what the bigger, stronger woman did to her. With her superior will and strength. Crushed her will and confidence, and made her her creature. Reduced her to something even less than what she had made Marlene.

Linda Cousin crawled into Tracy Kullman's lap, fondling her large breasts, sucking them. Tracy released a satisfied sound, a grunt of complacency. Linda moved her lips, speaking words only she could hear. Words of revenge and horrors and pain beyond anything, anything she could imagine right now. But it would come to her, she knew that. Tracy wasn't really here, so Linda spoke, cast her spells and her echoes across an unsuspecting world.

I thought it was only Ted I hated. I know, now, I hate Tilla as well. Tilla that I will destroy, slowly, painfully to nothing. I hate everybody, the entire fucking world, and it will pay. Pay for being alive.

Everybody.

2

The cold wind blew straight through the warm room. Linda stood before the mirror, putting on make-up, putting it on thoroughly and focused. She had seen, along with all the nieces and nephews a girl be whipped senseless for being sloppy. Every time Auntie paid her room a visit she curtseyed deeply and received the guest with the utmost honors. She did everything the others did, and much, much more. She had become Aunties Favored, with all the privileges and duties following that.

– You've become such a skilled and eager servant, puppet. I've trained you well.

– Thank you, Auntie, Linda replied softly. – Auntie is most kind.

Auntie lay down on her back on the bed, signing for Linda to join her. Linda did, crawling on top of the large body, eagerly performing the skills the puppet had been taught, that had been beaten into her. She licked the nipples of the gigantic breasts, sucked them with a zealous drive in her effort to please her cruel, demanding Mistress.

Yes, she was well trained. She imagined she was that puppet, moved by strings, remembering the theater in Denver. More and more she felt that way. Nothing was her. She was an animal trained to perform. And she pleased the person holding the leash with a satisfied smile frozen in her face.

But not the soul. Not this time. Nevermore the soul.

She pulled close to the warm, bigger frame afterwards, like a content animal. She remained in that position long after the Mistress had left her, left her alone.

Sleep almost overwhelmed her. She rose in bed, left the bed, with slow, lavish moves, having learned and learned well how to move, how to perform even when no one watched her.

She walked to the bathroom. She knelt before the toilet and stuck a finger deep in her throat. The buzz in her ears rose. She waited. Nothing happened. The finger, the long and slimy claw was pushed down the throat once again. She waited. Nothing happened. Blind eyes stared horrified at the wall, at the blank, blank wall. She rose, running to the mirror, expecting to see the horror and disgust written in her face, but there was nothing. There had been, at first, the first few weeks of her time here. And she had always been able to throw up afterwards, but not anymore.

A howl of anguish pushed itself from her shaking body, her calm surface, as she fell to the floor, utterly broken and defeated.

3

It was one of the nights, a Gala Night. An evening where important guests were given extended treatment, both in the salons and the rooms, a very appreciated initiative among Auntie's customers. Linda and the rest of the pleasure girls and boys stood in line in the hall, greeting the guests as they arrived, one by one leading them into the deeper halls of the lavish, shuttered palace.

Linda curtseyed before a man, one she recognized from before. If not anything else she recognized the nervous twitch in a corner of his mouth. He took her hand and followed her lead, not really there, not really seeing her, but she was used to that by now, and it didn't really faze her anymore.

They entered the inner salon. This was a costume ball of sorts. Even though not everybody had dressed up. Frank, she remembered his name in a flash, Frank Baxter hadn't really. She knew he wasn't really one of the bigwigs here, not one of the filthy rich, but more of a glorified employee, a messenger of sorts, passing notes between Kullman and whoever out there that had sent him. Linda had seen him in Auntie's office more than once.

He never paid, never sent a check to swell Auntie's accounts. Linda had seen them. And he came and went as he pleased, even beyond ordinary opening hours. She had seen him with several of the other girls, observing him from afar, not being able to actively seek him out. But tonight, he had chosen her.

Something stirred in her, something dead, something alive. She smiled to her companion for the night, the smile transforming her face. She read kindness in him, read cruelty.

The music played up, changing character, turning to a beat echoing pleasantly in her limbs.

– Dance? She asked him.

He nodded, not really saying much. They joined the other exalted couples out there, joined the stiff, formal dance, the groping and clinging, the seductive setup.

He was a good dancer, good enough for her not to need to hold back too much.

– You've come here… to play?

She sought close to him, her lips close to him, her huge eyes looking shyly into his, giving him the usual seductive, needy smile.

He pulled her even closer. She gasped in surprise and pleasure.

– I've been studying you, he said. – It's no good playing the silly goose in my presence.

She shook slightly, giving him a careful kiss on the lips.

– We are… told not to pry. Our task is to please the guests.

She lowered her eyes in the desired manner.

– Then please me, he growled, kissing her hard.

She released a satisfied moan, the stirrings inside suddenly turning to movements, to flows harsh and frantic.

They were among the first couples leaving the party. She sensed in him the same impatience she sensed in herself, and it pleased her. Her room. Suddenly her room looked completely different. She untied her bodice ripper in front of him, blushing like a schoolgirl.

– It's actually quite impossible to rip this off…
She reddened, writhing in his grip and under his groping hands.
– I know. He nodded. – Another unrealistic story element in many a storyline.
She… felt him, felt him inside of her, and she cried out in his arms. He took his time with her, and she gave him time, impatience raging within her.
– I've got a scam going, he told her, unprompted afterwards, as her head rested on his chest. – Not here, of course, since I would quickly end up in the river then. It is long term, in the south west, with a couple of old acquaintances of mine.
– Sounds interesting, she said, with just the right intonation of enthusiasm.
He looked at her. It was enough.
– Don't kid a kidder, he admonished her. – It's demeaning, and I won't have it. Do we understand each other?
– Yes, Frank, she said, big-eyed, sensing unfelt joy swell within her.
– It might lead to something, but it's a long shot. Even with the initial capital in place there are no guarantees it will ever work. There never is.
– Capital? She wondered innocently.
– Yes, you fucking virgin in jeopardy, he joked, he said seriously. – Even fraud and racketing need investments to work…
– Ah, she said, – you need *money*.
He looked at her. She returned the look. Something passed between them, even more than already had. She shook lightly, expectation rising in her. He saw it, and a light was lit in his eyes.
– Auntie owns this house… doesn't she? Linda said slowly. – This… business?
– Yes. He nodded, a mixed look of fear and anticipation dawning on his face. – All earnings go to her unabridged, except a small percentage to my employers, of course.
– That's what I thought. Now, she nodded and nodded decisively. – When we take over here, we'll have all the investment capital we need.
– Take over? Are you…
A kiss stopped his automatic response. Desire rose in him instantly. She had that effect on him. He was well aware of that already, even though they hadn't spent that much time together.
– You're so hungry, he stated. – One of the hungriest people I've ever met. And I should know.
– A question, she said, ever the practical girl. – Is Auntie protected in any way? Will there be anyone we will need to take care of afterwards?

– Not if those… taking over the business know their business, showing people that they can take care of things, no. Then there will be no trouble.

– I will take over here, she said passionately. – I'm gonna cut her heart out and eat it, and afterwards we will run this place together.

– I can pull in some of the guys, he suggested carefully, a bit taken aback by the glare in her pale eyes. – Support to make the takeover run smoothly and stuff.

She nodded and did so enthusiastically.

– I was right about you, she cried. – I was so right.

He was reluctant at first, not really believing it, believing it was actually happening, but when he decided to go for it, to take the plunge he turned eager as a kid, way too eager. She was calm as ice, no, hotter than any fire. She was patient, calming him down, cautioning him not to risk exposure. Especially during the late preparations, where the danger grew every day.

One day it almost went wrong. He rushed into her room just after one of her regulars had left. He grabbed her wrist and pulled her out of the bed.

– I can't stand it when one of those gropers… gropes you, he said. – I just can't.

– They aren't here, she whispered in his ear. – Only you are here. Only you.

And soothed him, soothed him, soothed him.

Until she managed to push him out of the door just in time for her next appointment.

He took her to dinner one day. Linda couldn't recall which day, but the light was so bright that it made water flow from her eyes.

– I'm sorry, she sniffed. – I'm hardly outside these days.

It wasn't suspicious that he took her out. He sometimes did take the girls to dinner, or to the movies or whatever struck his fancy. Auntie knew that. He didn't pay. He never did. Not for the girls and not for the food.

Linda knew that. She had been studying bookkeeping lately, both Auntie's official and unofficial bookkeeping, incredibly cautious.

The waiter brought the plates. They were in an expensive Chinese restaurant in Mayfair. Linda grabbed the eating sticks and began devouring the food, greedily and without pretense of elegance. She could be elegant if she wanted to. Auntie and her cronies had taught her that, too. She recalled the lessons vividly.

But she didn't want to.

– I follow her every move, she said, staring into Frank Dexter's eyes. – I know if she is in the building. I know exactly where in the building she is. She doesn't make a single move that I'm not aware of.

The air was sharp, even here, at the depth of the fluffy restaurant, far from the after all crude scenery outside. She looked around while feeding, at the theater, at the pretense.

– A lot of rich men take their whores here, don't they? She grinned.

– Yes, they do.

He nodded solemnly.

A light clad woman laughed a bit too loud over what her companion said.

He held back. She waited.

– That's why I was initially attracted to you, I think, he said. – Your brutal honesty. Not even Auntie has managed to destroy that.

But she had diminished it, though, Linda thought, diminished me.

– People like her are diminishing the world, she said.

And she sensed it, sensed the swelling inside him, the swelling between his legs, and it was all the same.

Someone played a flute somewhere outside, a black blade cutting right through her bones. In Mayfair, a luxury area of London, in a place where there were no beggars. She grabbed his hand, clutching it hard, digging her nails into his skin. He didn't cry out.

– I can see the future. She spoke intensively. – See it written in blood, hatred and guts.

And the future came. The future was there.

Auntie made her visit on Sunday, as she usually did. Linda curtseyed sweetly before her. The girl wore a blue t-shirt and panties - and in the bright light it was easy to see through it. The silver hair was split in two thick braids. Her face was heavily painted, looking like that of one of the dolls she had played with as a little girl.

– You've been good today, pet, Auntie told her with mercy in her voice.

– Thank you, Auntie. The girl curtseyed again. – Thank you so very much.

The voice was husky. She rubbed preoccupied her hands over the bulbs on her t-shirt, breathing faster, faster, faster.

Auntie got an expression of lust and greed in her eyes. She walked to the girl and grabbed her, lifted her up as if she was a doll, that little doll. Spittle flowed from Linda's mouth. Auntie put her on the bed. She stood there, towering above her for a moment, before she crawled into the bed. She moved, and Linda moved, as they lay there, on their side, front to front.

– I've used great skill on you, pet.

The disgusting voice, a voice thick with sadistic pleasure. Sickening. Linda's eyes turned clear, wide open.

– Truly gr…

A flash of shadow, a gasp. Linda stabbed deep into Tracy Kullman's belly. Pulled the knife back out. Jumped out of the bed, beyond reach. Auntie stared at the knife, the black blade as if she couldn't believe her eyes. Mesmerized by the red on black, by the sight of Linda licking the blood, she couldn't quite grasp what had happened.

– That's not a very big wound. You won't die because of it… for a while.

The voice was soft, innocent, like that of a little girl holding a doll. The serene face hadn't changed, in spite of the blood covering most of the body attached to it. The satanic, hateful quality of the voice was sort of beneath the surface, but not hidden, not anymore. Enraged and frightened Auntie attempted to rise from the bed. Linda kicked her with full force, exactly at the wound. And then Auntie *screamed,* even louder then Linda had been doing when Auntie had started her treatment of her.

– Now, you'll die faster. You were lucky there, Tracy.

– You're insane, Tracy gasped. – Beside yourself if you think you will get away with this.

– Away? Linda looked at her, curiously, like a predator in the wild would at the wounded game, tilting her head slightly.

She gathered a pool of blood in her palm and drank it greedily.

– Of course I'll get away with it, Linda snarled in contempt, in something beyond hatred. – But that won't matter to you anyway. You'll be just a pool on these exquisite silken sheets. And your death will be one, long *pain.* I'm being quite vicarious, now, am I not, you repulsive cunt.

The black blade flashed forward, cutting in the big woman's arm. It hung down along the side, useless. Auntie lunged at the lithe girl with the other arm. Linda drove the blade deep into the armpit flesh. She struck the wound again and again. The White Rose smiled then, in ecstasy and cruelty and expectation. Tracy Kullman gaped and gasped, and then she fell, fell so hard on the bed that a leg broke. She lay there, kicking about with her legs, her arms close to paralyzed. With a few, quick cuts her legs were close to immovable, too. Linda Cousin stood there above her, covered in blood, her hair close to red, the color of dawn and rust, her mask smiling.

And the screams began, screams for help, for mercy and everything, to no avail.

There was a guard, appearing in the door with his gun drawn.

– Get out! The ghoul's ghostly voice commanded him.

And he never even considered resisting it.

When Baxter arrived in the room some time later it was quiet. The entire building resembled a funeral or something even more horrible, perhaps a funeral and a wholesale slaughter rolled into one. And everybody waited downstairs, for the demon to appear. No one left, no one moved. There were large bruisers of men there, frozen in absolute terror.

Baxter knocked cautiously at the door ajar and looked just as cautiously inside. Linda stood by the bed, a creature in ruby and ice. He couldn't see her hands. She held them hidden behind her back. On the bed lay a bloody heap of what had once been a human being. At least Tracy Kullman had looked human.

But no longer.

He couldn't prevent a flow of bile from entering his mouth. He was no stranger to killing, to death. But he had never killed with anything remotely similar to her blood rage.

– I can handle it, he told her. – I know, now, the will burning inside you, burning hotter than any furnace. We will go far together, baby. I don't doubt that, not for a second.

– Everything is… fine downstairs?

He hesitated upon hearing her voice.

– Everything, he hawked. – We've done it. You've done it.

– I think you're correct, she said, speaking without tone, without inflection. – They're coved. They will do exactly as I tell them to do, and they won't need much in the sense of additional incentive either…

He would never stop wondering about how much life, in truth there was beneath the cold mask.

– When we show them this.

She held up the bloody fist, curled around the fist-sized meatball. Her arm, her body turned even a shade redder. With a hand pushed at his mouth Baxter could finally look, really look at the body on the bed and actually see details… look at the huge hole in its chest.

CHAPTER SIX

It was a strange morning. Ted walked through the streets accompanied by his brothers and sisters in arms. The first light had yet to appear in the east. Restlessness haunted them all, good and bad. None of them had been able to sleep much last night and everybody had woken up early.

The mime performed north of Oxford Street, as she often did, playing her daring game with the passing cars. Iris touched her belly, sensing the worry in Ted's restless mind, echoing her own.

They passed the mime. There was no face, but they could still see it. There were no eyes, but the woman still stared at them.

The eight of them stopped in front of a storefront window further south, casually browsing the baby clothes in the window.

– I want to kill him, Iris said clenching her teeth. – I do!

The doctor refusing to honor his pledge to help the baby be born. They had taken Iris to him, but he had refused to see her. And he had threatened to call the police on them, and they had removed themselves, anger burning in them, tears of frustration in their sizzling eyes.

There was a whining of breaks. A dump sound and some screams. They turned, and up the road, covered in blood they saw the mime. They rushed to her, reaching her just as she drew her final breath. The driver stood there, shaking her head.

– She just appeared from nowhere, she complained. – One moment she was there. The next she wasn't.

The police came and closed off the place, and took the mime away, and they never saw her face.

Shock and a kind of sorrow stuck in the travelers' guts.

Iris frowned and then suddenly pushed both hands at her belly, moaning, her face cracking in a strange expression.

– We must go, she insisted. – We must go home, now.

– You mean… Pete looked stunned at her.

She nodded, her face transformed into a smile. They hurried home, half pushing her, half supporting her, and they made it in time.

It was in the middle of November when the collective got its first truly young member. Iris gave birth to her child, a girl. Zoe Espershin had come to their aid, replying to their pleas for help. Zoe wasn't trained for assisting births. She hardly had more than a basic understanding of childbirths. But she offered a level head, as if she had been through this or something like this many times before. She was there. That was enough.

It was an «easy» birth. The girl appeared not much more than an hour after the first signs had manifested themselves. Virtually everybody was present, except those who «had to take a walk», who were too nervous to watch. When the first thin wails sounded, slowly turning to screams tears of joy filled many faces. The screams, the screams of life, of joy filled the building, echoed between its many walls, very much like the first light appearing in the east.

Iris stood, at the center of the circle, surrounded by happy friends. She held up the baby and these were her words:

– Behold new life, she cried. – Welcome Stella into our tribe.

– STELLA, everybody repeated.

– In death there is life, Iris sniffed.

Zoe Stella Espershin moved her lips, proud and with a catching in her throat.

Everybody sought to the circle's center, to the new mother and the soft, vulnerable thing she held in her arms. They forgot time and place and everything, forgot for a long time, while time moved outside, and shadows grew long and deep.

Zoe came to Ted in the ground floor training hall later. She seemed hesitant, not nervous, but clearly haunted. They all were, to some degree or another, but it showed on her today.

– How can you go barefoot on a concrete floor this time of year? She shook her head. – Your feet must be pure ice by now.

He stopped beating on the hard swinging heavy sack of leather, and turned towards her, startling her, startling her again.

– They burn hot as the sun, he said. – Feel!

He raised his right foot, balancing easily on the other. She did touch it, and she burned her hands, letting go almost instantly. He stood there, naked on his upper body as well. Evidently he wasn't cold, and he didn't sweat either.

Zoe's face changed from worry, to incredulity and wonder.

– I can't believe it, she exclaimed, sighing happily. – Iris named her daughter after me.

– Why shouldn't she? He said and once more made her breathless. – You came and helped us, when no one else would.

In the shadows in the room further inside the building Iris and some others danced, humming and chanting. Repulsion and attraction were both cut into Zoe's expressive face.

– Uh, I haven't seen Mark… uh, Stewart here…

– He left, Ted said abruptly. – Quite some time ago.

A thin, barely audible wail.

– Where did he go? I… need to speak to him.
It was quite clear why. To him and to everybody else watching her face. But he couldn't help her. Not now. Not ever.
– I don't know. No one does, to my knowledge.
I would very much like to know.
He took a towel from the wall, and dried what little sweat he had on his body.
Zoe stayed with them. She sold her apartment and moved all her furniture to their place.
– Don't think Mark will be back, Ted told her, to her silent query. – He won't be.
– I want to stay, she said firmly. – I want to learn, learn to live.
She blushed hard after the violent outburst, and even more when he studied her.
It was quite the moving day the day she moved in. The place she left wasn't that far away, and they carried everything by hand, through the streets, to the vast space where it was hardly noticeable.
They were done, and they sat down in the living room and welcomed her, surrounded and smothered her in the close proximity of their bodies and minds.
Hours fled like seconds, and in just the turning of the head was an eternity.
– Come, Tilla took her arm, – time for you to try on some new clothes.
Zoe grew aware of her, focused on her only with the greatest of difficulty. It was like they were swimming in a lake of thought, of mind, of heat. Tilla rose and led her away. It was night, late at night, so late that it should have been morning, but it wasn't.
Tilla led her into one of the large bedrooms. Zoe saw only the first few steps into the room at first. The only light in the room was the candle in Tilla's hand. Tilla moved further into the room with the candle in one hand and Zoe's hand in the other. Slowly, slowly the fire dispelled the darkness. Zoe stared ahead, and the texture of darkness brightened… until she could see the large bed and all nude bodies on it. They stared at her, smiled at her. Zoe turned thunderstruck to Tilla.
– Old clothes must come off before new can be added, the redhead shrugged.
Lips kissed Zoe's neck, an act making her gasp in surprise and pleasure.
And they both joined the swirling mass on the bed. And the darkness was filled with a thousand sounds and a million stars.

In the midst of desire Tilla froze, momentarily, as one of the males pushed deep into her, pushed life into her. She realized that they all saw what she did, that the experience was coherent, shared and real.

They all glimpsed the mime's face.

2

Zoe quickly learned, learned a lot about the world and how it currently worked, as they knew she would.

There was just a short walk to the hospital. She walked there in her new clothes. Looking at her self in various indistinct exhibition windows, it was hard to see any difference between herself and other youths she encountered on the street dressed in what had been branded «hippy clothes».

– They're so smooth, she said excitedly, – feel so pleasant.

– That's so true, Jane nodded. – I think one reason why people react so strongly to them, to people wearing them is that clothes just aren't supposed to be comfortable today…

Everybody stared at her, especially her colleagues at the hospital. Not just at the change in clothes, but more than anything the change in her. It wasn't just the hair, the loose hair, the purely physical appearance. Beneath it all, in ways they could only glimpse… she had changed.

But there was another side of the coin. Apprehension and guilt kept riddling her, and intensified when a group of bikers seemed to follow her. Their stares were clearly more intense then most of the other, random focus she was subjected to, and felt more than a little uncomfortable. The stalking, as she had begun to fear it was, kept up so long that she began to feel mildly threatened. Eventually, as she turned left, they turned right and vanished, and she released a sigh of relief, and felt silly.

Apprehension was far less, now, though, anyway, she noted, than in her old life.

She hurried home, into the warm embrace of the people she had just begun to know.

One day she had some time off from the hospital she walked with Pete, Veronica and Tilla to buy some hard needed supplies. It was hard, very hard, she knew, to distinguish between her and the others. Not to distinguish them and her as individuals. They were far more different from each other than those in the crowds surrounding them. It was virtually impossible, she knew, at least to those staring to see that she had been a normal, boring mouse only a few days ago.

I'm free, she thought happily.

She wanted to kiss Pete there and then, in full public view, to feel his body close to her own.

But she wasn't that free. Not yet. She bowed her head, briefly, in shame.

– It happened so fast, she said in amazement. – I moved in. I became one of you.

– Bombshells tend to do that, Tilla grinned.

And then, a tad more somber:

– And you've always been one of us.

– You've always been here, Veronica stated.

– I feel like I'm being held in a warm, soft darkness, Zoe said. – It's both pleasant and absolutely terrifying. I am myself, but I'm also a part of you all.

– In our group, our tribe you aren't required to surrender your individuality, Tilla spoke intensively, – but to strengthen it. What is good for you is good for the tribe.

– I love that word, Zoe whispered. – Tribe.

Tilla kissed her on the lips (in full public view), and it hardly bothered her at all.

– Look at us. Pete shook his head in amazement. – We walk through the street as if we own it. Our position in the current society is rather tenuous. We don't own anything to speak of. They want us to feel shame, but we don't.

– And that's precisely why we own *the world,* Veronica grinned and snarled.

And the short girl was so tall, tall as the world.

– We're stronger because we aren't dependent on a group, Tilla said. – And most current living humans are nothing but dependent. They need reassurances from peers to do anything. So they don't do anything, except what is generally accepted, in ways that is generally accepted.

– It's so *sad.*

Zoe shook her head in bewilderment. She realized that suddenly, she didn't understand most people anymore. That part of understanding suddenly eluded her.

All other parts blossomed like a flower, like a universe.

– It's such a fine day, she marveled, shaking her head in apprehension. – Cold but fine.

– I would feel the warmth from you guys in the coldest of pits, Veronica stated.

And they all felt the catching in the throat.

They reached the store.

– This is our favorite place, Tilla told Zoe. – They almost treat us as human beings here…

This was just a catch up trip. They had shopped en masse yesterday, with half the collective carrying stuff. But they always missed something. Bruce had elaborated quite a bit over that fact yesterday, called it his «missing pieces theory». It had caused a lot of hearty and healthy laughter.

Money was running out, and even though they had begun cutting down on even essential supplies, their funds dwindled.

They had begun extensive searches through garbage cans at night. Before that had been prudence and a certain abandon. Now, it was a necessity.

Zoe noted the nervous twitches in the corner of Tilla's mouth, her ever-moving eyes, and began doing the same, restless search herself. She realized they were all doing it, to a larger or lesser degree, and the cold she had felt turned to ice.

And she wondered about how they seemed to study the items they wanted to buy, with more than a casual glance.

– Better safe than sorry, Tilla said when she noticed her glance, grinning grimly.

They reached the cashier. They had paid and were on their way to the exit when a tall, large gentleman stopped them. He grabbed Zoe's arm so hard that it hurt.

– Would you four please come with me? He said, his apparent kindness very apparent.

– Why?

Zoe attempted to pull free. He increased the strength of his grip. She moaned in pain.

– There are some irregularities we must discuss…

– Irreg… But I… we haven't…

– We haven't stolen anything, Tilla stated angrily. – And we have the receipt to prove it.

They always triple-checked everything they bought… before they bought it.

– May I see it, please?

The gentleman's voice dripped with sarcasm and suspicion.

– You would just love that, wouldn't you? So you could tear it to bits.

The girl in the cashier seemed both confused and worried. Pete took the receipt and supplies and walked to her, showing her the receipt. She nodded.

– Will you please check everything? He said kindly. – So we can put a stop to this comedy, at least this particular act.

The girl was even more confused, but she recounted and checked the numbers. Twice.

– Everything checks out, she said aloud. – No *irregularities*.

Pete smiled. His three companions smiled. The girl smiled. They all turned towards the dishonorable gentleman.

– Accept my sincere apologies, he said rigidly. – I was wrong. Better safe than sorry, right?

There was a sick, twisted look in those wet eyes making them all uncomfortable. They sighed in relief when he disappeared back into the storage room.

– Do you risk being fired for this? Pete asked the girl lightly.

– Absolutely not. She rejected it with a broad smile. – I'm the daughter of one of the owners, and that guy has only been here a short while.

She considered that with a sudden incredulity.

– He was actuality hired only two days ago.

The four of them walked home, saddled in stuff.

– This is one of the aspects of being a free spirit in today's society you'll have to live with as well, I'm afraid, Tilla said lightly to Zoe. – Those in high places in today's society do not generally favor us…

They laughed themselves silly over that one. And occasionally, from time to time they choked on it, glancing at each other with flickering eyes.

On the corner of Charing Cross Road and Shaftesbury Avenue, by the Palace Theater Zoe turned for the third time. It had begun as a nervous twitch of the head, of paranoia, but had soon turned to certainty.

– It's them, she mumbled, so low that the others didn't hear her. Then aloud: – We're being stalked.

Pete turned without turning, casually and alert, as they kept walking.

– I can't see anything specific, he concluded, a bit patronizing, clearly feeling that if he didn't see anything, then there wasn't anything of notice.

– It's the bikers, Zoe cried. – They followed me from the hospital recently, the same way they do now. Not together. Spread across the street. They… scared me.

– I see them, Pete noted, shame notable in his voice. – I can't see how I could have missed them. Damn!

They all did, saw the bruisers move like they were connected somehow, interconnected like one, single being, even though they were nowhere near being in physical contact.

– You should have told us.

Tilla grabbed Zoe and held her, as their feet kept moving, as their senses kept sharpening, to a cutting edge.

– I *know*. But it all seemed to, seemed so…

– Unbelievable.

She saw how the three prepared themselves, stretching limbs, softening muscles, how already readied bodies turned even more alert, even more supple, ready for… ready for *war*.

– Six, Pete said. – They were four two seconds ago. They're coming.

Zoe looked swiftly behind her, observed how the six large men advanced, quickly shortening the gap between the two groups. She sensed how she was pushed forward. Cold by the building anxiety she let it happen.

Everything… moved, moved with them, around them, in a whirl of air and flesh.

Two of the «bikers» passed them on the opposite sidewalk, clearly intending to surround and corner them. The six were dressed as most bikers, in black leather and with insignia on their backs, this particular ones reading «Red Devils». But there was more than one thing that didn't quite… fit. Their black leather was brand new, straight from the store. They hadn't been driving very far with them, if at all. They were as fake as acid rain, and hardly even that.

The four were cornered at the corner of Shaftesbury Avenue and Wardour Street, a very public place.

– They want to make an example of us, Tilla said.

– A good idea, Pete nodded.

Zoe heard the anxiety in their voices, and easily saw it in their pose, beneath the light banter.

The six large men surrounded them, cornered them. Tilla and Pete stopped, and Veronica and Zoe followed their lead, perhaps not such a good idea.

– Look at the freaks, one of the men shouted, shouted aloud. – Look at how they dress, how they behave.

He made an effort to speak simple, like people expected of a man dressed like that, but his «cultivation» broke through like a sore, a very sore wound.

– I *told* you so, another broke in. – They're from the freak farm in Aldow Square.

– So this is the new act, Pete sighed. – What do you guys want?

– Where they're fucking like ravens…

– I'm willing to bet they're all sick, sick as sin.

– They should be ashamed of themselves. Contributing to the moral downfall like that.

The biggest stepped forward and stopped in front of Zoe.

– We should make an effort to understand them. They're only kids after all. Except this one. She's old enough to know better. Perhaps she's the one *teaching* them, leading them down the primrose road.

One almost just as big grabbed Veronica's jaw and made her look at him.

– This looks like a tasty lamb, even though she's probably worked over numerous times, like the rest of them. So, how much do you charge for a roll in the haystack, sweetie? Do we get a group discount?

She kicked him in the groin, that was her reply. He howled, a thin, thin childish scream and collapsed on the sidewalk like butchered meat.

Chaos and mayhem ensued, in motion of air and flesh and clothing and pain. The man touching Veronica had hardly more than hit the ground before she had jumped into the air and given another a paralyzing kick on the jaw. He fell as well. Tilla and Pete had seen it coming, and reacted far quicker than their opponents. Tilla grabbed an arm and broke it over her knee. Pete struck another of the bullies with a good old-fashioned fist to the side of the jaw. Zoe watched wide-eyed as the three took care of the six large men, beating them senseless in a matter of seconds. Before Pete had knocked his man unconscious Veronica and Tilla had vanquished the rest. Veronica struck down her third and began kicking him. Violently, savagely many times. Her face was a mask of hatred.

– You should have stayed out of it, she snarled. – I wanted to take them all, *them all*.

Tilla had to parry a fist when she moved towards Veronica.

– Hey, Vernie, she joked. – You can rest now. You've virtually cleaned the table, girl.

– Those bastards, Veronica cried out, shaking hard. – They deserve to die. DIE!

Hoarse, sore crying. Tilla pulled her close and comforted her. The shaking body slowly turned calm or calmer. Tilla dried the big, salty tears. There were still motion of air and flesh, echoes of what had been, slowly settling as well.

– Better?

Veronica sniffed and nodded. There was a smile or a ghost of a smile. She discovered that Tilla had a single tear in her eye and removed it with her index finger.

Pete grinned almost apologetically to Zoe.

– Isn't that a tough little fury…

Releasing all her anger, all her rage in one explosive outburst. Zoe wondered numbly what such potential could do during other, deadlier circumstances, if it was directed, if it was focused.

Three police officers arrived at the scene. Not much of a force. But clearly determined. That determination wavered visibly when they realized that the circumstances had turned out quite different from what they had envisioned.

– I'm Chief Constable Wilson, the leader declared brusquely, very full of himself. – What has transpired here?

– These men harassed and threatened us, Zoe spat, – after following us around for days.

– Forgive me if I have some difficulties believing that, Wilson brushed her off. He didn't feel that good anymore. – To me it seems like you have turned this upside down.

And in that he was undoubtedly correct.

– You won't get far with that, boy, Tilla grinned. – Not in a court of law or in an anywhere else even remotely impartial body. If you claim that the four of us attacked six big and strong boys like these you'll ridicule yourself beyond belief. Not even your friends in high places will be able to keep you from doing foot patrol service for the rest of your time in the force.

Wilson stood there, red and sweaty. Scowled at the four and the gathering audience. The crowd had stood still to this point, but now they began to mumble between themselves. Several stepped forward, clearly *excited.*

– I don't know about earlier, but things here happened exactly as the young boy and girls have said.

An older man angrily to the Chief Constable. Several voices agreeing loudly.

The cars in the street had stopped. Some of the drivers had even left their vehicles and joined the crowd. Everything looked stationary, but clearly not fixed. The intersection was blocked, and the situation deteriorated rapidly.

Wilson had considerable experience with crowds. This one was clearly hostile. He realized he could no longer do anything but to save the pieces, now. People had smelled the stench of foul play.

– Think about it, he cried, filled with righteous reason. – You might have gotten it all wrong. Think about who these four are and where they're coming from. They're not to be trusted.

– I live nearby, a woman spoke up, – and I've never found any reason to distrust them. And don't attempt any hokey pokey with me. I've got four children and my husband is a *lawyer*.

– I don't like radicals, another stated. – But I like you even less…

It slowly dawned on Wilson that he would indeed earn foot patrol if he didn't get away from this place at top speed. He prepared a hasty, but worthy retreat.

– One moment, Zoe spoke up, – what about these men, these wretched bullies? Is your intention to leave them be, for them to be free to attack us again?

– You impudent slut! He spat it out.

– I'm filing charges against these creeps, she cried. – It's my right.

– Do so, and see how far you'll come, he shouted back. – I'm certainly not taking a charge from people like you seriously.

He had lost it completely, now. Saliva flowed from his mouth. The two that had arrived with him held themselves strategically back.

A clearing of the throat from behind and he turned abruptly. Two men had entered the stage. He recognized Ted Warren, but not the other.

– A very strange precedent, if I so should say, the other, a cheerful, well-dressed man in his late twenties commented.

– Who the *hell* are you?

– Carl Palmer, attorney in law at the crown's court. A card was stuck into Wilson's hand. He crushed it unrestrained to a ball of paper. – May I remind you… Chief Constable, that you, too can be charged, for misconduct to boot. Yes, after what I've seen here, that isn't even the worst you might be charged with.

It was no more mister nice guy. When Palmer spoke again his voice was quite icy.

– My advice to you is to show a little appreciation of the public's concern in this matter. You've screwed up enough for one hour, don't you think?

With clenching teeth Wilson and party had to cuff the still unconscious bullies. They had actually brought six pairs.

Two for the road, then, Tilla thought.

She turned to Ted, her face brightening the moment she focused on his familiar face.

– I felt your approach, she said.

– I felt you, too, he said. – Your anxiety and need. You didn't really need us, though.

– I will always need you, she said softly.

A Black Maria arrived. Someone in the neighborhood had evidently called it. For once it wasn't a calming influence on Wilson's nerves.

– Stay away, Pete whispered to him a few steps away. – You don't get more than one change with us.

Wilson heard him, and his sweating increased, and they were confident he wouldn't sleep well tonight.

The «bikers» were pushed and pulled into the Black Maria. It didn't happen gently.

– How fast do you think they'll be released? Ted asked Palmer.

– I think their masters will let them stew for a few days, before posting a not too expensive bail.

Palmer shrugged.

– I've seen a lot of such things, he added. – I guess that's why Stewart «recruited» me in the first place.

– The posting of bail, Tilla began, lightening up, – is a matter of public record… right?

– It is indeed. He nodded. – And even though it's done by front men, it isn't hard to find out who's behind them either. I'll see what I can find out.

– Everything is basically known, transparent, Tilla swore. – But nothing is done about it. Nobody cares!

– It's time, Ted spat. – Time for us to do a bit more in the department of active resistance, time for us to be *proactive*.

They attempted levity, at least in the foundation of their voice, knowing fully well that this was only a reprieve. This was just one minor battle, in the long, hard struggle ahead of them. They felt little joy when the Black Maria drove away. Mostly a kind of sick relief, over the fact that they had persevered again.

Ted felt an impotent rage as he stood there, watching with the others. Nothing of the intoxicating sense of power that had earlier accompanied it. The arrogance, the deadly confidence was almost gone, to the point of him being almost like everybody else. There were times, like now, he desperately wanted it back.

– We do need *something,* Pete said, clenching his teeth. – Something tangible we can fight.

They pulled back. The crowd dispersed, slowly, but they still kept their eyes on the six at the center of their attention.

– Look at them, Vernie scowled at the crowd. – How they stare at us with their fish eyes. I can't *stand it*.

Ted looked at her. Then he looked at Tilla. And then back at Vernie, feeling something… something inside, a birth, a release. Zoe had learned,

learned of the world, and so had Vernie, good and bad. Vernie, at least had come through this in a good way, as more than she had been before.

– Stand it, he told her. She looked at him, startled. They all looked at him. – Endure. You, the three of you took the six bullies out, and you, Vernie could have done so alone. They know, now, the people in the pale, sickly shadows how lethal we can be.

Her eyes cleared. Wonder mixed with the rage.

– We're being looked at. Stand it. It's the way of the world. We're scrutinized, because of our experiences, precisely because of the horrors we've lived through and endured. Every time they look at us they know that the world isn't the rosy cloud they're being told it is. But more important… what's truly making us a threat to the walking dead sitting above, ruling the world, is that we're showing them, slaves and masters both, how the world can be, what Human Beings are. We're showing them, by our mere presence, *showing* them that the human spirit is still alive.

Tilla, big-eyed, grabbed his hand, took it in both her own. They all touched him, embraced him, as he embraced them.

– Your words, Phoenix, Vernie said. – They stir me, stir me far beyond words. Thank you. Thank you.

And they didn't see the look of pain crossing his face.

– Come, Tilla said softly. Let's go home.

3

After that day they never walked outside less than five in a group. Preferably they were seven or eight, close to ten. Not during the light of day, and not during their many nightly excursions, scrounging garbage cans for food or any other desperate mission during the shadow time.

The persecution continued unabated. Executed in slyer and more clandestine ways. The major attempts at putting them in a bad light stopped. The attacks were not so large scaled anymore, but they increased in numbers, and they stung, stung hard, drawing life's blood from their hearts. So small were the attacks, that individually they might not have been noticed at all. No more visible than shadows in the dark. It was impossible to fight back, at least effectively.

Persistent phone calls. Breaking of windows. Anonymous complaints to newspapers. Badmouthing on the streets. They kept the little money they had left at home. Making sure they got valid receipts on anything they bought, what little they were able to buy. Not throwing them away, even many months after the purchase.

But it was impossible to predict, to counteract everything that might happen, they knew that. The pressure… got to them, inevitably. They caught themselves wondering what would happen next, what insidious horrors had been planned for them. When. If everything was a preparation for something… horrible. The first began to leave the house. Some returned after a time, and others arrived. But all in all they shrunk in numbers.

Bruce bent over a garbage can a full moon night. Hands and face were dirty of all the garbage they had shifted through. The others easily saw the drawn lines in his face.

– I just wish I could wring a neck or two, he said.

They went to see a movie one day, *Jaws,* sneaking in among a crowd in a queue practically filling the entire Leicester Square. People sat on the floor all over the theater. An ugly mood entered the hall when guards attempted to empty the place, and the officials gave up, allowing the show to start, almost an hour behind schedule.

It stirred something within them, the sight, the experience of the savage shark did, something primordial and infinitely precious. The music was like heartbeats, drumming up thunder.

– The people making the movie… touched something, Iris said later, when they sat on benches in St James's Park in the moonlight. – They're probably not aware of it themselves, but they touched something deep… and profoundly human.

– Stories are heard through the blood, Sandy whispered, – and right now, it's roaring.

Ted and Tilla walked a bit behind the others, as silver trees passed them, as they passed those quivering strains of life.

They walked, back in the city now, the dirty neon lights. They visited a TV and radio store, not certain why, they just felt like it. The large group filled the store and put fear into customers and employees alike. A radio was on, way too loud. It hurt Ted's ears. He walked to it to shut it down. The moment he touched it, it sputtered and died. They walked back out, waiting for people to accuse them of destroying property, but it didn't happen.

– Did you see the look on their faces, she grinned. The two of them still walking a bit behind the others. – You have a knack for locating technology… and destroy it. And I think they, the people in there, realized that, somewhere deep down.

Her laughter stopped. It seemed to be stuck in her throat.

One of the reasons he had done it was to cheer her up. It had worked, but not for long.

– Do you know what, he said. – For some reason it made me think of the ship, of the time we spent there. I still have only dim memories of it, about a man they called the Mask. It's strange, I can remember almost everything else, but no matter how much I focus on that, I can't seem to get past the fog in my mind.

– It was a horror beyond belief, she whispered, – affecting even the strongest spirit.

She clung to him, clung hard

He looked worriedly at her. She was down. And it wasn't just the bad memories, not in itself. He could easily sense that. It was unusual. Usually she had to cheer him up.

She looked at him, instantly noticing his worry, smiling reassuringly.

– It's just so frustrating everything, she said, digging her nails into his palm. – Most people are so convinced they're free that they don't see the forest for the trees. And to top it off we're given the blame for all their woes, not those who are doing it to them.

– «No one is more enslaved than those convinced they're free», he quoted.

– It's true! She exclaimed. – Look at them.

He did and saw complacency wherever he looked.

– What are we going to *do?*

She dug her nails deeper into his palm, drawing blood. He yelped, couldn't help himself, couldn't hold it back. Her features softened, and she mumbled an apology.

He could feel her gloom. It was very unusual, and cut deeper than ordinary bad mood.

– The worst part of it is that it isn't really organized, he said slowly. – The persecution against us and others similar to us. Oh, there are some eager souls who want to «make an effort against unruly elements», but mostly it's a kind of sick automatic defense function of society against any type of outsider. Pretty «nifty»… and frightening.

She nodded, the bags under her eyes clearly visible. She had also spent more time in the bathroom in the morning lately. That…

Then he had it. It suddenly dawned on him, and it was so obvious. It swelled within him, the knowledge, what he should have realized much sooner. Everything, everything of joy and grief and fear.

– Come.

He rushed them both forward, eager like a kid, so they quickly caught up with the others. She looked at him, inquiringly, a burst of expectation suddenly, joyfully swelling in her.

They walked to the front, and turned. Everybody knew instantly something was up and stopped. They had become so sensitive to each other and to each other's needs and uniqueness, and that realization, in itself made them feel good. They looked at him, as he stood there, before them. He didn't have to lift his hands or do anything to get their compete attention

– I feel for a party tonight, he said. – We deserve it. Let's celebrate everything, the past, the present, the future, everything they're striving to steal from us.

He knew. Tilla stared big-eyed at him. Looking at him all her doubt was swept aside.

His excitement, and hers swept over them all, washing away their bad mood, their gloom.

They sat there, at their round table, in the dining room later that night, where there were no windows, where they couldn't see that night turned to day, cheering with the scarce amounts of alcohol they had scavenged, in the soft, dark lights of candles, and Tilla's confidence turned to certainty.

Ted rose. It was something so profoundly special about it that it made everybody smile, smile in the rain.

– Nothing can take away what we carry inside, he said forcefully, beyond passion. – Not if we don't allow it. They can lock us up in padded cells, and the unbridled fire will still burn. It just takes the tiniest stoking of embers to rekindle the fire.

His eyes did glow, but it didn't frighten them anymore. It warmed them, stoked their embers.

– You may not think there's a special reason to celebrate tonight, but you would be wrong. We don't need any such reason, of course, not to celebrate life, life in all its glory… But tonight we have one nonetheless…

With a dramatic gesture he grabbed Tilla's chair with both hands and lifted her up. Lifted it effortlessly and put it on the table. Tilla giggled like a young girl, like the young girl she was.

– We're celebrating the… he counted… – second, third, fourth… *fifth* very young upcoming new member of our gathering.

He put both hands on Tilla's belly. She smiled to him, the worry diminished. She wasn't alone anymore.

The cheers went through the roof.

– I felt it, he said. – Felt the extra life within you, but didn't know what I felt at first.

– I made Zoe promise not to tell, Tilla said, whimpering a bit. – I wanted… time.
– I understand why you were worried, he said. – Having a child in our position. But don't be. We can handle it, handle that, too. There's nothing we can't handle.
– And we'll get help, she said dreamingly. – From everybody here. It will be their kid as well.
– Sure, he said cheerfully. – He shouldn't be a problem, not a problem at all.
A slip of the tongue. He clenched his teeth, desperately wanting to take it back. But he couldn't. There was no way to do that.
Tilla grew aware of something she had noticed for a while, and especially tonight, after the film. She was certain the others had noticed it, too, though not to the same degree that she had. They could never do that.
Ted was in an over the top good mood these days, and he wasn't really like that, not the joker, the man lightening up the parties. He was deeper, much more brooding.
He was playacting, and overdoing it to an uncanny degree to boot.
Tilla turned seriously scared.

4

Ten of them walked on Bayswater Road the next evening. Ted wanted to be alone. For the first time in a very long time he felt… watched. Not by the idiots the government and various agencies, private and public sent after them, but *watched.* By one who was good enough to be able to not be close, and who didn't need to show himself more than absolutely necessary. No one else, no one mundane would have discovered anything, not even by random chance. The ten turned a corner. Ted wasn't the first, neither the last. There was nothing suspicious about the turning of a corner. The moment the corner hid them he stopped them, put a finger to his lips, signing for them to keep walking, and they did. He did, too, for five, seven, ten seconds, before turning back, running back the way they had come the fastest he could. He was a wind and they felt its power.
He turned the corner in a whirlwind of movement. And before the man there ahead turned and ran, he saw his face clearly, focused, frozen like a photograph. It was Chin, Scarface, the oriental, the observer who had followed him, followed them all, like a shadow… yes, perhaps his entire life. He brushed people aside as if they were cardboard statues (and they were), caring for nothing but the chase. Chin rushed on, at least as brutally effective, but much closer now. Ted was gaining on him, step by

step. Chin rushed into the street full of snarling fast running vehicles, crossing Lancaster Terrace by jumping from car to car. Astonishment mixed with rage in Ted as he followed him the same way. He felt like he would lose his footing at any time on the shifting ground, but it was like a dance, and he had learned to dance. Chin landed on the street on the other side like a ballet dancer, not breaking his stride the slightest. Ted felt a pain in his ankle. He rushed on unabated. Fall, *fall, damn you,* he thought, focusing beyond thought on the indistinct figure ahead, on its whirling feet, focusing on grabbing them with his fevered mind, with his power. But nothing happened, even though he desperately wanted it to. Scarface ran into Lancaster Gate Station, going right for the stairs, ignoring the elevators, the frantic calls of the guards. The narrow stairs going down, down, down. Ted could no longer see the man in front of him, but he heard him, sensed his breathing, sensed the blood flowing through his veins. It was like he could touch him, like he could… A train approached the station. Ted heard, swearing silently under his wheezing, but silky, easy breath. He reached the departure platform. He saw the train leave, watched as he kept running the last few coaches dive into the dark tunnel, watched Chin as the man held on to the sliding doors, as he forced them open, as he dived inside the moment before the train vanished into the dark, dark underworld. As Ted stopped just before he hit the wall, as he fell to his knees, howling in boundless frustration.

The others felt like they had been waiting for hours for him, there on the corner, but it was only a few minutes. He arrived with unruly hair and a slight limp, but seemed okay. They saw the storm rage within him.

– It was Chin, he said curtly.

And those among them who knew that name, knew what it signified, felt the chill in their heart. It was another riddle in the mystery they partly had been caught up in, partly chosen. There didn't seem to be an end to them, to the mysteries, the Mystery.

And during the dark night, in the attic Tilla and Iris watched him pace back and forth on the floor.

– I wanted to use my power to stop him, but I couldn't, and he got away.

– Don't beat yourself up over it, Tilla said softly. – It's amazing that you were actually able to run faster than he was.

– The power is gone, he said flatly. – I've tried to use it, but I can't lift a piece of paper or a feather. It's gone!

That silenced the two. They looked worriedly at him.

– I wasn't ready, he mused. – I didn't want to use my powers, didn't feel confident enough. I'm not ready. Not yet.

And they sat with him there, on the dusty floor, breathing in the dark, long after the candles had burned down.

They, the lot of them from the collective, watched a fifty pence rerun of The Exorcist a few weeks later. Except for them the theater was practically empty, and they easily negotiated a group discount.

In 1973, when the movie had first been released, horror and upheaval had visited the theaters across the planet. People had fainted and ambulances had been parked outside the theaters. Mass hysteria and religious panic had descended on an unsuspecting world.

The movie had practically played in London continuously, on various theaters since then.

Various national censorship authorities had banned it, and in some countries it had yet to be shown.

There was horror present in the theater. Perhaps others couldn't sense it, but Ted could. He had stopped believing in a god or a devil a long time ago, but he still felt the horror emanating from the screen, from the air in the darkened place.

He blinked. Something… shifted, faded in, and he found himself in a bigger theater, packed with people. A woman screamed and fainted. She fell to the floor and lay still. Ambulance personnel came running into the theater, carrying a stretcher. They rushed back out, carrying the woman on the stretcher, the stretcher with red, red sheets. Turning and looking around Ted saw that Tilla, and most of the others, was no longer present. Glimpsing in mist, straining in shadow he spotted only a few of his friends. And on the stage… And on the stage beneath the projector screen…

He saw Brian Garret.

The man spoke and spoke and moved his lips, but Ted couldn't hear a thing. Others could. He saw how they listened in awe to the transparent figure up there. Garrett wasn't really here. Yet he was.

The devil appeared in the film, and people screamed, screamed like hell and huddled together.

Ted blinked, and in that blink was an eternity, flashes before his eyes he could only glimpse pieces of afterwards.

– CHRIST! Bruce cried afterwards. – I'll be shaking for days after this.

Ted lifted up Tilla with a cheerful grin and let her sit on his shoulder all the way back home.

– This is *amazing*. She shook her head. – I can see so much better from up here.

So, there was laughter, there was joy. Mixed with the horror of both the seen and unseen world.

And both haunted Ted at night. His dreams increased in frequency and intensity. Others might have called his dreams nightmares, but what he called nightmares would have driven the ordinary citizen insane.

There was the road, the path to the mountain far ahead. The shadow creature was closer, now, contrary to what he had expected and hoped. He felt threatened. That was all he knew. He walked on the road. The shadow creature sat on the tall peaks. He and Tilla walked hand in hand on the road. It was Tilla, but it wasn't her, but her skeleton. There was another skeleton, a baby skeleton in her belly.

He woke up, and discovered that Tilla was shaking him, shaking him hard, as he looked at her with wild eyes, as sweat covered his body.

– We were at a cinema last night, weren't we?

His hands shaky, his voice hoarse.

– Yes, we were, she replied, rubbing him, rubbing herself softly at him, slowly calming him.

– I wasn't sure, he whispered. – I just wasn't sure. It seems so… so long ago.

He sat on the bed later, covered in blankets, but still freezing, staring out through the window, at the falling snow.

The year 1976 began in the Storm. 1976 - western, christian time frame. An explosive storm ravaging Western Europe. The wind reached 180 km/h at its peak. Fifty people died. Not a major disaster on a planetary scale, not compared to the truly devastating bad weather further south. But the technological human always turned insecure and frightened when technology failed. When nature showed man it was still part of nature. A part of its wiles and magnificent power.

In the warm, pleasant living room. His friends were there with him. But suddenly, terrifyingly they were not. He looked out of the window, and he was back in the bedroom, back in the theater. The possessed girl's head turned around and round and round. The woman in the theater gasped and fell to the floor. The men with the stretcher arrived, remarkably fast, Ted thought. He wanted to help. The two guys with the stretcher turned towards him. Both had horns on their forehead. He looked down at the woman. She had grown horns as well. The shadow called. Sent for him from afar. He was back on the road. The fire-spitting dragon waited for him to come, to come to him. He walked up the isle in a church with a girl, a girl with green hair. The dragon priest waited for them, called them to him. People sitting on the rows cheered. A wedding was a happy event. You may kiss the bride, the priest said, and he did. Kissed her lips to shreds. Greenhair waved. He turned to do as she did. That was when he turned to stone. All the people in the church were without heads.

He looked at Tilla, her soft hands touching his chest, her bony hands. NO! Her worried smile, the golden red hair covering most of her face. She didn't see what he saw.

– Nightmare? She spoke softly. – Poor boy. Let me take you in my fawn, let Tilla comfort you.

She crawled on top of him. Slid back and forth. Laughed giddily when he reacted to her caress. He put his hands on her belly, sensing him, the little dragon. She laughed more, and kissed him on the lips in pure joy.

– You've slept badly for many nights, now, she said a while later, lying close, with her head on his right shoulder, tight to his head. – There are hard times ahead… right?

– Yes…

He couldn't make himself lie to her. It would be useless, anyway, she knowing him so well and he carrying his fears on his skin like open wounds.

He played with her hair, let it slip through his fingers. She noticed how distant he was, had noticed it even during the fucking, and that, if not anything else would have made her pissed, if she didn't know him so well, if she didn't feel the fear festering in her gut.

She fell asleep again, too spent to stay awake, and he did, too, eventually, drifted back into the dreamscape, the mirror of all things. And he was still awake, lying there on the bed with the warm body close to his. And the nightmare began.

He and Tilla and many others walked through a forest, a dark and dense forest. The sky above was pitch black. The forest changed to a labyrinth. It reached far upwards, into the everlasting darkness. There was no way out. They walked and walked. Fed many times. Every corner they turned they met a wolf snarling at them. They walked unafraid towards it, and it dissolved into nothing. But at the next corner it was right there again. And again. And again. It faded and dissolved, but it never disappeared completely. It was always there, never leaving them in peace. And they grew tired. Every time it appeared they tired further. Eventually their clothes were so ragged that they were practically naked. Clothes that had once been new and shiny.

The trees in the labyrinth withered and died. He wanted to set fire to it, destroy it, but Tilla convinced him not to. She led them further, ever further. Instilled in them all a hope that they would eventually escape. Then another wolf appeared, far bigger, hungrier. It wolfed down Tilla, swallowed her whole, and many of the others behind her followed her in death. It was too late, but he threw himself at the wolf. Killed it in swoop of his own paw, and ate it raw. Digested it with long, sharp fangs. Tore it apart, and left only pieces of fur and flesh. He had grown large now, so large that he could leave the prison in one single step. Behind a fence at the center of the labyrinth a few stags graced. He devoured them as well. He sat there, content, licking his paws. It was then he discovered how hairy he had become. In a pond he could see his reflection, the wolf's head. He looked down at the enormous claws on his paws.

Pete and Vernie had guard duty that night. Most of the others were sleeping, sleeping soundly. Content in their life here, their relatively good life. The scream woke them up, abruptly and terrifyingly. Upon opening their eyes gooseflesh already covered their skin, from top to toe. The scream was loud, so loud that even people in the neighboring building fairly far away woke up. The howl of fear filled the air, quivered, vibrated and reaching far and deep. Perhaps people recognized the scream, even though they had never heard it before. Perhaps that's why they were so frightened? Pete and Vernie covered their ears with their shaking hands. It did them no good. They stared at their surroundings, incredulous and paralyzed. Objects fell from shelves, danced on the tables and in the shadowy air. They could hardly believe it, but the following day, if they hadn't wanted to stay quiet, they could have sworn on it, sworn that the entire building was shaking.

CHAPTER SEVEN

Born to run. Bruce Springsteen. Born to ruuuuuuuunnnnnnnn…

The red haired woman and the black haired man sitting back to back on the couch turned towards the large window. They saw it from below, saw only sky. Dinner. None of them had eaten breakfast. The Hunger burned within them both. He had broken every fork, knife or spoon he had grabbed. Finally, he had eaten solely using his hands.

None of the others had eaten much either. They didn't have much of an appetite.

– You must never go out, he insisted. – Not unless I'm going, too.

– Why she said. – Tell me why. That's all I ask. Tell me about the dream.

He stared at her. How could he? How could he tell her that he wanted to pluck the fetus from her belly, rip it to shreds, throw it in the toilet and flush it down.

– You do as I tell you, he told her.

– Is your intention to force your will on me? She asked sarcastically. – What is Master's intention if I don't obey his royal commands? You don't think I'll let myself be treated like a sheep without a very good reason, do you? Damn you!

They had kept it up like this for a while.

She fled the room, snarling and swearing in every move she made.

Iris followed her. Right by the stairs Tilla stopped. Lifted her hands above her head, fingers bent like claws.

– I know how you must feel, Iris said grinning. – I…

Tilla slapped her, a stinging slap. Iris gasped and touched her cheek. She turned scared and wanted to run away. Because she had seen the sadistic smile before, in a much younger Tilla.

She was grabbed and held in an iron grip, moaning.

– Poor little Iris. She still hasn't learned to be anything but a victim.

Iris couldn't make a sound. She shook too much. She stared at her friend's twisted face. Saw how the saliva flowed from her mouth.

– You'll never know how I feel. Never!

Tilla's scorn haunted the crying girl fleeing from her.

Pete had seen and heard most of what had transpired. He stared at Tilla with an open mouth.

– That was cruel, he cried angrily.

She laughed, scorning him with her every move, every nuance of speech.

– Poor boy, she spat, grabbing his jaw. – Can't take the heat, huh?

She made a slow, sensual turn in front of him, revealing herself from every angle, every part of herself, letting him see, letting him sense her close proximity. She ran up the stairs, light on her feet, leaving him, too in tatters.

Pete stumbled into the living room, where Ted sat alone.

– What was that about? He said angrily.

Ted didn't reply. He looked at Pete and spoke volumes, but didn't say a word.

– No matter what, Pete choked, – it's totally unacceptable, from both of you. I can take lovers' quarrels. I've had my share of them, but not like this. You've made everybody flee the building for fuck's sake.

– They're probably enjoying the nice weather, Ted grinned.

Pete froze, his face twisted in anger, his body crouching in pain.

– Was that supposed to be a joke? *Was it?*

– Yes. Ted shrugged. – It didn't work, though.

Ted's shoulders sagged. It was like he crumbled there and then. Pete's features softened. He sat down on the couch by his friend's side.

– It's all unraveling, Ted said.

– And you don't seem surprised at all, Pete replied, angry again.

– I'm not. None of us are.

That took Pete aback, made him speechless.

They sat there, the two of them, for a long time, the silence between them, the sounds from the outside tearing them apart.

– Thalama told me something once, Ted finally said.

– *Thalama?* Pete wondered thunderstruck.

– It was in the cabin outside Leadville, Ted continued in a distant voice, – just before we were… taken, taken away. She spoke to me, I guess, but she was really speaking to us all. And what she told us was this: «These are your first warriors, Phoenix. With these you will fail, succeed and fail again».

That silenced Peter Fallon. He understood, and the wrenching pain cut into him like a spiked saw.

– And you believe that? You all believe it?

– Of course we do. Ted turned to him. – We believe Iris. We don't believe she's acting or playacting or lying to us or anything, do we? And we aren't speaking nice to her, speaking down to her, saying that we believe she believes it. We *know* there's something to it, and we see it all unraveling, see the facts support the cards destiny's hand has dealt us.

Pete's shoulder's sagged, too. He opened his mouth to speak.

– But we can't allow that to stop us, of course, Ted added, – stop us from doing anything. Potential isn't certainty. Destiny is just the most probable outcome, not necessarily what's going to happen. It isn't fate.

Pete brightened. The ruby eyes cut right through him, and he was bathed in their warmth, and he felt their power.

– We'll fight that, the way we fight everything… with everything we've got.

Tilla showered, in the coldest of cold water. Needles of water hit her skin, penetrated it to her deepest pit, and it felt good, so very good. She felt strong and energetic when she stepped out on the floor and began drying herself.

The house was still quiet. Most of its «tenants» had returned, but the mood was still muted, subdued. Tilla dressed slowly, lavishly, in quick, confident, feverish moves. She walked directly to Iris' room, walked inside without knocking. The girl's timid expression turned even a bit more timid when she saw whom the visitor was. The beginning of a smile died on her lips.

– We're so far away from home, Tilla stated. – So very far away from home. Not from America. Not from the place we grew up, but a point in time and space mankind left behind long ago. We must stake our own place in this world, no matter the cost.

– I agree with t-that, Iris stuttered.

– Poor girl, Tilla said, tenderly touching her cheek. – You're good looking, skilled and everything. Why do you persist in behaving like an insecure brat?

– I know I shouldn't be, Iris choked. – I can see the admiration in every boy and man's eyes, but that isn't easy to live with either. They don't see me, only a woman they want to p-possess, to own. And the… insecurities of the past won't let g-go. The fact that I'm aware of my f-failings doesn't help me at all. I enjoyed d-displaying mys-self bef-fore. I d-don't anym-more.

She was hardly able to utter the last words, the stuttering almost taking her over completely.

– That's of no importance, Tilla said. – What's important is that no one is better suited than you to do what must be done.

I want to devour you, a man had said to her once. I want to swallow you whole.

Those words were very much with her as she walked on Strand with most of her skin exposed, wearing a daring outfit outdoing any daring outfit she could ever recall having seen. It was a warm January evening, so warm that her exposed skin hardly felt exposed at all. Heads turned as she passed. Admiring and cruel eyes registered her every move. The eager, the brave, the needy approached her, but she rejected them easily. She had grown skilled in denying those she didn't want. Earlier in life she had basked in the admiring glances men and also some women had sent her. Until she had realized they weren't truly admiring, but possessive. They wanted to own her, to display her as their own, as a trinket, a property.

Tilla followed her, at a safe distance, so far away occasionally that she couldn't always see her. Tilla, but not Tilla. She had transformed herself into a fairly unremarkable figure, compared to all the young meat passing back and forth here. She was quite proud of her disguise. The grayish wig, the blue contact lenses, light wrinkles on the forehead and tiny pillows in her cheeks, making her face bloated and older.

Middle aged career woman on the prowl. And she had done it all herself.

Iris walked down Strand in complete contempt for her surroundings. A group of young boys was so horny that they practically stumbled on to her. She dismissed them with a wave of her hand. The ease in which she did it pleased her.

Tilla discovered two men between her and Iris, very distinct from the rest. Even though they were dressed in ordinary clothes and made an effort to blend in, she easily recognized them as cops, easily recognized their kind.

Iris turned by Charing Cross Station and returned the same way she had come. There had been a few turns back and forth by now, and her feet started to feel a little sore in the high-heeled shoes. She saw that Tilla had stopped and knew something was up. The two men grabbed hold of her just as she was about to pass them. The two policemen that had been following her for a while. She looked at them more closely, able to do that, now, without rousing suspicion. She knew they were brutal and shallow men.

– Hi, honey, one of them greeted her, so parodic that she felt a strong need to giggle.

– Hello, she replied.

– You look like a girl who wants to have some fun, the other stated.

– You, too, she giggled.

The two men glanced at each other, for a moment slightly puzzled, but then they shrugged. They were used to girls being stupid as a breadbox.

– We're a bit curious. We've actually been studying you sweet thing for a while. You've rejected quite a few offers, and we wondered why.

– Either they've been single or they've lacked the necessary funds or both, she shrugged very deliberately, very arrogantly, patronizingly.

– We rather thought you would be too much for a single sucker. A grin. – And don't fear we're lacking in funds or in any other department…

– You seem both quite wealthy and able to handle yourselves, she cooed.

They had let go of her. She sought closer to them and stroked one seductively on the chest.

– Listen… we have an apartment nearby very fitting to our little soirée…

– There.

She pointed. They looked, followed the direction of her arm to the other side of the street to Strand Palace Hotel. They glanced at each other, a bit taken aback, clearly expressing doubt. Her lips curled in contempt. They nodded hastily.

– I prefer hotels, she declared. – Besides, my feet are so sore that I can't walk more then a few steps more. Not for a while…

They glanced duty-bound at her feet, feet just as lovely and tasty as the rest of her.

The three of them crossed the street. Iris smiled brightly to a driver being forced to stop with whining tires. He sat there, his face lit by a dreaming expression, until being abruptly roused from the trance by a row of angry horns.

Getting a room wasn't a problem. This would certainly have befuddled Iris. If she didn't know better. A police badge opened most doors.

– We also observed how a group of five approached you. Why did you reject them?

– Two is enough, she replied sweetly. – I'm not greedy.

What morons. So *stupid*. The way they asked and bothered her not even the most needy drug addict hooker would have had any problems exposing them. They could just as well have worn uniform.

Or did they feel so confident that they felt caution was unnecessary?

Inside the room they didn't wait long to push her down on the bed and start the pawing, the very rough pawing. It hurt and she had to release a yelp.

– Nothing personal, boys, she said with a little laughter, – but I am strictly a pre-payment service.

A police badge was pushed into her face.

– You see this, you fucking whore. He slapped her. So hard that her face started swelling instantly. – There is a number of offenses we might book you for. Many we can imagine as well. You better start cooperating or you'll be stuck in quite a mire… *understand?*

– Yes, she whimpered. – Please.

– That's a good bitch, he grinned, petting her cheek.

– How about a… floorshow to begin with? She wondered, giving them her best smile. – To… whet your… appetite. I can do a mean floorshow. Cops have always turned me on. I'll show you. Please?

– Sure. Why not? A mean laughter. – We've got time.

She slipped out of the bed, never taking her eyes off them, starting on her swaying, her lavish, sensual dance, while humming a melody. The men sat on the bed and stared hungrily at her. She kicked off her shoes in ongoing elegant moves. Removed the stockings slowly from her thighs and legs. Her hands sliding up her legs again afterwards. To the edge of the dress, under it, playing with herself a bit, before removing her panties, showing them what that small piece of cloth had been hiding.

– This is what you want, isn't it, boys…

She bent forward, displaying herself, showing herself, rubbing herself. Fingers turned wet, showering in her juices. She released a long, lust-filled wail. One of the men couldn't hold back anymore. He grabbed one of her hands and pulled her back into the bed, buried a fist in her sex. She moaned longingly. He removed the straps of her dress from her shoulders burying his face between her swollen breasts. She writhed her body, as if wanting to help him.

There was a knock on the door.

– Who's there? He wondered, with badly concealed irritation.

– Room service. The well modulated voice sounded clear through the door.

– We haven't ordered anything, damn it.

– I have, Iris said sweetly. – I always get so thirsty, you know…

– I'll get it, he who had been the most pulled back stated.

They had told her their first names, but she couldn't recall them. She didn't care about that, anyway.

He walked to the door. The other rose and placed himself before Iris. Fumbled with his belt. She sent him one of her husky stares, sensing how he was turned even more on, how his cock pushed against the fabric of his pants.

– You're a great whore, Iris, he mumbled. – One who likes it is rare. I'm gonna enjoy this to the max. You'll be totally spent when we throw you in the cell.

The door opened. A breath of wind, a hard piece of flesh hit the man on his way forward. A foot hit him in the chest and threw him gasping backwards. The indistinct figure was over him before he had even begun to regain his footing and his breath. Tilla hit him with a rock-hard hand in the neck and the brief, unequal struggle was done. He hit the floor and lay still.

An enraged Iris took care of the other. She kicked him in the groin with cruel precision. If she had had shoes on, there wouldn't have been much left down there. As it was he released a wail, and fainted on the spot.

– Now, you know a little of how I feel, Tilla patted her cheek. – Soon you'll know more.

They worked quickly and effectively, finding two sets of cuffs on the two cops. They put them on wrists behind the men's backs and put the two on their knees. Tilla found a roll of industrial tape from the plastic bag she had brought and taped the two around their arms and legs. Then their mouths. In just a minute or so they were completely helpless.

Bringing the metal garbage can belonging to the room Tilla walked to the bathroom and filled it with water. She returned and emptied it over the cops. One of them shook. Iris shook the other. Slowly, painfully, as they were brutally beaten by the two girls, they returned somewhat to their senses. Tilla drew a knife. Their eyes were locked on to the blade. She had their complete attention.

– Gentleman, she greeted them, – now, you'll lend me your ears or I'll take them. You will remain in the position in which we have placed you, on your knees, or you will regret it.

She turned to Iris.

– Pay attention, she admonished the two on the floor.

Tilla grabbed the other girl's shoulder strap and pulled. It snapped with a loud sound. Then she began slapping Iris. On both cheeks. A bit careful at first, careful, but not hesitating. Iris choked and choked, but didn't move. Tilla kept striking her. Harder. Many times. The face framed by the brown hair was slowly beaten up. Blood flowed from both nostrils.

– That's good. Tilla praised her. – You can remove your dress now, and lay down on the bed.

Iris obeyed. She lay down on her belly, shaking slightly, but she didn't hesitate.

Tilla turned towards the two men. They looked incredulous at her. She removed their leather belts, and brought them with her back to the bed. The two men shook their heads, and kept shaking them, as if they couldn't quite believe what they saw, what was happening.

Iris trembled there, on her belly, holding on to her dress.

– You may bite in the cloth if you want, Tilla told her. – We don't want you to scream, now, do we?

One of the cops shook his head some more, fought to open his mouth to speak, to protest, but he was helpless. Iris saw Tilla lift the hand holding one of the leather belts. The first strike fell on the unprotected skin.

Iris didn't scream, but there was a large bite-mark hole in the dress when Tilla had completed her task. She choked and spat pieces of cloth, bathed in blood from her mouth. The two cops kept shaking their heads, unable to quite grasp the horrible events unfolding before their eyes. Iris rose, picked up a knife from the plastic bag and walked to the two men, stopping before them with the knife lifted. They looked up at her with a dazed expression in their eyes. She had big trouble standing, but she did.

– You will speak, she told them. – You will sing long and well to us, and you will leave out nothing.

– Your hands will be full of her blood, Tilla told them. – Her skin will be under your nails. Who do you think will be believed, after all?

They looked uncomprehending at the two demons towering above them. Fear shadowed their faces. Their brutal demeanor was totally gone. They believed.

– You can't imagine it, can you? Tilla spoke hoarsely, unmoving like a statue. – You can't possible imagine how far we're willing to go. You're just little boys, begging candy from the adults. Such sweet boys.

She ripped the tape off their lips. A lot of skin followed. They didn't scream, didn't even attempt to do so. They were just wet rags, wrung and hung to dry, ragged dolls feeling the irresistible need to move their lips, to beg the smallest of favors and never stop. The two demons petted them, and comforted them and cajoled them as they confessed their sins, as they fell ever deeper into the hole there was no return from.

Sometimes during the deep night Tilla closed the door behind her to the room where she and her mate lived. It was pitch black. She lit a candle. Ted sat on his heels on the bed. Fully dressed. He hadn't slept. She walked to him, her hand a feather touching his cheek.

– I'm yours, she said humbly, proudly. – This was just something I had to do. I did what you couldn't.

– I'm proud of you, he stated.

He reached out a hand and *touched* her, and she felt desire rise in her like a geyser. Sighing happily she let herself be pulled into his dark embrace.

– We are birds, she said softly. – A bird in a cage is no bird.

– Birds flying in the dark, he said. – We can hit something at any time. The dark is filled with shards and great things, and we can't tell which is which.

She writhed in his arms, as she removed her top, as he started undressing, too.

– We got names, she said proudly. – They sang like canaries. I'm confident that at least one name, parts of their confessions are useable.

– How is Iris?

She wasn't really surprised that he knew. It just confirmed her dedication to him, her undying love.

– She heals fast. A shrug. – She'll be okay tomorrow.

She kissed him, mewing, writhing and moaning. He pushed at her, pushed hard.

– We've got something, she said ecstatically. – We finally got leverage, flesh and blood people we can target, something tangible we can use to fight the pale shadows.

There was abandon. There always was. As they fell on the bed, as they rolled back and forth, as they consumed their communion, as they howled in pleasure, as the candle burned down and the texture of darkness took over their perception, as their voice shook the Earth. But at the back of their head, no matter how much they wanted it to go away, was the apprehension, the cold voice talking, talking, talking and never letting go. Even in the moment of the most explosive heat, it was there, like a sword cutting through their hearts.

2

It was Friday the thirteenth. Ted stopped a bit upon waving Tilla goodbye. She was radiant, there in the shadows, whispering to him with her full lips.

John poked him lightly, grinning with the others.

The two of them, with Vernie, Kim and Bruce were on their way to Carl Palmer with their information. They didn't trust phones or mail or any method that didn't include them delivering it in person.

Carl's office was far away, in the worker class area in the South East. They had to take the Underground or they would have needed to walk for hours.

They walked to Piccadilly Circus Station. It was a fairly long stretch and they were submerged in the city, in the crowds, the streets between the old buildings. People stared at them. Even those who didn't know them or didn't know of them. They always did. Even in this place of variety and mystery they stood out from the crowd.

– Do we walk differently? Vernie giggled. – Do we breathe differently?

– Yes, we do, Ted nodded. – Perhaps not in any overt way, but there's something about us, about how we behave they notice, notice in the deep, atavistic parts of themselves, and that makes some of them embarrassed and even ashamed, others sore afraid, or angry, and others again… are all of the above. They see our dance, see at least a semblance of what we all once were.

– Thank you, Sensei. Kim bowed as she walked. – For the words of wisdom. I will always heed them.

He shook his head. She was speaking lightly and smiling, but he wasn't at all certain she was kidding.

Tilla gave the sandbag the hardest kick she could muster. Her foot hurt, but the sandbag hardly moved. She kicked it again and again. And again. Incredibly enough to herself and to those who watched she increased the strength in the kick. She had seemed to reach her limit quite some time ago, but that was clearly not the case. The rope connecting the heavy sack to the ceiling almost broke at the last kick, as she exhausted fell to her knees.

– Holy cow, a boy exclaimed. – That was amazing. How do you *do* it?

– By determination and passion, she replied, – by will, by making the body move far beyond its apparent limitations.

She rose and went at it again, kicking and hitting the current object of her focus in a series of power bursts. Her limbs and muscles hurt when she was done, as it was supposed to do.

– You're still better than Ted.

Iris handed her a towel, admiration clear in her eyes.

– I train much harder, Tilla replied. – I have to.

They all went to the showers together. One shower room, for all, boys and girls together. No modesty, no shame. They washed each other on the back and elsewhere. Sometimes that was an initiation of sex, sometimes not. It felt good, so very good. They played with each other, played and enjoyed themselves, screaming and laughing. So fun, so much fun.

A couple of boys made their intentions painfully clear to Tilla, but she rejected them today, kindly but decisively. She appeared from the locker room, fully dressed, with her sensuality burning on a low flame, feeling good about it. Right now, this day she wanted to stay aroused, to hold out the low burning flame, to wait for her mate, to «save herself» for him. The thought brought a smile, both ironic and not to her face. Her hand touched her belly briefly.

Ted felt heat flow through his body. He and the four others walked through streets where sights of houses closer to ruins were common. It was also far from the closest underground station. They walked a kind of gauntlet between crowds of youths, dressed in rags, gangs looking upon them as intruders. This was a classic urban disaster area with large unemployment figures and little hope of an improved future.

This was Carl Palmer's home. He had left for a few, short years, and then returned.

– I know why Carl stays here, Bruce commented. – All his rich clients have to come here and beg his favors.

Carl's portfolio had improved significantly in number and «quality» after Stewart had picked him. It had been the best advertising a man could ask for.

– He's got a lot of money in the bank, Bruce kept commenting. – But he stays here.

He hesitated, evidently considering something before continuing.

– I can't tell if he's very smart or very dumb…

– He's an idealist, Vernie said. – He wants to return something to the society that helped him forward.

– You know… Bruce replied, – … I can't decide whether or not you're being sarcastic here. My compliments.

They laughed, more warm, but brittle, hollow laughter.

The house stood out to them. They had never been here before, but they recognized it the moment they laid their eyes on it. It was no more or no less refurbished compared to the rest of the neighborhood, but it had the kind of distinctiveness they had learned to recognize… that of a fortress. It didn't look like one, but it felt like one.

He sat on the stairs, looking like he didn't have a worry in the world. When he spotted them he waved up a storm. He rose and grabbed their hands, grabbed their one with both his. Ted felt, recognized his touch, as familiar as a smell or a face.

– Come, Carl said, – let's go inside.

Tilla made dinner with Pete and Alex and Sandy. There was a lot to do, cooking for so many. The kitchen was hot and humid. It always was. They put in the spicy and meaty remains of yesterday and added some vegetables. As they would use the remains of this meal tomorrow. They never threw away anything.

– I've been thinking, Alex said. – There's a lot of unused furniture here. We can sell it at the markets.

She cast a motherly look at him. He was fairly new here. They always arrived with a plethora of ideas, which was good, which was great.

– You look into it, she said. – You see what can be useful and what won't, and the markets that can be useful and whose won't.

– You got it, he grinned.

His enthusiasm, thinly veiled, didn't hide the pain and darkness beneath the surface. In that, too, he was very much like the rest of them, she ventured.

– We shouldn't be feeding the capitalist machine, of course, he said, – but I don't see we have much choice here. We do everything in our power, striving beyond striving every day and night, and it isn't enough.

They looked at him with sympathy. He didn't say anything that they, themselves hadn't already thought.

– You shouldn't be too concerned about staying «true» to socialist «ideals», Pete said lightly. – Both capitalism and socialism are just two sides of the same coin. None of them offer a true way out of the perils humanity is facing today. The respective «leaders» and those running them in the East and West do this tennis match together, but they have far more in common than what's dividing them.

– I don't think anything is dividing them, Tilla nodded. – It's about power, that's all.

– It's so inspiring, living here, Sandy said abruptly.

They all looked at her.

– We *think* here, she said, a bit more shyly. – I wasn't used to that. The crowd I grew up with hardly looked beyond their own nose. Not my friends, or the adults or the «teachers». You're lucky, in the world as it is, if you find enlightenment in your immediate neighborhood. Most people don't. I surely didn't. You guys are great. You're all great.

And Tilla felt pride swell within, felt it in herself as she felt it in those around her.

Iris rushed through the kitchen with Stella in her arms, her face flushed and sweaty.

– She's about to…

She completed the sentence as she departed for the hall, clearly embarrassed, clearly joyful.

– She's about to pee on herself.

And Tilla felt a large, sticky ball catch in her throat.

Pete spoke, anger very present in his voice.

– And people living under the yoke of the tyrants have the audacity to attack us because we do what they don't dare.

Sandy's expression and eyes turned distant.

– There are times I think I can actually hear them out there, she said, her voice equally distant. – Hear their buzz and yapping, hear them say nothing at all.

Tilla imagined she could, too, sometimes, but when she focused on it, and attempted to listen on a conscious level, there was nothing there, nothing that she could discern.

She studied Sandy for while, studying her without studying her, as she had grown quite good at.

Sandy had changed, as had they all, since coming here. But there was something more, something undetermined, another thing Tilla couldn't quite grasp.

– I'm taking a break, she said. – Is it okay?

– Of course, Pete said. – Everything is proceeding on its own here for a while, anyway.

She shook her head as she left, a bit irritated at herself. She knew, like they all did, that she didn't have to ask, ask anyone permission to do anything, that they didn't ask before doing what they wanted. But she was distracted, not quite here.

Her feet moved her. She walked to the remote areas of the building, knowing fully well where she was heading.

The stairs were done quickly, effortlessly. She stood on the dusty floor in the attic. The room opened up to her, as she, herself opened. Turned slowly. Concentrated, focused on the whirling dust. Breathed. Someone was playing a guitar downstairs. The music rose through the floor until it hit her like wave upon wave of soft, tangible air. She turned slowly, and the dust turned with her. There was a pain inside her somewhere. She got tears of joy in her eyes.

The sound of the guitar downstairs filled her mind. Suddenly she was Pete, sitting on the couch, playing the guitar. It was her fingers touching the strings. Her eyes that saw Iris and Sandy stand by the door, listening, moving alike, humming alike, dancing the same steps. Something in Iris' mind. She knew something, but didn't know she knew. The cabin… Tilla shuddered.

The dust settled. The buzz faded. The room, the room filled with energy and shadow was just a room again.

Smell… She touched her upper lip. When she pulled back the hand, there was blood on it. Blood shimmering in strange hues of red and ruby. She gasped, totally overwhelmed by the experience.

Alex entered the room. She sensed him before she turned around and saw him.

– You look so… happy, he said, his voice faltering.

– Have you felt yourself being born before? She asked him. – Have you experienced strong colors and detailed textures for the first time, drawn your very first breath of air? That's exactly how I feel right now.

She danced to the music, moved in synchronicity with the dust particles dancing in the air.

When she looked again he had come close to her. He held a bottle of soda in his hand, offering it to her. She was thirsty and accepted, drinking greedily of the cold fluid. Handing the bottle back to him, half empty, licking her lips. He put it down on the floor.

– Your belly is still flat, he said hoarsely. – Just as desperately sexy as the rest of you.

He grabbed her, pulled her close and kissed her on the lips.

– Thank you, she chuckled.

There was no need for her to comment on his state of mind and body. That was obvious when looking at the considerable bulge on his pants, without sensing his churning, conflicting emotions.

It was at that time Ted began to show visible signs of distress. He began writhing in the chair in Carl Palmer's office, clearly showing more than mere discomfort. He touched his forehead. A thin film of sweat covered the ice-cold skin.

– I won't ask you how you got hold of this information, Carl said, shaking his head, – but it's dynamite, more than explosive enough to create a giant stir if being played right.

The others nodded in excitement and anxiety. This was important. They had been striving towards something like this for months, a breakthrough, a breach in the armor, the defenses society had put in place to deal with insurgence and insurgents. Ted tried to connect something to it, anything, but he couldn't. It was like he wasn't even here anymore, but somewhere dark and dank, where there was no way out.

He sat there with his eyes open, unable to shut them, to shut out what flowed through them from nowhere. Tilla danced, he saw her, and was there with her, but everything was so hard, as if she moved through quicksand instead of air. There were pale shadows surrounding her, first one, then more.

Alex began touching Tilla, pulling her close again. She freed herself with a giggle.

– Not now, she said. – You're very sweet and attractive, but I just don't feel like it for the moment. Later, huh?

She faltered as she took one step back, as she attempted to speak again. In a whirl of darkened air she glimpsed something in his hand. There was a sting of pain, and her eyes widened. A needle. She attempted to strike him, but it was a clumsy, ineffective attempt. Her vision blurred. Darkened air surrounded her and swept her off feet. He struck her, a fist to the ribs emptying her lungs for air, keeping her from crying out. He grabbed her and held her, pushed her at the wall.

– Do you know how dangerous you people are? He snarled at her, slapping her as he spoke, slapping her repeatedly, making her cheeks sting. – Young boys and girls come here, and you fill their impressionable minds with your filthy garbage, making chaos and anarchy and unrest and dissatisfaction grow in them.

He tied her up in short, angry moves. She felt rough rope tighten around wrists and ankles. Something was pushed into her mouth. Tears of fear and rage filled her eyes. The ropes were so tight and she was so weak. She had believed herself safe within these walls, foolishly believed she would only need to be vigilant in the streets outside. And now she paid the price.

Price pricepriceprice. Everything went fuzzy.

Four men gathered around her and Alex. Alex still smiled in scorn. Tilla didn't look at him. She stared paralyzed at the man by his side: Robert Tremblay.

A horribly silent scream assaulted Ted. He practically jumped out of the chair. The others looked at him, and they had never seen a stronger fear in any human face.

– You stay, he took the time to tell them. – I must… leave.

He ran out of the office, a whirlwind on the move. Left the door wide open. John had just glimpsed the terrified expression. It was enough. A moment's hesitation, and then he ran, too. The others remained, frozen on the spot.

Ted ran right into the street, in front of a cab. The driver had no idea what miracle had made him stop in time. A shadow jumped inside. And darkness jumped inside with him.

– Wardour Street, Ted shouted, almost howling. – As fast as humanly possible. *Step on it!*

A wailing banshee haunting humanity.

The driver wanted to ask specifics, but he held his tongue, and stepped on it, the roar of the engine sounding strangely tame.

– I hear you, sir, he mumbled. – I hear you.

The door stayed open. John managed to jump into the cab just in time. The door slammed shut behind him as the car took off on something at least resembling whining tires. John looked at Ted. His friend didn't seem to register him being there at all, with eyes staring into nothing. John knew they stared at something, something far away. He wanted to ask, wanted desperately to ask what was wrong, but he didn't dare.

Two other men appeared carrying two other women, Sandy and Zoe.

– Collateral casualties, my dear Tilla, Robert Tremblay told her. – I kinda like that.

Tilla was scared, and was unable to hide it as Tremblay, Bob, her childhood friend touched her. And she remembered what he had done to her, done to her when she had been his slave. He pinched her left cheek and she couldn't hold back the tears. Tears of rage, hatred and nameless fear.

– Our two bonuses will sleep soundly during transport, but you won't, dear Tilla. It would have been easier to tranquilize you completely, too, right from the start, but I wanted you to be awake, wanted you to catch everything, so to speak.

She was fuzzy, and sick, and nauseous, but she was awake. She shook with awareness.

He put his hand on her belly. She attempted to twist her body away, but they held her so hard, so hard. He slapped her. Many times. Alternately on the left and right cheek. It hurt, hurt terribly.

– I own you, he snarled. – You are mine! The sooner you realize this, the better for you and the freak you're carrying.

Her eyes widened slightly.

– Oh, yes, we know, he said. – Not just because of Alex here, but because we have kept tabs on you. I have kept my eyes on you, waiting patiently for the day we would meet again. And now the time is right. The time… is now!

All this time he had waited, waited for the time in his mind when this was «right». She trembled, couldn't stop trembling.

He lifted her up and put her over his shoulder, nodding to the others. Alex returned back down, joining the others, and they looked at him without reproach, without suspicion.

– FASTER, Ted howled.

The windows shook.

– With respect… sir… there are cars back and front, and nowhere to maneuver.

– Use the sidewalks. THE SIDEWALKS, DAMN YOU!

The man behind the wheel paled. The sidewalks were filled with people. In the mirror he saw two eyes… change, turn even freakier.

– That's it, he cried. – I don't have to out up with this. We've got rights in this country. We…

His foot was on its way to the breaks, when a sharp pain in the foot and throat *stopped* him. His hands were torn off the wheel. The door opened wide. He practically flew out of the car, as if grabbed by a storm. He landed awkward and painfully in the street. The door closed in contempt, snarling at him. He would repeat this story in the padded cell he would spend the rest of his life. «I swear, I had this monster in my car. I don't know how, but it did all this. It made it happen, brought all this horror to the world, to MY world, are you LISTENING, damned assholes».

The car turned abruptly towards the sidewalk. People attempted stricken to throw themselves to safety. Not everyone made it. Their blood and flesh decorated the windshield. John stared in terror-mixed wonder how the wheel moved by itself, how its every move corresponded with another flare in the ruby eyes. John wouldn't dream of disturbing the stranger sitting there by his side, rocking in his seat.

Another car charged them from the right, unable to stop. Ted managed to avoid a collision, but couldn't stop the cab from hitting the closest wall. The engine died in a cacophony of shrill sounds. John shook his head in incredulous silence. They were uninjured. He had looked at the speed just before the impact, fifty miles, through packed streets.

– I can't believe it, he exclaimed. – I saw it, experienced it, but I can't quite wrap my head around it.

The other acted as if he hadn't spoken, as if nothing had happened at all. The door was blown from its hinges. Ted jumped outside. John crawled from the wreck after him, in an attempt to keep up, realizing in moments how futile it was.

Ted ran past National Film Theatre. By then John was long gone behind him. He knew this place. His mind worked, in a kind of subroutine, beneath the roar of the storm. This was the place he had had his first touch of realization, of true realization, about who he was, realizing that there was no going back. He crossed Waterloo Bridge. And all the time the silent sarcastic voice cried «too late, too late» in his head. He increased the speed further. Eventually, another time, another place he would wonder about how fast he was running and how fast he would be able to move… if he wanted to. But not now. Now, everything was on autopilot, desperation and anguish filling his every waken thought.

The run from the bridge was only a blur, impressions he would never be truly able to make sense of.

Too late. He read it in every face he encountered when he rushed into the building, the place that had been his home.

Such a painfully long time.

He raged through the building, in a stubborn, beyond stubborn exercise in futility. Searching every corner and shadow. He stopped in the living room, where everybody present huddled in his presence. The table was set for dinner. He raised his hands above his head in limitless hatred.

– Where is she? WHERE IS SHE?

Peter Fallon cautiously appeared in his line of vision.

– They came and went through the roof hatch, he said. – Sandy and Zoe are also gone.

Ted Warren struck the dinner table. Broke it in a single strike. Food and plates and tools flew everywhere. It erupted in him, the rage.

– ARRGHH

A limitless frustration, The Power, and the sense of Power flowed in him.

NO, not yet. Too early, too early, too early.

He grabbed a chair and crushed it against the wall. Crushed another chair, and another. Then he attacked the wall itself. Struck it, struck a hole through it. He wasn't hurt.

– HAH! A cry in primitive triumph.

Hours later. Twilight. He sat on the couch in the living room, not really moving much. The others were there, too, but they didn't approach him and didn't speak to him. To the monster. The stranger. John had returned. Vernie, Bruce and Kim as well. He sat on the couch with his knees pulled up and back, staring at them all with a luring grin.

The eyes looked to them like fires of hell. To those who dared to glance at him. John felt physically ill. In the cab there had been both rage and fear. Now, only the rage remained. There had been a sense of warmth and protection. Now it was just rage incarnated.

The beast's eyes stared at them. Filled with hatred, contempt and superiority. It looked at them with a wolfish grin beyond any sane description.

A ball began bouncing, up and down, by itself, there on the floor. He stared at Iris, as if challenging her. Her right hand went to her face. Then she curled that hand into a fist. Another ball closer to her began bouncing. Pete walked right out there, between them, grabbing first one ball, then the other. Instantly two other balls began bouncing, bouncing harder, faster. Pete grabbed those, too, and another set, and another. It did him no good. There was always at least one bouncing, or rather jumping up and down in joy. He could almost see the smile, the horrible grin painted on their surface.

The fog covering Ted's mind finally lifted, but the need to crush, to conquer them all didn't go away. On the contrary. It increased to explosive levels.

– LINDA, he cried darkly, making everybody look startled at him. – The bitch. She's behind this. I should have known. She will pay. PAY!

– How do you know that?

Pete turned towards him, facing him, realizing that Ted's thoughts were more than a bit muddled now. Somebody had to put a stop to this.

– YOU! Ted was up before anybody could blink. – You know where the bitch is. You've always known. Tell me. TRAITOR. *Tell me!*

Pete was lifted up in the air by the invisible hand and thrown into the opposite wall. He hung there, his feet floating just a little bit above the floor. Sufficient for everybody to see. A collective gasp. Some of them had steeled themselves, ready to aid Pete. They remained in position, staring at the demon in their midst. The enormous creature that seemed to fill the entire room, fill all space available to them and strangle them. A creature even larger than what some of them had experienced little more than a year ago. And those from Denver who had experienced Mike at his worst could never have imagined something like *this*.

– *Tell me where she is!*

From one second to the next Pete was grabbed by a fear he couldn't escape, no matter how hard he tried. The only thought in the terrified Pete's head was to obey the terrible voice. The others heard stunned that he was actually stuttering.

Ted Warren let go of him, released him right there, and he fell to the floor, shaking like a leaf. The creature let him go - and forgot about him. The door to the stairs opened. Stopped abruptly before being smashed at the wall. Warren didn't say goodbye. He left them without a word. Forgot about them, too.

John rushed to the stairs and followed him with his eyes down.

– I'm going with him, he said, watching as others helped Pete back on his feet. – I owe him a lot. You keep everything together here.

– I don't think that's' possible, Pete said, hurt trembling in his voice. – Not after this.

He stared at Iris. They all did. She looked at them all, with a look of utter horror painted on her face. There was a choking sound, and she, too, ran out of the room. They heard her slam the door to her room.

John rushed down the stairs. He, too, forgetting about what he left behind.

Ted calmed himself with an effort as soon as he got outside. It didn't matter. It was there, with him, the Beast, and would be, until the very end of time.

People still walked in large circles around him.

John caught up with him in Wardour Street, gasping for air.

– I'm going with you, he cried. Then calmer, more decisively: – I'm joining you.

Ted smiled coldly. To himself. He hardly knew John was there. He sensed that he had never been more powerful than he was at this moment. He knew, with knowledge beyond knowledge that it was nothing compared to what he could become, the enormous potential resting inside him.

Phoenix was awakening from the long sleep.

Leaving only ashes.

CHAPTER EIGHT

The non-existing wind blasted the two men, ice cutting the heart.

It was quiet. They could hardly hear the close traffic, just outside the yard in the somewhat concealed building.

Ted forced himself to knock on the large, solid oak door. The ten seconds it took anybody inside to respond quickly eroded his patience.

A small hatch was opened. He saw a sweet, made up face.

– Hello, sirs, she greeted them sweetly. – What's your pleasure?

There seemed to be some sort of password involved somewhere here. He didn't give a damn.

– Isn't it obvious? He snarled. – We want in.

The intense stare made her take one step back, an act saving her life.

– I'm sorry, sir, she replied. – It's outside visiting hours. I must ask you to return…

Words were nothing to Ted anymore. He concentrated slightly. The door was blown off the hinges, blown off the solid frame. A mighty force pushed chips and pieces of the solid oak door far into the building. Some of the remains gained such a speed that they were crushed to powder on the far side of the hall. Unaffected he crossed the threshold. The girl had all her fingers in her mouth, terrified. Eyes turned to marbles in shock.

– I'm only asking once: Where is Linda, your boss?

She attempted to speak, but it just collapsed into babble. She pointed up with a bloody arm.

It was unnecessary. He had already looked up, to the top of the house' elaborate staircase. Linda stood there, Guards - women and men - appeared behind her and came running from all over the place with guns in their hands. Very organized, very deadly.

– STOP! She cried. – Don't try to keep him from doing anything. Let him come upstairs.

He studied her intensely. Flashes came to him as he ascended the stairs. He noticed her black clothes, similar to his own, hers being clearly far more expensive, probably tailor-made. This was another Linda, the one he had always glimpsed behind the youthful appearance, one that had changed, irrevocably. She was so… adult, such a paragon of confidence.

She brushed against him, as he passed her, her lips brushing against his.

– Not that they could have stopped you in anything, she whispered. – I just valued their lives, that's all. I wanted to see you, see what you have become, but I resisted the temptation. There will be time enough, time enough to see you in all your glory.

– Where is Tilla? He asked.

– Tilla? I don't know that…

She looks truly incredulous, Ted thought.

– Tilla has been kidnapped, John said cautiously. – With Zoe and Sandy.

– And you think I… She looked shocked at them both. – You can't possibly believe…

– YOU KNOW WHERE SHE IS. I DEMAND TO KNOW WHERE SHE IS!

He turned to her. She only looked calmly at him, seemingly totally indifferent faced with the monster towering over her. John and all the others got gooseflesh all over, but she just stood there, calmly enduring the wrath, the pure wrath it conveyed.

– You know I'm telling the truth. The thin voice had a slight quiver. – I know you can look right through me, sense that I'm telling you the truth.

– You're lying. BITCH!

He struck her, struck her so hard that she fell like a heap on the floor. The wrath faded again, as it kept seething within. She was telling the truth. But he still wanted to hurt her. Wanted it badly. He didn't need any other reason. The line of doubt was paper-thin. He knew that. She didn't move. Just looked up at him, calmly, excitedly awaiting her fate.

He turned to leave.

– But I can easily find out. Dwelling. He turned back again, focused on her again. – I believe, know we can find out who has taken her, and why… and where. Nothing or no one can stop us in anything.

He didn't help her up, but that was also unnecessary. She moved just as he did, like a cat on a prowl, a predator on the hunt.

They entered her office, the three of them, leaving the others behind, entered a lush and moody place. He saw that it had recently been extensively redecorated.

– How long will it take? He asked, visibly impatient.

– Not long, she assured him, adding: – I'll do anything to please you…

John closed the door behind them. She pushed a button under her desk.

She turned to Ted, her face a serene mask of a smile.

– You know… she said, the White Rose said. – I'm finally living my childhood nightmare. Except that it's no longer a nightmare, but a dream come true…

She posed for him, displayed herself to him, unafraid, distorting nothing.

There was cautious knocking on the door.

– ENTER, she snapped irritated.

The door opened. Ted recognized Marlene instantly. Even though she was now far more timid, pale and humble.

– Call a meeting, Linda bade her.

It was no order, really, more a casual suggestion. More wasn't necessary. Marlene smiled eagerly and rushed back out.

The meeting was brief. Ted watched it all from the background, curiosity flashing in the ruby eyes. Her underlings took notes. When they opened their mouths to speak it was to ask effective questions. They were skilled and they were obedient, and that was all that was required of them. Ted heard whispers of the Ice Princess, and he was positive Linda heard them, too. Admiration and respect, tinged with absolute fear. She smiled coldly. It was the same, now. No one asked why. She didn't give orders. Just told them what to do. And they did.

It took four hours. Ted was impressed. His ice-cold smile warmed her. By then they had the exact time. A description of the kidnappers, details just as thorough as a police all points bulletin and even drawings. The exact route from the collective, street by street, block by block.

One of the drawings they easily recognized. All three of them. At first glance.

– Bob, the pig, Linda swore. – Just wait till I…

– You've done well, Ted praised her.

His dry voice was just a thin veil hiding the wrath beneath.

– I want to come with you, she demanded.

Then adding, wheedling:

– Please!

– Just the three of us, walking into a well designed trap? He wondered. – Bob wants us to come, come to him.

– I don't care, she raged. – We'll make their poorly executed plan explode in their faces.

– Well spoken, he nodded.

The drawings were torn to pieces. So fast that it looked like they were just falling apart. Linda stared excitedly at the pieces whirling in the air above them, not falling, stared even more excitedly at the remains of the door below, as they left the house. As she did, too. Never to return.

2

They drove off in an old Volkswagen bubble. Linda handled the wheel. Ted and John sat in the backseat, checking the merchandize. John put an Irlim M-11 machine gun inside his coat.

– My father has this, too, in his ordnance, he said. And then adding puzzled: – Sometimes I imagine he has every possible weapon conceived in that cellar.

And then, after a while he added, a remote look in his eyes.

– How many do you think we can kill, before it gets to be too much for us?

– Each of us can kill dozens. Ted shrugged. – Together we should be able to take out hundreds. They will need an army.

It was the way he said it, so confident, so beyond doubt.

After just a few blocks Linda turned into a dark alley. They walked a short stretch before jumping into the next car. Ted's eyes flared briefly. It was sufficient. The engine started.

– You could get rich this way, Linda grinned cheerfully.

They drove and moved in large circles, But eventually in the right direction. They were heading north, inevitably north.

It took time, and they were given time to ponder, to reflect, and they kind of wished they weren't.

– I try to remember Bob's face, John said. – I can't really; no matter how many details I can actually call forth.

To Ted it was just bandages and an indistinct, inflamed expression.

– What happened to him, John cried, – to make him change like that?

– Nothing, Ted snorted. – He was always like he is, just very good at hiding it.

Linda passed the large estate at the safe distance. Its dark and ominous light was visible from far away. She stopped at the place where they could no longer see any of it and couldn't be seen from it.

They left the car. Linda gathered her hair in the neck and tied it up, putting on a black wig.

– Let's *move*.

– The tree of us against all of them.

John shuddered, strangely little afraid.

Ted, Ted Warren led them, into the deep shadows, into places of the modern city most citizens never saw.

A tall wall surrounded the place. A barb wired fence covered the top of the wall.

They chose a spot at random and approached it from darkened streets.

– I on your shoulders? John whispered, his eyes constantly moving, looking for hostiles.

The street remained quiet, empty.

– … no. Ted, frowning considered it briefly, before shaking his head. – The wall is rigged with alarms. The fence is electrical.

John suffered a violent chill. He couldn't keep it from manifesting. At the sight of Ted Warren, a man he didn't know crouching before him. Ted closed his eyes, evidently concentrating, and when he reopened them they were no longer eyes, but pools of dark fire. Hands curled into fists.

– The forest, Warren mumbled. – I can feel it. Stifled, temporarily tamed, but there.

John felt the quiver all over his body, and then… and then he was pulled into the air, by a mighty, invisible hand. He was levitating upwards, over the wall. John choked. He couldn't stop it.

– Have no fear. He heard Linda's soft voice. – We're flying, flying on Phoenix' dark wings.

And when he turned his head she was there, at his side, flying through the air like he was. Ted lifted them. He made them fly through the air, over the fence letting them go on the lawn inside.

He felt them land, felt their feet touch the grass. And it was so easy, not hard at all. Rage and joy continued to mingle inside of him. So hard to control. He had to, for the sake of those, for the one he wanted to save.

He took a few steps back, hesitated a bit, and took a few more. Measured the hurdle before him. Then he ran forward and *jumped.* A part of him feared the jump would be a ridiculous attempt. Another part knew it wouldn't be. He jumped over the wall, over the fence, high above. From John and Linda's point of view he saw himself as a dark shadow against the brighter dark of the night sky. He landed softly and effortlessly. As if the jump had been from a chair and not a flight over a hurdle impossible to cross.

The park-like estate was dark and quiet. The two looked at him with unlimited trust and admiration. John with fear. Linda with joy. Warren led them on, across the black grass, in-between tight bushes.

Ted heard the birds, heard them sing, heard their song vary and change, constantly, until a pattern emerged. He heard nature's tiny sounds, heard it everywhere these days, but never more than here, now. The main estate building was to the right, a couple of hundred steps over the rise. He knew, even though he couldn't see it. It was like he could see the entire area, as they crossed the open field. But it was so much, so much to focus on. He never managed to warn the others. The moment he saw an indistinct movement that to them was just darkness, the lights flooded them. His legs had already jumped, jumped far to the side. There was thunder from a number of guns, most of them directed at the spot where Ted had been, a moment ago. He wasn't hit. The little arrows hit far from where he was. They hit John and Linda and the two fell like they were being hit by an axe.

Neurological poison, Ted thought. It would have worked on me, too.

He ran off, through the forest, with single jumps covering a dozen steps. Mumbling to himself, cursing the enemies. They will pay. THEY WILL PAY!

He growled deep down in the throat, as he fled the light, fled into the darkness, into the ebony world of the night.

Linda and John lay unmoving on the ground. Men with guns surrounded them. Robert Tremblay pushed at their bodies with a foot. They didn't stir. He nodded, somewhat pleased.

– What the fuck happened? What excuse can you offer?

– Nobody understands it, boss, one said nervously. – We had them all in our sight. The trap had already sprung. One moment he was there. The next he wasn't. I've never seen anyone move so fast.

– Relax, Tremblay said relaxed, calming nervous, timid minds. – He will be ours soon. With the infrared cameras we've placed all over the place it's only a matter of time before he's caught.

– Nobody understand how they got over the wall, either, the closest confidante stated. – Do we post men along it to keep him from going for help?

Tremblay looked into the darkness with a smile covering his mouth.

– No, concentrate all the men close to the center of the operation. Send out search-teams, and be ready to give them immediate support the instant the traps are sprung.

He nodded to himself, content, elated and with this small buzz of hatred and fear filling his entire being.

– He won't run. Not until he gets what he came for.

3

Linda woke up hurting and weak on the cold concrete. She felt the ice-cold metal around her wrists. For just a moment panic rose in her, but she forced it back by an act of will. Fear was a luxury she didn't allow herself, had promised herself she wouldn't allow herself. She forced her hurting body up, making it stand, on shaky legs. Two separate manacles chained her arms to the concrete, just long enough for her to be able to stand somewhat straight.

She glimpsed, through flooded eyes John and Tilla, Sandy and Zoe chained like she was chained, like items on an exhibition. All the guards with guns. The large yard in front of the stately building. The crossing floodlights removing all shadows in a wide area. Robert Tremblay with an older gentleman, Rudolf Verheyen. Linda had seen pictures of him, and also seen him as one of the High Ones, even though she couldn't quite remember that. The sight of him sent waves of fear and hatred through her.

The two were not carrying visible arms.

– Hello, Ice Princess of Denver, Tremblay greeted her, so different, so much the same compared to the boy she had known. – It pleases me that you're all awake for the show we've prepared for you.

– What a pitiful attempt at deception and intimidation, Tilla snarled. – I've been awake for a long time. I heard you, even though I didn't need to. You hadn't planned on Ted getting away. He surprised you again.

Tremblay scowled at her, though quickly regaining his composure.

– You're correct, of course. He shrugged. – But you're also wrong. We hadn't planned it, but we've made contingency plans. We know what Warren is. Don't believe we don't. We know he's a freak of nature, an animal pretending to be human.

He stared at them with his marble eyes, his beyond rational contempt.

– We've got fifty men here. It's much more enjoyable this way. We can relax and savor the hunt.

– That's what tipped you over, isn't it? Linda stared at him. – Your professed rationality couldn't handle the beast in your world. There's no place for it in your reality. I remember, now, during the fight, Mike and Ted's fight… You couldn't watch. Not because of Ted's suffering, but because you just couldn't *handle* it. We all had trouble dealing with it, but you refused to.

– You're awfully certain of yourself… *slave*.

He snarled at her.

– Yes, I am, she replied, unbowed, returning his snarl tenfold. – We freed ourselves from your machinations, and you have no idea how strong that made us, you pathetic *excuse* for a Human Being.

He raised his hand in anger, laughing briefly, before letting the hand fall again.

– You will fall in line again. It's just a matter of time, and after this we'll have time, to set you right. And this time we'll make sure you remain cute little dolls, obedient eager soldiers for the rest of your life.

– You've got no idea what you've set in motion, Tilla said. – The forces you're playing with. Not the slightest idea. If you had, you would've fled to Antarctica or somewhere even further away.
– You're already dead, Linda grinned wickedly. – Stone cold. And your death will be unimaginably painful and last an eternity.
Sandy didn't seem completely awake yet. She spoke in a dreaming voice:
– It's the Angel of Death that's out there, that's coming for you.
Zoe blinked confused. John smiled encouragingly to her.
Tremblay and Verheyen and their henchmen stared sullenly at them. Bob laughed contemptuously, and deliberately turned away. A chill passed through him. They could all see it, and he kept staring into the darkness, forcing himself to stare and not closing his eyes, looking at the giant shadow moving out there, moving through the night, slowly becoming the night, becoming darkness, and becoming Shadow. Everybody could see Bob Tremblay's hatred like a palatable, tangible horror, there in the bright, bright light.

4

Ted slipped through the night like a cat on two legs, but also on all fours. Pride filled him, as he sensed it, actually felt the sense of destiny, of drama unfolding, like something alive inside and outside. It was present here, on this place, all around him, claws and fangs in the night.
Primitive pride cursed through him as he moved without making a sound, not any that others were able to hear. He passed behind the hunters' backs, the backs of many of those believing themselves to be hunters, and they noticed nothing. The dark fun of it all strengthened him further.
Hardly scaring him anymore.
The birds moved. They didn't fly up, but they moved in relation to the men with guns moving around. And that was just a part of it, a part of his amazing increased sensitivity. He felt the men move, felt the leaves rustle by their feet, felt the grass grow…It was too much. Focus, focus on what's important. He was pulled in a thousand different directions, when only a few were right. Focus on the hunt, the men chasing you, the men you chase. He avoided the men easily, but they didn't go away. They went away… and returned. They…
They *saw* him. He smiled, and he knew the camera caught it, the camera in the tree above him. His eyes flared, and the electronic eye sputtered

and died, and then abruptly, it was blown to pieces. Large and small remains rained over a large area. The sound echoed through the forest.

The men fired at the sound. The bullets didn't even come close to him.

– THAT WAS THE CAMERA, IDIOTS. A commanding voice cut through the night. – IT HAS BEEN RENDERED INOPERABLE. HE KNOWS. I THOUGHT YOU WERE BEYOND THE NERVOUS TWITCH FIRING-PIN STATE OF MIND, THAT YOU WERE SOLDIERS, NOT CHILDREN PLAYING WAR. HE'S CLOSE. *Find him!*

Another growl deep in the throat. The previous, minutes ago could perhaps have been mistaken for coming from a human, but not this one. The men hearing it shook hard. There was nowhere to direct the guns. The sound seemed to come from everywhere.

– What the *hell* was that? One of them cried, fear very evident in his voice.

– It's him, you idiot. There's no large animal here.

The shadow slipped away, out of their immediate range. There was a rustle of branches on the ground and they fired at that. A man cried out in pain. He had been hit.

– No, I repeat NO firing without direct visual contact, the commanding voice ordered sharply. – He's not going to decimate us by our own clumsiness, are you boys *listening* to me?

One thought he saw something, a creature on all fours between the trees. The next moment it was gone. He exchanged glances with his closest comrades. They were all sweating profusely, and it wasn't really a very warm night. Even for February the moist air covering the fields made it ice-cold. They were all sweating, constantly moving, looking for something that wasn't there.

Warren homed in on the sharp barking voice, slowly closing the distance between the commanding officer and himself. It was easy. It barked all the time. Warren heard only the electronic voice at first but then, like a weak pre-echo he began hearing the true voice. He rushed up behind the big man, ready for anything, putting his arms around the man's neck and breaking it in one, sharp pull. Nothing to it. He let go of the dying body with a silent, undetectable snarl. The face of the man falling to the ground hadn't even had time to change expression. Warren had begun to pull back when he noticed that the head rolled back and forth on the man's socket, and had almost loosened from the shoulders. The epiphany made the cruel smile light his face.

The others eventually noticed that the sharp voices had ceased barking orders, as they one by one stopped in their tracks, feet without a head.

Uncertainty changed to anxiety, to fear. As if by telepathy they gathered in groups. No one dared express their fears, but they couldn't deny the cold trickle racing repeatedly down their spines to themselves. They took their time, but after a lot of screaming and shouting they decided to go and find the team leader.

They charged anxiously through the dark, doubling back to the place where the man had last been seen. And they found him easily, almost before starting the actual search. He sat with his back to a tree. Or… his body did, what they were fairly certain was his body. The head was gone, torn off its socket. They spotted the torn sinews and muscles. The spine sticking grotesquely up. Two of the men couldn't hold back. They rushed into the bushes and threw up. Everybody could hear the half-choked sounds. No one could avoid hearing them. A few minutes ago those very sounds would have resulted in scorn and scornful laughter. No more. Now, a remarkable number of the hard men felt more than a need to do likewise.

An enraged voice sounded through the intercoms. Verheyen.

– What the fuck is happening down there, he roared. – Don't you have better things to do than to stay put and shout insults to each other?

– Nothing we can't… *handle,* sir. One of the men grabbed the mike on the former team leader's chest and responded. – You should just be aware that the object is a bit more… resourceful than expected, that's all. He took out the team leader.

– He... took out the team leader?

– Yes, sir. It will definitely take longer than expected to neutralize him.

Warren heard their whisper, laughing at them, scorning them, fighting with himself not to be too cocky. Fools.

None of them had any idea of what true neutralization signified.

Half an hour passed. Not much happened. Not at the command center, and not in the field. Small things, sounds from intercoms and from the darkness surrounding the circle of light. The ten guards at the circle's perimeter began pulling back a bit, further into the light. They scratched themselves, as if lice had suddenly appeared on their body, a sure sign of the anxiety haunting them.

– You and your thugs aren't worth much, Bobby, Tilla said sarcastically. – You can't even catch a single man. I'm ashamed you were able to create so much trouble for us that you did.

– We didn't really. Tremblay was just as calm. – We stayed mostly in the background. There wasn't much planning to speak of or anything. We only helped out a bit here and there. Letting the other fools that didn't even know about us do most of the work. You non-adaptable creatures aren't really appreciated. No one will miss you.

– It's you that no one will miss. YOU!

Linda spat the last word.

He wanted to strike her. They all saw that. But he reined himself in, infinitely patient.

A signal from operations inside the building distracted them. One of the white coats came rushing outside. Tremblay and Verheyen turned towards him.

– What NOW? Verheyen growled.

The bald man in the white coat was sweating, both excitedly and nervously.

– It's… the object, sir. During the last five minutes he has put five more cameras out of commission. Eight in all, now, sir. Increasing his intervals. If he keeps this up, very soon, now, there won't be any more left.

– And you have yet to make a profile of his modus operandi? Verheyen said, very annoyed. – You should get to it, Johnson. We're paying you extremely generously.

– That's just it, sir. Johnson breathed visibly harder. – The object is changing modus operandi constantly. He seems to be *learning*.

– Learning? Tremblay narrowed his left eye.

– Precisely, sir. It seems like he's the one with time on his side. Not… us. For every passing minute, every new event he gets better in what he does, self-organizing, turning faster, slyer and more dangerous.

He dried his forehead with a white cloth.

– But I believe I've been able to detect a weakness, a pattern…

Something dropped from the air, from the darkness. Landed on the lawn in front of them. A body without head. Johnson turned yellow. And then from the opposite side dropped another body. Blood flowed from the wound, the hole left by the missing head. The limbs twisted and writhed as if the body was still alive. Johnson fainted on the spot.

Linda clapped her hands enthusiastically. Tilla did as well. Zoe stood there open-mouthed and seemed to have totally forgotten where she was, forgotten her predicament. Her scientific mind in uproar. The large bodies had been thrown from the darkness, from two opposite sides. The space on both sides was much too large for anybody to throw them this far. And the way it had happened was even more incredible. Her mind connected everything that had happened, everything she had experienced the last year. One word forced itself to the surface: Telekinesis. Or psychokinesis. Words she and her colleagues had always had much fun with and always scorned.

– Cheap theater, Tremblay mumbled.
But he didn't sound very convincing, not very convincing at all.
– From now on everybody will fire live rounds, Verheyen shouted into the microphone with bulging eyes. – Fire at will, I repeat: fire at will, at anything that moves.
It was a totally unnecessary command. The men had gone to this level of alert minutes ago, on their own initiative. But there was nothing to fire at, except figures that were clearly their own comrades sneaking around, attempting to spot the creature.
They had begun with going two and two, when four headless bodies were found to the west. They blew their whistles and everybody gathered around the unrecognizable corpses. Shouting and reminiscing slowly died, and they started formulating something resembling a plan, or a tactic. Reduced from forty to thirty-two they began walking five and five, with one seven man group.
The dark laughter followed them wherever they went. But there was nothing to fire at, not even anything to point at.
– He isn't human, a man mumbled. – He just isn't HUMAN!
The seven-man group reached a spring-water fountain. The lights from the main building just about reached them there, through the trees. The men stopped abruptly. At the edge of the fountain there was placed a head. Its mouth was frozen in an eternal grin. The spring-water dripped and dripped on the head's top. Then one eye, one of the staring, staring eyes blinked, blinked insanely to them. Then they heard the voice, unable to tell if it came from the radios… or the head. If it could be called a voice. It resembled more what they imagined would come from the deepest, stinking moors of hell.
– Leave! Flee this place, now. If you don't want to stay here forever.
One of the men stood a few steps away from the rest, though far from any bush or deeper shadow. He just was unable to approach the grinning head. Suddenly he received three light slaps on his cheek. He jumped. Looked around, but there was no one close to him. Then there were three slaps on the other cheek. He screamed aloud. Hysterical. And he fell to his knees and began sobbing.
– I felt him, he howled. – HE TOUCHED ME!
The other groups charged through the forest and all gathered before the bodyless head. They all tried, while the cold penetrated their skin to get at least a few words of reason out of him, in vain. He just kept repeating the same words. Over and over and over again. Until he straightened with a face like a death mask, howling at his fellow soldiers.

– Don't touch me. You're all *demons,* sent to torment me and take me to *hell.*

– He's flipped completely, one of them shook his head.

Then the hair rose in his neck, on his head. Church bells tolled somewhere in the city, somewhere close. A loud laughter from the spring water made them turn, turn in a whirl of motion. The laughter came from the head, the insane sound making it shake. They stared openmouthed. Then it rose up in the air. Floated in open air. In pure panic and desperation they emptied their clips, shooting the laughing head to pieces. But the pieces didn't fall to the ground. The bones, the bloody pieces of flesh and brain mass rained down on them like hail, sticking to their skin like glue. They heard the laughter again, and this time it didn't come from any specific place, this time it was like rolling thunder. Some of them pointed with quivering, bony fingers. And there, as they turned, on the hill they saw the monster, a sight worse than any nightmare they had ever had. They made an attempt to process it, to make some sense of it, to gauge details in their mind, in vain. The monster… invaded them on all levels, scared them out of their wits.

– Be gone!

Some of them made the attempt at reloading their weapons, but their arms hurt so much, were so heavy that they had to let go of everything in their hands. Small burns grew on the skin, forming a mouth and a grin.

They ran then. A few managed to hold on to their weapons, but they were merely a heavy load, an impediment on their wild, wild flight.

A few hysterical, scared to death men ran to the circle of light. The many that didn't, ran like hell off the estate. They were four, only four, those brave souls choosing the circle of light.

– What the hell is going on? Verheyen shouted, scared and enraged. – I WANT AN EXPLANATION.

– The salary is good, one breathed. – Good enough for us to s-stay. But it isn't worth being butchered for. We're staying, but DON'T ASK US TO GO BACK INTO THE DARKNESS.

The others rushed towards the gate. Some of them even attempted to climb it, not waiting for it to open.

Tremblay took a few steps out on the lawn, shifting between rage, uncertainty and something beyond fear. It slowly dawned on him that the Ted out there was someone… something completely different from the boy he had known.

From far away he glimpsed the creature. Clearly, shimmering through the darkness. The glow in the eyes had grown so strong that it seemed to come from one single source. To Robert it seemed like it was towering above the trees. It set course directly towards him, like a magnet. Tremblay grabbed a machinegun from one of the shaking guards and fired. The figure vanished, swallowed by the darkness.

It turned quiet. No one dared breathe.

– I hit him. First he mumbled, then he shouted: – I HIT HIM!

It remained quiet. They slowly dared breathe again.

– Okay, let's…

One of the floodlights went out. Then another, and another in quick succession. Then all the lights in the windows.

– Money isn't worth being butchered for. The voice reached them from the darkness, the darkness itself reaching them, masquerading as a voice. – And I will butcher you, gut you like the two-legged pigs you all are.

Robert swore. He rushed to Tilla and grabbed her in a brutal grip.

– Okay, buddy, THE GAME IS OVER, he shrieked. – Surrender immediately or we start shooting the prisoners one by one. Tilla last. She will get it right in the cunt. ARE YOU LISTENING TO ME?

The only response was the cold, cold laughter. And this time it definitely didn't come through the communication system. But from the very night itself, from the darkest spots in their minds, the ancient memories they had all worked so hard to erase from their consciousness.

– I'll be there soon. Everybody still there then will die, but your death, Bobby, will be one long pain, a thousand times worse than that of the others combined.

– Don't call me Bobby! Tremblay shrieked incomprehensibly. – Damn you! DAMN YOU!

He threw Tilla back on the concrete. She didn't give away a sound. Only spat at him. He grew even more furious.

No, Bobby, Warren thought. Damn you!

Through hell, through a thousand hells he would have hunted Tremblay.

But it wouldn't be necessary.

He was here.

Through the darkness

closer

while the white light, the protection where the game huddled faded, faded ever more. He turned right, closed in on them all in a wide arch. There was no hurry. Time was on his side. His Shadow reached out, slowly devouring the minds of the shaking men ahead. Death itself closed in on them.

He smelled humans. Two of them. Easy to spot even without the sweat tearing at his nostrils. They had doubled back to fool him. Him. Death incarnated.

They hid, quietly, they thought. But he heard clothes rub against grass. He heard the quiet breath move through their throat. They waited for him, waited for him to emerge from the bushes. But long before he was even close to walking into their trap he had chosen another path. He circled around them and appeared behind their backs. They saw and heard nothing. He drew and cocked the gun in one single, fluid move. The sound was like death bells in the ears of the two lying there with their guns pointing in the wrong dircction. Making one desperate last-ditch attempt they hardly got more than a glimpse of the angel of death before two bullets hit them between the eyes and blew out their brains. John smiled, alternatively cold and warm, upon hearing the characteristic crack from the Peacemaker.

Two new floodlights went out, and a triumphant cry rose from his throat. At the edge of consciousness they all recognized the cry, from the time when humans had reason to fear the night.

The beast sniffed in the air, smelling, sensing no more live humans out there. They were all gone, fled from the demon in their midst. There was no one left, except in the fading light. Listening with fine-tuned ears he could hear them, hear them speak low and fearful, pathetically. He walked to the two dead, growling a challenge… and then he tore off the arm of the closest body. For every new arm he tore off, the horrible sound rose from his throat. It happened practically automatically now, an act a natural part of him. Robert Tremblay, paralyzed by fear and shaking in rage, was assaulted by a panicking Verheyen.

– There's a demon out there, the South African screamed. – A DEMON! You fool, who were stupid enough to compare him to the brother. You've fucked up completely.

Whispering:

– We've all fucked up.

Tremblay pulled himself free. His face beyond distorted.

– There's a man out there, he snarled, turned towards Verheyen and the hardcases yet there. – A MAN! Are you so easy to terrorize, so easily frightened beyond your wits?

Then the last remaining floodlights were smashed. All went out, except one, one directed right at the concrete. And right there, in the middle of the tiny circle it rained legs and arms and heads. The heap was built like a pyramid before the wide eyes. At the top was a head with bloody eyeballs and the brain mass exposed. There was one single shot. The large caliber bullet hit Rudolf Verheyen right between his eyes and blew out most of the back of his head. The men whirled around, towards where the bullet had been fired from, but there was nothing there, except pitch-black darkness. The body of Verheyen fell right into the pyramid, making the heads roll in all directions. The grown men screamed like children. They threw away the weapons and fled, they and the few lab technicians still in the house. Two hesitated visibly.

– This is your last warning, the ghostly voice thick with wrath warned them. – *Go!*

They obeyed, more afraid than a small child in the night. Tremblay stood there alone. And he saw all his plans and hopes vanish like a dream.

Fast as lightning he stepped behind Tilla and put his arm around her neck. The barrel of the machinegun pointed straight at her ear, steady and confident.

– You have the advantage, he cried wildly. – I admit it. You've truly come far since Denver. But you'll never be able to keep me from firing if I get an irresistible urge to do so. Never in a million years.

Silence. Burning silence and nothing but. It should have made Tremblay feel better. It didn't. The hatred in him burned a notch hotter.

– You blocked my path, he cried. – You and you alone. And you'll *pay!* Even if you're Satan incarnated.

There was a rustle in the bushes, no sense of movement, only the wind.

– There's something I've wanted to tell you, to share with you for a long time, Teddy, he said scornfully, as he breathed and breathed and breathed. – It concerns The Mask… our great leader. He didn't think I recognized him, but I did. If not before I did so when I saw that your eye color had also changed. Then everything suddenly made sense. Everything.

Ted froze. Blood flowed to his brain.

– When this enlightenment overwhelmed me I was convinced we had all taken orders from a ghost. I don't believe in ghosts, though. He was very much alive. It was Mike, Teddy. The Mask was Mike. Isn't that hilarious?

Mike. Alive. The avalanche of thoughts paralyzed Ted. The cabin. The strange feeling… *That was recognition.* When he and Betty had hidden in the lifebelt closet and the Mask had passed by. He had felt affinity, kinship. But he had refused to acknowledge the obvious truth, because he had been in denial.

MIKE

ALIVE

Tremblay heard the sharp choked gasp. In that very moment he moved the barrel of his weapon at Tilla's ribcage and fired. Ted rushed forward with a loud shrill. NO! All he seemed to see was the red hair spreading on the body. All he seemed to hear the horrible scream in protest and pain. Bobby smiled in triumph when he let Tilla fall and fired at Ted.

Ted Warren felt for the very first time bullets penetrate his skin, felt tissue be sundered. He lost the revolver and fell back. Gasping in pain and shock.

– You idiot, I knew you would appear from there, from that precise spot.

The revolver had fallen a bit more than a step away from his right hand. He reached for it. The machinegun cracked again. Single shots, now. The revolver was hit. Several times. It was pushed away from Ted and landed in the grass, way out of reach of his hand.

– What happened? Tremblay exposed his teeth in a grin. – Did you *loose* it? I knew there was something of the old, inexperienced boy left in you. That will cost you. You're gonna pay. Suffer. Feel how helpless you are.

He directed his gun at Tilla again. Let it briefly swap the others chained by her side. Ted forced himself up on all fours, glancing towards his gun.

– Try it, he was told, scornfully, encouragingly. – It isn't far. You can do it.

Then Ted smiled wolfishly. So viciously and cruel that it made all the old insecurities descend on Bobby's mind, paralyzing it.

Strength returned to Ted's limbs and mind. He threw himself to the right, away from the gun. Tremblay fired automatically at the place where the gun was. Ted jumped in the opposite direction. The Peacemaker flew up from the ground and into his hand. Just as the first round from the machinegun hit the ground - far away.

He fired again and again. Emptied his gun in the shaking figure. He kept pulling the trigger long after the gun was out of bullets. Far into death Tremblay pointed his weapon at those chained. It was torn so hard from his hand that two fingers were torn off with it.

The dust settled, cold and dank and dead.

Ted rose. It wasn't hard, wasn't hard at all. Upon putting one foot ahead of the other, he didn't stumble. There was no more pain. Not in the body. There were no tears. Only a pain somewhere making him wish he was dead. Even in the final, irrevocable defeat Robert Tremblay kept the grin around his mouth. Because he wasn't the only one who had lost.

– You shouldn't have DIED. With a minor effort of will Ted pulled the body high in the air. – Not so easy. You should have suffered and died a *thousand* times.

He let it fall. It hit the ground with a brittle sound. He kicked it. Kicked it. Kicked.

I lost, Teddy. But you didn't win. Perhaps you would have preferred to lose?

No! That time was over. But the pain. Not even the all-encompassing savage fury flowing through him could dull it.

He knelt down by Tilla's side. Broken ribs and pieces of broken ribs showed everywhere. Her life's blood leaked from her. Amazingly enough, she was still alive, but it was hopeless.

If Stewart had been here, with his ability to heal wounds, influence other bodies, she might have been saved, but as it was she didn't stand a change. Ted let his hand slide over the holes in his own body. The wounds might have been grave enough for an ordinary human, but to him they were nothing. He pulled four bloody bullets from his chest and side. The wounds had already begun closing. He could heal himself, but not her.

Their eyes met. Her lower lip quivered. She struggled a bit and managed to achieve something resembling a smile.

– You saw this, too, didn't you? She gasped. – You saw *this!*

– I wanted to meet Keller, he said hoarsely. – The scenario might have changed dramatically with him in it.

– He might have saved me…

She struggled to keep breathing, to keep speaking.

– You did well, she gasped. – Don't let this… ruin anything. Don't use it as an… excuse.

She grabbed his hand, and amazingly, held on.

Her lips were flooded in blood. She coughed several times. Her eyes flashed in green fire once, and then their light faded, and left only ashes.

He rose with his hands curled into tight fists. The other four stood there, sad and paralyzed. He tore their chains to pieces as if they were straws. Linda would never forget the look on his face just then. He stepped a bit away, as he stood with his back to them and lifted his fists above his head in anger and powerlessness.

– Get down, John said quickly.

The treetops began swaying. Hair blew back on the four's heads. The figure in front of them grew bigger, bigger, and turned misty and ghostly.

– ARGGGHH

The scream cut through the darkness. No one could avoid hearing it. Zoe noticed to her shock that the ground shook. It happened. She wasn't imagining it. Reality was the windows in the villa that were all being smashed at the same second, the unimaginable power emanating from the frail human figure. She believed.

It turned completely dark for a moment. Until fire rose from inside the building, began licking its walls and cast dark light and shadow over the five people. It was like a river taking them and carrying them away, a roar without mercy, making them all mute, death and blind.

5

On another estate, smaller, but just as empty a few weeks later. Ted shivered to the point of shaking when he walked against the northern wind. It surprised him. It had been a long time since physical cold had actually bothered him. He approached a crypt, a family burial chamber close by the large house. A part of the building showed above the ground. Most of it was hidden beneath it. The door was open. It was dark down there, even though the torches were still burning.

He walked down the stone stairs, descending into moisture, mist and shadows. The coffins were placed on shelves. There were four of them, four bodies. And they were all still there, he assumed. There was an inscription in front of each chamber. Simple. Nothing fancy, only names and numbers.

VIRGIL WARREN 1901 - 1944
NANCY STEWART 1903 - 1940
JAMES WARREN 1909 - 1944

And then, a brand new inscription, a bit away from the others:

TILLA WARREN 1955 - 1976

He looked closer at the other names and dates. All the three had died during wartime. Perhaps they had been killed in World War 2. Perhaps not. There were more shelves, but they were empty. This was it. There was no one else. Not before, and not until… long after.

He had visited the morgue, waiting for the authorities to release… the body. Waiting without waiting, not truly noticing his surroundings.

A man, very correctly dressed had approached him, a man clearly not employed there.

– Mr. Warren? The man had asked quietly. – Edward Warren?

Ted had looked up, a glimmer of interest being lit in his eyes.

– My name is Anthony Wilson, Mr. Warren. I'm an undertaker. I've been given quite an unusual mission.

– I'm quite busy right now, Ted had replied crudely, smiling cynically. – Are there so few deaths these days that you have to do personalized advertising?

– My employer predicted certain reservations on your part, sir. He assured me that you would understand. My task is to take care of the girl, and to take you both to a particular place. Would you please come with me, sir, so we can do the preliminary arrangements?

The good Anthony had been great, like Burke Adams before him at cutting through red tape. And then he had taken the coffin and Ted to that special place.

Here.
A place filled with the dead. No living beings resided here, except the older couple, the caretakers in the old house. They had lived here for twenty years. They were basically gardeners, and called in people to clean the house's interior now and then. They were given regular payments through an anonymous source, everything done through clandestine bank accounts, funds and other ways of obscuring everything. None of them knew anything of importance.
He walked back up, turned his back to the graves. Upon ascending the stairs he was once more caught in the wind. It surrounded him like a storm. The crypt was built on a mound, right by the worn rock fence. He cast his eyes to the gate, the rusty gate. Mike waited out there. And others like them. He hadn't succeeded in saving Tilla. In the crucial moment he had lost control, had failed. Because of his inexperience. He had let his training slide, hadn't trained in the use of his powers, his deadly powers, hadn't made them an instinctive part of himself. And Tilla was gone. He would never more stop using his curse, his gifts, even if he should happen to walk the Path of Power.
He was walking that right now, and it stretched out indefinitely before him.
Linda and John waited for him right outside the gate. He walked past the house, sensed how it pulled him in. The old couple had given him the keys, told him it was his. They had been given explicit instructions: It was his, to do with as he pleased. He didn't want that, now. It wasn't his.
Linda followed his slightest move. She couldn't hide her expectation from him. He saw his own flickering eyes in hers, the pained, haunted expression.
– What will you do, now? John wondered.
– Leave. Ted hesitated. – There's someone I have to see.
The girl drew a short breath.
– Not Mike, he assured her. A rough smile. – Not yet. But one day we'll... *encounter* each other. I know that.
John cleared his throat.
– Do you have any money?
– I'll manage. And if I don't, I'll just get more.
They looked at each other, forced a smile.
– Listen, Ted said, – can you wait for the old couple and hand them the keys? I have some things to take care of.
They studied him as he walked away, the cold stranger. To John he was. He turned towards the girl.
– Do you think he'll ever find the peace he seeks?

– I'm convinced he'll find what he's looking for, Linda replied. – It certainly isn't peace.

– It might take time before he comes to you.

He couldn't hide his worry. He couldn't hide anything from her.

– He will come, she stated. – But nothing keeps us from enjoying ourselves in the meantime, huh?

He pulled her to him. Enjoyed her lust for life with a catch in the throat. It wasn't for himself. He feared that she would never find any true peace, either. Even if Ted Warren should one day accept her into his grace.

Wind. Ice cold. The windows rattled in the old house. An almost silent sound from the crypt. They stared after their friend, ready to wave if he should happen to turn and do so. But he just continued, walked on, not turning, not a single time. He disappeared behind a corner. They didn't see him anymore, but he was yet there. The way he would always be. When they listened they would always hear him.

CHAPTER NINE
DISTANT BUTTERFLY WINGS:
New Orleans 1917

Nancy had been pampered all week. The girls had bathed her, oiled her and perfumed her. They had tried several dresses and costumes on her. Nancy had hardly moved at all, while the women and other girls had worked on making her presentable.

She felt the hands, heard the chatter. The others' excitement rubbed off on her. The constant touches and caresses aroused her, inevitably. The drugs they had given her today to calm her down didn't affect that. The combination made her both drowsy and uncomfortable. Desire burned in her, burned on a low flame, just as it was supposed to.

The Mansion Carré was fairly quiet, in spite of the hectic activity indoors, echoing that of Bourbon Street outside and the Vieux Carré, the French Quarter as a whole. There was an autumn storm brewing, but it put no tangible damper on the festivities. She heard the sound of drums, far and close. The beat affected her. She couldn't help it, help herself. The city of New Orleans prepared for Halloween, for the All Soul's Night.

They placed her in front of the mirror, so she could witness the final preparations, the end result of endless trying and failing. Her black, black hair, usually framing her face was pulled tight back, and bound to the head, a portion of it falling down right behind her right shoulder. The open face felt exposed, vulnerable. Her skin was as pale as it could be, after a summer spent in seclusion from the sun. The impression of dark marble wasn't vanquished, though. Not until they put on the powder, the rouge, diluting her color. She had to cough and instantly she was given a strike on her buttocks. It stung, and she wanted to cry, but her face remained dry, remained stoic.

– Young missus will behave, Estelle said. – Or we will make her regret it.

Nancy felt no anger, only recriminations directed at herself, not Estelle. She just did what she was taught, like everybody here. Nancy knew what a prolonged encounter with the stick or whip felt like. She experienced it regularly… like they all did, like they all had done from an early age.

The dress was white, striking white. Her brown skin, hidden by the powder covering her face, was easily exposed by her arms and thighs and legs, by her bare feet.

– Young missus will bring a high price and Master will be pleased with her, Estelle said, – pleased with us all.

Estelle was a large, striking African American. She and Nancy represented two of many colors and shades in the room. The segregation laws voted through in the nineties, strictly regulating interactions between the races had never had any bearing here. Not in Storyville and not anywhere else in the Vieux Carré.

Nancy was well read. She and everybody else growing up within these walls had been given an education. They were cultivated and could partake in a conversation when called for. Master saw to that. He saw to everything.

Nell entered the room. There was a rustling of skirts and dresses as the girls, Nancy included curtseyed deeply.

– This does indeed look promising. Let me have a look at you.

Nancy stepped forward, towards the woman, displaying herself, as she had been taught from an early age.

The face she looked at looked so similar to her own, so different, she felt.

Nell slapped her. The girl stiffened, but she didn't betray the slightest sound.

– I must be strict with you, Nell said softly. – Or you'll suffer for it.

The girls hurried to reapply the rouge, to erase the mark of the hand from Nancy's cheek, before pulling back again just as quickly, filled with respect for the tall woman in their midst.

Nell didn't really look any older than they, but she had the authority, the cruelty they all lacked.

A hand touched Nancy's jaw, carefully, hardly noticeable this time.

– I think you'll make quite an impression, young lady.

– Thank you, Maman. Nancy curtseyed. – I will. I promise.

– Remember, you don't speak without being spoken to, without being explicitly told to speak. You don't take any initiative if it isn't clear that it is desired. You're not being forward in *any* way and you certainly don't try to impress anybody with your wit. You're the object of men's desires, and that is *all* that is required of you.

– Yes, *Maman*. I know, Maman. I will make you proud. I will make Master proud.

– I know you will, dearest. I know you will.

The noise and shouts from the streets outside rose a few more notches, to a point of it being almost impossible to ignore. Nancy turned her attention to the window and regretted it instantly. She turned back towards a scowling Nell.

The girl straightened, her eyes turning glassy and misty.

– There is nothing outside, she recited. – There is nothing for us there. Our life is here, and only here.

Maman smiled. Nancy felt a sickening sense of gratitude.

– Very good, girl, Nell nodded. – Very good indeed.

Nell turned to all the girls present.

– Time is running short, she cried. – We still have a lot of work ahead of us. Let's get to work.

– *Yes, Maman,* everybody choired.

They grabbed Nancy gently and decisively, and brought her to yet another room, to the inner workings of the Mansion. The noise from the street grew distant, and as it faded from her ears and eyes, it also faded from her mind. This was her world. This was the world.

Nell clapped her hands.

– It's TIME, girls, she cried. – Time for the final preparations, time to transform this blossom into the delicious fruit she was born to be.

I know this is everything that is, mother, Nancy thought. You have told me that time and time again.

They did venture into the streets on occasion, on shopping trips and such, all of the girls. They had a household to run, after all. But that was merely another mandatory act.

There was a table ahead, one covered by flower petals and soft carpets. Nancy's dress was removed. It was an easy task, as it was made to be. They put her down on her belly, righting her with soft touches and caresses, and then the oiling and massaging began. It made her sleepy, but also awake. It awakened her to what was expected of her. She felt it, felt her desire throb and burn, as it rose to an unbearable need within her.

The hands, the delicate and clever hands awoke her, transformed her, elicited moans from her throat, a sigh from her entire body. She turned as they directed her, stretched as they told her to do, and everything turned so pleasant, a pleasant haze of red.

– How do you feel? Nell asked her.

– So good, Maman, Nancy mumbled. – I want this. I want this.

– Remember. Nell said. – Men's touch is cruder, more invasive, making this just a tiny ripple in the ocean, compared to the storm, and that's what you shall cherish. That's what you shall desire beyond anything for the rest of your life.

– I do, Maman, Nancy cried. – I DO!

– Good, Nell whispered. – Very good.

She was ready, her skin peeled. The dress was refitted. It felt like a second skin. The room had a hot, pleasant glow. Nell dried a little saliva from her cheek. Beloved mother.

The procession moved across the room, towards the open door, towards the murmurs and expectant talk. The girl's high heels, making her even taller than she was, silently touched the floor. She emerged in the outer room, to the scents of tobacco and sweat and juices. The many men assessing her with needy eyes, as the lovely price she was, as she made her way to the stage, to the dais there, to the table where the prize would be assessed, bid on and sold.

The smile was on, as it would be the entire evening. She knew that, didn't need the mirror to know that. She was that smile, was this delicious fruit, and all men loved it.

It was October 31st 1917. Nancy was fourteen, and her time had come.

2

Nancy knelt on the table, her eyes lowered, the lovely smile present on her face. The men passed by her, puffing on their cigars. They studied her, appraised her, making her feel wanted and appreciated. They studied her, from all possible sides, but they didn't touch her. She wanted them to. She feared they would, even though it wasn't customary.

One stopped. She didn't see it, but sensed it, her acute awareness, as always serving her well.

– Up, he commanded.

She obeyed, quickly but gracefully. Grace was rule number one, Nell had told her early in life.

– Turn.

She turned, revealing herself to him and to everybody looking, the lower parts of the dress lifting slightly, breaking contact with her thighs.

– Perform, he commanded, and now she could hear the slight hoarse undertone in his voice.

She did, dancing, not dancing on the small table, revealing even more of herself, even more of what she concealed beneath her skin and skull. She had no choice and she wanted to. It was the way she was trained. It was her. A sign from the man, almost imperceptible, and she stopped. She faced him for the first time, looking at him, but not meeting his eyes, still slightly, clearly lowering her own.

– What are your languages? He asked brusquely.

– I'm fluent in English, French, Spanish and German, Master. – I can also speak and understand Portuguese and some of the Indian tongues.

– German, huh. How is that?

– There was this old woman… she's gone, now. She taught me.

He studied her more, made her turn her head, showing her jaw and shape of the head. He was one of the most thorough she had seen, and she had seen quite a few of these séances, from a distant, different viewpoint.

But he never touched her. Not once!

– In position, he snapped.

She knelt, quickly, gracefully, his harsh command making her choke.

He left. Others kept filing past her. The smile remained.

The display finally ended, and she was once more alone on the stage. It felt… empty around her, even though countless eyes still stared at her with impunity from the room at large.

There was the sound of chairs moving over the floor, as the excited buzz faded and the room slowly came to order.

A man rose, holding up his hand, making the last of the room's chatter fade. Her eyes were drawn to him. He was one of the tallest and biggest men Nancy had ever met and the mere sight made her tremble.

– We seem to have drawn quite the gathering tonight, he declared.

He nodded pleased when that selfsame gathering applauded.

– Storyville may be gone, he cried, – but its legacy remains.

This caused thunderous applause.

Storyville had been the part of the city, of the Vieux Carrè where the city council had gathered the *vice* in an attempt to get it under control, but instead it had consolidated itself beyond any anxiety they might have had. So they had closed it down - again, but as the tall man had just bragged about - it was still here.

– I won't delay tonight's main event for much longer, but just restate what you've all been able to confirm with your own eyes the last few hours. And you know me. You know when looking at me that this is a man to be trusted, and I tell you the little flower you see here before you is the hottest thing that will ever be presented on these our exciting gatherings.

All the eyes in the room turned once more towards the kneeling girl on the table, and she felt their hot stares warm her face.

– Just to make this clear: We'll do this the usual way, and those of you gentlemen that are new in this better listen, to avoid more of the few unfortunate misunderstandings we've had concerning this. Those of you that so desire will bid on this sweet fruit on the stage, and the winner will have the privilege of spending one night - one night - with her, where he might not harm her, but aside from that do anything he wants with her. When the morning breaks she will be returned to her true owner, and take up her chores in this house as one of the adult household, and you will all have the change to enjoy her sweetness.

– She's a bit old, a guy from the back of the room commented, prompting laughter from the others.

– She is indeed, the tall man nodded. – And she's large for her age. This is a deliberate choice on my part, for reasons of my own.

And whatever those reasons might be, no one would know. No one would want to. No one would dare to. Nancy's trembling intensified for a moment.

The bidding began. Nancy didn't listen to it. She never did. And if she noticed that the exchange of words was a bit more heated than it usually was, she did her best to stifle the gust of pride within.

These were all mighty men, coming from all over the southern Unites States to partake in the New Orleans festivities on Halloween, and he controlled them all, made them eat from his hand.

She studied the men. She always did, even though no one could look at her, and say she did so. Their outward manner, their inner life, often so different from how they presented themselves.

– Never probe a man's true self, Nell had cautioned her early in life, – never expose their mask.

The room turned darker. Twilight descended outside and inside. Gaslights were lit, still used some places in this part of town, its soft touch casting its spell over the gathering.

Voices turned excited as the final part of the séance commenced.

The bidding ended. There were cries of disappointment and polite applause.

Heavy steps approached the displaying table, easily heard in the silence descending in the room. She recognized the steps. She recognized all steps. They were like voices and smells and signatures and faces.

It was the thorough man. He who never made a purchase without checking the goods first. She sensed him, felt him physically as he stepped into her room, invading it, invading her.

– My lady, he coughed discreetly.

She rose and reached out a hand. He took it like a true gentleman, and she stepped down from the table. She was tall enough to rival the height of most men in the room, but not him. He stared unflinching at her, and she finally looked at him under lowered eyelashes, heat rising to her face, making her happy for the make-up.

It was dusk. She was his to do with as he pleased, until dawn.

He brought her to the tables where other gentlemen and the female companions provided by the house sat. She smiled to him when he pulled out a chair to her.

She sat there listening, smiling, like the other girls. That was her purpose, their purpose. She wanted to speak several times, but held her tongue.

– … so in closing, the Great War is one of the most profitable ever, a man ended a longer lecture concerning his recent earnings and conquests.

– Companies producing weapons and logistics are indeed hot right now. Another nodded. – And will be for a long time. The trench war shows no signs of decreasing. They're just shooting each other to pieces over there.

– Our esteemed government's declaration of war against Germany was very unfortunate, of course. There's even talk about similar acts against Austria-Hungary and god forbid actual participation in the war.

– The idiots in Washington are surpassing themselves…

Nancy sat there, listening hard, noting every detail, every scrap of information being discussed. Most of the other girls were clearly bored, but she wasn't. She had always had a hunger for knowledge, hunger for just about anything, one ever so rarely sated.

The sudden catch in her throat made her glad she wasn't asked to speak.

She felt so astute this night. The clicking of the glasses, the puffing sound when the men smoked. She heard it as a cacophony in her ears. But also all the very, very distinct sounds. She could identify each and every one.

Her breasts stayed swelled, her nipples remained hard. The need grew so strong that she could hardly stand it, but she sat still, waiting patiently, suffering her unbearable need.

He looked at her, he finally looked at her, and she returned his look with misty eyes. He nodded to himself, and in that nod was everything she desired. She opened and closed her mouth in a hardly audible gasp. He took her hand and pulled her to her feet, and she stumbled and could hardly stand, and he had to hold her. There was distant laughter, but it didn't matter. Nothing mattered, but his smell, his closeness and the potent desire she smelled on him.

She sensed it, the moment before he made up his mind, before he rose and bid her to take his hand. He walked away and she followed him, her smaller hand disappearing in his larger paw. Then she led the way. She had to, since he didn't know the way to the room, the prepared room. The shift happened subtly, almost unnoticeably, the way she had been taught.

The room was on the upper floor. The walk up the stairs seemed endless. She made herself available to him, letting him know in a discreet manner that she was there, that she was ready.

But he kept up the appearances of chivalry all the time they were visible to others. Even the first few moments inside the luscious bedroom he did it.

Men are so repressed, she thought.

She had seen them, though, seen them cut loose, after too much to drink, too much temptation, and the memory still thrilled her, still scared her.

And her empathy allowed her to see their seething inner life, what they hardly shared with others.

She stood by the bed, displaying herself to him, letting him see her, letting him in, as she was trained to do, as she desperately wanted to do.

– Undress, he snapped, suddenly very impatient, suddenly wearing his inherent brutal need on the outside.

She began something she had done hundreds of times before, in her mind and in actual fact, but it was the first time she did it before a man. This is what she had trained for, and been trained for.

Trained, trained, trained.

Everything turned wet, wet, wet down below as she slipped out of her clothes.

– I'm yours, Master, she said huskily. – I've always been yours.

He sat down, and she pulled off his boots. She rose and pulled back afterwards, and kept performing. The last piece of her clothing fell to the floor, and she crawled onto the bed, as she kept moving, and every little move was in his honor. He removed his clothes in quick, excited moves. It was easy to notice how the sight of her nude body affected him and she moaned in expectation, and she observed how the veins in his temple bulged. He was pleased with her, so very pleased with her.

They were both in bed, now, finally. He moved on her. There had been pain. The pain lasts only a moment, Nell had told her. The joy is forever. She writhed and stretched beneath him, crying out to him, not only with her horny sounds, but with her entire body.

And he turned absolutely wild above her, moving hard and violent. And it was like an explosion of heat, and she sobbed in pleasure and pain.

He kissed her on the brow afterwards, and then, with that act of kindness her tears came, tears of relief and joy, and a pain inside almost overwhelming her. He lay there on his back, his large manhood resting on his thigh. A sign and she focused on it, grabbed it and played with it, as she had been taught to do. And when it hardened again, she, too, once more felt the heat spread throughout her body, and it was all so pleasant, and she had no choice but to please him. He used her many times before dawn, and it was amazing to her that this controlled man turned so absolutely savage during the night. He slept soundly, like the dead when the girls came and fetched her at dawn. Nell held a hand over her mouth, keeping her from crying out, and the others pulled her gently out of the bed. It was how it was supposed to be, how she was taught, and she followed them willingly.

They brought her to the girls' rooms, to her new life. She was one of them, now, one of the women set to serve the men of the house in all things.

– How was it? A younger girl, not yet a woman asked.

She thought about it, not certain how to reply.

– How do you feel? Nell asked her.

– I feel good, she whispered. – It was all so good, mother. I loved it. I loved it all!

– Good, Nell nodded relieved. – Very good!

The others kissed her and embraced her, welcoming her.

They bathed her again, and dressed her anew, and before the hour had passed she was back into the lower parts of the house. It was quiet, very quiet. The morning chores were easy, not very demanding at all. She just went through the motions.

There was a mirror, the familiar hall mirror, where she could see herself, see her new self. She stared at the strange woman there. Nothing had changed. Everything had. She choked. The old German woman had told her that the eyes were the mirrors of the soul. That if nothing else changed, they did. And they had. It was the same face, but her eyes revealed it all.

She passed the Master's office, and stopped, easily recognizing the two voices inside.

It was the Master of the house, and her Master the previous night, he who had given her the gift of womanhood.

– I *must* have her.

– As a… wife, you mean. The teasing voice of the Master penetrated her ears and soul.

The other one mumbled something, something she didn't catch.

– Are you sure you'll have her, and she not you? You need to keep her on a tight leash, you know.

– I can do that. It won't be difficult, not difficult at all. She's just a woman, after all. She belongs to me.

– *Will* you be strict with her?

– Aye, the reply came hoarsely, – I will. She will be mine!

She looked through the keyhole. The House Master, her eternal Master nodded after a brief hesitation.

– You will have her, but not yet. It's not yet time. She's not yet properly groomed, but she will be, trust me. The day I turn her over to you she will be the perfect meek wife. She will serve you in all things, and she will give you many strong children.

Nancy hurried off, not making a sound with her high-heeled shoes.

She hurried to her room, her own small private cubicle, and closed the door behind her.

– This is my world, she stated. – This is the only world I will ever know.

The girl in the mirror looked at herself. She brushed herself, and readied herself for the daily chores. Her lips kept moving, but there was not a single sound coming from her. She stood there for several minutes. She nodded, nodded again, and then she hurried back out.

The day had just begun.

3

Nancy walked with the other women. Twilight had just set. They descended the stairs from the upper floor; fully aware of the stares they drew from the men in the hall. The women were being looked at, studied and assessed. They were supposed to be. This was their lot in life.

The heat rising from Nancy's groin brought a smile to her face. They entered the assembly room, and the stares increased in both numbers and intensity. The night's festivities began with their appearance, and everything was all right with the world.

She was still the freshest and the most popular. Belle, the next girl in line, was still months away from her first night. Nancy wasn't the youngest. Francine, a few months younger than her had made her debut almost a year ago.

Nancy wondered about that, wondered about the Master's intentions for her.

– You are special, Nell whispered to her in the silence of the night. – Never forget that. Never say it aloud or act upon it, but never forget it.

Nancy wondered about that, too. She wondered a lot.

The women spread out in the room. Nancy stopped before a middle-aged man with a slight potbelly.

– Hi, she greeted him softly, as she curtseyed, as the smile widened in her blushing face. – My name is Nancy and I'm going to serve you tonight.

He was her designated master for the evening, and from the moment he cast his eyes on her, all her thoughts and attention centered on him, making her forget everything else. The room faded around her, only his bloodshot eyes and face registered in her mind.

The days passed in sleep, the nights in a daze of Hunger and need and release. Nell and Estelle made sure she didn't conceive, by regularly sticking the smooth prod inside her, assuring nothing stuck in there.

– Stand still, damn you, Nell swore.

– I'm trying, mommy, but it's so hard. I get… roused.

– And you're supposed to, Nell nodded strictly, – but you will still learn to stand still, young lady.

– Yes, Maman, Nancy replied cowed.

It was done rather quickly, even though it felt much longer.

– That's it! Nell nodded. – This should do it. Remember to tell me if your blood doesn't flow, and we'll do this again immediately.

She nodded as Nell pulled out the prod, not trusting her voice.

– Why can't I use herbs, like the others?

– Because that won't work on you.

She let go of the skirt and it fell back on her sweaty thighs. The sound from the streets once again reached her ears.

– And besides, the prod keeps you roused, and that's good. It's the way Master Lance wants it, especially tonight.

He had sent for them both. A thrill shot through Nancy, more powerful than any of her previous nights.

Her voice, when she spoke, was ghostly and thin:

– Herbs won't work on you either, right?

– No! Nell said.

It was night, and they were in Master's bed, in his powerful hands. His green fire warmed her skin, burned her insides so hard that it hurt. And when he was inside her it was as if the entire world was ending. His hot water reduced her to nothing.

Nancy and Nell rested on the bed, totally spent. There were still the sounds from the outside. Nancy always heard them, even when she didn't listen. Nell eventually pulled closer to Master, needy as a little child. He pushed her away.

She left the bed, her body crouched like an animal, an animal in a cage, wounded and filled with disbelief.

– Come back here, he said lazily.

– Damn it, Lance, she cried, – please make up your mind!

Nancy listened to the fluctuations in the air, the waves flowing between people and walls. She could always hear them.

Nell froze there on the floor, lowering her eyes as Master stared at her, glancing fearfully back at him.

Master turned to Nancy. She pricked her ears, attentive and eager.
– I would like your advice on something, Nancy…
– Sure, Master, she brightened. – Anything.
– What would, in your opinion constitute a fitting punishment for Nell's transgressions?
– Ten strokes, Master. Nancy attempted in vain to keep the catching in her throat from manifesting. – Perhaps fifteen. Nell spoke without permission. She even spoke back to Master and deserves to be punished.
The music in Nancy's ears hurt her.
Master nodded, pleased with her.
– Go to your post, he turned to Nell and commanded her strictly.
– NO, Lance, she sniffed. – Please. *Please!*
One mere look was enough. She ran to the wall with the chains, and put them around her wrists.
He rose from bed in lazy moves. The bed sighed in relief. His cock alternately struck the left and right inner thigh. He walked to the table and grabbed the whip. A small sign from him, and Nancy tiptoed to him, eager and attentively. He handed the whip to her. She took it without hesitation.
– Twenty strokes. Nell didn't obey my orders instantly and eagerly.
Nancy rushed to Nell and began whipping her, in hard and merciless strokes. Nell began screaming almost immediately, as if on command.
– But you do, he said. – You're a wonderful girl, born and forged in my shadow.
He walked to Nell, so close that the lashes, and the drops of blood and sweat jumping from her shaking body almost hit him.
– You'll heal fast, he said indifferently. – You always do.
It was done. Nell hung in the chains, weeping openly, totally out of it, but still there, still wide open for the pain Master had inflicted upon her.
– Attend me, Master told Nancy.
And she instantly did, as she tore her attention away from Nell's shaking form and soul.
He raised his hands, and then she stared. *A ball of fire* grew in the very air in the space between his palms.
– Existence is fire, he said, in a ghostly voice she had never heard before. – Fire burns and will burn the world. It's just as inevitable as night follows day. It speaks to us, and we speak back. We become it, and it becomes us.
She stood before him, drowning in his might. The fire faded, but she could yet feel the heat in his hands.

He grabbed her jaw, and squeezed. She moaned in fright and pain. His heat hurt.

– You're *open,* he snarled, – but you will be even more so, to the point of my essence filling you to the brim, and you're nothing more than an extension of my being.

Time passed, and it didn't seem to pass at all. He had become time, passing through her.

– I am a witch, he told her, – an age-old power that has been with the humans since our inception… and so are you.

The room faded before her eyes. Lance… Lance… filled her, not only her perception, but her everything.

– You're mine! He told her, chastised her. – I will teach you everything you know. No matter where you go, you are my pet, my creature, and you will obey my wishes in all things. You will do everything your mother never could.

Everything faded, even the very sight of Lance. But his presence didn't. If filled her, pushed her to a small corner of her own self, and kept her there, filling her mind with the secrets of his wisdom.

Daylight slipped into the room, the room, the bed in Nancy's room, where she woke up alone, with the almighty shadow by her side.

Nancy was pampered all week. She didn't serve customers anymore, but tried on wedding dresses, one after the other, in quick succession. She didn't see Lance, not with her eyes, but he was always there, always watching. The other girls switched around her, excited, and excited on her behalf.

– He took a fancy to you, Estelle nodded. – On your first night. That happens sometimes. But usually it just leads to a nice, quiet little house somewhere in town, and not to matrimony. Be happy it did and never look back.

– I won't, she assured the large woman, the child by her side.

Lance was giving her away, to the southern gentleman that had taken her cherry. But he would always be there with her, with them.

She heard his voice in the shadows, speaking to her from the fire.

– And one day I will come for you, he said. – And then I will teach you all the secrets, everything you yearn to know about yourself and the world.

She dressed with Nell and some of the girls, to go outside, to do the daily chores of providing supplies for the household. Antoine, Stephen, Laurent and Merrill, four big bruisers, bodyguards followed them around at all times. The girls dressed differently for the day, and for the outside world. No one would have been able to tell where they lived, if they weren't well known in the neighborhood.

Nancy shrugged. They didn't really stand out in any way here, coming from merely one of many «Mansions».

They walked through the busy streets, very much like other people, moving sedately, keeping their breasts and hips from moving too much, like the fine wives and mistresses that the men for some reason or not had brought to the Quarter. Nancy had learned these two very different approaches the same way she had learned everything, from an early age. It felt strange, like being a completely different person out here, in the sun.

– Why don't we move? She asked Nell.

Nell just looked at her, as she did every time she asked such a silly question.

– Why don't we *move* out here? Why move like the other females, hiding ourselves? It doesn't make us feel any different. Nothing is different on the inside, so why do it?

– Curious Nancy, one of the other girls giggled, properly covering her mouth with a hand.

– Because this is how it's done, Nell replied patiently. – This is how the world works. And you need to learn this once and for all, now, to not bring shame on your future husband.

And the familiar pain stung Nancy somewhere inside. She held her tongue like a good girl.

She turned her head, and looked behind her, suddenly wide-eyed and afraid.

After turning the next corner she did it again.

– Look forward! Nell corrected her sternly. – Don't turn your head like a *peacock*.

– You shouldn't worry so, Cherie. Estelle soothed her. – If there's danger our four strong men will protect us.

And Nancy looked at them, at the men. All four of them, big and strong, certainly seemed more than capable of protecting their helpless female charges.

They reached the large store on the corner of Basin and St. Louis, right by the First Cemetery. The girl both wanted and didn't want to look at it, to look at its wonders and horrors.

Nell gave the shopkeeper the shopping list orally, delivered it with an ease revealing her experience in doing it.

There were two doors to the store, one leading to the cemetery, the other away from it. Nancy turned her head constantly back and forth. Nell slapped her cheek, slapped her hard. She sagged, and stood still, absolutely miserable, and the buzzing wasps dancing on her back didn't go away.

The four giants by their side carried all the goods, fairly unhampered. Nancy didn't fear anybody would jump them. The Master ruled this town. It belonged to him. His will reigned supreme. Everyone testing that paid for it, and everyone knew it to be so.

The street people passed them by, from all sides in a whirl of motion, making her eyes hurt. There were some cruel remarks, but mostly it was the stares, the silent condemnation. Dust whirling in the streets made it hard to breathe, and she started coughing, coughing hard. She covered her mouth with a napkin, but it did her no good.

– Dust again, huh? Nell chastised her cruelly. – You poor baby.

Nancy stared hurt and angrily at her, for the first time not shrinking under the older woman's scrutiny. Nell noticed it immediately and the brief expression in her face was one of absolute terror. Nancy didn't understand that, didn't understand that either, and both anger and pity crossed her own features.

– You're so young yet, Nell whispered, tenderly touching her cheek. – So sheltered, after all. So very young.

And the naked fear in her eyes made the girl shake in horror. And she sought closer to mother, sought the comfort and protection of her space, and she couldn't be sure whether or not that hadn't been mother's intention all the time.

The other girls comforted her, in a thousand small and big ways. She let them. They surrounded her, isolating her from the surroundings, protecting her from the world. And she let them.

– The world is loud and rough and obnoxious, Nell told her. – You're wise to keep it out.

Wise mother.

The small group was close now, close to their home. Nancy was suddenly wet with perspiration, and she had no idea why.

They turned the corner. There was a whirl of motion. Nancy saw Laurent be struck down by one, single brutal blow, and then all-hell was loose around them.

It was over so fast, in just a few heartbeats. The four bruisers lay on the ground, beaten bloody and unconscious. Around them stood men and women with guns in their hands. Nancy saw her mother turn pale as a ghost.

– J-john, she stuttered. – D-desmond?

– With us are Nick and Carla and trusted friends, the tall man with gray hair at his temples said.
Nancy looked at him, looked at the other tall man with fire in his eyes. She felt joy, she felt fear.
– It's all right, Nell told Nancy, with a shaking voice. – These men are our family, our blood. I was lured away from them when I was very young. They've come to save us, and take us away from this place.
Nancy moved her mouth, but no sound came.
– Stay here, John bade them. – Desmond and Carla will protect you. Nick and I will *take care* of Lance.
Nancy gasped. She grasped the… finality of his words.
The other girls stood frozen on their spots. One of them opened her mouth to scream. The woman John had called Carla struck her down with one blow.
– We will take care of you all, she stated. – You won't starve, and you won't suffer anymore, and not be arbitrary treated by anyone.
John and Nick were gone, in a rush of dust and air.
Nancy studied Carla, studied her face, the confidence and strength she conveyed.
Then the first shot was fired inside. Nancy shook. There was rage, boundless rage inside. She felt it, like a blow in her belly. It was like the house itself shook.
– Remember, Carla said. – If you see him, fire and keep firing, until he lays still. Add even a few more bullets after that, and then we cut off his head, and burn him on two pyres.
Master appeared on the balcony, firing his weapon at those inside, backing off, hit by a number of bullets. Blood filled the air. He fell from the balcony, and hit the street hard, in a pile of dust, landing, amazingly on his feet. Nick and John appeared on the balcony, and the bullets from his gun, hit them. They jumped down, while they kept firing. John jumped at him, and they fought. Master struck him, and he fell backwards. Nick assaulted Master, and he didn't give any ground. It was like his hands were claws cutting into his enemy.
– Fire, Carla barked. – Don't care who you are hitting. Nick can take it.
And they did. Blood flooded the air, almost like floating water.
Nick struck Master down, and emptied his gun into his body and head.
More men, Master's men rushed the scene, and fired their weapons. Nick was hit by an onslaught of bullets and was pushed back and down. John fired at the men, with one revolver in each hand and killed a score of them. Nancy looked back at Master, and he was gone, leaving a bloody trail behind him. Nick walked in among his men, and killed them

wholesale. He carried five or six guns on his body, and when they were empty, and when there were no longer any more loaded weapons to pick up from his victims, he began killing them with his bare hands. It was a sight Nancy would never forget. It was as if Death itself had descended among them. They cried out in boundless fear and fled like rabbits.

John walked to one of the wounded men and lifted him up, shaking him like he would a rag doll.

– Where is he? He mumbled. – WHERE DID HE GO?

– I DON'T KNOW! The terrified man screamed, and died.

Red dust and fluid settled slowly. Carla rushed to Nick, speaking comforting words in his ears.

– It's all right. She whispered it over and over in his ears. – It's all right.

– I lived through the icy cold of the sea, he said, Nancy heard him say. – This is nothing.

And it was as if the icy fire of the far north was still with him.

– Take from them, Carla instructed him. – Take from those still alive, and leave nothing but withered husks.

He bent down and touched them, and they screamed in terror. His wounds knitted themselves, and they died in agony. Nancy saw the Glow surround him, saw him bathe in the death and life in the air. He went to John afterwards, but John stopped him.

– I'm okay. I can heal on my own, a bit slow, but good.

Nick walked to the wounded on the ground and touched them, and they, too, healed. Terror and gratitude and joy and everything visible in their faces.

What's happening, mother? Please, tell me what's happening?

– These men, these your brothers and sisters are Master's equals, Nell turned to her, sternly, softly. – And you are, too. I want you to never forget that. Because he will come for you. Sooner or later he will come for us all.

Nancy nodded, dizzy and shaking in fear and excitement.

– We need to get out of here, Desmond cried. – This is *his* city. He can gather hundred men in an hour here. Twice that the next.

John nodded.

– Let's go, he cried.

Horses were brought, a lot of horses. And they rode. Those that couldn't were tied on the horses' back. Nancy could ride. She recalled nagging mother as a child, until mommy relented. She sensed the power of the animal beneath her, sensed its muscles and it exhilarating moves. Her bare skin touched the horse, and it was as if she was one with the beast, with its power and majesty.

They rode, all very aware of the Shadow rising in their tracks.

4

New York, during Christmas. Nancy was still hot, still in New Orleans in its hot, southern moisture. The snow didn't… matter somehow. It was just more hot water on her cheeks.

She had a snowball fight with her distant cousins, Virgil and Susan, far into the large, wonderful Central Park.

– Look at them, she heard Desmond say to John. – It's like they're brothers and sisters, and have never been apart.

She didn't hear John's reply, only sensed his worried frown.

Susan fell. Virgil was there instantly and helped her up.

– Are you okay? He wondered.

– I'm perfectly all right, she replied. – You shouldn't fuss over me so.

Nancy saw a tear on her cheek, sensed the pain of the hurt and sense of betrayal dominating her perception.

The snowball war ended. Virgil stared at Nancy with something resembling hatred in his eyes. She would always remember him like that, hurt and bewildered by the world.

Nick walked up to her from behind later. She shook. She hadn't sensed him.

– So, how are you coping? He wondered gently. – It's a silly question mostly meant for polite conversation, but I want to ask it anyway.

She giggled, looking up at him in awe. He was taller than Master, the tallest human being she had ever met.

– It's strange, she acknowledged. – The really weird thing is to be… covered, and not necessarily coveted.

– It is important that you're aware that you don't need to perform for every man desiring you anymore. He nodded. – But I think you'll always be coveted.

She blushed. She actually blushed, like the petite schoolgirls she had observed walking with their parents.

– It's so silly, she said, actually glancing shyly around her. – I feel… awkward by the glances the young men send me, almost like… almost like Sue.

– Sue is a frail flower, Nick said. – You aren't. But you're still only a child, hurt and bewildered by the world.

She looked at him with wide eyes.

– Pray that you will always be that.

There was something, something in his voice. She realized startled what it was.

– I hear fear in your voice, she said.

– That's good, he replied.

They headed home, home to the large Mansion.

As they walked she sensed the armed guards, mostly unseen, move around them, and she swallowed hard. They entered the large, safe house, and she still didn't feel safe.

She came to him later that evening. He sat in the library. He spent almost all his time there, when in the Mansion, before heading back to his dank apartment.

– I feel much more at ease with you, you and Carla than the rest. Why is that?

– Probably because we're different, even among the different, he said.

She paused a bit before speaking again.

– Why is James living here, and you aren't?

She sat down in the chair right in front of the desk he sat behind.

– It's an unsafe world. He must be here. I'm not comfortable here.

– Give him a hug before you leave tonight, she said. – He needs that.

– I will.

They sat there in silence for a while. She kind of enjoyed that. There was no pressure, no demand of performance. He read a book. It had no title. It looked old, decrepit.

– What are we? She asked with her childish voice. He often forgot that she was no more than fourteen, but not now. – Children of the Gods?

– I don't know, he replied after a brief hesitation. – People like us have certainly been mistaken for gods in ancient times.

She paced back and forth for a while, before her eyes focused on what was in his hands.

– Which book is it?

He smiled and handed it to her.

She opened it, and on the first page she casually opened it on, there was a drawing of a woman shooting lightning from her fingers. Under the drawing was a text:

THE RAGING WITCH

She turned the pages, devouring its content, like she had always done with all information, all knowledge she had ever encountered.

Carla stuck her head inside.

– We're ready, she informed the two, before vanishing.

Nancy reluctantly handed the book back to Nick.

He closed it and put it away, and rose to his full height.

– So, how do you like Christmas?
– Master punished me for the very first time during one, she said harshly, harsher then she had meant. – For speaking without permission.
He walked around the desk to her, touching her jaw tenderly with his hand. It felt strange to her. A man had hardly touched her, except in desire, and he clearly didn't do that. She would know. The warm snow in her face didn't disappear.
She pulled back, startled.
– Sorry, she whispered, hurrying back into his reach.
– Look at me.
She did, shame and fear visible in her eyes and stance.
– You will no longer be punished if you «misbehave». We don't do that here.
– I understand, Nick, she nodded, smiling assuredly, doing her best to mask her emotions.
It's hard for me, Nick. I've been taught from an early age, to behave, to be pleasing to the eye and encourage male interest.
– Make an effort, he insisted. – You may strive with this your entire life, if you can't liberate yourself from your upbringing.
– You're so young, sir, she whispered, joked, – and so wise.
He was twenty-seven. He looked ancient to her.
Almost the entire, extended family watched the play «Why marry?» at Astor Theatre, Dec 25th. Nancy laughed in several places. She laughed a lot, tears in her eyes. Her eyes glued to the stage.
During the intermission they gathered in the vestibule. She looked at herself in the large mirror, the red, happy face.
– This is so great, she marveled. – I can practically feel what's happening on the stage, and it makes me *think*.
– It's just a play, Virgil shrugged.
And they all laughed some more. Virgil reddened under her direct stare.
Virgil was sixteen, tall and skinny and incomplete. He and his sister always walked side by side, as if they couldn't bear being apart. Sue was nineteen, but still skinny, pale and not yet whole.
– I need to pee, Nancy said straight out. – Where is the… restroom?
She said that with just the right amount of irony. There were more smiles. They were all in high spirits.
– Me, too, Sue just said. – Come with us.
Virgil followed her, of course, and Nancy followed them both.
– I need to pee *badly*.
Nancy grabbed their shoulders and held on. She blinked, breathing hard, letting go.

Nell met them close to the entrance, startling them.

– You come with me, she said, and turning to the others she continued: – You two, too.

Nancy followed her without really considering it, used to, as she was to obey her mother explicitly since early childhood. The other two joined them, obeying Nell's commanding voice.

They passed the restrooms, walking towards the entrance, walking outside, into the cold, cold winter night.

There was an alley, dark and foreboding and moist and windy.

It hurts, mommy, it hurts terribly.

Master stood there, right in front of them. A number of men surrounded them. Nancy stood still, very still. The men grabbed Virgil and began beating up on him. Sue attempted to scream, but her scream died in the wind, in palms covering her mouth and brutal strikes against her body.

– Come, Master commanded.

Nancy walked, followed him in mother's footsteps. They walked fast, towards the harbor, towards the cold, freezing dark water. There was a ship there, a large ship, its engines already roaring.

Master stopped. Everybody else stopped.

He drew a gun, and shot Nell through the head, the bullet cracking it open like an eggshell. Nancy gasped as her mother fell in the snow.

– She was of no more use to me, the tall, imposing man said evenly.

He turned to Nancy. The girl couldn't breathe, couldn't think. Everything had turned into a dark, dark void.

– No marriage for you, my girl, he told her. – You had your chance at that. A quite different fate awaits you.

Everything turned black. Her entire reality turned numb and dead.

And only hours later, chained along her kin and many others in one of the ship's storage rooms, when she discovered she had peed on herself, was Nancy able to cry.

«[The] assumption that it is the aim of the [American] public school to fan the intelligence and to produce large numbers of alert and curious youths of both sexes is foolish. The state maintains its control of elementary education, not primarily to reduce illiteracy and turn the eyes of the plain people toward the stars, but to make sure that they are not taught anything that is subversive. Public education is thus a police measure. The goal it moves toward is perfect standardization, perfect discipline, perfect imbecility.»

- H. L. Mencken
Baltimore Sun
February 23, 1924

«You must adjust... This is the legend imprinted in every schoolbook, the invisible message on every blackboard. Our schools have become vast factories for the manufacture of robots.»

- Robert Lindner

«My schooling did me a great deal of harm and no good whatever; it was simply dragging a child's soul through the dirt.»

- George Bernard Shaw

«And what is a good citizen? Simply one who never says, does or thinks anything that is unusual. Schools are maintained in order to bring this uniformity up to the highest possible point. A school is a hopper into which children are heaved while they are still young and tender; therein they are pressed into certain standard shapes and covered from head to heels with official rubber-stamps.»

- H. L. Mencken

PART TWO
ELIZABETH

CHAPTER TEN

When she was ten…

The autumn the same year Ted had come to them.

– He's weird, isn't he? She had said to her father that early spring. – So pale and scrawny. He isn't sick, is he?

And daddy had looked at her with a strange relief in his eyes.

– But he's smart. She nodded self-consciously. – And I am, too, much smarter than the other children.

She had known she was different, but not to what extent.

Suddenly, in one stroke, everything changed. She knew the day and the hour when that was. On the afternoon October 31st, Halloween.

Her mother had been over her like a hawk for days, literally sniffing and probing her. The girl was dressed in the dark and expensive dress she had been given on her birthday six months earlier. She had gone to the low hill the way she, June and Linsey did every year to hollow the pumpkin. But mother joined them this year, Ted joined them, and everything was different.

Little Elizabeth was very conscious of her feet touching the ground, of the edge of her dress blowing in the wind around her knees. Mother hollowed the pumpkin, expertly, quickly. She held it in her hands as the fire rose on the hill. And she was singing, or rather chanting a strange song, with indecipherable lyrics. Little Elizabeth heard music, and she was positive that June and Linsey and Ted did as well.

It was as if that rose from the ground, too, like the fire, with the fire. Trudy Kendall's voice eventually faded in the wind, but the music remained.

– I've been amiss in your education, the grown woman said. – It's about time I remedied that. Look at this as your first class of many.

The children sat down in the dry grass, the strangely dry grass when one considered how moist it was everywhere else. They looked attentive and fascinated up at the unknown woman.

– Existence is vast, she told them. – This is just one hill in the tapestry that is the world.

Elizabeth understood the strange words. She nodded to herself. All the children did.

There was no further warning beyond this, beyond mother's strange behavior. Suddenly Elizabeth had felt a sharp pain in her lower parts. Her panties and her inner thighs had turned wet and sticky. She knew what was happening. Both mother and the older girls she had befriended had described it in detail to her.

– May I be excused? She said to them with a blinding smile. – I need to go to the bathroom.

– Sure, honey, mother said. – We're practically done here, anyway. You run along.

It dawned on her, now, why mother had been chasing her the last few days. She did the best she could to keep a straight face. There was something deeply disconcerting about mother's behavior. So the girl kept her mouth shut and rushed down the hill to the house.

The bathroom was quiet compared to the rest of the house. Halloween was an American tradition, after all. There was hectic activity to prepare for the evening's celebration.

She stopped before the mirror, looking at her own uncharacteristically pale and sweaty face. Shaking hands sought the edge of her dress, sought the soaking wet panties, and pulled them down the thighs. She stood there, staring at the bloodied cloth in her hand.

Trudy entered the bathroom. Elizabeth jumped high.

– So, young woman, you thought you could deceive me that easily, huh?

– No, mommy, the girl whimpered. – I just…

– You must not be this stupid. It was evident to everybody, even to your dull-witted brother, what happened. You bled all over the hill, consecrating it, making it the Place of Power it has always been.

The strict, foreboding woman scared her, and she bowed her head in confusion and misery. Mother grabbed her hand and pulled her with her, led her down the hall, towards the stairs at the far end of the house. The girl opened her mouth to speak, but Trudy put a hand on her lips, harshly and decisively.

She was taken to the cellar, taken beyond the area of bedrooms and wood, and into that of concrete and twilight and dust. There was one single lightbulb in the shadowy hallway. At its end was a huge, heavy door, locked with a tick bolt and three monstrous padlocks. Mother produced three equally monstrous keys and unlocked it all. The bolt was heavy. Mother strived with both removing it and open the door. Elizabeth had expected it to creak, to give off some horrible noise as it opened, but it didn't. It swung open, on hinges smooth as velvet. There was no noise at all.

Inside was another, narrow hallway. It was totally dark in there, until mother lit a torch. The girl cautiously touched the walls. They were solely made of soil, hard, hard soil, but soil nonetheless. The way led to a room, a square room. Its walls were soil, too. It was dry and hot in here. Little

Elizabeth wondered where the ovens where. She wanted to ask, but the intense expression in mother's face discouraged her.

– *Now,* do you see anything?

The girl looked around, turned her head, turned her body, staring hard at the naked floor and walls, prompted by mother's insistence. Mother seemed to move with her, scrutinizing her, looking for something on her, for something… something to happen, with her face, her eyes, but Elizabeth just felt uncomfortable and bewildered, slightly nauseas. She wasn't afraid. The worry was caused by mother's strange behavior, and intensified when Trudy grabbed her in the arm and asked eagerly:

– How are you, girl? Do you feel something… something… *special?*

– How am I supposed to feel, mommy? I don't know…

– *What* do you feel?

– Pain… down there. And on the shoulders. You're squeezing so hard, mommy.

Her ears were ringing. The heat in the room smothered her. She felt weird under the onslaught that was the unknown woman's stare.

– Nothing more?

Little Elizabeth shook her head, a bit afraid by now. She couldn't decide whether or not the unknown woman was satisfied with her answers.

Seconds passed as eternities while fire and shadow played in Trudy's face. Finally she straightened, her face softening.

– Okay, honey. A motherly pat on the cheek. – Let's go back upstairs and have you changed, so you may go and play Trick or Treat with the other children.

While they stood in the bathroom and her mother scrubbed her clean the child's face presented a thoughtful expression.

– Mommy…

– Yes, honey?

– I was wondering… Mommy, almost none of my friends have started on their… periods. And they who have are far older. Why is the Blood coming to me so early?

– Our family is early. Mine started when I was your age.

– Why… are we early?

– If I had known that I would have told you, but I don't, Trudy snapped, clearly irritated over the child's ability to cut through red tape. – And it isn't that unusual among others either. Relax, now, so you can go back out. You do want to have fun with the others… don't you?

Elizabeth swallowed hard and nodded, crushed by the rejection. She allowed herself to be rubbed with the towel, cuddled and clothed in spite of the fact that she had long since found it humiliating.

They stood in the hall. Trudy appraised her, doing the final touches on the costume.

– That's it. Now, you may go and scare people shitless. It will hurt below for you tonight, but it won't be so bad that you won't forget about it all when you get other things on your mind. And don't soil these clothes, too. I'm your mother and you will obey me, understand!

– Yes, mother, the girl replied meekly.

Mother put on the mask, and put her before the mirror.

– Now, look at yourself, she commanded.

Elizabeth obeyed, even though she found it rather a strange command, since she could hardly see herself. It was only the hair, and the mask and the eyes and…

She blinked, and jumped back into mother's safe clutches, and refused to look into the mirror.

It took several minutes for her to calm down.

Outside. The warm autumn wind moved her hair. A rather large group of smaller and bigger demons waited for her.

– Off you go, mother said, giving her a light tap on the back, an encouraging nod. – Be a brave girl, now.

She ran with the other children through the valley, from house to house, calling people out on the porch or stairs of their houses, begging candy, performing for them, and all in all being nice little mongrels.

– I'm a demon, she declared, – come from hell to take you away.

And mother might have noticed something then, if she had been there. The girl did, in herself, in the flickering eyes of the man in front of her, of Mr. Grey, the schoolteacher.

They returned to the farm, walking among the tall adults, like tiny trolls on the prowl. And the little girl felt very much like she was prowling, grinning wildly behind the mask.

Her mother and father were shouting to each other. Elizabeth didn't quite understand that.

– Why do they speak so loud? She whispered in Claudia Cornwall's ear. – They can't have trouble hearing each other, can they? In fact I know that mother and father have excellent hearing.

Claudia looked at her, giggling behind her mask.

Elizabeth felt sadness, without truly understanding why, even as she threw herself into the ongoing fun and games again.

Mother never took them to the hill again after that.

The younger children were put to bed early, and Elizabeth was, to her great chagrin counted among them. She and June were tucked into bed by their mother, given a kiss on the brow and left alone in their room, far away from the festivities taking off on the other side of the house, far, far away, only a distant rumble. Elizabeth lay there, set on not falling asleep.

– I will wait until everybody is asleep, she declared, – and return to the hill, and cast my spells.

June, lying still in the other bed didn't reply. Even more insulted Elizabeth demonstratively closed her eyes… and fell asleep in a second.

At night she came rushing into her parents' bedroom. Her hair fluttered in the air around the nude body and her eyes were large and wondering.

– Christ, girl, father exclaimed. – Where's your gown?

If she hadn't been so upset, so excited, she would probably have seen fit to point out the fact that both he and mother lay there stark naked, even without a blanket, sweaty and breathing hard, entangled in each other, and with a strangely pleasant smell emanating from them.

– MOMMY, MOMMY, there are lots of strange people outside our window. And mommy, June has turned blind. I woke her, and she saw *nothing*.

She stood tripping before the bed, torn between sensationalism and worry. Father stared alternately at her and at the wall, incredulity and other, less savory emotions written all over him.

– She means right outside, he said, turning angrily to mother.

– I'll take care of this, mother said softly, and she kissed him on the lips, visibly calming him.

Mother led her back to the bedroom. June slept soundly, still tucked in peacefully in her bed.

– I woke her up. I'm positive I shook her and woke her.

She turned even more agitated when she looked through the window and realized how far it was down to the ground.

– I could see them clearly, even when I was in bed.

She lay down in bed. It wasn't possible to see the ground from there. No way! She choked.

– I knew it. Mother looked at her in unfathomable ways. – I've been watching you, you know. I knew you were not the rather dull-witted weakling you pretend to be in your father's company and among the other children.

The girl looked up at the regal woman like a whipped dog.

Mother knelt by the bed, took her hands and squeezed them softly. The girl let her, feeling a strong need for being comforted.

– Listen to me, Liz, she said, – and listen carefully: What you experienced was a dream. You were dreaming. Not exactly like other dreams or how other people dream, but close enough. As you grow older you'll understand more, much more.

Mother had regained her intensity. The girl's fear remained, but it was mixed, now, with something else. She looked hungrily at her mother, as she waited for her to continue.

– I both envy you and feel sorry for you. You'll have a lonely, but remarkable life. No matter how much I would want to, I can't say more. You must walk your path alone.

Trudy clutched her, taking the smaller body in her fawn. The girl thought it was she who was shaking until she realized it was the woman.

The girl slipped out of mother's grasp and then it was she who grabbed her around the shoulders.

– You're sad, Elizabeth said pointedly. – Why are you sad?

Looking at Trudy with her penetrating eyes.

– You will understand, when you get older, her mother said. – Believe me, you will understand and you will learn many things. That includes things you might not want to learn. Understanding, my child is a many-edged sword and all the edges cut, cut deep.

She embraced the daughter affectionately, and the girl clumsily returned it. Liz imagined that mother dried a tear from an eye.

Out in the darkness the voices reached out, carried with the wind from the dark corners of reality. Mother was gone. Elizabeth was alone. The celebration continued throughout the night, on the farm and elsewhere. She saw them, saw the masks dance around the fire. The tall little girl stood by the window, confused, frowning, very aware this time, over the fact that she was truly in bed, sleeping soundly, dreaming, dreaming the night. By the almost burned down fire by the hollowed pumpkin on the hill, a tall, skinny figure crouched painfully. The girl on the bed was warm under the blankets. She slept, but remained restless, writhing her body ceaselessly. The voices kept speaking, unintelligible, but strangely clear. She knew she would, they would one night be able to listen to them and *understand.*

2

She understood Ted ever better as time passed. They were the same. The signs she saw in herself she also discovered in him. They both changed, changed a lot during the about eighteen months towards what she silently called the Time of Separation. No one could call any of them skinny anymore. But they were both outsiders, strangers in this place and most other places. They were… they were *different.*

When she was twelve…

– I miss him already, she told June, in one of their confidential conversations on their room. – He's so silly. Can't he see how we well we fit together, that we're one?

June had no answer to give. Little sister was called down to the kitchen to help mother, so eager to help, so eager to leave.

Elizabeth was alone, lying in bed, fuming. Her hands hurt. They were curled into fists. Yes, outsiders, even among those called friends and family.

Her thoughts drifted, drifted back to the barn, to Ted's beyond naked expression, to the naked fear in his face.

Why bother, why bother wasting regret on those two assholes? Ted held back, because of Mike, she knew that, but the pain, the ravaging pain remained.

She drifted into another restless sleep. Upon waking up she realized that she, too, needed to be a little careful, careful about wishes and horses. Her blanket was spread unevenly around the room, torn into hundreds of small pieces. She looked incredulous at the mess, wondering if she was really that strong. Looking at her nails she found no threads there, no signs that she had ripped the blanket at all.

The Cornwall's and the Davidson's deserved to be punished.

– Damn you, she swore at the picture, the picture of the dark boy. – Why are you being so unreasonable?

The dream had been about Claudia Cornwall, about the girl lying bound on a table, and Elizabeth had stood over her with a large bloody butcher knife in her hand.

Liz shook, suddenly so very cold. She fell back on the bed and attempted to cover herself with a part of the blanket that was still somewhat whole, and she cried herself back to sleep.

3

When she was thirteen…

That spring she disregarded completely her father's orders about not swimming naked in the river. The cowboys saw her and the rumors spread. And she did fear that those rumors should return to her father somehow. Shame and regret and anger and sadness warred within her, and worse of all… there was no winner.

The yellow bus brought her and the other kids home from school. She walked home from the stop at the edge of the farm's land. It was raining, but she didn't care. She had turned wet ten steps after stepping off the bus. Most of the children without an umbrella or raincoat ran off as fast as they were able, but she didn't change pace at all. The rain flooded her face and it felt all right somehow.

The farm was visible from far away, and now, this close it seemed to loom over her. The road made a turn right where the terrain started rising. She stopped there. It felt… right. She stood there, already cold and wet, watching the valley below. Rain flooded her eyes and made it hard to see. She was wet and cold and hungry, but she stayed. The ground here… She bent down and touched it. It felt similar to… to that of the hill.

– Ah, daddy, she said aloud, grinning – this land isn't quite what you think it is, is it?

Then she felt it, something very similar to an electrical charge in her fingers. She sensed it spreading to the rest of her body, a pleasant, pleasant sensation impossible to ignore.

She blinked, and she saw them, down in the valley, the children playing, covered by blankets. It seemed to be some sort of game. She stared, absolutely fascinated.

There was the sound of hooves against the ground coming closer. She turned. One of the cowboys, Logan Dysart approached her on horseback. She briefly turned her attention back to the valley. The kids were gone.

– Are you okay, girl?

His voice was rough, but pleasant enough.

– I'm fine, thank you, she replied, giving him her best of smiles.

– You should get home and out of those clothes, he said sternly. – It's quite chilly today, and you can catch a cold.

He bent down and brushed a hair lock off her cheek.

– I will, thank you, she whispered, suddenly so very, very short of breath.

He rode off. She stared after him, stared at the rider fading in the rain. Everything had turned so hot suddenly. She attempted to take one step forward, but stopped practically at the start of the step, gasping loud, very loud.

– Oh, god, she cried.

It was almost like she was suddenly sore down below, and it hurt so much. It felt so good. She wanted to touch herself. Shame rode her as she realized that everybody would see her, and the worst of the terrible need subsided. She made her way home, somewhat, walking in a manner she was certain would give her away. The entire experience was shocking to the point of being paralyzing. She knew what this was. Her older friends had given her vivid descriptions about this, too, in whispers and giggles. It was like for a moment there, she had lost all control of her own body and of herself, of her very self. Fear riddled her. Need riddled her.

She rushed right up the stairs to her room.

– You need to get out of those clothes, Trudy cried after her.

– Right away, mom, she replied.

The clothes were so sticky that it felt almost impossible to get them off. Using force was no good. She had to coax them off her, wriggle her body a bit, then pull, wriggle a bit more, pull a bit more. And to boot it was all that more difficult because of her shaking hands and body.

She dried herself with a towel, dried her hair first. It was so long that it was always difficult to dry, reaching her to her hips. Then, tentatively she began on her body. And had to stop almost immediately. The moment she touched one of her breasts the heat shot through her, and she fell to her knees on the floor. She began drying and touching herself, drying herself in lavish deliberate moves, not holding back any longer. Somehow she made it to the far, far bed. Tucking herself in in bed everything turned so very, very hot and so very, very good. She touched herself below and moaned aloud, very loud. And having finally done that it was as if a kind of calm strangely enough settled on her. Even in the red, red haze that had become her mind, she could slouch there and have time between the moments to actually enjoy it all. Seconds, minutes passed, she couldn't tell. Everything was immediate, was a horrible, prolonged torture, before the moment her entire body stretched and turned rigid, as she bent her back backwards and the sheets turned even wetter, and she fell back on the bed, totally spent and in a state of absolute, profound joy.

There was a school dance that evening, with supervisors, all of it sickeningly proper. The girls wore dresses and the boys wore suits. Elizabeth decided on a whim to go. June helped her with her dress and her hair and make-up. The child, Elizabeth noted, a bit patronizing, knows far more about such things than I do.

June was a nice and obedient daughter, her father's jewel.

– You look *so* nice. June clapped her hands with shiny eyes. – I wish I could go.

Liz looked at the well done hair, the blue eyes, the visible brown skin, her growing body, and nodded shyly.

– Your time will come, little sister, she joked. – In time boys will eat you up. They love that innocent look of yours.

And it was true. Liz, being very conscious of such matters had seen the looks already. June was only a bit late, that's all, at least compared to her one year older sister. Liz nodded self-consciously.

Boys danced with the tall girl in quick succession, most of them not very tall at all, and they had to look up at her. She felt a bit lonely then, and in a rut of self-pity she didn't leave or didn't voice her discontent in any way, and she came to worry about her state of mind. She worried a lot.

A tall, big boy danced with her. She smiled to him in a sickening bout of gratitude, and he turned red on the ears and several other places besides. The music was slow, more to the adults' liking than to the kids, as expected. The Rock revolution had basically passed this area by so far, at least officially. It was boring as hell, but she suffered on in silence.

Then the lights went out. The music was cut off. The dance stopped. All the dancers stood there in the darkness holding on to each other. Some time passed. The lights didn't return. The boy was panting in her ear, and she realized startled that he was groping her. She almost laughed… until… until she felt the pleasant warmth rise in her again. A silent cry of protest remained silent. He kissed her on the lips and she melted in his arms, finding herself responding to the kiss.

The lights came back on, fortunately with a slight sound of warning, and they managed to disentangle before everyone saw what had happened between them.

The rest of the dance, and indeed the evening happened in a daze. She made all the right moves, curtseyed before inquiring adults and behaved so suspiciously proper that she was positive she gave herself away, that they just had to see the kind of state she suffered.

– Jessie Lorenson groped me, she said enraged to June as they went to bed that night. – I don't even like him, but I still reacted to him as if he was… *Elvis* or something.

June sat there, by her side, on Liz' bed, somber and sympathetic. Very sympathetic.

– I tried to resist him, Liz said in despair. – I really did, but all reason just left me, and if we had been in a backseat on a secluded spot or something…

That was also something the older girls had communicated *in detail* to her. She giggled nervously.

– … I would have given in. I'm sure of it. And given myself a lot of potential trouble to boot. And do you know what the worst part of it was? I found myself glad for the chaperones, glad that we weren't in that secluded spot.

Insane eyes glared at little sister in true despair.

June giggled.

– That *is* horrible, she grinned.

And they both laughed themselves silly. Liz dried a tear from her left eye, very emotional.

June patted her head, giving her a bit of comfort.

– It's the *blood,* Liz said. – We, both Ted and I have such strong urges and are therefore vulnerable.

She stepped out on the floor, pacing there for a while, pacing a lot.

– This can't go on. It just can't.

June sat there nodding, not really following her.

Big sister turned towards her, her face an image of determination, very «adult». Somewhere outside an owl was howling, and she trembled.

It was an owl, even though owls were hooting, not howling. She was positive.

– I need to be done with this, Liz emphasized. – I need to get it out of my mind.

And June's eyes widened when she realized the implications of her sister's words.

– Yes, that's it. That's exactly what I need to do, but on my terms.

She sat back down on the bed, touching June's jaw with feather-light fingers.

– I can always speak to you about anything. She kissed little sister's brow. – Thank you. Thank you.

They spoke a little more before going to bed. Spoke a bit afterwards, as they lay there in the dark.

– Look at it, Liz cried. – Look at the dark.

Knowing well the smile forming around her mouth.

– I don't see anything, but the dark, June said, clearly shaking her head in confusion. – What's good about not seeing anything?

– Because it isn't empty, Liz corrected her, a bit sharper than intended. – Only to those who can't see.

And they slept - and dreamed. Liz writhed on the bed, and the sounds coming from her kept June in a pitiful sleep, until silence finally claimed them both, and the night turned truly black.

4

The river was green and cold because of all the melted snow from the mountains. She found it refreshing in the hot, hot day. And it felt so good to let the water surround and flow around her body, to feel its power, to feel one's own slowly awakening from its slumber. She studied the skin on her arm. Even though it was still early in the year she had already turned a darker hue. Not much sun had been needed.

She let herself drift down river, and then, after a while, she swam upstream. It was hard, but not so hard as the first or second or third time she had done it, and it was easier every time. The light from the sun blinded her, and she dived under the river's unruly surface, towards its murky, peaceful depths. She floated down there, upside down and let herself drift, and got caught in its power, and screamed in delight, there, below the surface. Large bubbles of air erupted from her lungs.

Her body grew supple and strong that spring. Aside from the swimming she ran and took long walks and journeys in the mountains. Running flat out one day she undressed the last few steps before she reached the riverbank and dived into the frothing water. There were clutches of trees and bushes where the river turned. She knew it was there they hid and watched her. It didn't make her feel bad anymore, but rather caused the now so pleasant and familiar sensation to course through her body. She realized with a happy sigh that she enjoyed exhibiting herself, enjoyed the sense of power it gave her. But she also knew she was vulnerable, and she never allowed herself to forget that fact.

– I'm going for a ride, she declared in the afternoon, after dinner. – A long ride in the mountains.

Everybody heard her, everybody present in the yard and in the stable as she fetched the horse.

She threw herself on the bare horseback, and rode away, best speed, towards the fairly distant mountains.

Later she slowed down, took long breaks and made sure it was evident that she followed the river upstream. She camped by an old tree at dusk. It felt oddly appropriate and she easily understood why. The old tree seemed to speak to her. She recognized the place as one of Ted's camps and the very thought echoed pleasantly within her.

Fire rose in the sky as the dry wood burned and the sun cast its final rays across the Colorado landscape. She looked downstream and spotted the rider early, recognized him easily. It was indeed Logan Dysart, one of daddy's season cowboys.

She had danced with him on occasion, under the strict supervision of father, she herself behaving so proper that she wanted to puke afterwards.

He reached the plateau and spotted her. She began undressing, slowly, deliberately, with light, soft movements, throwing her clothes away. Throwing them she didn't know where. He looked calmly at her. There wasn't any signs of him being nervous or anything. She smiled and walked into the river. The water splashed against most of her body. She gasped in delight.

– Join me, she cried. – The water is great.

The water closed around her. She submerged herself below the surface, where there was virtually completely dark. Only the fire above lit up her vision. She felt the powerful currents play with her body. When she reappeared above he had dismounted and began undressing. The muscles on the hairy, broad chest was covered in sweat and glowed in the light of the fire. She stood with water to her knees, close to the river's edge. She almost fell. Her knees almost gave in under her. Without really consciously noticing it she began rubbing her breasts. She spread her legs, wanted him to see as much as possible of her, posing for him, and it felt right.

– You've chosen quite a place, he said hoarsely. – There's quite the current here.

– I like powerful currents, she replied boldly.

– Come here, he commanded.

– You come and get me, she called back sullenly, acting hard to get.

Then he pulled down his pants and underpants, and her mouth opened. She attempted to close it again, but couldn't. He was big, so very big, and he pointed right at her. She attempted to speak, but found herself completely unable to. He walked into the river and grabbed her. Unresistingly she let herself be pulled close to him.

– Give me a kiss, he commanded.

She obeyed, unable to meet his eyes.

– You're just a little girl, after all, he stated indifferently.

He lifted her, put her on his shoulder like butchered meat and carried her on land to the spot of soft moss. She let him. He rubbed her below, casually, without the slightest consideration to her needs. She moaned.

– Untouched, after all. And needy, very needy. I rather thought that to be the case.

The contempt in his voice made her feel even smaller. He put her down on her back, but never stopped exploring her nest. She moved beneath him, moved and whimpered in her terrible need. He lay down on her, and her smile was full of promise and her eyes twinkled strangely in joy.

– Good servant, she gasped. – Skilled and useful.

He pushed inside her and she moaned in pain. But the pain faded, and pleasure embraced her like fire. She thought she might not feel much, except him moving back and forth inside her, and the pain from the soreness, but then, suddenly the pain increased tenfold and a pleasure unlike anything, much more than she had felt during her own clumsy try-outs exploded in her groin and spread throughout her body in a single moment. She cried out, cried out like a wolf-bitch getting it in the forest. And she was. She moved under him, moved hard, not content, wanting more, more, *more*. There was a slight shift in pressure and they rolled a bit. She came on top. Her mouth moved across his face biting and chewing, drawing blood. Everything turned foggy, everything turned right. She moaned as she spoke, rolling words off her tongue, and everything turned good, good, *good.*

– I've marked you, my useful servant, she droned. – Marked you forever. I carry your blood in my body.

There was a flash of fear in his eyes, unmistakably. She turned wild.

– AHHH, she shouted, shouted in ecstasy.

He came, came in a rush. She got her second orgasm then by the time he finally got his. Her nails cut deep into his shoulder. He yelped in pain, in ecstasy. They fell, fell deep into the soft moss. The roar of the forest turned silent and everything turned still.

She kept herself on top of him, stretching her body in lingering, lazy moves, licking the blood off his shoulder.

– Christ! He cried, his fingers playing with one of her nipples. – If the boss only knew what a crazy bitch of a daughter he has.

– But he doesn't, she mewed, – and he won't. You won't tell, will you?

She looked at him with those weird eyes of hers. They were blue, blue like the night and the ocean both, but he thought he saw fire there.

– That would truly be crazy, he grinned. – He would kill me. He would torture me and roast me over open fire first, and then, after a million years or so, he would kill me.

– You're so wise. She kept mewing. – Such an incredibly wise and skilled man.

His cock twitched. They both looked at it. A happy, expectant smile crossed her face.

Her body moved, and she let it. She was her body, after all. The happy realization hit her, a wave of hot water in the stream in which she floated. She sat up, sat up on him, with one leg on each side of his body, and she began humming, and the humming turned into a mantra. And she sensed it, how something strange but strangely familiar rose inside of her.

I feel it, she told him. I feel the power. The power is eternal.

Her hand panned across his body. Her palm and finger, wet of blood rubbed his skin, painted on his skin.

– I paint you with blood, Logan Dysart, she hummed. – With my blood and yours. I make you mine. I devour you, leaving you only with pieces. You are mine, mine, mine.

– Fucking witch, he moaned, he spat.

She grabbed his cock, and the moment she touched it, it returned to full power. The fire in her eyes turned stronger, more pronounced. She licked her lips, and she looked down on him with her predatory eyes.

Her hips moved forward, without the slightest effort, his cock being pushed between her thighs, and then, in a soft continuation, inside her.

And she began moving on him, moving with slow, lazy movements, slowly changing pace. Blood exploded in her eyes, and she cried out. The wolf howled again, and the entire forest replied.

It was early next morning. They sat on their horses, ready to ride back, to part ways.

– And I trust you won't tell your old man or anybody either? Even if I'm only a part-timer in Kendall's employ his money is good.

– Don't bc silly, she grinned.

He was sore all over his body. The scratches ran from head to toe. He felt a little woozy, too, a little weak. She had truly done a number on him, that little wildcat.

She practically danced on the horseback. What was left of the soreness below was only a minor itch compared to the power coursing through her body. It was as if every single one of her cells were burning on a low flame.

– Why did you pick me? He wondered. – Because I'm leaving tomorrow?

– Only partly correct, she grinned again, even wider.

It actually made the experienced man blush, and it made her feel even better. She felt good, good and better than good. It was like she couldn't get enough air. Even if every breath filled her up, it was never enough.

– We both did everything right, he nodded. – We will both do the right thing.

They parted ways. She took the longer path back. He would be gone by the time she returned.

She realized that she had indeed chosen the right man. They would part. Without longing or remorse. Exactly the way she wanted it.

5

She was fifteen. Fifteen and almost eight months. She would be sixteen in spring. In the death-sleep season, in winter, in the dark season, her body grew, everything in her grew, and she began in earnest to learn what was hiding within her. She filled out her clothes in ways she had never done before. Even though she grew taller, her forms, her femininity were clearly more pronounced.

– You should have accepted the bra, Trudy coaxed her. – Your father's Christmas gift wasn't totally without merit. You can see his point, can't you?

She could. It was impossible not to, studying herself in the mirror. Her breasts pushed against the clothes, as if threatening to burst through them at any moment.

– It was too small anyway, she snorted. – D-cup, big size, and too small.

She added, somberly.

She was taller than her mother, now, taller than Linsey, taller than her father, taller than anyone she had met, except Ted.

And she was big.

Father had given her a Christmas gift designed to benefit him, and not her. It was his concerns that were behind the «gift» and it wasn't meant to please her, but him. She had returned the gift… to his face, and left without a word. They had all looked stricken at her.

As she enraged had passed the mirror she understood better why. Her eyes didn't look blue anymore, but more like violet, blue mixed with fire. She looked larger than she ordinarily did. The mirror seemed to bulge, and a bell tolled without her being near it, ringing so very loud in her ears.

Her room, quiet and empty. She had moved out of the place she and June shared the year before, after one of her many quarrels with her father. He seemed to increasingly echo the sentiment that women didn't have sufficient personality to warrant a place of their own, their own private space. *Damn him!* With hands curled into fists and tears of rage flowing from her eyes, she threw herself on the bed.

She wept. Her body shook in rage and despair. She fell asleep in her clothes, entering a period of pitiful rest, one of confused and jumbled imagery and whispers.

There were always whispers.

Silence greeted her when she woke up in the middle of the night. Time had passed. Rest of a kind had passed. But the storm still raged within her, being fed by something, something she couldn't identify. She sat up, left the bed, changed her mind, sort of and sat down at the edge of the bed. The girl sat there, sat still in the chilly room. If someone had seen her they would be tempted to say she was sleeping, sleeping with her eyes open, with eyes staring at nothing. She had been sitting still for a while when her attention was called to the framed photograph at the night table. It seemed to pull her to it. Her eyes glossed over and she bent sideways and reached for it, but it was beyond her reach. She swore and stretched further, to no avail.

Then something happened, something *extraordinary*. The photo *jumped* from the table and into her hand. She shook in astonishment and almost dropped the frame in her hand. Eyes cleared. She stared at what she held in her hand. Rose. Put it back. Sat back down, out of reach. She couldn't possible have reached it, as she couldn't possible do so now. Her hand reached out. She wanted to feel its weight in her hand, wanted it more than anything right then.

Right here and now.

The frame just slipped through the air and into her hand. She had made it do so. This was real. This was true, not a result of her imagination or any wishful thinking. A lucid light lit her face. She felt it, the stirring in her body, on her skin, beneath her skin, inside her heart, both concrete and insubstantial, in her toes and fingertips. With an almost boundless eagerness she directed her attention to a rubber ball on the floor. She breathed in and out, focused to *make it* levitate. It was her entire world. The ball shook a little at first, making her stare in apprehension.

Then it rose from the floor. Just like that. The incredible sight made her sit still with an open mouth. The ball kept floating, kept fulfilling her wildest dreams.

Higher, she thought. Higher.

It rose to about half her length, no higher, no matter how much she concentrated or wanted it to. It started to slip, slip from her «grasp». She focused on keeping it where it was. Five seconds passed. Ten… Sweat poured from her brow. The ball fell and rolled across the floor. The girl let herself fall back on the bed. She had a headache, but that dissipated quickly. She was tired, but most of all happy. Hell, she was *ecstatic*. She kissed the photo devoted and jubilant.

– You, too, she mumbled. – You, too.

During breakfast the next morning she wolfed down the food, reminiscent of a big bruiser after a hard workday.

Eugene stared at her with his usual condemning face.

– I'll never be the Miss Congeniality you want me to be, father, she said slowly and deliberately, returning his stare with one far more focused and determined.

But in spite of her harsh words she flourished that morning, leading the conversation with the joy surrounding her like air. And that seemed to reduce father to an even fouler mood.

She walked to her favorite place on the hill and stayed there the entire day, until June came and told her dinner was ready.

– You interrupted my thoughts, Liz said with the chill in her voice. – Disturbed my peace. Don't ever do that again.

June shook as she was being subjected to big sister's cold rage.

– Sorry, she whimpered.

She ran away with tears in her eyes.

Liz sat in the living room, staring at the Television screen, hardly hearing or seeing anything but the voice and the image from the little box ahead of her.

Father's family came on the usual Sunday visit. But she had no time for them, no time at all, even less so than she usually had. There was a newscast, a rerun of 1974 events. There was a remark from father's sister in law, an idiotic remark that ordinarily wouldn't even make Liz twitch an eyebrow. But now it made her jump from the chair and crouch on the floor, making her look like she was about to attack the poor woman.

She returned to the chair, as she kept staring at the screen, hardly ever taking her eyes off it.

Ted was gone, truly gone. Since August. Vanished into thin air with his classmates and friends. No one had a clue where they were or what had happened to them.

She was alone, more so than ever before.

Her mother had turned distant. She couldn't talk to her anymore. They conversed about trivial things, but they didn't truly speak to each other. She felt a strong need to shake both her and father, so they could understand. Sometimes she felt she *hated* them. That realization shocked her less and less. She stayed away from the visitors. Rode a little. But she quickly exhausted a succession of three horses. They were all breathing hard after just a short ride. She didn't want to harm them. So she ran instead. Sat on the hill a lot. «Elizabeth's Hill». Linsey approached her once, handing her an apple. She accepted it… and crushed it in her hands. Her brother quickly left.

The unrest persisted. As expected it didn't help her that the relatives finally left. They were just an excuse anyway, a way for her to vent her frustrations. She exercised her mind powers on her room, made the ball pack up and down on the floor and from wall to wall for minutes, but then she was so exhausted that she felt totally gone for hours afterwards. The way she wanted it. But eventually she grew less and less tired. She discovered that the more frustrated and angry she felt the easier everything was.

On New Year's Day she packed her small suitcase, fully intending to leave the coming night. The decision caused strangely little upheaval inside. It made sense, that's all.

She walked downstairs. The house was strangely quiet. Except for the sound of the television, she heard no voices. It was as if everybody had left the house and left her alone, truly alone. She smiled in bitterness.

Then the sound from the speakers began penetrating her fog of indifference. She listened and could hardly believe what she heard.

– LIZ!

June rushed at her from the living room. She ran straight to Liz and embraced her.

They all gathered before the TV, before the news, the startling news, alternately warm and cold or both simultaneously. Nothing seemed impossible then. Liz didn't take her eyes off the screen. When there was nothing more on the TV, she turned on the radio. She threw herself over any newspaper she could find that day. Usually she hardly read them. The next morning Linsey drove her to Trinidad to find more. He attempted to hide it, but he was just as stunned and eager himself.

They sat in the living room, reading, hardly speaking. Liz listened to her father and mother speaking, far away; in a place they believed she couldn't hear them.

She saw them, was there with them, her sense of them being very distinct, almost as if they were truly physically close, and it excited her, it thrilled her.

Displacement, she thought. *Farsight.*

Trudy moved close to Eugene, touching him softly, suddenly uncharacteristically bold, coaxing him with her every move, her every word and intonation.

– You see how it is with her, don't you, Eugene? She needs this, need to find out what happened, see for herself.

Her carefully crafted argument persuaded him. It usually did. To a point.

Liz returned to her room in a daze. She sat down on her bed, not frustrated, not angry. The small suitcase caught her eye again, so different, so much bigger.

She stared at it in joy.

6

Elizabeth Kendall walked through the arrival hall of Stapleton Airport. The place was filled with people. It had a busy, restless spirit that appealed to her. Behind her was her plane, her way of traveling the world. In a way that was quite funny she felt a strong need to turn back, not to continue the return. To the anonymity, where the humans were dead to her. But she kept walking, and not too long after that she sat on the bus to Trinidad.

She had done it, she, not yet sixteen had traveled across the big sea and done everything she had set out to do… except the one thing she had set out to do. She bit her lip, attempting to keep the lump in her throat from manifesting.

Mark had sent her away, easily, like swatting a fly. She wondered if she shouldn't have acted more resolute, insisting on seeing Ted, demanding for Mark to explain himself.

But the image of Tilla always stood in the way. That and the hot stab of jealousy in her gut.

She wondered about Tilla, wondered about so much.

The sun was shining outside. Her eyes were sore. She felt grateful for the dark windows, protecting her from the bright light. There weren't that many passengers in the bus. She had placed herself at the center of the backseat, the only seat in the bus where she could actually stretch her legs. Everywhere else was made for dwarfs or masochists.

In her lap and in both the adjacent seats lay heaps of newspapers and clippings. At the front page of them all she saw the image of the same person. Mark Stewart's eyes stared at her. Even in black and white one couldn't avoid noticing those eyes.

A man moved back to her from one of the seat in front. She looked at him with distrust and annoyance. He studied her with impunity, not looking away like she was used to the boys at school did when a girl stared back.

– Hi, he said.

– Hi, she heard herself say, sensing the first stir of interest within herself, sighing silently on her own behalf.

– Why does a cute kid like you travel alone like this? He wondered in mock interest.

He wasn't interested in her mind. She knew that much.

– I'm not a kid, she replied, very much like a young, insecure girl, in style with his expectations.

She knew she looked like both a girl and an adult woman. It depended much on the expectations of the person looking.

– No matter, you're very pleasing to the eye…

Language, she thought unprompted, what a load of shit.

He wasn't very good looking or didn't have a nice built or anything. But he had *something*. And whatever that was, was exactly what made the heat rise in her like a rocket. And the fact that he was fully aware of the impression he made on her didn't make him any less attractive in her eyes.

He sat down close to her. Just like that. The warmth leaped from his thigh to hers. She sighed again, relenting. It would be a waste not to take advantage of this opportunity. On the farm and near it she wouldn't have anything like the freedom she enjoyed right now. And she hated to hide herself, hated it. He waited a bit, but when she didn't move away he went right to it. His right hand touched her cheek and sought down her body to a breast. He squeezed and rubbed it, revealing great skill. She closed her eyes and sighed happily, quite audible this time.

– I knew it, he stated curtly. – I saw the signs on you the moment I first laid my eyes on you.

She turned in the seat, seeking even closer to him. Kissed him on the neck, seeking his lips, grabbing his thigh, fumbling with his belt.

– Hey, horny one, he grinned. – I think perhaps a little bit of patience is called for here. With the fireworks you'll make we would be thrown off the bus in ten seconds. We'll rent a room, okay.

With a few well-placed words he had reestablished control. He was good.

– Okay, she shrugged. – I thought all boys were impatient, that's all.

– Boys might be that, but men aren't.

Such arrogance in his voice, in his very posture. He was clearly used to handle innocent, inexperienced girls.

On a stop in the afternoon he rented a room.

– I must be home today, she said. – Or there will be hell to pay.

– Don't worry, you will be. As I said, this is a longer stop. We'll have time enough.

– But you rented the room for the night, she insisted. – And the manager didn't object. What will he do with the room after we've left?

– Ah, the naiveté of youth. The man shook his head. – He will have it cleaned, and put back up for rent, of course. And if anybody should stay the night? He gets a percentage of the bus tickets sale as well…

She nodded serious minded, learning about the world.

They reached the room. He closed the door and locked it.

– I *am* horny. She nodded. – And I want you. I want you very much.

She undressed in quick, feverish moves.

– I know, he grinned, as he too undressed. – I have that effect on women.

Her eyes flared in anger. He didn't see it, was too busy with looking at himself in the mirror. Where did he get off?

It was different this time. Her anger didn't dissipate. She began to feel wonderfully clear minded. Felt it many times stronger than after a cold spring bath.

They moved on the bed. She noticed it as it happened, also in her most feverish moments: She felt the energy in him where they touched skin to skin, felt it leave him… and flow into her, an undeniable fact, a sensation transforming her skin, turning it into fire.

His grip on her arm loosened. He just didn't have the strength to hold on anymore. She put him down on the bed, far stronger than him, now.

She moved over him, looking at him with glowing eyes. He gasped in fear.

– You thought you could be my teacher, she said, – but you were mistaken. I'm the teacher, the Master. You are my pet.

Afterwards. She stood by the bed, fully dressed and looked down at his still form. He slept. He would sleep a long time, and definitely miss the bus.

– You couldn't do it more than once, she spat. – You deserve this. Overachiever.

She smiled to the mirror. Studying the blushing face in there. And the eyes that should have been clear as water, but was muddy. It was like watching an underwater fire. She giggled. In wonder, in happiness. She could do anything now. Anything.

That arrogant shit would wonder a lot when he finally woke up, that's for sure.

The day was no more than a dark red line in the horizon when she stepped off the bus. They were all waiting for her. Eugene, as well. She was the only one leaving there. They rushed towards her. Linsey and June embraced her.

– Jeez, little sister, how you have grown, she joked.

– You haven't been gone for more than a week, you know.

Father's voice had an edge probably no one but her noticed.

– That was a week funnier and more interesting than any I've previously experienced, she declared.

She saw father frown, but just shrugged. It was nothing he or anyone could do right now that could ruin her mood, ruin the boiling joy within. She knew now, beyond doubt what she was.

To this day she had basically played by the rules. A few sidesteps and missteps didn't change that. But no more! She laughed loudly over something Linsey said, but couldn't hear the words. The sound of boiling blood in her ears kept her from doing so. No one would decide for her anymore what to do or not to do. Certainly father would not be allowed to form her in his image anymore. He had tyrannized her long enough, under the pretense of being a loving, caring father. She saw straight through him, now.

She would hide no more!

CHAPTER ELEVEN

The path stretched out indefinitely before her.

She walked through a landscape dark and bright, mysterious and dangerous, its clouds and mist trembling in anticipation.

Her first day back at school, her first hour was led by Howard Grey, the biology teacher. It was a pure coincidence, really, she told herself. She hadn't thought about it in any conscious way and could have returned any day, using the various excuses she had concocted. But she had returned today, and that was Howard Grey, the biology teacher, the same person who had «taught» in Denver, taught Mike, Ted and Linda.

She stared out of the window, at the landscape illuminated by the pale sun. The highway stretched on as far as her eyes could see. A girl and boy kissed each other passionately before jumping into the car and racing off. An eagle sat on a field. She knew the others couldn't see it, but she could. A headless figure approached and wanted to capture her. She looked at it in contempt and flew away, took off with ridiculous ease.

Her journey across the Earth, across the ocean already seemed like a distant memory. Her recent experience of the boiling of blood and spirit, the power within, however did not. It was a perpetual living thing, forever a part of what made her what she was, and could never be parted from her.

Judy Davison nipped her in the sleeve. It angered her to be distracted like that, but the other girl didn't seem to notice. Judy was way brighter than her two brothers, but she wasn't exactly the most sensitive person in the world.

– Don't turn around, Liz, dear, but old Ash is staring holes in your back. He has hardly done anything else since we sat down.

– I don't mind. Liz shrugged. – He's the only boy in the class reaching above the mediocre.

Judy giggled as silent as possible. She didn't offer her opinion, but Liz easily sensed her reluctance. Ashley Griffith was an African American. It didn't dissuade Liz in any way, but it still meant a lot to most honorable white skins, and here they weren't exactly less intolerant compared to other places.

Liz didn't turn. There was no need. She felt his eyes in her back, and they warmed her.

– And now we'll cover today's lesson. Grey's nasal voice interrupted her pleasant thoughts. – Elizabeth, will you come up here, please?

She felt the rage instantly, like something physical, a living thing.

– I most certainly won't! She pinched herself in the thigh in an attempt to keep the rage in check. – As you know perfectly well I have no idea what «today's lesson» is, that I didn't return until late last night.

– From your travels, oh, yes… I completely forgot.

He hit the blackboard with his pointer, did so very deliberately. Liz wanted to close her eyes. She didn't suffer. It was just so frustrating everything.

– Your travels, indeed. Won't you tell us what you happened to be doing on that journey? How it feels to cheat to get a week off… You know very well, young lady that such permits are given with the explicit understanding that the student is keeping track of the lessons.

– «Within reason», Liz quoted. – You forgot that part. Are you turning senile, Howard?

Nervous laughter crackling through the classroom.

She got to him. She sensed it. Saw his entire figure crouch and snarl.

– What a truly great example of an irresponsible youth you are. Grey sadly shook his head. Only Liz could spot his thick aura of triumph. See the eyes shine in pure sadism. – Tiring your father with your antics and never go to church. Godlessness and irresponsibility usually go hand in hand.

– Tell me, Howard, she said calmly. – How fanatical a man of the church are you? How many centuries back does your view on life go? You probably see all the scientific theories from Darwin and on as heretical and godless and thereby fake, don't you?

– You're scum, Grey frothed. – Poison of the Earth.

– You bloated asshole, she said softly.

She was in front of him in a second. Towering over the plump man. Somebody gasped, having spotted the change in the girl's eyes. Grey raised his pointer with a shaking hand. Liz quite simply pushed him, and he fell backwards, his ass hitting the floor with a loud, smooching sound.

Good for him that he didn't get to strike me, she thought upon collecting her stuff. If he had struck me, then, then…

She calmly left the room. A few of those present laughed, but most of them looked at her in disbelief. There was a loud crack as she closed the door in their face, hard enough and loud enough to be heard all over the school.

– Please, Elizabeth, Stevie Fulton, the student's counselor told her later, – you have to understand you can't call Howard Grey a bloated asshole.

Stevie let out a giggle, realizing what she had done and attempted in vain to hide her smile with a hand.

– But he can say whatever he will about me, right? The girl spoke quietly, not hiding her grin. – And I just have to take it lying down. Isn't that great? The great American school in a nutshell, I suppose…

– He is a mouthful, Stevie said admittedly, – but he has the support of the board. They feel that he's a necessary counterweight to certain parts of the youth rebellion… an assessment I tend to agree with.

– Are you out of your mind? Elizabeth blurted out. – If you know your history you know that the now extinct German «nobility» used similar tactics of appeasement to deal with Adolph Hitler. I guess they never saw it coming, huh…

– You need to apologize, girl, Stevie said, clearly strained, – and you need to be nice about it.

– Have you read your Mencken lately? Liz said pointedly.

– What? Stevie looked totally blank.

– H. L. Menken, Liz emphasized. – In Baltimore Sun February 23, 1923?

And she recited flawlessly.

– «[The] assumption that it is the aim of the [American] public school to fan the intelligence and to produce large numbers of alert and curious youths of both sexes is foolish. The state maintains its control of elementary education, not primarily to reduce illiteracy and turn the eyes of the plain people toward the stars, but to make sure that they are not taught anything that is subversive. Public education is thus a police measure. The goal it moves toward is perfect standardization, perfect discipline, perfect imbecility.»

It turned quiet in the room, very quiet. Skin turned red.

– You teachers don't really know much, do you, Stevie? The girl said softly.

Stevie Fulton looked at her with an expression of absolute horror in her face.

– Howard Grey belongs to a group of people that will gain ever more influence in the world in the years to come, silently supported and appeased by you and your kind. He's my sworn enemy and I *won't* apologize to him, publicly or otherwise. On the contrary I will keep telling him and you exactly what's on my mind.

She earned a week's temporary expulsion.

Great, she shrugged happily, another week off.

But she wouldn't let herself be caught napping anymore, ever again.

So she went to Allan Kendall, her cousin. He was quite the bright light at school, paid attention enough to make her puke. That included Grey's classes.

It was he who met her in the door. He did ask her in. It wouldn't do to not accept kin in the house. Bad form.

They had been sitting there with the books for a while when he couldn't hold it back anymore.

– You're throwing it away, you know…

– What's that exactly?

Her cold eyes revealed that she didn't have to ask him to explain himself.

– Listen, he said embarrassed. – We're family, right? So I would be amiss in my duty if I didn't tell you what a mess you're about to make of your life. You're very gifted. I think everybody sees that. You'll ruin your chances of a good life if you keep up this stubborn rebellion of yours, that's my honest opinion.

There was a break, a moment where they both sat there breathing.

– «And what is a good citizen? Simply one who never says, does or thinks anything that is unusual. Schools are maintained in order to bring this uniformity up to the highest possible point. A school is a hopper into which children are heaved while they are still young and tender; therein they are pressed into certain standard shapes and covered from head to heels with official rubber-stamps.»

She quoted, recited, like the most innocent of choirgirls. He stared at her, beyond shock.

– You haven't attempted to see it from the opposite perspective, have you now? She said softly. – That it's in truth the conformity that will destroy me, like it's destroying you and everybody else, not the opposite. Have you really understood anything, anything at all?

She jumped up. He shook in something very akin to fear.

– My words have shaken, you, she noted. – That's good. That means there is still hope for you.

She let go of the books. They hit the floor with a dump sound. She walked away, and left the front door open.

– You need a lot of fresh air, she shouted.

They stood in the window, staring at her as she faded into the darkness, the strangely distinct figure and the twilight shape, standing there, present there for quite some time. Long after she had vanished from their sight.

2

It was late afternoon. She sat on her hill, with her back to the sun. What little was visible of it through the clouds. She could see far from this vantage point, farther than before. Her vision had improved to an uncanny degree lately.

Below was the farm, with all its activity, reaching long and far. Its activity integrated in that of the valley and also the world outside. Eugene had managed to keep the land in a time when most had to decrease or halt one's commitment. He was good at this, to a point.

She moved her eyes over to the Cornwall estate, a modern, effective factory of plastic and metal, making her wretch inside. A grotesque example of modernization. What that meat contained she didn't want to think too much about, at least not in her darkest moments.

To the west was the Jimenez estate, and its reclusive owner Emilio. Liz felt something akin to nausea every time she ventured close to it. The school and public offices and the cluster of houses where the general population lived were not far away from it, so she passed there often.

To the east Thomas «Doc» Kennedy held on to his unfruitful land, with his rocketing bills, too stubborn to quit. She kind of admired that, in a way.

And beyond it all… was the mountains, the still untamed wilderness. The sight of it, its vastness and mystery played within her, echoed pleasantly in her deepest core. Nowhere near any kind of romanticized surface emotion, but tangible and true, and pulsing like a heart.

Below… she sensed the power of the Earth. She did wherever she walked, but stronger here. This had been a place of attraction, of worship for eons. To the Indians and perhaps to some of the first white settlers as well, some of the sages and witches fleeing from persecutions in Europe. Like the Indians they had worshipped snakes and eagles and celebrated life in all forms. Such hills, such places were found in Europe and throughout the world. Different in both form and use, she suspected, but they had in common that people like her sought them in their loneliness and desire and need. Sadness stirred within her. Defiance burned even stronger.

When she looked at the form from below, she imagined she saw a much bigger hill, a dark one covered with trees, and the sight triggered a pleasant feeling within.

She returned to the main building, towards what was supposed to be her home. In one of the windows in the smaller houses she glimpsed Lucy Barker, a quiet, timid woman. They were all here, Liz' extended family. Linsey hammered something in the tool shed. Him she sensed easily, his presence glowing in her mind.

Something drove her on, something that wouldn't be denied. She increased her speed, setting course for the horses' enclosure.

There was only one horse there, Blackie, Scott Thompson's horse. He was always alone there. No other horses, and certainly not males were allowed near his royal presence. She jumped easily over the fence. He straightened. Didn't neigh, just stared rigidly at her. The muscles hardened and swelled in his neck, his suddenly very tight neck. He stood still, but she sensed easily how tense he was. She walked closer, with a strange smile around her mouth. Then, right before he would have jumped away from her and run off, she grabbed his reins. It happened fast as lightning, even for the animal's senses. She pulled hard and merciless. Blackie rolled his eyes in terror.

– You're obstinate, she mumbled into the large ear. – You don't really want to be that way, do you? Not in my presence?

She rubbed the strong body. It was already covered in sweat. There was no saddle.

– Your weakness attracts me like a lighthouse in the night.

Without warning she threw herself on his back. He reacted instantly. Jumped and shook like a wild horse. She pulled in the reins. He ignored them and rushed off in a desperate run. Stopped abruptly, and kicked his rear legs in the air. Liz hung on, her legs tightening so hard around his ribs that they threatened to break. Her laughter was loud and scornful, and she knew he understood. Breathing hard he sat out towards the fence. She tightened her grip around his mane, and twisted his head brutally to the side, forcing him to turn. He tried one more time, on the other side. She twisted his head a bit more. He returned to the jumping and shaking for a while. She hung on, feeling the rush, turning stronger by the second. His strength faded, and faded fast, now, as her soared. She had won. As she had known she would. She growled in triumph deep down in her throat, and then she laughed, a laughter like thunder.

Blackie stood there with bowed head and labored breathing.

– You aren't that tired, are you? She spoke softly to him, while rubbing her body teasingly against his, soaking up power. – I don't want you to be hurt. I just wanted you to learn your place. And you have, haven't you?

She moved her heels lightly. He began moving forward, still with his head bowed. She bent forward and kissed his brow. Her hair fell forward and covered his eyes. There was no discernible reaction. She stretched her arms above her head, fully aware that she was being watched, caring shit.

Strong, so very strong. The intoxication flowed through her. Shadows sparked from her fingertips. This was… indescribable. And the sensation increased, increased far beyond what she had imagined it would feel like. The horse began to stumble beneath her. She caught herself, pulled herself together enough for her to jump off him, to… *to save his life*. Realization hit her, and the shock flooded her mind.

Scott Thompson observed how she landed, graciously like a cat, and moved away from the horse. She saw herself through his eyes, something that wasn't hard for her anymore. At least not now while power flooded her body and mind. It was broad daylight, but what she saw in his eyes was a shadow creature, one surrounding her human form. She had looked at herself in a mirror under similar circumstances, but then she hadn't felt half as good as she did now.

– I know what you are, he said darkly.

Scott Thompson confused her. It was as if he wasn't really there. No matter how much she studied him, she couldn't get a solid look at him. Not now, with her improved vision.

She realized she saw beyond the normal specter of reality, saw a place where everything was mist… and Shadow.

– But do you know what you are? She replied. – Have you looked at yourself in the mirror?

And she contemptuously left him there, the trembling figure in the form of a man.

She danced across the yard, seeing it in a completely new light. It wasn't there. Yet it was. By concentrating, by shifting her perception just a little she could choose what part she wanted to see. What she had done wasn't much, just a small thing. It had been so easy, like picking flowers. She was virtually in a state of ecstasy when she reached the large and tall house. Three full floors tall, including one lovely mysterious cellar. She looked up at the roof and the chimney. It hid the sun. It and the clouds did. She had to get closer, if ever so little. The porch, the thought flashed in her mind. She ran to it and jumped up on it - and then she jumped again, using all the explosive power in her legs. The roof was more than twice her height off, but she reached it, with her right hand's fingertips, and then with the other hand, and then with her right hand's firm grip. She pulled herself up easily. The roof was covered by pieces of turf. It felt soft and pleasant to the touch. She ran to the top, to the chimney, placing her feet on both sides of the ridge. Then she reached out with her arms, and stared at the sun… stared at the place behind the clouds where the sun was. And *then,* suddenly, shockingly euphorically… she was able to see the sun. She gasped. Everything turned tipsy turvy, upside down, inside out. It was like she was up there, on its glowing surface, experiencing the star in all its majesty.

The moment passed, fleeting, transitory. Its joy remained.

She smiled to June down on the ground. Liz can see June. June can't see Liz. Her vision faded and left only the lingering memory. Everything looked normal again. It was enough.

– LIZ, I know you're there. We saw you come.

June looked around with devious eyes, taking very deliberate steps as she began circling the house. Liz followed her with a roguish flash in her shining violet eyes. She saw something new in little sister then, and it was immensely interesting. Her mind reached out, playfully touching little sister, nibbling her ear, pulling the long, bright blond hair. June shook her head irritated. It evidently didn't occur to her that there was no wind. Liz sensed the wind. She had before, too, but not this way, like energy patterns in the air, like doorways into another world. Even though her extended perception had faded she could still remember it, remember the path, and Memory was everything.

The roguishness in Liz overtook her completely. She grabbed June's foot and held it, held it steady in the air. June stumbled and fell. Liz' laughter echoed across air and land and ears alike.

– Very funny, June cried. – A laugh riot, if you ask me, and YOU DID!

And she didn't sound surprised at all. She knew. And that did very little to surprise Liz.

Then June started laughing, too. And Liz laughed some more, and they both laughed themselves silly. Liz lost her footing. She grabbed the ridge just as she was about to roll down, in the nick of time. They lay there, laughing, laughing themselves silly, silly, silly, and it felt so good.

She heard the sound of running feet, first from far away, then close, close enough to make the ground shake, to make the ground in her shake.

Eugene arrived first of the three. He looked shocked at the two sisters stretched out on high and low ground.

– What in the hell are you doing up there? He shouted. – Get down immediately!

She rose grinning and began to walk to the end of the ridge, of the tall roof, dancing a wild ballet.

Alive. *I'm alive!*

– NO! Not immediately, damn you! He cried in sudden panic. – We'll get a ladder. Wait right there.

He was on his way before he had finished speaking, but was stopped by her commanding and ghostly voice.

– There's no need for a ladder.

Without acknowledging his desperate NO she jumped. Where it was the longest way down. She landed slightly crouched. It hurt a bit, but not more than that she easily hid it. She knew she did, saw it in her kin's thunderstruck faces.

She grabbed Linsey's hair and pulled him to her, kissing him hard on his lips.

– No need, she repeated, violet eyes stabbing Eugene.

Family dinner. Liz spoke incisively and incessantly. Nobody could avoid noticing her excessive good mood. She dominated the conversation in a way she never before had done.

– London was SO great, she marveled. – Even with a chaperone and within the limited structures of the tour guide arrangement it was *so* beyond words.

– Tell us more, June said eagerly, childishly. – What did you do?

– We visited many of the famous places, like the London Dungeon, The Tower and Madame Tussaud, Liz said dreamily. – But that wasn't it, really. What truly «sold» me was all the informal and daring stuff happening in the streets. There were musicians, performers and operating on key places all over the city, many without asking permission from *anyone*.

– The London Dungeon? Eugene commented critically, and with a clear taint in his voice.

– It's described as a medieval torture chamber. Liz didn't back away, not anymore. – But what it is beyond the fancy talk and sensationalism is a list of human atrocities throughout history, presented with surprisingly little of the usual hypocrisy and stuff.

– How did you manage to get to the military facility? Linsey shook his head, an admiring glance in his eyes.

– It was easy. I told a journalist that I was a relative of people inside…

She closed her eyes, smiling at the memory.

– I ditched him afterwards, not really telling him a thing. I guess he was so ashamed of being screwed by a teenage girl that he decided not to use the little he did know.

– But you didn't get to meet Ted? Eugene asked sharply.

– No, Stewart kept me from doing so, that shit.

– Thank God for small favors…

– I know you don't like him, Liz shrugged, – even if you pretended otherwise. What's the matter Eugene, wasn't he obedient enough for you?

– He brings discord and confusion to an otherwise orderly society, Kendall said. – He spent two years in our valley, and nothing was the same when he left.

– Things change, she said. – Have you ever thought about that?

– And you like London? He kept going. – I can't say I'm surprised you do enjoy such a cesspool of human degradation.

– Eugene! Trudy cried angrily.

– The last two nights I just ignored the stupid rules, Liz said dreamily, – and snuck out in the dark. I walked up Wardour Street, walked through Soho, among hustlers, whores and walkers in the night. I can't even begin to describe how great that felt.

– You spent most of your childhood and adolescence there, didn't you, mother? Linsey said quickly, taking the sting of Kendall's pointed stare.. – What do you think of it?

Trudy leaned back in her chair, a glow being lit in her eyes.

– The war was mostly spent indoors and afterwards there were mostly ruins, she said. – But it was still great, still had that special mood and quality I will never forget. I remember Grandfather Nick taking us children to the 1948 Olympics. There was so much hope then, so much hope of a better world.

She stared at Eugene, nailing him with a stare fare more potent than anything he could bring to bear.

– There's nothing inherently dangerous about London or similar places where thinking, living humans meet, except to those who fear ideas, fear variety and freedom.

Liz clapped her hands, an excited, childish happiness transforming her face. She knew immediately that it was a mistake, and all joy left her. Her hands fell and her entire body sagged there, on the chair.

The mood in the room turned sinister then. Something rose in Kendall. Liz sensed it in him, a poison beyond, way beyond mere anger.

Keep it up, she told him with her eyes, challenging him. No matter what you say, no matter how ugly it is, I'll keep my cool. You won't win!

– Your mother and I got a phone call from school today, he said evenly, casually. – What we heard wasn't very nice. Not only were you expelled. You also insulted a teacher.

– No, that's not what happened, she replied, clearly despairing. – *He* insulted *me*. Something he has kept doing since he first arrived from Denver and laid his eyes on me. I finally fought back and I'm glad!

– You were rude to your relatives, too. Does that make you glad as well?

– Well, yes, she nodded. – I don't have more respect for them then for Grey.

– Is that how you're thanking us for giving in to your unreasonable demands and allowing you to rocket across the globe?

Her hands whitened around the plate. The table shook.

– Damn you! She cried. – You're not *listening!* Don't you want to hear my version? Stupid me, you don't care *shit!*

She sought mother for support, but met only an unmovable face.

– You must earn the right to be heard, he said in a crushing blow. – And you haven't. You're nothing but a little kid begging favors from easily relenting parents, not fit to make your own decisions.

– You're so clever, father, she said, hardly moving her lips, – so skilled in twisting the knife. Have you ever been taught the art somewhere, or were you born with that skill?

She got to him. She knew she did. It was evident in the flickering of his eyes, the twitching of the mouth.

– And you've hardly touched your plate. You know what I feel about leaving food.

– Don't I ever? She grinned.

Than the mask fell. Her face turned naked and needy.

– I told you I wasn't hungry, she said, clenching her teeth. – But you insisted on me being the cute, polite girl and sit by the dinner table with you. As usual, not even considering my words.

– You impudent little…

A hand froze on the way up.

– I'm not hungry, she kept at it, a sickly glare in her eyes, nothing similar to the usual glow. – Therefore I don't eat. It's simple, is it not? I'm your daughter, not your slave. I don't obey your slightest whim.

– You didn't have breakfast today either, he insisted. – You must be hungry!

She blinked.

– You're afraid, she exclaimed, staring incredulously at him.

He lowered his eyes, unable to look at her.

– That's it. She spoke aloud, a shrill evident in her voice. – You're afraid of what you've given birth to. And you would be right. I am the demon you've always made me out to be, father. Congratulations.

– Liz… Linsey tried to break in.

– No, Lin, she cut him off. – I want to hear it. I want to hear him *say* it.

She looked at him, vulnerability and rage warring within her, cutting her up from the inside.

– I demand that you eat your food, Eugene Kendall shouted to her in a timid voice.

– I'm not HUNGRY! She rose abruptly, knocking the plate at the table. – You can go to hell!

She ran off in tears. They could hear her cursing and snarling, hear her strike the walls all the way up the stairs to her room. At one time one of the fists struck the walls so hard that the entire house shook.

It turned quiet, eerily quiet. There was no warning to what was coming. Eugene had faked a shrug, and grabbed his fork and knife when his plate rose in the air, rose all the way to the ceiling, where it stopped. Then it was as if it was thrown through the air. It hit the wall and was smashed to dust. The food and fine powder fell on them all. Three left the table while staring accusingly at Kendall. He sat there, sick and queasy, and nothing made sense anymore.

3

The ball jumped back and forth from the wall, hit by a flat pole. Steady, with no deviation in the power hitting it. There were no more tears in the girl's eyes, only fire. The long raven hair flowed around the body. She pulled it, caressed it, her rage like the pressure inside a volcano just before eruption. Her lips moved while cursing and swearing soundlessly.

Oh, why care? Why care about caring? She was different, alien to them. Nothing she would ever say or do would make them listen to her. Not until she made them listen.

That night she had her first dream about the shadow without a face.

It was the next morning. She stood before the mirror while the bright sun warmed her through the open window. She studied her eyes. They were still blue, but as she stepped closer to the smooth surface before her, she could glimpse the first, emerging red dots. The dots were clearly there. They hadn't been there before. She realized that they were permanent, that they would never go away. She began humming, humming a cheerful song.

The boundless frustration, the boiling rage had brought this on, brought on the final stage of the metamorphosis.

It made her feel better, so much better.

– This is my Time of Change, she told June later, – a very exciting time for me.

– Aren't you w-worried? Little sister wondered timidly.

– Why should I be? Ted and Mark and countless others have gone through it, and they're none the worse for wear. On the contrary. They're *better,* so much more capable of meeting the world *head on*. I want this!

And the change progressed, increased in scope and detail far beyond what she had once imagined it would. It wasn't only the eyes, as expected, but also her face and body, inside and out. On occasions she actually felt bones move and set into new and different configurations.

Her skin turned a darker hue, without the aid of the sun's rays. Her hair turned darker, virtually completely black. It grew thicker and its consistency changed dramatically over a few days' time. And she got more of it, all over her body, and for a while she was actually worried. But the change settled there, and she could breathe a sigh of relief, and keep enjoying what was happening to her.

She got stronger. Muscles seemed to appear all over her. Exercise brought quicker results. She was able to run faster, longer, and faster longer. Her body turned supple and ever stronger, seemingly every time her feet hit the soft ground beneath her soles. She often studied her face in the mirror and she could observe the changes from day to day. The dots in her eyes grew to spots. Her face turned even more distinct and fascinating, a jigsaw puzzle where no piece seemed to fit properly. It wasn't pretty exactly, far from it, as it was way too intense. She had seen other girls change from skinny skeletons to large, soft and enticing frames «over night». It was nothing compared to this. The smile transformed her face, making it beautiful, making it demonic.

– SPEAK, she cried jubilantly to June and Linsey at the far side of the house.

And they did, and her eyes glowed. Her ears vibrated, as they picked up on the changes in the air and the wind.

– I can hear you, she cried. – As if you're standing next to me. Whisper now. Whisper me secrets of times past.

At first she couldn't hear them. But then the wind shifted and practically carried their words to her.

Her smell was enhanced to the point that she for a time believed that something was wrong with the air. Everything was felt so strongly that she had problems dealing with it. She sensed people, sensed their moods and intentions to such a point that it approached mind reading. She experienced herself and the world in a totally new and exciting manner.

The three of them walked long trips into the wilderness, where she could excel in her newfound strength.

– Behold, she cried to big brother and little sister.

A large stone was torn from the ground and pulled into the air. Her two companions stared.

– This used to give me a major headache, she told them. – Now, I hardly need to strain anymore.

Sometimes she just had to cry out loud in her joy. It was real, real, *real*.

People noticed the changes, the visible changes. It was to be expected. But she wasn't worried. Most people, knowing so very, very little about the world, didn't make anything of it. Everybody changed at her age. It wasn't directly suspicious.

She began using shades, though, hiding the one thing she needed to hide.

And they fit my personality, she grinned.

Even in the dark she wore them. The eyes, her eyes were more visible then, not less. There was light in them, not merely a reflection. Only within the house' four walls, when there weren't any outsiders present, she didn't wear the shades. To her mother, sister and brother she had nothing to hide. Father she let see, just on spite.

Spite felt good sometimes.

At school she felt the stabs in the back worse than any physical reality. There weren't that many attempting to tease or bully her directly. They found out quickly that it was doomed to fail. She played up to it with burning scorn.

– Do you enjoy being such a peahen? They cried to her.

– Do you enjoy being such a gray mouse? She replied.

The indirect, less obvious stabbing she could do less to defend herself against. The silent group bullying. She was only one. They were many. She could have struck back in ways they could hardly imagine, truly punish them, but she hesitated. They weren't worth any effort on her part, anyway.

Hunter Cornwall invited to a party, another one of the valley's boring «family» get-togethers. But it was the only show in town, and Elizabeth, not feeling very picky, decided to go. Besides June had been after her all week because she wanted to go, and she couldn't go alone.

Trudy and June brushed her hair, her very long and very unruly hair.

– It's like it's actually moving by itself, June complained.

Liz had been a bit afraid that it was actually doing that, but had disregarded the thought. It was dead, dead skin. It wasn't alive, only unruly.

– It's actually falling beneath your hips by now, Trudy said with a critical look. – Not that it isn't… decorative and nice, in its own way, but I have to say it's totally old fashioned. You shouldn't stick your neck out more than you already do, if you ask me.

– I know, mom, Liz nodded. – I'll be all right. It's *me*.

June didn't say anything more. She had pretty long hair herself. Their mother grabbed the shades and held them up.

– You do realize you can't wear these forever, I trust?

– I use them because I want them, Liz replied intensively. – No one can make me do anything I don't want to.

Trudy touched the skin around the eyes. Liz let her.

– These you must wear forever… the eyes of the Beast. The symbol of your power and your curse.

Liz knew what she meant. She would never be able to hide, and those with knowledge would know her for what she was.

That both excited and terrified her.

She, June and Linsey walked through the dark underbrush wood towards the Cornwall building. Eugene couldn't stand the Cornwalls, and stayed away, and then Trudy did, too.

– Those shades… Linsey shook his head in laughter. – I can't for the life of me understand how you can walk without stumbling. I can hardly see the path.

– I can see the path easily, she mused. – I can see in the dark. Better for every new night.

There was the familiar quality in her voice then that always made the cold tingle trickle down their spine.

– How exciting, June exclaimed. – I wish I could do that. I wish I were like you.

– Not I. Linsey shook his head. He hesitated a moment, when the two kid sisters looked at him, before shrugging and joking about it. – I'm quite happy the way I am.

The three of them, like any guest, old and young were met in the door by Cornwall and son, Hunter and Paul. Paul held Elizabeth's hand and she felt the charge from his skin.

Inside she almost threw up on the spot. It didn't take more than a few minutes' exposure before everything had turned absolutely intolerable.

– This won't do, she mumbled. – This won't do at all.

– What do you mean? June asked innocently.

– Wait and see, Liz told her, suddenly suspiciously good-humored. – Just you wait…

Fairly casually she began her great work by presenting Linsey for Stevie Fulton (and husband).

– Stevie hadn't arrived in school when you moved on, Lin, she said innocently, – so you haven't met, have you now?

– A pleasure, Fulton mumbled, clearly not enjoying himself.

– What was that for? Linsey asked her, very suspicious as he pulled her aside later. – I *know* you. You don't do anything without ulterior motives.

– Such high thoughts you have of me, big brother, she grinned.

She held on to the silly grin even when he tightened his grip. Then she shrugged.

– This «party» is boring me to death. I need *something* to do.

He seemed content with that explanation, letting her go with one last admonishing shake.

She mingled. There wasn't much of a pond to mingle in, so she threatened to go stir crazy. She sought out Linsey after just a few minutes and pulled him aside.

– What's the matter with you? Little sister is doing you a huge favor, and you're just pulling back and throwing your gift away.

– What do you mean? He said irritated.

– Don't play coy with me, she stonewalled him. – I know you've conquered a looong line of the valley's little beauties lately. In fact you've gained a reputation as a champion in the number of completed *fucks*. So what's the matter, afraid of taking on bigger game?

He looked astounded at her. Then, slowly his eyes sought out Stevie Fulton and her husband.

– You're crazy as a loon, he said nervously.

– It is a challenge, she said admittedly. – Stevie and hubby have been married for ten years, since college…

He turned aggrieved towards her. And she couldn't hold back an expression of astounded surprise.

Yes, she was convinced she noticed anger in him… *and also something else*.

After he had left her Liz just had to sit down, a look of absolute astonishment painted on her face.

The world had just turned upside down… again.

An image came to her, one she found incredibly funny, about Linsey covering Stevie Fulton. She giggled insanely, and knew people looked at her, and she didn't give a damn.

– What's so funny?

June sat down beside her, looking quite full of mischief herself.

– Nothing, Liz grinned. – Nothing important.

She looked closer at the tall blond girl.

Liz realized with a shock that little sister had also grown the last year, to the point that she was hardly little anymore.

– Dance with me, big sister, June said impulsively, shyly.

That surprised yet Liz again, and she let herself be led to the dance floor in stunned silence. June seemed a bit reserved at first, but she loosened up quickly, and Liz noticed that she, too, did. As the music rose to a crescendo in her ears, she noticed she gave in to the reckless abandon breaking her surface from beneath. June was a natural dancer. Liz sensed life's rhythms in her, and enjoyed it. They weren't the only girls dancing together. It was fairly common that girlfriends did that, «to ward off the big bad wolf boys». But people studied the two sisters, inevitably, as they came to dominate the floor.

June kissed Liz' lips. It happened so sudden that Liz couldn't stop her, and she wasn't sure she wanted to, finding herself responding to the sultry kiss. She sensed the surge among the spectators, the outrage, the beyond shocked interest.

– You'll be blamed for this, too, June giggled darkly. – You've always been more high profile than I…

The shocks seemed to be well supplied tonight. For once Liz Warren was speechless.

The music to this point had been quite lame. The established generation's music or a few, current, not very dangerous tunes. But then somebody started up Bad Moon Rising. The beat and music and words surged in Liz' limbs, and she responded, unable and unwilling to hold back.

They want a show, she thought. Let them have one.

A little taken aback at first, Liz began to feel greatly encouraged. The two of them *danced.* And the others stopped at their feeble attempts at doing so. There was movement. Liz felt it, felt it in every limb. And she saw the burning interest being lit in every male's eyes, as they watched the two females perform on the floor.

The dance ended. There was stunned, polite applause. The two sisters curtseyed and kissed each other's cheeks, all very proper.

– You're so very, very impatient, June told Liz, briefly touching her cheek. – That will cost you one day, cost you dearly.

No one else heard.

The two of them parted. The music turned silent. Everything seemed out of whack to Liz, in more ways than one not real.

Liz decided on a whim to be patient, devilishly patient that night. She enjoyed herself while dancing with boys, watching June with her innocent smile dance with boys.

She looked at it all from above… a powder keg about to blow.

There was a long queue of boys waiting to break in and dance with the sleeping beauty. June smiled and they stuttered and they stumbled, and weren't quite in charge of their own faculties anymore. Liz waited, waited with infinite patience.

After being passed over several times Butch Davison finally got to dance with the young fairy princess. June danced with him, as she had done with all the others, with infinite sweetness and grace, keeping her distance.

The dance ended. June disengaged from him and wanted to leave the floor, but Butch held on to her.

– Would you like some p-punch? He stuttered.

– Thank you, Butch, she fluttered. – I would love to.

– W-wait here, he told her and rushed off.

When he turned his head halfway across the room, she was still there, smiling encouragingly at him.

He returned with one glass in each hand. On his way towards the awaiting June he had to pass the table where Allan Kendall sat with his feet placed comfortably on the floor. As Butch passed him Liz made one of Allan's feet move. It was so enjoyable. Butch stumbled and hit the floor with a loud boom. The glasses broke and the fluid flowed on the dance floor, and made (with Liz' explicit help) a couple slip on the slippery slope that was the floor. They fell on their backs and remained there, gasping for air.

Butch jumped to his feet in a flashing speed. He grabbed Allan by the collar and lifted him up high, shaking him like a towel.

– You're meat, skinny, the butcher snarled.

– I didn't do anything, Allan howled. – I DIDN'T FUCKING DO ANYTHING!

One of the guards entered the fray. It was Hunter Cornwall.

– What the… goes on here? He cried, almost forgetting himself for a moment.

– I didn't do anything, Allan whimpered, still hanging from the butcher's hook.

– He put out his foot, June said anxiously. – I saw it.

And Allan looked at her, a very hurt expression evident in his eyes.

Butch turned even meaner. He lifted his free hand to beat the other senseless. A warning cough from Cornwall put a stop to this tempting notion. The large boy shrugged and let go of the meat. Allan landed on his backbone and released a thin wail.

The ruckus ended there, unsatisfactory, but promising. Liz didn't feel cheated.

She walked to the punch, sipped it, and emptied the glass in one single gulp.

Linsey approached her and removed her shades.

– You look very pleased with yourself. Toasting with yourself, are you?

He felt the heat from her and the strange quiver it created in him. She recaptured the shades and put them back on.

– It's shit, she said in contempt. – Not much stronger than soda.

– Like the party, he nodded. – Not much to write home about… except for a few bright spots.

– Thank you, big brother.

She kissed him on the still soft cheek. He didn't mind. She sensed that clear enough.

Everybody saw them, but he didn't mind. And that pleased her, pleased her immensely.

She walked out on the empty balcony, half on half hoping and expecting him to follow her, but he didn't. When she turned he wasn't there. She stared stubbornly up on the full moon. The sight stirred something in her, something profound she couldn't fathom. It irritated her, like everything beyond her reach.

Paul came to her. She didn't move, didn't in any way acknowledge his presence.

– You like this house, don't you?

He told her, in his very confident manner. She didn't reply.

– Perhaps not the house itself, but what it represents, unbound freedom, unlimited potential.

She turned towards him, acknowledging his presence.

– You've got a seriously warped view of those things, she replied.

He just kept looking unfazed at her, ignoring the implied insult, the stark challenge.

– You're good, he nodded. – Skilled and strong. There isn't a girl in there that is your equal.

She had played poker with him and the boys once, and bankrupted them all, but not him. He had been neutral, indifferent, to the point that she hadn't been able to read him. And she had read the others like open books.

She had won a lot of money, and put them aside for leaner days.

– What a sexist remark, she remarked.

– No false modesty. He nodded pleased. – I like that, too, in a girl.

– I don't see your sister here, she said casually, very casually and innocently, eager to sense anything other than the smoldering desire he didn't hide in him. – Won't she return soon?

Claudia Cornwall had left the valley for unfathomable reasons four years ago, creating the wildest speculations.

– Claudia is actually married, he replied lightly. – She and her husband live in Costa Rica. He's one of our executives. We have a project down there.

He was so smug, as if he looked very much forward to something. She couldn't help but wonder what that was, and it stirred a fear in her.

He was good-looking, and not a sheep like most others she knew. It was a good thing she knew him so well. So she wouldn't be fooled. She detested him and everything he stood for.

– I've always loved the full moon, he said softly.

She had, too. When the forces and desire flowed freely through her. When everything seemed possible and… He stepped close to her, taking her hand, giving her every chance to pull back. She breathed faster, the anticipation ravaging her like a storm. Breathless she let herself be pulled into his fawn. He took her shades and threw them off the balcony. She heard them hit the soft grass far below.

– I love your eyes, he said.

He met her eyes, and pulled her tight. Her lips quivered. He kissed her and she responded, couldn't help herself.

Not him, she thought, a sore catching in her throat. Anybody but him.

She liberated herself from his strong grip.

– I'm not one of your tramps, she said icily.

– I know, he stated. – That's why I'm so patient.

That word again. It twisted and burned within her.

He left. She remained there for a while, under the moon, motionless and vulnerable, so fucking vulnerable. Almost subconsciously she reached a hand into the air beyond the balcony. The shades rose from the darkness and into her hand. She put them back on and instantly felt much better, not realizing what a mistake she had done, not until she had left the balcony and returned inside.

Fuck, he didn't know. It wouldn't even occur to him. He had distracted her, made her careless. Damn him!

Molten rock flowed through her veins, and once again she wanted to reveal herself, to cry out her rage to the world. It made her weak, and she had to support herself on one of the pillars.

The desire to break, destroy, oppress… It was always there. Even when it rested some dark place within her, it was always there. Humans were ants she could crush under her heel.

Ants could easily be stepped on, but they were so many. So many.

She dried her tears from her eyes. They never truly appeared beyond the moist fire. She curled her hands into fists. A demonic smile transformed her face.

Very few realized what actually went down that night. The party was off to a good start. The youths being very polite and attentive, not really causing any kind of trouble. There were a few skirmishes, but then again, there always was. Nothing serious. Everything proceeded smoothly and excellently. No one could step forward afterwards and state with any authority what had happened.

Something… happened. The mood was slowly, unnoticeably poisoned. A dark angel, one no one noticed in such a way, walked among them, stirring the pot, causing skirmishes where no one was, showing great skill, making old scores grow raw and testy. Only one very sensitive person could do such a thing, pick emotions people were hardly aware of themselves.

It was almost too easy.

Rupert Fulton grew more and more irritated for every new dance his wife had with Linsey Kendall. For a while there it seemed like she was practically clinging to the boy. She had looked quite shocked at her husband afterwards and told him she had stumbled in something. But how plausible was that, out there on the naked floor?

He had some punch. Right after that he returned and had more punch. Three, four trips more like that and he began to grow quite *agitated.* He stared at Hunter Cornwall through a very foggy vision, more than wondering if the prick didn't look accusingly at him.

Fulton saw that Stevie and Kendall had begun another dance, and he joined the longest queue of the evening, the one making the lucky stiff fall into June Kendall's lovely arms. Suddenly, shockingly he was there, and he pulled her out on the floor, no longer caring about dispersing the red haze obscuring his vision.

– You're something of the sweetest a man can know, he declared, he drooled on her and spoke through his nose.

She just kept smiling, giving no indication that she had heard him or acknowledged his words.

– You have the sweetest smile, he said aloud.

Before he even knew what he was doing he had kissed her. With the image of Stevie clinging to Linsey with rotating hips stuck on repeat in his mind he doubled and redoubled his efforts.

Butch broke in and pulled June out of his arms.

– C-can I break in, he stuttered.

Slightly disoriented and more than a bit dizzy Rupert grabbed June again and attempted to pull her back into his arms.

– Really, guys, June grinned. – I'm not a tug of war you can pull.

Allan Kendall, feeling very noble and protective towards the virgin in need, filled with righteous chivalry took a step forward.

– She's right, he sniveled. – Stop *bothering* her.

Butch growled deep in the throat. He struck Allan with a right hook, sending him across the floor. Hunter grabbed Butch with both hands and lifted him high up in the air. Butch' brother Kevin, feeling he had something to prove put a hand on Cornwall's arm… and kicked the large man in the groin.

– It felt very right at the time, he confessed with lowered head later on.

Cornwall fell squealing to the floor. The guards rushed to the rescue. Butch met the first with a fist sending him right down to his boss on the floor. The other wanted to talk some sense into Butch, but he slipped, and his foot hit poor Butch in the belly. Fulton, a bit discouraged pulled back, looking for Stevie. He spotted her with Linsey. She pushed herself at the wall with an ecstatic look on her face and the boy had a hand on one of her breasts. Fulton recognized all the signs of mindless desire in Stevie, the empty eyes, the tongue licking her lips and the rapid breathing. Seeing red, he rushed forward and hit Linsey right on the jaw.

Linsey went down. Felt the pain from the strike in a distant, strange way. Saw the world through a red haze. Wrath raged uninhibited through him. It puzzled him. He had never before felt such a totally pure rage.

He was on his feet like a cat. And before he even realized what was happening he had grabbed Fulton by the throat. He raised him up like a rag doll and held on. He struck him. Struck him in the belly, and at the side of the head, struck him hard, again and again and again. The grip was so firm that the hard strikes didn't make it slip. Fulton wasn't yet unconscious, but he was completely defenseless. Linsey struck again. Harder…

The various fights turned into an all against all ruckus. The fights spread from the dance hall to adjacent rooms and even upper floors and outside.

June managed to get away with just a few bruises. She sought the higher ground where Liz had already taken position. They sat there, shaking their heads, watching it all from relative safety.

– Look at it, Liz grinned. – That's a disaster of biblical proportions for you…

The eyes behind the shades glowed in excitement. She had done this, and not really by using her powers at all. It had mostly been the divide and conquer-method, but that didn't make it any less enjoyable. On the contrary. The two girls sat there and giggled and giggled and couldn't stop giggling.

The dust took days to settle, and the valley's various affairs would never be the same.

4

Valpurgis Nacht, Cuckoo Mass, Beltane, Witch Sabbath, Witchnight…
Dear and feared child had many names.
Heat arrived with spring. Elizabeth gathered all the information she could find, which wasn't much. She scoured the land but found nothing truly useful. Not in any schoolbooks or library she could find. What she did find was mostly generalities, displays of intolerance and hearsay she knew to be wrong or grossly inaccurate.
An example of the quality or lack of thereof, was «Myths and Pseudo-Science of the Modern Age» by Anton Berkowitz.
She felt lonelier than ever.
– He's commenting on everything from alien abductions to telekinesis… ridiculing it all, reducing it to nuts and bolts, she raged to Linsey. – He's a real class act.
She paced back and forth on the floor, making holes in the carpet.
– Listen to this: «Telekinesis is supposed to be about mind over matter, but such a noble pursuit can never take such a banal path. Science itself is the true Mind over Matter».
– That is remarkable mimicry he gaped, he joked. – You sound exactly like him.
She threw a pillow at him.
«The system of psi-classification», she read, alone in her room, «developed by J. B. Rhine and Karl Zener at Duke University in the twenties, failed miserably to achieve any kind of scientific legitimacy».
Below the good *Doctor* Berkowitz had listed the four main classifications, keeping to his dry sarcasm, of course.

Telepathy - so called mind reading. Mental contact. Empathy. Sending and reception.

Clairvoyance - literally *clearsight*. Sensing without known senses.

Liz added the word «known».

Precognition - psychic abilities. Mystical knowledge of future events.

Telekinesis or **Psychokinesis** - movement by mind power. Mind over matter.

She closed the book neatly, and put it away on the shelf beneath the night table.

Impatience and frustration evident in the body writhing on the bed, it finally settled and sat up, settling some more, never truly settling. She paced back and forth in the room a few times before nodding to herself.

She headed downstairs and right for the kitchen, where she smelled her mother's cooking.

– Mom. Trudy looked up and to the side, acknowledging her presence. – Are there writings from the family anywhere in the house?

As she spoke she grabbed mother hard around the bare arm. She had surprised Trudy, not given her time to prepare.

I'll know if you're lying, she told her mother with a challenging stare.

The girl stiffened before Trudy had collected herself sufficiently to reply.

Her twisted face revealed how hard she concentrated.

The question had inadvertently made Trudy to think about the answer, even if she perhaps wasn't willing to give it. It didn't matter anymore.

There was a jolt, a ripping sound, of a veil brushed aside, a moment of dizziness, of utmost clarity. Elizabeth knew she wasn't a mind reader, but she was empathic, able to receive impressions, emotions and a wide range of sensations. And now she did! A memory from childhood, a girl being led through a long, dark tunnel. A special day.

The Blood Day.

Darkness. Heat. She looked down on herself, didn't need to, to feel the warm, red fluid flow down her thighs, down on the kitchen floor.

She stood there frozen for a moment, for seconds, for days without number.

– I'm going to clean the floor, Trudy said, her voice akin to a whisper.

– Thank you, mom, Liz cried, and rushed off.

It was as if a hole opened up in reality itself, as if she reached the dark, moist cellar long before she ran down the stairs, before she touched the three locks and unlocked them with her mind and euphoria embraced her.

She grabbed a flashlight from the table and walked inside, apprehensive and excited beyond words. This was it. It had to be. The place where mother had taken her, where none of the other children had tread.

The dark surrounded her. The flashlight seemed to only cast a pinprick of brightness. She hesitated, but then turned it off and threw it away.

– Useless, she mumbled.

She stopped, waited. Slowly, slowly her sense of the room improved, until she could actually *see* it, and walk further in. She was light and confident on her feet, but the apprehension persisted.

The room was huge and… and empty? The disappointment made her curse under her breath. Slowly, deliberately she curled her left hand into a fist, and sure as rain… the rage came.

The room *changed.* Its very air danced on a different frequency, and she was *aware* of this as it happened. She grew aware of the same atmospheric mood she had been five years ago. A sinister scent. A warning, an interest, an invasive… sweep. She sensed the presence, and in the adolescent girl there was no doubt. She sensed nothing from it, from It, no thoughts, no purpose or mind, except that it was here. And it wanted her. The shaking began, imperceptible at first, then full blown. She wanted to fall down on her knees, she wanted to run, to flee with her tail between her legs. She stood her ground, on shaky ground, but she stood.

She registered the heat, the dry air. The soil making up the walls was wet, but the room was dry. Dust and shit danced in the air, but the room was clean. The contradictions passed her by, as the whispers, the insistent and invasive whispers rose in her ears, incomprehensible and terrifying.

– Oh, God, she whimpered, tears forming in her eyes.

The dust… the sound of bells. There was a beam of light following the dust. The bells grew louder. Then it abruptly *stopped.* And her vision turned foggy or clearer, she couldn't tell. Eyes stayed wide open, as she crouched in nausea and fear.

– You want me to kneel, don't you, she snarled, drying saliva off her jaw, – like a good dog? Or to run, until there is nowhere left to run. But I know, I *know* if I do that I will have nowhere left to run.

She saw herself kneel in the dust, feeling his hands around her neck, feeling the cold metal of the collar as he put it on her, as he made her his. The scared little girl ran to the end of the world before she finally stopped, exhausted and broken, turning towards him, begging him to put the collar around her neck.

She straightened, and it was like a very heavy load was lifted from her, from both her mind and body and soul, and at that very moment she noticed spots of red on the floor, growing more distinct as she watched, forming a circle covering half the room.

There was an impasse, a resistance when she attempted to step into the circle, no matter how high she lifted her foot. Even her hand had difficulties breaching the invisible demarcation in the air. This was a three-dimensional dome, not a circle. She broke the circle. There was pain, as more blood flooded down the insides of her thighs, and fertilized the ground. There was a shimmering, both familiar and unknown. And then she saw, saw what had been hidden, the stables of cardboard boxes seemingly growing out of the very air itself.

Reality reset itself, into new and unseen patterns. She shook her head in amazement and wonder. The world was so big, so very big.

She bent eagerly forward, reaching for the closest box. Before she could lay her hands on it her arms turned heavy and weak, and fell down, completely devoid of strength.

What a fucking *thoroughness,* she thought enraged.

The girl, her anger serving her well, as it always did grabbed the box and tore it open. It was easy. Just a minor, final resistance and it was done.

Her eyes glowed in excitement as she searched its content. There were books there, and a folder. She recognized the names of several of the books and swelled in joy. One stood out: «Magick in theory and practice» by Aleister Crowley. She had looked for it in London, but it had been sold out or been «unavailable» everywhere she went.

She opened the folder. It contained only one sheet, but writing covered that single sheet on both sides.

«I greet you, young female witch. I welcome you, Elizabeth Warren, to the Janus Clan».

A thrill, a cold tingle shot through her spine. Whoever had written this had known, known that she would find this, known that she and no one else would find the books.

– Elizabeth Warren, she said aloud.

She tasted the name on her tongue, savored it in her mind.

«You have opened Pandora's box. There is no turning back, now».

– No turning back, she said.

«This isn't really sufficient to cover your need for knowledge, but it's a beginning, setting you on the path, the many-faced path you're born to walk. The Time of Change is upon you, and you will be changed, as you change the world».

She flipped the page and looked down at the signature at the bottom.

Nick Warren 1955

Her great grandfather. He had known a young witch with beastly eyes would find this.

He had put all this here twenty years ago. He had known her name four years before she was born.

– How much do you *know?* How powerful *are* you?

Weak-kneed she wanted to kneel in the mud, to expose her neck to his mercy.

«I don't require your subservience, but your strength. There are enough of those who would welcome and force your blind service, though. Beware! And beware the distant shadow without a face».

Sick relief and fear made her cringe in self-contempt. She recalled the dream in vivid detail, recalled the revulsion and attraction.

There was a sound of steps on the soft ground. Liz whirled around. Trudy stood in the opening with the flashlight in her hand. The strong light hurt Liz's eyes.

– He made me forget, Trudy said tonelessly. – But now I remember. Now I remember everything.

She stepped into the circle. There was no hurdle anymore. The circle was broken.

– Nick? Did Nick do it?

– Yes. He came here in a truck, a few weeks after Linsey was born. He left the next day. I never saw him again.

They went through the books together, kneeling on the ground, treating the books like they were relics.

– Many of these are first editions, Trudy choked, with tears in her eyes. – I remember them from our house in London.

Mother had always looked younger than her actual age. Now, this was even more pronounced.

– Great grandfather can't still be alive, can he? Liz said cautiously, breathlessly. – He was old already then.

– He was sixty-five. Trudy grinned and shook her head. – He looked like twenty-five. We've always died young in our family, but that was usually caused by injury, grave injury, not old age.

She paused a bit, smiling.

– He might very well be alive.

– And is that… good or bad? Liz whispered.

Trudy thought about it.

– Before you asked that question I would have said «good», she said softly. – But I'm not sure. He was always deep, always strange, even compared to our «standards». He didn't exactly treat me gently on his visit here. And then there was…

She held back. Liz wanted to push her, but she felt weak, felt drained.

– Come, Trudy said, taking command. – We must clean you up. And you must rest. Not even you can take punishment like this without repercussions.

Mother led her out of there, in spite of her protests, her feeble resistance.

– This will be here when you return. It has always been here.

Mother bathed her, as if she was a little girl again. She put her to bed and sang to her, a lullaby of peace and quiet, where no peace and quiet was, lulling her to sleep.

And Liz Warren fell into a deep well of peace and quiet, sleeping like the dead.

5

Liz slept for three days, totally exhausted, almost in a coma-like state, a death-like sleep without dreams, plagued by horrible visions.

The place reeked of horror. Cleaned skeletons were seen everywhere, on the ground, hanging from ropes. Skulls had been stuck on poles. Poison-ridded smoke drifted in the air.

– They killed all the men and older males, and took the females as slaves. The boys were incorporated into his army.

The woman with a wolf's head spoke to her in a strange tongue, but Elizabeth understood every word. It was hammered into her like nails.

Liz stood on a field, a field of chopped down trees. The roots were still fresh, but dying, dying, and it made her feel bad beyond belief.

– Jahavalo came to this place and changed everyone, living and dead, molded them in his image, like he does everywhere he walks.

– Jahavalo, Liz said softly.

She sat up in bed, shaking in horror, soaking wet by cold, cold acid sweat. It burned and hissed on her skin.

It was as if the entire room trembled with the echo of the name.

She still smelled the stench from the field, still saw the horrible sight. She couldn't get rid of either.

The room kept trembling, kept opening. She was opening, and the pain was joy, and she trembled.

There were words. Memory. Of the future, of the past, she didn't know.

She spoke, and what she heard was a male voice, so much like her own, but an octave or so lower.

– «Perhaps my eyes are really closed, after all, but I can see still?»

The mirror… the mirror was her.

The spring equinox. How many days had passed she didn't know. Neither how many she had spent on the hill with the pumpkin. The pumpkin grinned at her. She concentrated, concentrated hard enough to make sweat flow and nourish the dead spring grass.

– Spirits of the Earth, of times past and times coming, sssspeak to me sssecretsss of Power.

And her words echoed throughout the valley, and she imagined everybody heard her. She was long past the cautious stage.

But there was nothing, no response, no sense of the elation following success.

– Life isn't a garden, the female wolf told her, – so would you *please* stop being a hoe.

She opened her eyes, tired and exhausted and frustrated, forced them open in the vain hope that insomnia would bring her what she needed, what she craved.

In vain.

– Don't *look* at me! She snarled.

In a fit she smashed the pumpkin. Her father had cried from the yard and she had a faint notion that she had turned towards to him, and snarled at him, and he had backed off the fastest he could, shaking like a leaf. She threw herself on the ground, rolled down the hill, where she came face to face with father. She smiled to him, a smile she knew to be terrifying.

She ran off, a howling lost soul. When she returned she was dirty all over, and her clothes were shredded beyond repair. She stood in the yard, breathing. Nick's words echoed within her.

«For your burning heart there is no peace».

She seemed okay. She felt okay. Trudy and Linsey came and led her inside, bathed her and groomed her. She let them. It felt so good to just sit there and do nothing.

What had she seen? What had she caught through her father's eyes?

She began shaking and couldn't stop. Tears filled her eyes. Trudy and Linsey held her, sang to her. Both did, and their voice embalmed her anxiety, her restless spirit.

The spirits are whispering in my little girl's ear.

Trudy sang.

The spirits are speaking to my little girl.

About the hidden world.

About times past.

And times future.

And ages untold of.

These are the horrors.

These are the dreams.

These are the joys.

Filling her life.

The girl staring into the mirror is pale, at least to her standards. The brown skin has turned ghoulish and gray. The hands clutching the clothes shake. The now so bloodless lips quiver and burn. Determination shines in her huge eyes.

The news arriving from the distant land of Vietnam was strangely comforting and elating to what Liz sat out to do. She and Linsey spontaneously embraced when they heard that the United States personnel had been forced to flee in choppers from the embassy roof in Saigon. It was completely accidental that they did it in front of their father, but Eugene left the room and closed the door hard behind him. Liz felt neither pleasure nor sorrow. The restlessness devouring her rescinded all other priorities.

– It does frighten me, she told Linsey, Trudy and June. – It should. There is ample reason to be frightened. But I'm not backing off. I must know!

It was night soon. Midnight in the wild garden.

– Life isn't a garden, she mumbled, – so stop being a hoe.

It was Beltane. The night of witches. The night to May first.

– During the middle ages there was a persistent belief that this was the night witches made their offerings to Satan, and consummated their service to him…

She turned to the three.

– What crap! I don't believe it, don't believe any of it. There's no Satan, no God. Karl Marx said religion is opium for the people, and in this he was right. It's self-evident, really. Those believing in God don't believe in themselves, and in their lack of confidence in their own power, they doom the world.

– Your eyes are glowing, June said, endlessly fascinated.

– Good, Liz stated. – Very good.

She stepped before the mirror, completely naked. June and Trudy began painting her, painting her face and body, and then she was naked no more.

– This is a dangerous night, Trudy said. – An exciting night, a mirror of our dreams and nightmares. It's older than the church, older than christianity and any form of religion. According to legend it's a time where the borders between worlds are weakening and occasionally also breaking. It leads to a place in our soul. A core we've always known and will never forget. The transition is hard, always hard, and one way or another it's something you must all go through. This is who we are.

And her daughters and son looked at the strange, unknown woman and a geyser rose in their soul.

– I made these colors in sweat, Liz incanted, as she painted the last few colors in her face and body herself. – I made them in blood and shadow. I paint myself with fire. I weave myself in spells.

The words from Nick's instructions, mixed with her own inventions echoed across the room.

The raven hair spilled around the strong body, the supple limbs. She painted green lines where the black hair painted its own line, around her thighs circles of blue. The breasts and buttocks she covered in brown.

– There's a sense of alienation, inevitably, she said proudly. – Tonight I embrace evil's beauty, and say goodbye to it forever. I'm a demon. I'm a witch. Tonight I part with all I've known. I do it alone, on my own recognizance. Let no one but me fall victim to its consequences.

She giggled as she made a pirouette before the mirror, before her kin.

She slipped into the dark and silent night - alone.

The creature moved catlike across the torn landscape of light and shadow. There was no longer any sense of her kin. She saw not a single star. Black clouds covered it all. Somewhere she heard distant thunder.

The thunder rolled towards her, through the air, through the ground. It was like one step took forever, like she had already spent an eternity out here.

– I can feel it, she mumbled.

The world sizzled with power. She picked electricity from the very air. Her fingertips sparked and burned.

The bull pulled in the thick chain she had bound it with. The pole shook hard as he doubled and redoubled his efforts. She walked to him, walked to the tamed beast, feeling both sorrow and hunger, regret and triumph. He attempted to spear her on his horns. She avoided them easily, drunk with expectation, attempting poorly to not let it make her overconfident.

– O'Minotaur, she called throatily, crying at the sky, at the ground, – come to me, embrace me. Do your best. Do your worst.

She rubbed herself at his hide, keeping in contact, as she circled him on rubbery legs. And as she sensed his strength leave him, her strength grew exponentially.

– You need your strength, she said softly. – At least for a while longer. I can't carry you, stupid.

His breathing turned labored. She bent forward and kissed his brow, pulling back easily as he made yet another feeble attempt at piercing her. The dark laughter cracked with the thunder.

She loosened the chain brimming with strength. He noticed the change and tried to run, but she pulled hard in the opposite direction, pulled so hard that he almost fell.

– Come with me, she cried, – and let's set loose the dogs of *war*.

She pulled him for a while, but then he stopped resisting, and it was like walking a dog. And he followed her, eager like a dog up the hill. She knew he would bring her no more trouble.

– Poor boy, she said softly, – all the fight gone from you, but we will bring it back. We will bring it all back.

There was a heap of dry grass awaiting her on the hill. She concentrated, focused. Nothing happened. Sweat poured down her brow. Nothing happened. But she hadn't really expected that, either. She had attempted to light fires several times before without succeeding.

She placed the bull on one side of the hill and walked to the other. He stood there, breathing hard. She sensed him, sensed how his fear and lethargy was slowly replaced with a smoldering rage. She felt it build in herself.

The midnight darkness closed in on her, on them both. He stepped his feet at the ground. She did the same.

Unshaken hands put on the mask, the demon mask.

– This is my face, she cried. – This is my shadow.

Feet moved in the dance. Hands painted the air.

She cut through the air with her claws, her midnight claws.

– I CALL YOU, LILLITH, she cried. – I call you, master of silver moonlight and the shadow night. Your daughter calls you, demanding her birthright.

She kept moving her claws through the night, drawing patterns, lighting fire. Her face, twisted and demonic revealed an ecstatic grin as she sensed the tingling in her fingers. Eyes widened and were lit by fire.

She began singing, and it was as if the sound didn't come from her at all, but from some point in the air, either at her front or her back.

– The bowl is the pot, she hummed. – The pot is the cauldron, the volcano in our belly, rising up from the depths to the shaking surface. I sleep, and I dream I'm awake. I stir the ancient pot. It explodes in my face, tearing it off.

And the words turned intelligible, more like chant than words, but not quite.

– I want… *Power*. Not just for tonight, not just for a thousand years, but *Forever*.

Thunder rolled, within and without, as midnight hit. The bull leapt. She stopped it in the air with a single focused thought. He hung suspended there, frozen in her mighty grip. She leapt at him. Her claws cutting through the night, cutting deep this time, severing his throat in one sweep, and she bathed in his blood, like a hose was directed right at her. His death cry and hers in triumph drowned in each other. She gathered her hands in a bowl and filled it, filled it up, and lifted it high above her head and let it flow like a waterfall on her shivering body. And she drank deep. As she refilled the bowl. As the hot, sweet brew swelled within her. Fire-eyes sought the dry heap of grass and it lit up, lit up in dark fire, its smoke and tongue seeking her, caressing her in its brilliance. She didn't back off, but bathed in it, in its heat and burn.

The bull yet lived, but died a bit more every time his heart beat. She lifted it further up, bleeding it dry. The blood nourished the fire like gasoline, didn't put it out. The smoke surrounded her. She let the dry husk fall into the fire, and the flames reached up and out to all sides like wildfire. And even though she lost all control over it she kept staring at it, endlessly fascinated. She knew it would come. Control would come.

She ran down the hill with steps so light that it felt like she was flying. She ran to the house in a wide circle, up the shingle trek, feeling every pebble under her soles. There was no pain. Quiet and supple like a large cat she jumped up on the roof. She reached the top in three jumps.

Standing there, at the mountaintop she surveyed the world. Sniffing the air she smelled the Earth.

Her eyes sought back at the hill. Something… She began trembling. Whether or not it was in excitement or fear she couldn't say. Thinking about it later she would say it was both.

Something happened. Something incredible, something topping even what she had already experienced. A crackling in the air, and a bolt of lightning struck the hill, struck it with such force that the ground shook and the first thought that struck her mind was how she would have fared if she had still been there.

She blinked, blinked continuously for a long time. The hill had been cleansed of everything, everything but the single black spot of singed ground covering it. There was more lightning. And then the wind and the torrential rain. The girl laughed madly as she held on to the chimney. The entire landscape was lit in an endless, ongoing bright flash. The girl laughed, curling her raised hands into fists, crying out her challenge, defiance to the Storm. She walked to the place of the roof where it was the longest down, and jumped, just like that, without any hesitation. The landing didn't hurt. She landed and kept walking. Nothing to it. She stopped after a few more steps, looking at the three huddling in the Storm.

– This is my Earth, she cried to them. – The way it should be for everyone. Feel the slumbering giant. This is the power making most people cringe in terror. It has grown beyond imagining in me this night. *Feel it!*

Her attention was drawn to the forest, deep, secretive. Before there was any noticeable conscious decision made, she was on her way there, the winds and water whipping her from all sides.

She ran to its most remote, unattainable parts, waving branches and other hindrances away with her mind power. Awareness increased by the second, by the moment. Everything… dilated, expanded in her mind, and in truth. The vast wilderness turned infinite around her. It was as if there was an entire new stretch of ground wherever she directed her eyes, in addition to what she could actually see.

There was an animal somewhere ahead of her, she sensed it, she saw it, even with all the trees separating them. She chased it eagerly and playfully, feeling fully the pleasure of the hunt. There were twigs and roots in her way. She avoided them elegantly and easily, without thinking or needing to think twice about it.

She stopped abruptly, distracted to the point of paralysis. She heard something. Not with her ears. She saw something, not with her eyes. She smelled something. Not with her nose. She tasted something. Not with her buds. What she sensed was far beyond the senses of her skin. *The bush.* She saw the bush… and it wasn't a bush. It changed into mist and shadow, melted away like mercury, and behind the fading bush and trees were a field. And she realized that she didn't even look straight at the bush, but stood with her back to it. The singing of the birds and of the forest itself had stopped, or faded into the background. The field was deep and wide. It was as if it extended far beyond the forest, far beyond even the mountains. Thoughts raced through her mind, concepts and theorems she knew she couldn't know, she had never read about anywhere, but that she knew as the back of her hand.

Is this four-dimensional space? Is this the world as it is, infinite?

She spoke without moving her lips. Her words echoed in the vast emptiness. There, behind the tree, was a shadow, a powerful built figure, a man. She tore the bush aside and it vanished under the onslaught of her attack. The laughter of a woman faded in the wind. A chorus of patronizing laughter rocked with the thunder.

– Spirits, she said aloud. – You're spirits, but you aren't dead.

There was a buzz, an invasive whisper, hurting her, making her writhe and twist, in anger, fear and curiosity, before that, too faded and she was once again alone in the forest, as she perhaps had been all the time.

The birds and the forest's song returned. Her nose twitched. She picked up the scent and trail of the animal, and before she knew it she was moving again. It was there, the animal, somewhere ahead of her. She heard it, even when she crossed a field where sounds were muted by thick fog. More than ever her instincts led her on. The bare feet drummed against the forest bed. And all the time, both exalted and terrified she sensed the presence running by her side. She could almost make it out, a blur, a shadow, a demonic mirror image smiling to her.

There were wolverines in this area, she knew that, she had seen them, feral beasts ravaging her mind and soul. One hunted, hunted her prey. Both animals were close. She exposed her teeth, snarling deep in her throat. The wolverine caught the prey, sank its teeth into its soft flesh, and she felt it, she tasted the blood, she bent down and devoured the prey, tore it to pieces and devoured the tasty flesh. And when she some time later knelt by a pond she was covered by fresh blood and pieces of skin and meat.

She ran to the top of the mountain. It happened easily, as if it took no effort at all. She looked down at the valley. Focused eventually on the modern buildings of plastic and steel. Her burning eyes were constantly pulled there, inevitably. She walked through the forest again. Passed the Castle of Despair. While approaching the Marble Manor. She heard the sounds of humans and froze, snarled a challenge before her mind once more overtook instinct. There were three there ahead, having a conversation. The talk stopped. She stopped and hid, lay there quiet as a rock, until she heard the voices once more. They hadn't come any closer. She continued forward on all fours. It was… was weird how easy that felt, how easy she moved that way. The bright light hurt her eyes, and she had to force herself, force the beast to advance further. The lamps from the house dimly lit the rain and the trees.

Her eyes glowed stronger than any light reaching her. Something had risen within her tonight, something dormant since birth.

It was so strong, so much, so pervasive that she could just barely handle it, even barely had a handle on handling it.

I am wide open.

All the hounds of hell were out tonight. She more than sensed them. Even if she didn't believe in them. She felt them gnaw at her innards.

A stretch away she saw three men. No, to say that she merely saw them would be doing her current incredible sight a huge disservice. She saw the men in heavy raincoats, that was true, but more than anything she *experienced* them all, as if the raincoats weren't there, as if the walls covering their thoughts weren't there. She saw straight through them, opened them like peeling an apple.

They pulled their coats tight and crouched in the harsh weather. She laughed watching their helplessness. The Storm was her friend, not theirs.

The three of them hurried into the stable. With curiosity written all over the beastly face Elizabeth rushed closer. She slid to the closest of the windows. Waited a while until she heard them talk in there, making sure she heard all three, before peeking in. The three, Terry Williams and Cornwall senior and junior looked quite chummy, quite the buddies. The witch's glowing eyes retained the look of cold surprise.

It was dark inside. The only light came from one lamp far up in the tall ceiling. She strained to hear their voices, but the roar from nature and the many machines inside made it next to impossible. Good hearing meant next to nothing during such strenuous conditions. It was like standing in a phone booth with a lot of traffic outside. She only got a few words and pieces of sentences here and there. Shit will float.

She sensed intent, vicious and cold,, but that wasn't exactly surprising.

– … need to worry…. contrary… everything goes…

It was *him*. She listened breathlessly, reaching out… and suddenly heard crystal clear beyond the noise:

– Certain people can turn impatient, Williams said. – If too long time passes the money flow may stop.

The horses began neighing, and jump up and down. One of the mares knocked her head at the wall. Elizabeth pulled back, drew breath sharply and pushed her back at the dark wall.

– What the hell…

– … don't like… weather, Senor.

One of the help. She hadn't noticed him. She froze, but not because of him.

The oldest… a snake, but teeth not very sharp. *He* much more dangerous. A dragon, a *devourer*.

And the fact that he had piqued her interest, made her reach out and listen that much harder, that made her feel even colder.

– Everything… all right… find… Jimenez… no rush… looks good.

– First Allan… one by… THEN WE CAN BEGAN IN EARNEST

The words screamed in her ears, and just then, as her senses were at its sharpest, it happened.

The horses neighed wildly. They began kicking the walls, and it was like they were screaming. The lightning struck, and in that very moment, as close as a heartbeat, there was the subsequent thunder. Animals and people screamed, walls crumbled, parts of the roof fell, and in the midst of everything was heard an inhuman shriek.

Silence finally replaced the horrible ruckus. There was no more lighting that night. All the thunder had pulled back into the darkness it had originated from. Of the building of plastic and shiny metal remained only rust and ruins. Most of the surviving cows and horses kept running through the night, seemingly set to keep on going forever. Humans rushed in from all sides, artificial lights in their hands, in a hopeless attempt to curtail the ongoing chaos. Riders and other employees came to as well. Both the crew and those barking orders eventually stopped in their tracks and stood motionless in front of the smoking ruin.

– I heard a scream, Paul insisted. – From a person.

The father looked at the son. No more was necessary. No more had ever been necessary between the two of them. In that look rested all the possible displeasure a father could convey.

Paul shrunk under that stare, as he always did.

The cleaning up began. Strong lights seemingly brightened every corner, every little shadow. The electricity returned. The emergency aggregate was supplanted by the main power, and the lights turned even brighter.

But no one spotted the crouching creature gathering all the darkness into its body.

The face was twisted in pain and hatred. Still crouching it crawled towards the forest. It was like the storm and muddy ground meant nothing to it, nothing at all.

Before long it disappeared between the trees.

CHAPTER TWELVE

Distant cracks of thunder in Elizabeth Warren's ears, echoes of the night.

The morning sky was deep blue, completely free of clouds. The water in the wet grass had already begun dissipating. A light breeze brushed at her. The trees whispered low in sore ears. She stood straight on the roof, facing the rising sun.

She was quite a sight, covered with mud and blood and dirt. The mask was gone, ripped off without leaving any mark or residue. Her hair was sticky, one single sticky mass. Only down by the hips it blew fairly free in the wind. The painted colors were one, singular mush. But they were still there. That small fact encouraged her further, and she laughed hard. The laughter tinted with a distinct, eerie tone.

It hurt in her ears. Pain shot through her brain. She grabbed her head, inevitably yelping. The eardrums were yet not completely healed from the thunder that had come while all her senses had been open and screaming for input. Her throat was still raw after the beyond loud scream of pain, and she still had little dots obscuring her vision while blinking.

She jumped down from the roof, supple like a cat. Humming she took one step forward and made a series of gymnastics across the lawn. Spring smelled great to all her senses. Totally undisturbed she took her time walking to the main entrance. She was fully aware of how scary she looked, but right now, at least right now, others' reactions to her appearance were of such unimportance that she could just as well have been invisible.

Lucy Barker walked out with a bundle of clothes in her arms. She cried out and the bundle fell from her hands and down on the dirty ground.

– I'm so sorry, Miss Liz, she apologized, – I didn't recognize you… just now.

Elizabeth kept walking, ignoring Lucy completely.

– Jeez… Linsey stood in the kitchen door. She nodded to him.

Father stood there in his underpants. She ignored him in the same sovereign manner she had shown Lucy.

She reached her room. The door opened without her touching it physically. It was second nature, now, this, this her command over matter. She walked inside, walked to the mirror. There was noise, disturbance from below, but she wasn't disturbed.

The creature grinned to her from the mirror. She stared at the smooth surface, at the moving image in there, laughing giddily. Linsey appeared in the doorway.

– I look completely ridiculous, she stated, shaking her head. – I look damn near impressive, don't I?

– Yes, he said hoarsely, almost unable to speak.

And then, then there were the eyes, and they were no laughing matter.

They were fire and nothing besides. A deluge of worry and exaltation assaulted her. What had been blue was now completely transformed.

The iris was now fire, a fire dancing like wings in her shadows. Her Time of Change was now complete. She knew that, even before she walked to the shower and turned on the water, cleaning herself, before returning to the mirror, before witnessing her changed body and face undiluted. Hands moving by themselves grabbed the hair and pulled it back, revealing the face. She still felt every drop of water on her sensitive skin, felt the water flow down her body, her face now so alike how she imagined Ted's, far more alien than Stewart's.

She stretched that body, familiarizing herself with it anew, and it felt so good. Bending backwards her hair, having grown visibly during the night touched the floor. Confidence flowed through her, confidence beyond confidence, beyond arrogance. She walked to the bed, grabbing the shades at the night table, crushing them to dust in her hands. Fire-eyes stared into the air, at the rising sun, at the morning, the new morning, as the powder fell to the floor.

She was reborn.

2

Friday, contrary to habit she walked early to the bus, with June, not chasing after her. She experienced it like her feet hardly touched the ground. She greeted the other kids in an exuberant way that stunned them.

The bus moved under her. The engine sputtered and died a hundred times, but kept it going somewhat. It shouldn't have, deeply unnatural as it was, but it did.

She had eaten today for the first time in two days, taking it slow, because she knew from experience that a stomach tended to be unruly after a long time of misuse. Her stomach objected a bit, but basically behaved.

– Just the act of waking up in the morning feels great and very special, she told June. – I don't need to blink, and in each blink there's an eternity. I'm wide-awake, and I haven't slept more than four hours, tops tonight. And I've got time for other things.

She had spent the time bathing in the river, sitting down in the cellar, chanting unknown words that slowly gained meaning. Linsey and June had tasted her spicy herb soup and politely kept from plainly revealing what they really thought of it… She had taken her time before the mirror this morning, tied her hair in three thick braids and dressed herself in a loose skin suit, very Native, and also other acts emphasizing her looks, not hiding them.

The two sisters stepped off the bus, into the warm spring sun, free as birds. Liz studied June, attempting to imagine her with dark hair. And in a brief flash she did, a cold trickling down her spine. The innocent, open smile seemed to fade, to turn moody and brooding.

They watched as Howard Grey arrived at school with his brood, his oldest son and daughter. He had many children, and he drove them all in a minivan to the various schools, where they remained until he picked them up in the afternoon.

– I don't feel sorry for Neal. Judy Davison had sneaked up behind them and spoke conspiratorially. – He's his father's mug multiplied, but Sue Ellen always looks so sad and lost.

Not so strange that, Liz nodded. With the discipline the girls in the family «enjoyed». They followed the words of biblical Paul to the latter there.

Sue Ellen suffered under her father's rule, that much was obvious. She wore a dumb look to most of the others, but Liz easily saw the flower beneath, desperately attempting to blossom.

Liz turned to Judy, studying her, looking for any sign that the girl noticed her physical changes, but there was nothing. Judy remained the superficial, blonde bombshell.

There were stares from others, but Liz had expected that, and prepared for it. No one seemed to be any wiser. Perhaps she had worn the shades for so long that people weren't really sure what color her eyes had been. Liz settled for that. She had been forced to settle for less.

There were archives, of course, but she would deal with that, too, eventually.

And it was only the eyes, anyway. That was the only overt change, the one alert people could look at and say: these were blue.

Nobody cared. For once the current superficial world worked to her advantage.

For once she looked forward to Howard Grey's classes. The expectation boiled and sputtered inside her like a living thing, and she had to pull herself together by an act of will to not go totally overboard.

He arrived with all usual posture and belief in his own superiority. Stopped a bit outside to survey his kingdom. Everything looked fine. He took the decisive step forward, to enter his domain… and stumbled in the threshold. All his desperate attempts to stay on his feet were for naught, and he hit the floor hard. Very bewildered, very confounded he fought himself to his feet, greeted by loud laughter. A laughter quieting quickly when he directed his icy glare at the class. He dumped his books on the desk, and opened the one on the top, preparing to give the bastards a lesson they would never forget.

Then the wind began to blow. He stared at the open window as if being personally insulted. The pages began turning, turning rapidly. He attempted in vain to grab them, to hold on to the unruly paper. The book closed with a bang, almost catching his fingers in the bargain. He reopened the book with an effort. It stayed open a few seconds, giving him a bit of a false hope… before closing again. He imagined it stared at him with vicious eyes.

He rushed to the window and grabbed it. He strained. Everybody could see that. He strained to close the window with all his might, but it wouldn't budge. It most vehemently refused. Liz giggled. The father signed to the son. Neal rushed forward, ever the obedient and eager son. With a lot of effort and coaxing and will the two of them managed to close the obstinate window.

They both stood there, breathing hard, their hair in disorder, a flow of sweat making them stink.

The window reopened, reopened wide, seemingly stuck to its opposite position. Grey stared at it. Neal did, too. The facial expression of both father and son was so infernally comical that the laughter turned hysterical and scornful. Liz registered with glee that Sue Ellen had to cover her mouth and fight to not join in on the fun. To this day, this moment Grey had enjoyed a tremendous respect at the school and in the rest of the community.

That's over, you old geezer, Liz thought. From this very moment on.

The rest of the class proceeded in a somewhat somber manner. But whatever Grey did there was a persistent suspicion that things were… off. The chalk wasn't where he put it. When he reached for it, his fingers caught only air. He was convinced the pointer writhed in his hand… like a snake. And the wind was there all the time, not always infernal, but… *sentient,* grinning to him in his weakness. When he dismissed the class he was merely a shadow of his usual self.

I'm not through with you yet, Liz thought. Don't think that for a minute. I'll never be done with you.

In the free time she followed Sue Ellen to the restroom.

– Hello, she enthusiastically greeted the timid girl.

Sue Ellen first looked worried, then suspiciously at her. She wasn't used to be treated with other than scorn. Liz did feel a little guilty because she approached her with ulterior motives.

– Father says you're the Devil's Spawn, Sue Ellen said.

He might very well be right, Elizabeth thought.

– Do you believe that? She replied calmly.

Sue Ellen hesitated, before slowly shaking her head. Fearfully looking around, as if her all-mighty father overheard the conversation.

– I know, Liz said, and kissed the other girl on the cheek. – We'll talk more later.

She left the restroom, jumping on light feet across the floor, leaving the confused and hopeful beyond hope daughter of Howard Grey.

Grey himself was on the prowl in the schoolyard, still nursing a very lousy mood. It was quite a hot day. All the girls walked around in light clothes. He stared at them. Liz knew he was allowed that privilege. Other males might have come under instant suspicion, but not he. He was above suspicion and reproach.

She focused on him, now, not his immediate surroundings, easily sensing the desire burning in him, what he might not acknowledge, not even to himself. He did notice his stiffening cock, though, and it bothered him, bothered him terribly.

He observed Stevie Fulton (or rather Stevie Marsh) in her tight pants, challenging and sinful, as her hips danced on her thighs. She danced every step as she moved across the yard. It was obvious she was thriving after her recent divorce. Liz noticed both his smoldering rage and lust as he watched her. She was everything he despised, everything he desired.

Liz stood there, uncomfortable and sweaty, suffering in need, one only increasing by her contact with Grey, that fucking closet passionate. It had to end, end now.

Grey looked down, prompted by a sudden cold draft around his hips. His eyes widened in shock. He was completely naked from his hips and down to his ankles. His cock stood straight out, long, thick and hard. People pointed at him. Every eye in the schoolyard pointed at him. Liz leaned against the wall, a storm of mixed emotions, hard, accentuated laughter and uncomfortable, undeniable need.

– No wonder he has fifteen children, huh, she cried to Stevie.

The teacher's eyes had a dazed, irrational quality, one she shared with the rest of the teachers present in the schoolyard that day.

– He can't talk himself out of this, the girl cried triumphantly.

It took several seconds before Grey was able to pull himself together enough to bend down and pull his pants back up.

He resigned on an administration meeting later that day, both as a teacher and from his position in the local congregation. Liz heard it through walls and could hardly contain the infernal boiling within.

Perhaps he's right, she thought, in a moment of sobriety.

She couldn't stop giggling on the bus on her way home.

– Private joke, she told the others, before collapsing in her seat.

She stood at the bus stop, breathing. June waited for her, a bit perplexed even though her little sister knew very well the reason for her exuberance.

– You run along, Liz told her. – I'll be right there.

– Are you sure? Little sister wondered.

– Sure, Liz replied. – Sure as rain.

Liz waited a bit, watching June walking up to the distant houses, before taking a detour. She was still headed back to the ranch, just taking a slightly longer route.

A car passed her on a lonely, fairly backward, overgrown stretch of a shingle road and stopped a bit ahead. She recognized it instantly, long before Paul Cornwall stepped out. He sat down on the hood, waiting for her. She quickly dismissed a fleeting desire to turn around and walk back the same way she had come, and tentatively approached him.

– Hi, he greeted her.
– Hi, she mumbled shyly, despising herself.
– What about joining me for a drive? He wondered, playing all out his disgusting handsomeness.
– Sorry, I'm on my way home.
Short, to the point rejection.
– Quite a detour you're taking then.
– I just needed to stretch my legs a bit, she shrugged deliberately, curling her lips.
– Yes, he said. – I know.
He reached out with a hand and touched a braid.
– What's the matter with you? Don't you like fast cars?
– I'm not carrying any animosity towards them, if that's what you mean, she said inflamed. – But in this case the owner leaves *a lot* to be desired.
– You're such a prize. He just grinned, seemingly totally unaffected by her harsh words, also to her enhanced senses. – I'll see you around… Squaw.
He was quite similar to the man she had met on the bus a while ago. But his confidence was only a façade. Paul's, in spite of his issues with his father, wasn't.
He jumped back into the car, started the engine, waved and drove off.
She caught herself waving back, distantly touching the braid he had touched.
Suddenly she felt very small and helpless.

3

That night she masturbated for the first time in a long time.
She held up the picture of Ted with one hand, while making the itch in her groin grow sweeter and sweeter and sweet with the other.
– You must come, she mumbled. – You must hurry.
She crouched in bed without anything covering her. The moonlight detailed the supple body. Lips were parted. The tongue tried constantly to wet them, in vain. She breathed faster and faster. The sight of Paul on the hood faded in and out, blocking the view to the photograph.
– Curse you, she snarled. – Why won't you HURRY!
A prolonged moan. She exhaled. The framed photographed fell on her belly. The body stretched and turned slack. She slumbered, but in her pitiful sleep she found no peace. She crouched there, twisting throughout the night. In frustrated, desperate despair. She dreamt she walked down in the basement, spending all her time there, as she also did when she was

awake. The walk through the dark passage seemed extra long and hard this time. She dreamt she drew a circle on the floor and knelt in it.

– I'm yours, she said.

And she dreamt she was with the shadow without a face.

4

The Storm came, and no one could see it. It was quiet, now, as it often was in the prelude to its arrival. Only the very sensitive could gauge the changes in the air.

The day began quietly. Warm. Dry. Cold. Linsey Kendall stepped into the baking heat. He saw his father stand at the end of the yard, surveying the property, as he often did in the morning. An envelope was stuck in his back pocket. Linsey walked to him.

– Everything okay? He greeted the older man lightly.

– You mean with the extension on the loan? Eugene smiled. – Of course, kid.

Linsey had joined him on the visit to the inner offices of the bank for the first time. The meeting had been kind of strange, but also strangely exciting.

He had noticed deceit in the bankers and also in his father. Later he had cautiously mentioned that about the bankers, knowing fully well what Eugene felt about extended «sensitivity». But Eugene had only laughed.

– Well done spotting that on your virgin tour, he had grinned. – Don't worry about it. Every banker I've ever met seems to have greed superimposed on his personality.

– Father, is it common with loans? Among farmers, I mean.

– As common as the grass on the ground, son. Virtually everybody has one. It's almost a tradition. Many of the loans are remains of the original mortgages dating back generations.

Elizabeth sat by the dining table. Trudy made dinner.

– Why do you play the obedient and good wife, mommy? The girl said thoughtfully. – You've done so in all these long years. *Why?*

– Be aware that you're treading the line, now, young lady…

– You're not anything like Lucy, Liz kept it up, – she agrees with her dear husband even when she doesn't. You aren't like that. You've spent twenty years with Eugene, giving him three children…

– Do you think I've given him anything? Trudy asked softly.

Liz was taken aback. She looked at her mother with new eyes.

– You're mine, Trudy said. – You're all mine.

She walked to the table, and sat down by her daughter's side.

– Besides, she said, – things aren't the cut and dried case you're making it out to be. Eugene took me in during a time I truly needed someone. He cared for me when I couldn't care for myself. That's why I held out with him for twenty years.

There was a mystery here, yet another mystery. Liz guarded herself, measuring her own reactions.

– He gave us you, Trudy said softly.

– Us?

Liz had learned to listen at an early age, not just to her surroundings, but to people, and Trudy's careful wording right now, and the way she spoke made the girl jittery all over.

– Look at you, Trudy said softly, very, very softly. – How you're evaluating everything, how you're prodding and measuring, how your mind is constantly working overtime. I can sense it, you know, sense your Power. It sings to me like a beacon. Others will sense it, too, and they'll come to you, and they'll be yours.

Her eyes… they changed, not into fire, but they stretched, turning oblong and eerie. Liz gasped and felt pain. She touched her lips, and when she looked at her fingers there was blood on them. It flowed freely from her nose.

– A Janus Clan mother is the greatest nurturer the world has ever seen. I would protect you, if I thought you needed it. But the best way to protect you is to let you take on the world on your own terms… and let the world take on you.

Her words… they made sense, a horrible sense. The catching in Liz' throat wouldn't go away.

– I've slept for twenty years, but no more!

Her entire face and skin seemed darkish, alien, her smile scary. She pulled back and slowly she returned to normal, or what went for normal.

She headed for the door. Liz stared after her, feeling the first sting of resentment rising within.

– What happened?

The mother turned as the daughter spoke, giving her an attentive smile.

– Yes?

– What happened… twenty years ago.

– Twenty-one, twenty-two, twenty-three, Trudy hummed, as she turned and left the room. – I loved a man and he turned out to be the devil himself.

– Figuratively or literally? Liz called after her.

But there was no reply or if there was, it was lost in the wind, in the sigh of the house.

Liz sat still, like stone. The pain in her nose lingered for a while, before fading, fading quickly. She hardly noticed when June entered the room.

– Is dinner ready? She wondered brightly.

Liz looked up and to the left, at the boiling kettle.

– I would say so, she shrugged.

– Then… June made a dramatic gesture, – why has no one made the table?

– Perhaps because it's *no big deal*.

Plates flew off the shelves and landed nicely on the table. The drawers opened. Forks, knives and spoons rotated in the air. Just then Eugene and Linsey entered the kitchen.

– WOW! June applauded.

The performer curtseyed before her attentive audience, making a dramatic gesture, a wave of a hand, with eyes hardly glowing. This was no exertion for her. It was easy to track and control the different objects in the air. Glasses joined the knives, forks and spoons, and all of it finally settled on the table with their fellow plates.

Trudy joined them, kissing her husband on the cheek. They sat down. Later Elizabeth, second-guessing herself, wondered if everything that had happened could have been avoided.

She had showed Cummings' drawing, caricature of President Gerald Ford to Linsey. He had seen it before, but still almost collapsed on his chair, as he began laughing to the point of exhaustion.

– I see you've done it again, Eugene noted. – Weakened the respect for our government in this house.

She froze, the joy dying in her eyes, as she directed her full attention at him.

– The way I see it, she said, eerily calm, – the Unites States of America has no respect left to defend, and has never had any, really. Like most tyrannies it has been a disaster from the start.

– I saw how you enjoyed yourself when we had to flee from our representation in Saigon. It wasn't pleasant to watch.

– Don't do the «we»-thing, she snorted. – Not with me, not with the five hundred thousand boys that will never return because of your various madmen heroes in the government.

– Father, she's right, Linsey said carefully. – People in the government aren't immune to greed and power lust, but are rather the kind of people feeding on it.

– Nixon is a hero who was framed, Eugene sniffed angrily.

– He is a first-class prick. June nodded.

– He's a criminal, Linsey noted. – Far more a murderer than anyone convicted for it.

– And Ford pardoned him, Trudy emphasized. – Saving him from the years in prison an ordinary person would've been given.

Kendall rose so quickly that his chair tipped over and hit the floor. He made a fist to them.

– All of you. Oh, God. He turned and raised finger at Liz. – This is your fault. Yours and those satanic writings in the cellar. I should have b-burned them a long time ago.

Elizabeth struck the arm reaching for her, shaking hard, very emotional.

He wanted to rush around the table, to charge her, but then Linsey was there, blocking his way.

– Look at her, he said. – Look at your daughter, what you have *done* to her.

Kendall looked, but only because he felt compelled to do so. He saw the tears flowing down Elizabeth's cheeks.

He looked at her with a smug grin Linsey couldn't help but picking up on.

– You want to break her, he said thunderstruck to his father. – You want to make her into a compliant, «sweet» girl you can mold.

– Don't be silly, boy, Kendall said patronizingly.

– But she's too strong for you. Linsey's voice rose in volume and anxiety. – So you had to resort to trickery. Are you… *out of your mind?* How can you do something like that? Do you know what? You're just a tiny, sniveling *racist*. To hide your own insecurity you're attacking your own daughter, because a «creature» like her doesn't exist in your ordered world.

Kendall stared at his son. He had never seen the boy like this, and what he saw made him gasp.

He turned to the only person in the room he still had faith in, looked into her brown eyes.

– I'm not the lily-white, naïve girl you think, daddy, June said. – Fortunately not. In your world it would be an advantage, but in the true harsh world the innocents are going down wholesale.

Where did they get their words from? No kids could speak like that.

– The CELLAR! He roared. – When I'm through with the shit there will be only ashes left.

– You're behaving like a lunatic, Eugene, Trudy said to him. – A little bit more of that, now, and you will also break the chain of kinship - forever.

He didn't listen to her, but turned on his heels, filled with a seething resoluteness.

– STOP!

A voice, so very cold and commanding. But he kept going. The door closed with a loud crack in his face.

Totally off his rocker in rage he turned to go the other way, but he remained on his spot. Elizabeth stood there, blocking his path. A monster stood there. It was like she was… growing as he looked at her. Her eyes glowed stronger than ever before. Tongues of dark fire seemed to reach out for him. She stared at him with her anger. Fury stared at him. He was lifted up and virtually pushed at the ceiling. The eerie, horrible half-smile paralyzed him.

Elizabeth felt the Song of Power as the ultimate joy. She shook the heavy man like a piece of cloth.

– Listen to me, old man. What is stored in the basement doesn't belong to you. It's mine! Mine! Do anything, the smallest thing to destroy it, and I assure you... you'll wish you were dead.

Completely beside himself he attempted to strike at her. It was like hitting an invisible wall. He screamed over the pain in his hands. She threw him away in contempt.

– You don't speak like that to your father, he whimpered. – You just don't. You lack respect, even more so than other young disobedient creeps.

– You speak as if you own us. Liz spoke in a choking mix of sorrow and triumph. – That's what you have always believed, isn't it? Most children and also adults let themselves be run over by parents and society as a whole, but you should know by now that we aren't in any way like the average crowd.

Trudy put a hand on his shoulder.

– You've been unreasonable beyond words for so long, now, she said, – but it's not too late to reconsider, to become the person you could have been. It's never too late.

He struck her. Blood flowed from her mouth. A howl echoed through the room. Not from her, but from Linsey. He charged his father, grabbed him and hit him, hit him, hit him and hit him. Elizabeth pulled him away. Held him. Spoke softly to him, calming the wounded beast. Slowly the glow in his eyes faded.

– It's over, now, it's enough, now.

Little sister's words were like the sound of tranquil wind in his ears.

Kendall sat up, while pushing a hand at his cracked lips.

– You will leave, now, all of you, he snarled, filled with hatred, Liz felt sorry for him. – Take your shit with you and disappear.
– This is just as much our home as it is yours, Trudy choked. – We're *staying*.
– I'll have you thrown out, he mumbled. – Incarcerated. Yes, behind a heavy steel door in a padded cell, yeah, that's it.
– Don't try it. Chilly and calm. – You'll lose.
Elizabeth knew that she had won. They would never more take his side against her. But she didn't feel very victorious at all. There had never been much of a fight from her side, mostly despair that through the years had slowly changed to quiet resentment and anger. The father's relationship with his family would regain a kind of equilibrium, a tolerable level, but no one called him «father» anymore. Never ever.

5

Elizabeth embraced what had been her hidden self. She spent ever more time reading the recipes Nick had left her, and spent ever more time down in the cellar, inside the circle she had drawn, first in chalk, then in blood. She kept seeing her own blood boil and steam on the ground, and she wondered if she was anything even remotely human.
The unrest had taken root in her, like a rock around her neck. Eventually even the freedom in the confines of the cellar wasn't enough for her, and she left.
She emerged back in daylight. It hurt. Her eyes and her entire body. She looked at her watch. It was broken, black and ashy.
– How long was I gone? She asked June, hating her cracked voice.
– Two days, June shrugged. – We thought about sending out a search party, but then you've been gone longer before, so we didn't.
It was Sunday morning. She could have sworn it was Saturday. Somewhere, somehow in the darkness down there, she had lost an entire day.
Later that day, after she had showered and dressed up, and eaten a healthy dinner, she paid a visit to Ashley Griffith. His parents were on holiday and he was presumably alone in the house. He opened the door and froze slightly when he saw who it was.
– Hi, she greeted him sweetly.
– Hi, he swallowed hard.
– I wonder it you would help me with the catching up on homework, she said, and held up her books. – I've read with Judy so far, but I've decided I'm in dire need of some male guidance…

He swallowed very hard.
God, did I really say that?
– Come in, he croaked, and she feared he would croak, right there on the spot. He repeated himself, a bit more indelible. – Come in.
– Thank you, she said huskily. – That's so very kind of you.
She passed him on her way in, rubbing herself against him. It felt so good to have him close, so very good.
May eight she celebrated her sixteenth birthday. She traveled to Trinidad with Ashley and Trudy, Linsey and June. Late at night, after Eugene and most people had fallen asleep. Just before they reached the Highway Sue Ellen came running towards them. She wore the clothes Elizabeth had given her. They didn't fit Liz anymore, anyway.
– Why are you being so kind to me? The girl had asked her.
Liz had touched her jaw and raised up her head, making her hold it high.
– Because friends can be found in the most unlikely of places, and friends are important, and life is too short to be wasted.
They watched pleased how the slight encouragement made Sue Ellen grow and glow on the spot.
– It was so easy sneaking away, the still timid girl giggled, in a sudden burst of euphoria and courage. – The old man has been so *lax* lately.
She glanced around nervously, fearing that someone had heard her little statement.
Once inside the van it was strangely enough, the end of her brave front. Further away from her father and the life she had known than ever before in her life, she clammed up altogether. She sat quiet as a mouse during the entire ride and for every look Ash or Lin sent her she reddened deeper than a tomato.
Trinidad was a small town compared to other American cities. But it was the flashpoint of southern Colorado, and there was no problem finding pretty wild places within its boundaries, and they sought the wildest one, the hottest one, and if the place they found wasn't that before, it was after this night.
They found a table close to the bar. It was a noisy place, but they didn't care. This was a joyous night. No one wanted to be reminded of he who had left them. Trudy flowered with impunity on this night, the first in a very long time she had experienced without the hawk-eyes on her.
Elizabeth and Ash danced. She was half a head taller than him. To compensate he was extraordinarily broad shouldered and well built. She rubbed his muscles, clearly pleased, though irritated because he looked at Trudy all the time.

– Tell me, Trudy is far younger than your father, isn't she? Is she your stepmother?

The irritation fading because she now knew the reason for his interest she got even chummier.

– Far from it, Liz grinned. – She has given birth to all three of us.

– I find that incredible, he exclaimed. – She looks like your older sister.

She kissed him on the lips, tasting them, savoring the close contact.

– She's born in 1933. Don't think twice about it. I wonder about it myself. Relax!

Elizabeth could clearly sense his nervousness over her close proximity. It just made her bolder. She stretched her arms above her head, wriggling her hips and moved in on him like a barracuda. She kissed him again, hungrily, filled with passion. He was too paralyzed to respond.

They had initially wondered how the guards could let Sue Ellen in, very young as she looked, until they entered and saw there were a lot of clearly younger teenagers here.

– This isn't a very respectable place, is it, the very nervous and incredulous and scandalized Sue Ellen whispered to Linsey.

– Clearly not, he replied, and grinned to her.

«You have such large teeth, grandma», he expected the girl to say to him.

The place' lack of respectability didn't concern him much, not anymore. The final piece of respect he had had for the older generation and its values had gone up in smoke the previous week.

The music picked up. Its beat seemed to turn heavier, its melody deeper.

I'm a savage witch, and I want to fuck you.

Liz moved her lips. She knew her voice drowned in the crescendo, but also that he heard her.

Trudy drank beer with a rather large redhead bruiser. He was lively, but not drunk like most of the others.

– You're married, he said, and touched her ring.

– In name only, she replied and stared naughtily at him.

Her thoughts drifted back, to a much younger Trudy, like her three children hungry for life, unafraid and vulnerable.

Mother has always been here, Linsey thought. Hardly more than furniture, But that's changing now. That, too.

Liz and Ash found a dark corner of the room, and began making out. She moved in his lap and she *felt* the dance, the dance of life. It moved through her like a curse, and she felt its pain clouding her mind.

– HI, NIGGER!

The loud voice reached Liz' fevered brain from far away. She sighed.

– I thought we would be left alone tonight. Silly me…

The two of them kissed again, deliberately ignoring the distracting voice.

– YOU FUCKING BROWNIES NEVER LEARN, DO YOU KNOW…

The man charged them, and grabbed Ash by the collar. The moment he touched Ash Elizabeth attacked him. She grabbed him and lifted him up in one sweeping move, her face twisted in rage. She dumped him brutally on the table without letting go, without the slightest effort. He was just a feather she moved. The Beast had suddenly found them all. They all felt its claws, felt blood leave them through gushing wounds. Saliva flowed from the female's long and sharp and flashing fangs. She was the personification of wrath as she bent slightly forward, looking down at the terrified man caught in her grip.

– *What sewer did you crawl from?* The voice wasn't a voice, only a series of beastly sounds. – *A typical good-looking dumb shit, ain't you? Born with two brain cells. One died of neglect and the other of loneliness.*

Absolutely terrified the big bruiser attempted to free himself. He writhed and pulled and pushed in her merciless hands, everything totally useless. She lifted him up again for a second and then pushed him back down, pushing all air from his lungs, breaking several of his ribs.

– Can I trust you to think twice or even thrice next time you consider behaving like a pig on two legs, instead of a human being?

Everybody heard the soft voice. Someone had turned off the speakers. The room had turned deadly quiet.

The man attempted to breathe, desperately attempted to speak, to nod, to communicate his fear, respect and servile agreement, while tears drowned his eyes.

– Good, the Beast whispered. – Very good.

She let go of him, and turned to the others, his buddies who had been ready and eager to follow up on what had been supposed to be his initial softening of the prey. There was a small amount of blood on her finger. She licked it off, keeping an eerie, unwavering attention on the men.

They pulled back visibly, relenting.

– C'mon, guys, we don't need any kung fu chick to ruin our evening.

It would have stopped there… if Linsey hadn't rushed forward and snarled:

– You do manage that perfectly on your own.

He didn't understand himself. He had become so immediate, so reckless lately. Merely the slightest provocation made him go off.

– That's it, one of the bruisers mumbled. – A man can only take so much.

He rushed forward.

Linsey struck him so hard that his jaw broke. The pain in his hand felt just wonderful. During the next few seconds, violence erupted all over the room, chaos spreading like wildfire, and he welcomed it. The volcano, cold for so long, erupted. He pushed a head into the wall. Many times. A fist came from nowhere. He avoided it *easily*. Mayhem dominated a place that had been basically peaceful not that long ago. He witnessed in a flash June kick a man in savage glee. There was another flash, and there was Trudy, making mincemeat of two opponents. He saw her lift up one of them and throw him across the room. She seemed bigger, stronger, wilder, not really how he had learned to know her at all. He got distracted, and was almost hit by a large fat woman charging him from nowhere.

The fight quickly deteriorated into a free-for-all ruckus. People and objects flew back and forth, people both with and without contact with the ground. A man slid across the floor. June struck him with a bottle, and he lay still, bathing in firewater. The girl grinned and jumped right up and down in pure excitement.

We're good at this, Linsey thought. So very good.

Then there was another flash, and it froze in time, stretching into forever. The sight of Elizabeth strangling a man burned into his mind. She tightened her scarf around the man's neck and her expression was totally insane. It wasn't really an expression at all, but an animal's unmovable face. A predator, focusing exclusively on the kill. Linsey hardly thought, but rushed over to her, swooping away people blocking his path like he would dust.

He had no idea of how to stop her. In fevered desperation he grabbed her shoulder, he pulled something from his vast Depth and cried

stop

– STOP!

And she stopped. The pressure loosened around the man's neck and he fell to the ground. She turned limp in Linsey's arms. He shook her. No reaction. Eyes were dull and her body slack. She didn't respond when he shook her. He looked worriedly at the blank face. It was like she truly had stopped, disconnected completely.

He put her, the heavy, slack body, with some difficulty on his shoulder.

– Let's go, he shouted to Trudy.

She heard him. In one way or another she did hear him. Ash, looking anxiously at Liz was there by his side, before Trudy, and then June, too. The three of them formed a guard around him, as they made their way to the exit. Sue Ellen joined them, and then finally they came to think of her.

She had a few bruises, but not really that much more compared to the rest of them.

They ran out in the darkness. No one attempted to stop or follow them.

– What's wrong with her? Ash asked, very protective.

– I think I shut her… I think I shut her down.

Linsey replied, with a voice very strained.

Elizabeth began shaking, shaking hard, as they made their way to the van, and he had to have help holding her. Slowly, only very slowly her eyes cleared, and the fire returned.

He put her down. She stood there, on shaky legs.

– What the hell happened? She asked, her voice much darker than usual, very close to the ghoulish variant they had known her to use during her more scary moments. – I had a blackout, didn't I?

– Some blackout, June commented cheerfully.

– You had a total savage episode, Linsey told her pointedly, in a shaky voice, attempting very hard to meet her eyes, determined to keep the steel in his visage. – I turned you off.

– You… turned me off?

He nodded, too dry in his throat to voice a reply, really rejecting it all. She sensed it, how he turned himself off.

– Good going, brother, she grinned, briefly touching his cheek.

He pulled back.

She began shaking again.

– Everything is a blur, she said, chilled to the bone. – It's a good thing you did stop me, or I would probably left a string of bodies behind.

She clutched his hand, still shaking. He nodded, his expression softening.

Ash wanted to give her his jacket. She said no thanks with a smile and a soft touch.

– I don't feel cold, actually, she said, wonder in her voice. – Rather amazingly relaxed and wonderfully warm.

They hurried into the car. Sue Ellen cast long, worried glances back at the club's entrance, but no one appeared. The… *noise* inside continued.

Flashes came to Liz in infrequent intervals on the long drive home, like they always did, but tonight they were like a blade cutting her mind. She shuddered, couldn't help it, couldn't control herself at all. The man in front of her, in her grip was dying, and she looked very much forward to the moment… the moment of his death when… when…

She crouched there, on the seat, putting her head in Trudy's lap. And mother sang to her, stroking her head, calming her, calming the wounded beast.

– Warm, I'm warm, the girl mumbled. – It's like I'm burning up inside.

No one spoke much on the way back. Linsey drove the van, and stared at the road ahead, and hardly anything else.

Sue Ellen left first. She jumped out of the van quickly and unceremoniously when it stopped across the field and on the other side of a bundle of trees from her current place of residence.

– I'll follow her «home», Elizabeth said, and jumped out before anyone could react. – Don't worry, I'll always land on my feet, you know that.

Just a few steps, and she vanished in the night.

Sue Ellen changed to her nightgown just before they saw the Grey residence in their line of sight. It was best that Elizabeth took care of the clothes. Sue Ellen looked down when she took her hands.

– Don't look so down. Elizabeth attempted levity. – It was fun tonight, even though it was fairly early and abruptly interrupted…

Liz nodded to herself when the other didn't respond.

– You're afraid of me, aren't you, little girl?

– Father has read for us, Sue Ellen whispered. – About minor demons and… witches.

– You should make up your mind. An exasperated sigh. – That is pretty far from your last claim. If I were you, I would stop believing the superstitious nonsense.

– Besides… there was a sisterly embrace when she saw tears flow down the pale cheeks, burning eyes drying them, – we witches are cursing no one that hasn't been deemed worthy of our special attention. Get it?

Like your asshole of a father. A fact you should be deeply grateful for.

A cheerful wink and then she was gone, one with the darkness.

Ash returned to the darkened house. The door was ajar, in spite of him having the only keys. He couldn't decide whether or not he felt fear when he continued inside without turning on the lights. She sat on the large couch in the living room. He saw her eyes.

The door closed behind him. He jumped high. A few lights turned on by themselves, creating a darkened, soft light. He turned abruptly from the sight of the naked figure on the couch.

– You're a witch, he choked.

– I knew it. You hid while Sue Ellen undressed…

Was she what he called her? She had used the words loosely in her mind before, thought about what it signified. The unpleasantness had never passed. Not until this moment. She pondered his words, his silence a few seconds before nodding.

– You're absolutely correct, I am a witch. What are you going to do about it?

Her words… both an invitation and a challenge.
– I won't tell anyone, he assured her, assuring himself, his words accompanied by a brittle laughter. – And even if I had tried to tell anyone, no one would have believed me, anyway. It would have been a tremendous expender of energy and totally wasted.
He heard that she moved and turned back towards her again. He swallowed and swallowed repeatedly. She slipped catlike off the couch and slid toward him. He inadvertently took a step back.
– Afraid? Don't be. If Elizabeth wishes to harm you there's no place on Earth you can hide.
She grabbed him and put him on his back on the carpet, after literally having clawed the clothes off him. He was bleeding from several of the scratches and she licked them clean.
– I can't believe it, he cried, – my virgin fuck, and I'm doing it with a true to life witch. Please don't turn me into a toad afterwards, huh?
She corrected his disrespectful chiding with a slap on his thigh. She began moving on him. There was little doubt about who was fucking whom, but she sensed his quivering power and eagerness and was pleased. She liked him and managed to hold back sufficiently to not make him too exhausted too fast. She got to enjoy his hot flow twice before his body turned absolutely slack and he fell asleep. He slept well the entire night, like she used to do. This night she twisted and writhed constantly, dozing off and on.
They had fun together for several weeks. She, too. He managed to satisfy her well enough. For a while. Until a night when everything just… overwhelmed her. She spent the darkness hitting the pillow with her fist. The nightmares returned. And the worst part of it was the joy she felt throughout it all. She was a wolf consuming people. Until the she-wolf noticed she wore a collar and was led in a chain… by a firespitting dragon.
She began masturbating again.

CHAPTER THIRTEEN

The sound of the harmonica reached through the warm air. It was at the height of summer. The grass grew tall and green where the cattle had yet to grass. Linsey sat on the Hill, playing. Elizabeth observed him from the kitchen window on the very hot and humid day. The girl stood naked in the otherwise quite chilled house and sweat poured from her skin. In a fit of hurried movements she dressed in a shirt and shorts, and walked to her brother.

He stopped playing when he saw her come. The distant, remote look softened.

– You're playing like a god, she breathed.

– Many thanks, Your Highness.

He managed to bow while sitting.

She nodded mercifully, almost automatically, but he noticed how rushed the movement was, how… charged she seemed, like she had been the last few weeks. Her eyes practically burned through him. It dawned on him that she was studying him incessantly, penetrating his hide and mind like a diamond drill.

She had just returned from days in the wilderness, more gone than ever. During the summer holiday it was even less holding her back from what she sought.

– May I ask what you're staring at? He asked, unintentionally coarse.

He doesn't know, she thought. He hasn't realized it yet, or he doesn't want to.

Every second since the party at Cornwall's, where she had seen his eyes glow, she had wanted to tell him the truth, but hesitated because it would complicate his life further, too. And if she hadn't been convinced before, she had been so after the evening in Trinidad. She had hoped he would come to the conclusion on his own, but time passed, and she could wait no longer. Anxiety fluttered like wings when she steeled herself.

– In case you're wondering, you're like me, she stated. – And like Ted, Mark, Mike, Nick. You're born with paranormal powers.

– You must be kidding, he replied strangely fast. – That can't be.

– I've seen your eyes glow on several occasions, she said firmly. – You're in denial. There's absolutely no doubt.

He turned away from her with tightly woven fists. She could sense his fear, uncertainty and confusion. He slowly turned back to her, facing her.

– The thing about the eyes doesn't have to mean anything, he protested. – The eyes can perfectly well be a hereditary trait unrelated to… to the other stuff. Mike never showed signs of being able to do any of… that.

– I'm fairly confident that he, given more time, would have done «that», as you put it. She smiled both sweetly and sarcastically. – And more importantly: I could, and you could, too, point to several milestone events that more than clinches it, proving that you know far more than civilization has taught you, but I won't do that. I'll let you demonstrate it yourself, beyond doubt, by prompting you to do something that I've never been able to do, even though I've certainly tried hard enough.

She stepped behind him and began rubbing his shoulders, pushing him gently but decisively to sit. She touched him under the jaw with feather-light fingertips. She pulled him deep into her eyes, but he didn't feel the cold emanating from her, as he had done before.

– Lucy, you fancy her, right? Round and generous limbs, tempting, desirable beyond words…

He found himself nodding.

– I want you to call her here, to us, without saying a single word. Your mind will bring her here.

She took a few steps back. Stared at him with infinite interest. He returned the stare, uncertain, irritated, but then he gave it up. He breathed deeply, closed his eyes, rubbing his temples, attempting to imagine Lucy Barker. It was true that he wanted her, desired her. But only as a thought experiment. He didn't want to complicate her life.

– I don't feel anything special. His voice seemed to come from miles away. – I'm supposed to feel something, right?

– Concentrate. Play!

The instrument pushed against his lips. The harmonies flowed through the ether. He heard himself play. Thought he had never before played this well. He really wanted Lucy to hear it, everybody else, too. No, only Lucy. God forbid.

Then he heard a door open and close.

He heard the sound of light steps on the ground approaching. He opened his eyes, and witnessed how Lucy ascended the hill. He stopped playing and put the harmonica away. Lucy kept walking towards them. Elizabeth smiled radiantly to him. Lucy didn't stop before she reached the top, and stopped hesitatingly.

– What are you doing here, Lucy? He wondered.

– Here? She blinked. – Oh, I just wanted to see the view, I guess. I have… I have never been up here before.

– You know you're not supposed to go up here, Lucy.

– Yes, Mr. Linsey, I forgot, it won't happen again.

She returned the same way she had come. Her thin nightgown, practically revealing everything touched the ground and soil stuck to its edge.

– Only witches are allowed up here, Elizabeth stated.

– I knew, he said quietly. – I've always known. I was afraid.

He recalled several events, now, that he had consciously or subconsciously pushed away.

His cousin on his father's side, Linda, in Washington DC before they had made love, before they had fucked. She had quite unceremoniously told him that he reminded her of Ted, and had then proceeded to undress. Christ, was it only a year ago?

When Ted had attempted suicide. Eugene had believed that he, Linsey, hadn't been able to stand the sight of blood. Instead its sight and smell fascinated him.

He had seen his younger witch sister bath naked in the river. He had felt such a need to jump her and fuck her that the entire thing left him absolutely terrified. He had hardly dared look at girls the coming years.

But he had caught up quite well there.

And then…during the times the dark witch had done her rituals on the Hill, and he felt helplessly attracted to it.

– What made you know… what… *convinced* you?

– It was the evening in Trinidad, she said. – I… you were inside me. But it wasn't very difficult, really, with all the chicks you've conquered lately. And you called me just now.

– But I didn't call you. I hardly thought about you.

– You did. She breathed deeply. – From deep inside. For the same reason I let myself be pulled. You wanted to touch a like-minded creature.

He easily caught the desperate subtext in her voice. She had been slovenly and inattentive for weeks. And if it was something she wasn't, that was it. Something did bother her.

– I'm… losing control, she said hesitatingly. – It can take different forms, but I feel like I'm sliding down an icy slope, unable to stop.

There was an overwhelming sense of cold and heat both. Her insides devoured him, submitted to him. He turned seriously scared.

– Come, she said, taking his hand.

He followed her apprehensively, reluctantly and curiously down the hill. Before he really understood what was happening they were in her room. There was a board on the table, a cardboard wall dividing the two halves. There was one chair on each side, and two widely different decks of cards placed on one side.

– You've bought Zener-cards, he said astounded. – Where?
– In London, she replied lightly. – Where else?
They sat down, and they could no longer see each other, and he abruptly felt very lonely and left out.
– Zener-cards? She prompted him teasingly, – Very few call them that today. It's mostly ESP-cards these days.
He stared right ahead, stared at the brown cardboard, and it was a mirror, staring back at him.
– You can sense me, she said forcefully. – You can feel my shadow in your mind.
And it was true. It was as if the wall between them didn't exist.
Elizabeth put on The End by The Doors. He saw her dance, dance in the sunset somewhere, turning her body around and around.
– This is a sacred ceremony, she tuned in and out in the long, long shadow tunnel. – One initiation of a witch.
At night she drew forms on his naked skin. They sat on the hill, swaying, swaying to the music, the ancient dance. The Sun and the Moon rose and set, rose and set.
She prodded him, pulled from him stings of blood and power, laughing thrillingly.
– The Wave, she mused, – the X that marks the spot, the Star we all are, the Circle, the infinite path and last the Square. We shuffle the card deck of the mind.
And he saw her do that, saw her hands and the cards becoming interchangeable, becoming one single, blurry movement.
– Let's do some Telepathy, she said, her voice clear for the first time in days. – I've found that I can receive, but not send. I'm an empath. We know you can both send and receive. The question is to what degree.
They sat by the table, facing each other, not facing each other facing the cardboard wall. She pulled a star from the deck and put it on the table.
– Now, big bad witch of the forest. What have I here in my hand?
– Star, he replied without thinking.
She held up the star for him to see, and his eyes widened.
She pulled a wave.
– Wave, he said decisively.
He saw it in her hand, as she held it up for him as a trophy, and a shot of electricity was fired from everywhere in his body. There was a thrill unlike anything he had ever felt.
Star.
– Star, he said.
X

– X.

When she had done the entire deck of twenty-five cards he had only missed a few times, and after two hundred cards he had only missed a total of sixteen times.

– This is far beyond probability, she declared excitedly.

They continued a bit longer. His results turned increasingly irregular.

– You grow tired, she said. – It makes sense. You're not used to using your powers consciously.

They walked through the forest. Every step felt clear, felt strong.

– There's no doubt, she said. – You're telepathic. We could have proven that in a court of law… if we chose to.

They reached a clearing. It was in the middle of the day, sunshine, warts and all, but there was still a misty quality in the air.

– Can you sense them? She asked enigmatically.

– Sense what, he said irritatingly.

– The spirits, of course, she said, as if it was the most natural thing in the world (and it was). – They're all around us.

He stopped, focused, concentrated and squinted an eye.

– I feel something, he admitted, – a presence, a… why?

– Why are they here? She grinned. – I'm not sure. There is probably a number of reasons. One is simply that there are spirits, and spirits Travel, for the sake of travel itself. Some might be conscious about it, others might not be. They might be curious or protective… or they might want to take a look at the… competition.

Her voice turned frosty, her eyes fearful and this astonished him.

– There might be *Secret Chiefs*, ancient witches who have foreseen and «guided» human development for millennia. Aleister Crowley and Helene Blavatsky, among others believed or believe they exist. I'm not sure I do. But it stands to reason there are some people out there who are at least aspiring to the title…

– Why? He repeated, sweat covering his brow.

– They're very much like us, she said in hushed whisper, a loud, proud voice, scouring the terrain with roguish eyes. – They can sense destiny, and those touched by it.

After a few days' break they returned to her room and the table of inquisition.

They sat by the table for a long stretch, without having any interest of measuring time. She removed the wall. That surprised him, it really did.

She put the deck at the middle of the table.

– Tell me what card will come up, she said.

– Tell you…

– Tell yourself. Don't doubt. Do it! You do have the dreams, don't you?
– Dreams…
And it was as if he was really dreaming.
– Star, he heard himself say.
She turned the card on top, and it was a star. They both gasped.
– Wave, he said.
It was a star.
– Circle.
Circle.
They did it hundreds of times, like the other day (if it truly was the other day).
– You score ten out of twenty-five times, she finally said. – Well above average, what's seen as statistically possible, but not that great.
She looked at him, with even more than usual her strange glare.
– Now, you shuffle the deck, she said.
He understood, and did as she asked. He shuffled the deck thoroughly, taking his time, before putting it down.
– I feel both anxious and excited, she said, a slight tremor in her voice.
– Star.
She said.
And the turned card was a star.
Several turns later, her efforts showed about the same results as his: ten of twenty-five.
She shuffled the deck again, and he sensed her unrest, sensed it double in himself.
– What are you…
– Shush. She put a finger on his lips.
– I'm tired, he insisted. – It's dinner soon and I'm dead tired.
She kept shuffling.
Hours later he saw in mist, in haze her bony hands shuffle the deck and put it on the table. They also tried on the ordinary fifty-two cards deck. That was a little bit more awkward at first, but then it turned out to be as easy or as hard as with the Zener-cards.
– My head hurts, he complained.
– *Heal yourself, witch.* Make the pain and fatigue go away.
He concentrated, he focused, but the axe splitting his head remained in his skull.
It was in the middle of the night when he looked up, startled.
– My head feels unstuck from the head, he cried.
It felt light, like it danced on hot airwaves.
– Queen of Spades, he heard her say from far away.

Her beautiful, dark-skinned hand turned the card, and there it was, the Queen of Spades. The constant trickle down his spine intensified to a waterfall of ants.

She grabbed his hand, and *she held on*. Her smile spoke volumes. He sensed fear in her, and it doubled in him. There was… a charge in his hand, and obviously in hers. Both bodies shook. And a ghoulish voice choired the words:

– *I see everything. I can see the Phoenix rising.*

And there, in the night, they saw a bird of Shadow and Dark Fire rise from a blackened Earth, and they shook in fear.

– Everything, Elizabeth Warren mumbled.

There were jumbled flashes of images not even close at making sense. It slowly coalesced into one single image: that of a dark, dank room.

They walked, walked down the stairs to the cellar, walked through the dark hallway to the deep, deep room.

– What's that?

He pointed at the broken circle and the signs on the floor that made it tingle so pleasantly in his fingers.

– For protection, she replied. – And to keep unwelcome visitors and intruders away.

He didn't notice anything when he stepped into the circle. Neither when he sat down on his heels to grab the cardboard boxes. He wanted to raise his arms, but they were suddenly, unexplainably completely paralyzed. He was unable to raise his arms towards the unopened boxes. All other directions went without a hitch, but not there. Enraged by her knowing smile he spat a curse.

– What the fuck is this?

– Nick did it. Her eyes glowed. She tore open a new box easily. – It is as I thought. He knew that my powers would be far stronger than yours. The circle was made for me to break it.

This particular box was nearly empty. When they looked down in it, it seemed almost infinitely empty. Far down there, in the infinity of space waited three small boxes. Elizabeth reached for them. She took two and let the third remain. She cast a challenging glance at her brother. He pushed his hand down, but it was like he had to reach up, and that the remaining box was farther away the more he strained. Finally his fingers closed around it. He had made it. It had been hard, so very hard. He had succeeded in spite of that.

Hidden in the boxes were rings, three of them altogether, one in each box, with fire-colored stones.

– Jeez…

It came out very meekly coming from Elizabeth. She looked perplexed at the rings.

– What in the world… This isn't… This doesn't look like any valuable stone I've ever heard about. There's a shell of glass or something covering it. Then there is… I'm no expert, but…

She cut him off, speaking with a hollow, dreamy voice.

– Don' you see what it is?

Slowly, ever so slowly she lifted the two rings to the level of her eyes, until four almost identical points stared at him.

– But… that's impossible.

– I think preposterous is the word you're looking for…

She grinned, flashing her fangs.

– You're correct in your fears, of course, she said calmly, almost resigned. – It's the eyes of the dead.

– And what are we supposed to DO with them? He cried. – We can't wear them on any finger, that's for sure.

She didn't seem to hear him. She pushed one of the rings onto her left ring finger. It fit perfectly. The other, on the other hand didn't. She had to wear that on the thick middle finger. It was still too large, but it wouldn't easily slide off.

He pushed his ring on his finger. It didn't surprise him that it was a perfect fit. It was like he was born with the ring on his finger. He saw what happened then. The ring glowed, as sure as night follows day. Abruptly he felt a strong need for completion.

– The redundant ring, he commented sarcastically, – what do we do with that?

She looked at him, very aware of his, unexpected, expected changed mood, of the desire in his eyes. He moved close to her. She took a step back. He covered that extra distance instantly. When he grabbed her she didn't protest. When he kissed her she didn't object. He started fondling her breasts. She grew very aware of the bulge on his shorts. The sight and sense of his muscles… Even more sweat flowed from the already sweaty bodies. She knew he used his power on her, but she was so tired, so tired of fighting. Was unable to fight him, to oppose his burning will. She sighed and turned limp in his grip. He put her down on the floor. She writhed and stretched her body as he covered her. He covered her and she hungrily returned his kisses.

– ELIZABETH. LINSEY. Are you two down there? DINNER!

Trudy's voice made the rage flow in him. He knew, now he could make her go away with his mind. He pushed a hand at Elizabeth's mouth and began pulling her shorts. She threw him off in one, single act of force. In less than a second, very much like a cat, she jumped up and faced him in a defense position. She kissed the two rings.

– The other belongs to Ted. A snarl of a smile dazzled and paralyzed him. – *No other!*

She blocked all his power, dwarfing him, showing nothing of her insides. Therefore he didn't see how weak and empty she truly felt.

They left the dark room, the hall of shadows, and entered the bright-lit cellar. It was the middle of the day. She looked at the ring again, touching it, making certain it was real, glancing at her brother from the corner of her eye, a sore pain festering in her throat.

She had sent him off on the Path of Power. It wasn't easy to say how it would end. She had enough with herself, her own problems, she couldn't take responsibility for him as well. The hope she had carried that he would be able to help her was ruined now. In his way he was just as dangerous for her as Paul was. They weren't enemies, but they were no longer brother and sister.

2

«The Kendall family» invited to Fourth of July barbecue party. Elizabeth had skulked demonstratively in her room the whole day, during all the speeches, ever more inflated as the day progressed. She sat naked in the window and let the sun warm her, not giving a fuck if all the participants saw her.

It was dusk. Time to join the party. It usually began at this hour. The most interesting part of it, anyway.

She clad herself in a lace dress originally belonging to her mother. Trudy had given it to her on her birthday. It was a very beautiful dress, and she loved it. It was a bit too small, but she loved that, too.

The evening was hot and dry. The grass broke under her nude feet. Ash joined her the moment she stepped outside, like the eager boy he was.

– Abysmal, he commented, indicating the gathered crowd.

– Tell me about it, she said exasperated. – If people in this country had any ideas and ideals of freedom two hundred years ago, they're long gone by now. It is as if the inferiority complex they're all carrying is muted on days such as this. Humans are helplessly dependent on tradition.

She had come to dislike the human in herself.

Eugene walked around and practically rubbed his hands in enjoyment. She sensed his self-righteous attitude and was almost physically sick. Events such as these were milk and blood to him.

But there was a furrow on his brow these days, for several reasons, and Elizabeth couldn't assure herself she didn't enjoy that.

There was his family that he just couldn't rule anymore, no matter how hard he tried.

Then there was the matter of broader concerns in the valley.

His old friend Thomas Kennedy had finally given in to the creditors. He had sold his property and moved from the valley. That had led to general distress in the area. Doc Kennedy hadn't moved and left the daily administration of his land to a proxy. He had sold. The first forced sale in the valley for decades. There was a persistent rumor circling the circuits about a tougher attitude among the creditors, and if so, many more properties would soon be in jeopardy.

And there were the unspoken whispers: No one had moved there. The animals had been removed and the buildings demolished. No one seemed interested in actually living there.

So Eugene was troubled. Elizabeth didn't fault him in that. She was troubled herself, for her own reasons. He waved to her, clearly to booster his own spirit. She didn't return the greeting. She never spoke to him anymore, except in the most rudimentary ways, out of pure necessity.

She hummed something, something turning into words, words she didn't understand.

– Again?

She turned, spotting with swollen eyes Linsey sit on a wooden stump, playing his guitar.

– Can you run that by me again? He grinned.

The words came easy, flowing between her lips like the silver-tongued demons they were.

I do want this anger burning in me.

It's so hard without it.

So hard to be free.

He began playing and singing, and it made gooseflesh erupt all over her body.

– You're getting good, she whispered. – Very good.

She hurried on, not looking back.

Linsey had been so busy or made himself so busy the last few weeks that she hadn't seen much of him. But enough for her to study him, to see him coming to grip with his new reality. It didn't seem to faze him much. It didn't mark him like it did her. He did struggle with the smoldering rage inside, but not compared to her, not in such a destructive way. The calm and harmony emanating from him wasn't pretence, even though it was slightly misrepresented.

He had formed a band recently, and they had been practicing, rather loud in a barn a bit outside the valley. Elizabeth had, along with a slew of others played an enthusiastic audience to their bungling efforts.
– Creating and playing music helps him, she told June, – helps him… cope.
June didn't say anything, but just studied her sister intently.
– I've tried similar things, Liz continued. – I wish it would help me.
The band had placed their gear on the Hill the previous night and covered it up. She had watched them from her window, unable to sleep.
They had written a rather large note on a white paper attached to the black plastic:

KEEP AWAY. PRIVATE PROPERTY!

Eugene had asked about it in the morning.
– It's a surprise, Linsey had replied grinning.
And gotten away with it.
– Good luck, she had told him, in the morning, with at least a bit of her old wit and roguish self. – You're gonna need it. The older generation doesn't exactly appreciate surprises…
Better safe than sorry Linsey and bunch had kept close to their stage most of the day, controlled the rather extensive wiring running from the closest house, nervous like rats hiding from cats.
It was almost dark when they revealed their «surprise» to an astounded crowd. And it wasn't hard to tell that it did indeed come as a shock to the rather rigid gathering. Several of the valley's influential citizens wanted to stop it. Kendall and other seniors stared at it all in a state of shock. You could just see them standing there in their tracks, ready to jump forward, and rush towards the writhing snakes in the grass and pull the plug.
But they didn't.
Flickering lights were lit. Linsey Kendall made his first really public riff with his electric guitar.
They opened with Ohio by Crosby, Stills, Nash and Young, a tune well known, also among the establishment in the valley, and not very favored there (to say it the least).
A boy sat by the mixing table, desperately attempting to handle the rather slippery buttons and knots. June and Elizabeth joined him there, and he turned even more nervous.
– Why are they allowed to keep it going? June wondered, smiling sweetly to the boy, to take the sting from her words.
– I guess they play so bad that no one perceives them as a threat…
Elizabeth shook her head with a grin wide enough to reach both ears.
The first song ended. There was sparse, polite applause.

– This marks the end of us poor souls being entertained by old, bloodless jazz bands, Linsey shouted into the mike, the words being distorted almost beyond understanding. – This is a new age, and our blood is boiling.

Thc other guitarist played low-key (sort of), while Linsey spoke.

– It's funny how things are turned around in just a few, short years. Ten years ago you would probably have shot us for doing this. Things are improving somewhat…

The drummer kicked the large bass drum, kicked it hard. It almost turned over as he did an insane solo.

It turned quiet again, for a tiny moment as Linsey shouted his words of declaration.

– We are *Mystic!* Hear our song!

They played a heavy Black Sabbath tune. The grass bent backwards and the ground was shaking. Linsey shouted savagely into the microphone.

A deputation formed instantly, as if by mind reading. The local christian majority, and a few more self-righteous people. They charged the mixing board, where Elizabeth and June had a great time with the flustered, distracted boy.

– What can we do for the Ladies and Gentlemen? June stretched her body coquettishly.

– We want you to put a stop to this satanic music, the local priest ordered piously.

– Why not tell the musicians? Elizabeth challenged them.

Her words mixed with the loudness from the band, making it hardly audible, but the self-appointed cultural deputies heard her.

– Turn off the damn noise, the school's principal growled, and grabbed her around her upper arm for the purpose of shaking the unruly girl, shake her hard.

She kicked him in the belly (oh, well, a bit further down then), and he fell whistling to the ground.

There was a quality in her expression while she turned to the rest making them very jittery and fearful.

– I'm the spawn of Satan, and if you don't leave this place this second, I'll transform you into toads.

They rushed off the fastest they were able, with her scornful laughter echoing in their ears, far longer than it was supposed to, when the loud music should have blanketed it.

The principal stumbled straight to Trudy, she standing by the barn rocking to the beat. The others were way too paralyzed to give him the necessary moral support.

– Mrs. Kendall, he yelped, – your daughter *assaulted* me.

– On the contrary, Trudy corrected him, – you assaulted *her!* If you don't want to hear anything more about that, I suggest you keep from yapping more about it.

– Mrs. Kendall, the priest's wife said pointedly, – I find all this absolutely scandalous.

– Absolutely not, Ruthie, Trudy replied cheerfully, – it's justice. After countless years of suffering through thoroughly boring parties, where you guys have decided everything it's more than about time for a change.

And she gave them the finger and joined the jubilant youths in the yard.

Mystic played Deep Purple's Child in Time, with Linsey sounding like a horrible parody on Ian Gillian. This both haunted and exhilarated Elizabeth.

There was danger everywhere, open and concealed for the witch. And something, something rotten was happening in the valley right now.

While she removed herself from the music and sought the quiet darkness, the image of Linsey's ring on his finger appeared in her mind. There was no sign of change in his eyes, but the ring had glowed the entire time on the stage.

She felt pride on his behalf, over what he had done, challenged them all. But she felt heart-gripping sadness as well, because she could no longer count on him or even trust him.

Elizabeth Warren sought solitude behind the Hill, beyond tonight's populated areas. She finally stood in darkness, alone, breathing easier, calmer, the night being a valve on her wounded soul.

There was a rather large rock buried in the ground in front of her. She struck out with her hands. The rock rose from the ground and high up above her, levitating there, as if there was no gravity in this place. The two rings glowed, mirrors of her eyes, she knew, and she rejoiced. The rock fell and burrowed deep into the ground. The rings made her feel so good, so good, beautiful as they were. And now she would know instantly when her eyes glowed. Whatever caused the glow it was as active… now… as it had been when the content in the rings had been a part of living people. People like herself. Horror coursed pleasantly through her body.

She went past another hill. So far that she could hardly make out the sounds from the party anymore. The dark landscape created a threatening silhouette against the electric light from the distant civilization. The Moon slipped in and out behind the clouds and its silver light created a strange, ghostly glow in the borderline between the bright and shadow ground.

A lost bird in the dark, she thought.

She reached one of the shingle roads. There was a bench there. Her father used to sit here, looking at the land, enjoying the afternoon sun. Lately he had been sitting here a lot and enjoyed it a lot. She sighed and sat down there and waited. Ash appeared fairly quickly. He hadn't been that far behind her.

He stopped right in front of the bench, glaring angrily and hurt at her.

– Why did you invite me? He asked. – I've hardly seen you the entire evening.

– Why shouldn't I invite you? She wondered. – You're my friend. You've got more right to be here than most.

– I want more than that.

She looked at him with her frank, direct stare.

– Please go, she told him. – You should go, now. We've got nothing more to give each other, you know that.

– I know I'm not the right one for you, he choked, – but who is? Won't you let me try? I would like to.

Her body stiffened. Somewhere inside her a knot was tied.

– Do you want to die?

The witch's voice was distorted to a point of being unrecognizable. Its honesty ripping him apart like a piecemeal wind. It made him pull back, made him back off, back off, until he only could glimpse her white dress. Then he turned abruptly and ran until he could hardly breathe anymore. Even with his eyelids closed tight he saw her face, saw Evil's Beauty, a sight that would haunt him for the rest of his life.

The girl didn't watch him flee. Out of sight, out of mind she forgot about him. She lay down and stretched out on the bench. Its surface was cool against her hot skin.

She regretted quickly that she had chased him away. He would have been useful, at least a while longer.

A hand lingered on her thigh. Without putting any conscious thought into it, she begin rubbing the skin just under the edge of the dress. It was like an explosion of heat, and she bit her lip.

A shape grew out of the darkness. She recognized Paul instantly. The way he walked and moved, and the rounding of his shoulders was so very familiar to her. She sat up and swiftly fixed her dress, pulled its edge back down her thighs.

She wanted to stand up, but she couldn't. Her legs shook beneath her. She hadn't heard him or known he was coming. Just like before she could hardly read him at all, even when she looked straight at him.

– It was sensible to send Griffith away. He nodded graciously. – He's much too weak for you. Admittedly more than strong enough for most, but you're something special, girl.

– And you are? She said inflamed. – Strong enough?

He sat down beside her, grabbing her arms, pulling her close.

– I know I am, he stated.

He pulled her tight and kissed her.

– What are you *doing?*

Her attempts at protest were feeble, pathetically weak.

– Taking what's mine.

He kissed her again. This time she responded and without reservations. He went right to it, pushing a hand under her dress and began *touching* her. She gasped, and then, shortly afterwards, she moaned, and softened in his grip. Her breasts swelled, her nipples hardened. Her skin turned enormously sensitive.

– That's better, that's so much better.

He let go of her and rose. She looked at him through a thick haze of helpless desire. He walked a bit away from the bench and sat down in the grass, the soft, pleasant grass. She swayed on the bench, unable to control herself.

– Come here.

He tapped the ground.

The ground was dirty. She would soil mommy's dress.

She hurried to his side and sat down in the grass, clinging to him.

– You and I have much undone together, he nodded. He took her under the jaw and turned her head towards him. She remained thus. – We can go far. You agree…. Right?

– Y-yes…

She hardly recognized her own voice, so thin, so needy. And his was so strong, no apparent crack there at all.

He began touching her again, so confident, as he pushed up her dress, and exposed her weakness. The stench of the sweat covering her skin tore into her nostrils. He took his time down there, circling in on the place she wanted, she desperately wanted him to go. Then he pushed fingers into her wet bush. She gasped and wanted to pull him closer. He grabbed her wrists. She didn't resist him very much before relenting completely, and allowing him to do as he wanted. He held her arms up while pulling off her dress. Her hands and arms were half bent and seemed to have lost all strength. She writhed on the back on the ground and watched him blindly as he undressed. The grass felt hot and alive beneath her.

– It's a good thing you don't care for that nationalist bullshit, he said. – I don't either.

She smiled to him. The music in her head rose to overwhelming levels when he lay down on her. His cock was large and swelling, but he waited patiently. The Moon vanished behind a big, black cloud. He bit her nipples. She writhed beneath him, eager for him to gain even better access. To her. She waited and waited for the rage to come. It didn't. He took her and her pleasure increased to insane levels. He smiled hard as he studied the willing and entreating female. He paused a bit and grabbed her right hand, and removed one of the rings. Ted's. He took Ted's ring.

And put it on his own finger. A little whine of protest rose from her, quickly drowned in her needy moans. That was all.

– So beautiful, he said, while caressing her hair. – And so beautifully vulnerable.

He moved his hips hard, ruthlessly. And while her arms fell behind her head, completely powerless… she became his. More and more for every move of surrender. She felt his heat spread in her. From the hole and to the rest of the body. She came choking and helplessly, and smelled the harsh scent of conquered female and conquering male and sniffed in despair and love. They stretched out on the ground, as the ride ended, as everything exploded and ended in a rush of need and pleasure. She lay still. He kissed a few of her tears, and then he pulled out, grinning like a devil. The female was deflowered and conquered. She belonged to him, now. She was his to do with as he desired… whatever he desired. Because he had taken the ring, the Beast's ring.

Time passed, but she didn't move. The Moon slid forward from behind the dark cloud. She lay still, waiting for his command. What he had taken was in truth a part of her soul.

CHAPTER FOURTEEN

DENVER.

The large suburbs, the tall skyscrapers in the middle, the wilderness not far away. A well composed image of human development. Linsey couldn't decide whether or not he liked the city. It wasn't large compared to several of the Unites States' mega cities, but the pollution was easily detectable to him. Both the physical and the stench from big money and power hunger. It was a *city*.

Linsey was registered democrat, fairly prominent compared to his young age. His presence in Washington DC the previous year had somehow gained him a legendary reputation. Now, during this gathering of delegates he could easily sense his elevated status. He met again many friends - and as he discovered - many enemies. And also total strangers that for some reason wanted to shake his hand. He was seen as an up-and-coming man, and some people kept special track of such things.

He also discovered that some of his friends were more like former friends as far he was concerned. A lot had changed. Most of all he, himself had changed. He discovered that he had major problems concentrating during the meetings.

– It's all so… bleak, he complained to an old «friend».

The man looked strangely at him.

The year before Nixon had been the big bad wolf, and it had been unsavory - even at closed meetings - to express ambitions. Now everyone spoke about the election in 1976, and everything was back to the old, old thing of power and politics that had been temporarily banished during the early seventies.

Gerald Ford's popularity, if he had ever had any, had kept falling since he had personally pardoned Richard Nixon. It was a sure bet that he would lose the election. Whoever was chosen as the opponent had a free pass.

After a revelation akin to an epiphany Linsey went to a masquerade, a Bal Masque dressed as Dracula.

- Great costume, another old friend said cautiously.

There was a question mark at the end of his words, hardly noticeable.

- I find it quite fitting, Linsey said. – They're all bloodsuckers here.

Someone had truly done his homework this time, and created quite a set up in both the hotel's lobby and great festivity hall (and used a lot of money doing so). No expenses were spared when it came to major political conventions. Behind all the masks hid many of the most influential people in local and national politics.

He studied them all, as he focused on them, and he could easily see behind the masks.

A group of women sat by the table, exchanging gossip and news, laughing their hearts out. He recognized Yvonne Garrison immediately. She was dressed as Catwoman, her dark skin almost impossible to divide from the dark fabric each time her face slipped into shadow. Her laughter, her moves, and the way she held her head. He believed he would have recognized her even without his increased sensitivity.

His increased sensitivity…

It was only in this place, so far away from his birthplace that he had given himself time to think. About everything that had changed. His wanderlust that pulled him away from his birthplace, the farm he had always assumed he would run one day. That made him uneasy, uncertain. But nothing compared to what he sensed in Elizabeth, what frightened him.

And what had happened in the basement hadn't been her fault, but his. What was in her was in him as well.

He stared at his eyes in the mirror every day, filled with apprehension, but they didn't change.

– Dance? He put a hand on Yvonne Garrison's shoulder.

So far the five girls by the table had rejected any offers, any potential dance partner.

Not you. You do want to dance, dance with me. You want nothing but to dance with me me me me me

It worked. She did allow him to take her outstretched hand and lead her out on the floor. Four angry pairs of eyes stared after them.

The slow rhythm took them, pulled them in: he led, she followed.

She was a big African American, almost as tall as him, and he sensed her strength and determination without really trying. She knew who he was. He had sensed recognition in her. Not instantly, but after just a few seconds. After all, she, too, was a keen observer.

– Perhaps I should feel flattered, he told her lightly.

– Uh, why? Her coal black eyes twinkled.

– You've rejected dance offers from several sons of top party officials, but you accepted me. I do feel flattered.

– Oh, that was just a bit of nonsense on our part, she shook her head, giving him her best smile. – We weren't supposed to dance with anybody the entire evening. It seems rather silly to me, now.

I'll bet!

They left the floor after just one dance.
– I can't stand jazz, he told her.
– Come to think of it, neither can I…
She laughed seductively and clung to him.
They sat down by his table, a small one, in a corner in the deepest part of the room. He ordered wine to them. It arrived quickly, with hardly any waiting at all. The waiter poured the bubbly white wine in two glasses and left.
– Cheers, he raised his glass, and she did the same.
– Cheers, Linsey, she said softly.
Glasses met and parted. They drank.
Yvonne was hot after the dance, in more ways than one. He knew that, didn't even need to scan her much to confirm it. Her breathing, the excitement in her eyes and posture made it more than clear to him that she was attracted to him.
She moved her chair to his side of the table, brushing an arm against his. He grabbed the arm and pulled her to him. She gasped. He pulled her tight, taking his time. He had all the time in the world.
He kissed her swollen lips. She responded, and he tasted her, tasted her lips, her fragrant, and she was pulled totally into his space.
She pulled back, laughing softly and shyly. And this was Yvonne Garrison. This would have astounded her friends and confidants.
– I don't know what you're expecting to get from this evening, Linsey, she said, clearly blushing.
– That one is easy to answer, he said, touching her cheek, taking her hand. – Hot, senseless fucking until dawn.
Sit! Sit still, damn you!
She took a sharp, deep breath, her mouth open, her eyes wide.
– You're so direct, sir, she said coyly.
That calmed him, calmed him almost beyond reason. And what she saw as his indifferent restraint merely served to excite her further. His charm had grown beyond any expectation the last few months. If he hadn't been convinced of that earlier, this evening made him a believer.
– I have to tell you that I don't believe in sex on the first date, she said, more determined, clearly shaken, filled with contradictory emotions. – I don't believe in it and haven't practiced it.
He listened, to her wording. He was a good listener, just as his sister, and Yvonne's wording came off pretty clear.
– You're just so damn sexy in that suit, he said. – Irresistible, I'd say!
– Flatterer.

She laughed, clearly flattered, giving him a quick kiss, before quickly pulling back.

I have her. The realization hit him like a flood.

The evening progressed to him like a river of expectation, as a reflection of her eyes, twinkling in the light from the candles.

– Fortunately there are no more shitty meetings, he said, a bit over nine. – They bore me to death. Now, there's only the fun part, the social… intercourse left.

– I love the meetings, she said with conviction, slapping his hand playfully. – There's so much power gathered there. The get together afterwards is boring or usually so…

That word. It stirred and festered inside him.

– So, why are you here, then? He asked calmly. – The masquerade is just a variation of the predatory dating and fucking game. Everybody knows that.

– Oh, connections are made here, too, she said excitedly. – Connections very valuable for the future.

He suspected she didn't truly realize how loose lipped she had become. Ninety percent of the delegates felt that way and acted that way, but they didn't give voice to it, didn't usually expose themselves like that.

The music, the insane, inane jazz pretending to be music played on, adding to Linsey's frustration, Linsey's irritation, Linsey's rage.

– You're renting a hotel room, I gather?

– Sure, she shrugged, – the girls and I. It's not as if we're from around here.

– I am, sort of.

Her mouth formed an O, adding more silly behavior to her already long list.

– I have a house. Hotel rooms are boring. Why not spend the night at my place?

– You're not renting a house, are you? You don't have that much income from that farm you're inheriting?

– It's really the property of my father's sister, my aunt, but she has been away for a long time. We use it whenever we're visiting these parts.

– I don't know…

Hesitatingly she glanced over at the far table towards the exit, where her four friends had been joined by four eager males.

– Bring your friends if you want, he stated. – The house has many rooms, very available. Let's have a party.

– No! She quickly shook her head. – I don't need any chaperones. And besides, I want you for myself.

Besides, he thought.

She spoke briefly to her friends. They cast looks at him and laughed, and then the two of them left the hotel, and the nauseas ball stuck in his throat loosened just a little.

He brought her to the white house by the river. It was old and in dire need of renovation. He had known how it looked, and had therefore arrived here in advance of the convention. The paint had been missing on large parts of the wall and the garden had been overgrown. He had been at it from dawn till dusk. Mostly to have something to do, to take his mind off things. He had painted the house' outside walls and fixed the worst of it, been at it until his arms hurt.

But the hard, boring work hadn't been enough.

It was always a strange experience to cross the threshold here. Linda's parents had left without taking anything with them. Left without a word. The furniture hadn't been covered. Everything was, he suspected exactly as it had been when Ted and Linda had last seen it. The walls were filled with photographs, things, memories. Memories not his, but still his. Important.

Two photographs hung on the wall by the attic stairs. Mike above, and under Ted and Linda, while they were still children. Had Mike ever been a child? Linsey could hardly remember him. The image of Ted blocked his recollection. Just a slight sense of unease, that's all.

He followed her up the stairs to the nearest bedroom. She giggled and curtseyed when he opened the door for her.

– Thank you, good sir.

– This was the parents' room. As you can see there's only one smaller bed here, now. I've moved the big bed down in the living room. I kinda think it belongs there.

– You carried a heavy bed down the stairs alone? Wow, you're strong.

He didn't comment on her flirting, which he knew infuriated her to no end.

– And you've got prospects, too, she nodded, more to herself. – I've heard you might be appointed to important tasks very soon. You made quite an impression on the meetings, more than confirming people's expectations of you.

He listened carefully for the slightest bit of irony in her voice. There wasn't any.

– I'm indeed on my way up, he bragged. She didn't notice the sarcasm. – I've got support from both the many and the few.

– An ideal candidate, she breathed. – You don't come across that too often.

He was fully aware that he was seen as important, a «coming man». He had been appointed to the right committees and knew the right people.

– Such a considerate man. She kissed him on a cheek. – Letting me stay here instead of in that dreadful hotel room. I'll see you tomorrow.

She wouldn't come to him tonight or let him come close to her. Not tomorrow either. She would keep him on arm's length, tease him, until she would be fairly certain of getting the advantages she desired so hard.

– Good night, he grinned, – and pleasant dreams.

That grin confounded her. His entire pattern of behavior was so atypical that she couldn't really get a handle on him.

He walked down the stairs, through the kitchen, to the living room. He undressed methodically, with very controlled moves. His eyes closed, and he could see Yvonne as if through a mist. She stood in front of the mirror, casting nervous glances around her. A person had been murdered in this room, and he took it for granted that she knew that, with the well of information she had gathered on everybody. There was a presence in the room. His presence. And she couldn't help but noticing. No one could. She shook her head and rejected it, rejected the reality of it, like most people do. She slipped out of the costume, letting it fall on the floor. Beneath she had a white silk top and panties. Her butt stuck out, brown and firm. He got a hard-on that very instant, seeing her with her eyes, smelling with her nose, tasting and sensing through her. Hearing the silk against the sheets as she went to bed. She didn't remove the silk, but lay there writhing restlessly under the blanket, leaving the night table lamp on. It was an incredible experience for Linsey. He was almost disoriented when he once again opened his eyes. It was hard to know which smells, sounds, tastes and emotions belonged to him and which were hers. He wondered if it could go as far as memories, if he had reason to fear it would mix up his recollection of events.

Memories.

He began flipping through the photo album on the desk, Rodney Cousin's desk, another great mystery man, another riddle cloaked in flesh.

Three photos stood out from the rest. He was incredibly astute at this moment, his mind clearer than he could ever remember, thinking, reasoning and concluding in rapid succession.

First there was a photo of the three children, Mike, Ted and Linda in front of the house. Then it was Linsey himself with sisters and Mike and Ted. Linda wasn't there. And then there was a photograph he had never seen before, a faded black and white image of three other children. A little girl that was almost certainly Trudy, and two boys, one with blonde and one with dark hair. The latter so obviously similar to Mike and Ted that Linsey felt the shock very much like an electrical charge.

Linsey - son of Trudy, great grandchild of Nick walked towards the bed. He fumbled in his pocket for the harmonica, but it wasn't there, and he recalled that he had left it at the farm, deliberately. The piano - Cindy Coogan's piano - called to him, but he resisted its call. He sat down on the bed, while opening and closing his fists, concentrating, raising something dark and scary from his depths. Linsey Kendall felt, in a very physical way, the power of the witch rise within.

Yvonne sat up in bed, shaking her head, out of breath, suddenly covered in sweat. She rose and stumbled towards the mirror, staring into it, at her unruly hair and open mouth. He saw her, felt her bewilderment, her rising desire, slowly turning to irresistible lust. She bit her lip, but unable to hold back the quiet moan for more than a few seconds. And she hurried, almost in a panic out of the room and down the stairs.

He sat crouched on the bed, with his arms around his knees when she entered the living room. She fumbled for the light switch, found it and pushed it, but there was no light.

– It's broken, he said. – Come here.

– But it's dark, she wailed.

It was completely dark. He had turned off the electricity, but he still saw her clearly, saw the entire room much better than he had merely a moment ago.

– Just follow my voice, he admonished her.

She caressed herself, in the mistaken belief that he couldn't see her do it, as she with cloudy eyes made her way across the floor. He didn't need any increased sensitivity to know that she was torn and confused. It wasn't supposed to happen this way. He should have come to her, making it that much easier for her to run him, to steer him in the right direction… her direction.

When he grabbed her and pulled her down on the bed, she was shaking so hard that she could hardly speak.

– It was so very long until morning…

It was merely a whisper, hardly audible.

He grabbed the straps of her top.

– No, don't take it off, she gasped.

He ignored her final attempt at resistance, like he had those before. Slowly and joyfully he pulled the top down her body, and when he reached the panties, he included them, too. She lay there, exposed, attempting to focus her eyes on him in the completely dark room, on her back writhing, while he touched her. He split her thighs easily. She released a loud moan and began moving harder, clawing at the sheet, spreading her legs further in exquisite sensual moves.

– You're so horny, practically begging to *get it,* don't you?

– Yes! YES! You're so strong, so manly.

Gasping wildly, her words hardly intelligible.

She never stopped. He laughed hard. Not in pride over her words, but in scorn. Fake bitch!

But her need wasn't faked. He knew that, beyond any doubt.

He took a firm grip around her muscular and round thighs and turned her over on her belly.

– Hey, what are you…

He put a hand over her mouth and with the other he grabbed her short, smooth hair. She fought against that, threw and writhed her body, to no avail. He descended on her and took her, hard and ruthlessly, penetrating deep within her. There were just a few thrusts before she stopped struggling and turned soft and compliant, her body forming itself according to his. She cried out and moaned alternately while a thick layer of sweat and musk came to cover her skin. When he emptied himself in her she would have screamed if he hadn't stopped her.

There were gasps of air in the closed-off room, and it had never tasted so sweet. He held around her hips and lifted them up, as he just kept going, hard again after just a few seconds, and he was stunned, hardly able to believe it. While she had her face buried in the pillow he pulled her with him down the river, the waterfall of his power, his irresistible power, and there was that word again, echoing within him. He squeezed her left breast. It was firm and large. She shouted his name repeatedly, while surrendering completely to him, to his… to his *power*.

She fell asleep like that, with her hips stuck in the air.

And his surroundings changed into a cool, shadowy place, a soft pillow with hard edges, and he changed into a bird of prey hunting in the darkness.

The sharp light of dawn greeted him, as he opened his eyes, and the night seemed short and futile. He sat there for minutes, taking it all in, taking everything in, taking a few trips around the house, slamming doors, carrying her costume from the attic, not bothering the slightest about being quiet, before once more returning to the bed. The song of birds outside. The whisper of cockroaches in the basement. He looked at his watch. It was as if its legs hardly moved. The seconds crawled as he felt the sun break the hard edge of the horizon.

He slapped her butt, slapped it hard, losing patience with her slumber.

She was still on her belly, with her ass stuck up. Her eyes opened wide, as she was brutally woken from her deep sleep. She rolled slowly over on her back, her eyes bewildered at first, before slowly focusing on him, as she stretched her luscious body and performed sensually before his predator eyes, and looked speculatively at him under lowered eyelids.

– That was *amazing,* she exclaimed in pure joy, more honest then she had probably planned. – I never thought it could be like that. I like you, Linsey, like you so very, very much.

There was a flash of temptation. She crying in his arms, broken, eating of his hand, his willing tool.

He raised her up, took around her and she kissed him hungrily. Several times. He held her arms in a firm grip and played with her like he wanted. While wondering how far he could take it. He knew he could take it far.

– You'll go far, won't you? She wheedled, giggling and with a hoarse subtext in her voice when he tickled her nipples.

– Sure, he replied with conviction. – I'll be President of the United States one day.

– I believe you will be, she said empathically, dreamingly. – I'm absolutely convinced of it.

She let him hold her, let herself be a pawn, a plaything in his hands.

He released the hold he had on her, and walked away. He began to dress.

– This house is surely tingling with history, she exclaimed excitedly. – The Cousin house. My God!

– It's coming out of the walls.

He held back an angry reply. Her behavior hardly deviated from what he had expected.

– You've got some famous relatives, she breathed.

She rose and reached for the ceiling, stretching her body gracefully, once more performing for him.

He pretended to overlook her. The ring on his finger glowed. In rage, not desire. She felt overlooked. Hot and needy she left the bed and slipped up behind him. She put her hands on his broad shoulders and rested her head in his neck.

– Come, she whispered, – let's return to bed. Its' still early.

Powerful arms pushed her back. Her arms fell down. He turned and pushed the bundled silk at her. Confused and paralyzed she put it back on. Her arms felt heavy and her movements strangely slow. She had trouble seeing clearly.

– I did something yesterday, he told her. – Something I've wanted to do for quite some time. I told the chairman and his puppets to go to hell.

– But… WHY? She gasped. – Why did you DO it? How COULD you? It…

Then, finally she discovered the sarcastic smile he had never attempted to hide. She froze, as understanding slowly dawned on her pretty face.

– You… tricked me! She exclaimed incredulously. – You didn't tell me. You never *told* me!

– You brought it on yourself, he said, he rejected her, the chill in his voice cutting into her like a metal drill a cold winter day. – Here's your costume. I took the liberty of fetching it for you.

He felt her anger burning under her surface, and it pleased him, pleased him immensely.

– You're both a male chauvinist pig and an *idiot,* she pushed between clenched teeth and lips. – You've acted beyond silly and ruined your life. What will you do now, return to that backward farm of yours?

His mood, riding high, plummeted a bit. He hadn't considered that very much. What he wanted to do with his life. He just knew a few things he wouldn't do.

– I'm just happy as a horse over finally having the guts to break my ties to you opportunists, he cackled and slapped his thigh.

– Is it because I'm black? She wondered, half choked in her anger. – Is that why you've done this to me?

– If it is of any comfort, he gasped for breath, – I would've done the same with your four friends and your like.

– Why? She shouted, totally out of it. – WHY?

– Because I can.

And the simple, ruthless reply, filled with contempt, made her speechless.

Enraged because he had seen straight through her, she charged him. He pushed her back easily, at the wall, but still so hard that it made her cry out in pain. She stared at him. Eyes burned in murderous intent. Both pair of eyes. She turned scared and backed off towards the door.

– Don't worry, he said calmly. – Both you and your friends will go far. Politics are like that. So is the world.

– Asshole of a saint, she snarled. – You suck dick! I wish I could've given you syphilis. Sodomite!

He heard her on her way out and far beyond, as she woke up the neighbors down the road. He opened the window and threw the costume after her.

– Hey, whore, you lost this.

She ran back, and picked up the skin, while she kept spitting the worst insults she could muster. He closed the window and released a content, relieved sigh, sending her a final, scorn-filled greeting. It was done. Finally. It was no longer necessary for him to pretend to be something he was not. He choked a bit, just a little bit. Then he fell on the bed and laughed himself close to tears.

2

Fall.

Elizabeth usually enjoyed it, enjoyed its death and decay. But this year it felt bad, as if it cut into her, and slowly ripped her apart. She wondered if she was about to turn insane, and a proud voice whispered to her that it wouldn't be so bad, that her power would increase enormously then, and nothing would bother her anymore.

She couldn't tell what bothered her the most, that, or the possibility that her power would stop working.

There were worrying signs. She had had trouble performing with the plates before dinner a few days ago, and she almost broke a plate when it landed too hard on the table.

Her mood fell to below zero. Not even Linsey returning home and telling her the amusing anecdotes from the discontinuation of his political career could cheer her up. It made her giggle and laugh momentarily, but it didn't last. She noticed her brother's worried glance, noticed easily the bags under her eyes every time she looked in the mirror.

And she knew he noticed it, too, but was uncertain whether or not to confront her with it. She knew how that was. She knew it very well.

– Is it only a trick of the light? She said with a horribly hollow voice.

– Excuse me, he exclaimed nonplussed.

– The hope of the world, she said strained. – The notion that there's something better out there somewhere. Is it just another illusion, something they're teasing us with, so they can more easily pull us back down, to make us even easier to handle?

He didn't have any answer for her, and she hadn't expected him to have any. She remembered her chiding him, cautioning him concerning his callous treatment of Yvonne, but it wasn't really any empathy behind her words, and she knew he sensed that, too, and felt even more guilty.

She walked the long, short road to visit Paul. He lived alone in the house, now, not counting the servants. His mother had been dead for a long time, and his father had already left for the winter. She was alone with him.

The butler - she called him that - received her in the door, as always.

– Good morning, Miss Kendall, he greeted her kindly.

– Good morning, Tremayne, she returned the greeting gracefully.

He sat behind his father's desk in the library. He flipped through heaps of papers. The Cornwall Empire included countless ownerships domestically and abroad.

– Have a drink, Paul told her.

– Shit, it's way too early for that kind of indulgence, don't you think?

– Have a drink, he repeated forcefully.

She shrugged and filled a glass without ice and consumed it. He always seemed to be irritated over the fact that she could drink more than him without being visibly drunk.

He rose and walked to the decanter and filled another glass for her. To the brim. Unmixed. He handed it to her and she flushed it down. And this time a pleasant warmth spread from her belly. He relieved her of the glass and pulled her close. The kiss burned far hotter than the alcohol.

– Oh, sweet mercy, she said cutely, clinging to him, the embrace being way too brief.

He let go of her, but they kept close, close enough to burn in each other's heat.

– I like this house so much, she said. – It's like a castle, a lap of the gods. Why can't I just move here, live here with you? I want to stay here, with you all the time. And I won't need to walk here every day.

She rubbed herself enticingly at him, and she sensed how he softened, how he relented.

– There's one simple reason, he said decisively. – We're not married.

She broke in a short, incredulous barf.

– I didn't know you were such an old prude, she said caustically, – not the way you fuck.

His palm struck her cheek.

She gasped and turned limp in his arms. He led her to the couch and put her on it. She stared unendingly at him.

– That was necessary, he told her in a very strict manner. – Don't believe it wasn't. You must be taught manners. We're gonna do everything right. We will frequent the finest circles one day. We will marry when the time is right. With you by my side nothing will stop me.

– What does words written on a piece of paper matter? She wondered. – Isn't it enough to love… to love one another?

– That's only the first step. He petted her on the inflamed cheek. – Other things are also important. Like our vaunted position in society, our power given to us to execute, the proof that we're part of the elite, the people born to rule. The woman who's gonna be mother to my children won't spit on this, on tradition and luxury and money, because without it, we won't achieve anything.

She wanted to say something, but he closed her lips with a potent and dominating kiss.

He put her hands on her butt, and pulled her to him. Desire awakened her again. She melted in his arms.

– Yes, she whispered. – Do it! Quickly! *Please!*

He pulled down the pants, hers and his own. Hard and ruthless he turned the shaking female, and put the upper part of her body over the chair.

– Such exquisite flesh, he marveled.

Gasping and defenseless the female lay there exposed, feeling the cold leather against her skin. Feeling the hard and hot thing enter her. And she died again.

They had dinner. Servants served the food. The two of them sat on each their side of the extremely long table. She did her best to eat properly with fork and knife. It didn't go well. She was way too nervous and shook every time she believed he was about to speak. His sharp eyes followed her every move with a reproaching stare.

– I see the new cow-house has been completed, she said with a caustic taint in her voice. – Much bigger, and with even more metal and plastic than the previous one, and that's how it tastes, too. Modernization to such a degree that the name «cow-house» is hardly representative anymore. The poor cows are certainly not happy there.

– Modernization is necessary. He shrugged. – You saw how Doc Kennedy fared. He couldn't adapt to changing circumstances and went down.

– Like Eugene's brother and all the rest that has been forced to sell lately?

– Absolutely, he nodded. – Progress cannot be stopped. Those who don't go with the flow are doomed to go under.

Thus spoke a devourer. A shiver passed through Elizabeth and she fell silent.

– By the way, how's your father these days? He asked lightly.

– Eugene? She replied with a voice totally free of flavor. – He's the same old geezer. He hasn't changed a bit.

He had changed - for the worse. She shuddered, unable to even think consciously about it.

– Come, Paul said.

She went to him. She was clinging to him, like a body lost at sea clung to the lifeboat.

– I've got a surprise for you.

He led her into the living room, a room more resembling a large hall. A tailor waited for them. In spite of her telling Paul time and time again that she wanted to choose her own clothes. She let the man take her measures, let Paul give him instructions and hardly ever spoke up in protest and never with conviction. As usual he got his way. She discussed less and less with him.

They picked a horrible white dress to her, told her it suited her hair and skin and eye color. She hated it, but knew she would wear it every time Paul wanted her to. He dominated her more and more, and she lacked the will, the energy to truly do something about it.

She went home and straight to her room. After closing and locking the door she focused on the ball on the floor. She frowned. Nothing happened. She tried again. In near panic she stepped closer and tried again, with all the effort she could muster.

Nothing happened. She just sat down on the bed and hid her face in her hands.

She spent days in her room. Concentrated until she got an awful headache. Stared at the ring for hours. There was not the slightest glow in it anymore. She couldn't even lift a handkerchief. She had to face the truth: She had lost her power. Why, if it was psychological or some other, obscure unknown reason didn't matter. It was gone, and she might never get it back.

The sensitivity was all that remained. But that was worse than nothing the way she was now, so down and so helpless, unable to take charge, over herself, over anything. She sensed suffering and turned even more despairing and submissive herself.

She caught herself in greeting the priest's bitch of a wife, a new low in a series of lows.

Even a trip to the forest failed to improve her mood. Sue Ellen met her there, and found her in tears.

That shocked her to the core. She was used to seeing Elizabeth as assertive and confident.

– What is it, she asked stricken, – what's wrong?

– Nothing, Elizabeth mumbled, hardly able to speak because of all the snot filling her nostrils and throat.

– Please tell me, she insisted.

There was hesitation, seconds passed, but when the words finally came, they came as a deluge.

– Daddy is hitting m-mommy, Elizabeth said. – Only when they're alone, and always on parts of the body where it can't easily be discovered, but I found out weeks ago. I witnessed it first-hand, and stood there, paralyzed, crouching in the shadows like a scared l-little g-girl. I've wanted to do something about it since, wanted to t-tell someone, but I haven't and feel s-so usel-less. I've waited to see if Trudy would fight back or ask for help. But she has been so out of it lately, even more than she used to be. As if she *enjoys* what the shithead does to her. I desperately want to do something about it, but I feel just as helpless myself.

– But can't you... what about…

– I've lost my power, Elizabeth sniffed. – Or I'm unable to use it, which amounts to the same.

The bigger girl's despair shocked Sue Ellen. She sat down and embraced Elizabeth, in an effort to comfort her. Elizabeth crouched there, with her head in Sue Ellen's lap, with the timid girl's hand stroking her head in a rhythmic, relaxing move. They sat there in the forest for hours, both very timid and very scared.

It was Halloween. Elizabeth sat on the Hill for hours in an attempt to feel something, to do something, but nothing happened. Nothing at all. And she cried most of the time up there.

She didn't feel anything special, and back in her room she threw the photo of Ted at the wall, broke the frame and locked herself in for the rest of the day, feeling even more ashamed.

– What's wrong with you? She spoke to the mirror image. – What's fucking wrong?

And even now there was no real anger, only the pretense of thereof, only bottomless despair, and she was unable to do anything about it. And she fell on the floor, breaking down in tears.

Paul came in his car at dusk, to take her with him. She didn't want to go, but her body moved, her hands fixed her face, and she dressed to his liking.

– You're not this timid, dependent creature, she told the mirror image. – You're strong. You can do this.

I won't fail this time. I won't!

– I'm not gonna be weak this time, she insisted. – I won't give in.

She passed Trudy on her way down. She didn't actually see mother, but she sensed her, sensed her hiding in the shadows, and the bile rose in her throat.

She approached Paul with a little smile, holding out a hand to him. He took it and kissed it. So elegant.

He held open the car door to her, and she gave him a radiant smile.

It wasn't a very long drive, of course. They were there before she even had warmed the seat. The sight of the marble castle, as always, made her feel small. The power it represented sent shivers of heat through her.

– I've got a surprise for you, Paul told her.

– A surprise, she wheedled, and kissed him in gratitude on the cheek. – That's so considerate of you. I love surprises… What is it?

She added innocently.

– You'll see, he grinned. – It's a doozie.

She sensed malice in him, but that wasn't unusual, so she didn't make too much out of it. And she had to agree with him… when Claudia Cornwall or Claudia Rawlins met them in the great hall. An adult Claudia, an even more vicious Claudia.

– Elizabeth, so nice. She reached out her hand. – Paul and you, huh? Things do change.

Elizabeth took the other's hand, but only because Paul pushed her in her back. She gave the other woman the most pleasant of smiles.

Someone played the piano somewhere in the house, mysterious, heavy chords quivering in floor and flesh alike. Elizabeth couldn't tell why, but it made her jittery all over.

Dinner. Claudia sat between them by the long table. Elizabeth believed there was hatred in the well-traveled woman's eyes, but she wasn't sure. She had practically lost her increased sensitivity as well. Or she second-guessed herself so much these days that she could just as well have lost it. It was like her senses hit a tall, imposing brick wall. And even though she hadn't had her sensitivity since birth it was like turning blind or deaf, a horrible, hellish experience. She hardly touched the food.

– Not very hungry, are we? Claudia said sympathetically.

Elizabeth shook her head timidly, unable to put up a brave front.

– You're a bit big here and there. Perhaps a bit more… conscious diet is good for you? I can give you a few tips.

– Thank you, Elizabeth whispered.

– We have so much in common. There's *so* much I can teach you… if you let me.

Elizabeth didn't comment on that. She wanted to, but her lips didn't move.

– I mean, I remember you as quite headstrong, but we must all grow up eventually.

– Ain't that the truth, Paul cackled.

The young girl stood by the window in Paul's bedroom, and stared down on the Hill, where the devil face of the giant hollowed pumpkin scorned her in her absence.

Paul and Claudia entered the room. She sensed them, and instantly regretted that she did.
She turned in a quivering, composed manner, building the mask of rage.
– What's she doing here?
– But what's this, Liz? Claudia said in a voice layered with honey. – Such an attitude towards your future sister in law?
– I can't stand the sight of you. Elizabeth raised a fist at her. – You know that very well. I can somewhat tolerate your presence at the opposite side of the house, but get out of here, and don't show your mug here a second longer.
– Okay, I'll leave. The ice-cold blonde held up a hand after a brief hesitation and the dark-haired girl had taken a step forward. – Jeez, I only attempted to treat you nice. I leave it to your future husband to teach you simple manners.
She left, leaving the door ajar. The minor rage left Elizabeth, as it often did. It had been fleeting, temporary. She felt numb, feeling nothing of the previous intoxication. The sense that it truly was worth it. Only ashes remained.
His eyes glared intensely at her, he wore the skewed smile around his mouth. Her shoulders fell.
– You insulted my sister, he said, very strict. – I can't allow it to go unnoticed. You must learn manners.
He went to the closet where he had his riding whip. He grabbed it and brought it out in the open for her to see, for her to tremble.
– NO! She backed off.
– We're gonna play a game, he said kindly. – There won't be harsh punishment this time, only a minor correction. You've come so far lately, and need no more than the slightest push in the right direction to learn what you need to learn. Undress, now, if you please.
I don't please, she thought.
She bit her lip and shook her head energetically. Eyes were large and wet. She sniffed heavily while imploring him.
– Don't do it. Please. Not that.
– Undress, he commanded.
She obeyed. When she stood there defenseless before him he put the whip down. She knew she had lost the moment she walked up here.
– I knew you would understand. He nodded. – I'm doing you a service, and you know that. I'm teaching you what you must learn to thrive in the world.

He forced her down on her knees. She didn't really resist him, resist his will. Eventually she didn't resist at all. He bent her forward until her head and palms touched the floor.

– Stick your cunt up. Offer it to me. That's the ticket…

He touched her and made her shrink further, squeezed the smooth, brown skin, until there was hardly anything left, and she felt nothing, was nothing.

– What a cute little creature you are. And you shall be such a good girl. There won't be limits to how good you will be.

– Don't do this, she wailed. – *Please!* You're ruining everything.

He wasn't interested. His callousness was felt like the prelude to the whip, poignant and horrible. She felt his wet hand on her skin, felt him deep inside. She died some more.

The very first lash made her cry out in pain and terror. It hurt. But far, far worse than that was the degradation, the shame whipping her mind and pride like a hot metal bar, leaving deep scars. She remained in the position in which he had placed her afterwards, unable to stop choking, when he was finally done with her. Her body had this thick layer of sweat and musk, and every spot of it hurt.

She grew faintly aware of the stronger draft from the door. There was the sound of steps. Claudia stood there, hovering above her, glaring triumphantly at her. She had watched the entire time.

– Now, the little girl has been taught a lesson. It was said with a sickening glee. – Haven't you?

The girl nodded blindly towards the elegant, suave woman.

– That's my girl, Paul said pleased, hardly out of breath, very controlled. – The time has come for your reward, your surprise.

This was it. What he and his sister had looked so much forward to.

– Michelle! He cried.

– A very appropriate name, if I may say so myself, Claudia stated.

Elizabeth crouched on the floor like a little child. A girl, about three years old stumbled on thin legs towards her. With wide-open eyes she stared at a younger version of herself. The same brown hair she had had at that age, the same features, the same virtually anything. Only the eyes were different. Gray, shimmering, virtually transparent. Elizabeth screamed and hid her face in her hands, hiding from the world.

3

Liz Kendall ran through the forest with branches whipping her face and unprotected body. She bled from several small wounds from her jumping through the bedroom window. Naked, senseless she fled from the marble castle. There were people everywhere. She hid from them like a wounded animal. Hid her nudity. Crawled on all fours to stay out of sight. She thought she might have heard people call her name, but she wasn't sure, and didn't care.

The house of her conception, birth and adolescence. She hardly saw it, noticed it, until she had sneaked all the way to her room. And it felt scary, alien, not comforting at all. She sat on the bed with the blanket wrapped around her, shaking in cold and emotional turmoil.

Michelle. Ted's daughter. Trapped by an accident of birth in Paul and Claudia's clutches. She felt she should do something about that, like so much else. But she didn't have the strength. She had enough with herself and her own concerns.

She showered, and the cold, cold water surrounded her body like a valve, and she slowly, miraculously regained the ability to form coherent thoughts. It felt so good. The very sense of joy felt brief. She felt it would always be. Paul - that shit. She had really known from the start that he hadn't been looking for a mutual relationship. He wanted to break her, forming her after his own head, and use her for whatever purpose he had in mind. She hadn't been aware of how much she had changed the last few months, how much he had changed her. Not truly. Not until she had come face to face with her own weakness, inadequacies. She struck her fist at the wall, and it did nothing but hurt. There was no satisfaction, no sense of justified anger, and she choked.

By the time she had dried herself, she felt remarkably calm. She dressed calmly, at least. Sweater, pants, socks, shoes, jacket. She found the little suitcase in the closet and packed it in an almost obsessively neat way, making room for so much more than first believed. The fire inside the large pumpkin on the Hill had begun flickering, dying.

– You're leaving?

She turned and stared, stared at June and the suitcase in her hand.

– Yes, she nodded. – There's nothing for me here anymore. And besides, as Ted once fled to gather strength against a for the moment too strong an enemy, I do, too. There's no shame. Not right, now, at least.

– I saw you arrive, and wanted to say goodbye, June said. – Now, I guess I better ask if you want a traveling companion.

– I would be honored, Elizabeth choked. – I didn't want to leave you anyway, but I had to.

– I've seen it come for a long time, little sister said. – And it helped convince me that there's nothing here for any of us anymore. This isn't our home. It's hardly a home at all, anymore, and the whole world is waiting for us.

And this was supposed to be June, sweet, timid June speaking. Well, she hadn't been so timid lately. Claudia was right. Everybody had to grow up eventually.

Carrying their light and heavy load, they stepped out into the darkness. No one saw them, even though they did nothing to hide themselves. They hurried to the stable, where Elizabeth found her little stack of money. They walked arm in arm down the road. Elizabeth turned one single time, casting her eyes below the house, towards the hidden cellar. There was one unopened cardboard box left there. The largest. But she wouldn't be strong enough to open that, now. No one else would either. It was safe. It could wait. She couldn't. With leaving.

– Where did you get your money?

– I broke up Eugene's safe, June replied soberly. – It wasn't hard, and I didn't feel bad about it. He deserves it. If I was in doubt about that before, I'm not anymore, not considering what he's doing to mommy.

Pumpkins lit every crossroads. A sight that would usually have encouraged Elizabeth to no end, but not now, not tonight.

The evening had one, final surprise in store for the two sisters. There was one more person waiting for the last bus. They recognized Sue Ellen. She rushed to them in a euphoria of joy. Elizabeth felt strangely comforted upon comforting the other girl.

– I *hate* him, she cried, mumbling in the other girl's hair. – I had to leave. I couldn't have stayed one more day.

Stevie Marsh had been «let go» from her position at the school, something not exactly alleviating Elizabeth's guilt. It was never explicitly stated, but everybody took it for granted that Howard Grey was behind it, stirring the waters, still influential, though no longer very visible.

Sue Ellen dried her cheeks and straightened her body.

– And then you're also leaving. It's almost too good to be true. Can't we travel together for a while? Just sharing some of your strength will help me a lot.

The worship in the other's eyes bothered Elizabeth, but the trust did warm her.

– If you haven't a special goal in mind we can be together for as long as you want, but you see, we aren't exactly very upbeat ourselves these days, so the help will undoubtedly be mutual. We're on the run, too.

June entered the bus first. She was the one leading on, the one somewhat harmonic. The northern sky was lit by a large meteor shower. They looked at each other in wonder, as they sat down, as they completed the first step on their Journey.

Sue Ellen fell asleep quickly. Liz started blinking quickly, too. She was so tired, so very tired. The pitiful sleep grabbed her by the tail, and held on. June sat there for along time, staring out the window, at the nothing out there, periodically striking her right armchair. She mumbled, gritting her teeth.

– There must be something we can grab hold of.

CHAPTER FIFTEEN

When they awoke, somewhat rested next morning, they were already well on their way south. They had long since crossed the border to New Mexico. The sun lit Sue Ellen's face when she opened her eyes. She stretched her body with a pleased sigh. The sisters had already straightened in their chair and looked inquiringly at her. She smiled brightly to them, assuring them she was okay. June returned the smile. Liz wore shades again, and made it hard to tell.

– We've left the state, June said. – We can relax, relax for now.

– We're free. Sue Ellen looked breathless through the rear window. – Free at last.

– Free at least, Elizabeth said with a grin tinged with apprehension.

She wondered if there was a place for them, a place they would truly be free. She didn't believe there was.

– The government won't look for us. June shrugged. – They don't look for anybody, except people who have broken their precious law. There are countless children vanishing all over the country, all over the world, without any effective search commencing. We, the three of us are on our way to create our own heaven, our own hell, like the one major parts of humanity live in.

Elizabeth surveyed the terrain, the lines in June's face. Little sister had evidently also, for some time carried unvoiced thoughts.

Her words chimed so very true. Elizabeth didn't understand the chill down her spine that moment. She didn't understand it at all.

The ticket they had bought was valid to Santa Fe, but they stopped a day in Las Vegas, New Mexico, «the original Las Vegas», a windy and dusty place filled with cafeterias and gas stations. A place used to strangers visiting, but quickly passing by.

They spent some time picking three auspicious hairdressers, all very well attended. They chose one each and asked for their hair to be cut very short. Elizabeth studied the young girl in the mirror while the black tresses fell to the floor. She was unable to look away from the striking, very striking visage. Fear and loathing and joy warred inside her, and all three won. The barber, an old white-haired African American had to stare as well. At the hair combed to the side, smooth and coal black, cut above the ears. At the eyes in a just as wild and alien face. At the broad and swollen lips, at the distinctive brow and bone structure. She attempted to smile, but it was hard for her, as it was impossible for many other animals.

– The missus has probably changed since the last time she had short hair, the barber remarked politely.

She gave him more money than he asked for and hurried outside, into the warm sunshine.

– We're all growing up, she said.

Before long, but out of sight of the hairdresser, she had put the shades back on.

Her traveling companions also stared, even though the shades camouflaged some of the dramatic changes. In June's eyes and posture she read endless fascination.

A seemingly endless time later they left the bus by a highway parking lot just outside Santa Fe. There were quite a few cafeterias there they could pick and choose from. A curious thing happened that Elizabeth noticed not long after they had left the bus. She and June began… scouting the surroundings. It was like something rose from deep below the surface and slowly emerged into conscious thought. They *surveyed* the place, checking it for potential hostiles. And they kept doing it, even after they had found no overt threat.

– Guys, Sue Ellen said nervously.

They looked at her.

– Your eyes are moving all the time. It's kind of unnerving, you know.

Even she noticed. That condescending thought was one Elizabeth smothered quickly. She looked at the other people at the lot. They didn't seem to have noticed anything.

The two of them stopped, stopped with an effort.

They walked to the nearest place, a steak house, didn't bother to pick and choose, stretching a bit after the long hours at the bus, but generally hurrying inside.

– Let's dig in, Sue Ellen cried excitedly, – I believe my stomach has forgotten what food is.

They had found a kind of freedom these days. Especially Sue Ellen that in truth had lived in a prison since birth. She had gone thirsty all her life, and now she was drinking the cup dry.

– Do you have a whole roasted chicken? Elizabeth asked the boy behind the counter.

– Of course, he replied, with his usual confidence in treating girls. – To share among the three of you?

– No, to me alone.

She gave him her cute half-smile. *Just try it, dummy!* The boy's confidence broke so hard that it was almost audible.

– That boy looked nice enough, Sue Ellen said while they sat by a table and ravenously nourished themselves. – Why were you being so nasty?

– Nasty, moi? A shameless grin. – I think I treated him nicely enough.

– I guess you did. The other girl nodded, in a somber way. – I know how you could have treated him… if he had truly offended you.

– Little Susie… She grabbed her friend's hand and squeezed, a bit harder than she had intended than what was pleasant. – There are things you must learn, and one is that most people you meet will look and sound nice. But the majority is wolves in sheep's clothing.

– Listen to Liz, the voice of experience, June stated.

Elizabeth sent her a pointed stare.

– That's right, she nodded. – You little girls should pay attention.

They laughed and the tense mood lightened.

Time passed. Elizabeth looked towards Santa Fe while drinking her large Coke in greedy slurps.

– Many nomads used to pass through this area, she said distantly. – Now, it's usually tourists, people reaching back into the past without realizing its significance. These days it's merely another dead place.

She sensed it, sensed the passing of time. The city had been a center for trade and travelers for centuries, and she sensed it, sensed the blood and death and life. She tried to lift the empty Coke with her mind, in vain, and shrugged.

They left the steak house, filled, content, and visibly giddy. Sue Ellen swore (sounding very refreshing in Elizabeth's ears) when she studied the bus' departure times. She threw an exasperated look at the other two. But a smile danced in her face, a devil-may-care attitude the three of them shared. The sisters studied a car ahead with open doors and a running engine.

And no one inside. The driver had rushed in panic to the restroom across the parking lot thirty seconds ago.

– Shall we…?

June looked at big sister in anticipation.
Elizabeth looked up in the air, at the air, tasting it, and slowly shook her head.
– No, she decided, – we might ruin the poor guy's car. There's such nice weather and quite a short distance to the city. Let's walk.
They walked arm in arm by the roadside in the hot sun, not that bothered by the searing heat. That was how they arrived the city of Santa Fe.

2

Everything shining and glimmering, Elizabeth thought. She walked with her two companions down the neon lit streets of the large Las Vegas, Las Vegas, Nevada.
Fremont Street, where the casinos rested side by side opened up to them.
The three of them had traveled through New Mexico and Arizona, either by bus or by hitchhiking. Through the mountains, forests and dry, open land and eventually the Nevada desert. To the glitter and glimmer city, where the hatred, grief, triumph and falseness hit them like a wave. She recalled her fits of rage, her continued disappointment over the fact that it hadn't become something else.
She recalled in Flagstaff, where the Interstate road split in two, and one direction led to Phoenix, to Phoenix, Arizona. It was just a name, a name for a city and nothing else, but she did feel something then, a stirring, a treacherous hope.
There had been nothing more.
It wasn't that hot, really, here, at this time of year, not at night, and they wore coats covering their rather revealing dresses. The desert winter wind caressed their bare legs.
They chose the Golden Nugget Casino for the evening, having tried most other places. Three men blocked the entrance, meeting the girls with grins and a rather patronizing attitude. Elizabeth welcomed the anger, like she had done so many times during their travels, in the hope of once again feeling the surge, the rush inside.
– What's your *problem?* She snarled at them. – Do you enjoy standing there, with those silly grins painted on your faces, displaying your fucking imbecility?
Shame and anger visible in their features they stepped aside like the whipped dogs they were. She enjoyed that, and it had been so easy, so easy to overpower them, exert her will over theirs.

But it was just anger and nothing more, like all the other times. She realized she had sought trouble all those times leading to this place, in a hope of regaining her lost power.

The glittering lights inside welcomed them, the same way those outside had done, with a fake smile and a treacherous attitude. They scouted the roulette tables for a few minutes before going for one with a lot of space. Elizabeth and Susie handed June all their chips, and she began placing them on assorted numbers. The wheel was spinning. Elizabeth sensed that, even before the little ball was released on it.

She wanted so hard to steer, to decide where the ball halted its journey, to bend the rules of chance. She didn't notice she had bit her tongue until blood filled her mouth. The ball jumped up and down, from one number to the next. She wanted to grab it, to put it to rest where she wanted it to rest, but she couldn't feel, couldn't feel it like she had felt the ball in her room or the large rock and other things she had moved with her mind.

Last night she had tried the card tables, with scant success. This was it. It had to be. She rubbed her temples. No more bets, the croupier announced. The white ball and the spinning wheel seemed to hypnotize her, making her dizzy. She almost lost her footing, had to grab the edge of the table not to fall. Zero, the house wins. They had nothing on zero. THOUSAND DEVILS.

They bet on three, only on three. Susie bit her nails again. Elizabeth wanted to do the same. No more bets. ZERO. The house wins again.

Bet. It had to be there, somewhere inside her. She had juggled heavy rocks with her mind, damn it.

There was a nudge in her mind, involuntarily, but she realized it wasn't directed at the table, at the spinning wheel. A man stepped up beside her. He put his chips, all his chips on Zero. Zero again? She looked at him with flickering uncertainty in her eyes. He grinned back, a very dangerous grin, and she felt compelled to smile. She put the few chips she had left on zero.

She won. They won, both of them, together. She experienced the thrill, the danger of winning.

But that was all. Both lost the next two attempts. She noticed how ragged he seemed, unfocused. Something bothered him, something not necessarily connected to the game at all.

Elizabeth gathered what little she had left and the three girls left the table.

– It isn't working, she swore to her two companions. – I just can't make it work.

The catching in her throat was almost audible and the tears in her eyes were almost visible. There were horror and despair in her windows as she looked at the two other girls.

They made their way to the exchange counters, striving to hold their heads high.

Something happened. She heard his steps behind her, certain that it was indeed his steps. She heard the wheel turning.

She whirled around to face him, and for the very first time he saw straight into the wondrous eyes, and he was totally captivated. For the rest of his life.

– Same fate, same pale comfort, he said lightly. – We must simply get to know each other.

Since she didn't dislike him at first sight she felt he deserved further consideration. And then there was the buzz in her mind, drowning everything else.

– The first or second part of Stairway to Heaven? She said.

– What? He exclaimed nonplussed.

– Stairway to Heaven by Led Zeppelin. Which part do you like the most?

– Ah, he grinned. – The second, of course.

– Of course, she whispered.

He was young, just over twenty. His eyes were by the tip of her nose. His face was a mix of recklessness and arrogance. It reminded her of one she had seen before, at the front pages of newspapers, but she couldn't recall which.

– Are you here often? She asked, in an attempt to match his light tone.

But she felt empty, drained.

– I am, he nodded. – I'm especially pleased that I was here tonight, though.

She reddened. She actually reddened, also ashamed because he so easily, with a few well placed words was able to evoke emotions in her.

They stood there breathing, their surroundings turning quiet and breathless.

– Philip. A melodic voice, a neat hand. – There's a phone call for you.

– Not now, Barbara, he said, dismissing her.

– It's your father.

And Elizabeth saw the light die in his eyes.

– You must excuse me, he said abruptly to Elizabeth, dismissing her, too. – I'll be right back.

She knew he wouldn't be. She turned, turned away, and rejoined June and Susie outside.

They walked back to their motel, their sleazy motel room, like wounded birds in flight. The two younger girls sat down on the bed, quite down and exhausted from the continuous ordeal of being on the frontier, of being carrion birds, looking for trinkets. Elizabeth paced back and forth in the room. Occasionally she mumbled something, words, curses the others couldn't understand. Suddenly, without warning, with a loud snarl she kicked a chair into the wall.

She began trashing the room, trashing it in a violent, mindless outburst of abandon and violence and rage. The furniture was old. It broke easily under the slaughter. She struck and kicked the walls, making large dents and holes, beyond reason, beyond caring. When she was done she fell on the carpet, totally spent, feeling nothing of the previous rush, the now so unfamiliar surge of power.

The girls took her to bed and comforted her, took care of her, until she stumbled into a less than tranquil sleep.

The nightmares began. They hadn't diminished, either in frequency or in intensity, but steadily increased both ways, as time passed.

She was back in the forest, running, fleeing the wolverine, one of the most dangerous predators in existence. She ran, until she realized he would eventually, and soon, catch up with her. She turned around and met him, torn him apart, destroyed him in a glorious fit of rage.

She discovered she had become a wolverine herself, far larger than the one she had killed. But the worried brow kept moving in her face. And when she finally reached the end of the forest, she faced a wolverine that was even bigger than she had become. It was enormous, and it waited for her.

He caught her, and collared her, and she looked at him with grateful eyes because he in his infinite mercy had chosen to spare her life. She ran down the road, led in the chain by the giant beast. But both the beast and the collar and the chain faded away. She kept running towards the distant mountain. So mighty a mountain that it seemed close. A road through the remote wilderness without any possibility of hiding. The shadow of a firespitting dragon appeared on the mountain wall. It changed to a large face. To a man with fireeyes. Ted's face.

As always June was there when she sat up in bed with wide-open eyes and covered in cold sweat, holding and comforting her big sister as she shook and trembled. It took minutes, hours today before she stopped trembling.

– It's growing worse, isn't it, June said softly.

Elizabeth nodded, unable to speak, to articulate in more than rudimentary ways the worry, the horror that haunted her.

She showered, feeling dirty, very dirty. She stayed under the shower forever.

The two girls, her only friends in the entire world dried her with a large towel, rubbed her sensitive skin until it was able to notice minute changes in the air passing it.

– So what's wrong with your powers? June asked softly, afterwards, when they had had breakfast and the world looked a bit less menacing.

– I don't know, the dark girl said hesitatingly. – It is as if they one moment quite simply… decided to leave me. I thought it was somatic at first, caused by my uncertainty and nagging doubt, but I'm not so sure anymore.

She noticed the ambiguity of her own words, and laughed, a brief, shrill laughter.

– I haven't had them since birth, but it still feels like I've lost my sight or hearing, like a horrific hell.

– Poor girl, June said, stroking her hair.

– And without it there's just no chance in hell we'll be able to pull off a win at the casinos. And my sensitivity is useless in poker until I get better at it.

– We haven't much money left, Susie whined. – What do we do?

Elizabeth hated that. It was too much of a mirror of her own exaggerated fears and worries.

But the look at their situation wasn't exaggerated. It was grim, and turning grimmer fast.

– I'll tell you what we should do, June declared. – We should entrap one of the fat pigs and rob him.

Elizabeth looked at her, as if in shock. It was so simple, so gloriously simple.

– That's right, she stated, her eyes turning vicious and cruel. – We should have done something like that long ago.

June's words incited her, readied her.

– Isn't there anything else we can do? Susie asked. – We can work or something.

– Without ID? Elizabeth snapped at her. – No, little one, you know well there's only one type of job we can have in this town. Do you want to do that?

– No… Lowered eyes. – B-but can't you two do it, the two of you? You'll do fine.

– Perhaps, the wicked witch nodded. – But that isn't the point. You won't leave the dirty work to us? You will pull your weight… won't you?

– Yes. It came out hardly audible. – Of course I want to.

– Good girl. A kiss on the cheek. – I knew you would say that.

– Besides, we do need you. June pinched the one-year-older girl in the other cheek. – You're such a treasure, sweetheart, so innocent. You will be our decoy, luring the dirty old cat to the wolf's den.

Sue Ellen began shaking. June pulled her tight.

– Don't worry. We'll tell you what to do. Trust me. It won't be hard, won't be hard at all.

The day passed in a rut. They cleaned up the room the best they could. It had been done before. They could easily discern that. There were old pieces of furniture in the closet where they put those recent. The room turned unbearably hot as the day progressed. They showered again, as the desert twilight approached, dried each other carefully and without too much effort, dressed in their best effort… and went hunting.

Elizabeth and June's eyes moved constantly as they embraced the predator within, as they scouted for prey. The evening passed, as they found what they initially deemed suitable candidates, as they hesitated and pulled back, as fear stopped them from making the final, decisive move. They had to eat. Elizabeth devoured the juicy, beyond fat and unhealthy burger in frantic, savage movements. It ruined her lipstick, make-up and nails, and she had to redo it all. Her hands shook as June helped her with the nails.

The time approached three in the morning. Life in Las Vegas went on 24/7, but mostly indoors at this hour, and there were fewer people in the streets. The girls wore their dresses like always, but had made some crucial changes, among them discarded the high-heeled shoes. They wore running shoes, now, and were instantly far more mobile. June carried a club under the coat.

Elizabeth's night vision still worked. Crossing from the neon lit streets and into shadow her eyes adapted instantly. The shades didn't hamper her in any way.

– Your eyes are big as silver dollars, June giggled. – If we encountered cops right now, they would think you were on something.

– I'm different, Elizabeth said. – I will always be different, no matter what.

And she couldn't and wouldn't conceal the pleased tone in her voice.

Sue Ellen carried her coat on her arm. The dress's cleft was extra wide. Almost half the rounding was visible. The make-up was slightly overdone to make her skin even paler than it was. She looked and was quite vulnerable.

They waited, in the darkness a fair distance from the casino. Many left, but they left in cars or taxis or were found either too big or too small.

– We've got time, Elizabeth instructed her charges. – We can wait nights for our perfect prey.

The impatience raged within her, the tongue almost falling out of her mouth, like that of a dog.

Finally, when they had almost given up hope a well-fed man without bodyguards, boiling with arrogance and self-importance crossed the road. Like predators they smelled their prey.

– Him, Elizabeth nodded.

She felt the hunting instinct tear at her insides, awake in the wild parts of the brain, but she didn't need June's hand on the shoulder to restrain herself.

The man approached with a steady rhythm of steps, a casual walk. June frowned, shook her head and sent big sister an apologetic smile. She comforted Susie and whispered in her ear.

They stepped out from hiding, with Susie in the middle, and revealed themselves to him.

– Hi, man! Elizabeth called scornfully to him.

– Beat it! He growled. – I'm not interested.

– Not in something… special either?

They pushed Susie forward. He stopped and cruel eyes focused on the girl sucking on her thumb. The other two had worked well with her. The big man licked his lips, suddenly very interested.

– No one has touched her?

– No one! Elizabeth confirmed. – If you doubt my words… an experienced man such as yourself can easily call a bluff, am I right?

They bent her forward and stuck up her butt, lifted her dress, revealing the white, stocking-free thighs. The man stepped forward and stuck a hand into her cunt. A huge, expectant smile spread on his face.

– And what about you two?

– We're available, if that's your choice.

He shrugged and nodded, hardly able to contain himself.

– Hundred, in advance, June said, holding out a hand.

The negotiations would continue upon arrival, he knew that, but didn't care. It wasn't a matter of money, not to him.

– Okay, okay. He nodded and peeled off a bill from a thick roll.

June closed her hand around the large, green bill and put it down between her breasts.

– We live over there. The hand with the ring pointed to a dark block. – We can walk around if you're… anxious.

He grinned and stated with sickening satisfaction:

– You girls can feel perfectly at ease. Only lunatics tired of life will even think of robbing me.

Even though they didn't let him see it, they once again felt uncertainty rise to a potent level. There could be more to anyone than what met the eye, they knew that.

Then he grabbed Elizabeth in the arm, and it was too late. He laughed harshly as she whimpered in his hard grip.

– Give us a kiss, he grinned to her. – You're the big girl. Show us what you can do.

They reached the deep shadows then, and in that very moment she struck him as hard as she was able in his belly. He bent forward, and she rejoiced. June hit his neck with the club. He fell and hit the ground hard. She hit him again, wild and without mercy. She kept striking him until he no longer moved. Elizabeth pulled the thick roll of bills from his pocket.

Sue Ellen stood there frozen, staring at the unmoving man on the ground.

– We must *go!* Elizabeth grabbed her.

– It's the Police Chief, Sue Ellen said quietly.

That stopped the other two. They looked incredulous down at the man.

– Yeah, June nodded. – I remember now. He was in the news. There were allegations of ties to organized crime, to the mafia.

June looked up first. She stared at her sister. Her voice didn't quiver.

– He got a good look at us. We must kill him.

– No, not kill. Elizabeth shook her head, closing her hand around the roll of bills. – We move on, we leave this fucking hole of a city.

They fled, but not without looking back.

Back to the motel, gathering their few, modest belongings. The helpless rage stayed with Elizabeth the entire time as they sneaked through the shadows out of the city. Once again fate had caught up with them. Of all the people they had thought of robbing, they had to choose the worst possible target, yet another power hungry man using the law to crush others. The irony was almost too much.

At a gas station and tavern by the highway they sneaked inside a truck. There was no way they could take being discovered by the driver at this point, and they hid in the back, in a wet and drafty room he probably used as a kind of toilet, the way it reeked of shit.

That was how they left Las Vegas, Nevada.

3

In the tree on the branch above the river sat a sixteen-year old girl. The wind turned the water in South Platte River black. The light of the pale afternoon sun was reflected in the relatively newly painted white house behind her. She watched her eyes in the water. They didn't reflect the sun, not more than the horrible ring stone did. She stared down river to the spot where it made a turn.

The three girls had arrived Denver on Interstate 70 a week ago, on December fourth. To Elizabeth it felt like they had arrived at the journey's true goal, as if it was all preordained. They had traveled through Utah, the Mormon state, an experience not exactly making them friendlier inclined towards religion. It had been hell for her, and for Sue Ellen - Susie - it had reminded her of all the long years in what had been, for all intents and purposes captivity, what she had now put behind her. To save most of the money until finding a place to settle down, they had lied and stolen throughout the entire state. They had just about crossed the mountains when a violent snowstorm had begun and blocked all the mountain passes.

June had shown no particular emotions. Little sister had changed rapidly lately. She had taken the lead in many ways, far more resolute than her older sister, that didn't feel very resolute at all these days. It was June that had suggested they kill the Police Chief, a fact Elizabeth didn't allow herself to forget.

Elizabeth had studied little sister's eyes to see if there was any change, but there wasn't. Except for the fact that the girl was growing up, there was no outward sign of her change.

June was the beauty of the family, that's for sure, more so for every passing day. She was a late bloomer, but now she bloomed in full. That unmotivated thought sent, for some reason shivers through Elizabeth's body.

Elizabeth sat there barefoot, completely dressed in black, in pants and top only. She was freezing. Grabbing her shoulders and rubbing them intensively didn't really help much. She jumped down in an attempt to get some heat in her body. It did her no good, of course. She got snow on her feet and turned even colder.

She studied her feet. They were kinda bluish, but there were no signs of frostbite.

Hot, cold, it didn't really matter. She hadn't been sick a day in her entire life, not even had an ordinary cold. She knew of no one on her mother's side that had.

She danced towards the house in an in vain attempt to cheer herself up. Covered in snow the garden seemed ghostly and barren. They had, to the best of their ability attempted to do further repairs on the house, both outdoors and indoors, but it couldn't be too much of that until spring. And she didn't believe it would count for much then, because they would no longer be here. They had money, now, but even at minimum expenditure their «fortune» vanished like snow… in spring. At this speed they would be broke in a month. She was certain, knew there were ways to increase their amount of money without high risk, but the inertia hadn't left her. She felt so helpless. They would have to steal again, and they would have to run - again.

Wet eyes blinked. She halted in her tracks, and there it was again, the creature without face and body and soul and blood. She was back in the basement, and it was there with her. There was a whimper, as she fought to regain her composure, her sense of Self. She raised a fist, the ring hand against it, against anyone that was against her.

– I won't give up, she said softly.

It started snowing again, so hard that the flakes felt like hail. She fought herself forward, against the wind, towards the house. The sun was gone.

4

The next day they received their first visitors. After breakfast they went outside to shuffle snow from the stairs and driveway. They had kept it going long enough to get red blossom cheeks when they discovered two men making their way from the forest. The three girls suddenly felt very vulnerable. Elizabeth detested the feeling, but there it was, making her breathless, turning her stomach inside out. She turned halfway around, scrutinizing them.

Both filled out their clothes and looked very fit. The tallest filled out a little too well, being fond of cookies, she surmised. They were familiar, but she couldn't place them. She turned completely, facing them. Both shook, and she realized why.

– We heard people had moved in here, one of them said hesitatingly. – We thought it was Ted…

– A quite understandable mistake, the other said. The forced cheerful tone didn't conceal the intensity of his being. – You're Liz, right?

– I am, she confirmed. – This is June and Sue Ellen.

– I'm Frank Forester, the tall one said. – This is Eric Carr. We…

Frank looked at Carr for support, but Eric just kept staring intensively at Elizabeth.

– Now, I recognize you, she said happily, and filled with sudden expectation. – Come inside. There's *so* much you can tell us.

They put down the shuffles and led on into the house, all of them looking tentatively at each other.

– I'm so excited about meeting you, guys, June said, flirting with lowered eyelashes and stance. – I've read everything I could find about the collective and your time in London.

Sue Ellen didn't say anything. She stood half turned away, clearly embarrassed by the intense scrutiny everybody subjected each other to.

Elizabeth fell into brooding, letting little sister take control. She thought about the airport, Stapleton, how close it was, how close she had been to give pride the foot in the butt it deserved, and fuck Stewart, and his grim tidings, and head for London… and Ted and Tilla. But she recalled vividly the sense of terror, the clear warning he had conveyed to her, he had instilled in her, and she stayed put.

June played the host, the sweet and engaged young girl. Elizabeth fell deeper into passivity and despair.

They sat in the deep chairs in the warm and cozy living room. The day passed incredibly fast. Eric and Frank told tales from the collective. About the physical and mental training, *preparation* there. About Ted and Tilla. About Linda. About what Frank's mother and stepfather had done. About the terror. When they had threatened Iris' child. Sir Wolcott, the proof of where the authorities stood in this matter. In this matter, too.

– You should teach us, as you did them, the dark one told Eric.

It wasn't a request, but a royal command. His eyes focused even harder on her.

– They have all the forces of the established society against them, Frank said, this fact clearly weighing heavily on his mind. – It will be a miracle if they don't fold under the pressure. And I haven't been able to help them much. I'm afraid my mother has me by the balls, and that situation won't change anytime soon.

There was laughter, with him, not of him.

Forester senior had written a secret passage in his will, what was for all practical purposes a profit clause. If Frank invested in «unprofitable projects» and lost money over time, Regina could take over the administrative duties and privileges of the firm and fortune for a year. This could happen time and time again for as long as she lived.

– I would like to meet her, Elizabeth said, giving Frank a wink.

She felt his eyes on her and smiled innocently. She felt Eric's eyes on her as well, and they penetrated her.

It was time for dinner. It was delayed because they had so much to talk about, and they felt the first hunger pangs. No one remained by the table, screaming for the food to arrive, but helped in its progression. Frank realized that Sue Ellen stared at him, and smiled uncertain to her.

– Sorry for staring, she said shyly, – but I'm not used to men helping in the cooking or doing anything in the house.

– Neither am I, really, he grinned, with a touch of gallows humor. – Even if my dear mother never did much. But in the collective we quickly cleared up such misunderstandings.

They all laughed together. It was all in all remarkable how they enjoyed each other's company, since they, after all, had never met until a few hours earlier.

– My father is a very strict and intolerant and ignorant little man, and if he can find me, society still give him legal power over me, and he will have that for two more years

Elizabeth shuddered. That also held true for her, and even more for June, concerning their father. And considering how cowed Trudy had been when they left, she would probably not voice any objection to whatever Eugene did during any circumstances.

And the girl felt vulnerable again, and scared and very young.

The five of them sat down by the table in the living room. The large bed that Linsey had moved down here, that the girls shared was still here, but there was no lack of space. The living room was quite large.

– Great place this, Frank commented.

– Yes, isn't it? Elizabeth looked around excitedly, with shiny eyes. – So filled with mood, shade and mystery.

– Great food, too, Eric acknowledged. – My regards to the chef.

There was more laughter. It came easy, unrestrained.

The two sisters focused their attention on Eric, though. He had a very expressive voice. His face didn't betray *anything,* but his voice was… His voice revealed a lot.

– Not that I'm complaining, Eric, June said sweetly, – but what are you doing in this great city? It can't be that much to write about, and you've even been here for quite a while.

– There's a lot here, Carr assured her. – At least to me.

– Eric is writing the Great Novel, Frank cautiously cut in.

– Oh, that sounds worthy of attention, June kept at it, – what is it about?

– Stewart called it the Tapestry, Carr replied. – That's just as good a name for it as anything else.

– It's about *him*. Elizabeth suddenly got very intense, too.

– About them, Eric said. – About you all, really. About the Janus Clan, past, present and future. About destiny and fate and coincidences and how it all mix, about how distant butterfly wings can eventually whip up a storm.

He hesitated.

– It's all happening so easily. I've never written so effortlessly before. The book is practically writing itself. I just lack some crucial background material.

– About us, perhaps, but you, too. Elizabeth told him. – You've been involved for a long time, at the very least since you met Patrick. Perhaps that's why you're so taken in by it all. *You must know*.

And he didn't take his eyes off her.

A dark day turned to a black evening. Not even the white snow seemed to have any influence on the eternal night. Eric didn't take his eyes off Elizabeth. She followed his every step.

They danced in the snow, the five of them. Frank, June and Susie wore shoes. Elizabeth and Eric didn't. It was show and tell. Eric moved, and they moved with him. It began like a series of clumsy moves, but he showed them, showed the three girls how to move, how to dance, how to dance death. Elizabeth moved in on him, but he avoided her easily and gave her a light tap on the jaw, and blood filled her mouth, and she smelled its sweet flavor. She made a murderous charge with her foot, but he avoided that, too.

– Learning the moves is fairly easy, he told them. – It's like learning how the pieces move in chess or the rules of poker. Learn only that, and you haven't really learned anything. The truly valuable information comes later, as your body, your very self learns, and is eventually able to move, to play, to dance instinctively, without conscious thought, without thinking, without reasoning, except in the most rudimentary way.

His intensity hammered them, taught them, and he found willing students, because they all, like him and Frank had their own experiences of pain and hatred and passion.

He showed them, shared his reality with them, shoved it down their throats and they learned, because it was their own reality, what they had learned intimately from an early age.

– And beyond reason, beyond thought, beyond everything is the most basic of truths. He sang his shrill song. – Beyond reality, beyond manifestation is perception, is the Shadow, the tapestry of reality…

Sue Ellen stood on one foot, doing the practicing, moving her arms, stumbling, standing, moving.

– Focus, he shouted quietly to her. – You're flesh, but you're also beyond flesh. Your body is an instrument. It's not the player. The player is You, peeled to your essence, independent of physical reality. This is who we are.

Elizabeth stood on her toes, repeating his words, doing his words, his thoughts, making them her own, stumbling, standing, dancing.

They returned inside. But the words and what they evoked remained within them, whispered and roared within Elizabeth. She sat in front of the fireplace, striving to deal with the pain, attempting to defrost her ice-blocks of feet as the sensitivity slowly returned to her skin. Eric stood by the window, still barefooted, seemingly totally unfazed after hours in the snow.

Susie hesitated, but finally and determined she walked to him. He turned to meet her, silent as a ghost.

– This is SO fantastic, she cried excitedly, gratefully to him. – I can feel myself *awaken*. I can't even begin to describe what it means to me. Thank you. THANK YOU!

– You're welcome, he replied dryly. – But any teacher worth his mold teaches himself as well as others, so it's really nothing but petty self-interest…

– You're funny, too, she joked back, surprising herself with her daring and forwardness.

They stood there for a while in silence. He had turned back towards the window.

– What are you doing? She wondered.

For a while, for several seconds it seemed like he wouldn't answer her, but then he did.

– I stare into the darkness in hope of seeing the fire. Stare long and hard enough, and you will see it.

He smiled a bit, and turned back towards her again, touching her jaw, very charming.

– Tell me, have you known Liz and June long?

– I've been Liz' classmate since first grade, but no, I haven't really known them for more than a few months. It feels like forever, though. It's been the *best* time of my life.

– My bet would indeed be that you've experienced a lot…

He formed it as a kind of question. They stood a bit away from the others, very convenient. Sue Ellen glanced at Liz, correctly interpreting her indiscreet cough.

– I wonder how you can stay here for so long, she cleverly, desperately, close to hysteria turned the conversation. – Have you borrowed money or something?

He sighed, relenting.

– I'm freelancing these days, he explained. – I don't want to work for a single employer anymore, but for some reason they're absolutely wild about my articles and stories anyway. I think I could have written about a rock in a rock bed, or sand in the desert for that matter, and they would still print it. Incredible. I'm enjoying my ass off these days.

And then casually, before she managed to put a word in:

– What about you? Money is scarce, isn't it?

– We stole and robbed ourselves throughout the entire state of Utah, Elizabeth broke in calmly. – In any way we could.

She realized fully what Eric was truly after. He had spent a lot of time with Mark and Ted, and he did see the Tapestry, and was chasing the missing pieces like a dog in heat. Sue Ellen was a lousy liar, an amateur when it came to prodding and cloak and dagger conversation. She would Fuck Up in minutes, if not less.

He came to her, as she knew he would.

She was flipping through the old photo album.

– Old memories? He wondered.

– The Tapestry, she threw back at him, making him wince.

She turned the pages slowly, letting him see. He reacted like she did, at the sight of the two pictures burned into her memory. That of Linda and the two brothers, and the other of the five where Linda wasn't with them.

– Why isn't Linda with you? Do you remember?

– Nope. She shook her head.

– Let me see if I get this right, he began. – Linda isn't the brothers' sister, but she's your cousin. Your father and her mother are brother and sister.

– Half brother and sister, she grinned, not bothering to hide that she was teasing him, leading him on.

– On the other hand, you and the brothers are obviously closely related. Stewart implied that they are the sons of one of your mother's lost brothers. Are they?

– Your guess is as good as mine, she shrugged, feigning an indifference she was a long way from feeling.

– And what about the picture missing in front?

He kept speaking as if she hadn't spoken at all.

– I've wondered about that myself, she told him bluntly. – I've never seen it. I wish I had.

She rose, handed him the album, and headed for the kitchen.

– Feel free to browse to your heart's content. She stopped in the door. – You *will* tell me if you find anything of importance, right?

He threw the album away without bothering to check where it landed. June saved it from the fireplace in the nick of time. He hurried after Elizabeth without looking left or right.

She stopped in the hallway, by the stairs. He closed the door behind him. They were alone. She turned and faced him.

– Sit down, she told him huskily.

– Why? He responded curtly.

– Hush, she whispered, and put a finger on his lips.

He sat down on the next to lowest step.

She sat down on her heels, and grabbed one of his feet. She began rubbing it in fast, furious moves.

– You're so cold, she said weakly.

– It's nothing, he said indifferently, rejecting her plea, her opening statement.

She slipped forward, letting herself fall on her knees, partly into his lap. Soft lips touched his, feather light, giving him a touch, just a touch of the delights to come.

– It seems to me that you're also very much in the dark concerning your origin, he said.

He meant that he was also very interested in her origin.

You fool, she chided him in her thoughts. You easy to read fool.

– You're making me out to be a very mysterious person, she laughed softly, while touching his cheek. – I like that.

She smiled enticingly to him, very conscious of how attractive she was. She sensed a fire in him she desired. And she knew now she could twist him around her little finger any time she wanted, so it didn't matter whether he knew or not.

– Nothing of this will ever reach print, he said furiously, shaking her, madness lit in his eyes. – I just have to know. *I must understand.*

A cough. Frank had torn open the door.

Eric released her and sent Frank an ugly stare. In a flash he had grabbed his coat and disappeared out the door - without his shoes on. Elizabeth shook her head in wonder.

– My hero, she said to Frank from the floor, displaying herself willfully.

– What was wrong with him? Frank lent towards the wall, quite stricken.

– He took on more than he could handle, she said graciously to him from the floor, giving him a look that turned his face tomato red.

She wriggled her butt and writhed her body sensually as she walked ahead back to the living room. It felt so good, so good to… let go. Sue Ellen looked astonished at her. June with something akin to admiration. June the virgin and the apparent innocent. Elizabeth wondered if little sister had played a game since early childhood to better gain advantages. She wondered if June had ever fought the horrible she carried within. Elizabeth had, and she was sick and tired of it. It felt so much better… to let go. The will to resist had withered through the years of suffering and pressure, and now it was gone. She realized she was about to lose.

5

There were no signs of June's eyes changing. There just weren't.

– You're curious, June said solemnly, catching her in staring. – I can understand that. I'm quite curious myself.

The cemetery field was ice-cold. The trees' naked branches cut through the two of them like black blades in the night, hardly seen, but clearly felt. To Elizabeth's overactive imagination they resembled burned out skeletons.

The tombstones were all covered in snow… except his. The simple writing had faded a lot. No one had looked after the stone in the four years since the funeral.

MICHAEL COUSIN 1952 - 1971

She didn't feel much one way or another, except for the weird tingling in her back.

– How can you stand it? June inquired.

– Excuse me?

– How can you hold out all the… the bad stuff without crumbling, without falling apart?

Little sister didn't seem very observant here. Elizabeth had feared she would crumble quite a bit lately.

– Sometimes I just want to curl up in bed and tune everything out, but that isn't a solution. There isn't really any alternative to *not* do that, so I just keep going.

There was a catch in her throat she couldn't hide.

And she felt watched. There was no other explanation for the tingling, and the strong desire to turn and look behind her.

She felt cut off from everything. It was a feeling she got a lot in cities, but here it was worse than ever.

They spotted a man by the gate. He approached them openly, without any sort of guile. A small man in black pants and leather jacket, wearing a rather gigantic scarf around his neck. The association that the two girls looked at a rat, a large and nasty rat was almost inevitable. There was something in his appearance, beyond his appearance, somewhere in the sticking eyes that actually gave Elizabeth the creeps.

– I bring a message, he told them in a quirky way.

– What message? June replied angrily, to mask the fear.

– To Ted Warren. Tell him that the time of reckoning is coming.

Elizabeth knew instantly what this was about. She experienced both fear and anticipation.

– Go to London and tell him yourself, she replied calmly, adding as much sarcasm as she could muster. – You don't think he's hiding in the house while us three defenseless girls are exposing ourselves openly, do you?

He studied her.

– Perhaps you're telling the truth, he eventually said, grinning sickly. – Perhaps not. But it will still prove interesting with three girls in the house.

He left them, leaving a place even deader than he was the same way he had entered it.

– That was Ray Channon, Elizabeth told her sister, visibly shaking.

– I know, June nodded, very pale. – Keith Lampard's sniveling lackey. Ted ruined Lampard's hand beyond repair, and he's now using a metal hand with a hook.

The sisters left the cemetery in a hurry. But there was no relief outside the stone fence, no respite from the terror ravaging them.

They hurried to Eric's house. Elizabeth didn't want to go inside. They talked to Eric on the stairs, witnessing how his lips stretched into thin lines.

– This isn't good, he said. – Lampard and Channon are bad news. They would be, even without their prevalent power base in this town. They can command hundreds of eager lackeys if need be.

If he wanted to intimidate her further, he succeeded quite admirably. She strived to pull herself together, to not reveal the emotions terrorizing her inner self.

– I can keep an eye on the house now and then, he suggested. – That might deter them, at least initially, until something can be done.

– That's mighty generous of you, sir, she replied and gave him her sweetest smile.

She hated him, hated herself, filled with contempt for the sniveling, dependent creature inside.

They sent him more grateful smiles and waved as they walked away, as they headed home the fastest they could.

She sat in front of the fireplace, unable to be get rid of the cold stuck in her. She sat close enough for her hairs to be singed, but it did no good.

– So, what do we choose for dinner today? Sue Ellen asked brightly, putting up a brave front.
– I'll be having dinner at the Farley Mansion with Frank and his mother in an hour, Elizabeth said. – A car will come and pick me up shortly. You two will just have to make it without me today.
– Good going, sister, June nodded, more admiration visible in her twinkling eyes.
There wasn't much talk after that, mostly generalities and one-syllable words. The car appeared in the driveway at the stroke of five, exactly as promised. The two girls embraced her as she left.
– You have a good time, now, you hear, sweet little sister told her.
– I intend to, stern big sister assured her.
Elizabeth approached the car. The driver waited for her and opened the door for her. She liked that, couldn't help it, and she sent him a reward, a gracious smile.
The car moved, through Southern Denver, and headed north, closer to the city. The drive wasn't long, but she made sure she enjoyed every second of it. The seat felt so soft, so comfortable. She stroked a palm over the fabric, sensing the texture as if it was living skin.
Farley Mansion was far bigger than the Cornwall's modest summer castle. After his marriage with the Forester widow Farley had added another wing, making it one of the biggest and most stately buildings in the Rockies.
Elizabeth was received by a whole set of servants. They took her coat. They welcomed her with all kinds of obvious and non-obvious honors.
And she enjoyed it.
Regina received her in the inner hall. Like a queen she took the girl's hand.
Elizabeth curtseyed before her.
– Cut that out, Regina barked. – We both know you're not the usual empty-headed hen. You're not like the other chicks he's brought home.
– No, I'm not. Eyes cleared and the girl straightened.
– Your excellent perception can take you far, the queen said, while holding the girl's eyes. – I know we'll get along just fine. As long as you know who's the boss.
– I know. A nod. – I've got time. I can wait.
– I rather thought so, the older woman nodded pleased. – Come; let's see how you handle yourself and the fool of my son.
Kent Farley and Frank had already gathered at the table. Farley was an impressive man in his early forties. With his hair combed back and his long nose there was something hawkish about him. Elizabeth felt even

smaller when she shook his hand. She kissed Frank on the cheek, and sat down quietly.

Regina clapped her hands, and the servants brought in the food. Elizabeth studied it all, every minor movement and mimic. The working relationship between the man and the wife was very clear. Farley ruled outside these walls, but inside the house the Queen was all-powerful.

In some ways it was very subtle, in others painfully obvious.

The dinner did have a certain solemn quality. Elizabeth was quite cheerful about it all, but she didn't show it. She was so meek that she wanted to cry. Naturally there was no open subservience to Regina. She did respond in kind to Regina's scornful comments and attack to impress Frank, and he rejoiced. But she never crossed the line his mother had made for decent behavior. She was humble, but not servile. She was ashamed, but did everything for the Queen to be pleased with her.

There was so much she couldn't say or do. She was unused to restrain herself this way. No one could be favored by Regina without compromising herself, without major concession of self. She felt like a fly in a spider's web, so very helpless and timid.

When the over-the-top dinner was done Regina rose with a generous smile.

– Now, my dear Kent, I believe we should retire and leave the ground to these outstanding youths.

Farley rose and took her hand. They left in a very controlled walk. Frank released a hardly audible sigh.

Regina turned half through the door.

– This was quite enjoyable, Liz, she noted, very patronizing. – You're such a sweet girl. We must do it again some time. How about we meet one day without the men and give each other our piece of mind?

The girl smiled brightly. She knew Regina was pleased with her.

– Thank you, I would like that *very* much.

Regina vanished into the hall, but she didn't go away.

– What was that about? Frank wondered.

– Oh, your mother is just curious, Liz dismissed it. – She wants to control all aspects of your life. You know that.

Regina was present everywhere, in the very house itself, her spirit visible in every piece of furniture and commodity. She had seen fit to tell the girl that she had personally seen to the redecoration in every little room in the building, in the palace. And as Liz followed Frank around, looking at all the wealth, all the power her eyes turned all shiny and wet.

– Let's go a place where the walls' ears aren't that big, Frank said brusquely.

They went to the lower floor, where he had his office. It was quite the simple décor, modest and functional compared to the rest of the palace. He pulled up a big key from his pocket and rolled aside the heavy carpet under the desk. On the naked floor there was a hatch. He unlocked and opcned it while putting a finger to his lips, revealing a fairly spacey hole. There was only one item there, something resembling a transmitter. He pulled it up, and began pacing around the room, directing the instrument against walls, ceiling, floor, furniture and shelves, and even some distance outside the room. He was clearly relieved when he closed the door behind him.

– No bugs, he stated. When he saw her incredulous visage he added: – Believe me, she's making sure they're put everywhere. It's quite the effort tracing them.

They sat down on the couch. She studied him, openly, frankly, making him blush again. He hadn't lost all the fat he had reportedly once had, but it was so scant that you wouldn't know about it unless you knew about his rather bloated past.

He took her hands, abnormally brave. A jolt shot through her nerves.

– I've done everything in my power to help the collective with money, he began, after a rather roundabout session of small talk. – It's hopeless. She has blocked all my options of direct withdrawal of cash. I can buy things for limited amounts, but it's just a pee in the ocean compared to what they need. Fortunately it's sufficient to help you girls over the worst, but aside from that she's… got me.

– It can't be that bad. She crawled up on the couch and began rubbing his neck. – You just need to be patient. In less than a year you're in control again.

– It isn't that simple. He jumped up in an abrupt move. – When the year is up it is I that have to prove I'm fit to run the company and administer the fortune. And I'm willing to bet my last cent that she has bribed people on all levels. And if I against all odds should succeed she might regain it at any time. If I could just… strangle her, but that's impossible, impossible to get away with. She has left everything to me, that… dragon. They won't even bother with a formal trial.

He was almost touching in his trust. He had even touched upon his fears that women only wanted him for the money.

– Next time you'll be prepared, she told him. – Next time you'll have her by the balls.

He ploughed his hand through his hair, pulling himself together.

– You're right, of course. We will vanquish her and that shit Kent.

He squeezed her hands, and it felt so good.

– There's something you should know, he said, – something everybody should know.

He let go of her, and got on his feet, pacing back and forth a bit, before continuing.

– I overheard a conversation between Regina and Kent a few days ago. It confirmed what I had already heard from several sources… about events brewing in «your» valley. They've got business interests there.

The tingling increased. She knew what he was going to say before he said it.

– The two of them, with local forces and other investors plan to turn the valley into an enormous amusement park and industrial park combined. A kind of center supposed to be self-sufficient, where people will work and live practically without moving. A place where there are only a few steps from their apartment to their workplace, where the leaders will have full control over production and the workers' life. They've used every dirty trick in the book, from extortion to financial pressure, to force previous owners to sell or give up their property. They control banks and can thereby control loans. They've sabotaged the daily run of the farms, terrorized people that wouldn't give in. Perhaps they're even killing people for all I know…

Kennedy's land abandoned. All the others… It had to be true.

Probable.

– And that will be quite profitable, I gather?

– Precisely, he said enraged, not registering the touch of interest and excitement in her voice, probably figuring she was being ironic. – They'll make themselves even richer and more powerful by stamping on you and many others, and they'll never stop. Their kind never does. Only public opinion and outrage might be able to stop them. The politicians can't or won't. We need to publish everything, but we also need solid proof for as many of their «misdeeds» as possible. This is the wave of the future, Liz, the very dream of the industrial overlords, a barren place where *generations* will suffer, and if we don't stop it here, it will spread everywhere.

She made the driver stop down the road and walked the final stretch home through the dark forest. She sensed the now so familiar eyes burn in her back. Whoever was following her wasn't from the biker's gang. They wouldn't have concealed themselves, but on the contrary made sure they were seen to intimidate her. It was the same person that had watched them at the cemetery. He she hadn't seen, but only sensed. The Observer. She had retraced her steps in the snow once, in an effort to track him, but all trace of him had ended in heavily trafficked public streets. She imagined she heard silent laughter. But it was a living human being, a physical body.

June waited for her on the stairs.

– I sensed you were coming, little sister said. – It was like a buzz growing louder in my head. The day was successful, I take it?

– Quite so, Elizabeth nodded. – So many possibilities opened up to me, so many options of Power, even if my powers should never return.

And the expression in June's eyes made her just marginally uneasy.

They walked inside and Sue Ellen waited for them. There were food and wine. More food and wine. Elizabeth drank, and in spite of the distinct burning in her stomach, the alcohol affected her less than ever.

She held out her hand. Studied the ring thoroughly. It was faint, but it wasn't a mirage or wishful thinking. She looked in triumph at the two girls.

The ring stone glowed.

6

They trained with Eric or alone or the three of them together. The three bodies were hardly visible as more than a whirl in the snow, touching, not touching each other. She whispered Eric's teaching to the air. The three of them echoed them, like a mantra.

– We've become *lethal*. Sue Ellen fought to breathe and speak. – And in such a short time. Eric is such a *fantastic* teacher.

And there was intoxication and hunger even in her voice.

They heard Eric speak.

– Your progress will seem almost miraculous at first, because you've taken the critical step towards self-awareness, and that is always crucial. Muscles and parts of the mind hardly in use awaken…

Elizabeth actually sensed it, felt what happened in every cell, every time she moved. She had run through the wilderness for years, but this was different, another sort of realization. Speed and balance… liberated her.

– It's easy to see why he's so right about this, she told her two charges. – We live our lives asleep, and once awakened it's like a waterfall of understanding.

One day she knew Farley and Frank were gone she went to Regina. The Queen was on her way out in her Rolls Royce. The girl was waved into the luxurious vehicle.

– Liz, the woman said, – so nice of you to come.

– I've been looking forward to it, the girl mumbled, while half curtseying, half stepping into the car's wide backseat.

She wondered where they were going, but were wise enough not to ask, focusing her attention at the older, regal woman.

Everything was huge here. The car's interior gave her the impression of a small living room. The windows, which was black from the outside revealed a wide panorama from the inside. She looked through the back window and caught a glimpse of Farley Mansion as it disappeared around the curve.

– A stately view, isn't it?

– Yes, Mrs. Farley.

– Call me «mother», sweetheart. A pat on the hand. – You might not be able to marry my son until you're eighteen, but it's pretty clear it will eventually be official, isn't it, my dear?

Liz understood what she meant, in the subtext between her words.

– Yes, mother. She smiled. – I'm keeping him at a distance, and he grows more eager every day. I'll soon have him exactly where I want him, mother.

The car made a turn, towards the central parts of Denver, to the tall business buildings. The skyscrapers, the heavenly houses, where humans were piled upon each other and stocked sideways like cattle. The girl shook imperceptibly. Because of that and the Queen's presence.

– Excellent. Regina moved closer to her. – I understand my patient search is done. I've waited a long time for you, Liz. You have no idea how long. I will teach you, you see. Add my knowledge to your nascent baby steps. Because there's a lot to learn. My family has married to larger and larger fortunes through the centuries. We've always been the perfect climbers. So imagine my horror over having given birth to such a good-for-nothing son. He does have a certain talent, admittedly, but need someone to polish it. He needs you, my beyond talented girl. Your family doesn't have any fortune worth mentioning, but you have other virtues that are just as valuable.

Liz sat there and nodded, eagerly listening to the lesson.

– Poor Frank. He walks around in a dream state all day. You've certainly made an impression on him. I believe you might influence him in similar ways I did with his father. He was also quite soft in his youth.

That made Liz cold to the bone. Thomas Forester, one of the highest-ranking members of the Abraxas Omega, a devil in human form. She couldn't picture any similarity between him and his son, but they *were* father and son. Frank had some parents, all right. She wondered if not at least some of it had to taint him, making him susceptible to his inheritance.

Like she herself obviously was to hers.

She wanted to leave the car, wanted to throw herself out even though it was moving. But she had no more places to run. She realized that, and remained seated.

Regina grabbed her arm.

– You do want to learn, right?

– Yes, mother. Of course I d-do. You know that!

– That's my girl. Your teaching begins this second. What you've picked up so far is hardly more than half-cried glimpses of the real thing. I was on my way to my friends' party anyway. It's boring as hell, but you'll learn the hard way. First we must make a detour to get you some adequate clothes, though. You can't make a house call to the city's elite in your poor man clothes.

The girl looked guiltily down at her simple dark fabric and nodded in agreement, admiring Regina's elegant, expensive threads.

They parked in the garage inside an exclusive shopping mall. The driver opened the door for them.

– I can get used to this, she giggled, and nodded mercifully to him.

There were guards dressed in livery there instantly, meeting them, receiving them like royalty, leading them the short stretch to the elevator, taking care of everything.

Even down here the walls were covered in expensive oak panels. There were red carpets from all parking spaces and to the elevator. Merely the act of cleaning them probably cost a fortune.

Nothing was said. One of the guards, servants pushed a button on the outside and the door closed and the elevator headed upwards. When the doors once again opened, a polite, servile woman met them, one fully aware that this customer could have her fired in a second. By a stroke of the hand or a phone call.

– Good afternoon, Mrs. Farley, she greeted the customer submissively, but engaged. – What can we do to help you today?

– A full treatment, Brigitte, of my sweet companion here. It's quite necessary, I'm afraid.

– I see what you mean, Mrs. Farley. Will you both come with me, please?

Brigitte attempted in vain to hide the fact that she reacted like most people - both men and women - with at least mild shock upon encountering Liz for the first time.

The woman led them further inside the establishment. It turned ever more luxurious the longer they advanced into the gilded castle. They were in a kind of hall. There were no clothes on display here. Along the wall there were large, separate rooms where Liz could glimpse other people.

Aside from that it all reminded her in a sick way of one of the haunted houses or castles she had seen in horror movies. They were led inside one of the largest «cubicles». Their guide snapped her fingers and a flock of girls flowed towards them.

It all happened with overwhelming efficiency and style. Liz was grabbed from all sides, measured and prodded from head to toe. They began undressing her. She resisted a bit at first, but then she relented and let them do their thing. They undressed her completely, removing every little piece of clothing. She cast bashful glances around her. She, who had never been shy, felt herself blush in shame.

The guide studied her, pointing a bit here, pinching a bit there.

– We'll take care of it, the woman said. – Take care of everything. One skin impurity here, one there, until they're no longer visible, leaving only soft, unblemished skin.

The very young and vulnerable girl could see herself in the many mirrors. The girls squeezed and patted her, some hands more invasive than others. They made her feel hot and queasy, but she knew Regina wouldn't stand for any exposure of the discomfort she experienced. With practiced ease they lifted her up, and put her on a table. They bathed her with wet cloths, did her hair in a wash by the table's head, removed her many body hairs, and finally oiled her. She bit her lower lip when a hand got too close to her weak, weak spot. They made all her moves. There was nothing left of her but the puppet dancing in strings. She felt very much like a pet being prepared for an exhibition.

It took time, everything did. She was fed as well. They did everything for her. She chewed and swallowed without really tasting the food and fluid they put in her mouth.

She tried on dresses, a long, long row of them. And jackets and pants, the works. Not once did they ask her what she thought. They only discussed between themselves and with Regina, of course. They moved according to Regina in everything, orbiting her sphere.

– The clothes are great, aren't they?

– Yes, mother, she heard herself whisper.

And she had never even seen such clothes before, far less been near them or worn them.

Regina spoke to her in a constant flow of words, instructing her in etiquette and proper conduct, without giving her a second's break. It was so calming, so seductive, and Liz found herself unable to resist the mesmerizing voice.

– You will not curtsey for those we meet, not even for older people. That's out these days. Only servants do that. But there are rules to be heeded and obeyed, of course. You don't lead on in the conversation between adults. You won't speak until being encouraged to do so. You may well joke, but not about certain serious subjects.

The girl looked at her teacher, now, but only politely, attentively.

– Politics is an okay subject to joke about. As long as the joke is at radicals and liberals' expense. Criticizing the arms' race is a big no, no. And you can't mention the poverty.

– So there is poverty? Liz wondered.

– Don't be cute, beauty. To be a realist is certainly a strength, but only if you follow my lead. You see, some of those we will encounter are stupid enough to feel guilty about the state of the world, over the way the sheep is shepherded.

– Yes, mother. The girl lowered her eyes.

– Such striking eyes, Brigitte said when they had put the girl in the make-up chair. – But we should mute them somewhat, mute them quite a bit. Them… and everything around them.

There was no longer any mirror for Liz to see herself. It was just the thousand eyes studying her, nodding in appreciation of their work. They were almost done. Only the final touch remained. She sensed the brushes and pencils, but it didn't feel like they touched her skin at all, only a reasonable facsimile thereof.

They were practically done. Liz finally stood in front of a mirror. Just the final touch remained. She was sweet this girl in the mirror, docile like sheep or a pet dog. They, with their scissors and brushes, pencils and clothes had transformed her, her body and face and everything about her. To a point she looked only like a girl, now. Her eyes seemed as dead as pearls. Her old self diluted, diminished to the point of not being there at all. Liz was gone. She wondered where she had gone. She wondered what had happened to her pride, her self-esteem. She felt… tamed.

– *What should we do about these… clothes?*

– *Burn them. She doesn't need them anymore*.

– That's better, Brigitte said pleased. – Much better.

– What do you think? Mother asked her.

– I look… beautiful, Liz whispered in awe.

She turned, admiring the sweet thing in the mirror. The crowd removed themselves with sighs of envy and joy, and she was alone with Brigitte and Regina. Brigitte escorted them back to the elevator.

– Have a nice evening, Mrs. Farley, the guide said politely. – We may even have the pleasure of seeing you again soon?

– After this work of art, I think you can safely assume that, Regina nodded mercifully.

Inside the elevator Liz touched her skin. To her it seemed smooth and soft like that of a newborn. Regina studied her, studied the clay she worked.

– Yes, you are beautiful, sweetheart. And you're so big that you'll be able to give me a bunch of grandchildren. You will do that for me, won't you, sweetie?

– Of course, mother. I'll love having children.

– This has been… educational… has it not?

– Very much so. An eager, sincere nod, large, somber eyes. – I have learned so much about myself, about everything.

– And you're being so willing to learn, to a point that frankly amazes me, beauty.

The girl hardly noticed the trip back with the car, her mind being a tumbling chaos of conflicting emotions. Inside, outside the car was the same, only a series of indistinct rolling images, she could make no sense of.

– You will meet a lot of bungling boys where we're going. Regina patted her hand. – I know I don't need to give you an advice when it comes to them, that you can handle them easily. Just note that flirting is allowed, and it's also a way to achieve advantages, both for yourself and for your future husband.

– Yes, mother.

Regina carefully dried a wet spot on the edge of the girl's eye.

– No tears, beauty. We won't have time to fix you again. Remember not to overdo the flirting. There is a number of women and men as well, that has climbed the ranks that way. They don't enjoy being reminded of that fact.

She patted the hand she held one, final time.

– I have high hopes for you, Liz. You better not disappoint me, not ever.

– I won't, mother, Liz stated with a humble certainty that made her seem far older than her sixteen years. – Trust me. You've given me so much.

Count on me to one day give you and yours tenfold in return.

She glanced at her ring and at the weak glow, and almost turned ecstatic in joy.

– We must spend a lot of time together, Mother said in a very commanding way. – But not as long as Frank is in our orbit. He might turn suspicious if he witness too much of the obedience and respect you show his hated mother.

They were received with all honors, when they arrived at Mortenson Manor. William Mortenson was another big man in Denver, very big in oil and mining. Regina presented her for the company as «my future daughter in law», and the smile in Liz' face turned wide and filled with bliss.

I deserve this, she thought. I've been hunted long enough. I will never more be a victim.

If there were only two roads possible to her, she knew which she would choose.

The adults evaluated her with critical eyes, and the youths by patronizing interest. But she handled it all «quite excellent», as Regina told her afterwards. She got confirmed to herself what she had long suspected; that she was indeed a chameleon. She could, if necessary fit in anywhere, in any crowd or surroundings.

– How is it like to grow up among cows and bulls, Lizzie, a naughty rodent of a girl, which father had millions in the bank wondered.

– It's called a ranch, Cinderella (laughter). It's very profitable, and you get a lot of exercise and you don't need to suffer through a lot of useless health cures. If you get my drift…

Liz walked around and relished her own fast lips, her ability to crush any opponent's gambit in its infancy. She had fun.

But at night she dreamt ever more often about the dragon with the face of a man.

She sat by the window one morning, staring out in the garden, at the river and the naked tree. It was June's turn to shop, and she had already left for the nearest grocery store. Liz spoke to Sue Ellen, but most of all she spoke to herself.

– The meeting with Regina confirmed my worst suspicions. I've got the same inborn weakness Ted has… a weakness, something almost approaching a need for self-destruction, to total docility. Either that or total dominion. There's no middle ground, not to us. I don't know if it's genetic or learned, nature or nurture that has made us this way, but it's there. Most people are a mix of these two, but like with everything else it is that much stronger in our family. I realize that there isn't any use for me to keep running. It will be the same no matter where I go. Regina has a hold over me because I let her… and so has Paul. I have Ted to compare with. He, too allowed himself to be cowed for a while, to a certain point… before becoming what he has always been; born to rule.

– I don't understand, Sue Ellen whimpered.

– Of course you don't, Susie. The dark girl rose and kissed the other on the cheek. – How could you? You have seen and experienced human cruelty, but you've never truly tasted it, tasted its fire, felt it like a scar on your body.

She celebrated Christmas Eve at Farley Mansion. There were no guests that day, except her. The ball would be tomorrow. Regina gave her a warm smile of welcome.

– Ah, Liz. You arrive just in time. I would like your opinion about a matter. Come with me, please.

She was led up the stairs, to Regina's bedroom.

The girl hung in ropes tied around her wrists from the ceiling, her toes just reaching the floor.

– This is Lois, Regina said. – I caught her stealing this morning. I had her tied up and left to hang. What do you think we should do with her, my dear?

Liz felt the stirrings inside, as she studied the girl hanging in the ropes. The maid still had a stubborn expression in her face, but it was waning after hanging like that for hours.

– I think she should be harshly punished, mother. If we let her off too easy the other servants will soon entertain the idea that such behavior is acceptable.

– My thoughts precisely, Regina nodded pleased. – Will you do the honors?

Liz looked at the whip on the chair, looked from that to the shaking girl hanging from the ceiling.

– I would be honored.

Liz walked close to the servant.

– Good afternoon, Lois. I'm a witch, a shaman, a sorceress, and a priestess of the dark arts. What you call it, call me don't matter, but I have the power of the gods, and I will punish you for your transgressions.

Lois' lips curled in a scornful smile.

Liz sensed it then, sensed the stirring grow.

Lois began shaking. Liz saw her eyes and Shadow in the other's eyes. It was remarkable, and it felt like it was the first time.

– Ah, I see you're well versed in the old legends.

Lois shook so much in the old and cold room that she had trouble speaking. She attempted in vain to twist her body away from the predator claws sliding over her thin skin.

– I had to s-steal, ma'am. My family is starving. My little sister…

Liz grabbed the whip from the chair.

– I'm positive concerning one thing, Lois: You've been very disobedient, but I am confident that it will never happen again, and soon, very soon… you'll be, too.

The scream echoed throughout the house and joyfully in the witch' mind.

– So, what have you ladies been doing today? Kent Farley asked the two of them. They spent time in the smaller living room by the library with him and Frank. – You seem very pleased with yourself. Pleased to the point of being… smug.

– Let us keep some secrets, will you? Regina purred.

Liz glimpsed what her future in this house would be. The men in the front line. The women influencing events from the shadows. Regina had never learned any other power than what came from «female wiles». Behind every influential man there was a woman.

Lois carried four glasses of wine on a tray. She walked towards the table in a stiff, unnatural manner. When she put down the tray her hands shook so hard that the glasses almost turned over.

– Is something wrong, Lois? Frank wondered astonished. – You're usually steady as a rock. Is there something we can help you with?

– No, Master Linsey, the girl stated with conviction. – I'm so sorry. This won't happen again.

– She's a little bit down, poor thing, Liz informed him. – Her family has come down with a serious contagious disease and she can't go home for the holidays. If things turn out to be very bad she won't be able to go home the next holiday either. But she will happily work for us instead, won't you, Lois?

– Yes, ma'am. Certainly, ma'am.

Liz knew she would hardly dare move a finger without explicit permission, and the witch was close to ecstasy when the maid left the room.

– She seemed unusually down, Frank noted. – Can't we at least help her in some small way?

– Oh, stop it, Frank, Regina replied pointedly. – We don't give the servants any special privileges, you know that.

– They're people. Frank shook. – At least as much «worth» as we are.

– Dear Frank. Liz rubbed him seductively on the arm. – She said she didn't want help, remember? Perhaps we'll be insulting her by pressing the matter further?

– Okay, okay. He calmed down looking into the eyes of his wonderful beloved.

Kent and Regina went to yet another social occasion, leaving the youths alone. Regina meant the time had come. Liz agreed.

All the servants had gone to bed. Liz was alone with Frank in front of the fireplace.

– Alone at last, he breathed a sigh of relief. Glasses met and parted. – The less I see of that… that hag, the better I feel.

– Seconded, Liz replied with a pearly laughter.

They drank bottoms up.

– But that having been said, I definitely think we should change tactics towards your mother, fooling her into believing we're coming along, to more easily crush her and take what is ours.

– I believe you may be correct, he said hesitatingly, too taken in by her to notice the careful subtext beneath her wording. – She has been hard on you, hasn't she, patronizing and cruel while you bought clothes.

– I can take it. She grabbed his hands, smiling sweetly, seeing her teasing flash as a reflection in his eyes. – I can endure anything to get what I want.

He stared at her, helplessly captivated, reaching clumsily for her.

She slipped closer to him, allowing herself to be caught. Laughing happily while he loosened his belt and pulled down his pants and underwear, gasping in true heat as his slowly hardening cock was revealed. She pulled back a little, deliberately, letting him see her as she stretched her body in the tight dress. The visible skin glowed even more golden in the light from the fire.

– What's wrong, my love, have you never done it on the carpet before?

The innocent, seductive smile removed his final inhibitions. She helped him remove her dress just in time, before he took her in arms and pulled her down on the soft, soft floor. She felt the heat from him just as strong as that from the fireplace. She gasped in surprise. This was pleasant, so very pleasant. Her laughter mixed with the rising sounds of pleasure.

She felt it, literally, his impatience, the result of his long chastity. He grunted and was incredibly active and vigorous. Her eager, slow moan wasn't pretend, but completely true. Everything turned out to be incredibly good, good, good…

The more the better.

And the face with the firespitting eyes came ever closer.

And she heard the many sounds of the whispering and roaring desert in her eyes and her mind.

CHAPTER SIXTEEN
DISTANT BUTTERFLY WINGS
Sahara 1918

«God has opened our mouths to put two things into them, either food to live or sand to die».

Tuareg saying.

The streets of Timbuktu whispered to them through the wind and the sand.

A toothless man sat with his back to a wall, speaking in a mix of French and Arabic to the four strangers, the woman and the three men.

– «Sahara means The Wasteland», John translated the old man's word. – «The souls of the dead are hunting the living in the desert. People disappear in there, among the dry sand dunes, never to be seen again».

– I can understand him, Nick said. – I don't understand the words, but I know, beyond language, what is on his mind.

– You have grown further. John nodded. – Your Power is growing. That's good. That's very good. You'll need it, need all of it.

Nick straightened, sniffing the dry, arid air.

– This is so different from the ice-cold north, he said. – That air can be still, completely still. This is always moving.

He sniffed some more, opening his mouth, as if tasting it, tasting the very air he breathed, its many spices.

– It's all the same.

– The extremes of the Earth are yours to enjoy, John stated. – You will never tremble faced with the ruthless nature.

The old man kept speaking unprompted. John didn't translate, but looked at Nick.

– Blue Men, Nick wondered. – I see them in his mind. Is he speaking about blue men?

– The Tuareg, John said. – He says the Blue Men are the messengers of the gods, the souls of the dead hunting in the desert.

– They call themselves Imashaghen, Carla said. – «The Free».

And in that moment she looked more mysterious than they had ever seen her, and she had always looked strange to them, even to them.

Desmond dried his forehead with his sleeve. The other three didn't sweat that much, at least not while standing still, but he did.

– So the Tuareg has taken them, then, if they're not here, brought them further east?

– They're the main users of the old Trans-Saharan trade route, slave route. John shook his head. – And they are slave traders, at least some of them are.

– So «The Free» enslaves people, Nick snarled. – That makes sense! That makes perfect sense!

His eyes flared, and the old man trembled, and mumbled something, something totally unintelligible, making the sign to ward off evil spirits, shaking uncontrollably. They left him there, on the dusty and windy street.

Everything was beige, parched yellow and white here. They saw some blue men, dressed in blue, but Nick sensed no ill intent from them, no duplicity and they left them be.

The large house wasn't really that hard to find. It was on a corner, at a crossroads, and they would have found it even if their sharp senses hadn't led them there.

Nick drew his gun with a snarl.

– Put that away, John told him. – We won't need it, not yet.

– What do you *mean?* Nick said, pain evident in his voice.

They stepped into the chill of the house. There were no doors, only a wide doorway. The «reception hall» was empty. Nick heard people pretty far off, but their walk was not excited or anxious, clearly non-threatening. They searched room by room and finally met people. But those people hardly even acknowledged their presence. The chill in Nick's bones advanced further. He sensed something, something…

Bad.

John asked a man about something. The man pointed down a staircase.

– What was that? Nick asked.

– I asked him where the merchandize is.

Nick froze. There was a quality in John's voice, in John, one of steel that Nick had hardly experienced.

– I reach back, John told him, – into younger years, when the relative tranquility of the last decades wasn't mine to enjoy.

They walked down the stairs, into the murky, twilight cellar. Nick felt it, felt it overwhelm him, the prevalent stench of mind and body. And then he saw them, saw the people sit by the walls and stare at them, stare at nothing with empty, like wounds eyes.

There were several rooms with half-naked and naked bodies without minds.

– We just walk in here, Desmond said, – without resistance, and nobody seem to guard these people. Why don't they leave, escape? They're not even chained.

– They're not exactly in shape to make any independent decisions, or to go anywhere, John replied. – And where are they gonna go? They'll be «recaptured» the moment they step outside or not far outside the house, even if they weren't reduced in physical and mental strength.

Nick felt the black rage rise in him, and for once he welcomed it, welcomed its purification, its fire.

– I feel so helpless, he mumbled. – I feel so damned helpless.

– But you're not, Nick, Carla stated. – None of us are.

His eyes burned at her, and something passed between them, an understanding beyond understanding.

They left, and they were not looking back. They crossed the town and jumped on their animals, their camels, and they rode out, rode in a cloud of dust, riding into the desert. It swallowed them, devoured them whole, and they faded away into the sand and violent heat.

2

Nancy walked and walked, and she could do nothing more than putting one foot in front of the other. Memory was faint, but it still continued to haunt her.

The cargo room was dank and hot. Moans rose from the young males and females chained there, on the hard floor. The ship moved, moved out at sea, moved them all away from everything they had known. Nancy stared blindly at all the faces. They swam before her eyes, turning indistinct and unreal. Some still shook and rattled their chains, but most had given up and lay still on the floor.

Nancy walked in the searing sun, and her head felt as if it was about to blow. The fever visions came to her constantly now, assaulting her like knives hammering her from above. She lay on the hard floor on the cargo ship, writhing and moaning with the others, but she saw nothing, nothing but the endless dunes of sand ahead.

She heard a sound, the sound of the large metal door opening.

– No, she moaned. – No.

– What is it? Sue wondered anxiously, tenderly touching her kin's skin. – Are you ill?

Men entered the room, many men. They filled the room, and they were all naked. Their cocks were all erect or about to become erect. Nancy shook her chains, and several others did, too, realizing to their horror what was about to happen.

Nancy fought. She did so in a sudden frenzy, realizing that these men didn't care about her smile or her grace or anything. They just wanted pleasure, and they wanted to hurt her as much as possible while having it.

They turned on the boys and girls equally. A boy realized this startled, and cried out in protest, sounding almost wronged, like a minor injustice was being done to him.

The man holding Nancy struck her, hitting her in the ribs and face, making her pliable. He lay down on her and then he brutally pushed her thighs apart and pushed his large cock inside her. Nancy heard Sue's scream turn to a high pitch, just before the sound of her own horror rose towards the ceiling.

The first man finished with her. He slapped her face a few times, making sure it hurt, before rising, before leaving his spot to the next in line. Hundreds, she thought. There are hundreds for each and every one of us.

And then her mind shut down, and she lost count of how many they were on her. For some reason she remembered only Sue's white face afterwards, the tiny, tiny whimpering sounds coming from her quivering lips. A man pushed her down and pumped on her, pumped, pumped, pumped, and it never ended. They were all raped repeatedly, and when the endless line was done, another began.

Insane sounds filled the room. Silence filled it. Nancy lay still, her mouth open. She reached out a hand, first to Sue, then to Virgil. Sue was totally unresponsive. She didn't respond to touch or anything.

– DON'T TOUCH ME! Virgil shouted.

Nancy broke in tears, and she was so grateful to her kin, so grateful that he had been able to reach her.

– I'm sorry, he sobbed. – Sorry, sorry, sorry.

They touched hands, and it felt both comforting and sickening.

Nancy writhed in pain, there on the floor. Her groin felt like it was on fire, and she knew very well why. She had been taken so many times that her skin had become inflamed. She was so sore and ashamed and scared that she just wanted to sink into a hole and die.

Sobs and insane howls kept rising to the ceiling, and it never ended. Semen and juices and blood and vomit mixed on the floor, creating a sickening smell. And it stuck in their nostrils, forever.

The door opened again. There were just a few men this time. The prisoners lay still and timid, not moving an arm or a leg or an eye.

They were fed. Pieces of smoked meat were thrown to them. They grabbed it with shaking hands and wolfed it down.

Those not moving, unresponsive boys and girls like Sue were brutally whipped until they moved. But some never did. Nancy noticed gratefully that Sue did move, and did feed. Her eyes didn't move, but her body did.

Nancy crawled close to her afterwards, speaking into her ear.

– You're going to live, she whispered. – Blue-eyed and blonde and tall girls are popular in Asia. You won't be seriously harmed, like the rest of us might be. You're going to live, do you hear me? No matter what they do to you, you'll live.

There was no reply, no response, nothing giving any indication that her kin had heard her. Nancy rested her head on Sue Warren's pale and soft skin, and fell into a terrible, tense sleep, so exhausted that she had no choice but to sleep and dream, and she moaned in those horrifying nightmares, moaned like a little girl.

And she felt like one, like that little girl afraid of the dark and just about anything else that might come her way.

The pain below woke her up, and there was no respite from it, nothing even resembling relief. If anything, it grew worse during the day or whatever time there was.

There were two possible outcomes when the door opened. They were either being fed and punished, or they were being raped and punished. It turned into a kind of routine on the endless voyage. Sometimes scores of men came and raped them repeatedly. Or there were just a few, taking their time, savoring it more. It was all the same.

There was no resistance anymore, no one protesting the slightest when they were given the kindness of attention and affection there on the floor.

Nancy began looking forward to it, instead of being alone, alone with her thoughts.

There were dead bodies down here, now. Some of those unresponsive carcasses. They weren't removed, but began to smell. A sweet perfume never leaving quivering noses, mixing with that of the stools and urine flowing freely from their openings. Nancy stared into those open eyes nearby, unable to look away.

The masters put a glass of water to her lips and she drank. The water was laced with poison, making them all even more unresisting and delirious. Nancy smiled to the man above her, but he just kept beating her, kept punishing her. And she cried out in despair and pain, moaning in need, and she despised herself.

She and Virgil lay there, staring, not staring miserable at each other.

– I thought… she whispered. – I thought I had found safety among you, found a true home. But that's how the world is… right? First it gives you hope. Then it brutally takes it away.

He had no reply for her. She had wanted that, wanted him to deny the hopelessness, the broken soul she saw mirrored in his eyes.

Nell Warren had served the Master to her last breath, unable to free herself from his influence, and he had disregarded her, thrown her away like garbage.

Nancy slept, and there were no dreams. It was like she was dead.

The chains were removed, and they were whipped on their feet, and driven to another room. Some had trouble staying on their feet. Some fell. They were brutally whipped until they got back on their feet. Everybody was pushed at a wall. A hose were directed at them, and they were hit by cold, cold water.

They lay there, gasping and spitting, desperately attempting to breathe. There was no respite, never that, only a continuance of the brutal, ruthless treatment, the same uncaring faces filling their vision. They were inspected. Hands investigated their bodies, and they could just as well touch dead wood, for the interest they displayed. Nancy was dry, now, her skin was dry, now, but she kept freezing in the hot room. The man… assessing her seemed utterly disaffected and inhuman, and she shrunk under his alien stare.

Another man was working on Sue. Nancy noticed it in a distant, disaffected way. They were treated like commodities, like merchandize, and they were, of course. But…

But then something happened. She noticed it immediately. Something, a glance, something else passed between the two men. Both girls were grabbed at the leg, where the faded mole was. Nancy noticed it in a dull, bland way. They nodded and pulled the two girls on their feet.

Nancy and Sue were brought into yet another room. The rest of the captives were left behind. A carpet covered the floor there, and there was a large bed. The men threw the girls on the bed and left them there. Nancy moved as soon as she heard the door close, moved to the unmoving Sue.

– Listen to me, she said.

There was no discernible reaction in Sue's face.

Nancy slapped her on the cheek. Sue yelped and looked astonished at her.

– You will smile, Nancy told her. – You will treat the man coming here as you would your future husband. You will be attentive and eager to serve him. *Do you understand?*

– Y-yes.

– Good! Nancy whispered and kissed the other girl's lips. – Very good.

There were towels on the wall. Nancy grabbed two of them, and gave one to Sue.

– Dry your hair, she commanded. – Rub it hard.
And she did. And Nancy did, too. The towel was soft and pleasant. She almost dreamed herself away as the hard rub changed to a slower, more flexible pace.
She combed Sue's hair with her fingers. Sue combed hers.
Nancy placed her kin on her knees on the bed, facing the door, and then, somewhat content joined her there.
– Remember to look down, Nancy said. – Never meet Master's eyes unless on his explicit command.
– M-master? Sue whined.
– Yes. Nancy nodded. – Our current high master, he who rules us, decides our life and death, he who we must obey in all things.
She put one hand on Sue's butt, and the other on her own, letting both slide down, into the cleft between thighs. It was dry there, dry as wood. Sue stiffened, a moment, before relenting, before a few tears fell from her eyes, before a few fell from Nancy's as well.
We must prepare, the dark girl told her kin. We must be eager and pleasing, please our Master in all things.
It hurt, forcing them both to bite their lower lip, but Nancy kept it up, rubbing and caressing and teasing their lower parts, and the pain faded, as heat rose in them, and the pleasant pain, the need rose in them. Nancy's hands fell, and both girls sat there, waiting, suffering, waiting.
– «We are the Janus Clan», Sue recited. – «We survive and thrive anywhere, also in a world of death».
A thrill trickled repeatedly down Nancy's spine.
And when Sue repeated the words, Nancy joined her, and they kept it up for minutes, until the words faded, and only the waiting remained.
A man entered the room. Nancy couldn't recall seeing him open the door. One moment it was simply open, and the man was there. Nancy saw him, without seeing him, as she was trained to do. His skin was white. He had sandy blonde hair and he was nude. His cock alternately hit his left and right thigh, as he advanced towards them.
He stopped right before he reached the bed, studying them intensively.
– You look quite presentable, under the circumstances, he commented. – Why is that?
– We're strong, Master, Nancy replied softly and docile. – Our blood is strong. We can endure rough male affection. It's our lot and joy in life.
She knew they didn't look good, but knew they looked far better than the girls and boys on the floor out there.
And she knew she got to him, finally got somewhere, knew it before she saw the first twitching in his cock.

He turned to Sue, snapping.

– And what about you?

– She speaks, truth, M-master. – We're trained from an early age to endure male interest.

He touched her, and she reddened all over her body, and he laughed hard. And as he kept touching her, she began moaning and gasping. Nancy closed her eyes briefly, relaxing, letting go, melting into his embrace as he joined them on the bed.

– And what's this? He grabbed their legs, touching the faded mole. – One of my Arab colleges was both excited and freaked by it. It was a remarkable sight. I couldn't get him to speak to me about it. The tough thug was spooked out of his wits. Imagine that.

– It's our Mark, Sue intoned. – The sign of our wretched blood. The Arab, the Traveler in the Wilderness knows of us from old times. Our great grandfather John told me the story when I was a little girl and sat on his k-knee.

– So you're valuable then. He nodded pleased. – I rather thought so.

Nancy wanted to say something, to protest or to wheedle, to convince him of her eagerness, as a docile slave, but the constricted throat kept her from speaking.

The man fell on Sue, and Nancy leaned against them both, offering herself, offering to give up what was already his, what was no longer hers to give, and the catching in her throat wouldn't go away, not even when mist covered her eyes and everything melted away into the nothing of the pleasure and pain assaulting her.

Sue sat in a chair, brushing her hair in front of the mirror. She hummed a melody. Nancy knew it, somehow. It made her eyes sting.

– We did what we had to do, she said in a whispering voice. – We're well fed, now, and is able to gather strength, instead of being among the poor things in the cargo room, but don't make the mistake of believing that this… this good thing will last. We're only Master's playthings and when we reach our destination he will sell us, like the merchandize we are.

Sue kept humming. She didn't seem to have heard her distant cousin's words. Nancy sat down on the bed, feeling the fine silk on her skin, attempting in vain to cleanse herself of the numbing fear.

Weeks and perhaps months passed. The ship landed in Africa somewhere. She knew that, had known that that was their destination, even if she hadn't wanted to admit it to herself.

The two girls were brought to shore, to the harbor with the rest, all the rest. It seemed to come as a shock to Sue at first, but then she accepted it the same way she accepted everything, with a distant smile on her lips. The two walked, while the others stumbled and was pushed and pulled.

The surviving captives were taken to a storage room inside a hot, humid building. The air, both inside and outside, was so hot, far hotter than even New Orleans. Each breath was a strenuous, prolonged gasp. He who had been their most recent master was given diamonds, a lot of diamonds, and then he left, left them to their new owners.

Sue choked, obviously beyond distressed, as they sat there with their fellow slaves, surrounded by hard, cruel eyes.

– Hush, Nancy whispered in her ear. – Hush…

She kissed her kin's cheek and rubbed her back. It worked somehow, calming Sue's distress, the hysteria that had almost claimed her.

– WHAT IS THIS, Virgil suddenly, shockingly shouted enraged. – What kind of people are you? I'm an American. We're all Americans here, and we DEMAND to be freed.

He jumped up. Nancy's heart jumped in joy when she saw and sensed the strength in his body, one hardly diminished by the long and hard voyage.

They beat him with sticks, beat him until he lay still. They dragged him to the wall, chained him there. He hung on the wall, his feet hardly touching the floor. They came at him with whips.

Nancy jumped up, too, running a few steps before quickly kneeling before the angry men, staring humbly at the floor. She sat there on her heels, waiting for the first sting of the whip.

One of the men nodded, giving her permission to speak.

– Allow me to punish him, she said in French. – Please, Master. Let him be my responsibility. He's headstrong, but I can… can fix that. I know how. I've been taught how from an early age.

He signed for her to rise, and she did.

– The next time… he said, handing her his whip, – … the next time he steps out of line, you will feel the whip in his place.

– Thank you; Master, she replied humbly. – Thank you very much.

Virgil's eyes widened. He understood, understood enough, and he looked at her in horror and despair. She walked to him.

– It's all right, she said to him. – Don't feel bad. It's all right.

She walked to him, comforting him, rubbing his shaking form.

– My arms are not as strong as theirs, she whispered in his ears. – I can't hold back. They will notice that immediately. But my whipping of you will be lighter. Please!

He nodded, or she imagined he nodded, and the catching in her throat, the deadness inside intensified.

The first stroke hit his back. And the second and the third and the forth. He gritted his teeth at first, but the screams eventually erupted, inevitably, tears and blood mixing on the skin of the young, supple body.

Nancy lay on the side in the corner. Sue comforted her and hummed to her, her nervous, twitchy rubbing strangely comforting.

During the next few days, there were more rape, more torture, more feeding. There were no resistance, no more rebellion left in the boys and girls.

The slavers used a kind of smooth prod, similar to that Nancy had grown accustomed to in the whorehouse in New Orleans. She felt it be moved back and forth inside, felt the first stings of arousal, and she smiled and moved in heat, and the other girls took after her, and the masters were very pleased with her.

– We are not distant cousins, she told the two one day, a quiet day. – You are my brother and sister. Never forget that. Never forget.

They didn't reply with words, but she believed, she hoped that they heard her somehow, and understood.

These masters left the prod in place, to keep the girls in a permanent state of heat, and to widen the boys' opening, making it ready for better use. It would be very easy to pull it out at night, when no one was watching them, but no one did. The prod was pushed into them all, and kept in place by straps fastened around their hips, and only taken out every time it was time for them to be used, to be used extensively.

They were given a lot of food, obviously being fattened for a long journey, fattened for sale, and Nancy made sure she and her distant cousins, her brother and sister got enough of it.

A new man, a stranger came for a visit one day. One of the men brought him to the sisters and brother, grabbing the leg, showcasing it, and in the stranger's impassive face Nancy sensed both interest and horror, and a need, a possessiveness making her throb and shake.

They spoke in Arabic, even though only the stranger was an Arab. Nancy didn't understand it at first, but it slowly began making sense to her.

She learned fast. She always had.

As she heard it more and more, as they were being skipped inland, far inland. As they were brought North East, on barges down a wide, wide river, as the jungle gave way to the ever more invasive desert.

Sahara, Nancy thought.

I can't stop thinking. I wish I could. I wish there would be no more thoughts.

They were given clothes, or at least simple covers to protect vulnerable white skin against the sun. It felt strange being covered again. It had been so long. They wore a simple collar around their neck and were tied together with one long chain fastened to the collars. The masters didn't bother with chaining their hands and feet. Why should they?

– We're chattel, Nancy cried quietly with her head in Sue's lap. – Chattel doesn't have thoughts, any thoughts, except the need to serve their masters. I wish it would all go away.

And the older, less experienced sister comforted the younger with her silence, with her empty eyes.

They reached the old city of Timbuktu at dawn. One more stop on their way east, on their way to oblivion, to the endless void of their bothersome mind.

3

The four riders didn't look any different from any other group crossing the Waste, not even by a closer scrutiny. They were dressed pretty much like many were out here, covered in the traditional Arab white clothes. For the casual observers nothing separated them from other travelers. But to those who knew about such things, there were clearly distinct differences. They *moved* these four, both compared to each other and to the desert. They were hunters, hunters in the wilderness.

Sometimes one of them jumped down from the camel and ran ahead, was «point man». Sometimes it was Carla, sometimes Nick.

– It's scorched, he mumbled, – scorched Earth.

– It's the muted fire of the Earth, she mused. – It's wonderful.

She came more and more into her own the longer time they spent out here. They witnessed it, they experienced it, as they moved and breathed with her.

– Such majesty. Desmond shook his head. – I never dreamed such a place existed. The New York scene certainly seems quite distant, now, almost as if that was the dream, and this is the reality.

– This is! Nick stated.

They rested somewhat, slept a little in an oasis.

– I can *smell* them, Nick said to John at night. – Smell the blood in the grains of sand coming my way. I need to know, John, know more about what I am.

– I don't know much, John told Nick late at night, – but we'll find out as much as we can, find out together. We should have begun doing this many years ago, when you were a child.

And Nick trained, exercised his Power, in intense ways he had never before approached. He moved the sand, moved the water in the cool pond, lit fires in the sand, in the air itself, driven by John and his own inner demons. He read the minds of those present, penetrated ever deeper, becoming one with their murky depths. Except Carla. She didn't consciously attempt to keep him out, but her mind was such a jumble, such a chaos of thoughts that he felt like he was right in the middle of Times Square.

Carla helped, too, with small suggestions, minor hints, and the three of them looked at her, as she, in increasing and ever more pervasive ways, seemed to tune in to her surroundings, to become one with it, to actually become the Desert.

Nick strained, as cold sweat broke on his brow. Sand and dust danced in the air at his command, but that was it, really, it for long hours, long days and nights.

He rested. He began again.

Then, one night, one hour something happened. There was a pain, a release. He gasped. Colors seemed to fade, fade from the very air, from the reality surrounding him. The others were caught in it, caught in his fervor, his

– DUST, he gasped. – They called it Dust, but it isn't really. It is…

Surrounding them, in a kind of vision was a landscape of mist and shadow. They saw shadows. The air was filled with shadows.

It was just a moment, before it faded, and once more form was just form and air was just air.

Nick focused on Carla, while sweat kept pouring from his brow, and strength coursed through him.

– You know what it is, he told her. – Tell me!

She smiled to him, radiant and true and enigmatic and beyond mysterious.

– It's a realm of the dead, she said, – of the soul and of Dream, a world of shadows, added to this one by humans through the generations. I've seen it grow and multiply, become important, become crucial. And you broke through its veil, Nick, in your rage and need and fire. We all touched it, because of you. We're Changed, now. More than ever we walk the shadows. We're the Shadowwalkers.

It stayed with him, stayed with them all, throughout the night, and the many dark and bright days ahead.

They sat there as the day dawned, as they were ready to move on.

– There aren't that many oases along this trail, John insisted. – Not that many paths they can take. We would have found them even without our special abilities. We will find them.

– I can smell the water, Carla said, the fire dancing across her face, – smell it under and over the ground.

– I can sense her, Nick said enraged. – Sense her fear and utter desolation and growing resolution. And I see her tormentors through her eyes. There's no place on Earth they can hide from us.

And the fire in the sand and in the air, where one would think nothing would burn, reached for the heavens, far into the dark sky.

– We should have taken the fight with Lance Powell in New Orleans, Fireeyes swore, – eradicated him and everyone else of his kind from the very face of the Earth.

They heard him, even when he wasn't speaking.

And they rode on, in darkness and in bright, bright sunshine. People observing them would think the devil was both behind and in front of them, and they would be right.

The pale riders rode on through the everlasting Waste.

4

They stumbled on across the dunes, up and down, up and down, chained together in a long row. The moment someone fell, their captors were beating up on them until they got up, until someone stayed down and stared at the sky with sand in their eyes, and everybody got a break, a respite from the cruel walk. They began looking forward to the deaths, like they would a hail of rain, and it made them feel even worse.

The boys and girls of the chain was a diverse group, of all colors, Americans and Europeans and Africans of all races. Nancy sensed how it all mingled inside her, and wished it wouldn't. Her increased empathy did her no favors.

When the day finally ended and they reached an oasis and a lot of water was poured into her mouth she felt a sickening gratitude, and she smiled and she performed for them, her masters, and they ignored her like the despicable low life of the Earth she was.

This was a large oasis, the biggest and busiest she had seen. People hurried back and forth, almost like on a trading post.

Then it hit her: She recognized this place, recognized its trade. It was like the display room in the Mansions of New Orleans, only bigger, much bigger.

She realized this long before they were actually put on the display, on the pre-sale block. There was no bathing, and only the minutest grooming, as was evidently the custom in the desert. Nancy knew how to stand, to display herself, and she saw how Sue took after her, mimicked her in all things. The potential buyers walked between the blocks. There was no talk here, no communication, except the most rudimentary between masters and slaves. These men didn't care about her education, about her vocal skills, but they did notice her smile, her stance, her eagerness to serve, she knew that, sensed that, sensed both the men's cruelty and desire, and their assessment of her as merchandize, of course.

Sue and the other blonde and fair-skinned girls drew most of the obvious attention. It was exactly as Liz had heard in the brothels in New Orleans: Arabs saw white women as a rare price. They «valued» variety. Bile stuck in Nancy's throat. Only her long experience kept her from exposing herself.

Hours and hours passed, as the evaluation continued. The merchandize stood there, in their chains, beyond exhaustion, beyond pain.

And then, just as the display was about to end, one of their masters called the attention of the potential buyers. There was something he said… making the crowd turn quiet and stunned. They stared at him in absolute disbelief.

Nancy understood enough, understood the words «People of Legend».

It was a part of the story Great Grandfather John had told Sue, that he had told her, about the lost North African tribe of wanderers, predating the Arab and the Gypsies.

The master lifted Nancy's leg, exposing the Mark, creating a stunned murmur from the crowd, one that only intensified when he repeated the procedure with Sue and Virgil.

Everybody, all the various peoples of the desert, came forward or tried to come forward simultaneously, with spectacular results. Finally, after a few chaotic minutes an extra round of inspections was organized.

– These three have walked through the Waste, one of the masters cried. – They have endured hardship and been treated harshly, as slaves are, and they hardly look any worse for wear. Compare them to the rest of the stock. Pay attention and know what a price they are.

Nancy understood almost everything, now, and what she didn't get exactly right, she pieced together.

He was right. It was as if the long journey hadn't happened. Physically they weren't really bad off at all.

– Make no mistake about it, the man said. – They are broken. Their spirit is crushed and they have become docile slaves, eager to serve, but don't they look more than presentable, don't they look magnificent?

And shortly after that the three of them was brought forth as one package, and the bidding began. Nancy looked into the faces of the people in front of her. She saw fear there. Some pulled back, uncertain, paralyzed by the rampant superstition and awe, the force of their legends. But greed and hunger, a desire to possess what frightened them mattered more in most of them. They believed. She saw that, in their eyes, in their every move.

Then one man, surrounded by bodyguards, stepped forward and raised his hand, and the bidding stopped, as if by Magick. Everybody pulled back, swearing and mumbling in their disappointment.

Nancy understood. Either no one could match the man's bid, or they didn't dare to.

But her former masters seemed more than happy, happy on the verge of being ecstatic actually.

The brother and sisters were pulled down from the block, and led away, sold to yet another Master. Nancy looked at the man without looking at him, smiling in bliss. They belonged to him, now.

They were taken to a large tent, where a score of other purchases lay in chains.

Nancy waited, waited until the guards had left them, left them alone with their brothers and sisters of the chain, before blurting out:

– Who is this man purchasing us?

A woman looked at her in contempt, as if she was feebleminded or something.

– That's Sultan Al Rashid, she said proudly, clearly in awe. – He owns thousands of slaves and hundreds of wives and concubines.

Nancy silently repeated the name, savoring it, tasting it on her lips.

She heard the auctions continue outside, but it didn't concern her. It wasn't important anymore. She lay down on the hard ground, as she had grown well used to. The loud sounds faded into nothingness. She grew tired quickly. Her eyes closed and she slept.

And she awoke, as she had grown accustomed to, to the sound and feel of the whip. All the slaves, far higher number of them than when Nancy had fallen asleep hurried up on their knees, eyes down, legs spread. The prod moved within her, and she grew aroused in a matter of seconds.

She saw most of the other females squirm, but she didn't.

Sue didn't either. Not anymore. She moved pretty much like Nancy, now, sensual and enticing, having caught up, learned fast, like all Warrens.

I'm a Warren, Nancy thought.

It's just a name, meaningless, except the realities behind it.

She sniffed, quickly drying a tear from the corner of her eye.

They were fed again, eagerly gathering around the present master for more nourishment.

After the feeding Nancy was singled out and taken away. No one reacted much to that, not Nancy either. It wasn't her place to question. It never had been.

She was taken to the big tent, pushed through its opening and left there. Her eyes quickly adjusted to the darkness, as they always did. The Sultan sat there, not far away. She quickly knelt in the dust, awaiting his command.

He signed for her to approach, and she did. She rose and ran to him, kneeling right in front of him, awaiting his word.

– What is your name slave? He demanded.

She had trouble breathing in her anxious fear.

– Nancy, if it pleases Master, she replied.

She still spoke with an accent, but it was hardly noticeable anymore.

She sensed he was pleased, and she shivered in joy.

– And your family name?

This was highly unusual. Slaves were usually encouraged to forget their roots, their old life.

– It's just Nancy, Master. I grew up in a brothel in New Orleans, the city of pleasures, learning servitude from an early age.

He saw her sincerity, saw it with all his experience. A slave lying for a master was severely punished.

– And your brother and sister?

– Their name is Warren, Master.

She held her breath, realizing that she had, in fact been lying, by not telling the whole truth. And he could see her anxiety, her shame, in every move she made.

– How many of you are there? He snapped, suddenly impatient.

– Just a few more, Master, a handful in America, and one in… Australia, that's all. I was with them such a short time, Master. I don't know much. They freed me, and took me to their home in New York. I lived there a few weeks, before my distant cousins and I were taken, and brought here.

He fell silent, clearly considering something, hardly able to conceal his excitement, and certainly not to her that could see through any guise. She waited.

– I will breed you, of course, especially the boy. The man in the large chair gestured, deliberately shrugging. – He can impregnate scores of females, and during just one generation I will have an entire people under my thumb, at my full disposal.

She saw it, saw Virgil be brought females day out and day in until he fell asleep on a rug. Until it all began again the next day, and the next and the next. She saw rows of women with growing bellies. She saw herself and Sue among them.

And worse: She saw herself become the truly willing servant of the Sultan, becoming the teacher of the children, the teacher of servitude.

She began shaking uncontrollably, couldn't help it, could no longer hold it back.

– Poor slave, he said, his voice thick with expectation.

He nodded, as he with his experienced eye witnessed her every emotion, her every thought, and he nodded again, nodded in exalted triumph.

– You can be broken, he cried. – You're all broken, and eager to begin your new life in my service. Allah be praised. He has truly smiled upon his son on this day, bringing the children of the gods into my grasp, grinded under my will.

He looked at her. She knew he did. Looked possessive at her.

– The People of Legend left this land long ago, but now they're back, and now they'll never more leave. Now, they'll live out their days in grateful servitude.

That word again. It hit her like a hammer. She sniffed and bowed her head deeper in acknowledgement of his power over her.

There was one more day of rest, gone in a whiff, before they were moved on, back to the dunes and merciless sun. Days and days in the endless Wasteland. This is the world. This is who we are. She stopped, startled. Immediately the whip was there, biting into her skin. She kept walking. Sleep at night. Walk during day. Walk and sleep.

The land hardly changed around them. There were only variations, and hardly even that. At night, there were inspections, lessons in obedience, submission and servitude.

– You better learn, now, one of the masters said casually. – Once we reach the palace, there will be no more lenience, no more patience with you not being pleasing in all things.

Sit, kneel, stand, turn, sit, kneel, stand, turn. Everything hammered into them. There were two slaves traveling with the caravan, one male and one female, obvious instructors, advanced tools for the masters. They had been taught the skill of teaching other slaves. If the Sultan's men were his hands, those two were his fingers, his nails. They were old, with dry skin and dry minds, old in the Sultan's service. Nancy shuddered, seeing herself in the female's place.

In some ways she was already there. The Sultan had a plan with her. She *knew* that. He had brought her to his tent. He had marked her, even though there was no visible scar.

A dog sat down before a master, its tongue sticking out. It was wagging its tail and eagerly begging favors.

Nice doggie, Nancy thought.

She was given the whip, on occasion. The sun made the masters lazy, and she was given the task of punishing displeasing slaves, and she was hardly punished herself anymore, not beyond strictly corrective measures, hardly punishment at all. And shame and eagerness warred within her. She felt it, felt it every time the whip hit unprotected skin, every time a slave cried out in pain and horror, and the prod moved within her, and pleasure ravaged her.

Good dog, she thought feverishly. Very good dog.

Hot, so hot. Sweat covered Nancy's skin all day long, as the ordeal of crossing endless dunes constantly assaulted her. But…

There was something, something she had yet to quite grasp.

I feel good, she thought.

And she pondered that feeling, fearing it, filled with apprehension, looking outside, looking inside.

She noticed that Sue's skin turned darker, day by day, even hour by hour, and that even her hair turned a darker hue. It happened so fast that it was easily recognizable. The slavers, the Sultan's men noticed it, too, and covered her up almost completely, but it did little good. The change persisted.

Virgil's skin and hair darkened, too. Nancy looked closer at him, fearing there was nothing there, beneath the blank stare, the shell of a body. She hardly even felt his emotions, felt him. There was just a black, black hole where his self, where he had been.

But he never stumbled anymore, and neither did the two girls.

Nancy sat close to the fire at night, pulling the two closest in the chain with her. They whimpered and tried to pull away, but couldn't resist her strength, her *will*. She sat close to the fire, the heat, and it didn't burn her.

She rose and walked away, dragging the others with her, before they had time to rise, without even thinking about it. A master sat by the tent. She knelt before him.

He nodded to her, giving her permission to speak.

– May I dance, Master? I am a skilled dancer.

He nodded, and disconnected the chains from her collar.

– There's majesty here, she said aloud, while walking to the spot between the fires. – The desert has a majesty all its own. I didn't know that. Before I came here a desert was just a desert, an inhospitable place, unfit for humans to live.

And she danced. First the western and American Native styles she had learned, but then it changed into the type of dance she had observed in Africa, and among the Sahara dunes. There was no music, except what beat and played inside her, but it didn't matter. What was inside erupted to the outside, and her movements increased in speed and agility. The flames licked her body as she passed close to them, and it was as if the fiery shadows of the night surrounded her and embraced her.

She fell on her back in the sand, laying still there for a while, before twisting and turning, performing there, before the slavers, and they came to her, they all came to her… and she welcomed them. *She welcomed them.*

They were done, and she sat there afterwards, back in the chain, the smooth prod reinserted into her. She sat there through the night, unable to sleep. Eyes were wide open, taking in the Night. They all looked at her the next day. She felt their eyes on her, prickling her skin.

She was brought back to the Sultan's big tent as the caravan settled at dusk, fresh as a mare. He beckoned her forward. Trembling in excitement and vigor she knelt down before the Master.

– The desert sits… well with you, he nodded.

– Yes, Master, she marveled. – It beckons me, calling me Home.

– You were not given permission to speak, he said sternly.

She smiled.

– You know so much about us, she said softly, – more than we know ourselves. I'm so grateful, Master, so very, very grateful.

She reached out to something, and seemed to touch that something, touch the very air in front of him, and something very similar to an electrical current shot through her. Touching her from outside, inside, a hand formed in the mist and shadow close to the hand she reached out with.

Nancy rose, and took the two final steps against the man sitting in his large chair. He opened his mouth to cry out. She raised a hand, and silenced him. Not a sound, not even the smallest yelp flowed between his lips. A knife on the distant table behind him began to spin, spin, spin.

– You recognize that sound, don't you, Master? You would recognize that sound in your sssleep?

And with that lisp the knife jumped into the air and into her outstretched hand.

She jumped at the Sultan, stabbing him in a frenzied, savage attack, stabbing him twice, stabbing him thrice. The third time she let the blade linger there, in his belly for a while, before twisting it, pushing it upwards towards the heart, and the moment it reached the pulsing, blood-filled muscle both the big and smaller form clinching there, in the large chair began shaking.

– You're just one, one Master, she whispered to him. – Among the thousands destroying the world. You'll have to do, though… for now.

Blood flowed from Sultan Al Rashid's mouth. He died there and then, died in terror, his last gasps a series of undying pain.

She sat there, sat on her knees in his lap, watching as his eyes turned gray and dead. There was a quiet click, and the collar fell off her neck and hit the floor.

– Death comes for me, she whispered in a strange, terrifying, ghoulish voice. – It *speaks* to me, and LIBERATES ME

She licked the blood, licked it off the knife, bending forward, drinking from his fountain.

Flashes came to her, that instant, and in that instant were many. To the north somewhere, was an old woman. She walked the modern streets of Egypt, but she was ancient, and Nancy felt such kinship with her, such familiarity that she laughed in joy. Nancy also sensed Nick, ancient Nick, and Carla, ancient Carla, not far from here, running, sensing her, sensing what was happening. The shadow hand she touched, she grasped grew to an arm, to a head, to a body.

– … *Shadow,* she cried, she gasped, turning towards the door.

The two guards charged her. She raised her hands, and stopped them in their tracks. One heartbeat, two later… they burst into flames.

– It speaks to me, she howled. – THE FIRE SPEAKS TO ME

They ran out of the tent, surrounded by the dark flames, screaming so loud that it torched their lungs. Everybody saw them, saw the tent combusting into an enormous pyre, saw the small human form leave it, saw an unearthly shadow fire embrace the form, making it grow, grow to a giant in their eyes.

Nancy Warren, ancient Nancy, spoke in tongues. First they didn't understand her, but then she spoke in their tongue, and they did understand.

– «We are the true Imashaghen. We are the ancient nomads foretold to return. You are nothing but despicable slave traders and your day is done».

They fired at her. During the first few shots their hands shook so hard that they missed by a mile, but they did get the hand of it, and the bullets buzzed closer to her. Then it was as if a *bubble,* one of air and mist grew around her and caught the bullets.

– The People of Legend have returned to North Africa and we have come as *conquerors*.

Shots were fired from behind, taking the slavers unaware. Four creatures seemed to grow out of the desert itself, attacking them from behind. One burned, as did the shadow in front of them, and they burned, too, and it dissolved them into nothing, while the two demonic forms charging them just burned stronger. They were not that many, the men of the caravan, twenty tops. They were hardened men, but they had ruled by terror, and now the terror was returned to them in ways they had never even conceived of, not in their worst nightmares.

Their worst nightmare was now, charging them relentlessly, coming at them in a never-ending wave of death. And they ran, threw away their guns and ran like little children, paralyzed by the terrors of the Night.

The bubble burst, and a bullet hit Nancy. She did stumble a few steps back, but she didn't fall. Her blood colored the sand red as a sea.

The four approached her. They were unharmed. She smiled to them.

– It stings a bit, she said. – It's all right. I'm all right. I've never felt more right.

As they watched, the wound knitted itself and closed, leaving only the color and not the tiniest mark.

There was a series of clicks. The chains, all the chains loosened and fell off the slaves huddling on the ground. The smooth prods were pulled out. A snapping of fingers, and they were freed.

The camels, on the verge of panic pulled in their ropes, but they didn't pull free. Carla walked to them, sang to them, and the others could swore they smiled to her.

– I wish it was true, Nancy said passionately to Nick. – I wish we did come as conquerors.

She kissed him, kissed him hard. Her touch burned, but he could take it.

– One day, he said lightly, too lightly.

She walked to the people still on the ground, still attempting to stand up.

– You're free, now, she stated, – as free as anyone can be in this world.

Sue and Virgil rushed to her, embracing her, and she embraced them in return. Everybody embraced each other. It turned into a free-for-all hugging, and Nancy Warren felt a great lump grow in her throat.

– Some got away. Desmond stood there with his smoking guns, wild and stark in appearance, so different from the civilized man she had experienced in New York, and even New Orleans.

– Good! She spat. – I want them to know that the People of Legend has returned, that the Shadowwalkers have come.

And she and Nick and Carla, forming a triangle, glanced at each other.

– There's a ship waiting for us in Dar Es Salaam, Desmond said. – I don't know for how long.

– It's outside the direct Arab influence. John nodded. – We should be somewhat safe there.

Safe is only a word, Nancy nodded.

Her tears were dry as the desert itself.

– We can't go back the way we came, she said. – The Sultan's family will certainly offer a substantial reward. Half the population in North Africa will be after our heads. The other half will be their ears and eyes.

Many were clearly afraid of her, overshadowing the doglike gratitude in their eyes. She ignored it, ignored them. She felt wasted, empty, her fire only burning with a low flame.

They set out South East, removing themselves from the looming Arabian peninsula in the North East. They took the camels, a few tenths, and what food and water they could find.

Nancy Warren looked back one single time.

It won't be your whip, she snarled.

So they headed south and east, out of the desert, towards the jungle, towards the sea. It still didn't feel right. Nancy wanted to turn north, and set everything on fire. Their passion said north, their reason south, so they headed south. Exhaustion claimed many of the freed slaves before long. They had to stop, had to rest.

– Share with them, Carla told Nick.

– How? He wondered. – I can't keep healing their body and mind indefinitely, can I, not without eventually making everything worse?

– Give them your blood.

He stared at her.

– Blood is the life, she said. – Life is the blood. And yours is infinitely more potent than that of others. One drop is enough for each person. It won't keep them going forever, but it won't need to either.

So Nick walked to them.

– Open your mouth, he said gently to the first in line.

Nancy stared at him, wondering if this was the same savage she had seen fight.

The man did as he was told. Nick's skin opened, and more than a few drops fell on the man's tongue. In a blink of an eye it filled his entire mouth. He began coughing, gagging, and couldn't even swallow it all. It was as if the red fluid… expanded the moment it reached the wetness of the mouth.

Nick got the hang of it rather quickly, and managed to leave only about one drop each time.

Nancy wanted to go to them, too, but Carla stopped her.

– You can't, she said. – Your blood only burns. It doesn't heal. Neither does your touch, like his does.

Nancy looked at those Nick had given his gift, his gift of life, and felt an irrational stab of jealousy. They… grew, grew on the spot. She felt it, how the blood spread to all their corners, strengthening them, making them glow in joy, true joy.

She and Nick stood on a high point at night, under the full moon, clasping hands, night and fire mixing at the contact points. They scouted the terrain on all sides, never losing eye contact.

– We will burn the world! She said passionately.

– We will! He nodded.

– But… the world is so big, she wailed, letting go, turning away in despair.

– It will take time, he said. – But we have time.

– Yes, she agreed. – A lot of time.

– I'm sure John has some good ideas. He's a smart old wolf.

– Smart old wolf, she repeated.

She sat down in the sand. He looked at her, waiting, seemingly the paragon of patience.

– It still feels like a dream, she said. – I felt almost outside myself when it happened, at least at first. Then I was inside, more inside than I can ever remember being. I feel such Hunger, Nicholas. I can't be human!

– Vengeance is yours, he said. – Vengeance is human. You've been a victim your entire life. The dam broke and the deluge washed away everything in your presence. The animosity burning in your gut is perfectly natural and very, very human.

He did look strange then. Perhaps he wasn't only speaking to her.

– I know, she acknowledged, – but it's more than that, more… fundamental. I don't know which is worse, the detachment I feel at first or the involvement with everything around me when I'm… burning.

Nothing feels beyond my grasp, Nick. Nothing! When I weakened there, at the end, when I turned human again… it almost felt like *dying*.

And her tears stayed dry, stayed remote.

The next morning, when they came down from the low hill, Sue was there.

– Give me some, she begged Nick. – I need it, just as much as the poor wrecks we drag with us.

With eyes like open wounds he reached out a hand, and she grabbed it, and began sucking violently, gagging when the red river turned into a waterfall. He pulled his hand back, tearing it from her grasp. She fell to the ground, her eyes shiny as glass.

– I feel it, you know, she said, – the desolation, the lifeless Waste of the world. I feel it now, feel it burning in my veins.

Her watery, hungry eyes never gave Nancy peace.

They pressed on south, reaching the River Nile, the River Styx, the river of life and death, knowledge and understanding, ancient father and mother. They walked a while along its shore before finding a boat, one to take them upstream, take them further south, into the damp jungle. Finally they reached the jungle. Dry air changed to wet and moist, and it was too much, like Africa always was. Breathing air, resembling water felt incredibly difficult after the dryness of the north, of the Sahara. And all the time their eyes at the back of their neck burned and fizzled, scouting for those who would persecute them.

Nobody died. Nobody during the entire journey. Nick and Carla healed them when that was what it took, and generally, to a point took care of all their woes. Nick using his warm hands and his blood. Carla using more indirect ways, like herbs and everything the jungle might provide. It was amazing to see her work, to observe her confidence and skill. She was very young, hardly looked more than twenty, but she seemed much older.

As do we all, Nancy thought.

The two of them sat on the riverbank after the lot of them had been dumped from the boat, close to a British military outpost, watching the river run by.

– How do you think they'll cope, returning to their homes? Nancy asked.

– Some of them will cope, Carla replied. – Some won't. That's life!

– I wouldn't expect such philosophical mumbo jumbo from you, Nancy retorted angrily.

They sat there for a while in silence.

– You know… Carla finally spoke. – We aren't far away, now, from the Great Falls, and the Great Eastern Plains, where people say human life began.

There was a dreamy quality to the other woman's voice and expression, one of longing and passion that appealed to Nancy, appealed a lot, and her anger relented a bit.

– I would like to see it again some day. Now isn't a good time, I know that. I just wonder when there will ever be a good time, you know…

They walked to the outpost. It wasn't that many soldiers there, most being busy in the world encompassing *unrest* up north. John spoke to the commander in a low, friendly voice, treating him like a buddy. It sounded like a typical conversation between two Englishmen.

– We had some trouble with the Arabs up north, he said. – A lot of trouble.

– I've had a few run-ins with those chaps myself, the Commander nodded capriciously. – I think the best way to deal with this is to get you all out of here as soon as possible, and I know just the ticket.

Two hours later they sat on the back of two trucks, heading east. It was refreshing to once again feel the wind in the face, something at least resembling a cool breeze at the skin. They couldn't recall the last time they had actually done that. The engines gave away a beyond terrible noise, but just now it didn't matter. And they didn't care that they weren't able to speak. All of them had enough with their own thoughts, their own noise.

Dar Es Salaam seemed incredibly busy to them, to the human beings that had practically lived in the wilderness for so long. Their time there already seemed like a dream, faded, forgotten.

– All the people throw off my senses, Nancy said frustrated to Nick. – I can't focus. How can people *live* like this… so crowded?

– They can't! Nick grinned wolfishly. – Hopefully they'll realize that one day.

The city was standard classical European colonial style, architecture and otherwise. It had been ruled by the Portuguese, the Germans and now the British. And by the late Oman empire. It was a classic European, Arab and African town.

Oppression was visible on every street corner. They had become very sensitive to such matters. But it was also a port, a gate to the wide world, and thus it made the Shadowwalkers feel welcome here.

– I think we should go right for the harbor, Desmond said.

– I think you're right, John agreed. – I think it's prudent not to be pussyfooting.

Nancy heard people speak in hushed whisper. They spoke a local dialect she didn't understand.

– «The People of Legend have returned home», Carla translated. – «I heard so. And its Wrath is terrible. My cousin saw the scattered remains of Sultan Al Rashid's caravan. There were blackened bodies and body parts everywhere. No animals were slain. There were no animals there at all. It was an eerie, horrible sight, he told me, as if the gods themselves had returned to Earth».

Hot and cold waves shot through Nancy Warren, as some of the rush, the sense of Power from that day in the desert returned.

– Makes sense, she cackled. – They can't imagine that the gods would need camels…

And she looked ancient just then.

They passed a building, and she sensed it, felt it, what was happening in there.

– That's the British administration building, Desmond looked at her.

– They're torturing people in there, she said, chilled to the bone. – I can hear the screams. They're doing it, right now.

Everybody stopped, glancing at each other.

– We can't afford to make enemies of the British, too, Nick said slowly. – Not, now, when we're vulnerable.

Suddenly Virgil was there, facing the two of them.

– We won't need to, he snarled. They could feel his rage, his crystalline hatred. – Use your Power.

Nancy and Nick stared at him.

– Touch hands, join forces, he said, with a hand curled into a fist. – Haven't you noticed, noticed how much more powerful you become when you are in close proximity or touching?

His rage also fueled theirs. They grabbed each other's hands, as they passed the building and walked on to the harbor. There was a man inside a dark cellar room beating up on a prisoner bound to a chair. Suddenly the torturer grabbed his throat and gasped, gasped for air. His eyes bulged and he fell to the floor, writhing in painful cramps.

Another of the torturers present took a step forward, and he, too, gasped, and fell to the floor.

The ropes fell off the prisoner's arms. He looked astonished at his freed hands.

– *Walk out of here,* a voice coming from the very air told him. – *You won't be harmed.*

The door opened behind the guards. They all heard the eerie click, and they stared at the dark opening. The prisoner looked a little unconvinced and the guards could see that he didn't have anything to do with this, with what the hell was going on. Then a resolute attitude came over him, his jaw tightened. He began his walk, his walk to freedom. The line of guards split in two, dividing so he could walk through the door.

He kept his bewildered face as he entered the dark corridor and saw that all the cell doors had been opened. A few of the prisoners looked outside. Most remained in their cells.

– What are you? The man cried, with a voice rising to a powerful current. – Mice or men? Are you free men or do you indeed belong in prison?

So some of them joined him, and quite simply walked out of the building. Guards and soldiers alike just stood there and stared, a dazed and fearful look in their watery eyes.

The former prisoners walked out the gate, looked around and at the others, and then they ran, in all directions, escaping their confinement with loud, triumphant cries.

– That felt good, Nick said, as they made their way towards the harbor.

– That felt *fantastic,* Nancy giggled.

Her burning eyes warmed them all, warmed them more than the tropic sun above.

They reached the outskirts of the harbor, where people to an even larger degree rushed back and forth. There was vitality here, undeniably, but beneath, like in all modern places was despair.

– The ship has WARREN printed on it with large letters, Desmond said. – I don't know how smart that is, but it will make it easy to find at least.

Nancy recalled her «conversation» with the Sultan, where she had given him their mortal name. A hand of ice and bone grabbed her.

– DOWN! Nick howled. – Get…

Shots were fired. Nick ducked, and a bullet passed right above his head. John was hit in the brow, and dropped like a stone. Nancy witnessed it, how his head was blown to bits by the large caliber bullet. She screamed. They crawled behind the nearest corner, in the nearest door, while bullets hailed around them. Several of them was hit and remained in the street, laying still. Those still able had their guns drawn, directed both into the room and out of it, at the street, where people ran panicked in all directions. The large room in the building was empty. Nick fired at the other corner, and a man sticking his arm and gun out was hit. He knew where every man firing at them hid, and he killed them one by one with deadly precision. They ran, but this time he didn't let them go. They burst into flames, and screamed their heart out as life slowly, very slowly left their burned-out carcasses.

John's body and three others of their companions lay in the street.

– Pull them in, Nancy said. – Use your Power! But don't go out there. I don't know if even you can survive a headshot.

– There's no need, he said flatly. – Our enemies are gone.

He rose. They all did, and hesitatingly followed him to the street. Nick stiffened then, and Nancy and Carla, too, in the grip of the shock rattling them.

There were still screams from the other side of the street and adjacent streets further away, as people succumbed to the flames enveloping them.

John's ethereal body levitated above his flesh.

There were also others, friends and enemies, but they faded fast.

Carla held Nick back.

– Half his head is gone, she said, filled with sadness. – There's nothing you can do for him.

– Don't be sorry, Nick, John the ghost, the shadow said, from the air, its mouth not moving.

Sue had been hit. She crouched there, in the street, moaning in pain.

– No! She wailed. – NOOOOOOO

Nick healed her, in the blink of an eye. He healed all the wounded without touching them. Nancy held his hand. She sensed the current, as she looked around, sick to her stomach.

– They knew, he said. – Knew our weakness.

– It's up to you to you, now.

John the ghost said to the wild man with the fireeyes.

Nick glanced over at Desmond.

– No, to *you,* Nick.

And a freezing cold rattled the large frame.

John faded away, lifting his hand in one last greeting, smiling, and then he was gone.

Nick pulled himself together, straightened himself. They saw it, witnessed it with everything they were.

– Come! He cried. – Let's get going.

Their weapons drawn, the group of travelers, a storm in human clothing walked, they actually walked towards the harbor, to the waiting ship. It felt good, so very good seeing the name on its side.

They hurried onboard, anxiously glancing behind them, but no one was coming, no one charged them. There was no one wearing a uniform in sight.

– I guess the British is busy with a certain prison breakout, Nancy giggled.

There was only sand on her cheeks, still only sand.

– Zanzibar is right outside here, she said in a small voice. – Once an important center for the east coast slave trade.

And she looked very young just then.

– Set sail! Desmond shouted to the waiting crew. – Set sail immediately!

It was an old expression. Even though the ship had sails, it also had large, powerful engines, growling as the travelers walked below deck, as they posted sentries above, still jittery, forever on guard.

The *Warren* set out from Dar Es Salaam, leaving Africa behind, setting course across the Indian Ocean, towards the Pacific, towards the American West Coast.

Susan Warren laid still in bed, pale and frail, her once powerful frame wasting away.

– Her wound has healed, Nick insisted. – And it wasn't much to speak of anyway. It would have healed on its own. But she is dying, dying inside, more so for every breath she takes. No matter what I do, what I say to her, what I try, she's just wasting away.

– She's even eating, Virgil said anxiously. – But she's growing weaker day by day. How's that possible?

Nancy pulled back a little then, and Virgil noticed, and stared at her.

– She's throwing it back up, Nancy said, staring at the floor.

– WHAT? He grabbed her, and shook her.

– She goes to the bathroom, at night and when no one sees her, and sticks a finger in her throat, and she throws up, all of it into the bowl or sometimes walking to the rail and let it go into the sea. I wanted to tell you, but she made me swear not to tell. I've tried to make her stop, but I can't. I'm sorry, *sorry!*

She stood there, worse off than they had ever seen her. They all pulled her to them, embraced her, and she felt somewhat comforted.

Virgil never left his sister's side, not even when there were others present. They made sure she was eating well, and made sure it stayed in her, and it worked. She gained weight again. She gained color again.

But her eyes stayed dead.

It was early one morning. Nancy sat by her bed, beside Virgil.

– You need sleep, he said, stroking her greasy, unwashed hair.

– No, she protested weakly. – I…

– Go, he said. – Carla will be here soon.

Nancy left, subbing her feet across the floor, very young and very vulnerable.

– Poor Nancy, Sue whispered.

– Don't worry about her, Virgil told her. – You worry about yourself. Focus on getting better. You must get better.

Nancy heard them, as she made her way to her cabin.

The room was filled with silence. Nancy heard it. She saw how he attempted to speak, but couldn't, the worry written on his face.

Then he heard his sister's voice, as if from far away, from a world away.

– Can I have some water?

– I'll get you some. He jumped up. – I'll be right back.

He rushed out of the room with a glass in his hand. Nancy saw him set course towards the bathroom. Nancy turned and walked towards one of the openings, on one side of the ship. Then she stopped and turned, feeling compelled to do so.

Sue's ghost levitated in the air before her.

– I can't take it anymore, the ghost whispered. – Please forgive me.

A chill never before felt overwhelmed Nancy. The revenant faded, revealing Sue, the other Sue at the end of the hallway, on her way out the other door, to the other deck. She disappeared around the corner.

– No. Nancy shook her head, shook it repeatedly. – NO!

She ran.

– TURN OFF THE ENGINES

SHE SCREAMED

Virgil entered the hallway from the restroom, just as she passed him. He looked into the cabin, at the empty bed, and there was fear beyond fear engraved on his face.

They ran, ran so hard that the tongue felt like sandpaper in their mouth. They saw her at the back rail. She turned once, and then, as they blinked, she vanished. Nick and the others came running. Nancy and Virgil stopped by the rail, almost falling off in their high-speed momentum.

– She, the fifteen-year-old gasped. – She…

And she could say no more.

And as they all stared down at the sea all that was left was the red spot on the surface, down there in the frothing water. All that was left was the rose.

Carla, shockingly began crying. Nick embraced her, holding her close to his heart. Everything was silent. No one spoke. Sound was dead. Sound had died.

Only the sound of the wet, wet mist was heard. And no one spoke anymore.

Nancy looked at Virgil, at his frozen features, and realized in horror that his sister's life wasn't the only one that had been lost to the sea this day. She knew, beyond words, beyond certainty, when looking at him, that everything valuable in a human being had been lost to Africa's bloody sands, to the dry, dry Sahara desert, to the wasteland of mankind.

She pulled back, stepped back, step by step, until she could no longer see him, see the shell of a man. She ran to her cabin, to the comfortable darkness, and stayed there all day long, until there was no longer anything but darkness anywhere.

CHAPTER SEVENTEEN

February in the new year came with heat and early spring. Only on a few evenings during the week did the cold wind drift in from the north and made mist form along the river.

Every time June Warren went shopping with Sue Ellen she led them past Eric's house. They always went two and two these days. June whistled, walking with light steps. She was lightly and brightly clad. The hair was combed back by the ears and covering her brow. There was little doubt that she looked very sweet and innocent.

The house was in a quiet street, split in the middle by a row of trees.

When they reached it in the early afternoon they could easily hear the tapping from him writing on his antiquary typewriter. Some days they heard him strike the punching bag he had installed in the attic. They went shopping and when they returned the tapping was supplanted by the punching, and as they slowed down, hesitating they witnessed the bag fly through the closed window in the attic, confirming their suspicion.

This particular day June had dressed in thick, white stockings, pulled over a blue dungaree shorts. The top was a bright red sweater just about reaching the edge of the shorts. More like summer attire, really, but it was a warm day, and she was increasingly less bothered by either heat or cold.

Sue Ellen, in contrast, was quite covered and was sweating in her extensive clothing.

It had turned quiet. No tapping, no punching. June had stopped, turned towards the house. Sue Ellen stopped, too, and looked curiously at her. Eric appeared in the entrance door. He walked barefoot and was naked on the upper part of his body. The sweaty body wasn't particularly heavyset, but precisely for that reason the muscles seemed totally over-dimensioned. The hair covered the brow and gave him a menacing visage.

– I need a bit of inspiration, he said curtly. – Come inside.

June pushed her arm inside Sue Ellen's and pulled the quite resistant friend inside the dangerous man's house.

It was dark and dirty and dank in there. Refraining from speaking he filled two glasses with orange juice and handed to the two girls. Her eyes dwelling on his frame June raised the glass and had a toast with Sue Ellen.

– Why don't you use an electronic typewriter? She wondered. – It's much faster, isn't it?

– This is an excellent way of hardening my fingertips since I'm sitting still, anyway. He shrugged. – Besides, I've got time.

He took the cardboard juice box, and emptied the rest of it in one slurp. He didn't take his eyes off June.

She felt the heat from his eyes, felt the pricking of her nipples, felt the increased stirrings of her own heat.

– Anything you could tell me to add to my story would be great, he said casually, not being much in the way of casual at all.

– I was quite young then, June said bashfully. – I don't remember much.

– You're just a year younger than Liz. You must remember something.

Eric turned eager, as if he was about to jump her at any time.

– You don't look much younger either. Not anymore.

– I remind you of her, don't I? June said softly. – And of Linda, too.

He struck a fist through the wall, the same wall where there were already several similar holes. He stared right through Sue Ellen. She had frozen still, there, by the door.

– Uh, Susie, June said casually and neutrally, – can you carry the things home alone today? I would appreciate it…

Sue Ellen smiled thinly and uncertain, and hurried out of there.

– But I am myself, June told Eric. – I'm not any of them.

He stepped quickly forward and grabbed both her arms. She laughed coquettishly.

– Relax, she whispered. – I want it, too. But you must be kind to me, my love. I'm untouched and innocent, you see, and can't handle too much of your vaunted strength.

He nodded and held himself back. At least a bit. He could have been more cautious when he kicked the typewriter from the table and out the window, when he put her on the table and more or less tore her clothes off her. There were a few swift moves as he rubbed his hands over her body. But she felt it, felt the heat increase, growing quickly to become *unbearable*. Just the opposite of what she wanted. There was a little sting of pain as he penetrated her, broke her virginity, but afterwards there was just the sweet itching and the overwhelming ecstasy. *No!* It wasn't supposed to happen this way. She wasn't supposed to feel anything.

The only reason she moved her hips was to encourage him. She couldn't, wouldn't feel. Damn him! It's nothing what I feel. He's nothing. I hate him!

Then the hot, lukewarm tide swept her away…

She returned to the white house at dinnertime. Liz wasn't back yet. She probably had dinner in the fine house, as usual. Sue Ellen stood in the kitchen and stirred a kettle. She didn't comment on or showed that she noticed her friend's rather shabby look.

– Food is coming up right away. You sit down, and I'll come to you with it.

June sat down by the window, where she could see the old tree and the river. Vegetation and rocks covered the riverbank on the other side.

– It looks horrible, doesn't it? She mumbled.

– What?

– It's nothing, June Warren said. – Nothing important.

Trees blocked the view. The fifteen-year-old girl curled her hands into fists under the table, around her own heart.

Sue Ellen put the plate before her. June fed. She chewed the tender meat to pieces.

– So did you make love? The girl asked excitedly and hesitatingly.

– We fucked, June said curtly. – I wish I could give him a disease, that shit.

The smile died on Sue Ellen's lips.

– He made me feel. Don't you understand? I wasn't supposed to feel anything. I just wanted it over and done with, like taking a trip to the toilet and get rid of shit, you know. Do you understand?

Her eyes were still a well of bright brown, but there was something in them making Sue Ellen shudder.

– Uh, June, don't be mad, but can I ask you something?

– Ask away, June replied, totally indifferent and evenly.

– Is it serious on your part? It came out even more hesitatingly, timidly. – Or do you just want fun… or something else?

– Are you implying that I fucked him with a purpose in mind, is that what you're saying, little Susie?

The timid girl didn't reply, not with words. June laughed a shrill laughter. There was something in that voice, that laughter, making the other girl shake, and shake hard, suddenly and horribly.

– Sure. I sure as hell didn't care about him or his motivations for fucking me. He was fucking Liz or Linda or Tilla anyway, and not me.

– It's just that Eric has been through a lot, Sue Ellen said, – and that he deserves a little peace and quiet, now. I spoke with his neighbors, and they like him, even though they think he's weird. So I think you should give him a chance, that's all.

– So that's what you think?

June Warren rose. Crouched a bit, so Sue Ellen had the intense brown pools on level with her own eyes. June took one step forward. Sue Ellen backed off until her legs hit a chair and she dumped down in it, an unexplainable fear cursing through her. June sat down on the armchair and grabbed a shaking hand.

– The thing is, sweet Susie… A hate-filled confidential tone of voice. This was different from Liz' tantrums… *worse*. – There are only two types of people in the world; hunters and prey. If you're not one, you're the other. And you, little girl is a prey sweet enough to eat.

– June, please, don't…

June clutched the slack hand harder. With her long nails buried in soft flesh she clawed five long lines in the exposed back of the hand. Sue Ellen opened her mouth in a silent scream.

– No tears? That's good, my beautiful pet. And we won't mention any of this to the fucking witch, huh?

The paralyzed Sue Ellen shook her head hard, while sniffing and sniffing and being totally unable to stop sniffing.

– *Yes*… There was a hiss, a triumphant hiss. – I scare you more than both Liz and your father do, don't I? That's so cool, so very cool.

And the terrified girl was unable to give voice to her fear, so she nodded, nodded and nodded.

Liz arrived home half an hour later, fresh and bubbling. Then Sue Ellen sat by the kitchen table. June did the dishes.

– Is anything wrong, sis? The dark girl said astonished.

– No. June considered it a second before shaking her head. – Why do you say that?

– You're doing the dishes, Liz pointed out.

– Oh, that. A shrug. – Well, Susie made the dinner all by herself today, so I thought it's only reasonable that I do my chores, don't you agree?

2

The nightmares progressed to the point that they threatened to tear her apart. June and Sue Ellen comforted her late at night, when there was nowhere to go, no way to alleviate the wind blowing through her.

It was Friday 13th. Liz awoke slowly, filled with dread and fear. She walked to the mirror in the kitchen, staring at the black bags under her eyes, feeling like she was about to burst. Something inside her pushed and pushed and couldn't get out, a dam keeping water from flowing.

– Today is the day, she stated at the table.

– But it's just a day, June protested. – A random day in a calendar.

Liz shook, as if awakening from a dream.
– What did you say?
– Poor Liz, June laughed. – So confused.
She kissed her sister as she rose to get more slices of bread.
– You feel something, don't you? She said excitedly when she returned to the table. – Today is the day?
– Yes, I…
Liz just trailed off.
And then she screamed, and grabbed her hand. The other rushed to her, grabbing her, holding her tight.
– My *hand*. It…
They watched, in horror and fascination how something moved under the skin, how the very bones seemed to stretch and reset themselves. It ended, the pain ended slowly.
– I'm okay, she said, kissing the other two on their lips. – It's passing, passing, passing.
She headed for the shower, stumbled in something on the floor before stumbling on.
The shower was a strange experience. It was as if she saw, in a dreamlike state every drop of water falling through the air towards her. She imagined it hissed as it hit her skin, evaporating in the merciless heat.
I'm dreaming. I'm aware, aware, aware.
She stumbled in another blockade of mess on her way from the shower. That prompted her to look around her, at the untidy floor.
– How did it become so bad? She wondered.
– You may not be aware of this, June grumbled, – but we've been talking about cleaning up here for weeks. Enough is enough, right?
– Okay, Liz shrugged, – let's do it.
She touched her skin. It stayed soft and smooth. She went to the beauty parlor twice a week to remove body hairs and retain her stylish look. The people there were so skilled and it was all so very, very pleasant, and she loved looking at the doll in the mirror.
She dressed slowly, and afterwards she did her face and hair in front of the mirror. It was fairly easy, maintaining most of it on her own, and she was getting ever better at it.
June and Sue Ellen did most of the cleaning. Liz was preoccupied all day, listening to the buzz, the gibberish inside. There was nothing there she was able to understand and she desperately wanted to.
She lifted some of the heaviest furniture. It wasn't hard. She had always been abnormally strong. But she wasn't really present, wasn't really there.

– There's something about today… She sat right down on the spot by the window, with the brush in her hand. – There were no signs, no dreams. I just woke up, filled with… with unrest. And it doesn't *stop!*

She stared out of the window, at the river. She blinked and she saw the short man stand on the opposite riverbank. The oriental, Scarface.

And she was positive it was him, to the point of her not really needing to look. The man that had followed in Ted and Mark's heels. The Observer. It was he who had followed her, his tracks she had seen in the snow. She blinked again, and he was gone. She blinked again, and he remained gone, and she couldn't say for sure if he had ever truly been there.

– Liz, can you help out a bit here?

– Yeah, sure, she responded sleepily.

– LIZ, can you at least help us with this drawer?

And minutes had passed.

– Yes, don't fuzz, she said irritated, while she kept staring out the window.

– LIZ, TURN AROUND THIS SECOND. The other two choiring.

She turned, noticing the stress factor in their voices. The large drawer levitated in the air before her. The moment she focused on it, it fell and hit the floor with a loud crack. A brief but intense joy assaulted her.

– It has *returned*. June clapped her hands enthusiastically.

Sue Ellen applauded, too.

– Can you get this load off our back, then? It gets to be a bit of a bother.

She tried to, concentrated all she could, but to no avail.

– It's there, she finally said, – but I can't access it somehow. Perhaps because it's not quite here yet, but it's on its way, I *know* that. I can feel it, feel the storm inside.

She kept staring out of the window. Apprehension and unrest kept riding her. Then… then…

Liz Warren moaned.

It just happened, without her doing anything to make it happen.

Existence… invaded her, assaulted her on all levels. There was a song, a beat. She hummed and danced to it, and didn't even have to move. The crawling unrest escalated minute by minute. Wonder cut into her, making her bleed. Everything she sensed, from the trees, from the walls, from the very air, and the animals calling her name. Chairs and tables moved, cups and plates floated in the air. She stopped it by a moment's concentration. But shortly afterwards it started again.

– It's so strange, she cried, – so familiar. The light and the darkness and the multitude, the myriad of levels of complexity. How the very air is vibrating… can't you *feel* it?

– We can't, June said curtly. – You know that.

Danger is coming. Darkness is coming. The coming darkness is here.

She was damned. Damned!

As the day faded the clouds pulled together, enormous, pitch-black clouds, covering the sky. The wind stopped blowing, stopped blowing completely. Everything turned quiet. There was no song, no dance. The cold air pulled in from the north. Dots of mist passed the window. Something would happen, something crucial, but her inexperience made it impossible for her to identify the onslaught rattling her. The dark arrived early this day, and it would last an eternity, she knew that. Liz was cold enough for her teeth to rattle, and they did, and she feared she would never be able to make it stop.

The doorbell rang. She jumped in the chair. Remained there with her arms embracing her deadly cold body, shaking, shaking her head. June had to go out. Liz wanted to stop her, but didn't have the strength. She remained in the same position when Frank entered the room. Not what she feared. Not yet.

– What's wrong? He asked concerned. – Are you sick?

– Sick? She rejected his silly worries. – Of course not. I'm never sick.

There was an echo in the ether, a sound tearing at the fabrics of reality.

He looked worriedly at the cold sweat covering her face. The inflamed skin around her eyes. The nervous, rapid eye-movement.

– You mustn't see me like this, she cried.

By an act of will, she rose and pulled him close. That stunned him. She never used to do this except when in heat.

– I just have a bad day, that's all, she assured him. – Don't worry, Frank, beloved Frank.

But she didn't really touch him, she never did, and he certainly couldn't touch her, her skin being impervious to his clumsy advances and comfort.

She looked into the mirror, at the luring, hate-filled, contemptuous eyes. The stupid shit! She didn't need him. Not now. Not anymore, when all the heavens and hells of the Universe opened up inside her.

She pushed him away and began pacing the room, kicking furniture and anything coming in her way.

– You don't understand, she shouted. – None of you do.

He took one step towards her, but stopped. Her hair stood straight up. The face in the mirror smiled beastly and cruel and demonic.

Liz fell asleep on the bed, having burned herself out. She remembered falling, remembered him catching her, and put her to bed, surrounding the shaking body in blankets, in a vain attempt to keep it from shaking. She fell asleep, but didn't sleep. Her mind, her cognitive reasoning worked perfectly. It was actually burning within her.

– I should call a doctor, Frank suggested hesitatingly.

– Nonsense. June grinning. – Liz is healthy as a horse. In fact she's healthier than ever.

Frank still walked to the phone intending to use it. He was so sweet.

– The line is dead. What the fuck?

He put the receiver back on. Tried again. The line was just as dead.

– The line is hanging straight down outside.

That was the girl with the claw marks on her hand. Liz wondered, not really interested, where those marks came from, who had made them.

Liz' eyes opened, clear and cold. June and Frank sat on the bed close to her. She jumped or rather slid to her feet, moving smoothly, without the slightest visible expenditure of power.

– Where's Sue Ellen?

– She left, less than a minute ago, walked to the neighbors to get a doctor. June grinned ironically. – You don't seem to need one. I rather thought that to be the case.

The unrest quite simply boiled over in Liz, but what she saw when she closed her eyes was the streets of London, where a giant wolf was hunted by the firespitting dragon. And then in blink after blink after blink she saw a giant bird rise from its nest of ashes.

– LIZ, HE…

The scream was cut off.

– SUSIE! Liz shouted.

In long jumps she hurried outside.

The moment she caught the bright light in her eyes she knew she had failed. All three of them stumbled in a tightrope struck across the stairs. They rolled down the stone steps. Liz felt the pain shoot through her body, but she managed to land on her feet. June did as well. Frank stood on all fours. Blood flowed from a wound on his head.

She realized that she had indeed been dreaming, that she had been a fraction of a second ahead of herself all day. But now, now, she was waking up. She stared around her. Resembling shadows in front of the strong lights stood a half circle of people. Men and a smaller number of women.

The bikers. The leatherjackets.

Everything cleared in Liz. Everything turned crystal clear.

A bit in front of the rest stood a red-haired man, with one brown and one blue eye. All the lights made his right hand shine.

Keith Lampard.

– Look at her, he said, venom in his voice. – Not so strange we mistakenly believed Ted was back in town.

– Hello, Frankie, Ray Channon grinned widely. – Long time, no see.

Frank fought himself back on his feet. He was clearly unsteady, but he stood. A crying, terrified Sue Ellen was pushed to their side of the half moon. June seemed almost indifferent, but she wasn't. She kept her eyes on her sister.

– What's the meaning of this? Liz asked calmly.

Not that she had any doubts in that regard. The grins of gang members, in front and behind her, both male and female, left little confusion as to what their expectations were. Liz was just stalling, checking out the battlefield.

– We've come to take you with us, Lampard stated ironically, visibly irritated because the girl showed no fear. – Make you ours. Voluntarily or not. The hard way or not.

– So, we do have a choice? June clearly giggled. – So gallant of you…

She's teasing them. She wants it to happen, happen to me.

They would come to her one by one, right to their death.

– So what do you have to offer prospective new members? She said lightly, striving to keep the pure practicality prevalent in her voice. – Do you, for instance have equal rights between the sexes?

Channon was about to say something, to charge forward. Lampard stopped him with a wave of his hand.

– That's true, he nodded graciously. – Other biker groups may not practice equal rights, but we do.

– Let me get this straight, she said sharply. – Except for you being the leader, everybody has the same rights, male or female?

– Everybody we don't have to… convince into joining. Lampard exposed his teeth in a horrifying grin. – If you know what I mean. Male or female doesn't enter into it. We even have a pension plan.

There was laughter.

– I was gonna ask about that next, she nodded.

There was more laughter, patronizing and cruel, but with a taint of curiosity.

She had seen the big pictures long ago these minutes, and she shuddered.

– If you had only known what was before you, she said, shaking her head in regret. – You would have run away like the deer for the wolf.

– And you're the wolf, I take it.

Lampard kept his good mood. There was only a slight wrinkle on his forehead to signal that his patience was coming to an end. He wondered where this game was going, and he found it increasingly less funny.

– What I am saying, in case you're wondering, the girl said pointedly, – in case I've misunderstood is that girls can become the leader, too? I guess you need to have been a member for a time to be able to achieve such an outstanding honor…

Christ, now I'm fucking with them, too.

She turned ever less afraid of them, ever more of herself.

– So you would fight me? Even his soft laughter sounded ominous. – Yeah, you're correct in the time-limit thing, but I'm willing to make an exception in your case. You will become such a valuable member of our flock… once you've learned respect.

– Yeah, I will fight you. The girl flashed her fangs. – I will pummel your bones and flesh to powder, and dance on it. I will show you what happens to those fucking with the *Janus Clan*.

There was a rush of murmurs, of whispers. It meant something to them, to him, and she rejoiced.

– And I will conquer you, he nodded, – after you've shown yourself worthy of my full attention.

He snapped his fingers. A woman broke the line and rushed eagerly to his side, focusing her total attention on him.

– This is Sharon, your test.

– Your tame bitch, Liz said in contempt.

Sharon snarled, but stood her ground, obediently waiting for the signal of approval from her Master. Liz studied her, her bulky frame and yet fast moves, showing she was a force to be reckoned with. In a place inside Liz her fighting instinct made a wheel of joy. And the terrible black dark that was no longer so deep within her did the same.

– NO, stop this! Frank shouted. – For the love of God.

A storm or protests and scorn hit him like hail.

– Go home, Forester. To your millions.

– Go home, Frank, Liz told him quietly.

He turned and looked at her. It was as if he looked at her for the very first time.

– I'm staying, he stated firmly.

– Okay, Frankie Boy wants to watch, Channon said. – C'mon, girls, we don't have the whole evening.

Liz stabbed him with her knives resembling eyes, and the hatred in his eyes intensified some more. He was a person hating everyone and everything. It was his only reason for existing. She would have shuddered if she wasn't so geared. So filled with rage and hatred herself.

Liz Warren threw away her jacket to June, giving her an ironic grin. She had no doubt about what Channon had meant when saying «watch». Sharon threw her jacket to Ray, equally ironic.

The two of them began circling each other, in a circle of about five diameters. They moved constantly, checking and counterchecking each other. Liz was very aware over the fact that she had never been in a fight before, that training could never compare to the real thing. But it didn't feel like that. She felt confident, easy on her feet and she felt lethal, as if she had fought a million fights.

Sharon charged. Liz tried to hit her, but missed by a mile.

Her face took a hit, and she dropped into the mud. It didn't really feel like it hurt. Irritation jumped at her, a gruesome irritation. She kicked Sharon, making her fall, too. Both jumped to their feet, snarling and spitting in rage, while the spectators were cheering. Sharon was so quick on her feet that Liz missed with her next blow, but Sharon missed with her kick, too.

They seemed to be evenly matched, the first minute or so parrying and exchanging blows in equal manner.

But then something amazing happened. Liz seemed to… change gear. Those who watched saw it, almost felt it like a palatable change in the air.

Liz slapped Sharon with a flat hand, so hard that it looked like an ordinary blow. The girl flew backwards as if she was being kicked. Sharon sat on her heels, shaking her head in dizziness and confusion. Liz could have advanced, but didn't do it.

– C'mon, prey, Liz snarled. The glow in the fire-eyes made the cheers fade. – Make my night.

Tough as nails Sharon froze to ice. The all saw it.

Sharon rushed her opponent in a fit. Liz twisted her body, easily avoiding the fast as lightning kick.

She grabbed the foot and twisted it brutally. The onlookers gasped in horror at the loud crack, and the subsequent WAIL of pain. Liz held her up for a moment, before throwing her at the ground. She hit hard and gasped for air. Liz kicked her in the ribs, and took all the fight out of her. Liz smiled and bent down, and began *hurting* her, kicking and beating her in slow, deliberate moves. The fight was long since done, but Liz kept at it, kept punishing the screaming girl. Sharon was used to pain, but not like this. She wasn't used to being kept awake, while the ongoing punishment reached new levels as Liz invented newer and crueler methods as she went along. Until the once so deadly Sharon lay in the mud and cried, and begged for mercy, for anything to end the torture.

Liz grabbed the long, curly hair and pulled her after it to Lampard, throwing the slack body contemptuously at his feet. He acknowledged her presence with an admiring look.

– Cruel and brutal, cunning and strong, he nodded. – Yes, you're indeed fit to take Sharon's place at my side.

Liz stood before him, hardly breathing any faster, practically unmarked by the battle.

She considered his words, she did, weighing possibilities, for one second, two, three, before rejecting them.

– And if I want to fight?

– The result will be the same. You will be mine. But the punishment for disobedience is that you must be at the disposal for anyone desiring you, and that, my dear, as yummy as you are, is quite a few.

She saw herself sit behind him on his bike, saw them go to his tent…

She was convinced he would eventually give her to the gang anyway, «to teach her respect». Perhaps she would be able to hold back at the first, or second or third… but then…

But perhaps he would show mercy if she surrendered now, humble and sweet. She was certain that Sharon had been his tame bitch. That she had fought him and lost. Then become his slave. She had been broken and molded in his image.

And there was the other alternative that perhaps scared her more.

Her deepest, indistinct dreams. Crystal clear memories. The man on the bus she had wanted to cow, and crush into submission. Who had fallen asleep shortly after his orgasm. And Ashley. Like the horse. They hadn't been sick. She had… drained them of energy, of life. She feared what would happen if she took it all, took everything they, a given person had… what would happen to her.

She stepped close to him, clinging to him, kissing his cold lips, lowering her eyes, not exactly sure what she was doing, why she was doing it. He grabbed her, holding her in a brutal grip. She turned limp, letting him do whatever he wanted, letting him roam her body at will. And her mind as well.

– I've looked my entire life for someone like you, she said.

– You've looked for someone strong enough for you, he laughed, – and now you've found him.

He let go of her and turned and walked away, and she followed in his tracks. She hardly heard Frank's cries of protest.

Lampard turned by his bike.

– Okay, grab the girls and let's get going.

Her eyes turned big and hard as glass. He frowned while watching her as she backed off.
– I was showing respect, she whispered aloud. – I would have been respectful. Let my friends go.
– Anybody who isn't anyone's bitch is free game, you know that.
– You had your change, she said. – You still have. I had decided to be sweet, to wait it out, see if you were worth betting on…
– Don't be foolish, sweetheart…
– But obviously you're as dumb as you're unreasonable.
She… *let go*. Irrevocably.
His eyes turned yellow. At least that was how it looked like to her, to her vivid imagination. He smiled then. A horrible, expectant smile. He threw his jacket to Channon. Liz pulled slowly back with all her muscles tensed like tightropes.
– Bare hands?
– I have no interest in killing you, she glared at him, filled with hatred.
– I won't kill you, either, bitch…
Now she saw clearly the gray rings encircling his iris. And she shook under a look so sadistic that she had hardly sensed its like. This was the man she had almost chosen.
– I'm gonna tame you, crush you totally, and you will hold the first knife cutting Ted's flesh.
She growled, a sound so real that it could just as well have come from an animal. She reacted to the challenge, not the threat. The beast charged him, clawed him and bit him, drawing blood. He struck her, she struck him, and didn't seem to notice his affectionate caresses. It had all happened so fast. The audience was struck to silence. There was a savage quality beyond reason in the girl's attack they could never have imagined her being capable of. A crouching predator had supplanted the proud girl.
He hit her with a flat hand of his steel fist, and she hit the ground hard. She lay still while clutching her head and whining softly. He bent down and began touching her breasts and groin.
– Now, bitch, you will learn.
– Get your hands OFF me!
The contempt in her voice pleased her, and it increased her already boundless fury.
She grabbed his arm and took advantage of him being out of balance, and threw him over her head and into the wall, and as he hit it there was a loud crack. He released an uncontrollable yelp of pain. Both fought themselves on their feet, swaying as they fought to stay up. There was a thud, thud, thud in her head. Blood flowed from her open mouth. But the

salty taste only invigorated her. He was clearly cautious now, fully aware of the fact that it wasn't an ordinary weak female he was facing, but a roaring lioness. She grinned openly, teasingly, triumphantly. He struck with his steel hand once again, and she only managed to avoid it with a breadth of hair. She struck him in his belly, giving it all the power she had, but without visible effect. This wasn't a fat Police Chief, but one who had fought for his life since he was a very young child.

He struck her with his left hand, the one she had damaged. It hurt. She struck him with her left in perfect balance. His head was almost split from his shoulders. He retreated several steps backwards before regaining his balance. She smiled or she grinned or she sent him a satanic grimace, it was impossible to tell which. He would have turned seriously scared then, if he had had a single bit of imagination in his bones.

Sue Ellen held onto June for bare life. June stood there laughing. Frank and the bikers stood there paralyzed. They had seen the fight between the two brothers. This couldn't quite match that, but in some ways it was worse. Not because one of the combatants was a girl, but because this was a battle totally derived of anything even approaching mercy.

Liz changed gear again, speeding up her moves further. Lampard struck her as she moved in too quickly, recklessly. She hit a tree, her hand being bent between her body and the trunk. A banshee wailed in pain. And there was surprise in the twisted face. He matched her speed. It dawned on her, shockingly, suddenly. He was… Whatever she was…

He was, too.

That stunned her.

He launched an attack. She ducked, and kicked his knee. It wasn't a clean hit, but he clearly had trouble moving afterwards. She laughed, a thrilling laughter defying any description. The rage almost exploded in her. She wanted to finish this, to attack him, but she held back, patiently, cunningly. She could control her rage. She could make it work for her, turn it into a lethal, unstoppable force.

And she did. The song began screaming inside her. Dry sand roared in her ear.

He lashed out with his metal hook, ripping off her right earlobe. A line of blood flowed from the soft, broken skin. It was a desperate move, one that stunned his underlings. The girl could have been seriously mauled by that move, if it had hit her face like he had intended it to do, and they knew he wouldn't have done that if he hadn't felt that he had to.

She hit him with her injured hand. It hurt, hurt so much. She screamed in fury and pain.

The sound made them all want to take off running and not stop until daybreak.

Lampard stepped close to her, hitting her with an elbow in her ribs. Something broke in there, and she coughed blood. She struck him at the side of the head with both hands in a vice. An incredible powerful blow that made him fly across the road. She was stronger. She knew that, now. Stronger than the devil in man's clothing she fought. Only his experience made this a somewhat even match. He swung at her and missed. She kicked him in the ribs, and a lot broke in there. His fist touched her head, and a lot of hair and even skin loosened. She didn't back off, but held her ground. There were more growls. She struck him on the jaw, and he staggered backwards, and managed to keep himself from falling only by pulling on his final reserves. She grabbed his stones, and his eyes turned almost white in pain and fear. She let go. He tried to hit her with the metal hand. She grabbed it before he could even begin the strike… and then she pulled it off its socket, tore it loose from his arm, and struck him with it. The metal broke his jawbone. She pushed him up against the tree before he fell, grabbing him and lifting him high above her head, her claws tearing into his skin. He wailed in absolute misery and incomprehensible pain. There was no regret in her, and no pity. There was just the grin of blood and triumph. She turned with him in her grasp, displaying him for the crowd, shouting in contempt. Before throwing him at the wall again. He slipped down the wood with blood leaking all over his body. When he desperately attempted to draw his knife and use against her, she kicked it lazily out of his hand. She wanted to stop, to hold back a little in triumph, revel in her victory, but the cold volcanic rage pushed her on. She struck and kicked him, kept striking and kicking him, until there was hardly a spark of life remaining in the bundle she easily kept standing by her strength alone. There was nothing left in him for anything. Then she finally let go, and forgot about him.

She straightened slowly, still wild and crazy in appearance. It was the calm she projected that made the look in her eyes even more terrible. She exhaled, as she looked at each and every one of them. To truly scare them out of their wits she wanted to lift Keith. High up, above the trees.

Nothing happened. Fuck. Phoenix' flames. She stared at the crowd of humans with something that didn't just resemble hunger, but actually was. She realized that now, upon her victory, was her true test.

Thunder rolled in the distance. Distant lightning created images creeping up on her. Haunted her. She saw herself. Most of those present accepted what had happened. Either because they thought that she as the new leader would serve the group's interest much better than Keith and the clique around him, or of pure, undiluted fear. She saw herself offer herself to them, with smile and promises. They would come, as the moth to the flame, Wondering, a bit scared, but irresistibly pulled towards this beauty, this horrible beauty. And they would meet Death, meet her, evil incarnated, a thing that destroyed without any goal beside that. She got her first vision when being fully awake then. She flew, rose from Denver in sovereign contempt, leaving ruins and death. Just ashes, no fire.

Looked down at Keith Lampard. A creature of hatred. Like he was. Through eternity. She backed off, literally, deeply disturbed, becoming for a moment just another, ordinary sixteen-year-old girl. She wanted her powers back, wanted it so bad that it hurt. But not like this.

But there would never be any kind of peace, she knew that. There was no sense of calm, relief, rectification, that her struggle was done, after making this decision. A part of her still wanted evil's beauty.

– Are you okay? June touched her shoulder, respectfully, apprehensible.

– Of course.

Even June shuddered when meeting the luring eyes, seemingly containing all the world's contempt.

Elizabeth Warren took a long, hard look at those who surrounded her, that she surrounded. She had rejected absolute power. For their sake? No, she wasn't that stupid. She had done it for her own sake. So there would still be a choice.

– It seems like you made a mistake by coming here tonight. She pushed the corpselike body on the ground with her foot. – At least this wreck did. And those who still feel they have anything remotely in common with him.

Before things could progress further there was a sound startling them all: A weapon being cocked, Eric appearing from the river, from the mist.

– To confirm what you already know, this is a twelve-shot automatic shotgun, he grinned.

– I've got everything under control here, Eric, Elizabeth told him. – This isn't necessary.

– You *see?* Ray Channon used the opportunity to cry out. – Do we take this standing? These are *enemies*. They've got nothing in common with us. When did it become our way to listen to enemies? Let's just leave this place. He won't fire at us then. We can always return later…

Ray attempted to slip into yet another open space, the last. The flock mumbled between themselves. Some agreed, most didn't.

– I can't believe you *listen* to this creep. Elizabeth jumped forward enraged. There was something horrible there, making an impression on them, just as much as the fight itself had done. It made them listen. – He, with a few other sycophants among you, has dominated and terrorized you for years, and you have accepted it. I don't know your reasons for doing so, but I imagine you've got problems at home and elsewhere in the shit of the world surrounding us. What I don't understand is that you were so stupid that you ran from one tyranny and willingly into another.

– DIRTY WHORE, Ray shouted, just as unctuous as any preacher.

She looked at him with humor, with death in her eyes.

– Will you oppose me, Ray? Share your master's fate? That isn't very *wise* of you, Ray. I'm warning you, you fucking sheep. You don't want to annoy me further. I'm telling you this one time. You will BEG for DEATH!

The desire to charge him and tear him apart was nearly overwhelming. Ray stared frozen to the ground into the beast's face. The first close lightning flared and exposed the fangs of the creature in front of him. There was a cruelty there that he would never be able to fathom. There was a loud thunder, and he shrunk in his tracks like a small child. He had his back to the wall now, and he knew that, with all the cunning he had acquired.

– It's beneath me, he mumbled with as much fake dignity he could muster.

He received only scorn. Even from his closest associates. Everything was lost. With a caught animal's desperation his fear changed, revealed his insane hatred. Directed at the reason for his final defeat.

There was lightning and thunder followed instantly. Eric shook, inevitably because of the tearing sound. Ray drew his gun. There was once again instant lightning, instant thunder, the instant Eric fired and Ray Channon's existence came to an abrupt end. In the blinding light it was as if his body disintegrated and was reduced to a lump of flesh and blood.

They who had rallied behind Ray shook visibly, waiting for the next rain of hails. Elizabeth stepped calmly forward.

– Well done, Eric. Give me the shotgun, now.

He did it, reluctantly. But an extra hard look from her made him obey. She threw the weapon in the river, and then she walked in right among them. She thought about Ted. About the collective. She had to be insane. These? She nearly broke into hysterical laughter, but pulled herself together, a bit ashamed. She didn't exactly feel qualified to judge these people.

– I'm your leader now, she stated. – My word is Law.

It wasn't a question, but it was still said in a manner that made it clear she expected a reply.

Mumbling agreement from some, loud from others. Just a few refused to acknowledge her. Those were the roughest, most brutal and sadistic among them, those who had led on and did most of the attacks on the defenseless. A bit odd, considering her recent performance.

– Those who don't think they can accept my leadership may leave this very moment. I certainly don't want you around. Vamoose and don't let me see you assholes again, not ever. And take the cadavers with you.

They split from the majority with hateful, uncertain looks. Because the eyes meeting theirs were without mercy.

– No, not her, she said, when they wanted to include the awakening Sharon. They let her go without protest and carried off the dead Ray and Keith that might still be alive. – Because you don't want to be a tame bitch anymore, do you?

She knelt down by Sharon and grabbed her hand.

– Hell, no!

The girl looked anxiously after the disappearing leatherjackets.

– You won't be afraid of them or him anymore.

Elizabeth helped her up, taking her in her arms when she was unable to stand on her feet.

– It hurts so much, the girl choked, as she folded her arms around Elizabeth's neck. – Thank you. Thank you.

Nervous, but not vicious laughter. Elizabeth let it pass.

But the voices within didn't let up.

– I'll take her inside and fix her up. You will wait here.

– Let me come with you, Eric said. – I must speak with you.

She nodded, granting his wish.

– Okay. She looked at him and them, and there was ice in her eyes. – Listen up. No matter what happens you will remain here. No one goes inside.

They nodded and they remained frozen in their tracks.

With Sharon in her arms, light as a feather, she walked inside, with Eric lurking behind.

– Some speech you made, he said when they reached the living room. – Great stuff!

She put Sharon on the bed and went to fetch a bizarre-looking pouch from a drawer. It had been there since their arrival and she hadn't touched it in six months. The pouch contained the powders and small boxes Nick had put in it, and the additions she had done herself during her excavations in the wilderness.

She dissolved something in water, stirred it with a finger and put the glass at Sharon's lips.

– Drink, she said softly.
– W-what is it? The girl stared at the fluid with the disgusting green color.
– It will make you sleep, Elizabeth replied. And then commanding: – Drink!
Sharon drank in three large slurps. Elizabeth took the glass from her weakening fingers. The sedative worked fast. It didn't take more than seconds before the girl blinked, and only a few seconds more than that to make her doze off, but she was still conscious when Eric and Elizabeth pulled her foot back in place. She moaned a few times, but then she breathed evenly.
– You'll feel better when you wake up. Elizabeth patted her cheek. – You'll go to a doctor tomorrow.
Elizabeth coughed a bit. There was still blood there. Her ribs hurt, now, when the rush faded.
She changed then. Her body crouched. She turned snarling towards Eric.
– You were there all the time, without interfering. Don't you realize what could have *happened* because of your damn need to understand?
– You don't have my experience, he replied calmly. – Mobs like that must be softened before making the move I made. And you did that excellently, as I knew you would.
– You worm, she said in contempt. – If you had known what you were playing with, you would have dug your own grave and stayed there.
– I've taken a look at old school and police records, he said intensively. – No matter what Stewart says, he had blue eyes two years ago. Both you and he and Ted had a totally different eye color the summer of 74 compared to now.
She didn't say anything, but she kept her eyes on him.
– There are ancient stories told about you, he said darkly, – legends so old that they're thought to be nothing but myth. You're a chrysalis waiting to become a butterfly, waiting to become an eagle, waiting to be *transformed*.
There was a loon crying outside. A loon or a raven. Her attention was diverted for a split second.
– I've studied the subject, you see, studied it intensively. I must know. I must!
He moved incredibly fast. Before she realized what happened, what he was doing, he had cut the large vein in her arm. Blood rose from the wound like a geyser. She stared astounded at the wound and at him, and the large knife in his hand.

Then it was as if she woke up from a long sleep. Half a year or more she had slept. The power once again hummed within her. The Song of Power. Was it too soon? Was she ready now?

She was ready now.

And if she wasn't, it didn't matter. It was here, surging through her veins.

She held him with her eyes, with their fire.

I should thank him. He has shown me the way.

– Was it this you wanted to see, little man?

The blood stopped flowing. Just a small amount had found its way to the floor, but it hissed and spread there. The hand wasn't even covered in red. Her ribs didn't hurt anymore. Her head didn't hurt anymore. And she smiled. The knife was torn from his hand and flew to the wall at the opposite side of the room. Then it was pulled back and flew right back to the place inside the jacket Eric had pulled it from. He stared at her. Seconds passed, and then he acted. He grabbed her and pulled her to him, feverishly kissing her and tearing at her wet shirt.

– Stay AWAY from me!

Her mind sparked and she used it to throw him into the wall, so hard that the house shook. And when he crouched on the floor, gasping and trying to clear his head, she grew to a giant before him. She raised her arms to the sides, and her hands sparked.

– You're a… Goddess.

He fought himself to his feet. He was thrown at the ceiling, making a large dent in it. She made him hang upside down, letting him see straight into her face, her Fury.

– Be warned, mortal man. Trying my patience more than you already have would be very foolish.

He was thrown through the window and out in the yard, landing like a sack of wheat in front of the astonished leatherjackets.

– I have to get in there.

Frank rushed up the stairs and into the house.

– Old Frank has finally snapped, one cried.

June understood what he meant. You just didn't fail to obey someone who was able to handle Eric Carr this way. She studied the bloody and shaken Eric. She felt pride.

Frank walked through the seminal darkness. There were no working bulbs. Smoke rose from the fuse box in the hall. The only lights came from the bikes outside. He heard the voice, the voice from his worst nightmare.

– I must go.

A voice reflective, wondering, but eerie.

She waited for him in the living room, right inside the door. The moment he stepped over the threshold she turned him around and pushed him at the wall. She wasn't anywhere near physically close to him. Pieces of the broken window danced in the air. He swallowed and swallowed and couldn't stop swallowing. Couldn't take his eyes from the demonic face.

– Did you know?

– No. He shook his head. He managed that much. – But my feelings haven't changed. They never will.

– I'm not for you. She released him, let him down, let him go. – Not for anyone.

– I know that, but I won't give up.

– Then you're an idiot!

She turned her back to him, heading for the window at the back.

– Everything is so clear to me now, he said excitedly. – Everything with Ted, and that I always felt so weird when Stewart touched me. The desert walk… You should have been there. It was fantastic.

– Death... Grave? Is that…

It looked like she had completely forgotten him. Her body turned slowly round and round. Her eyes were closed, but the face wasn't less eerie. Her wounds were now very difficult to spot. He attempted to reach her, but the couch, the bed and all the furniture moved and blocked his way, without acknowledging that Sharon rested in its path. It seemed clear that the dark girl had thrown all caution to the wind.

She reached out her arms to the side, slightly up, the thumbs and index fingers touching each other. He imagined he saw a shadow by her side, but he couldn't confirm that to himself. A blackened human form, a shadow in the shadow. The window broke. The glass jumped outwards. Not a single piece remained in the frame. She jumped through it. It happened so fast that he for a moment believed she simply vanished, simply faded into thin air. He jumped forward and managed to look outside, just as she, a fast-moving dark form, disappeared between the trees.

He believed he knew where she was headed.

It's insane, he thought, but what isn't?

If he was wrong he wouldn't know where to look for her, and that was far worse.

It was raining, ever harder, as he rushed down the stairs to those waiting, pulling tight together in the mud. He jumped on one of bikes.

– I'm borrowing this.

The closest of the bikers nodded his approval.

– Is she hard to hold on to, amigo?
– You have no idea how hard, he mumbled darkly.
The laughter was drowned in the roar of the engine. It surprised him that he managed to start it at the first attempt. He had never done it this easily during all his previous attempts. He jumped forward and slid in the mud, but then he got it under control and charged headlong into the forest.
– Let's go inside, June said aloud. – She'll be back. I can promise you that.
Eric fought himself up on two legs.
– People with torches will come for you, he mumbled, – and as has always been done, they'll hunt you to the end of the world.
– Are you coming?
June rubbed his arm. Led him like a dog. He followed her, but the rigid eyes followed the lines of exhaust in the mist.

3

There was running. There were confused thoughts and imagery and emotions raging through the female's mind as she ran to her goal through the empty city streets. No human beings ventured outside in the water and fire, but in many a home the curtains moved fearsomely. A lonely cab strived to overcome her speed. The driver stared at her, stared at the speedometer, stared at her again, stared right through her.
When she turned at the next corner she easily spotted the small churchyard, and the old church. What made her come here she didn't know, but she knew she could have found her way completely blind. All her instincts, her psi were soaring this night.
Between the graves she slowed down to walking. Yet it felt as if she was sliding across the ground towards Michael Cousin's grave. She wondered if she would encounter a ghost or a walking, grinning, decomposed body. The distant, mighty roar from the powerful engine didn't faze her. Her eyes were like glued to the black flower at the top of the gravestone. She blinked and it was gone.
– LIZ, LOOK OUT!
The bike slid more than rolled into the cemetery, and turned over several stones.
Elizabeth whirled around, knew instantly that Frank had warned her about something behind her back. The Oriental stood there, balancing on his toes, his entire body in perfect balance, like her own.
– WHAT DO YOU WANT? She shouted through the rain. – Why are you here? Why now?

– Do you need to ask that? He said softly. – Look at yourself. Look at the chrysalis flapping its wings, at their fire and smoke.

The grin made his face even uglier. He didn't speak loud, but his voice still carried strong and far.

– You came here to see what's hiding in the ground. Why don't you do that? I'll stand here… and watch.

He pointed, but it was unnecessary. It was like he said. She had come here to open Mike's coffin.

Watch? Her eyes narrowed to slits. There had been something clearly patronizing in his voice. She raised her arms in a raging move. Stones and soil were pulled up and away. In an even stream the soil slipped into the air and formed a large heap on the ground quite a distance off. It felt absolutely remarkable, as if something was sucking the soaked, heavy stuff up and away. She didn't grow tired either, not the slightest bit, even though it took some time before the worn coffin was revealed in the large, unnecessary large hole she had made. The most remarkable about this was the fact that it didn't feel remarkable at all, but… expected. She lifted up the casket carefully and put it down a safe distance from the edge of the abyss. And now she felt something, like a string quivering inside. Impatiently she tore off the casket's cover, and most of the rotten wood broke into lots of tiny pieces.

She looked first at Scarface, then with burning eyes into the coffin. Except from a bit of dirt and a few bugs… it contained nothing but rocks and air.

A paper sheet wrapped in plastic had been placed beneath the largest stone, what was supposed to represent the head. She grabbed it and put it in her pocket without looking at it.

– Will you go looking for him? The little man wondered.

– Who are you?

– You may call me Chin. He bowed. – At your service.

– Jeez, Frank exclaimed for the fourth or fifth time.

His eyes had turned wide and large when he had first looked at the content of the coffin. His constant theatrics razzed her.

– Is this the man you've chosen as your mate? Chin said, beyond scornful. – Quite a bad choice, if I may say so.

– You may not, she said arrogantly, moving closer to him. – No one has given you permission to do anything.

That little shit, what did he think he was?

She turned to Frank to give him a sweet, mitigating smile, and then Chin made his move. He went for the nerve at the side of her neck, but something, an instinct beyond anything remotely conscious made her duck, and he hit her head instead. She tumbled backwards and fell into the grave.

So dizzy… can't concentrate… took me with my pants down, that asshole.

Water… mud covering her. In her face, in her eyes. Air pushed from her lungs.

He's gonna get it, and I'm gonna give it to him. Before she was consciously aware of what was happening she was up on two legs again, water splashing around her feet, and with all her senses burning and ready for the upcoming fight, trailed by a halo of water and mud, she had taken a giant leap out of the pit.

Chin was gone. Frank lay unconscious in the grass. Only seconds had passed, but the oriental was gone. She looked around her several times to assure herself of that fact. Then she relaxed. Slowly, consciously she directed her attention to the south.

– I must return, she said aloud.

As she had realized quite some time ago, she had Ted and his experiences to compare with. He had been compelled to do the same: to confront the nightmares of the past, to better face the nightmares of the future.

She knelt down by Frank's side. He breathed evenly. There was a small mark on his neck.

– I would have destroyed you. You will do better without me.

She faced the storm. Soaked like she was she should have been cold to the bone. She was dirty through and through. Her face and hair and clothes totally ruined. Regina should have seen me now, she thought. Seen my savage demeanor. She shouted a challenge echoing through the flooded streets.

Wild and untamed like the storm.

4

The Sun
Shone
Right
at her face. She had feared she would never see it again.

Half the sky was blue. Heavy and dark clouds covered the southern sky. It was afternoon the next day. She stood outside the house with a lot of leather-clad people surrounding her. Eric, Sue Ellen, June and Frank, as well. The little suitcase rested by her feet. Sharon supported herself on a

crutch. She was smiling. Elizabeth Warren tied the suitcase to the seat of the large bike.
– If Lampard and his remaining lot come for you, then take them on together, not one by one. She admonished them. – Remember that the need for a «strong leader» is nothing but stupid.
– We heard that he's left town, Sharon said. – We won't see him again. And if we do… we'll *deal* with him.
– Be careful. June kissed her goodbye on the cheek. – I'll look after things here.
Of that, dear sister, I have no doubt.
Smiling she mounted her new bike. Frank had given it to her, as a parting gift.
He knew that her smile wasn't just for him, but for them all.
That was also why a catch grew in his throat. Not for himself, but for her.
She used neither gloves, helmet, nor protective glasses. They thought she looked great in one of her old skin suits. She had kept what little she liked of Regina's gifts. The rest she had thrown into the river.
It had been like a ceremony, a catharsis.
Eric was surprised at how calm and relaxed she seemed. He knew it was a front, a pretense but was still impressed, like he was by everything about her. It was he who had given her a crash course in driving and elementary traffic rules. He enjoyed the speed in which she learned, and even more how sovereign she broke those selfsame rules. He wanted to go with her, but she had been *very explicit* when she had shown him that she didn't want him to.
Elizabeth felt she had done some good with Sharon and the other present leatherjackets, in spite of it all. She hoped that what she had left behind would last for a while, but she didn't really believe that.
The engine started on the first attempt. She let the bike roll down the shingle road, through the forest. Hesitatingly speeding up the moment she reached the highway.
She put Denver behind her.
At sunset she stopped at some dark cafeteria to eat. She sat in a deep corner of the dank room and ignored the usual staring. She looked at the paper she hadn't looked at before now. It was a message, quite brief:

TO EDWARD WARREN:

I KNEW YOU WOULD COME HERE, BROTHER.
MICHAEL

CHAPTER EIGHTEEN

The dark clouds chased something across the sky. Time flied, so fast that she was unable to catch its breath. She took her time, cruising and enjoying the Colorado scenery, until she, about forty-eight hours later reached her childhood's valley. The closer she came the worse it looked. The signs in the sky had turned darker and more ominous. There was no wind now. The rain fell straight down. She saw that, outside the suction that was her moving vehicle. She was freezing, she who never froze. In the clouds she imagined she saw all kinds of horrible forms. Her eyes glowed feverishly under the soaking wet mane.

She could hear the large, noisy machines from far away. See the dust from the torn Earth. She saw the bulldozers destroy the topsoil, and hammer, push the oxygen out of it. Many of the valley's people stood behind barrages and barbwire, and shouted and raised their fists. Policemen and what had to be private guards protected the destruction with their clubs and helmets and shields, as if they were actually, factually born with it all.

She had kept up with the events. Only two of the farms were still owned by people not part of the consortium: Kendall and Jimenez. It dawned on her that she had never counted Cornwall among «the remaining». She had always suspected them.

It felt wondrous to reach fairly untouched land, Kendall land again. The borders had been diluted, almost non-existing before. Very few had cared about them - until now. She looked back at the wasteland and felt the rage and the surge come, welcome as rain.

Linsey stood at the base of the Hill and cleaned a small, congested river and still pond. He was still fighting.

– Why haven't you done anything? She shouted to him, while driving by in mud and roar, and he heard her.

She drove across the fields to the house. Eugene and Trudy stood in the yard, and she couldn't hide the violent hatred she felt towards them both.

When she stopped she slid sideways. It rained shingle and soil, landing very close to the two.

– So you return? Eugene snarled bitterly. – What rudeness.

– That's enough, Eugene, Trudy snapped. – Shut your fucking mouth!

Enraged he lifted a hand to strike her. Then he screamed loud in pain, and his hand fell down, weak and powerless. He stared at somewhere in rage and desperation, but Elizabeth hadn't done anything, and she realized he looked past her. She turned and saw Linsey crouch by the pond, and then she understood. He straightened and headed towards them. Eugene turned abruptly and rushed inside the house. Elizabeth pushed the bike into the barn, and as expected her brother followed her inside. He stood a bit in silhouette in the opening before joining her among the horses and scents.

She recognized at least a little bit of her own restlessness and intensity in his still normal eyes.

– I have done something, he said nastily. – I visited the bank director and told him what I would do with him if he made any attempt, any attempt at all to foreclose our loan.

A grimace.

– That was before Christmas. I know he believed me.

– I'm sorry, Elizabeth said softly. – My mood is rather bad these days.

– The thing with Eugene was harder, he said thoughtfully, while scratching his jaw. – I had to repeat my attempt several times before it really took, but now I've achieved *contact* all right.

– I'm not quite sure how to interpret your cocky manner, she grinned. – It does feel a bit forced on me, but I feel your anger and it pleases me. Still, you're yet not comfortable with your gifts.

– I can feel the change in you, he said. – But I don't quite know what to make of it.

– «Gift» is just a shitty description of it as «curse», of course, she spat. – We haven't been given anything, good or bad. A witch is born, not created.

And then she turned sweet again, moving close, touching his cheek with a feather-light hand.

– Linsey, she said suddenly, grabbing his arm, his naked skin. – Is Trudy hitting on you?

She had hoped to get some kind of answer by their skin-to-skin contact, but he had been ready for her. He had taught himself a lot. All she got from him was a kind of unpleasant feeling.

– What are you saying? He exclaimed shocked.

– Please! She laughed. – You don't fool me more than I fool you.

– It's mother you're talking about… talking about as if…

His voice just trailed off.

– You have had to comfort her a lot lately, huh? And she's been very motherly, hasn't she?

– What's the foundation for your allegations? He kept going. – Your wild…

He fell silent, brooding at her.

– It's strange where your thoughts take you when you have a lot of time to think. She nodded. – She has been after me since I had my first period. At least that long. She seems more than fairly obsessive about us, don't you think?

Linsey could have told her more about the reason. He wanted to tell her about the photograph, and he wondered why he didn't.

Elizabeth looked at Trudy, still standing at the same point in the yard, studying them with eyes so luring and speculative that it gave her experienced daughter fits of frost. A long time's brooding over frustrations and pretence exploded.

– She has always been a better mother than Eugene has been father, right?

– Yes, he replied automatically, without really considering it.

– But *why?*

– Why… what do you mean?

She nodded sadly. He couldn't fathom it, couldn't go where she was going.

– You've borne two ringbearers, mother, she cried scornfully. – You must be proud!

She wanted to rush to her mother and shake her, force her to reveal everything, but she relented.

– I know what you're thinking, Linsey said.

And suddenly her suspicion against him, towards his motives was roused as well.

She struck her left hand through the barn wall, feeling a little better. It had felt as if she had been strangled.

– Welcome home, Liz, she cried bitterly.

2

She entered the main building, the house where she had been born and had lived most of her life. It did feel familiar to a certain extent. Nothing had changed much, really. No chair or table had been moved. It was a static place, filled with memories, some of them even good. It was a dead place, inside as well as outside. Looking through the window she saw a lot of cattle, but very few cowboys, and this was the start of the season.

– Where is everybody? She knew that Linsey had followed her inside.

– There isn't much work to find in the valley this spring, he said. – So fewer seek out here. And most of them work at Cornwall's place. It pays a lot better. And people we've been able to hire tend to quit fast. There are many *accidents*. Not very improbable if you only look at one isolated case, but when you study them all quite the clear picture emerges.

In the coming days they both threw themselves into the work. There was a lot to do, and they worked themselves to exhaustion, knowing fully well it didn't do much good. They just felt they had to do something, anything, against the new kind of corruption that had entered the valley.

Elizabeth fell on the bed every night, falling into a dreamless sleep.

She healed, awakening fresh and bright and strong the next morning. The two of them had breakfast together. The other two in the house weren't present. Both ate like horses, but she ate the most. It was like she could never get enough, as if her consumption resembled that of a human black hole.

They walked outside in the fresh morning air, and they felt it, in every breath they took.

The horses were restless again. She was unused to that, now, when she had learned to control herself, to hold herself back, now, when she no longer held herself back.

She picked up the saddle, and was about to strap it to the horse… when she noticed something chilling.

The strap was cut half off. And that sinister process would have been complete after a few minutes of riding.

– I've never seen the need for the fucking saddle anyway.

She shrugged. And he smiled his dangerous smile with admiration in his eyes. He unsaddled, too. And they rode out in a cloud of dust.

It was easy now, when they knew there was something, someone to look for, to find the person in question. They circled him in and found him in minutes.

She rode right up to him in front of the other riders, and grabbed him, pulled him from his horse and over on hers.

– Why? She snarled.

– They said they would h-hurt m-me, he stuttered like a small child.

– *Who?*

They didn't present themselves.

– So you do what?

– I cut the horse's saddle strap, he sputtered.

She threw him down

– Are you totally out of your mind? For the sake of your precious safety you're willing to harm others?

He didn't reply, except by bowing his head in boundless shame.

– Get lost! She spat.

And he did, fading away long before he had walked off the property.

The days passed in a daze of clarity.

Eugene lay sick in bed. He had caught a bad strain of the flu, one of these epidemics that reared their ugly head every other year or so. Many in the valley and elsewhere got sick, but as usual neither Elizabeth, Linsey nor Trudy. Eugene looked old and ugly as Liz passed by his room.

– None of you have ever been sick, he cried darkly. – Not a second of your wretched lives. Do you come straight from Hell or what?

They didn't care about him anymore. Lucy Barker had to nurse him. She ran around as an even bigger slave, ran the whole day long.

Elizabeth's dreams resurfaced after just a few nights. It didn't matter how exhausted she was. They still assaulted her in waves.

He's coming, the young girl in the strange room said.

Ted was coming. Elizabeth didn't know why, but he came alone. She wanted to both laugh and cry. The Storm was coming. Whether it came with him or just simultaneously, she didn't know. She just couldn't tell.

But she shivered in her cocoon as she floated through eternity.

She finally told Linsey what Frank had told her. She had held back for several reasons, but she needed someone to share her despair with.

– You're right. He shook his head. – We're pretty defenseless.

– No, we aren't! She said inflamed, with smoldering, staring eyes. – Not if we can find out who all the implicated are, those truly pulling the strings. We can seek them out then, and *deal* with them. We'll stir the pot, smoke them out of their lair, delay their precious project, making it so costly for them that they will fuck up.

– Time is on their side.

He kept shaking his head.

– *No!* She shook him. – Under ordinary circumstances that would hold true, but we aren't ordinary. They've got the power of money and social position on their side, and only that. We're walking *Power*. It's a part of us, *is* us, interchangeable.

– It's not that simple, he insisted. – There are all kinds of trouble. Getting supplies and equipment, selling our meat. Age-old contracts are being cancelled. Many people don't even want to *talk* to me.

– That's just tools, technicalities. She spoke softly, whispering like an approaching storm, and he felt it. – It's nothing compared to what rests inside the Human Being. We're the greatest creative force the Universe has ever seen, and the so-called overlords are demeaning it every step of the way. But they've never tasted true power, and we're gonna shove it down their throat.

He looked like he was going to say something, to object, at least in part, but he held his tongue.

– Yes, she said triumphantly. – You feel it. You know I'm right. You're as pissed off as I am, but you refuse to acknowledge it. You've never been a rebel, but now your contempt for society knows no bounds. Your contempt makes you dig your nails so hard in your palms that you're drawing blood. Do it, little brother, *let go*.

They worked late at night. They patrolled the premises like sentries. They guarded the place like hellhounds.

A cow was stuck in the bushes by the riverbank. They freed her without spooking her too much, and then they began cleaning the area, a task that had been ignored for years.

It was hard work, but it didn't really tire them. The dirt and mud didn't bother them. They kept working in a frenzy of energy and desperation.

Elizabeth heard the sound of people approaching and grabbed her brother in the right arm, signing for him to be quiet, and pulling him into hiding. It wasn't difficult. They just slipped in between the bushes and became one with their surroundings, the growth and mud and dirt.

We're the invisible people, she thought. It's only in civilization we stand out as a sore thumb.

The two people approaching lit flashlights upon reaching the cleared area. It was Judy and Butch Davison. They looked very nervous, very tense. Elizabeth and Linsey stepped forward from their hiding. Flashlights were directed at the faces with the beastly eyes and a twin gasp erupted from the visitors' mouths.

– What do you want? Elizabeth asked tonelessly.

– S-speak to you.

Butch couldn't quite control his voice.

– We overheard Paul Cornwall and Terry Williams having a conversation on our land, Judy said quickly. – You're done with Paul, aren't you, Liz?

An empathic nod.

– That's great! Butch said. – We, Judy and I think we youths should stand together. The older generations can't handle what's happening. They're used to seeing things in black and white.

– Why isn't Kevin with you? Linsey asked sharply.

Judy and Butch exchanged glances.

– He was with Terry and Paul.

That didn't exactly come as a surprise to Elizabeth. She had always disliked, truly disliked Kevin. Butch tended to act first and think later, more unthinking than downright vicious like his brother was, easily led.

– The bank has already foreclosed our land, Judy said, clearly upset, beyond upset. – Cornwall senior offered us… «an amicable settlement», but daddy wasn't sick then, and threw him off the property. The land was supposed to be sold on forced sale April 1st, but there is a clause in the contract we had with the bank. Any foreclosure has to be warned a year in advance, and they gave us just a month. So daddy has taken the case to court, and we're sure to win that… eventually.

– But in the meantime there's a lot of unpleasantness. Elizabeth nodded.
– Unknown and ugly voices on the phone, accidents, unforeseen cash flow problems and such.

– They're threatening us. Our people quit. The sheriff, the shit says he will investigate, but we never hear from him. He's crooked as a broken bone.

– Paul, Terry and Kevin spoke about the valley, Butch choked. – About the changes they were going to make, about all the sheep they were going to shepherd.

– Kevin is with them fully and completely, Judy said. – I'm positive he tells them everything we do, every strategy we come up with. How can he?

– He has chosen side. Elizabeth took one step forward. – And so have you.

There was hope in the two others' eyes. She knew that, without looking at them, and she sensed no duplicity on their part, and she would have. They were as transparent as clean glass.

There were five heaps of dry branches spread around on the somewhat flat riverbank. She found the lighter in her pocket and lit them in all fiery, deliberate moves. The flames reached for the heavens and seemed to transform the landscape around them.

– The Devourers have ruled the Earth for so long now, she said. – They've made the rules and the laws, to serve themselves, and everybody must obey those selfsame rules and laws… except them. They've remade the world in their image all this time. It's time for it to stop. It's time to put a stop to a lot of things.

She looked… mighty where she stood between the heavenly fires. The three others listened.

The other three slept. It was late at night. She sat on her heels on a cliff above the river. There was some sort of peace, but the hard knot in her belly didn't go away and yet another time in her young life she felt as if she was choking.

She had a clear line of sight to both the Cornwall and Jimenez properties. There was a lot of activity on both places, a lot of light and sound. She heard it as easy as she saw it.

Old Jimenez wouldn't the Cornwall Consortium manage to rock much. He was too rich, way too rich to fuck with, and they had nothing to offer him. There was no crack in his armor they could exploit. Since his daughter had vanished he had turned his land into a fortress, where only his most trusted men gained entrance.

She turned her attention back to the camp. The fires grew to enormous infernos in her eyes. She heard the brother and sister snore. But Linsey didn't snore. He never snored.

Hearing the sounds of the wilderness had become second nature to her now. She didn't even have to listen consciously, and when she did all her senses listened and interpreted and lived. Her senses penetrated the shadows, saw beyond the known, sensing what was hidden.

Something distracted her. There had been moving shadows, shapes there in the darkness, and then her attention had been pulled back to the Jimenez place.

She focused on it, on the lights and the sounds. She imagined that Linsey spoke to her from the fires, from his sleep, but she didn't hear him. Her eyes began to twinkle like the fires and the stars. Something happened over there…

3

The dark trees surrounded her on all sides. The needles on the ground pinched her feet. She had been away for so long, and it took time to get used to the forest again. Its sounds and presence invaded her, and there was joy. She moved in on the Jimenez property against the wind. It carried the sounds even easier to her. Her ears were pricked and moving. A few humans were able to move their ears while concentrating, but she did it like an animal, without effort.

There were dogs there, of course. She knew they would eventually catch her scent, and they did, and as expected went totally apeshit. The guards had to strive hard to not loose hold of their restraints. She sneaked through the forest, and was ready to act on a second's warning if the men gave the barking, giant mutts free reign. Given the change they would tear her apart in seconds.

She moved on all fours. The guards' eyes were primed on something of human height, and passed her merely a few steps away without being close to discovering her. There was an ever-shifting maze to cross before reaching the open yard, but she did so easily, and she allowed herself a touch of pride.

The main gate was open, a very strange sight on this place, at this hour. Something made the creature hidden in the bushes stare down the road, and there it was, a lone vehicle climbing towards the armed guards posed in the yard.

The car turned and stopped on the small parking lot outside the gate. A group of masked men rushed outside, Men, on each side of the gate, faced each other as enemies. A man, Emilio Jimenez appeared in the doorway of the large house and stumbled towards the two groups. He seemed far older than Elizabeth recalled him. The century old «dignity» was also diminished, to the point of being almost gone.

The leader of the «visitors» was Terry Williams. Elizabeth recognized him because she didn't see just with her eyes, and could easily look beneath the mask, to the emotions and personality lurking there.

Williams nodded. Two men brought a half unconscious woman out of the van, and supported her.

Maria Jimenez.

– Dios, Emilio moaned. – It is she! But… but what have you done to her?

– We had to restrain her. Williams shrugged. – But she's here now, and now it's your turn to uphold your part of the bargain.

Jimenez was given a paper and a pen, and he signed the document without looking at it. Williams gave a sign, and Maria was handed over to Jimenez' men.

– You're not so stupid that you will keep opposing us. I know that. You know we're the strongest. Three days and you will be gone from here. Crawl into a hole and stay there, one far from us.

The visitors left, their short welcome outstayed, for now. Elizabeth hurried after them, taking just a few cautious steps before running full speed after the car, throwing all caution to the wind. Jimenez and his men might have caught a glimpse of a black shadow there on the open road, but she doubted it.

The car made an early turn towards the Cornwall castle, her dream house, without really bothering to hide itself. She slipped into the forest again, taking the shortcut to the metal and brick place ahead.

She sensed the predator in the forest. The wolverine. It howled to its mate. She howled back, certain that no human ears could hear the difference between the wolverine's howl and her own.

The van had not quite reached the outer gate when she jumped the final fence and settled inside a clutch of trees a few steps from the clearing. It stopped outside this gate, too. An unmasked Terry Williams jumped out.

The van turned and left. Williams strolled up the asphalt road as if he owned it. Cornwall senior met him on a secluded spot.

Elizabeth strained her ears to listen in on their conversation, but she was too far away. She ran on all fours across the field to the barn, the horrible, newly reconstructed steel barn. No one had cried out, and now she was once more safe in the shadows.

– … went well? She heard the sickening, arrogant voice of Hunter Cornwall.

– Smooth as a newborn's butt. One more down.

They stood there talking a while longer. It was mostly a stroke feast, where they were congratulating each other with their «success». Elizabeth was very close to throwing up.

They finally walked inside, leaving her alone, to recover her wits.

Sweat kept flowing from her skin, and she couldn't seem to be able to stop it, no matter how much she managed to calm herself.

She turned, feeling the cold draft in her neck, and there he was. Paul was.

He approached her in a relaxed, completely non-threatening way.

– I told them. He walked to her with his blinding, terrifying smile in place. – I knew you would return, return to me.

A set of handcuffs was dangling from his hands. He grabbed her, and kissed her. She found herself responding. He pushed her away, held her at arms' length, turning her around, pulling her arms behind her back. She felt the cold metal around her wrists.

– What are you *doing?* She asked incredulous.

– Your disobedience must be punished, he said strictly. – You will thank me for that, for that, too.

He pulled her with him towards the house.

– But first I'm gonna show you something, and after that is done, the punishment will probably be quite redundant.

He looked at her with love in his eyes, and she cringed. How could he do that? How could there be love?

– You always hurt those you love, he said. – Haven't you learned that yet?

And she winced in his grip.

– I'm not scared, you know. I don't need my hands to kill you.

He didn't reply, not with words anyway.

Apprehension did ride her, as he led her into the empty castle. She knew there had to be others there, but she saw no one. They had left it to Paul to deal with her. She had been so confident in herself, in her ability to deal with things, after Denver. With one stroke he had made it go away. Her eyes tried to stop looking at him, but they couldn't. She was helplessly attracted to him.

The lights. In the hall and hallways. In the entire, shining domain. It was so strong that one had to look hard to glimpse the heaps of dirt in the corners. Elizabeth did, but it did her no good. She was just as helplessly fascinated by the glitter.

I wish I could see the sun right now. This place is so dark and dank.

They walked down the long staircase to the lower floor. She knew of it, had heard the servants whisper about it. Only the most trusted of them had access here. The huge room below opened up to them. She almost laughed. This house had no cellar, nothing resembling the «lower floor» of ordinary houses.

– I…

He stopped, stopped them both in their tracks.

– You can *sense* something, cant you? He whispered.

– Sense something? She said incredulous. – What the hell are you…

There was something down here, something in the air, in the walls.

He brought her through a long, dark corridor. Small fires burned on the walls there. It was night forever down here. They were about at the center beneath the house when they encountered a large door of dark and solid oak. Paul opened it. It didn't quirk. Filled with wonder and apprehension she followed him inside.

Something nagged her, something she hadn't been able to catch… until now, when she saw the interiors of the room.

He knew.

The room was darker and even emptier than the room outside. At the center of each of the five walls burned a candle, a black candle. At the center of the floor was drawn a pentacle, a five-point star in a circle. And there were black candles there as well, at each of the five points. Michelle Warren lit them with an oozing torch. Elizabeth looked at the girl in the white nightgown and felt even weaker. Damn catch in the throat. The smell of blood assaulted her and dizziness almost overwhelmed her. It was on the floor, on the walls, in the ceiling and fucking everywhere.

– That's very good, Michelle, Paul said. – You may go to your mother upstairs now.

– Okay, uncle, said the little girl. – May I, auntie?

Elizabeth nodded faintly. She was somewhere else entirely. Michelle blew out the torch in one powerful breath and padded out of the room. The smoke from the put out torch had a sweet, sickening smell.

– You killed someone here. Elizabeth's voice rose. – You s-sacrificed him.

Images of Claudia flickered before her eyes. Stronger imprints than she had ever experienced. She practically saw Claudia stab the bound man on the floor with a large, shining knife, witnessed how he expired in a heap of fading gasps.

– We consecrated the room, he said, – made it ready for you, for you to consecrate it for you. This is your room, your domain. It has waited for you.

The very room focused energies. It strengthened her. It sickened her.

– This is my room.

He opened the door going further in. Bright light flooded them, and the radiance of the past faded. Elizabeth's eyes hurt and tears flooded them.

This room was also a pentagon. Computers and modern communication-equipment covered it from wall to wall.

– The absolute latest, he lectured her. – The monitors' clarity is truly amazing. With stuff like this you can easily control many people's life. Not to speak of how it will be a few years from now.

Elizabeth felt cold and heavy when she stared at all the blinking lights and the monitors, the surveillance screens. They showed the castle both inside and outside, and the surrounding terrain, both in ordinary light and infrared. Paul activated the keyboard and pushed a button. Then the images showed the school, everything interesting there. Another push. The bulldozers and various machinery. Where they were active day and night to destroy the valley and its people. The next image was of the Kendall main building, from all four sides, the surrounded fortress.

– I've always been interested in film and photo. There has been a rapid progress in the area, but there will still be moments when one has to resort to the good old one-picture method. This is especially true if one is heading far into the wilderness, far from people and electricity.

He typed a codeword on the keyboard and hit RETURN. The reaction on the screen was instantaneous.

There was a fairly recent picture, followed by a lot of text, of information, and it stunned her.

SUBJECT: ELIZABETH WARREN
BORN: 1959-04-30
CLASSIFICATION: **Homo Magi** (commonly referred to as *mutant*).

Subject is born with paranormal abilities. In her case Telekinesis and increased empathy have been confirmed…

The words turned into a jumble of confusion.

– I'm not born in April, she said weakly.
– Yes, you are, he grinned. – What your parents told you and what is the reality are two different things. My people made a thorough check on things. You wouldn't believe everything they found…
More images, more words.
Three sharp color images side by side. The first a school photograph from before the Time of Change. The other during it. And the third afterwards. Everything presented in such a striking way that it struck her mute.
More photos. One taken the moment she lifted the large stone with her mind. One of her on the veranda, as she called back and grabbed her shades from the dark below. A twilight picture of her on the Hill. One of her on the roof.
And there were others.
– I've got a souvenir from that night. A plaster cast of your beautiful foot.
Finally the computer showed a film of her as she chased the van from Jimenez. Numbers showed average and maximum speed. It showed clearly how she, at least for a moment there, kept up with the car.
She saw the hunter's eyes, the hunter's pose, and realized perhaps for the very first time that she truly was a hunter, that she always had to hunt *something.*
– I have been obsessed with you for years, he willingly confessed. – From my early childhood I've known I'm better than everybody else. Only in you I found my equal. And I eventually discovered that you would be more valuable than even I could dream of. I was reluctant to admit the stunning truth at first, but no powerful man has gone very far by denying the facts, and a lot have changed in the valley since then hasn't it, my love?
He punched a few more keys
She looked at the plan drawings appearing on the screen. She looked startled at them.
– A pyramid, she whispered, – a pyramid of fear.
He grabbed her again. She didn't resist.
She faced him, speaking slowly and deliberately to him.
– I heard Terri and your father talk, heard them brag to each other. It felt completely alien to me.
– Soon it won't be, he assured her.
– It isn't strange you're saying that, she spat. – You've learned nothing else since early childhood. But you're so bright that you should have been able to deny its truth, not willingly fall into the same pool as your parents.

She hesitated, her voice shaking.
– You've chosen to be what you are.
– Many are confusing intelligence with kindness, he said with his face close to hers. – They believe one follows the other. What fools. One with greater capacity needs more to fill his mind to not grow bored. I've always been at my best when I have confirmed my superiority, every time I've demonstrated beyond belief that I'm the greatest and best. And now, my love you're here to share my joy.
– At least you're being honest, she said contemptuously.
She managed that, at least.
– You aren't ready yet, he noted, nodded to himself. – You do indeed need a steady hand.
He was like Regina, being honest with himself. He wanted the power, and it was the goal, not the road. It was everything he wanted. He wanted monetary wealth beyond anything, to shine even stronger, at the expense of as many as possible.
– You're talking about growth… That is what you're talking about, right? I'm familiar with quite a few manners of growth. I know there's more than one way…and I don't care much for yours.
– You will, my love. He grinned, very solemn, very convincing. – And in the meantime you should thread carefully. May I remind you that we have the means to reveal how amazing you truly are? Please don't take this as a threat. I would never hurt my woman.
– I'm not your woman!
She shook in his hands, close to shaking.
– You're my woman already. It's just that you have yet to convince yourself of that fact. Don't worry, you will soon, and then we can began in earnest.
He kissed her. She responded to him without measurable resistance. There was a table at the center of the room. It felt amazing to her that she hadn't noticed that fact before.
– Who was the sacrifice?
– He was just convenient. He shrugged. – It doesn't really matter, does it?
He put her on the table, lifting up one of her legs, grabbing the foot, picking a few needles from between the toes. The toes itched pleasantly. She had never imagined a touch there would feel so good.
– Such soft skin…
He pushed a hand up her leg and thigh. She resisted, but it was only half-hearted and very, very ineffective. He loosened the belt, pushed the willing body down on its back on the table and pulled off pants that now

seemed so very, very tight. She wanted to use her power, to punish him, to draw blood, but being totally unable to focus as she was, nothing happened.

She cried out in need, in mindless lust. He smiled, and his smile was so pretty. She had always loved his smile.

– That's it, he said triumphantly. – I know you'll eventually realize I'm right. You will realize everything, everything important.

– NO… PLEASE! She wheedled, she begged. – You're killing… my *soul*.

Her face mirrored the greatest of pleasures when he removed the remains of her clothes. She writhed in his arms. Her denials changed into soft, longing moans of surrender. She pulled in the cuffs, but there was no force or intent behind it. There was no movement but what resembled the wings of a dying fly. She moved beneath him begging favors, mumbling fever-hot words. He captured an even bigger part of her dying soul.

CHAPTER NINETEEN

And then Ted arrived, imperceptible. So quietly that he was hardly noticed at first. Still… to most of those looking right at him he looked totally insane. Eyes burned without pause. His clothes were mere shreds. They had several bloody spots. He had minor tears on his hands and face, and all over his body. The workers along the road had been recruited from the toughest crowds in the country, and were used to just about everything. They were proud of their rough attitude and resilience. But now they hardly dared look at the ghoul passing them, and suddenly they felt very much like scared and cold little children. The Sun no longer warmed them.

He walked on the narrow shingle road up the hill to the house. Elizabeth and Linsey groomed the horses outside the stable. She had felt… worried, even more so the night before, and had drowned herself in work since the morning. Shock rattled her when he came closer. He was changed, very changed, even from the newspaper clippings.

Even… from a few weeks back. It suddenly struck her. At the time of her last day in Denver he had also experienced something horrible, and the weight of it struck her like nails of ice. She froze in the warm wind.

Trudy had also spotted him. She was first by the entrance to meet him.

– I've been expecting you, Edward, she said, strangely smiling.

– You're the second person to use that name in a fairly short time, he said. – The first was a secretive undertaker in London. I can't recall having heard it more than once before that. It was sometime during my early childhood, and I believe it was you then as well.

– Where's Tilla?

Elizabeth understood, and felt the pain like a blade through her own body.

– Tilla is dead.

His voice was strangely distant. There was no sign of sadness, only desperation.

Linsey put his hand on his shoulder. The distraught dark man didn't seem to notice it. His eyes were locked on Elizabeth. Nobody said anything.

Eugene appeared, taking one single look at Ted, before leaving without a word.

What does he want, this stranger? Elizabeth wondered.

That one was easy to answer.

Ted Warren wanted Elizabeth Warren.

She had realized that the moment she spotted him. If he had just arrived a year or even a week ago… But now it was too late.

– It is a good thing you came to us, then, Trudy said kindly. – To your closest family.

She touched his cheek. He flinched. She removed her hand.

– You've traveled far. She nodded. – Dinner isn't quite ready, yet, but I can make some food to you.

I'm not hungry, he replied curtly. – But I should change clothes… if you have any.

– I believe some of Linsey's largest threads will fit you somewhat, Trudy said cheerfully. – Even though they, too, will be a little tight.

– How did you manage so far without money? Linsey asked hesitantly.

– I had some at first. Ted shrugged. – Then I stole, wherever there were time and opportunity.

Elizabeth felt the hollow place within herself. She understood him so well.

It was twilight, twilight already. Linsey stared through the window from his bedroom at the valley and the ongoing destruction there.

– The lights from the damn machines will very soon be the only lights here, he said, – if they aren't stopped.

Ted undressed. He practically ripped off his remaining shreds in slow, deliberate moves, leaving them in a heap on the floor.

– I mean, Linsey continued. – I felt helpless before I discovered my powers, but now I feel, if possible even more so. Even the three of us combined haven't really a change of putting a stop to this… this travesty.

Ted stood naked before him. Linsey's lips quivered when he saw the countless small wounds.

– Jeez, how did that happen?

– I had to throw myself through a window last night. Another shrug. – It isn't like in the movies.

– Why didn't you use your powers to break the window before you jumped through it?

– I forgot.

The simple reply rendered Linsey speechless. He felt ill under the terrible direct stare.

He watched as Ted let a hand slide over his body, perhaps not touching it. When he was done he held a small collection of glass fragments in his palm. Linsey swallowed hard, realizing that Ted had pulled them all from his skin. Ted held the hand over the wastebasket. All the fragments dropped into it, falling from the open hand.

– We should do something… about the wounds.

– There's no need. They'll be gone soon.

Ted turned to leave.

– Uh, the shower is…

– Down the hall? I know.

Linsey brought a bundle of clothes to Ted's old room, the place Trudy had kept tidy all these years. The bed was recently made. The room smelled fresh and inviting. Ted entered it behind him. Linsey shook as he turned to face the specter. He couldn't recall noticing the water had stopped flowing in the hallway.

It was true about the wounds. They had already visibly mended on the muscular and hairy body. They had closed and some were already fading. In the morning, Linsey suspected, they would be gone.

Even the old scars from the severe whipping he had endured as a boy, had paled significantly, to the point where they could almost be mistaken for skin discoloration.

– Yes, the scars are… going away, Ted said. – It began recently, just after Tilla's death. I'm no longer keeping a lid on my powers, no longer… holding back.

He dressed slowly, standing there, reaching out to the clothes with his eyes closed, not really noticing much around him, not really here.

The eyes opened. They didn't blink. One moment they were closed, the next open, aware.

– Your father seems to have degenerated further in my absence, he noted.

It was almost an accusation. Linsey kept his cool.

– I totally agree with that, he replied. – He has become an asshole of the first order. If there ever was anything there worth bothering with, there isn't anymore.

– Five years ago I kinda admired him, Ted said. – At least enough to listen to him. We had a chat just before I left. I believed his drivel, at least subconsciously. I even sort of aspired to it, to his ideals, to society's fake ideals for good conduct. He instilled a sort of naiveté in me, I let him and society do it, and it almost destroyed me.

Linsey nodded, and nodded some more.

– We're on the same page here, he said hoarsely.

– Eugene has lost his illusions, Ted added. – And still he's clinging to them for his life and allowed himself to be destroyed. I won't allow that to happen to me.

And Linsey Kendall froze in the cold twilight.

– The rings, where did you get them?

– We found them, Linsey replied unresistingly. – In a box in the cellar. Great grandfather Nick left them for us. There's one more, one meant for you.
– And your mother hasn't turned more communicative lately, I trust.
– Both Elizabeth and I have tried to make her talk for years, Linsey said frustrated. – But she just won't open up. I think we need to use torture to get essential information from her.
She's like Stewart. Ted nodded passionately. – Lying by telling the truth.
And now, suddenly he was here. Now, there was passion.
Eyes locked on to the glow on Linsey's finger.
– The third ring, where is it?
– Paul Cornwall has it. Linsey was defensive, experiencing fully the unpleasantness of it all. – Liz… gave it to him. She's in love with him, I think. At least she was. I can't tell for sure. But I know that he exposed her, exposed… us. He has photographs, proof of her powers, and they know about you and Stewart as well.
Ted nodded, but he seemed strangely disaffected again. It didn't seem as if the threat of exposure, of full disclosure *worried* him. Linsey feared that nothing worried him anymore.
– I've traveled half around the globe, the witch said. – Nothing is different. Nothing is changed.
They kept talking. About other things. But the conversation, the audience was done. It slipped into more mundane themes. Linsey wanted to discuss their origin, their destiny, but right now, Ted didn't give a shit about that either.
Linsey couldn't do anything about it.
It wasn't him Ted wanted.

2

The fire lit up the night like fireworks. Everybody could see the embers' dance above the burning inferno that had been a house.
Elizabeth woke up with smoke in her nostrils, jumping out of the bed in a fit of fright. She cast long glances around her, sniffing the air, as she rushed out in the hallway, rushed to the window to the other side of the house, as her family gathered by her side, as she sensed Ted's close proximity, where she saw the fire.
They all dressed in the hurry and ran through the night. She stood in front of the burning inferno, her back cold, her front sizzling from the heat. People coming from all over the valley stared and gasped.

The Davison family home disintegrated before their eyes. It was surrounded by flames, totally unrecoverable. There were sirens growing louder as the firemen and police arrived, obviously way too late to do anything good. There were screams from inside, deafening in its pain.

A figure threw itself through a window. In a beyond strange way everybody recognized Judy Davison as she flew through the air and landed, landed hard on the ground right before the gathered neighbors. Smoke rose from the sizzling body.

The firemen finally arrived, with their cars and hoses, spreading water on the raging inferno. But it was useless. First, for a very long time the onslaught of water didn't seem to have any effect at all, but then the building quite simply crumbled to ashes as darkness and smoke slowly supplanted the fire.

Kevin appeared, looking very shocked and sad, but Elizabeth easily saw through his act. In fact the majority of the people present did. They stared at him and condemned him, and he glanced at them with luring, insane eyes.

Judy's parents and her brother Butch succumbed in the fire. The girl lay still and pale when Elizabeth and Linsey visited her on the hospital the next day. There was no movement there on the bed, no sign of life beyond the somewhat even heaving and lowering of the chest.

– It's amazing, isn't it, how she half dead jumped through the flames and the window, to relative safety. The will of the human being knows no bounds.

Elizabeth spoke in burning sadness, with a hardly contained rage, strangely comforted by her own words, deeply ashamed by her own feeling of inadequacy.

– I can't get her to respond to me, Linsey said, shaking his head. – I have tried and it's like she isn't really there. Perhaps I'm not doing it right or is too afraid to fuck her up further.

– She needs healing. Elizabeth touched his shoulder. – We can't give her that. We can only grant her revenge and justice.

He looked at her.

– Call your people, she said. – Call all of them.

3

Linsey called everybody he knew in the radical and environmental movement, both domestically and abroad. It was a frustrating experience. He slammed the receiver down more than a few times.

– Most of them have kids and nine to five jobs *already,* he said angrily and incredulously. – I mean, I suspected it was headed that way, but not so fucking soon.

But he did get some, the frustrated, the angry, the stubborn, those growing more radical, not less, and they arrived in the valley like a trickle from a punctured wound.

Judy slipped into a coma and didn't wake up. Kevin declared that he was dropping the lawsuit, «to not keep ripping open bad memories».

– He can't do that, can he? Elizabeth protested. – Not without Judy's consent. They're both equal heirs.

– Not yet, no, Trudy said. – But eventually, if Judy doesn't wake up, he will be named her legal guardian.

Early one morning, when the sun burned hot both the arrived strangers and what remained of local protesters made their way to the construction area.

– It looks bad, one exclaimed. – In fact it looks horrible. How can they do things like this? How can they even imagine it?

– This is happening everywhere, another shrugged, – and has for some time. It's neither better nor worse than what I've seen elsewhere.

– I close my eyes, the other said, – and I imagine it's gone. But it's still there when I reopen my eyes.

The heavy machinery made the ground shake. Elizabeth shook, too, the reason for it eluding her.

Another busload of people arrived the moment they passed the bus stop. There were a lot of people recognizing each other, old friends and fellow warriors.

Ted walked behind Elizabeth, looking more than a little indifferent concerning everything happening. He was only interested in Liz. She knew he followed her practically every second of the day. He seemed confused like a neutered dog over her efforts of avoiding and ignoring him. If he only knew.

She wanted to be close to him. It was nothing she wanted more. There was so much she could have told him, and he her.

But she couldn't.

It was like she was paralyzed, as if she could do nothing but going through the motions of complacency.

This was nothing. She could do so much more. She wanted to.

But she couldn't.

She lifted her hands above her head, and it turned silent, the buzz faded.

– Welcome, she greeted them all, also those she had already greeted, feeling very much like a cheat, a charlatan. – We're about to confront the enemy head on. But remember, even though everything may turn a little… hairy there must be no physical aggression on our part. Not unless they're actually attacking us. We will do this. We will stop them, stop their mad rampage, and we will do it by peaceful means, and thereby show others that it is possible to stop industrial giants from destroying the world.

Her words inspired them. She sensed that, and felt a little better, seeing the young, innocent, spunky girl from their perspective.

The gathering began moving, moving like one single coherent mass against the monster ahead. The brother and the sister walked in front.

– It's invasive, Linsey told her. – I sense… it's like everybody, all the people here and down there are inside my mind. All the hatred, despair and rage… are overwhelming. I don't know how long I can take it.

– You can and will take it, she snapped. – We need to be strong, and *we will be!*

She showed him nothing of herself, nothing of the fluttering wings inside, portraying a confident and calm front.

– You must learn to focus, little brother, to concentrate, she insisted. – Then you won't have to risk being overwhelmed by others' thoughts. Use your own emotions. Pull your powerful rage from your depths. Touch its currents and be *strong*.

The power of suggestion worked. She felt the determination in the air echo within.

There was no rain from the dark sky today. There was only the wind. One of despair, seemingly blowing from all sides, assaulting, rocking them all. The clouds rushed across the sky in a turbulent, violent pattern.

The small group of people stopped right in the large and fear-inducing machines' path. A roar of rage rose from the engines. It was more than clear that at least a few of the drivers pushed harder on the gas pedal. Dirt and small rocks were kicked in the air by the practically spinning wheels, and the distance to the unprotected people was shrinking fast.

– They're gonna run us down, a man cried in a panicked voice.

– Hold your ground! Linsey admonished them, and they obeyed the strangely compelling voice, the one that didn't seem to belong to him at all.

He rushed forward, directly in the line of the bulldozers, raising his hand in a stop signal.

Three people with cameras stood on the Hill, a safe distance away, documenting it all. He saw himself from there, from above, from a weird viewpoint that didn't seem to be that of the camera people at all.

– STOP! He cried out in such a way that his voice seemed to echo through the valley. – We want to SPEAK to you, just speak. Stop the machines and LEAVE THEM.

The rage and passion was there, in his voice, in the very air carrying its sound, and he felt its power.

Some did slow down, some stopped and jumped out of their vehicles, but not all. The front machine didn't slow down at all. Linsey concentrated, focusing on the driver, but it had no discernible effect.

Ted turned his back to the cameras. The eyes lit up. Loud sounds of calamity erupted from the engine. It stopped abruptly in its tracks when the pistons shot through the vertical hood and almost hit several workers. The driver's head hit the wheel. He fell out of the vehicle and hit the ground. He didn't move. The others stopped and turned off the engine, leaving their seats very quickly.

It turned strangely quiet. The howl of the winds roared in their ears.

– Blessed luck, Linsey grinned, keeping his anger, his edge, staying focused. – Now, we can talk.

The workers and the drivers gathered in tight formation. With a firm hand on hammers and tools they faced the protesters.

– What the hell is there to talk about? One of the drivers, he who had been behind the wheel of the second front bulldozer, asked, suspicion and distrust evident in his pose and face. – You will stop us from doing our job and earn our pay, that's what you're doing.

A cry from the others supported him.

– Doing what precisely? Linsey asked sarcastically. – Destroying people's livelihood, forcing them from their homes? That's the «honest work» in which you're taking part, guys. You must have witnessed things, grave things not quite right even seen by the blindest of the blind. Yes, I know that many of you have been recruited from deep core poverty to salaries you could hardly dream of, but that doesn't excuse anything. It even makes it worse in a way, because you know, you know how it is being at the mercy of the lords of this world. You may claim it's no one's business who you are working for, but that isn't true. Your decision, or rather lack of decision, of resolve, affects everybody else.

– What *are* you talking about, man? The man in front shook his head in confusion and dismay. – Say, you aren't one of those radicals, are you, out to destroy our vaunted way of life?

Disbelief and frustration raged through Linsey.

– The guy is totally clueless. Elizabeth turned to Linsey and shook her head. – He wouldn't know the truth if he stepped on it.

Linsey shook his head in despair, before determination shook his form, and he turned back to the workers.

– You've *seen* things, he stated. – It has happened right before your noses. How your bosses, your masters have treated people, how they've stepped on them, and eliminated from consideration those standing in their way. Do you think they truly value you? What do you think will happen eventually? How do you think life under their heel will be?

He stressed every word, spat out every punctuation as if it was a curse, and he sensed them, saw them react.

– He's right, one said hesitatingly. – I've been here so long that I should know. I have just been remiss in realizing it.

– Shut up! The current front driver snarled. – He's just attempting to confuse you. Don't listen to him! I'm warning you…

– I'm listening to him. A man straightened. – I've lived long and seen a lot, but I've hardly witnessed the kind of bad stuff executed around here.

A cry of support followed his words. In a moment or two the mood had seriously changed. The crowd that had been instrumental in destroying the Earth split in two. Almost half of them suddenly looked at their clubs and tools in disgust and threw them away.

– You're risking dismissal, they were warned, – and if that happens you know you must look long and hard to find another job… to Alaska and back probably.

New uncertainty and hesitation. They were threatened with blacklisting, and they knew how powerful their employers were.

– You can work for us, Elizabeth said kindly. – The season begins shortly, and we're so far behind with the preparations that there's enough to do for everybody. Move to us, bring your families, there's more than enough space.

She paused a bit, before continuing. Now, the voice was harder and clearly more accentuated.

– I know you've been promised life-long employment in the pyramid that's supposed to *supplant* the very valley. Hopefully you have at least *started* to realize what an enslavement that will be.

– You're considering the overwhelming power of what we're opposing, Linsey nodded.

He seemed in many ways… impressive where he stood and stared them down. Convincing. Those in the crowd looking closer at him feared there was something wrong with his eyes.

– It does seem invincible, doesn't it? But we can never know that for certain, can we, as long as we don't fight them? I for one believe that what Cornwall and his colleagues are doing can't stand the light of day.

There was a commotion. An… unrest spread among the gathering, protesters and others alike.
Hunter Cornwall appeared, leading his son, Kevin Davison, the sheriff, with deputies, security guards and dogs.
– Sheriff, he began arrogantly, – please have these people removed from the premises. They're blocking legal and important activity.
The sheriff looked like he didn't quite enjoy himself. He was sweating and glancing nervously at the men with cameras on the hill.
– We? We haven't blocked anyone? Elizabeth enlightened him, very helpful. – You need to sweep your peepers, Hunter. Your machine collapsed. We didn't damage it or anything.
– Be careful now, girl…
– No, you be careful, she shouted, knowing fully well what he had meant. – Not to go too far with your extortion, fires and murders. Perhaps you'll eventually encounter someone not giving a fuck about you or your threats. You big wart!
Cornwall managed, by an act of will to refrain from reddening. Many laughed, even a few among those who had worked as drivers, as his lapdogs.
– Get the machines running, Hunter screamed. – Keep working.
There was hesitation, but not for more than a few seconds. The drivers moved first, returning to their machines and jumped inside.
But when they turned the ignition the engine wouldn't start. Everything was dead. There weren't signs of life. The drivers struck out their arms, bewildered, as if saying they were sorry, as if they were responsible for the lack of fire in the engines.
Then the engines did start, start by themselves, without anyone being anywhere hear the ignition. The one at the rear started first. The number of the engine's revelations increased dramatically in mere seconds. It rose and kept rising… until several pistons jumped through the hood of several vehicles, and flames rose high.
– RUN!
People had just reached a somewhat comfortable distance from the ruckus when the first engine *exploded.* Then there was another, far louder crack as all the rest went up in flames simultaneously.
The smoke from the intense fire covered the ground and the people like a blanket, smothering them. There was a lot of coughing and hurting.
– SABOTAGE! Cornwall cried.
He had definitely lost his cool and the wound on his forehead didn't make him look any better, making him look old and tired.
– The culprits will *pay!*

– Don't make an ass of yourself… Contempt glowed in the girl's eyes. *I could have killed you,* they enlightened him. – With that iron wall your soldiers has made around this place for days there's no way we, or any others can get even close, not even if we had been invisible. So you better pull yourself together and stop throwing accusations around. Don't blame us for your equipment being faulty, man.

He breathed and breathed and breathed, and his eyes bulged.

– Yes, feel anger, she told him. – Feel helplessness to the point that you may approach what we're feeling over your brutal ways.

He did once again pull himself together by an act of will. She saw it, sensed it, how he regained whatever center he might have. He wasn't done. She had feared he wouldn't be. This was a giant snowball gaining momentum as it rolled down the slope, one that wouldn't stop for anything until it reached the end of the trek.

– This is the American Way, he stated proudly. – Those opposing it are opposing America. I'm appealing to all good citizens: Reject the lies you see before you. You know that the radicals and the communists use any trick in the book to cause unrest and brand industrial leaders as crooks, and they never come up with so much as a shred of evidence.

– He's right, one among the protesters nodded, seemingly reluctantly. – They're not to be trusted.

Elizabeth turned towards him. His eyes began flickering the moment she did.

– So you haven't quit your job at Cornwall after all, she said icily. – I rather thought you hadn't. Christ, you people are so stupid, believing your old methods of fooling people will work indefinitely.

She grinned, and the man that hadn't quit his job and Cornwall himself felt ice form around their hearts.

– May I have your attention, ladies and gentlemen? Linsey handed out a document to protesters and workers. – Here's your proof that this man was indeed employed in Hunter Cornwall's firm, until he officially quit three days ago.

Loud laughter. Pointed stares.

Kevin stepped forward, stopping between the two groups, looking as if he wanted to say something, but Ted stepped forward, too, and Kevin paled and held his tongue.

The laughter faded, and a wall of hostility took its place. People reminded themselves why they had come here.

– Mr. Cornwall… An older man wearing glasses stepped forward. – Are you aware of the harm you and your brethren are doing to nature, to the planet and all life on it? Recent and older studies are more than suggesting that this kind of behavior is far more dangerous to mankind and the world as a whole than The Bomb, you know.

– Another Doomsday Sayer. Kevin let out a barf.

– I've got America's people and laws on my side, Cornwall said, dismissing it all with a wave of his hand. – And I've never allowed garbage like you to stop me in anything I wanted to do.

– And you can all forget the journalists that were supposed to «cover» this, Kevin cuckled. – They've been hopelessly delayed.

– Stop the filming, Hunter barked. – Confiscate the cameras. This is private property. No one has given anybody permission to film anything.

Three people belonging to the security detail rushed up the hill.

– You truly believe you can get away with anything, Linsey said incredulous. – There's a far stronger reason to incarcerate you and equals than there is the worst murderer.

– You've managed to anger me, Cornwall clenched his teeth, – but believe me when I say that that will cost you. I'm going to kick you out of the valley, and there won't be many places in the world you can avoid my wrath.

The guards rushed confident towards the men with the cameras. Until suddenly, half up the first stumbled and the other two stumbled in him. They rolled helplessly back down, the suddenly so very steep slope. Jumped back up in determination. Grabbed their belly screaming and fell again. This time they remained on the ground, while clutching their belly in wordless pain.

– Get the fuck up! Cornwall screamed. – I don't employ children.

His confusion was evident, as he stared from the men to Elizabeth - she smiled scornfully - and back to the men. One of them fought himself to his feet, but he kicked his ankle right at a rock, and fell again. Blood flowed from his wound and colored the grass red. Now the laughter was loud and almost heartily. The three men were so clumsy that it seemed almost beyond ridiculous. The other guards scowled, as they exchanged glances, angry and ashamed.

The large group of journalists and photographers finally arrived. The men attempting to climb the slope seemed totally out of it. They waved and hit the air, as if there was something there, attacking them. Elizabeth approached Hunter. She spoke just loud enough for Paul to hear her.

– We are the Janus Clan. There is no place you can hide from *us!*

Leading the newshounds was Eric Carr. They all gathered in front of Hunter Cornwall like bees before the honey.

– Mr. Cornwall, a journalist initiated. – May I ask how many public servants you've bribed in order to play king the way you do?

– You better watch out, kid. As a matter of fact I own the paper you work for. You're working for me.

They all saw it, the shadow of doubt, turmoil and determination crossing the journalist's face.

– Very wrong, sir. I just quit. None of this will be hard to sell, you see. People have a well-developed nose for foul play these days.

Watergate and Vietnam were still so recent, so fresh in people's mind that newshounds could write the actual truth far more often than before. Linsey and Eric had still encountered some difficulties recruiting journalists known for not easily being intimidated.

– Mr. Cornwall and his like are like predators, the older man with glasses said. – They must be stopped before they manage to destroy every reason humans have to live.

– SHERIFF, Hunter screamed, – remove these freaks from my property!

The sheriff liked being here less and less. This hadn't turned out as expected. Not at all.

– Or you can forget about being re-elected.

A stunned silence and incredulity greeted his words.

– Don't you know sheriffs are in fact elected by popular vote in this county and not appointed, Hunter? Eric wondered curiously. – May I ask how you intend to fix that one?

Now, people stared equally at Cornwall and the sheriff. Both were sweating heavily. There was an expectant mumble. Everybody knew they were witnessing something extraordinary.

– I've got something to say, the sheriff began nervously. – This man has threatened me for years. To make me close my eyes for all his disgusting acts. He ordered his henchmen to beat up on my little daughter…

Fast as lighting, before anybody really noticed that anything happened Hunter Cornwall drew a gun and shot the sheriff. Twice in the head. The large body fell to the ground, and hit it, heavily and dead, dying in cramps. It turned very quiet. There was the weak howling of the wind and hardly even that. Everybody stared astonished and paralyzed at the bizarre and shocking scene.

Paul took one small step away from his father, a very telling act. Linsey believed his face mirrored both shock and pleasure… no, not pleasure…

It was pure coincidence that Linsey, from his position could also see Ted and Elizabeth's faces then. There were the same contradicting emotions of shock and triumph there.

The sun set on the valley.

Elizabeth and Paul walked alone, hand in hand in the machines' tracks.

– Hunter will get away from this one, too, you know. Perhaps not totally unscathed, but rest assured he will.

– I don't doubt that, she nodded.

She didn't really comment on his words, seeing them as fact, as truth.

– What I don't get, he said, shaking his head, – is why you're fighting so hard for this little spot when you can have the world.

– I don't like being hassled, she replied angrily. – I won't stand for it. Tell your father that.

– Well… He just laughed. – If you wanted to display your worth, you've certainly succeeded. It was quite the performance you and Teddy gave.

They arrived at the burned out wreckages of the machines.

– There's a meeting in our consortium in ten days, he said. – Everybody is keen on seeing you. Will you come?

– I'll think about it, she replied, and shrugged, very deliberately.

– As stated, you've shown your worth, he insisted. – You don't have to fool around anymore. The world is at our feet.

– I know that…

She kissed him on his lips, a quick, tempting touch of affection, looking at him from beneath the lowered eyelashes.

She knew she could do it, agree to his offer and give in to his overpowering will. The dizzying offer. They would complement another. He would lead on at first, steering her ever further. But she knew beyond reason that she would… would leave him behind, that she would grow to a princess of evil that would dwarf his. A nightmare wherever she directed her attention. And she would have to fight Ted and god knew how many others. Or perhaps she and Ted would join, then. No matter, there would be nothing left of her inside that seething, wicked creature.

What was she supposed to do? No matter what she decided it would be wrong, one way or another. She had been pushed to the brink.

She just didn't know.

4

Eric Carr stood on his dais, looking at the sea of journalists and blinking flashes below. His publisher, Otto Danforth spoke to the gathering with a voice and attitude well versed in occasions such as this, speaking his bullshit and sweet words.

– When I now present to you this young man, it's not just another presentation of another promising author. Mark my words well; this is a man who will blaze a long and honored trail throughout the United States and the world… Ladies and Gentlemen, I present to you the long since distinguished journalist, the writer of the New York Times number one bestseller The Defenseless… ERIC CARR.

Eric took his place behind the microphone, accepting the accolades of the gathering, wavering to fainting women and admirers.

The applause lasted for minutes, before the ruckus eventually faded, and there was time enough left for a few questions, just like Danforth had planned.

– So, Eric, a women Eric had never met or spoken to before asked him, – how does all this *feel?*

– Well, Marjorie, Carr grinned, – I have to tell you… it feels great, great for me to be able to bring this important story to the public's eye. A shroud of obscurity buries too many similar stories, but *this* won't be.

Elizabeth looked at it all from the living room. It was as if she could see nothing but the small screen there in the corner.

– So, Eric, a man said eventually, – is there anything more you would like to share with our readers?

Carr hesitated a bit, there on the dais, before nodding, before holding up a copy of the book.

– The Defenseless is a story about hope in a world without it, about the human spirit, and raging will power seething under the surface. There's one man I would like to thank in particular. Sadly he isn't here, as he was taken away before his time, by the very people we both fought against…

One more hesitation before raising the book even higher.

– This is from Eric Carr. With gratitude and deep admiration to Andrew Benedict. My friend.

5

Ted stood on the Hill, frozen. The Sun rose high in the sky, but it wasn't really visible. The wind ruled everywhere, except on the Hill, where the Storm ruled supreme. Only a thin line of light broke through the dark clouds. Elemental powers tore at the frozen figure.

Elizabeth had gone to bed in the middle of the day, after watching the television. She lay there fully dressed, looking at him through the window. She watched as the pumpkin rose in the air and was blown apart in a burst of power. There was movement, independent movement as she walked to the open window and jumped through it, without considering her balance or anything. It looked like it would go all wrong, but she twisted in the air like a cat and landed softly on her feet.

He waited for her. At first he didn't acknowledge her presence, but then he did. Their eyes met when she was half up, and they remained such.

– Hi! She greeted him lamely.

He didn't reply, not with words, but she sensed the Storm rage within him. She walked to him, touched his head and coddled his hair.

– You know, he said painfully. – My summer with Tilla in London was just an illusion. A horrible nightmare, now. When I woke up I lost my footing. There's nothing left, except hatred and contempt towards everything and everybody. No hope, only expectation of worse things to come.

He laughed, and his laughter was hollow, as hollow as his voice and everything about him.

– But ironically it was hope that brought me across the ocean. Desperate, blind for everything else. Lethal beyond words…

– I need someone suffering like me, she said softly. – That's my only change.

– I must have the ring, he said, forcing himself to say it, closing himself off to her, knowing fully that he had to.

– Paul is wearing it on his finger, she said quickly. – Why don't you go and *fetch* it.

– No. He shook his head. – That's not my task. You gave it to him. You must take it back. Or you will never find any sort of peace.

He reached for her. She stepped back.

– Peace is for the grave, she cried.

He rose. She took another step back.

– None of us will ever find peace, she said tired. – Our enemies know that, and they're taking advantage of it.

– Or perhaps they have underestimated our resilience, he noted. – I think it's quite stupid of them to meet in one place… the way they do the coming Saturday… don't you agree?

A door slammed open in her mind.

– Is that what you're reduced to, she snarled, – sneaking around eavesdropping on people's private conversation?

– Poor little girl. He grinned diabolically, leading her further down the path. – You still need someone to hold your hand.

She attacked him, attempting to claw at his face, to flay it from his bones. He deflected her attack easily, slapped her and made her fall. She renewed her attack, but he just grabbed her, put her flat on the ground and held her there, held her hard. A long time. Every time she attempted to fight herself free, he strengthened his grip, twisting her arms, making her cry out in pain. He held a hand at the back of her head, pushing her face into the dirt, making it hard for her to breathe, showing her beyond doubt who was the boss.

He let her up and rose, waiting in a relaxed pose, one that didn't in any way hide the snarling animal beneath the surface. She rolled half around, baring even more of her neck to him, waiting. He didn't take her up on her desperate invitation.

She looked up into the ruthless face. He had come further than her. On the Path of Power.

– We're pitch black inside, she whispered. – And it grows stronger. The more we fight it the stronger it becomes.

– You must realize who you are, he said. – To truly learn one must also seek in darkness.

Yes! A glimpse of hope.

– A light in the dark isn't necessarily a symbol of hope, she said, her voice an open wound.

Then his cruelty wasn't that strong anymore. Her weariness and hopelessness made his shrink.

– Stewart… once told me that there was a soft spot in me that I had to work hard to get rid of, he said slowly. – I believe he was right, and that the same holds true for you.

– And so what, she spat. – We've worked hard on it, both of us, and there isn't much left of anything in there by now, is there?

A tiny ember perhaps. One that could be extinguished by the smallest breath. She began sobbing. But he didn't. He was done with that. And it was also one of her last times.

She jumped to her feet and ran away in despair, hoping to run away from him, her mirror image, knowing fully well that even though that might be possible, she could never run away from herself.

The last line of light in the sky vanished and darkness embraced the land and all its people.

CHAPTER TWENTY

The storm clouds gathered, as all choices narrowed down to one.

– There is a choice, the young, frail girl insisted, sitting on her bed in her dank room, staring at the wall. – There always will be.

A very predictable turn of events proceeded the next few days. They had managed to get an injunction, a stop in the construction work, granted by one judge because one of the entrepreneurs was under investigation for murder.

But the next morning another judge, one obviously under Cornwall's thumb, in his pocket rejected the case against him, on grounds of self-defense. Many had come forward, swearing the sheriff had turned insane and had gone for his gun. The movies were rejected as evidence, even though the judge made sure to point out that the sheriff's waving *could* be interpreted as proof that he had indeed gone for his weapon.

The district attorney hadn't filed for an appeal. He, too was on Cornwall's payroll. It was a joke, all of it.

– It's like we're playing roles in an old western, one of the protesters stated to a national newspaper. – Except this is real. This is actually happening in the United States today.

– And listen to this: Another protester cried from the stairs of the court building, laughing himself silly. – The judge is commending Cornwall for acting swiftly and saving lives…

The bank had sent out a final debt-collecting letter to the Kendall farm, without warning. The same day the director went on «a lengthy holiday».

– I realize now, what I should have realized long ago, the young, frail girl told the wall. – It's impossible to stop people like this with human means. The end can be postponed, but not stopped.

It was Saturday, the third of April 1976, a totally ordinary day. Elizabeth sat on her heels at the roof by the chimney, watching Limousine by Limousine, an entire line of rich men's cars rolling into the large yard in front of the Cornwall Mansion. They had finally come, all of them, showing themselves openly, reveling in their power.

Elizabeth knew the cameras watched her.

– Yes, watch me, she mumbled. – Watch the inhuman witch perform her tricks.

She cursed under her breath, repeated words until they became chanting, until they became curses.

– Damn you, she muttered. – Damn you all. The witch curses you. Know that you are damned. Wherever you go, wherever you turn your eyes the witch's eyes will burn holes in your rotting carcasses, your putrid soul.

Slowly, but inevitably Paul, with other people she had encountered and known had killed her emotions. Driven her to the final recourse. She would accept the invitation. Let whatever happens, happen. Because she could no longer hold out the pain inside. She would rather walk the Path of Power.

Ted and Linsey waited for her in the yard as she arrived downstairs. Without words, without visible acknowledgement, they began walking. Trudy and Eugene stood in the window, watching them go.

– There they go, he spat, filled with hatred. – The spawn of Satan.

– You idiot, she cried exasperated.

He slapped her. Linsey was busy with other things, now. He couldn't keep anything from happening anymore.

She rushed to the kitchen. With an expectant, silly grin he chased her…

And stopped abruptly at the sight of the large knife in her hand. For the very first time he saw her show her full savagery, just like her children had done.

– One more step, she grinned. – I besiege you, good sir. Take one more step…

He wanted to cry his poison, hurt her, burn her over open fire because she had mislead him all these years.

– You believe you're being treated unfairly, don't you?

She spoke softly, even with a touch of pity, putting down the knife.

– Yes, I…

Taken aback, he didn't quite manage to convince his legs to charge her, the way he burned to do.

– You think I've behaved badly, that I deserved every injustice, every indignity and cruelty you've visited upon me?

The sarcasm made his rage boil once more. He took one step forward and stopped, stopped in shock, beyond shock.

In a breath she grew taller. Not much, but enough. Her face changed. The tone of her skin changed. Her always-visible muscles swelled some more. He stared at the horribly strange creature looking sweetly at him. Stared at him with its eerie, horrible inhuman eyes, in his eyes resembling more those of a fish, instead of those of a human being.

– What's the matter, Eugene? Don't you love me anymore?

Even her voice had changed, becoming something thick and horrible and unrecognizable.

He began backing off, and he kept doing so, until he hit the wall at the far end of the kitchen, and then he turned and ran, never to stop, with her scornful laughter ringing in his ears, ringing in his ears forever.

The three of them headed straight for the Cornwall estate. Mist surrounded them, danced as they danced whispered as they whispered, as they chanted their song. There was something timeless over this night. They sensed that this was something that could happen and had happened at all times. Something fundamental. They had been and would perhaps always be lost birds.

Linsey felt uneasy, unable to help it. The other two looked so at ease, so casual, like a stroll in the park. He feared for them, he did. Feared.

– Let us go with you, he begged her. – You shouldn't go alone.

They had stopped fifty steps away from the building or so, behind that bundle of trees. The castle was dark and quiet. Light was lit in only a few windows. Elizabeth turned to Ted, ignoring Linsey.

– This is my problem, she said, dead as an autumn leaf. – Wait here!

Slowly, but decisively she continued forward. She didn't turn and didn't wave. She had turned her back at them. Ted's hands were forever tightly woven.

The house remained quiet. The servants had left it earlier that day. She had seen them, had observed the spectacle from afar. Only a few trusted maids and the three ugly bruisers remained. There was no one by the entrance. The large welcoming hall looked dark and remote. Or… She tilted her head to hear better, and amazingly she did. There was someone breathing rapidly under the stairs. She looked into a pair of round eyes, rough by curiosity, Michelle's eyes.

With a pained laughter she knelt down by the girl. There was very little warmth left in her by now, but the child prompted what little remained.

– What are you doing here? She asked, very strict and solemn.

– Mommy wanted me to go to bed early, the little girl whispered eagerly with eyes filled to the brim by sensationalism. – But I wasn't sleepy at all. I waited by the window and saw you come, and I *rushed* down here.

– That was a very smart thing to do, little one. It came out harshly and cruel, but the little girl didn't look afraid, didn't look afraid at all. – Listen closely to what Aunt Elizabeth tells you.

Ted saw the small figure emerge from the house's shadows. A dark girl in a nightgown already too small. He hesitated a bit, before waving to her. She instantly changed course and ran to him, to them. It swelled in his throat. He had understood the connection the moment he caught eyes of her.

– Christ, Linsey exclaimed, understanding very little.

– I'm Michelle, the girl exclaimed unafraid as she stopped before the terrifying man. – Aunt Elizabeth told me that you're my daddy, and that you will protect me. Auntie looked so strange. I got *scared,* daddy.

She smiled widely and didn't look scared at all. Ted patted her on her head, distracted, fighting to stay alert.

– Claudia, Linsey said, his voice shaking. – I didn't know. If Liz knew this she kept it from me as well. And people in the valley have never even *seen* her. She looks nothing like Claudia. The rumor mill would have started immediately.

The girl looked just like Elizabeth as a child. And the eyes were a more perfect version of Trudy's. Linsey had seen them before, in Jack Warren's face, on the old, faded black and white photograph, the one in Linsey's pocket.

The first doors to the large living room were locked. Elizabeth could easily have *opened* them, but she shrugged and didn't. She calmly continued into the long, dark passage at the end of the hall, to the library. She smelled and heard the three heavy men easily. To her just as heavy and slow as elephants. She opened the door and walked through it. They grabbed her arms and neck. She let them, waiting patiently.

Paul came through the door from the living room and approached her.

– Sorry about this, he said with a sweet smile. – There are people inside that don't want to be recognized quite yet.

He tied a thick, dark scarf around her head, covering her eyes. She felt a crude rope tighten around her wrists behind her back.

– I don't mind, she assured him.

She wondered what he would have said if he had known she could see him easily, that she could see just fine.

They led her to the dinner table. She giggled. The thugs squeezed a little harder, and she had to suppress a yelp of pain. They didn't enjoy being made fools of.

She saw Paul's skewed smile. It melted her heart, turning her all mushy inside.

– You're just in time for dinner.

The thugs let go of her. He grabbed one of her arms and led her to the table. She let him believe it was necessary for her to be led. He let go and pulled out a chair for her. Kind and cheval Paul. She sat down and had to restrain herself not to send him a grateful smile.

Except for her and Paul there were eleven people sitting by the table. Some she knew, others she didn't. They were Hunter Cornwall, the new sheriff, Terry Williams, Howard Grey, Kevin Davison, strangely enough, and Regina and Kent Farley. She couldn't truly see them. Her «sight» was detailed contours, features, textures. She assumed it was a kind of radar that her brain interpreted very much in the same way as it did eyesight. There were no colors. She recognized these people because she knew them so well, and because she had actually experienced them earlier in her life with her eyes closed.

The rest she didn't recognize, even though she probably had seen them in the papers and on television and would recognize them as soon as the blindfold came off.

She turned her head a lot, making a point of it, getting a feel of the room. The three thugs took their place by the door. Two maids served. She knew them as well, knew them as servants loyal to the household.

– Is this The Last Supper? She joked.

– This is just temporarily, Hunter assured her. – Until the cabal gathered here tonight has taken a closer look at you. In the meantime, if you're hungry I'm afraid we'll have to feed you

– Thank you, she said sweetly, – but that won't be necessary.

The large plate with the cut steak rose from the table and levitated above it, stopping right by her plate. Two pieces seemed to jump from the big to the small plate. The knife and fork moved, cut and pierced. With a pleased, smacking sound the girl put the meat into her mouth, and began chewing.

– Not bad, she acknowledged. – Give my regards to the chef upon his return.

There was no audible response. No one spoke, and they hesitatingly began eating. They were unable to look away from the seemingly quite ordinary dinner table, and the levitating food and stuff.

– Liz, Paul said kindly patronizing. Her ears moved. She knew they did. – We have a scientist here tonight. We want you to tell us about yourself. We all have very high expectations of you.

Cooperate. Remember what I've taught you.

He was like an ocean she swam through, so far out at sea that she could no longer see the shore.

– One actually accepting what he sees with his eyes, then, I hope…

The jibe worked. She could sense the man's anger instantly, directed towards her like daggers. He didn't enjoy the knife being twisted in his wound, his eyes still being locked on the levitating dinner plate.

She began speaking, concentrating, focusing on the processes of her mind, learning about herself even as she spoke.

– I don't know what I am, what we are, not exactly. It is mostly guesswork. I stem from an old… line, one that has kept a racial uniqueness through the millennia. I can't imagine how old. There aren't that many of us. There never were, I guess. We're born with paranormal powers. We carry all human characteristics in our blood, from one side of the spectrum to another, and we are more, more than humanity's sum of the parts. More than anything we're good and evil and the yin and yang, both duality and the colors of the rainbow, the many-faced Beast. We are the Janus Clan…

Clarity came to her as she told her story.

– I called my cousin Ted Janus when we both were very young. Janus is an old god, not just with two faces, but with many. We're the guardians of the gate, the beginning and the end, the face in the mirrors. Yes, some of us were gods. Quite a few times during human history one of us has stood before others like I'm standing now. People like you have always wanted to exploit our kind. Some succeeded, others… didn't. These are thoughts I've gathered on my path from childhood. I gain strength from them. I know they'll sustain me.

– You said you've had these… powers from birth, Hunter said, – but when did they manifest? It can't be too long ago.

Since you didn't discover them, you mean. The thought pleased her.

– Since my first period, she stated cheerfully, – and that happened when I was ten.

There were waves in the air around the room. She sensed them, and she sensed more. There was something… something she couldn't quite identify.

She kept eating, a bit distracted, with the fork and knife moved by her invisible hands.

– There's my telekinesis, as you guys can clearly see, she noted. – But that's just one part of it, one manifestation, more like the visible part of an iceberg, if you will. I have senses, and then I have *senses*. The normal five are enhanced. My touch, smell, hearing, sight and taste is growing stronger year by year, even though I still have a way to go before catching up with a wolf and/or any other truly wild animal, really.

She frowned. Her blindfold moved.

– And there's more. There's always more.

And an uncomfortable silence settled in the room.

– You've probably realized that we're into big things, Liz, Cornwall said after a while. – We're doing business all over the globe. This valley is merely one of many where we're making our influence felt.

– Yes, I've noticed, she said, devouring a strawberry, making a head start on the desert, a piece of its red juice settling on her cheek.

The nervous chatter they weren't aware of doing rose to a buzz in the room.

There was something in the room, a presence, almost something tangible, something she could almost touch. It scared her. It terrified her. It excited her.

A shadow blocked her sight for a moment, turning everything totally black. She shivered and shrank there on the chair.

– Paul has told us many good things about you, about how clever you are. I've seen for myself how… resourceful you are, seen it more than once actually. Around this table you'll find people commanding their own, unique power. Power of business, of spiritual matters and other forces dominating the world. We want you on our team. We believe you'll belong here quite soon.

– Thank you very much, but I know I already belong here, she stated dryly.

Heartfelt laughter, or their particular version of it. But these people had put such things behind them long ago, like Paul was about to do.

– We're about to expand our power base, he informed her casually. – Picture it in your mind. What we're about to build here, we'll also build other places, after a few years of… of extensive testing. Let's say you're the missing link our chain needs to be extraordinary strong.

– I can picture it in my mind. She nodded. – I can see us begin it all, and our children's children continue our great work, until it's everywhere, and there's nowhere to hide for those opposing it. I would certainly see to educate my children, making sure they would make the right choices in life.

The laughter turned nervous, turned uneasy.

I'm too much for them. They're like ants to me.

I used to throw a fit of rage upon encountering injustice and people like these. When did I stop?

– The world is built on suffering she continued softly. – Endless rows of it. People have always cried out for an answer, and always picked the first, easiest solution, the first person telling them what to do, how to live, how to sleep. Most people are sheep, easily led. And now, in an age where people can be registered in files everywhere, it's easier than ever to put a collar around their neck and lead them around like dogs in chains. It's almost too easy, isn't it?

– I'm certain we will all benefit from your inventive talents, my dear, Paul said hoarsely.

– I know you will, beloved, she replied.

He was taken by her. He didn't want to be, but he was. Impressed to the core. Seduced by the promise of ultimate power.

– I will take you the final distance, my love, she told him. – I will show you beyond anything… what Power is.

They looked at each other. They couldn't stop doing so. And they kept glancing at her, unable to look for very long at the time, at the glowing sun in their midst.

– How about it, Regina, do you want me to send you the salt?

And then they were stunned, were paralyzed.

– Oops, she grinned.

– How did you do that, he who in all probability was the scientist asked. – We haven't spoken. We have hardly moved.

– I could say I recognized Kent, Howard and Regina's scent. A patronizing laughter. – Like I've marked all your scents in the case I ever encounter you again. And that would be true as well…

Sweat turned to musk, as the outpour from their skin increased.

– But that would, in any case not be totally accurate. I will probably be able to do that one day, but I'm not quite there yet. But my sixth or seventh or perhaps eight sense, my radar sense managed admirably. I can see you almost as good as if I didn't wear this stupid blindfold. It itches, you know.

She pulled it off her head, and color and the rainbow returned to her senses. Her sight opened up to the bright room, the burning candles on the table, the blinding electrical lights, and she wondered what were the purpose of the candles when one couldn't see the fire.

The bright light stung her eyes, and pools of water inevitably formed there. She blinked several times, blinking away the tears.

– These fucking ropes, too.

Her muscles tensed and ripped the rope to pieces. It fell to the floor, slowly through the air. The act hurt, but she had no intention of sharing that detail with them. She knew her face didn't reveal anything.

– Hello, little fox, Regina said, very relaxed, not worried at all.

– Hello, bitch, Liz replied.

She felt joy when the Queen's face didn't quite highlight the same calm.

– No matter our differences, I've still got high hopes for you, Black Beauty, the queen nodded gracefully.

– We all have, the Scientist cried. – I'm confident that with our help you will be able to develop your… gifts to an uncanny degree. They will be useful in so many ways. In quelling rebellion, during interrogations and industrial action and such. And we will certainly come up with new uses in time.

– Malcontents are on the march everywhere.

The new sheriff had a fanatical glow in his eyes.

– Communists and other ungodly creatures are infiltrating our community and our way of life, Howard Grey chanted. – They shall be crushed like ants on the ground.

– I can kill, Elizabeth said innocently. – I can kill with a thought. There's no protection against my power.

– Let's not get ahead of ourselves here, Beauty, Regina said. – There's plenty of time.

– But I *can* kill, the girl insisted. – You know that… right?

And their unease intensified.

– Yeah, that's it, she said, frowning. – I can be the greatest assassin the world has ever seen. Picture a car filled with people, a room far away, a scared man or woman locked inside a vault. It won't matter. He or she will die, quietly or screaming.

She straightened in her chair. Something dangerous appeared in her eyes.

A knife rose above the table. It began spinning there, until it stopped, until it was thrown at the wall, and quivered there, like an arrow.

– That could just as easily have been flesh, she pointed out. – You're not in control here, you know.

Her eyes began glowing, and Regina put a hand to her mouth.

– I am! The girl stated proudly. – You will follow my orders. I won't obey yours.

– What are you talking about? Williams said irritated.

– You guys think you can do anything, right? Stamp and keep stamping without anybody stamping back?

– Do I hear a little protest in your sweet voice? Regina wondered, back on familiar ground as she once again sensed vulnerability in the girl's voice.

– A major protest, the girl exploded, letting go of all pretense. – I won't join you. I will crush you, like the bugs you are.

– Don't be silly, girl, Cornwall admonished her, like a father. – If you aren't with us, you're against us.

– You don't get it. The girl looked exasperated at the ceiling. – You are silly. You have, by you all coming here tonight totally exposed yourself to the enemy, and you don't even fucking *realize* it. The resistance you have previously encountered can't have been much to speak of, for you to grow so *complacent*. I sincerely hope that you believe me when I tell you that this time, you do have something to fear.

Some laughed and others drew a smile.

– I can *sincerely* say I hoped to avoid this. Cornwall sighed, very patronizing. – But it's obvious that you need to be *convinced.*

He didn't give any obvious sign, but Elizabeth knew two of the guards stood behind her. The third blocked the door, the open door, presumably to keep her from escaping. She giggled. Then she kicked backwards and hit Right's foot. He screamed. She whirled around towards Left. He gave her a crushing blow to the skull. She slid light as a pillow across thc floor. Stopped abruptly against the wall with a loud crack. The crack was her shoulder breaking. It *hurt!* She cried enraged. Right and Left rushed towards her, very determined, but not really scared or even worried. They looked unstoppable. She sensed them, their confidence, their sick, foolish confidence…

Then they stopped, stopped as if they had hit an invisible wall. They moved forward one moment, and the next they stood still, unable to move. It looked like Right jumped into the air. He hung there suspended for a few heartbeats, as the girl in front of him studied him with her little smile frozen on her lips. Then he was thrown headfirst into the wall - the skull quite simply crumbling like mush. The other remained suspended, obviously hanging by the head. He turned blue in the face, and then he turned black.

– A man sits by his desk, the girl sang. – No one sees anything, suspects anything. Suddenly he grabs his throat, gasping for air. He dies there on the spot. People rush forward, attempting to help him, in vain. He dies screaming, but there's no sound, nothing but the gasps of horror fading into black, black, black…

Left fell to the floor like an empty sack. He crouched there, gasping for breath, gasping, gasping, gasping.

Elizabeth headed for the twelve. The man by the door stood there frozen. The fear in the big man's eyes pleased her, pleased her immensely. The twelve… she had shaken them, but still they studied her, arrogantly and patronizing.

One of the maids, obviously skilled in martial arts rushed her. Suddenly a knife buried itself in the woman's throat. The woman dressed as a maid fell to the floor, dying as the knife was pulled out and her lifeblood flooded the floor, painting a rose around her shaking body.

– That's enough, Cornwall stated, almost exasperated. – You have proven your worth to us, and we our value to you. Why don't stop horsing around?

A neigh rose from her throat, a perfect imitation of a horse, making the people at the table shake some more.

– You aren't LISTENING, she shouted at them. And then, suddenly, calm as death: – You have underestimated me completely, underestimated the peril you're in. I can kill, close up or from a distance. There's nowhere you're safe from me, and from my kin. Don't you fucking *get it?* Convince me that you will leave the valley and us alone, and we will also stay away from you.

But the catching in her voice revealed her inner turmoil, and it sickened her when she sensed how their confidence once more ascended to previous levels, how her weakness strengthened them. She had fucked up. By appealing to their common sense, to their humanity she had only succeeded in convincing them of her weakness. She spat on herself. Spat

Their laughter was a bit more uncertain this time, but still filled with scorn, with contempt.

– You go too far this time, Beauty. Your value isn't that high.

– She goes evil's errant, Grey nodded pleased. – She needs chastise and pain.

– Convince them, she appealed to Paul.

In his eyes she saw the ever-stronger glow in her own.

– That won't work. He shook his head.

It was no use. She should have known that and acted accordingly. Nothing else would work. They were all here now, at her mercy, at the mercy of a creature without mercy, without conscience, without pity. These people ruled their empire from their dark offices. They lived and grew in tune with the sick society. She and Ted, Mark and Linsey, and the others would be hunted, not they. There was just one thing she could do, just one, final choice available to her.

Oh, whom was she attempting to fool? Herself, only herself.

I was a fool that didn't realize that sooner. *A fool!*

I *choose* this. I choose this willingly and eagerly, and I embrace my path.

She had gone too far to turn back now, and she didn't want to. She longed for release, and it came to her. The molten flow of hatred erupted in her core.

The candles on the tables… its fire turned dark, and the room turned dark, and the cold burning place within her swelled and multiplied.

Let suffering end. Let it turn into something else.

The voice wasn't a voice, but a snarl, a growl rising from the very ground deep beneath their feet.

– Then be damned!

Ted had played in the grass with Michelle. He had seemed almost calm on the surface while Linsey had paced back and forth, and hardly taken his eyes off the house. Now Ted Warren rose with eyes hardening like glass. Linsey couldn't tell if they moved in the sockets as he turned. It was eerie.

– Go and take the girl!
– Go? Linsey looked confused at him. – Why… Not without you… Liz…
– Run! As far away as possible. Take Trudy, too. Go to the bus stop or wait in the car, I don't give a shit. You'll know if you must go.
Flee.
They heard a horrible roar from the house. A window was broken by something unrecognizable that only had a faint resemblance to a human flying through it. It hit the ground and remained there, lifeless and still. Michelle looked up at her father. He managed to convey a stiff, somewhat relaxed smile. He roughed her hair, not really very cautious, and used his mind to lift her up, and into Linsey's arms. Linsey Kendall fled, holding on to the little girl. He ran faster than he had ever done, knowing beyond knowing that he would never dare to look back.
Ted faced the front of the house. Stood like that for a while. Then his fingers began glowing and sparking.
The last guard attacked Elizabeth. She lifted him and turned him around in the air. Levitating him above the table. A few seconds. An eternity. His head began twisting. Eyes bulged in desperation, and half-choked sounds were pushed through his glued lips. Something broke and he turned limp. The head kept rotating. Round and round. Slowly at first, but then faster and faster until it fell off and dropped into the soup bowl. The body followed and hit the table with a soft crack.
A gun was fired behind her. She heard the sound, seemingly from far away. When she looked down a tiny dart was buried in her thigh. She experienced how its poison paralyzed her body. Imagination worked overtime as she visualized how she dropped to the floor, unconscious and at their mercy. How they brought her to a horrible place on a hill and began working on her. She turned and saw Claudia grin at her with the gun in both hands. A grin fading fast when Elizabeth crouched only slightly and pulled out the dart, and discarded it, giving them a contemptuous grin. It was wonderful to feel how her body took care of the poison, how it was cleansed from her system in a matter of seconds. She seemed to be growing to a monster in their eyes. She stretched out her arms and her fingers sparked.
– Idiots! Did you believe this little dart would stop me?
Claudia was thrown through the window. The broken glass cut her to ribbons, destroying her.
The twelve sat there unmoving. Cornwall was unnaturally pale. Every time he attempted to move or speak pain ravaged him.

– You will burn in hell, Grey cried. – Like the whore masquerading as my daughter. I know where she is, now, you know. I'm going to take her home, and punish her. And you shall be made to watch.

Elizabeth directed her attention solely at him. The sheriff saw it and drew his gun. But he was still too late. The witch stabbed him with her eyes. And he turned to stone. The barrel pointed at her, but when he attempted to pull the trigger, it couldn't be moved.

– Problems with your tool, sheriff? How sad…

And her voice wasn't a voice, but a collection of growls picked from the very air around them.

A pull, and the barrel pointed at Cornwall. There was thunder and his head cracked open everywhere. Wild, panic-stricken howls filled the room, and everybody threw themselves off the chair they sat on and away from the table. They rushed towards the only door not locked. Kent Farley tore at the handle, in vain. Neither the handle nor the door moved an inch. The sheriff remained on his chair, sweating and shaking hard. The inhuman laughter thundered in their ears like a distant echo, and they turned totally bonkers. It reminded them of something from a nightmare they didn't remember. They, too, carried atavistic memories from ancient times.

The gun fired and fired. The poor sheriff choked harder every time another bullet left the barrel, and headed for the pack. Two missed. Farley and another were hit.

– One bullet left, sheriff.

It seemed like the man voluntarily pointed the gun at himself and pulled the trigger. By then Elizabeth had practically forgotten him.

Farley crawled on the floor, leaving behind a broad trail of blood. It didn't matter. He wouldn't get anywhere. Elizabeth brushed the candles off the table, pushing them through the air to the curtains and wall carpets. Greedy flames started licking the walls. Knives from the table danced in the air in front of her, a wild, wild dance echoing the full-blown inferno in her eyes. Those with weapons drew them feverishly. She saw that only Williams could handle them. The knives flashed forward. Williams fired his Magnum 44" and it was like an invisible sledgehammer hit her chest. Two knives speared his chest. She took two steps back.

– NOW! Kevin shouted. – Let's get out of here.

He managed to take two more steps before another of the large meat knives penetrated his upper body. Regina grabbed Williams' Magnum. Elizabeth brushed it from her hands. The flames licking the walls paled before those in the demon's eyes. As if the hellfire in there was nourished by something quite different from any physical flame.

The inner wood had caught fire fully, now. Burning pieces were torn loose from the walls and without mercy they cut into the panicked humans. And something surfacing within Elizabeth jumped in joy.

She stopped a bit to enjoy the view. It was a whopper. Her face was without expression, nothing but a mask filled with a serenity not of this world.

Only Regina, Grey and the scientist were still standing.

– It isn't possible, the latter cackled insanely. – It isn't posssiiiiiiible

There was only one escape route yet available - the broken window. He and Regina ran towards it. Elizabeth cut their throat with two pieces of glass. It happened way too fast. Elizabeth had wanted to make Regina suffer but grew too eager.

Grey fell to his knees among the dead and wounded. She walked close to him.

– You didn't really believe your own words, huh? That *I am* a spawn of Satan?

She broke his thighs, an almost impossible task if not for her godly mind power. It was easy to freeze one part of his body and move the rest. Tears of pain and the ultimate fear dropped on the carpet when he attempted to crawl away from her.

– This is such fun, she grinned. – It extends my wildest expectations.

She broke his legs, in one place, two…

– Crawl, you snake. Crawl for your life. But I wouldn't bet much on your changes to crawl fast enough… before the flames of hell catch up with you.

Kent Farley crouched on the floor while life flowed from him.

– Let me live and I'll give you *anything,* he gasped.

– I have everything, she replied distantly.

Paul still sat by the table, as he had done all the time. He rose and walked towards her.

– You're wounded, he said.

– The bullet… didn't really penetrate very deep. I… caught it.

She reached out a hand. The bloody metal fragment rested in her palm. The wound in her chest hardly bled. Her ribs hurt. Probably a sprain. The pain in her shoulder was now only a distant memory.

– Idiots! He shook his head in acknowledgement to her. – I kept warning them about your potential, but they wouldn't listen. They didn't realize that I knew you better than any other. But this is quite a fortuitous set of events. I would have taken them out eventually anyway. It just happened a bit sooner than expected.

He glanced at the flames while pulling her tight.

– I'm gonna miss this house, but we can build another, one much, much larger.

He kissed her on her lips. She responded. Blood mingled between them.

The blood hurt him. She could easily sense that. Like acid it was, on his lips. She quickly stifled the touch of pity.

– Nothing can stop us, now.

She freed herself from his grip, just slipped out of it like quicksilver.

– You had me, you know, she said softly. – You had me cowed. Your goal was my goal, but now your modest aspirations are beneath me, really.

– The cowed thing was just to force you to learn, to realize life's realities. That's obviously no longer necessary. Now, we can feel together.

She smiled, and knew very well it was the most terrifying thing he had ever seen.

– After what you've DONE to me… Do you truly believe I have any softer emotions left? I? Being born black inside? You're just a little shit I brush off my heel, my love.

She towered above him. High above. Then he finally glimpsed the nature of the fire he had played with. He was like a little child.

– DON'T BE SILLY! He shouted. – Have you any idea how powerful we can become together?

– You have no idea what Power is.

A knife buried itself in his chest. He choked and fell on his back, and protested silently while his attempts at pulling the blade back out weakened by the second.

– Behold, behold Evil's Beauty, she whispered. – It's blinding, isn't it?

His eyes stopped flickering. She looked down at him without feeling the slightest sting of remorse.

The room had turned into a sea of fire. The smell of burning flesh stuck in her nose, stuck in her nose forever. Burning pieces of wood began falling from the ceiling. It would have fallen on her if she hadn't protected herself. She directed her attention at the large double doors. They disintegrated in one single burst of power. She smiled viciously, joylessly, without expression.

The thorns in her side were gone. She had become the sea. An ocean of sand. So thirsty, so filled with Hunger. They were all dead. There wasn't a shred of life remaining in any of the bloated carcasses. Why the hell hadn't she saved at least one of them? There were no one here she could feed on. She had to. Feed. She left the dead, left them behind. Her eyes looked straight ahead, hardly seeing the burning ruins, hardly registering the enormous heat. Burning wood dropped to the floor everywhere, but not on her. She turned one single time. The ring flashed on Paul's lifeless finger. She pulled it to her. It slipped from his steaming meat, through the air and onto her left long finger. In a moment it glowed as strongly as her own did. The flames reached Grey and the others. She watched as the fire consumed them all. The serene mask remained, as she stepped out of the room, walked through the corridor, through the welcoming hall, as she left the total inferno the building had become.

Ted should have become frightened as he spotted the demonic creature, but he had also come too far to feel terror.

Elizabeth knew how she looked, with the fiery hellfire behind her. Good. Excellent. People would be terrified and they wouldn't even dream of stopping her, of opposing her. No one would stop her in anything. No one!

Ted or something resembling him blocked her path. Something resembling how she had imagined Satan in her nightmares. She stopped.

– Mankind will once more discover why they fear the night.

She snarled at him.

They guarded each other with fingers stretched like claws.

Energy flared. They used all their powers to strike down the other. Nothing happened.

– *Let me pass,* the she-devil hissed.

– *Give me the ring,* the devil hissed.

– *Come and get it,* she challenged him. – We are One. Let's hunt together.

He didn't do anything, didn't say anything.

– Yesss, she grinned, – you're tempted. The need burns within you.

He longed to do it. It was evident in his pose, in the way he curled his claws. To take the final step. To conquer her. Put out the final ember of warmth in them both.

A crystal clear memory came to him. Warm hands. Gray eyes, but yet sparking in fire. Tilla. Her words to everybody in the collective.

– You're thinking about Tilla again, the creature chastised him. – I can tell. Can you still feel the lashes, the pain, the humiliation, the hatred?

He took one step forward, his fangs flashing.

«We have something here… something indescribably precious. That we must never allow to die or fade. We must hold onto it with both hands. This real, this true inside. And never let go…»

He could never forget that. He could never allow himself to forget that.
– No… you must give it to me, he stressed. – Voluntarily, no coercion. That's the only way we can both be free.
– I am free! She cried. – Join me or not, but let me pass.
He merely shook his head. Striving to hide how pressured he was.
– I am the one who have to convince you, he said. – I won't force you. With Tilla I got a taste of how life might be. You never did. We can only be free together. You must believe that.
If he had only believed it himself.
– *Hope?* The scorn and venom in her voice hit him hard. – Stop bullshitting yourself. Be the Beast, My Lord, and let us hunt together.
Saliva flowed from her mouth, as she was bearing her fangs.
– You're so clever, he acknowledged.
She smiled proudly.
– Such a clever girl.
Her smile vanished.
– I went to your room, he said, with a voice that could be mistaken for soft. – I found Nick's writing. I read it. It was written just as much to me. You should know that, but you've forgotten what you once knew intimately, what I refused to admit: that we belong together. No matter what. No matter the path we'll *choose* to follow. Forever!
He was reaching her. He felt it in every nerve.
– But I'm Hungry, she wailed, – so Hungry.
– I am, too, he cried in despair, no longer able to hide his need. – I've fought so long, and it has been so hard. Time is running out.
Her lips quivered. Eyes were open wounds.
He reached out his hand, spreading his fingers. The other hand was curled into a hard fist. She crouched a bit, but only for a brief moment. She reached out with her left hand. It sparked. The ring slipped from her thin finger to his perfect fit. Then both hands sparked. A brief moment there was a thin beam of fire between them. Then it faded. The eyes flashed simultaneously.
There were smiles, frightening to others, perhaps, but not to them. Uncertain, flickering in the four winds, but there.
And the rumble in the ground rested.

Other upcoming novels by Amos Keppler from **Midnight Fire Media**:

The Janus Clan - (ten chapters about the Wild Man in the modern world, a world balancing on a razor's edge):

The Defenseless
The Slaves
Birds Flying in the Dark
At the End of the Rainbow
Lewis of Modern York
The Werewolf of Locus Bradle
The Valley of Kings
Eye in the Sky
The Iron Cage
Phoenix Green Earth

At the End of the Rainbow

There is a treasure at the end of the rainbow, or so the legend says, a place, an El Dorado, a Xanadu, a paradise, a heaven where all wishes are granted, a lush and peaceful garden people have been searching for since time immemorial.

Ted and Elizabeth Warren have finally, at a terrible cost claimed their name. They leave their fairly safe haven in the American Rockies, and they begin their tour, their Journey across the Earth. They cross the United States on a motorbike, first traveling west, stopping in Las Vegas, playing the stakes, throwing the dice, then traveling east and south, ending up in New Orleans, the City of the Dead, where they find more mystery, the mystery that is their life, find Life and find Death, find David Gidman, find Mark Stewart locked in a horrible battle of supremacy.

An eccentric millionaire invites them to accompany him on a treasure hunt in the South American jungle, and they go, go into the moist and hot jungle, to old and new pyramids, hiding terrible secrets. And everything else is traveling with them, every ghost, every shadow. Old enemies and friends… or both, join them there, in the lush, green and lethal surroundings. Ghosts of the past, ghosts of the future, and it's all one.

Death, tangible and true, awaits them in the pyramid of fear.

To be published October 31, 2012

Shadow Walk

The world is changing. They know this, in their core of cores, where everything moves and shifts. Night and fire have followed them all the days of their lives.

What they carry inside has always scared them, always intrigued them...

They have always felt different, apart from the crowd. And here, now, they get the confirmation they have always wanted, always yearned for, that they are truly different, a breed apart. The metamorphosis begins. Their minds, their bodies are changing in shocking and unpredictable ways, as what's on the inside is brought to the outside. And as they themselves are changing they are also changing the world.

Danger awaits them, Life awaits them, in the small, backward New England town. Magick and Mystery may be found beneath unturned stones.

People, young and old, are descending on the small, insignificant town of Northfield, New England.

Boys and girls, students at the school of Life, Seekers, yearning for what's different, what's hidden.

They're seeking within and without, high and low.

And here, in this dusty, remote place they're finding it, turning the stone, finding the strength within themselves to be themselves, to break out of confines, to the world beyond. And in time, after the initial, tentative steps, pushing down paths new and undreamed of.

And the present day order sees them for what they are... Agents of Change, a threat to any establishment, any imposed reality. The heatwave, the worst in living memory, is nothing compared to the boiling within the human heart. The Indian Summer heralds the twilight of mankind.

To be published October 31, 2011

Your Own Fate

From The Book of Fate:

In the Book of Fate there is everything. Every incident, all times, everything that has been, that is, that will ever be, everything that might be, everything that could have been.

But who is writing it? Who is penning it? Who is turning page by page, too many to be counted, blowing in the wind? Does it perhaps write itself, with a pen moving across the yellow sheets? Or is it a hand moving the pen, one unseen, one stretching back into the past, back to the time before everything was created, creating itself from nothing?

Timothy Joyce is an enigma, a man without a past, appearing from nowhere, to go on a rampage in an astonished world.

Jeremy Zahn is hunting Timothy Joyce. It seems like he has always been hunting him, from old London, from the island of angels, where it is said they met for the first time, to the city of angels, California, the new world.

Here, on this shaky ground, following confrontations spanning the globe, its time and space the two will fight for the last time.

And the world is watching, its people shivering in their frozen hearts.

ISBN 978-82-91693-05-7

Night on Earth

This is said to be the age of enlightenment and reason...

A culmination of thousands of years' development and illumination.

The hunters are dying off, they say. Their day is done, in favor of the new, enlightened time of neon lights, technology and civilization.

But a hunter is stalking the streets of London. A creature without form, eyes and skin. In a city on the brink of chaos, of social and economic collapse, it is stalking cops, killing them in ever more horrible ways.
Sheila Watts is a hunter. She's a cop.

Sheila is lost, losing herself further by the second. She's losing herself, finding herself, as she's closing in on the creature of the night, as it is closing in on her.

Sheila Watts can taste the sweet blood in her mouth...

ISBN 978-82-91693-07-1

Complete Poems 1989 - 2003

Venture into existence with Amos Keppler, into the rainbow, of red and green, shadow and pitch black. Experience Life through ShadowWalker's many senses.
That's all, folks.

Contains eight collections of poems, the first 291.

The Green Rose 1989 - 1993
Cry of the Jester 1993
Poems of the Hot Wind 1994 to 1996
Travels And Revels, Life and Magick, Tales from Hell and Beyond - Aleister Crowley 1995 - 1996
The Infinity Cycle 1995 - 1998
Chronicles of Our Dreams 1998 - 2001
Diary of a Traveling Man 2002
TheBeautifulExcitingWorldinPieces January to August 2003

Also included are author's remarks and background material.

ISBN 978-82-91693-06-4

Dreams Belong to the Night

New, emerging urban rebel guerilla groups, freedom fighters, called terrorists by enraged authorities are overwhelming Europe.

What is, in truth terrorism? Who does it to whom?
How much can a human being take of bondage, injustice, degradation and destruction of spirit... before being fed up?

Present day society is a wound not closing.
In a modern world society destroying everything making life worth living there are those, who, through coincidence and fate, have decided not to take it anymore.
And as they are making that decision, together and as individuals, they are also starting on a journey, a journey back to humanity's roots.
Judith, Sivert, Kim, Willhelm, Anya and many more.
A handful of people against an entire world.

This is their story...

To be published June 21, 2011

The Defenseless

The two rivers meet and join in the city of Denver, becoming one...

The two dark brothers, growing up with their sister Linda in a mundane, average suburb, a place well entrenched in modern United States and the world, have since their moment of birth been at odds with the world... and with each other.

Mike and Ted Cousin are not who they are. There is a mystery here, one of birth and upbringing, one of fate. Violence and death, blood and fire follow them all the days of their lives. The fire is resting somewhere inside... waiting for the Spark.

Their parents know something, but are not telling it. The policeman Mark Stewart and their aunt Trudy do, too. Everybody knows something, pieces of the whole, but nobody knows the whole truth, nobody telling it.

The ancient power is returning to the world, a world massively suffering from physical and spiritual poison, on the brink of collapse and a collective tailspin suicide run without its like in human history.

Magick is returning from its long exile. Thus begins the story of the wild beasts rising from their ashes.

The Spark is struck, horrible and terrifying.

First book of ten in the Janus Clan series: Ten stories of the wild man in the modern world, forty years of wandering, before the Phoenix is rising from its ashes.

ISBN 978-82-91693-08-8

www.ingramcontent.com/pod-product-compliance
Lightning Source LLC
Chambersburg PA
CBHW060604310726
48982CB00008B/1230/J

* 9 7 8 8 2 9 1 6 9 3 1 0 1 *